O.M. Wills
Presents
ERTA
The Complete Series

Author's Note

When you day dream of someone you like, it's a hot, beautiful flash of lust, passion, hunger, and desire.

This is what I want you to experience when you read my books.

So I encourage you to please cut lose, enjoy, unlock, and embrace your primal desires in the safety of your mind.

~O.M. Wills~

Table of Contents

Table of Contents
(Continued)

O.M. Wills
Presents
ERTA
Book 1

Prologue

Road Trip: Day Two

Date: Friday June 2nd 2017

Time: 2:00 am

Location: On the outskirts of Missoula, Mt

"Ah! Ah! Ah Shit Nate! Yeah! Yeah! Fuck me like that! Oh! Oh God Yes!" Jay heard a woman scream through the cheap motel wall, causing him to wake.

"Is that Rayya? I heard her say Nate."

"Oh God, your dick! Fuck me! Fuck me! Yes! Fuck me!" he heard the woman scream, panting and gasping as if she were about to cum, followed by loud smacks.

"Yes! Spank me! Spank me like I'm a bad girl! Oh yes! Spank me daddy!"

"That is Rayya! Holy shit, I'd never expect to hear that from her! Or expect those two to be so freaky," he thought, feeling his dick starting to grow as he shifted in the bed, looking at his wife Karman, whose eyes just flicked open.

"Ooh, ooh yeah, fuck me harder baby! Harder! Harder! Harder! Ayeee!" he heard Rayya scream, this time groaning and whimpering as if she were cumming with every fiber of her being.

"Goddamn she sounds good. I wish I could watch them," he thought, smiling at his wife whose hand was sliding down his boxers, taking a hold of his dick.

"Ah! Yeah baby! That's my pussy!" he heard Nate grunt, followed by more spanks.

"Yeah! It's your pussy! Fuck your pussy baby! Fuck your pussy!" he heard Rayya gasp and moan.

"God," he whispered from the feel of his wife's hand as she began to stroke, and from what he envisioned happening next door.

"Oh! Oh, shit yeah!" he heard Nate grunt, followed by a long deep howl, through which he could hear Rayya groan, "Ohhh yeah! Baby, cum in your pussy! Cum in your pussy for me! Yeah, give it to me!"

1

"Man, he's getting that pussy," Jay whispered, picturing Rayya's beautiful Lebanese body covered in sweat as Nate fucked her from behind.

"Yeah, he is. It sounds really good, huh? Does baby want to make some of our own noise?" he heard his wife ask as he continued to imagine the scene where Nate was now filling Rayya to the brim, with their mix rushing out all over the bed.

"Oh, shit that's good," he replied from the visualization, and from the feeling of his wife massaging the tip of his dick with her thumb, using the pre-cum that'd leaked out for lube as she continued to work her hand over the rest of his cock.

"Is that a yes?" Jay heard his wife whisper, as more groans and moans came through the wall, causing his dick to grow harder.

"You don't even need to ask," he replied, pushing his wife onto her back, pulling down her pajamas and thong, smiling at the scent and sight of her arousal.

"Fuck baby, that looks yummy," Jay whispered, lowering himself, drinking in more of her scent before running his tongue over her entrance and clit.

"Mmm, how do I taste?" he heard his wife whisper.

"It's so good, but not enough," he replied, running the sweet, honey like flavor over his tongue, watching intently as she grew wetter from his words.

"You sure? I think you're lying, not that I care…Come, make some more," he heard his wife whisper.

"Oh, I'm planning to," he replied, kissing and sucking his wife's inner thighs before moving his lips over her clit.

"Oh, baby is such a fucking tease," he heard his wife whisper as she began to squirm.

"Am I?" he replied, tracing his tongue around her clit then down over her inner and outer lips.

"Yeah! You like torturing me," he heard his wife reply.

"I do, don't I?" he whispered, running his tongue over her entrance, coating his tongue in arousal.

"Baby likes my taste a lot doesn't he!" he heard his wife gasp.

"Uh-huh," he intoned, moving his lips over her clit, sucking hard, hearing his wife gasp and say, "Stop!"

"Stop?" he asked, flicking his tongue over his wife's clit before saying, "Why stop?"

"Baby! Baby?" he heard his wife gasp.

"Humm?" he intoned, sucking her clit again, making sure he added more and more pressure.

"Oh shit, your tongue! No! Don't stop!" he heard his wife gasp, working her hips up and down in rhythm with his tongue.

Seconds later he heard Rayya scream, "Oh yes! Fuck my ass!" through the wall, quickly followed by Nate grunting and saying, "yeah! Such a tight little fucking ass! You want me to fuck it? I'll fuck it! I'll fuck it real good!"

"God, I love listening to them. They sound so fucking good," he heard his wife whisper before saying, "suck my pussy baby. Make me cum on your tongue. Make me scream like her so they can hear me."

"Word, for sure baby," he replied, sucking and flicking his tongue harder and faster, causing his wife's entire body to quiver, letting him know he was about to receive a mouth full of cum.

"Oh! Baby! Your tongue! Ahh!" he heard his wife scream as her pussy throbbed and erupted, filling his mouth with hot, semi-sweet cum, which he greedily drank down.

"Oh God, you're nasty!" he heard his wife say, panting out of breath.

"You know I love it when you cum in my mouth. Why? Does bad girl not like it when I drink her cum?" he asked, feeling drunk off his wife's scent and taste as he inched his head back, watching small streams of cum continue to leak out of her pussy.

"Mmm, you know I love it! Do it again!" he heard his wife whisper, pressing his head down, working her hips, running her soaking wet pussy over his lips.

"*I love it too!*" Jay thought, extending his tongue to run across her lips and clit as he heard Rayya scream, "Ahh! Yes! Fuck my ass! Fuck it! Yeah! I feel it! I feel it! Yeah, cum in my ass!" through the wall, causing him to think, "*Never in my life would I have imagined this happening. There's no way I would've pictured these two as freaks, especially not after that car ride.*"

Chapter I

Why?

Road Trip: Day One

Date: Thursday, June 1ˢᵗ 2017

Time: 2:30 pm

Location: Bellevue, Washington

"Why the fuck did you have to invite these fucks with us on our road trip. Tell me, huh? We're supposed to be de-stressing, not adding more stress," Jay said to his wife Karman as he kicked pebbles into Lake Washington.

"Baby, stop being such a grump. Nate and Rayya are nice people. Plus, we need help driving to New York. Remember what happened last time we tried to make the trip? We almost died," he heard his wife reply, patting him on the ass, causing his frustration to grow even further.

"How many times do I have to tell you, I hate it when you touch my ass like that?" he mumbled as he thought, *"Every time we get too close to our couple friends, they start judging us, which leads us to fight! That, or somehow everything turns into a stupid competition. Now I need to be ready for war from Bellevue to damn Chicago. Oh 'It', this is going to suck!"*

"I know you hate it, that's why I do it. Anyways, they're almost done putting their stuff in the car. Please stop being an ass," he heard his wife whisper, rubbing his shoulder, kissing him on the cheek, which was her sweet way of telling him she was running out of patience.

"I'm not being an ass. I have a reason to be defensive – called being too close to our couple friends always causes you to overanalyze our life," he said, turning towards their SUV, which was across the street from Lake Washington, when he heard the trunk close.

"Baby, please?" he heard his wife mumble, waving towards the couple, while gripping the back of his arm with her other hand.

4

"Fucking annoying," he thought, knowing her grip meant he'd now crossed her annoyance threshold, where she'd become super pissed if he continued to bitch.

"You know it's true…And the only reason we need help driving is because you always damn near fall asleep at the wheel," he continued, growing even more aggravated by the bright smiles the couple wore as they waved back, giving him the feeling that they'd already planned their whole reign of couple's domination.

"Cut it out, baby, please?" he heard his wife reply in a venomous tone, causing him to bite his next words and say, "Okay my love. Let's get going then."

"Thank you," he heard his wife, Karman reply, letting out a low sigh, sounding relieved as he took her hand and began to walk - slowly towards the SUV.

"No prob," he replied, playfully moving his shoulder into his wife's before saying, "Besides, you're going to make it up to me with lots of sexy time."

"Am I now?" he heard his wife respond, gently shoving him back.

"You bet," he replied as they crossed 'Lake Washington Boulevard', thinking, *"I hope so. It's the only thing that'll keep me from going crazy."*

"Hi guys! Thanks again for inviting us!" he heard Rayya say the moment their feet touched the sidewalk, causing him to grit his teeth, thinking, *"Oh please! You know it wasn't me!"*

"Of course! No problem! This is going to be fun!" he heard his wife reply, sounding just as cheerful, causing him to grit his teeth even harder, thinking, *"For who!?"*

"Yeah girl, it'll be!" he heard Rayya reply, moving towards Karman, giving her a hug and kiss on the cheek before moving towards him, presenting him her cheek to kiss.

"You guys are so fucking boring. How can we even attempt to have fun?" he thought, pecking Rayya on the cheek, then nodding his head to Nate who was standing by the passenger door with a strange, unreadable smirk.

"Dude's so fucking weird. He's always smirking at something in his head," he thought, noting the fact that Rayya smelled amazing, and looked extremely attractive in her hot-pink, spandex booty shorts, and white tank top.

"But maybe it's because he knows she's hot as fuck," he thought as he stepped past Rayya who was already moving towards his wife with open arms for another hug.

Arriving a few steps in front of Nate, he reached out his hand and said, "You ready to go bro?" as he thought, *"You're a handsome dude. I'll give you that. Tall, and got that perfect gym body thing going on. But I really don't see what she sees in you. It seems like she has the personality for both of you, and that's if she bothers to actually talk about something other than celebrity gossip."*

"Yeah man. Can't wait," he heard Nate reply, taking his hand, yet looking past him, which made him turn and trace his eyes to Rayya's ass.

"Holly Shit! She's not wearing panties. No thong, no nothing! Fucking 'It'! Why the fuck did he look at her just as he took my hand. It's as if he wanted me to check her out. Are they up to some kinky, voyeur shit? No way! I don't sense a freaky bone in their bodies! Yet, her outfit, and his leading stare just now. Is it possibly my amazing people reading skills have failed me!?" he thought, quickly snapping his head back towards Nate, hoping he didn't catch him looking.

"Yeah, this is going to be fun," he heard Nate say right after, in a soft sleepy tone, still wearing the same smirk as before, but this time gazing directly at him, making him feel self-conscious.

"Well, he had to have seen me look. He's the reason I looked. But his demeanor's off. If he wanted me to look, wouldn't he just do what normal dudes do and just give me the head nod…or hell, the head tip? Or whisper something like, 'check out my boo, she's not wearing any underwear!' What's up with the quiet, creepy smirk?"

"Come, sit in the back with me, let the guys sit up front," he heard his wife say, interrupting his chain of thought as he tried to read Nate's passive demeanor.

"Sounds good girl. And I love your summer dress, it's so cute. It looks like the one in my magazine, you know the one that…umm, what's her name is wearing. Oh crap, I can't believe I forgot her name," he heard Rayya reply.

"Lord 'It', this is going to be torture," he thought, head nodding Nate as he walked to the driver's seat, hopping in.

"It's okay girl, tell me in the car," he heard his wife reply before saying, "And let's do our nails!"

"Oh, I'm happy you said that! I left my Nail Kit out, hoping you'd want to!" he heard Rayya respond, opening the passenger door on Nate's side, hopping in, giving him a bright smile before turning to watch as his wife jumped into the seat behind him.

"Oh man...I can see everything. Her fucking shorts are pure see through," he thought, looking in the rear-view mirror, tracing the thin landing strip of hair running down Rayya's pussy as she flicked off her sandals and folded her legs Indian style.

"You okay?" he heard Nate say in a somewhat knowing tone - causing him to look to his right, finding that Nate had already gotten in and buckled his seat belt.

"Yeah man. Why, what's wrong? I look a 'lil' sick? It's 'cuz' I have allergies to Cedar and that other hellish tree that's trying to kill all of humanity," he replied as he thought, *"Did he just bust me checking out his wife again? Fuck! I want to stop, but I know I can't. This ride is going to be torture for two reasons!"*

"Yeah, it looked like something was in your eye. Allergies though, huh?" He heard Nate respond, and when he looked over he could see him bobbing his head up and down as if he agreed one hundred percent.

"Yeah, I took the pill and everything. But it still gets really bad. It's fucked bro. You know, essentially the trees are literally face fucking me. You know, blowing their load in my face," he said as he thought, *"His smile, his tone, he knows damn straight what's up! Oh! Oh shit! I just saw wifey take a peak and she's never been the bi-curious type. This shit is crazy!"*

"Bwaahahaha!" he heard Nate burst out laughing with a snort, looking at him with wild eyes.

"What!? Face fucking? Who's face fucking who?" he heard Rayya say right after.

"Oh, the trees," he heard his wife reply airily, before whispering, "He always says the trees are face fucking him when he gets allergies. He uses the same jokes."

"Well, I've never heard it. That's funny!" he heard Rayya reply, looking to Nate, who was still cracking up laughing.

"Alright, let's get the fuck outa here," Jay said, feeling some of the tension and reservation he had about driving with the couple start to ease.

Approximately seven hours later

"Fuck my life, this guy shuts down every conversation in the history of man fucking kind!" he thought, reading the sign for Missoula, and praying the six or so miles they had left to get there would go by with light speed.

"So, you don't watch Hockey or Football?" Jay asked, annoyed at himself for not wanting to sit in the passenger seat in silence and just leave Nate's awkward self alone.

"No, no I could never get into sports," he heard Nate reply, without even a single head gesture to indicate that he would say anything afterward.

"Oh my 'It'! What would it take to make this 'fuck' talk! Talk about any fucking thing! I don't give a shit! I can't fall asleep like these two goofs in the back. So 'It', please spare me and make him fucking talk!" Jay thought after the fifth silent minute rolled by in which Nate sat perfectly still with his hands at ten and two on the wheel.

"So then, what do you get into?" he finally asked, being sure to hold back every ounce of aggravation from his tone.

"You know, a few things here and there. I like to work on games and what not," Nate replied, turning to him with the same smirk he always wore.

"Games? Like video games? Board games? What kind of games?" he asked, feeling the last of his strength drain out of his body.

"Cards mostly," he heard Nate respond, before making a sound that indicated he wanted to say something.

"What?" Jay pressed, desperate to kill the silence.

"So, how 'bout' you? What do you do other than sports? Or watching sports? Or talking about sport cars? Or talking about your car? I mean, don't get me wrong, this SUV is amazing. V-Eight, leather seats, and ummm, I do think it's cool it can be manual or automatic. But, well... what do you and Karman do for fun?" he heard Nate ask, sounding slightly pensive.

"Um, we go on road trips to Portland, Vancouver, sometimes to San Fran and San Diego. And if I feel like seeing my 'peps', we go to New York, like we're doing now. And since we're dropping you guys off in 'Chi Town', we'll probably poke

8

around there a bit," Jay said, grateful some form of conversation was starting up.

"Poke around. What kind of poking around? What do you guys do?" he heard Nate press, sounding somewhat annoyed, making him think, *"What the fuck else does poking around mean? It means look around, eat shit, and get dragged into shopping sprees, where you're forced to hold all the wife's shit for hours on end. Is life really that different for you?"*

"You know, shopping, eating and stuff," he replied, studying Nate's face for cues when Nate whispered, "Shopping and eating…right…right."

"Yeah, what else is there to do?" he asked, wondering why Nate's smirk changed to a look of pure perplexity.

"A lot of things," he heard Nate respond, giving him a look as if he felt bad for him, before saying, "Finally we're here, well the outskirts of here. 'Wanna' just stop at this janky motel? We just need to catch some 'Zzz', right? Nothing fancy right?"

"Yeah man, sure," Jay replied, staring at the motel Nate was pulling up to with pure disdain.

"Cool, I know it looks a little rough, but if the ladies are going to be driving tomorrow, I want them to have a better rest than sleeping in the car," he heard Nate say, placing the SUV in park.

"Na' man, I agree," he replied, staring at the blinking, broken sign that read, 'M tel' in cursive, as he thought, *"And this is where my wife and I die. Someone's waiting in there to cut us up and hang dry our bodies. Why the fuck am I going along with this? Oh right, because one more second in this car with this fool and I'm going to jump out and kill myself anyways."*

"Hello ladies. Wakey-wakey. We're stopping for the night," he heard Nate say, turning and tapping Rayya's legs, which were draped over his wife's.

"Mmm… where are we?" Jay heard his wife ask, yawning and stretching her arms.

"We're on the outskirt of Missoula, Montana," he replied, smiling at his wife, remembering the last time they were in Missoula.

"Nate, what is this place? It looks scary," he heard Rayya say, yawning and stretching, then smiling between the two of them before saying, "So, did you guys bond?"

"Yeah," he heard Nate reply quickly before saying, "Come, let's get our rooms. Unlike you two, we haven't rested. And I want to stretch my legs."

"Bonded my ass," he thought opening the door, coming around to his wife's side of the car.

"You okay boo?" he asked, taking his wife's hand, giving her a small tug to help her out the car.

"I'm okay Papi," he heard his wife reply when her sandaled feet touched the pavement, giving him a hug right after.

"Good, good," he replied, watching as Nate went to the back, taking out bags, before heading over to Rayya, giving her a small peck on the lips.

"Mm-hmm," he heard his wife mumble knowingly.

"Mm-hmm what?" he replied, watching as the couple then headed over towards them.

"Here ya go brother," he heard Nate say with a smile and head bob, passing him he and his wife's overnight bag.

"Thanks bro," he said with a short head bob, wondering why both Nate and Rayya wore such odd expressions on their face.

"Wasup?" he finally asked, seeing Rayya open her mouth, then bite the bottom of her lip in obvious contemplation.

"Well, this place is kinda creepy. I don't want to be alone here," Jay heard Rayya say, seeing her look between he and his wife before looking down towards the ground - seeming shy.

"We're not alone, right guys?" Jay heard Nate say, nodding his head, giving he and his wife a bright smile as if they were the best of friends sharing a secret.

"No, you're not alone, we're here," he replied, giving his best – 'it's going to be okay' smile to Rayya as he thought, *"I'd offer to share rooms, but the last few times we did that, we always found out through the couple friend's grapevine that they thought we were swingers, trying to fuck them. I think I'll spare us the agony this time. Even though this time, I really think we should."*

"Yeah girl, we're here. I'm with you though, I'm kind of scared," he heard his wife say, looking around dubiously before

10

playfully hip checking him – which he knew meant she wanted him to say something.

"What do you want me to say? Please don't tell me you want me to say, 'let's share a room'. It's that or you want me to talk to Nate and tell him you don't want to stay here. Fuck my life, now I 'gotta' figure it out before you get pissed off at me," he thought as he said, "What's wrong boo? Too creepy? You don't want to stay here?"

"No Papi, why you say that? It's late, we're all tired," he heard his wife reply, sounding way too casual for his liking before hearing her say, "I think we should share a room with Nate and Rayya, it'd make us two ladies feel way more comfy."

"Oh really?" he replied, looking between Nate and Rayya, trying to read their faces, noting that Rayya looked somewhat anxious, and that Nate held a perfectly neutral face for the first time he'd seen since the trip began.

"I don't think they like that idea at all. Plus wifey, aren't you tired of being burned?" he thought as he said, "I 'dunno', isn't that imposing?"

"No, not at all," he heard Nate reply in an extremely easygoing tone before saying, "If the ladies feel better, it's for sure cool with me. I'm sure we can get twin beds and share the room."

"You sure?" he pressed, feeling like he was being cornered, before saying, "Umm, I umm, you mind if we don't? Not to be rude, it's just."

"No, no, you're not being rude," he heard Rayya cut in with waving hand gesture, giving Nate her own hip check that didn't look so playful before saying, "Anyways, your room will be on us, a thank you for taking us to Chicago."

"Hey, umm, no, it's okay," he said, feeling sweat starting to form under his armpits.

"Na, we got it bro," he heard Nate reply, before saying, "Just wait here, I'll go get the keys."

"Alright," he replied as his wife leaned into him, which he knew was her way of telling him that he should not stop what was in motion.

"Cool, be right back," he heard Nate say, pecking Rayya on the temple.

11

"So, what did you guys talk about?" Jay heard Rayya ask as Nate walked past them towards the motel office.

"Umm, sports, and umm, like hiking and hobbies and stuff," he said thinking, *"I talked, he deflected with his famous line of, 'I've never taken much interest in that'."*

"Oh," he heard Rayya reply with a face that said, 'poor you' before moving to his wife, giving her a hug, saying, "Girl this place is scary. What was my baby thinking, stopping here? If you get nervous, you two come to our room, okay?"

"Wait, what? I'm 'hella' good at reading people, and she did not seem like she wanted us to come. And even Nate wasn't wearing his 'perma' smirk. So why invite us?" he thought as he said, "Yeah, I promise we'll come if she gets nervous."

"Good, good," he heard Rayya reply, patting him on the shoulder as Nate returned and said, "alright guys, got the room keys. Let's get in and get some rest."

"Perfect," he said, allowing his wife and Rayya to walk ahead of him, taking the key from Nate's hand when he stepped up on the sidewalk.

"Look man, I didn't mean to insult. It's just, wifey and I, we've been on road trips with couples before, and sharing the rooms turned out to be…yeah," he said when the women were somewhat out of ear shot.

"Na man, it's cool. To be honest, Bellevue is small, Rayya and I have mingled with some of the people you're speaking of. We heard the stories, but man, we know it's nonsense. We know people make up shit and are immature. And even if…," he heard Nate say, trailing off.

"Even if what?" he pressed, watching Rayya open a room on the ground floor, then both women enter, followed by both saying, "Eww," simultaneously, which made both he and Nate go to investigate.

"Eww what?" he heard Nate ask, stepping into the room, looking it over, mumbling, "What's eww? Where?" after a few more seconds.

"Nate, they're freaking out over the 'it-thingy' over there by the lamp," he said, pointing to a 'Daddy Long Legs' next to the floor lamp placed in the center of the room.

"Oh, I didn't even see it. And no Rayya, I know what you're going to say. I told 'ya', I'm not killing things for no reason," he heard Nate say, shaking his head, giving him a look that said, 'this woman'.

"But, but it's a spider, why won't you kill spiders for her," Jay heard his wife ask, making a pouty face at both himself and Nate.

"Come boo, give them their space, and I'm not killing it either. It's not even a damn spider, it's more like a scorpion and the things don't even got teeth or fangs. Hell, scientist can barely observe them eating. So, leave the damn thing alone, for at least science sakes," he said, shaking his head, wondering why almost every woman he knew wanted him to be a walking executioner of anything that crawled.

"Bae, bae it eats people," he heard his wife responded dramatically, backing up towards the door in a slow exaggeration of fear as if at any moment the insect would lunge across the room.

"Unn-huh…you guys have a good night with Mr. Long legs. See y'all tomorrow. Just knock on our door when you guys are awake," he said with a wave.

"Alright bro, sounds good," he heard Nate reply.

"Cool, here, I'll close the door for 'ya'," he said, closing the door, then giving his wife a, 'what the fuck' look before walking towards the next room over, opening the door.

"Why that look baby?" he heard his wife ask the moment she stepped through the door.

"Close it, lock it…then put the chair…wait our killers can just burst through the window. It was nice knowing you," he said, kicking off his shoes and socks.

"Well if you feel that way, why didn't you just share the room with them, it's cheaper," his wife growled in a low voice before he cut her off and said, "Cheaper? Who gives a fuck? We're not broke by any means. And, we both know we're not really scared of this silly ass place. So, it all boils down to me thinking, do we really want to risk returning with even more rumors we're swingers? It's bad for our cover, 'ya' feel me? Plus, like fuck! Real talk, we've never even had a fucking threesome, how the fuck can we be swingers? Fucking lying ass people.

13

Sometimes I think it's worth showing those fucks who we really are, popping them in their bitch ass faces."

"Calm your ass down Papi, we can't live our life like this. Not everyone's the same!" he heard his wife reply in a harsh, low voice.

"Shhh, don't whisper yell. It's still loud when you do that. I don't want them to hear us fight. See, whenever we deal with so called couple friends, we fight! I don't want to fight, I 'wanna' make loveee. Want to, want to?" he said, wanting to lighten the mood, tugging down his pants and boxers.

"No, I'm not in the mood, you piss me off. And you're not in the mood either. I know you're not scared, but I know you really don't like and are creeped out by this place, or you'd already be hard," Jay heard his wife respond, causing him to burst out laughing, realizing her observation was correct.

"Damn, what can I say? I'm not a small, outskirts, bubble fuck town kind of guy. This place got my internal body watching out for danger," he said, pulling up his boxers before saying, "So sad, last time we came to this city, we had good sexy times! Wait, if we did stay in there with them, how could we do our thing, even if we weren't creeped out? Humm?"

"I 'dunno'. Maybe quietly?" he heard his wife whisper.

"Huh? You know damn straight you can't hold your gasp," he replied, feeling butterflies erupt in his stomach, having never expected to hear his wife suggest such a thing as she'd always been a private person when it came to their love life.

"Anyways, last time we came here we stayed downtown...and I didn't see any man-eating spiders. It was much easier to get in the mood. Maybe, you need to do something to change my mind," he heard wife reply, giving him a loving, sarcastic look.

"Dude, you're from the damn jungle. Full of man eating spiders!"

"Did you just hear what I said? And Oye! Papi, that's different," he heard his wife say with a warm-hearted giggle.

"Yeah, yeah, yeah, I heard what you said. But wait, I'm thinking about something," he mumbled, unable to concentrate on his wife's naughty suggestion due to a nagging thought in the back of his mind.

14

"What, what's up Papi?"

"Hey, do you think, do you really think they wanted us to come to their room?"

"I 'dunno' baby. Yeah, sure, I think they did. I think it would've been fine. Why? I'm not going over there now, they've already paid for our room," Jay heard his wifey reply, walking towards him, spinning, with her arms raised.

"Yeah, I know, it's just," he said, pausing as he lifted off her summer dress and undid her bra, "It's just, I get this feeling from them. Like what's with her shorts? She's got no panties on."

"Ah, so, you were looking?" he heard his wife ask, sounding amused as she went into their bag, digging out her pajamas.

"Well fuck, how could I not? It was so obvious! And you were too!" he replied defensively, somewhat expecting her to be angry, surprised at her tone and smile on her face.

"Baby?" he asked, taking off his shirt as his wife went over and flicked off the light, having still not said a word.

"Huh? Yeah, I was looking. She's, she's very sexy, I have to admit it hubby. But hubby, you have to remember something. I go with her to get the Brazilians. I've already, long time ago seen everything," he heard his wife say teasingly as she slipped on her Pajamas, heading over to him with her lips puckered for a kiss right after.

"Well now me too, 'cuz' seven hours of her sitting Indian style, legs wide open counts as long time ago, yup, yup," he said, pecking his wife on the lips and forehead, tugging her down to sit on the bed before saying, "Do you think, do you think they're actually swingers? I mean they must have something going for them. If not, then damn I feel bad for them, 'cuz' Nate's lame as fuck. He doesn't do shit, talk about shit, and the most I've heard him laugh was when I said the tress were fucking my face. He laughed the most at a sex joke. You know, that's telling me something."

"I 'dunno' baby. And who cares if they are. Let's get some sleep, I know you're tired," he heard his wife reply, putting her hand on his chest, pushing him back so that he would scoot up onto the bed, then laying her head on his chest as he laid back onto the pillows.

"Baby, she had no thong on, no nothing. Her booty shorts were pure see through. And when Nate took my hand he…" he began, trailing off, thinking, *"Am I over thinking?"*

"He what?" he heard his wife ask in a groggy voice.

"Nothing. Wait, fuck! I was supposed to do something to change your mood," he replied.

"Nope, too late, moment came and went, go to sleep," he heard his wife whisper in a voice that said she was already drifting off to sleep.

"Damn it brain, why you always 'gotta' over think and fuck things up for me?" he whispered, feeling his eyes grow heavy, drifting off to sleep before he even knew it.

Chapter II

Hear That?

Road Trip: Day Two

Date: Friday, June 2nd 2017

Time: 2:04 am

Location: On The Outskirts Of Missoula, Mt.

"God, I'm so fucking happy we woke up to them fucking!" Jay thought, as his wife pressed his head down harder so that his tongue ran across her pussy.

"Yes! Lick my pussy! Oh God Yes!" he heard his wife scream as she came.

"I love this!" Jay thought, tasting and feeling his wife's cum fill his mouth and splash all over his face.

"Mmm, you taste good, cum for me again," he whispered, taking hold of his wife's thighs, pressing them back, driving his tongue into her entrance.

"I can't! No more! No more!" he heard his wife beg as he worked his tongue in and out, feeling her pussy squeeze, almost forcing it out.

"Yes, you can. Squirt for me again," he whispered, forcing his tongue in deeper despite the pressure.

"Aye!" Jay heard his wife scream, feeling his tongue forced out followed by the taste and sensation of her cum splashing all over his mouth and face.

"Mmm, yeah, there we go my little squitter! I know you can squirt all day," he whispered, moving back to look at the mess he'd help create.

"I need your dick, Papi, I need your dick," Jay heard his wife reply, moving her hand to her pussy, rubbing her clit.

"Oh! Oh Yeah! Ride that dick, ride that dick, with that tight little ass!" he heard Nate blare through the wall.

"Damn baby, you hear that? He's fucking that ass. You want me to fuck that ass?" he asked, running the tip of his dick over his wife's entrance down to her ass then back up again.

"Yeah, you know I like it there," he heard his wife reply, setting his blood on fire, while simultaneously hearing Rayya scream, "I love it! I love it when you fill my ass daddy! I love it! Yes! Fill my ass daddy!"

"Mmm, that sounds good Papi. You 'gonna' fill my ass?" Jay heard his wife ask, giving him a mischievous look as she took hold of his dick, guiding his tip it into her entrance.

"Yeah, you know I will," he replied, thrusting slowly, gasping from the sensation as his dick slipped in deeper.

"Mmm, I can't wait," he heard his wife reply, parting her fingers over his dick, rubbing her pussy, giving him another mischievous smile.

"Wasup' 'lil' freak? What you thinking?" he asked.

"Oh nothing," he heard his wife reply with a giggle, bringing up her hand, licking her cum off her fingers.

"Like the way your pussy taste?" he asked, watching his wife bring her hand to her breast, massaging them.

"Yeah. And you know what would make it taste better?" he heard his wife reply, biting her bottom lip.

"No, tell me," he replied, taking her by the thighs, flipping her to lay on her right side.

"Oh! Oh, shit baby! You know I can't take it like this!" Jay heard his wife plead, placing her hand on his stomach as if she were trying to push herself free.

"We'll see about that. Now, tell me what you think would make that pussy taste better?" he replied, placing her left leg over his shoulder, thrusting hard, and deep, where at every end stroke he could feel her heart beat at the tip of his dick.

"Aye! Fuck baby! Baby!" Jay heard his wife gasp, pressing harder on his stomach, with her other hand gripping the sheets as if she were about to fall off the bed.

"Yeah, take that dick! Take that fucking dick!" Jay grunted, feeling her start to tremble under his thrust.

"I can't! Oh, God baby! I can't!" he heard his wife gasp.

"Oh, you can take it! Yes! You can fucking take it!" he grunted, watching his dick slid in and out, loving how wet and tight her pussy felt.

"Mmm! Baby! Yeah, fuck me deeper! Deeper!" he heard his wife beg, leaning up on her arm, pushing herself down on his cock.

"Shit!" he gasped, loving the feeling of his dick pressing as far as it could go.

"AYE!" he heard his wife scream less than a second later, feeling her pussy squeeze and erupt, forcing his dick out.

"Yeah! Cum all over that dick! Cum all over that dick!" he gasped, looking down at the clear stream of hot cum rushing out, reveling in the scent and sensation as it splashed all over his dick and body.

"God baby! Your dick!" he heard his wife gasp, quaking and shivering as she inched forward on her side, as if she were planning to take a rest.

"Where you going? My dick what? And, you still haven't told me what would make that pussy taste better," he replied, flipping her onto her stomach, pulling her ass up so that he could stare at her leaking pussy before driving his tongue into her entrance.

"Mmm, your cum baby, your cum," he heard his wife groan, wagging her hips as he began to suck and lick her pussy.

"My cum huh? You want me to cum in that pussy?" Jay whispered, inching back to gaze at his wife's pussy, spreading open her lips with is fingers.

"Yeah, in my pussy, and my ass," he heard his wife reply, moving her right hand back, gripping her ass, pointing to the two places she wanted his cum with her index finger.

"Shit, I love you baby," he responded, sliding his fingers into her entrance, working them in and out, spreading them wide before slipping them out.

"I love you too baby," he heard his wife reply, wagging her ass again before saying, "come, fuck me baby, she's hungry for you."

"Oh? She's hungry for me huh?" he replied, licking his fingers clean before lifting up, taking hold of her waist, pressing his tip into her entrance.

"How's she feel now?"

"Stop teasing, give me more," he heard his wife whisper.

"More? Like this more?" he replied, pressing himself as deep as he could go before starting to thrust.

"Baby, baby! I can't!" he heard his wife scream, bucking herself back with his every forward stroke, causing him to lose his breath as the warm, tight sensation fully registered in his mind.

"Mmm, you always say you can't take it! But look at you, coming for more!" he gasped, slapping her ass as she continued to buck back.

"Yeah! Spank me! Fucking, spank me!" he heard his wife plead, pressing her ass back, immersing his entire length within her.

"Shit!" he gasped, smacking his wife's ass again, feeling her pussy clench and body shudder.

"Yes! More!" he heard his wife beg, causing him to smack again and again, smelling and feeling her pussy grow wetter with each blow.

"Oh, fuck! Oh, fuck!" he gasped, loving the what he saw and felt, spanking his wife's ass again, hearing her scream, shudder, then bounce and wind on his dick.

"Baby!" he gasped, feeling himself going over the edge.

"Yeah, hubby likes it when I do that huh? You like watching it go in and out, don't you?" he heard his wife ask, winding slower, then faster, not allowing him to get used to the pace.

"Oh, fuck yeah! You know I love it!" he gasped, continuing to spank her ass, now added his own thrust to her winding rhythm.

"Ou! Baby! Then cum for me! I need you to cum for me!" he heard his wife beg, all of a sudden squeezing her pussy with every turn of her hips.

"Fuck! That feels good! You want me to fill that pussy huh, baby?" he gasped, inhaling deeply, wanting to get even more drunk off the scent of his wife's sweat and arousal.

"Mmm! Yeah! Give it to me! Give it to me!" he heard his wife plead, bucking back harder and harder, no longer bothering to wind.

"Ah! Fuck!" Jay groaned, losing control, feeling himself shake as he came inside his wife's pussy.

"Yes! Oh my God, yes!" he heard his wife gasp as he continued to cum, filling her to the brim where he could see their mix rush out, coating her pussy and the base of his cock.

"Mmm…that's some good pussy!" he groaned, curling forward, wrapping his arms around her as he continued to empty his load.

"Yeah, that's your pussy. She likes it when you fill her," he heard his wife whisper, squeezing her pussy, sending shivers down his spin from the sensitivity.

"Sshh…Shit!" he groaned, bringing himself up to watch and feel as their mix flowed out over his dick before sliding out, running his tip over the rim of her ass.

"Oh, is baby going to fuck my ass now?" he heard his wife whisper, squeezing her pussy, seeing and feeling her asshole flex on the tip of his dick.

"Yeah, yeah I am. Is baby 'gonna' squeeze her pussy like that when I fuck her ass?" he asked, watching more of their mix run out, catching it on the tip of his dick, then placing it back to her asshole.

"Un-huh, you know it," Jay heard his wife reply, pressing herself back so that the tip of his dick ever so slightly slipped into her ass.

"Damn, that ass is tight," he whispered.

"You like?" he heard his wife reply, flexing her muscles, allowing him to sink in just bit further.

"Yeah, I love…Ohh, good girl letting me in," he whispered, enjoying the warmth and tightness of her ass as he inched himself in deeper.

"Unt-unh. It wasn't all me. Someone added lube," he heard his wife reply, flexing her ass, allowing him to fit more than half of his eight-inch length within her.

"Shit, baby. Feels so good!"

"Deeper, I want deeper," he heard his wife reply.

"Oh yes, I will baby, but I 'wanna' take my time," he whispered, stroking as slowly as he could, taking in every detail as he fucked her ass.

"Yeah? But I want deeper," he heard his wife reply, pressing herself back until his full length was within her.

"Shit! Your ass! So, fucking good," he gasped, feeling his wife begin to bounce, and grind on his dick.

"I love deep!" he heard his wife moan, feeling her squeeze his dick, grinding hard.

"Baby! Baby!" he groaned, taking a deep breath, barely regaining control.

"Yes?" he heard his wife ask, sounding mischievously innocent, pausing her hip movements.

"You're being a bad girl, almost making me cum too fast," he whispered.

"Whoopsie. Was it from this?" he heard his wife reply, winding and squeezing his dick again, sending shivers down his spine.

"Fuck! Oh, is that how it is? Fine then, I'll punish you like a bad girl," he whispered - only after he'd regained control for the second time.

"Oh, really? You're going to punish me? How Papi 'gonna' do that if he can't even take it?" he heard his wife reply, bouncing and winding even faster, letting out a giggle as he tried to inch back.

"Huh, where you going Mr. punish me?" he heard his wife reply, feeling his dick slide deeper as she followed him back.

"Oh! You'll see! I'll fucking control it," he whispered, gripping her waist tight, taking long, slow strokes as he worked his hips.

"Baby!" he heard his wife plead.

"Yeah, you see? Slow is dangerous," he replied, sliding his dick almost all the way out, leaving just tip, then driving himself all the way back in as slowly as he could.

"Baby! Oh my God! Baby!" he heard his wife scream, starting to quake.

"Yes boo?" he asked mischievously, doing it all over again, but increasing his pace, stroking harder and harder as she continued to tremble.

"You! AH!" he heard his wife gasp, grabbing his wrist as her pussy erupted, shooting out wave after wave of hot cum all over his balls and thighs.

"Me what?" he replied without even a pause in his thrust, causing her to scream at the top of her lungs as she erupted again.

22

"You! Not fair!" he heard his wife gasp after catching her breath, tapping his wrist, begging for him to stop.

"Oh! I'm not going to stop till you say it! Me what? I want to hear you say it!" he said, giving her a spank as he thrusted.

"You! You! You!" he heard his wife moan.

"Me what!?" he grunted, thrusting and working his hips even harder.

"My ass! Feels so good! Feels so fucking good!" he heard his wife gasp.

"Yesss! I'm fucking that ass real good huh!?" he grunted, feeling a surge of primal energy course through his body, reveling in the sight and sensation of his dick sliding in and out of his wife's ass.

"Yeah! Feels so good!" he heard his wife reply, groaning as he fucked her ass even harder.

"Baby!" he heard his wife scream, feeling her squirt again.

"Yesss! Fuck, smells so fucking good, looks so fucking good! I got that pussy leaking!" he groaned, inhaling deeply to drink in the scent of sweat and cum rising from between her legs before saying, "This is my ass! Say it! It's my ass!"

"Yeah Papi! It's your ass!" he heard his wife moan, driving herself back, harder and harder with his every thrust.

"Shit!" he gasped, feeling himself on the verge cumming – suddenly hearing Rayya say, "Oh! Listen to that!" through the wall, followed by Nate saying something along the lines of wanting to watch them.

"Shit, I fucking wish!" he thought, imagining the couple being right beside them, causing him to thrust even harder.

"Oh! Oh God!" he heard his wife scream.

"Oh yes! Listen to them baby!" he heard Rayya moan.

"Fuck! I'm 'gonna' cum!" he gasped, wanting the couple to hear, now feeling his dick throb and pulse so hard he could no longer even breathe.

"Aye! Baby!" he heard his wife scream, squirting and shaking so hard he could feel the vibrations in his dick even through his own orgasm.

"Fuck, this is the best!" he thought, wrapping himself around his wife, hugging her tightly.

"I love you," he heard his wife whisper, adding even more layers of pleasure as he continued to release his load.

"I love you too," he whispered, feeling his dick starting to pulse less and less with each passing second until his orgasm finally came to an end.

"Baby?" he heard his wife whisper.

"Huh?"

"I can't wait to see this huge mess we just made," he heard his wife reply with a soft giggle.

"Oh yeah," he replied, uncurling from around her, looking down as he slowly inched his dick from her ass, which instantly began to leak cum.

"Yeah baby, it's a lot, you'll love it," he whispered, now gazing down at the soaking wet bed sheet.

"Mmm, let me see," he heard his wife whisper, rolling onto her back, looking down at the sheets as she ran her fingers over her soaking wet pussy, slipping them into her entrance.

"Ohh, so wet," he heard his wife whisper, sliding her fingers out, showing them coated in their mix before bringing them up to her open mouth.

"Yeah, taste it," he whispered as she sucked and licked her fingers clean.

"Mmm, it's yummy baby," he heard his wife whisper, returning her fingers to her pussy, slipping them in for more.

"Oh yes! Give me more!" he heard Rayya moan through the wall seconds later, causing both he and his wife to laugh.

"Hey, guess what? I, actually want a couple's competition for once in my life," he whispered.

"Really? How so?" he heard his wife ask.

"I'm thinking; we can't let them beat us…You up for some more?"

"Humm, I agree, but are you up for more?" Jay heard his wife reply, biting her bottom lip with a mischievous smile.

"Oh, you know it!"

"Then come here," he heard his wife whisper, spreading her legs, summoning him with her index finger.

"Baby?" he whispered, moving over his wife, kissing her deeply.

"Yes hubby?" he heard his wife moan, breaking their kiss as he slipped his cock in her ass.

"I'm going to show you the literal meaning of, 'that ass is mine', and I'm going to make them hear it?" he whispered, feeling her arms wrap around his neck.

"Yes, make me scream, make them hear us baby," he heard his wife gasp, kissing him deeply, feeling her legs wrap around his waist and ass, pulling him deeper as he began to thrust.

Chapter III

The First Suggestion

Road Trip: Day Two

Date: Friday, June 2nd 2017

Time: 10:30 am

Location: On The Outskirts of Missoula, Mt.

"Yalla tnam …Yalla tnam…Yaaa llaaa…Yalla tnam," Nate heard his wife Rayya sing softly, feeling her fingers trace along his back and shoulders, causing him to shift closer to her touch – opting to keep eyes closed, enjoying the moment just the way it was.

"Oh Lord, help my Nate sleep. Help my Nate sleep," he heard Rayya continue to sing, this time in English causing him to smile and open his eyes.

"Good morning my love," he heard his wife whisper, moving her lips to his, pecking him softly, then rising to sit up in the bed Indian style, with a somewhat puzzled, yet mischievous look on her face.

"Good morning sweetie. I love your voice, I can listen to you sing forever," he whispered, sliding the sheets back to look between her legs, smiling at the mess caked up on the landing strip of hair, running the length of her pussy.

"Hummm, I've been thinking to sing for you more in Arabic, since I think you're getting much better at understating me," he heard his wife whisper, giving him a warm smile as she lifted her arms expectantly.

"Lier, you know I still suck. In all this time, all I know how to say is - Oh Lord. Shut up. Asshole. Come eat and ummm, what's the one your mom says because she hates me?" he replied, scooting himself down, laying on her thigh, inhaling deeply, drinking in the sharp, musky scent of their mix, before saying, "abn … something abn maz."

"Haha! Don't worry about it," he heard his wife say, giggling as she rested her arms over his body.

"Her level of hatred for me, it's honestly the best," he replied, half-jokingly, with a snicker, turning his head to look between her legs again, taking another deep breath, holding it to keep the scent as long as possible.

"Oh please, don't act like it's just towards you, she hates both of us. And I can feel my father's hate for us from the grave. A Lebanese, marrying an Israeli. He's probably trying to find his way back, just to rip us apart," he heard his wifey say, feeling her mood change to cold and dark before returning to normal, now hearing a soft giggle.

"Well, they shouldn't have made such a beautiful, sweet, and wonderful daughter for me to fall in love with then," he replied, taking his third deep breath before saying, "God, I love that smell."

"Those things you just said, are those the only reasons you fell in love with me?" he heard his wife ask, sounding mockingly disappointed as she gently ran her fingers through his hair.

"What if I said yes?" he replied, turning to gaze up into her hazel-green eyes before moving his hands to her breast, softly pinching her nipples.

"Then my love, I'd have to remind you of the other reasons," he heard his wife whisper, biting her bottom lip as he continued to play with her nipples.

"Wait, I'm starting to remember," he replied lifting his head, taking her nipples in his mouth one by one, causing her to gasp and lean back on the headboard.

"Mmm, but I'm starting to forget again," he whispered, settling his head back down on her thigh as he thought, *'I was a little worried about last night. I knew they'd be guarded. But it was worse than I thought. Those other couples really left a bad taste in their mouth, especially Jay. I'm glad hearing us fuck helped them open up a little bit. I just hope it stays that way, or its going to be an even more awkward car ride than yesterday."*

"What's your thoughts on last night my love?" he heard his wife ask, gently lifting his head, parting her legs so that he could lay between them, knowing he wanted to continually drink in the scent of her pussy.

"Hummm, do you know how happy it makes me when you know my train of thought? And truth, I'm not really sure my love," he replied as his wife scooted herself down, spreading her pussy, allowing him to see her creamy arousal just as it was starting to run out.

"It's not their fault they're on guard. Especially Jay, he's just trying to protect them. Those immature fucks got to them. It's annoying," he heard his wife whisper, sounding genuinely annoyed, causing him to glance up and study her face.

"Yes, it's very annoying. Those two, they're sexy as fuck, right?" he asked, seeing a fire in his wife's eyes, knowing she was envisioning scenarios where they would've taken the road trip with Jay and Karman before the other couples made them feel uncomfortable.

"Her lips, those sexy Latina lips. And that fat little ass she's always hiding in her loosey-goosey, conservative clothing. And she has perfect tits, just absolutely perfect," he heard his wife whisper, running her hands over her breast and stomach then back up again - undoubtedly picturing herself touching Karman.

"Just her?" he asked teasingly, staring at her entrance expectantly.

"And him, don't get me started. He doesn't know how sexy he is. Half Black, half Asian mix, with that curly fucking hair, curly fucking eyelashes, and that beautiful smile," he heard his wife whisper, seeing more of her creamy arousal run out, so much so that it was now touching the bed sheet, forming a thick, cream pool.

"Yes, go on, don't forget his lips. And remember, I told you I saw his dick at the strip club. It's big and thick. I'd say an inch and a half bigger than mine. He was so hard he couldn't pee right away. And baby, I think I forgot the part where he had to stand far back to keep his dick from touching the porcelain," he whispered, keeping his eyes locked onto her entrance, watching her pussy throb, followed by more arousal, which slowly ran down over her ass, colleting into the pool on the sheets.

"Fuck, it's not fair! They ruined it for us!" he heard his wife mumble, running her fingers over her pussy, coating them in arousal before bringing them towards his lips.

Opening his mouth, he sucked her fingers clean one by one, taking his time, enjoying her scent and taste, then replied, "Baby, don't be mad at immaturity. Think about it, if it weren't

28

for those peoples' lies, we wouldn't have even thought to ask to ride with them. They must've done something to give off the swinger vibe, and they obviously don't do it all the time, or we'd have seen it. If they are really giving off that vibe, maybe that's their inner them trying to escape, and maybe, just maybe, they'd be the perfect vanilla couple we could flip," he whispered.

"Do you think we really have a chance? I'm a little nervous," he heard his wife reply, inching herself down, bringing her pussy directly in front of his lips.

"I understand, I'm a little nervous too. But did you hear them last night? That's the vibe right there. They were calling to us. Begging for us to listen to them as they submitted to their primal desires. That, that has to mean something my love," he replied, laying a small kiss on his wife's pussy, closing his eyes, inhaling deeply, feeling his already hardening cock grow further.

"Yes, yes I heard them. That's why I'm nervous. Before last night, I wasn't sure I cared if we lost them. But now, now I care one hundred percent," he heard his wife whisper, running her fingers over her pussy, bringing them to his mouth when they were fully coated in her arousal.

"Oh, you're spoiling me today," Nate whispered, sucking his wife's fingers clean.

"Yes, of course my greedy one," he heard his wife reply as he moved his lips to her pussy, flicking his tongue over her clit.

"You taste so good, I'd hate if you didn't spoil me and give me my yummy," he whispered.

"So, you're starting to remember the other reasons why you love me? Me, allowing you to be greedy? Me, being your yummy?" he heard his wife ask with a moan.

"Hummm," he replied, with a soft chuckle, moving his tongue to her entrance, then back up to her clit, sucking firmly.

"I'll take that as a yes!" he heard his wife gasp, feeling her hands run through his hair, pressing his head down, causing him to suck her clit even harder.

I could never forget why I love you. You're my everything," Nate thought, feeling his wife squirm, hearing her gasp, "I love you my little pervert. I seriously love it when you always come and smell and taste my pussy."

"Mmm," he moaned, inching back, flicking his tongue over his wife's tender clit.

"Yes, my greedy one! You heard me, I love how you love eating my pussy! This is your pussy, you hear me my little pervert? This is your yummy!" he heard his wife gasp as she squirmed even more.

"I hear you baby," he replied, lifting his head, wanting to see the look of pure pleasure on his wife's face, before whispering, "What about Jay and Karman, isn't it going to be their pussy too?"

"Fuck, I wish. Last night, they sounded so fucking good. Mmmm…babyyyy. What are we going to do?" he heard his wife reply, wrapping her arms around her eyes as she placed one of her legs on his back, tugging so that he'd come eat her pussy again.

"Haha," he chuckled, rising and sitting Japanese style with her leg still on his shoulder.

"Hey, where's my tongue? And what's so funny?" he heard his wife ask, lifting her arms just enough to peek at him.

"Remember when we thought they were the most boring; 'vanilla' fucks we'd ever seen. Now we're head over heels with lust for them. It's too funny," he chuckled, kissing the inside of her calf.

"It's not! I want them! And I don't want to be stuck in the car with people I can't have for however many days we have left to get to Chicago," he heard his wife reply, moving her leg back, bringing her toe to his mouth for him to suck.

"Well, whatever we do, we're not going to rush them," he said, taking her big toe in his mouth right after.

"I don't want to rush them. I want them to come to us. But yesterday," he heard his wife begin, trailing off as she laid her arms down over her eyes again.

Sucking her toe just a little harder, he then slipped it from his mouth and ran kisses all along the rest of her foot, then asked, "But yesterday what?"

"Yesterday, he barely looked at me. I sat Indian style in that chair for I don't even know how long, and you know how many times I caught him trying to look?" he heard his wife ask, sounding genuinely sad.

"No baby. How many times?" he asked, inching closer, lifting her arms from around her eyes.

"Four, only four times did he try to steal a look at my pussy. After all those hours sitting like that. Mmmm, my fucking legs went dead I sat there so long. I did all that and only four times he looked. Baby, I think he still really doesn't like me," he heard his wife whisper with a pouty face that almost made him feel desperate to do something to rush Jay and Karman.

"Aww, baby. That's so not true," he replied, lowering his head, laying kisses over her pussy before bringing his head up again.

"Really, how do you know?" he heard his wife ask, raising her arms up in the air so that he'd come hug her.

"Because," he began as he inched himself up, "He was using the rear-view mirror to look at that sexy 'lil' pussy. And come on - Karman, her eyes were glued to your pussy the whole time you did her nails," he continued after she wrapped her arms around his neck.

"Really? The rear-view huh? And yeah, I saw her. At one point, I even saw her bite her bottom lip like this," he heard his wife reply, mimicking the way she'd seen Karman bite her lips.

"Yeah, you see, they like you. Don't worry about a thing," he said, taking hold of her thighs as he ran his dick back and forth over her clit.

"Sss-so good, oh, okay, I won't worry about a thing. We got this," he heard his wife whisper, taking hold of his dick, guiding it into her soaking wet entrance.

"Shit! I never get used to how good you feel," he gasped, shivering from the warmth and tightness enveloping his cock.

"Mmm, does that mean you're not going to hold back, and just cum for me?" he heard his wife ask, softly squeezing her pussy as she wrapped her legs around his ass, pulling him deeper.

"Oh God!" he gasped, feeling his dick surge with the temptation at her request.

"Yes baby, cum for me, don't hold it, just give it to me," Nate heard his wife beg in his ear, working her hips in circles as she continued to pull him deeper with her legs.

"Fuck! Baby wants me to fill that pussy huh? She wants to feel it leak out all day long, doesn't she?" he whispered, kissing her deeply as he released control, allowing himself to cum with such force he could already feel it surging past his shaft, running out all over his balls.

"Ah, yes!" he heard his wife gasp, feeling her hand grab his ass, while her legs released their grip.

"Oh, opening your legs...you want more huh?" he whispered, feeling his wife squeeze his ass and press in response, causing him to thrust.

Within seconds, a sticky, wet sucking sound filling the room, which made him say, "You hear that? That's us, that's our mix."

"Yeah, I hear it baby. And fuck, we smell so good," he heard his wife groan, pulling his head down, kissing him deeply as she ran her hands up and down his back.

"Yeah, I love it," he groaned, thrusting harder and harder.

"I love it when you cum in me! Give me more, you know it makes me cum, when you cum," he heard his wife whisper.

"More?" he asked, thrusting even harder.

"Yeah! Give me!" he heard his wife gasp, squeezing her pussy as she wrapped her legs around his ass, pulling him as deep as he could go.

"Ah! Shit I'm cumming!" he screamed, loving every ounce of warmth and tightness, releasing all control, feeling his cum rush into her again.

"Fuck! Baby!" he heard his wife scream, feeling her pussy throb on his dick.

"Yeah baby, cum on my dick! Cum on my dick for me," he replied, kissing her hungrily, as the both continued to cum.

Feeling both of their orgasms ease, Nate broke their kiss and moved his lips down to her breast, sucking them one by one before coming back up, making out with her again. After a few moments past of just kissing and grinding, purposely stirring their mix, his wife moved her head and began to giggle.

"Wasup' baby?" he asked.

"I wish Karman and Jay were here...I want to corrupt them. See if they'd eat my pussy, messy just like this," he heard his wife whisper, wrapping her legs around his ass, rubbing gently up and down his back.

"Mmm, I'd love to see that. Humm, do you think they would?" He asked, kissing her deeply again.

"I...I think maybe Karman would, I get the feeling she's just as freaky as us," he heard his wife whisper.

"Tell me what else you want," he whispered.

"I really, really want to suck Jay's dick...and I want to watch you fuck Karman from behind," he heard his wife reply, gently pressing his head down, presenting him one of her breast to suck.

"Tell me more about how you'd suck Jay's dick in front of me" he whispered, tracing his tongue around her nipple, before saying, "Tell me, what will you do when he cums? Would you show me before you swallow?"

"Maybe, or I might get greedy and want every drop for myself," Nate heard his wife reply as he ran kisses over her breast up to her neck.

"Oh, that's not fair, I'd make Karman show you mine," he replied, moving his lips from her neck to her lips, kissing her deeply, teasingly working himself back and forth, enjoying the feeling their mix.

"That's because she wouldn't be able to handle how much you...," he heard his wife begin after breaking their kiss when he heard a soft tap on the door, followed by Jay saying, "Hey guys, it's getting pretty late. Umm. You guys 'wanna' head out? Or...Ummm, we can stay here for the day. Check this place out a bit, I 'dunno'."

"Hey Jay! Sorry, we're just waking up! We'll get ready right away!" he said, staring at the rickety off-white door, noting the restless shadow bobbing back and forth underneath the door.

"Uhh, alright. See you guys...see you guys soon," he heard Jay respond sounding anxious, causing he and Rayya to both sigh in unison before he replied, "Alright Jay, see you soon."

"Baby! Baby, he sounds nervous! Oh, my fucking Allah, I'm going to fucking kill those people," he heard his wife say in a low harsh tone, taking him by the chin so that he could look her in the eyes.

"It's going to be alright, baby. Trust me, it's going to be alright," he replied, placing his forehead to hers, pecking her gently on the lips.

"Oh, yeah? How the fuck is it going to be alright? Tell me?" he heard his wife ask, looking away from him towards the door, running her tongue across her teeth, making her look predatorial.

"It's going to be alright because," he whispered, thinking, *"Why is it going to be alright?"*

"Mm-hmm, you don't know, do you?" he heard his wife press, exhaling heavily before turning to face him with a look of pure aggravation.

"No, I don't know. But I know that what happened last night wouldn't have happened if they weren't willing to open up. We don't need to force them. We just need to convince them," he whispered, inching himself back.

"And how are we going to do that?" he heard his wife ask, pulling him back down with a, 'where are you going' look.

"By showing them that the way we think, and the way we're living our life is the best way," he replied as an idea began to form in his mind, causing him to smile.

"Mmm, my baby has a plan. I like that look on your face," Nate heard his wife whisper, wrapping her arms around his neck, bringing his head down, giving him a deep, long kiss before saying, "Okay, let's go."

Chapter IV

He Talks … A Lot

Road Trip: Day Two

Date: Friday, June 2nd 2017

Time: 11:40 am

Location: On The Outskirts of Missoula, Mt.

"What the fuck is taking them so long?" Jay whispered, pacing back and forth behind the SUV thinking, *"Why am I so aggravated? I know they were fucking when I knocked. And I know it takes a while to clean up. Hell, it took us a while too. So why am I so pissed? And where the hell is wifey, she said she was going to change a half hour ago,"* he thought, looking at his phone, then up at the blaring sun beaming down on him.

"Fuck, she was right. I should've brought my sunglasses," Jay whispered, squinting and placing his hand above his eyes, when he heard his wife, Karman say, "Here baby, I brought your sunglasses for you, I knew you weren't going to listen," from behind.

"Huh? Oh, hey boo," Jay replied, turning around, feeling his heart leap into his chest, taking in the sight of his wife's baby-blue, spandex booty shorts, which were almost just as reveling as the one's Rayya had on the day prior.

"Here baby, take the glasses, and stop staring at me like that, you're making me feel awkward. And sorry for yesterday, when I didn't ask you where you wanted to sit. I know I never ask, and just tell you what to do. So…" he heard his wife begin to say when he cut her off and said, "No problem, today, I'll sit in the back with Nate."

"Really? I know you hate sitting in the back of your own car, so if…" he heard his wife begin.

"Boo, you're being way too nice. I know you want to sit up front with ya girl, so you two can be booty short twins," he said cutting her off again.

"Huh? Nooo," he heard his wife reply with a bright smile as he took his sunglasses from her hand, placing them on his face.

"Yeah, whatever," Jay whispered, walking around his wife, checking out her features in her new apparel before saying, "In our six years of marriage, I've never seen you wear anything like this. Why today? What's up?"

"Mmm, nothing hubby. I just wanted to try it, I 'dunno'," he heard his wife reply, sounding annoyed as he ran his hand over her ass, tracing her thong from the small of her back down to the crease of her ass.

"Why you 'getting' annoyed at me. Why can't I ask what's on my 'wifey's' mind?" Jay asked, taking hold of her waist, turning his wife to look at the design of her thong through the spandex.

"Because," he heard his wife mumble, sounding almost childish as she turned her scowl to a teasing smile.

"Because, you think your hubby would get mad or annoyed at your choice of clothing? Psss...why would I? I love it. You look sexy as fuck. And I know why you're wearing that thong instead of no panties. And it's not because you're being shy, you've already gone too far to have cared. So, my thought is that something's leaking, huh? You needed a 'lil' pad huh?" he said teasingly, kissing her on the forehead, noting that for the first time since they'd been together, she was wearing a tank top – and had not tried to cover up her arms with a summer shawl.

"Unh-huh, it's messy," he heard his wife reply, taking hold of his arm, pressing herself to it, looking up at him with a cheerful smile.

"I had a good time last night. I really liked fucking you with them screaming and shit in the background," he said, kissing her softly on the lips.

"Yeah, it was really sexy. They really turned me on, especially hearing Rayya moan. It's, it's making me wet just thinking about it," he heard his wife reply, laying kisses on the side of his arm.

"Wet huh? How can you tell what's what with all my stuff in there?" he asked, thinking, *"And this morning, I could hear her begging him to cum through the door. God, I wish we could open up to them. But it's so hard to trust people."*

"Hey love birds! Sorry to keep you two waiting, we overslept and then it took us a 'lil' while to get ourselves together," Jay heard Rayya say, coming from around the SUV, walking directly towards he and Karman with her cheek already moving to the side for them to kiss.

"Hey girl? Ready to drive?" he heard his wife ask, pecking Rayya on the cheek as he thought, *"Oh, Holly 'It'! This is going to be more torture than yesterday!"* taking in the details of Rayya's white, see through spandex booty shorts, bright red thong, and bright red belly halter top, with no bra holding her C-cup breast.

"I'm ready, but you're driving first. Come Jay, kiss-kiss," he heard Rayya say, seeming to sense his hesitation as he slowly moved his head down to kiss her on the cheek, trying to completely avert his eyes away from her breast.

"Sure, I'll drive first, you lazy 'lil' Chica," he heard his wife reply with a giggle, all of a sudden hearing Nate say, "Hey guys, apologies...the hour it took us was all my fault."

"I highly doubt that. From what I've heard, both of you are to blame," he thought, feeling awkward, quickly pecking Rayya's cheek to get it over with, only to see a small, knowing smirk appear on Nate's lips before it vanished.

"Yup, you drive, and guys in the back! That's right I called shot gun," he heard Rayya tease, running to the other side of the SUV, almost losing her white, Glider sandals.

"Easy now 'Sanderalla'," he heard Nate say, chuckling as he nodded to him, shaking his head as if to say, 'this woman.'

"That woman is right. I think she's aiming to torture me! And now she'd influenced wifey to do the same!" he thought as he said, "Boo, pop the trunk so Nate can throw their bag in."

"K' hubby," he heard his wife reply, opening the driver side door, bending over to press the button for the trunk, sparking him to look over to Nate and bob his head towards his wife's ass, thinking, *"If you want me to look at your wife's ass, this is how you tell me you clown."*

In response, he saw Nate simply smirk - without even the slightest eye or head movement towards his wife's ass before saying, "Thanks Karman, got it," tossing the bag in the trunk before closing it.

"What's with this guy? I don't get it? Why didn't he look just now? His wife is blatantly being a voyeur. Two days of sexy, revealing clothes is not a fluke. And I've had all morning to think about his leading look and how everything went down with Rayya sitting cross-legged, directly in my line of sight for if, and when I turned around. So, what gives?" he thought, feeling annoyed as he opened the door, hopping in the back seat behind his wife.

"Seriously though, what gives? I'm certain they're voyeurs, feeding off of our energy. Hell! I'm even willing to bet that wifey and I being flustered over her outfit is what sent them into that fuck frenzy they had last night. Not that I'm mad at that. Hearing them and feeding off of it was fun. But why didn't he look just now? Was that a show of dominance? Like as if to say, he'll watch me lose control over his wife, but he won't give me the honor of watching him lose control over mine? Fuck! If that's what it is, then here we go again with another couple's competition!" he thought, feeling a flash of anger as Nate hopped in, hearing him ask, "Hey man, are you alright?"

"Yeah man, I'm alright," he answered, knowing he sounded absent.

"Wifey wants us to behave, but I'm getting tired of pretending we're nice. If these two really start becoming manipulative fucks, then...damn, Rayya smells good! Oh, fuck me! I've already reacted, and its supper obvious!" Jay thought, shaking his head in disappointment at himself due to the fact that he'd full on turned towards Rayya to drink in the warm, sublet scent of vanilla coming off of her.

"You sure man? We can stop at the drug store if the trees are fucking your face again," he heard Nate respond nonchalantly, causing he and both women to burst out laughing.

"Oh man! Shit! That caught me off guard," he said, still chuckling as he thought, *"Why am I so upset with the fact that they're playing voyeur games? How does it hurt us? Last night was fucking amazing. And if wifey wants to show off her sexiness because of Rayya, where's the harm in that? In the end, I'm the main person that benefits from it. Then it'd be them I'd need to thank for being the final nudge, helping her to step out of her comfort zone."*

"Actually, can we go to the drug store? I need thong, panty liners. I'm dumb, I realized I only packed one liner and the rest, might as well be diapers," he heard Rayya say with a chuckle, jarring him out of his thoughts, where he must've looked bewildered, because Nate tapped him on the arm and said, "Relax my friend. Now that you're getting to know us, you'll find that Rayya has no filter."

"I'm relaxed," he blurted way too fast for his liking as his wife started the SUV, and said "Use mine, I'll give you some when we get to the next rest stop, it'll probably be time for me to change mine by then anyway."

"Aww! Okay! Thanks girl! Ah haha! And after this morning, the rest stop needs to be sooner rather than later," he heard Rayya reply, flashing he and his wife a mischievous grin

"I bet girl, I'm right there with you," he heard his wife reply, reaching out, pinching Rayya on the cheek.

"Wow, this conversation is out of control, and I love it!" he thought, hearing Rayya say, "Trust me, I heard y'all last night, I know."

"See, no filter. Wifey, do you even check to see if everyone's willing to talk about their personal life," he heard Nate say in a 'tutoring' tone, feeling his hand rest on his shoulder in an apparent attempt to reassure him that he wouldn't let the conversation go too far if he was uncomfortable with it.

"I'm good," he replied, trying to sound calm, and in control.

"See he's good. And what's with this word, 'personal' as if Karman and I don't go get Brazilians done together? Also, do you think we wait for different change rooms when we go try on clothes or go to the spa? Pfft, all that personal stuff, most of the time, that is with you men," he heard Rayya say, pausing for only a short moment before saying, "So, girl was it good? We heard y'all and we were like, 'Yassss'! So, wait, maybe I should rephrase it to, did y'all get any sleep, 'cuz' when it's that good, it's hard to take a break!"

"Jay, really, please excuse my boo," he heard Nate say in a tone that caused him to look away from Rayya, finding Nate looking extremely apprehensive.

"Na man, seriously no worries. I'm from New York. This 'kinda' 'convo' is actually normal for me. Only when I moved to Bellevue did I start having to bite my tongue," he said as he thought, *"Every time we've opened up to anyone in Bellevue, it always bites us in the ass. I'm surprised 'wifey's' going along with this conversation. Does she agree with Rayya, and feel that because of the things they've done together, there's no need for boundaries right now? If so, then I don't get her logic. All the women who've back stabbed us before…they've all done the whole Brazilians, go to spas, and changing clothes together stuff too. What's different about Rayya that'd she trust her?"*

"Ah, true. Same in Chicago. Bellevue is a new city my man, with lots of new money. A lot of the people there, you have to give them the benefit of the doubt. New city, new life, everyone wants to appear a certain way to each other. You know what I mean?" he heard Nate say as his wife pulled out onto the open highway, gunning it, giving him a rush of excitement at the bottom of his belly.

"Yeah, at the expense of others," he said bitterly, keeping his ears locked in on the conversation between Rayya and his wife, hearing his wife say, "Noooo, it was you two who sounded good, we woke up and started playing because we heard y'all."

"Yeah man, at the expense of others. But that's human nature. I think it's just the way they're going about it that's pissing you off. In the cities where we grew up, everything was at the expense of others as well. But it was more straightforward. People held real weapons to our faces. Where we live now, it's all passive aggressive. And the guns and knives are lies and deceit, all coated with smiles and kind words. So yeah, I get you my man, I get you. Anyways, what I was getting at was…what was I getting at?" he heard Nate say with an absent look flashing across his face, causing him to laugh.

"You were worried about me being offended about Rayya and wifey talking about our sex life. And yeah, you're right about the new city thing, and where we come from situation," he replied, hearing Rayya whisper, "Was it a lot? Nate cums a lot, a lot, every…single…time."

"You don't need to whisper. I really don't care," he said feeling annoyed that he was being treated like he couldn't handle the conversation.

"Oh, okay then. Nate comes a lot. And it feels really squishy right now. Ah boy, I'm going to need to get a new liner even before we leave the city for sure," he heard Rayya say, turning and flashing him a mischievous smile before facing forward, placing her feet on the dash.

"This chick," he thought, shaking his head, laughing before replying, "You're something else."

"You're something else," he heard Rayya mockingly reply in the same dry tone he'd used, turning to look at his wife with a, 'Haha' smile, before looking towards him saying, "What's with that voice? You always like to use that 'you're in control voice' when you talk. I know it's not how you really sound, not after what I heard last night. Humm, if that 'in control voice' was your norm, last night Nate and I would've heard, Oooh, zero one, ooooh, zero one, Ohh, zero one, that pussyyyy, my circuits, my circuits, overload, overload."

"Pfft. Ahh Rayya," he said, trying to not burst out laughing – like everyone else.

"Okay fine, want sex talk? What do you guys want to know about us?" Jay said after everyone settled down, surprising even himself.

"Ouh! How many times did you cum? And how long can you las…" Jay heard Rayya begin when he heard Nate cut in and say, "Rayya," in a stern voice with an, 'I'm sorry' look.

"It's all good bro," he replied, shaking his head laughing.

"See, baby…Jay's fine," he heard Rayya say in a darkened tone.

"Okay, okay," he heard Nate reply, with a few head bobs and a hand gesture that said, 'fine answer her question'.

"Okay, ummm. Fuck, now that I'm on the spot, I'm answer shy. Can I come back to it?" he replied feeling a flash of heat as he tried to conjure up words for Rayya's questions.

"Sure, sure," he heard Rayya reply with a giggle, also seeing that his wife was laughing as well.

"Assholes," he whispered, smiling at Nate who returned it, but from what he could tell, held no truth behind it.

"Wasup' bro?" he asked, wanting to unkink Nate's mood.

"I, actually also have a sex question," he heard Nate reply in a low voice.

"Ohhh, okay bro, shoot then," he replied, trying to understand why he felt so many contradicting moods from Nate.

"What do you love about Karman?" he heard Nate ask in a neutral tone.

"Oh…ummm," he muttered as he thought, *"How the fuck is that a sex question!?"* feeling a flash of heat as the pressure to answer the question correctly quickly weighed down on him.

"Yeah baby, what do you love about me?" he heard his wife ask right after, adding even more pressure as he thought, *"What the fuck! Is this dude trying to dig me into an 'It' damned grave or something!?"*

"Nate?" he heard Rayya whisper in a soft, casual tone he knew from years of personal experience was her way of saying - 'what the fuck!? Don't fucking ask questions like that!'

"Yeah man, what the fuck is right. Even your wife knows this 'ain't' cool!" he thought as he said, "Umm her smile and her…"

"Here we go," he heard Nate cut in, sounding disappointed, placing his hand to his head as if he had a migraine before turning away from him, opening the window.

"Here we go what?" he asked feeling his temper starting to rise, sensing a high and mighty, judgmental vibe starting to rise off of Nate.

"Jay, don't mind Nate, he's just, he's just…" he heard Rayya say, without finishing.

"No Rayya, let Jay answer, I want to hear it," he heard his wife say, sounding annoyed, causing the small amount of words forming in his mind to disintegrate.

"Here we go what?" he pressed, realizing his New York tone and demeanor had slipped out to the point where he was now leaning forwards, tilting to the right as if he were about to attack Nate in the corner of the car.

"Excuse bro, I apologize. Truly, I apologize. And yeah, you caught me. I was being judgmental. But not to you, 'cuz'…" he heard Nate whisper, trailing off, giving him an apprehensive look, before gazing out the window.

"I don't know how to explain," he heard Nate begin again, so low in tone Jay felt he were speaking more to himself.

"Well you better fucking try!" he thought sitting back, taking a deep breath, allowing his mind to digest Nate's apology and tone for sincerity before saying, "Na man, it's cool. It's just…"

"It's just, you're real man. You know? You're one of the realist people I know. So, when I heard you begin to answer, I know there's more to it. And then I realized it's not any of my business," he heard Nate cut in, causing his eye to twitch.

"Well you're right, It's not your business. Sex talk, sure, I'm cool with that, but your question…" he began when Nate turned to him with his hands raised in surrender, causing him to stop.

"Hear me out, what I'm going to say is – well, it might be a little hard. Actually, you know what? For you and for Karman, it won't be. Just…"

"Alright, shoot, go for it," he cut in, titling his body towards Nate, showing that he had his undivided attention as he thought, *"By now…I'd have picked up some fucked-up intention from him if he meant ill will. But he's trying to really be chill. And if he really wanted to put a rift between wifey and I, there are way easier ways."*

"When you love someone, like really love someone, that's the sexiest thing there is. I mean, of course there are the external things too it as well. Like looks, smell, taste, and so on and so forth. But with those external things, there's the emotion. The real current of love, the real drive behind the sex, the real meaning behind the passion," he heard Nate say, nodding his head as if to say, 'thank you for letting me speak', before saying, "Does, does that make sense?"

"K', I get that," he replied, trying to process the true emotions he felt for Karman after hearing Nate's explanation.

"I know you do. That's why I got annoyed," he heard Nate whisper, raising his hands in surrender expectantly before saying, "And, although it's not really my place to put you on the spot and hold you accountable for that. I was really looking forward to enjoying this road trip with my guard down, and I figured you'd like that too. So, I was hoping, I was hoping that if I asked you that, you'd open up. Open up more than yesterday, with all that sports, bullshit talk. I figured it'd be easier if I asked you to talk about something – well I should say, someone you really love and are passionate about, and that I'd get to hear a real, heartfelt answer."

"How do I feel about wifey? What's the emotion below the surface? How does she make me feel? I love her to death. But she fucking frustrates

me at every turn. But then, if I'm not near her, I get lonely, I feel lost. And if I picture her dying or not in my life, I picture myself breaking down - lost and alone, unable to move on. And when I have sex with her, every time feels new - like I'm rediscovering some lost part of myself by being with her."

"I feel my body relax, but charge up all at the same time. I feel my mind go at ease, but sharpen to a point of perfect focus. Being with her, loving her, there's always this strange merge of opposites that somehow become one. Like the literal meaning of man and woman. Opposites, but together as one," he thought, barely hearing his wife say, "Jay? Earth to Jay! Jay!"

"Karman, sweetie," he heard Rayya whisper, followed by something inaudible because he'd already returned to his inner thoughts.

"I see, I see what you mean now. But, you have to understand. I get tired of opening up to people. Tired of being stabbed by smiling faces and kind words. Besides, what you asked, I really didn't have words for, till now anyway. But thank you for helping me. I think I can form them now," he said, taking a deep breath, nodding his head to Nate as he thought, *"There's no harm in saying what I want to say in front of them. Why not?"*

"Thank you for listening to me my man, giving me a chance to explain," he heard Nate say, nodding his head before putting his hand on his wife's shoulder, whispering, "Sorry Karman, I shouldn't have done that to either of you. Forgive me. I know after your past road trips, you two are having a difficult time opening up to people. And maybe now you feel on guard again, but…"

"What I love about Karman," he interjected causing Rayya to spin in her seat and Nate to pause and look at him.

"What I love about her. Huh, it's funny because what I love about her, I hate about her," he said turning his gaze towards the floor as he chewed his bottom lip, choosing his next words carefully.

"I love how she can sweep me off my feet and scatter all my thoughts. Yet, I also hate it. Hate it because in those moments, she's just taken control of me, and shown me that I'm not as solid and stable as I thought I was," he said, pausing for a brief moment before saying, "And I love how she feels secure in my arms, yet makes me feel insecure and doubt myself, all while she looks into my eyes for direction."

"Baby," he heard his wife whisper.

"Knowing she feels security in me, there's no greater feeling than that. Because she's my baby, my responsibility. She trusts me whole heartedly to take care of her in every situation, from the worst to the happiest. And for her to have that kind of trust in me, for anyone to have that kind of trust in me, well then, the words for that do become almost indescribable emotion," he said, looking up, focusing his eyes on the center of the head rest.

"So, what I love about her, is the fulfilment I feel in my soul when she shows me that she has absolute trust in me. What I love about her, is that she shakes my foundation, keeping me on my toes, so that I'm never complacent about my need and desire to be her foundation. She keeps me grounded, humble, and careful of our vulnerability to destruction from both outside and inside forces. Yet, she gives me the energy to protect her, and to protect us with that same trust. With that same instability," Jay said, feeling his voice crack and tears well up in his eyes.

"Baby, it's okay, you don't have to answer, I'm sorry," he heard his wife whisper.

"I love her because of her energy. Boundless, boundless fucking energy. You know? She's always like - baby let's do this, baby let's do that. I could never be bored or sit still even if I tried. And other than when she's being a fire-dragon, because she's a big ass brat, she's literally always happy. Always bright, when there's no reason to be bright. Giving me this, this energy…yeah energy is all I can describe it as," Jay whispered, taking hold of his shaky voice, blinking away his tears, looking up towards Nate, giving him a wry- 'that's it' smile.

"I, umm, that was," he heard Nate whisper, nodding his head, clamping him on the shoulder as if to say, 'I'm sorry.'

"Psst, you think I'm a wimp? Get off me, you ass," he replied, feeling like a weight he'd been carrying his whole relationship had just been lifted.

"No, not at all, I just…" he heard Nate say trailing off, looking towards Karman.

Jay heard no sob's but could tell his wife was crying from both intuitive feeling, and because she was no longer driving like her normal manically, speed demon self.

"Hey sweetie, pull over here, let's go to the store, get some drinks. And you know what, I'll drive for a while, with Nate in the front. How's that sound, 'K' sweetie?" he heard Rayya say, seeing her place her hand on his wife's shoulder.

"Oh, okay," he heard his wife stutter, with soft sniffle, causing the tears he'd been fighting back to reform in his eyes.

"Hey man, again, I'm…" he heard Nate begin.

"Na fam, it wasn't welcome when it came, but, thank you all the same," he cut in.

"Really, I meant the best when I asked you that question," he heard Nate whisper.

"I know fam," he replied, nodding his head, looking away from Nate, staring out the window, thinking, *"So, that's what it feels like to tap directly into love. As uncomfortable as that situation was, I'm truly grateful for it."*

Chapter V

Subtle Is Force

Road Trip: Day Three

Date: Saturday, June 3rd 2017

Time: 1:00 am

Location: Bismarck, North Dakota

"What did we just do? Nate, baby, thirteen hours. They barely said a word to each other or us in thirteen hours. Baby, baby, are you listening?" Nate heard his wife, Rayya say the moment they stepped into the hotel room and closed the door, but he was too lost in thought to answer.

"Never in my life have I been this excited by a couple. Their potential is limitless, and I want Rayya and I to be the catalyst to their growth and usher them into their new life. I can't believe this, but I'm truly frightened. They're at the very edge. The spot where they can step of the cliff and fly into the horizon with us - or plummet - plummet down into the depths of their mundane, stale existence. We must be careful not to drive them down, while still maintaining the same level of pressure, if not more, so that they truly become a diamond. We need, we need to be subtle. Yes, subtle is force."

"We need a distraction. Oh baby, that desk girl, she was flirting really hard, let's go try and bring her here so we don't need to think," he heard his wife say, cutting into his thoughts, bringing him back to reality.

"Baby, baby, get out of your head. I think we need a distraction," Nate heard his wife repeat, tugging him in front of the full-length mirror by the door as she looked herself over.

"I'm back," he replied, placing his hands on her waist, before moving his right hand over her belly, kissing her on the cheek and temple.

"What did my brainy come up with?" he heard his wife ask in a hushed voice, leaning back against him as he hugged her tightly.

"That you're the most beautiful woman in the world, and that there's never a need for you to consult with a mirror," he

47

replied, inching his hand down from her belly, underneath her shorts and thong.

"Aww, and what else did your brainy come up with?" he heard his wife whisper as he began to massage her clit, loving the feeling of her arousal and sweat coating his fingers.

"Brainy says that they're adjusting, because what Jay said to her was no small matter, and that they need time to absorb those type of emotions. In a way, they've fallen into a kind of love trance," he replied, bringing his hands to his nose, chuckling because he could smell her scent way before his hand came up.

"Oh Allah, that's pretty stinky. I need a shower after sitting that long. Baby, baby don't lick - never mind. Such a little 'perv'," he heard his wife say with a giggle, smiling brightly in the mirror as she watched him put his fingers in his mouth.

"So, how does, 'sitting in a car for way too long', pussy taste? And a love trance you say?" he heard his wife ask, turning to face him, smiling mischievously as he rolled his tongue in his mouth, loving her salty, sweet flavor.

"You're really, really yummy. Are you sure you need to take a shower? You know I like it when you're hot and sweaty," he said kissing his wife softly on the lips before pulling back, studying her face.

"Hubby?" he heard his wife ask with a curious expression.

"What did you notice about them the whole ride? Did you notice how peaceful they were? Or that she slept on his arm for hours at a time, while he stayed awake and watched her?" he said, smiling as he had a flash back of the couple.

"Yeah, I noticed. It was cute. Especially how he'd run his fingers over her cheeks, or how he gently stroke and move hair from her face," he heard his wife say, rubbing her head on his chest before tilting back so that he could kiss her forehead.

"My love, they didn't need to talk yesterday, not one bit. They were fully in sync with each other. Most likely feeling the way they'd felt when they first meet."

"I get it, but…How do I say this? Okay, I just have this feeling they'll hate us for putting them through that. I mean sure, they might feel good now. Or may even continue to feel that way. But to them, we might be the bringers of pain. People, myself included, don't like to feel pain, even if it's beneficial, and

48

will quickly disassociate themselves with that pain. If I were them, then I would definitely disassociate with us," he heard his wife say, forming her lips into a frown which made him kiss her again.

"You're not wrong. But let's be optimistic, and let's not over think. You're right, we need a distraction," he said, moving his lips back to hover over hers so that he could peck them over and over as he spoke.

"Yeah, let's go talk to the desk girl, I could tell she really liked us. Especially you, since she was eye fucking you the moment we walked in," he heard his wife reply, sounding slightly more cheerful.

"Yeah let's go for it. If not, then let's keep our eyes open," he replied remembering that the desk clerk looked as if she were about to get off work.

"Humm, did baby see someone else? You're always so observant, my little hunter. What would I do without you?" he heard his wife whisper, wrapping her arms around his neck, kissing him deeply causing his whole body to grow warm.

"I saw a few sleepy travelers heading to the bar, dinner place right next door. If the desk girl is busy, we can always go there and find us a sexy someone," he replied after their kiss broke, now seeing a look of concern play across his wife's face.

"My love, don't worry okay, we don't need to force them. We just need to guide them with suggestions. And then you'll see, they'll start making suggestions back. Let's be patient with them. Remember how we used to be before we met Ella and Carl?" he said, opening the door, guiding her out into the hallway.

"Oh Allah. Yeah, we swore we'd never speak to them again, and…and thank you baby! You always know just what to say!" he heard his wife shriek, hugging him tightly before turning and bounding down the hallway, leaving him far behind.

"I didn't want to disappoint her, but that desk girl seemed liked she was getting off soon. And that place next door has probably already wound down, meaning there's only the strange characters left. With any luck though, the desk girl is still there," he thought, seeing his wife come to a standstill where the hallway opened up into the lounge.

"What's wrong? Oh," Nate said to his wife almost under his breath, now finding himself nodding his head to Karman, who was sitting in a single seat lounge chair halfway facing them, and halfway facing the front desk as Jay came to her side with a Styrofoam cup of something steaming.

"That look in her eyes scares me a little bit. It's not exactly angry, but it's not exactly friendly either," he thought watching Karman bob her head back at him very subtly as if to say, 'I acknowledge your presence', but that's about it.

"Hi guys, what are you two doing out here?" he heard his wife ask, walking over towards the chair, giving them about four feet of distance.

"Her giving that much space!? My boo is spooked too," he thought, looking over towards the desk girl, finding her staring and smiling at him as she slowly placed her Tupperware and other effects into a plastic bag.

"Damn it, she's waiting for us to come," he thought as Jay made his way over to him and said, "Hey man, can I talk to you for a sec?"

"Sure, of course," he replied, tipping his head towards the woman at the desk, whose face went cheery to disappointed as he turned to give Jay his complete attention.

"Look, I wanted to clear the air a bit," he heard Jay begin, pausing and looking past him towards the woman at the desk, who he could feel was now burning a hole into the back of his neck.

"If I don't show him one hundred percent attention and I stare at her while he's talking, he'll sense it and think I don't fully care about what he has to say. And flirting with her on the off chance she'll come with us for a good time is not worth fucking this up."

"You okay?" he asked, sensing Jay had lost his train of thought as he continued to look past him at the desk clerk.

"Fuck, from the way my neck feels and from the way Jay's looks, she really would have come with us. But now, yeah, it's definitely too late. I just felt your look of death across my spine and Jay caught you giving it to me. And now he's watching you leave, wondering what we did to you."

"Yeah, umm, I'm okay," he heard Jay respond, looking him in the eyes.

"Good, good," he replied, letting out a slow breath.

"Look, when I say I wanted to clear the air. I wanted to say that - I'm not stupid. Well, that we're not stupid," he heard Jay say, without any trace of anger in his voice, causing him to involuntary tighten his stomach.

"Jay, I never said," he began when Jay rested his hand on his shoulder and said, "We don't like…What's the word I'm looking for? Humm. We don't like being controlled. We both know something's up with you two, and that's all well and good. But that shit you pulled, with that love question, that was a 'lil' over the top."

"Look Jay, I apologize," he began when Jay snickered and brought his hand back to his side, giving him a knowing, 'sure, whatever you say' look.

"I really meant no harm. I just," he began.

"Want to control us," he heard Jay finish for him, causing him to think and almost scream, *"To set you free!"*

"What makes you say that?" he asked instead.

"Oh, come on, you think we're blind? Rayya is almost naked, and you were leading me to look at her. You think we don't know what voyeurs are? Feeding off our fucking energy. You think we don't know what that sex in the room was about? You think we're dumb?" he heard Jay ask, finally showing small signs of aggravation but otherwise mostly keeping his voice and posture neutral or with a small smile.

"Jay…I'll admit. We umm, we do have a voyeur side and we…"

"Look man," he heard Jay cut in.

"Please let me finish," he said, finally growing annoyed at being cut off so many times.

"Finish, and say what? Something to manipulate me? If there's one thing I know since moving to Bellevue, with people that never completely show their emotions, is that the best way to control someone, is to lead them subtly to the conclusion they want the person to believe. So, all I really want to know is, what the hell do you two really want? The rest of anything you have to say is bullshit, pure bullshit. And by the way, if you want to look at my wife's ass, just look at her fucking ass. I'm for sure looking at your wife's fucking ass, and her tits, and everything else. So there, you happy? You voyeurs are getting the attention you wanted?" he heard Jay say while taking a step back, looking at

Karman, who was now talking to his wife, before turning back towards him with smile that looked more like a snarl.

"God, he's sexy when he's serious. That face makes me want to bite his lips. And I love how intelligent he is. No, how intelligent they are. They're all over us, sensing and anticipating our every move. But to what degree? I'd expect way more anger than the look I'm seeing now. And now that I think about it, that look on Karman's face was more a look of disappointment than anything else. Disappointment! That's what this is! They're both disappointed, not angry! Could it be that we're simply having communication issues," he thought looking between Jay and Karman a few more times.

"Okay, that's a start. Now you're looking at her. Yeah, that's a little better. Anyways, you two have a good night, and the food over there in that dive of a place is actually pretty good. Well, from the two bites we've eaten from our take-out. But hey, if you're going to go, go now, the waitress told us the kitchen was about to close," he heard Jay say, now sounding calm and happy, which completely confused him.

"Huh? Oh, oh okay," he said watching Jay stroll over to Karman with his hand out for her to take.

"And just like that, he swung back to calm, cool, and collect. And even offered friendly advice. This is a new side of him I'm seeing, and it's making me hot! God, I can't wait to tell Rayya this. She loves men with deep, dark sides just burning below the surface."

"Have a good night guys," he heard Karman say in a soft, almost shy voice as she took Jay's hand and rose from the chair.

"Have a good night," he replied almost in unison with his wife, who flopped into the chair right after Karman stood.

Afterward, he watched the couple breeze by him without either one taking even a small, side long glance.

"They're in perfect sync with each other. And right now, no one else in the world matters to them but them. It's absolutely beautiful!" he thought, walking up to his wife with a giant smile he couldn't suppress even if he tried.

"My love? Are we in the same dimension? How can you be smiling? They hate us," he heard his wife whisper, giving him a look of pure disdain.

"My baby," he whispered, taking a deep breath as he crouched down in front of her, taking her hands in his, kissing them softly as he looked in her the eyes.

"Yes, my love?" he heard his wife reply, leaning forward intently, keeping her eyes locked with his.

"They don't hate us. Not at all," he said feeling a tingly, butterfly sensation in the base of his stomach as he thought of the words to explain what his gut feeling was telling him.

"Well, I couldn't hear everything he said to you, but it didn't sound friendly. And my talk with Karman was her handling me in the calmest possible manner," he heard his wife whisper, moving her head down, kissing his fingers, hands, and finally forehead before saying, "But I trust you. So, tell me, if they don't hate us, what's going on?"

"Well, they don't hate us, but right now, they really don't like us," he said bursting out laughing, causing his wife to push him and tumble onto his back.

"Not funny, not funny at all! Tell me what's going on," he heard his wife say, flopping on top of him, tickling his stomach as he continued to laugh.

"Ahh... Ahh! Okay...stop, stop, stop! I'll tell you, just stop, stop, stop," he pleaded, laughing harder and she continued to tickle him.

"Tell me or so help you, the next time we go to Lebanon, I'm bringing you to my father's grave, so he can come out and kill you," he heard his wife say, biting his triceps and arm.

"Mmm, it was something he said that made me realize they don't hate us," he gasped from the pleasure of being tickled and pain of being bitten.

"And?" he heard his wife press, biting his triceps again.

"And, I think we're having communication issues," he said, forcing himself up, then tackling her to the ground.

"What kind of..." he heard his wife ask before he drove his tongue into her mouth, cutting her off, kissing her deeply.

"Hey love birds, you mind? That's what the rooms are for," he heard a male voice say in a horse, raspy tone, giving him the impression that the speaker was a smoker, and at least sixty years of age.

"Oh, excuse," he replied, quickly looking in the direction of the voice to find an elderly man who appeared to be a mix of native American and Caucasian glaring down at them with a look between amusement and annoyance.

"Excused huh? That you are. Take all this P.D.A to the room. If I wanted to watch porn, I'd bring it up on that tablet thing my son gave me for Christmas. If only I knew how to open the damned thing," he heard the man whose name tag read John say, trailing off towards the end, walking off as if they weren't even there.

"Okay, sorry John," he blared, standing up with his hand out for Rayya to take.

"You would be sorry, but I caught the last part of your little spiel with your friends and called over to the bar for you two love birds. I took it upon myself and ordered a bunch of wings. Can't go wrong with that can 'ya?" he heard John reply, not even bothering to look up from whatever he was doing at the desk.

"You ummm…thank you," he replied, pulling as Rayya tugged his hand and stood, staring at the man as if she'd seen a ghost.

"Un-hun, Un-hun. 'Any who', Reggie will be over in a bit, he'll drop off the food to your room. Can you two wait, with all the fooling around 'till' then? Pa-haha! From what I just saw, I don't even know why I bothered to ask," he heard John say, shaking his head as he laughed, still not bothering to look up from the desk as he moved to the computer, pecking the keys one at a time.

"Oh, okay. Wait, umm, we're in room one thirty-six, and thank you again," he said, feeling awkward as he began to walk towards the hallway with his wife still holding his hand.

"Yeah, I know what room you're in, trust me. I know what room you're in," he heard John say, finally looking up with a wicked grin as he raised a yellow post-it with the number one thirty-six, and a heart drawn around it.

"Oh, shit," he heard his wife whisper, sounding stung.

"Oh, shit, is right," he also whispered, tipping his head to John before looking away.

"This night is full of surprises and disappointment. But you can't always have everything go your way. If it did, then where would the fun in life be?"

Chapter VI

Work Up

Road Trip: Day Three

Date: Saturday, June 3rd 2017

Time: 1:30 am

Location: Bismarck, North Dakota

The walk back to the room felt fast and slow to Rayya, and as Nate opened the door, she felt the weight of the day fully settle on her shoulders. Staring at the empty bed, she wished they had at least one extra person to share it with.

"We fucked up big time. We got too excited and pushed them way too fast," she thought, removing her halter top, placing it on the chair beside the bed, letting out a, long, low, sigh.

"I love you boo," she heard her husband say reassuringly from the restroom, causing her to smile as she flopped down onto the foot of the bed, kicking off her sandals.

"I love you too," she replied, massaging her breast, looking towards the restroom as she heard Nate's final drops of urine splash into the bowl before saying, "Nate, baby, can you rub my feet, and can you tell me what you were saying about us having communication issues with them."

"Of course my love, anything for you," she heard her husband reply, emerging from the restroom with a bright, knowing smile as he came up to her and kneeled, taking her right foot in his hand, bringing it up to his lips, kissing it.

"You always know how to make me feel better," she whispered, closing her eyes, enjoying the sensation as her husband continued to kiss her foot several more times.

"But my baby doesn't feel all that much better," she heard her husband reply, working his thumb into the arch of her foot.

"I feel like we're off of our game," she replied, flopping back as the tension in her foot eased.

"I know! It's exciting isn't it? Nothing's going to plan," she heard her husband reply with an elated chuckle that made her prop herself up onto her elbows, looking down at him before saying, "No, not really…Allah, you're weird."

"It's Jehovah, thank you very much. And my love, I think we're actually doing just fine. When I say we're having a hard time communicating…well, you want to know the funniest part?" she heard her husband ask, taking her other foot in his hand, kissing the bottom before massaging it.

"I don't know…the cold shoulder they gave us? You tell me," she asked in a low voice, becoming groggy.

"We're trying to say the exact same thing. That's the funny part. Do you know what he said to me?" she heard her husband ask, placing her foot down, hopping onto the bed beside her.

"What?" she mumbled.

"He told me if you want to look at my wife's ass, just look at it. And he said, 'I've been looking at your wife's ass, you don't need to lead me to it'."

"He said that? I didn't think that was the type of conversation y'all were having. He sounded pretty aggravated. I'm surprised he'd say that. Yeah…Wow, I can't believe he said that," she whispered, feeling her body grow warm with the knowledge that Jay had been enjoying her.

"Yeah, he did. And baby, he has a dark side. A really deep, dark side," she heard her husband reply, moving his hand to her breast, softly massaging them as he inched closer.

"Oh yeah? Tell me more about this dark side," she replied, looking into his eyes as she moved her hands to his, massaging her breast along with him, then turning her body just enough to let him know she wanted him to suck them.

"Well, he had this fire in his eyes. The kind that said, 'don't fuck with me or my wife'," she heard her husband whisper, scooting down, running his tongue over her nipples.

"Oh? Tell me more," she replied, fully laying back in the bed, enjoying her husband's tongue.

"Wait, never mind, tell me later," she whispered, feeling her pussy begin to throb and grow hot as her husband began to suck her breast one by one.

"Mmm…baby, I'll tell you now. They want us. They really, really want us. And all we have to do to make it happen, is offer the opportunity in the same language they speak and understand," she heard her husband whisper, sucking her breast more passionately after he'd spoken.

"Oh, fuck yes," she whispered, feeling her arousal slip past her lips onto her thong, causing her pussy to tickle.

"Tell me more, what's their language? And suck harder. Fuck, I want you to do both," she whispered, bursting out laughing as the sensation between her legs intensified to the point where she could no longer contain herself.

"Oh, she's really wet, isn't she?" she heard her husband ask, tracing his fingers over her belly, down to her pussy, pressing into the spandex material of her shorts, that'd already become soaking wet.

"What? I don't know what you're talking about," she replied, moving her hands to her waist, beginning to slide down her shorts when she heard a knock on the door.

"Oh, fuck! The food. Why now?" she groaned, slamming her head backwards into the pillow a few times in frustration.

"Yeah, who is it?" she heard her husband ask, shaking his head as he looked towards the door.

"Yeah, it's Reggie, Reggie from the Bar next door. I have your wings here," she heard Reggie say in a deep, commanding voice.

"Ah, okay perfect! Be right there!" she heard her husband reply, giving her a mischievous look that said he was planning something.

"Baby! No! What's with that look!?" she shrieked, visualizing the man on the other side of the door.

"His voice! Oh, please I know you like!" she heard her husband reply in a hushed, energetic tone, giving her the brightest, 'let's have some fun' smile she'd seen come from him since the trip began.

"Okay! Okay! I know you have a naughty plan! What do you want me to do!?" she exclaimed in a whisper, shooting up to a sitting position, trying to anticipate what her husband was going to say.

"Umm, umm, Oh God. Wait, let me see if he's hot first," she heard her husband whisper, kissing her on the side of the head before leaping out the bed, quickly striding over to the door, looking through the peep hole as he said, "Just two more secs bro."

"Uh, alright. Um, take your time, I was umm…" she heard Reggie trail off, causing goosebumps to rise on her skin, realizing he'd come knowing they might be in the trawls of it, when Nate turned around and mouthed the words, "Oh my God! He's fucking hot! Hot! Hot! Hot!" all while doing a gesture to show that he had a goatee and long hair.

"Oh fuck! What do I do?" she shrieked, excitedly slamming herself back onto the bed then shooting up again, looking to her husband for instructions.

"Go to the bathroom…then come out after he comes in," she saw her husband Nate mouth as he pointed to his chest then her own, making a gesture to show that she should come out topless.

"Ah!" she replied with a giggle, giving him a thumb's up as she darted to the bathroom, thinking, *We're going to make this man go crazy! He has no idea what he just got himself into!*

"Hey man, thanks for bringing the food. You didn't have to, we could've come over there," she heard her husband say as he opened the door.

"Okay! Okay! Here's the hard part. You got this baby!" she thought waiting expectantly for her husband's next words, knowing this was the make it or break it point.

"Ah shit, how much does it cost? Here brother, step in, step in. My cash is in my bag and I don't want you to wait out here while I dig through it," she heard him say in a calm, yet commanding voice.

"Ohhh shit! Here comes the part where he might say, 'no its okay, I'll wait out here'. Come on baby, come on baby, you got this," she thought as Reggie said, "Uh…it's okay bro. I can wait here."

"Brother, you came all the way here to bring us food. Now you expect me to just leave you out here while I dig through my stuff. Come brother, it's all is good, as a matter of fact, have a beer with us, it's the least we can do to say thank you. Or are you more of a shot man? Come have a shot with us, and then I'll dig through all that stuff in my bag and get you, how much is it?"

"Twenty-five, sixty-four, but twenty-five is fine. And umm…" she heard Reggie trail off.

"Twenty-five it is, come brother, you want a shot or beer," she heard her husband say in a relaxed tone, seeing and hearing the door hit the stop as he backed up giving room for Reggie to walk past.

"Uh, are you sure? I mean, I'll take a shot. What do you guys have?" she heard Reggie say, hearing the plastic bag he was carrying rustle and his voice sound more inside the room than out.

"Oh, fuck yes! Yes! Here we go!" she thought, listening to Reggie's foot falls as they came deeper into the room.

"We have Vodka and we have a case of the local beer we picked up at the gas station. The clerk told us it was really good," she heard her husband say as the room door closed.

"And that's my cue!" she thought feeling a rush of energy course through her body as she stepped out of the restroom with a bright smile, instantly locking eyes with a now dumbfound looking Reggie who said, "Ah...um. Ah...it's really..."

"Is it really good or no, not so much?" she finished for him, in the calmest voice she could muster, making sure she was fully facing him so that he could take in all her details.

"It's...pretty good," she heard Reggie say in a low voice, seeing his eyes look away only to return and travel up and down her body, finally bobbing his head with a smile as if to say, 'hello, I was shocked, but I can handle seeing you now'.

"Oh, you can handle yourself, huh? Well, we'll see about that," she thought, taking in the details of Reggie's handsome, rugged face before moving her eyes down to his muscular arms and torso, showing easily in the loose, all black sleeveless shirt he wore.

"Man! You don't seem too convinced. I say you drink one first and prove it's not going to kill us," she heard her husband say, smiling and winking at her as he took out his wallet, pulling out twenty-five dollars, waving it behind Reggie's back, causing her to almost burst out laughing.

"What? It's not going to kill you. My grandpa is one of the main brewers," she heard Reggie say smiling at her, shaking his head as he turned towards her husband, who quickly jammed the money into his pocket.

"Is he now? Well then, we'll just have to see," she said wanting all of Reggie's attention back on her.

"Sure, then I'll have a beer too, what the hell," she heard Reggie say, shaking his head with a low belly chuckle, now turning toward her with a smile, this time making it obvious he was looking her up and down, causing a flash of hungry lust to surge through her, as he was now taking his time to take in her every detail.

"Yes, look at me. Enjoy me. I want you to want me. I want you to want to claim me. And then, I want you to act on it!" she thought, biting her bottom lip as she made eye contact, only to break it, purposely staring at his crotch so that she could catch the look on his face, which was now a perfect mix of 'oh my God, I can't believe this is happening, and, I'd fuck the shit out of you if I could'.

"Perfect, that's exactly how I want you to feel," she thought, walking towards the mini fridge, bending over, knowing her shorts would turn see through, wanting Reggie to see her ass, her thong and how wet she already was as she grabbed two cans of beer in her left hand and the bottle of vodka in her right.

"Hey Reggie, since we're having a drink, you mind throwing in your own two cents into a problem we're having," she heard her husband ask, causing her to glance under her arm to see where Reggie was looking.

"Good boy," she thought seeing his eyes locked on her ass as she pushed a third can of beer on top of the other two.

"Sure, I guess. What's up?" she heard Reggie reply, sounding slightly concerned.

Smiling, Rayya stood up and rested the hand carrying the beer on her breast, allowing the loose can to slide between them.

"It's about communication. I was telling …Oh excuse me, my wife's name is Rayya," she heard her husband say as she came up to Reggie, gazing into his eyes then down at the can of beer between her breasts.

"Oh, hi Rayya," she heard Reggie stammer in a low voice as she tilted herself forward, offering the can.

"And, I'm Nate," she heard her husband continue, winking at her as Reggie slowly brought up his hand, taking hold of the can.

"Nice to officially meet," she said, casually turning so that his hand and the can ran across her breast before walking past him towards her husband who was now kneeling in front of their bag - stuffing the money into one of the zipper compartments.

"Uh, nice to officially meet you both," she heard Reggie stammer as she bent over, placing a can beer and the bottle of Vodka next to her husband, who flashed her a mischievous grin, letting her know that Reggie had turned around to look at her.

"Likewise, so what was I saying? Oh yeah, we're having a communication issues with some people. And it's funny because we're saying pretty much the same thing, but we keep misunderstanding each other," she heard her husband say as she stood up, making her way to the bed, settling herself down with one of her legs up so that Reggie could look between them.

"I'm sorry, I don't follow," she heard Reggie reply, looking between she and her husband, swallowing hard before apparently choosing a spot to look somewhere in between.

"No, that won't do. What happened? You were being so brave just a second ago," she thought, opening the can of beer, taking a sip, placing it to her side before saying, "Reggie, I don't follow either. That's why we need your help."

"Sure, it's just, I 'kinda' need more info," she heard Reggie reply, sounding slightly anxious as he ever so slightly shuffled towards her husband.

"Look at me Reggie, show me your hunger! Show me that you want to claim me! I want my husband to see your desire for me! I want him to know that you'll give me your all when you fuck me in front of him!" she thought as her husband came and sat beside her.

"Well, here's the thing Reggie. People can be saying the exact same thing, but in two, totally different ways. And then there's a big miscommunication. For instance, right now…what's my wife saying to you?" she heard her husband ask, kissing her on the side of her cheek, taking the beer from her hand, giving it a sip, with a look of pure curiosity fixed on Reggie.

"I…well, she didn't say anything," she heard Reggie reply, with a truly confused expression on his face.

"Oh, I see. Baby you're a genius," she thought, realizing the point he was trying to make when her husband replied, "Oh, come now, sure she did. She's been speaking to you from the moment she came out the bathroom. So, tell me what's she saying to you?"

62

"Hey, umm, maybe I'm not the one to answer this… I…," she heard Reggie say, trailing off as she opened her legs, licked her lips, and gazed at his crotch.

"Really? I thought I was being clear," she whispered, biting her bottom lip, looking up into Reggie's light brown eyes, which she could tell were filled with hunger.

"I…I'm not sure" she heard Reggie stutter.

"Oh, I think you are," she replied, smiling at Reggie as she began to massage her breast.

"I mean, I mean…Hey, is this some kind of joke?" she heard Reggie ask, shooting both she and her husband an accusing look before shaking his head, sucking his teeth and saying, "Ah, I can't fucking believe this is happening. I just came here to deliver food, what is this shit?"

"And see Reggie, this is the exact miscommunication I was talking about," she heard her husband reply.

"What?" she heard Reggie ask, with a disbelieving huff.

"Reggie, please, this is not a joke whatsoever. So, now that you know that. Try for us, tell us what she's saying to you. And tell us what your rock-hard cock, you keep trying to hide with the bag is saying to us," she heard her husband say in smooth, commanding voice, that made her think, *That's right baby, take control, show him he can't hide from himself or us! Make him confess how bad he wants me. Make him confess how bad he wants to fuck me in front of you!*"

"Look, I get it, you guys are probably swingers or something, and you're looking for some fun or something, is that right?" she heard Reggie ask sounding hoarse.

"Oh? So, you do understand? So, then Reggie, why are you so confused? Am I not beautiful enough for you? Why do you keep looking away from me? Do you not see me calling you?" she asked, scooting herself further up on the bed, opening her legs wider, craving every ounce of his attention.

"I mean, I mean, when does this happen?" she heard Reggie ask, gazing down at her, with his eyes locked with hers.

"Well, right now. And why do you keep hiding your cock behind that bag? Don't you think I want to see it? I'm showing you my pussy through my shorts, why can't I see your cock?" she asked, moving her fingers to her clit, working them in wide circles, sending shivers up her spine.

"Well, I mean…" she heard Reggie begin, stopping and looking at both she and husband, then back at her.

"Ahh…I see. Too good to be true, huh Reggie? Now do you see why we're having communication issues? You know what Reggie? What could we have done to change this situation? Change it to where you could've understood and acted on it, almost right away? What language could we have spoken to make it completely clear that she wants you to fuck her? That I want you to fuck her. Was her body language not enough? Was her being topless or bending over, showing you her pussy not enough? What could we have done to alleviate your confusion, so that instead of you standing over there, gawking at us, hiding your cock, you'd be over here, maybe letting her suck it?" Rayya heard her husband ask, gesturing for Reggie to come closer.

"I," she heard Reggie mumble, taking two steps forward, stopping, shaking his head as if he were trying to break free from a trance.

"So, baby, you think they want us, like Reggie wants me?" she asked, biting her bottom lip, following Reggie's eyes to her breast, seeing them dart up, gazing somewhere above her head.

"Yes, my love, but they're fighting it, just like he's fighting it. But it's our fault, it's because we're not saying the right things to make them come to us. Kind of like we must not be saying the right things to Reggie, because he's still standing there."

"Humm, I see. So then, how should we speak to them?" she whispered, summoning Reggie with her finger.

"Earlier, I had said we should be subtle. But, I think I'm dead wrong. Jay seems to like everything spelled out. And as for Reggie…Reggie, what is stopping you? Is my wife not beautiful?" she heard her husband ask, feeling him come behind her, gently pulling her to lean back on him.

"She's beautiful. I never said that she wasn't," she heard Reggie reply, shaking his head with a chuckle, walking directly in front of her, stealing a peak between her legs, then looking up, into her eyes.

"So then, look at me the way you want to look at me. Don't hide the way you feel. I saw you looking between my legs.

Do you want to see my pussy? Do you want these shorts off?" she asked, watching Reggie bite his bottom lip in response to her question.

"I'll take that look as a 'yes'. So, move those sexy eyes back down and stop fighting it. I want to see how much you want me. I want you to show me how much you want me. As a matter of fact, put that bag down and let me see," she commanded, sitting up, resting her hand on Reggie's bulge, feeling the warmth of his hard cock through his light-blue jeans.

"Shit," she heard Reggie whisper.

"Shit is right," she whispered, squeezing ever so gently, loving the thickness of his cock.

"Baby, come, lean back against me again," she heard her husband say in a tone that made her instantly obey.

"Am I being too naughty too fast baby?" she asked, once her back was against her husband's chest.

"No, never baby, there's no such thing," she heard her husband reply.

"Oh, okay. Then I guess it's okay if I do this," she replied, sliding her hand beneath her shorts, slowly massaging and fingering her pussy.

"Yes, that's perfectly alright," she heard her husband reply, before saying, "I just want to see. I just want to know what Reggie wants to do. Aren't you dying to see what he'll do on his own?"

"Mmm, yeah I am. Reggie, what are you going to do? I'm right here, waiting for you," she whispered, looking into Reggie's eyes as she brought her hand to her husband's mouth, instantly feeling self-conscious as her full scent hit the air, reminding her that she'd wanted to take a shower.

"I want to…I want to," she heard Reggie begin, pausing to look down at her pussy, then back up as if he were suddenly confused.

"Baby, I should …I should…" she began when her husband ran his fingers across her cheek and said, "Reggie, she smells good doesn't she? She thinks she needs a shower, but tell her, tell her what you think. Doesn't her scent make you feel hungry? Doesn't it make you want to go down on her and have a taste?"

"Taste…Yes. I, I love the way she…the way you smell. Why, why would you need a shower?" she heard Reggie reply, biting his bottom lip, looking past her towards her husband, who was now sucking her fingers.

"Yes! That look of hunger!" she thought, resting her foot on Reggie's bulge as she whispered, "Oh? You want to taste me, just as I am? You don't think I'm stinky?"

"What? No, not at all. God, what would make you think such a thing?" she heard Reggie say, chuckling and shaking his head.

"See baby, both of us are telling you that you smell yummy," she heard her husband reply, feeling his arms wrap around her, with his hands softly caressing her breast.

"Yeah, yummy, that's the word. Real fucking yummy," she heard Reggie reply, awkwardly placing the bag of wings down, taking hold of the foot she'd pressed to his cock.

"Well, if you really want to taste me, then prove it. Come, show me how much you want me," she whispered, massaging Reggie's cock with her foot, feeling something wet and sticky touch her toes.

"Mmm," she intoned, feeling her mouth instantly water at the thought of what touched her toes as she slid her foot down, seeing a dark, damp spot where Reggie's pre-cum had leaked through.

Chapter VII

All For Me

Road Trip: Day Three

Date: Saturday, June 3rd 2017

Time: 1:45 am

Location: Bismarck, North Dakota

"Oh, look at that. Someone's really excited, isn't he?" Rayya asked, smiling as Reggie moved closer to the bed.

"How could I not be?" she heard Reggie reply, getting down on his knees, first looking into her eyes, then behind her, towards her husband expectantly.

"Baby, tell Reggie how bad you want to see him eat my pussy" she whispered, extending her right leg over Reggie's shoulder, pulling him closer so that his face hovered just over her pussy.

"Reggie, I'm dying to watch, go on, taste her," she heard her husband reply.

"Are you, are you sure?" she heard Reggie stammer, looking up at her, then down, between her legs, feeling the warmth of his breath brush against her pussy through her shorts and thong.

"He's giving me to you, I'm yours to take," she whispered, loving the tingle up her spine from both the sensation of Reggie's breath and from the look of pure, unchecked lust playing across his face.

"Yes, it just what she said. It's okay, you don't have to look to me for permission. Enjoy her. I brought you in here because I want to watch you enjoy her," she heard her husband whisper, feeling his right hand gently press down on her belly.

"Baby, you're not just going to watch, are you? You know I'm greedy. You know I want both of you to taste me, right?" she whispered, feeling the warmth and pressure of his hand spread down through her belly into her pelvis.

"Oh, trust me, I plan to," she heard her husband reply.

"Good," she whispered, now watching Reggie close his eyes, taking another deep breath.

"Mmm, you really do like my scent, don't you?" she gasped, becoming even more aroused, seeing how much Reggie desired her.

"Not like, I love," she heard Reggie reply, laying a soft kiss on her pussy through the fabric of her shorts.

"And if I said I don't believe you? That, that one kiss wasn't enough to be convincing?" she replied, running her fingers through Reggie's long, golden hair.

"Hum? If there wasn't something in the way, I'd give more kisses there to prove it," she heard Reggie whisper, looking into her eyes as he hooked his fingers into the waistline of her shorts.

"I'd say, get it out the way," she whispered, lifting her hips, feeling Reggie tug until her shorts and thong were off and on the floor.

"Oh, my fucking God, that's unreal," she heard Reggie gasp, staring down at her soaking wet pussy as he spread her legs.

"Taste," she moaned, raising her hips as Reggie lowered his lips, hungrily kissing and licking her pussy.

"Yes!" she gasped, closing her eyes, enjoying Reggie's lips.

"She's delicious, isn't she?" she heard her husband ask, followed by Reggie driving his tongue deep into her entrance, as if to say, 'Yes! And I want more!'.

"Oh shit! Yeah, you love the way my pussy taste, don't you?" she gasped, feeling Reggie work his tongue back and forth before bringing it down to lick the rim of her ass.

"You're fucking delicious," she heard Reggie reply, feeling the heat of his breath brush against her inner thighs before he pressed his mouth against her pussy again.

"Oh fuck!" she gasped, feeling him begin to suck and release her clit over and over again, causing her whole body to tremble.

"Yeah, just like that. Yeah, she loves that," she heard her husband whisper, feeling him gently inch himself back, allowing her to fully lay with her back on the mattress.

"Mmm, baby! Baby!" she pleaded, feeling her pussy begin to spasm as Reggie continued to add and release pressure on her clit.

"And you know what else she likes?" she heard her husband ask, feeling his hands take hold of her ankles.

"Hum?" she heard Reggie reply with a groan, sending vibrations through her pussy as she continued to cum in his mouth.

"She likes it when people share her," she heard her husband reply, feeling his hands slide down, firmly taking hold of her thighs, parting them wide where she could now see Reggie's face as he continued to hungrily devour her pussy.

"Oh my God," she gasped in anticipation as she watched her husband kneel beside Reggie, who'd inched his kisses over to the soft portion of her inner thigh, giving her husband just enough room to bring his lips to her pussy.

"Holy fuck!" she screamed the instant her husband's lips touched - as he was both gentle and strong, pressing his tongue deep into her entrance, only to slowly, deliberately take it out and run it over her clit.

"I can't! I can't take it" she gasped, feeling herself cum again.

"Yeah, there it is. Reggie, look at this, come lick this up, it's all yours," she heard her husband whisper, feeling Reggie's goatee bush against her thighs as he moved his lips over her pussy, devouring her with more hunger than he had before.

"Fuck!" she gasped, feeling herself on the verge of cumming again, when she felt Reggie slip two of his fingers into her entrance, hooking them right up to her G-Spot.

"No! Too much!" she gasped, feeling her body betray her words as she worked her hips, fucking Reggie's fingers.

"Yeah, now give it good shake," she heard her husband command.

"Hey! Wait! Wait!" she gasped, clenching Reggie's fingers with her pussy.

"Like this?" she heard Reggie reply, working his fingers faster and faster despite her clenching them, causing her to cum so hard she felt her toes curl.

"Wow!" she heard Reggie whisper, feeling his finger slip out, along with a wet, sticky sensation spreading down over her ass.

"Lick my pussy. Both of you, lick me clean," she gasped, propping herself onto her elbows, wanting to see.

"What did you say?" she heard her husband ask in a commanding voice.

"I said lick me clean," she replied, looking between both men, whose mouths were already glossy from her cum.

"You hear that Reggie? She's telling us what to do. Do you want to tolerate that? Or do you want to discipline her?" she heard her husband ask, taking off his shirt and unzipping his fly.

"I think we should punish her," she heard Reggie say, doing the same as her husband.

"Oh yeah, and how do you think giving me what I want is punishment?" she asked, bringing her hands to her pussy, spreading open her lips so that the men could watch her arousal leak from her entrance.

"Jesus," she heard Reggie whisper, inching forward, licking his lips.

"Unzipping your pants. Saying you're going to punish me, yeah, I'll take it," she said, tracing her arousal over her inner and outer lips.

"Nate, I'm tempted to do what she says," she heard Reggie whisper, licking his lips.

"Yes, you don't have to go through with this supposed punishment. Come Reggie, just lick me clean," she replied, dipping her fingers back into her entrance, removing them and using them to summon Reggie to come closer.

"Don't give in," she heard her husband say, watching him stand, with his rock-hard cock protruding from his jeans, but it was too late, because in that very same moment Reggie began to lick her pussy.

"Oh, you're being a real naughty girl, conquering Reggie like that," she heard her husband say, winking at her as he looked down at Reggie with a mischievous smile.

"She can conquer me all she wants," she heard Reggie reply, feeling his thumbs massage the lips of her pussy before moving up to her clit.

"Reggie, are you really going to let me be a bad girl and tell you what to do? Are you really not going to punish me for torturing you when you came through the door?" she whispered,

70

smiling at her husband as she took hold of Reggie's head, pressing him down to lick her pussy.

"Mmmm," she heard Reggie reply, kissing her pussy passionate and slow as if he were making out with it.

"Fuck, I love your tongue" she whispered, running her fingers through Reggie's hair, watching her husband move toward her with a look that said, 'you're a bad girl.'

"Hi baby," she whispered as her husband kneeled on the bed, taking her breast in his mouth, sucking hungrily, yet gently at the same time.

"Hi yourself, it looks like you have a new slave," she heard her husband reply, inching forward, taking her other breast in his mouth, before moving up, kissing her deeply.

"Yeah, I plan on draining him dry, and making you lick it from me," she whispered in her husband's ear after their kiss, tugging Reggie's hair, pushing his face down harder after feeling his tongue slip into her entrance.

"Oh really? And then what?" she heard her husband ask, standing up, walking over towards Reggie, keeping his eyes locked on her.

"And then I want both of you inside of me," she replied, pushing Reggie's head back to look into his wild, ferocious eyes as she pointed to her pussy, mouthing the words, "Fuck me. I want you to fuck me."

"Unnnnnn," she heard Reggie groan, sounding primal, feeling her heart skip a beat as he stood and undid his belt - allowing his jeans to fall.

"Oh, look at that cock," she whispered, bringing up her legs up, spreading them wide, letting him know she was more than ready to receive him.

"You want it?" she heard Reggie whisper, sliding his boxers down, stepping forward with his cock hovering just above her pussy.

"Yeah, give it to me," she gasped, watching and feeling Reggie's warm pre-cum drip down onto her pussy.

"I don't know. You don't sound too convincing," she heard Reggie reply, smiling at her mischievously as he ran the length of his cock between her lips, and over her clit.

"Fuck! Fuck me!" she gasped, trying to rock her hips so that the tip of his cock would slip into her entrance.

"Yeah torture her, make her beg for it," she heard her husband whisper, inching forward, staring down at Reggie's cock as he continued to tease, now working his tip over her clit in circles.

"No, don't!" she pleaded, reaching out for Reggie's cock as he again ran the full length between her lips, this time stopping with his tip resting right at her entrance.

"And why not? You tortured me," she heard Reggie reply, ever so slightly pressing his cock in before slipping it out, running it between her lips again.

"Oh shit! Baby, tell him to stop!" she gasped, feeling her pussy pulsing in anticipation.

"But I like to watch you squirm. Why would I tell him to stop?" she heard her husband reply, taking Reggie by the shoulder, whispering, "When you fuck her, fuck her hard, harder than you've ever fucked before. And when you cum, you cum inside of her. And even when she's overflowing, begging you that she can't handle anymore, I don't want you stop fucking her, is that clear?"

"Yeah, it's clear," she heard Reggie reply, feeling him take hold of her inner thighs, with his cock teasingly stroking between her lips a few more times before slipping into her entrance.

"Yes, fuck me! Oh my God! Fuck me!" she gasped, loving the feeling of Reggie's cock as he began to thrust, going so deep that the tip of his dick pressed into the farthest depths of her pussy over and over again.

"Ahhh! God Damn! So, fucking good!" she heard Reggie groan, tugging her thighs, pulling her closer as he thrusted even harder.

"Yes! Yes! Fuck my pussy!" she screamed, enjoying his long, fast stokes, wanting him to pound her pussy even harder.

"Unh!" she heard Reggie groan, falling forward, driving his tongue into her mouth as he continued to thrust.

"Yes! Oh God! Fuck your pussy Reggie, fuck your pussy!" she gasped, wrapping her arms around his neck.

"Shit, I'm going to cum," she heard Reggie gasp, feeling his cock throb.

"Yes! Cum! Cum inside me! Give it to me" she begged.

"No!" she heard Reggie plead.

"Yes! Give it to me!" she gasped.

"Ahhh!" she heard Reggie groan, feeling his cock surge and pulse, followed by a delicious rush of hot cum surging within her.

"Yes! Yes! Give it to me! Give it to me!" she gasped, loving the warm rush of cum and pulsing sensation of being filled, causing her to climax with every fiber of her being.

"Yes!" she gasped again, kissing Reggie deeply, feeling her whole-body tremble as she wrapped her legs around his waist, pulling him deeper, wanting every drop.

"Mmm!" she heard Reggie gasp, feeling stronger pulses than she had before, along with the sensation of even more cum filling her.

"Yes! The kiss always makes them cum again!" she thought, driving her tongue deeper into Reggie's mouth as she rocked her hips and ran her hands up and down his back, hungering to keep him cumming inside her as long as possible.

"You. What the fuck did you just do?" she heard Reggie gasp, breaking their kiss, gazing at her in pure trans fixation.

"Oh, nothing…I don't know what you're talking about," she replied, sucking Reggie's bottom lip as she worked her hips in slower circles, enjoying the feeling of his dick stirring their mix.

"Oh, God! I can't take it! Shit!" she heard Reggie gasp, causing her to giggle.

"Hey, when you pull out, I want you to watch my husband lick our cum from my pussy. Do you hear me?" she whispered.

"Yeah, I hear you?" she heard Reggie reply with a slightly puzzled look on his face which made her laugh, knowing what he was thinking.

"Don't think about it, just watch. Will you do that for me?" she asked, unwrapping her legs as she pressed him up ever so slightly, looking down, drinking in the heavy scent of their climax and sweat as it rose up from between her legs.

"Yeah, I can do that for you," she heard Reggie reply, smiling at her with a slightly dubious look on his face before gazing down between her legs.

"Smells good doesn't it?" she asked, taking hold of his chin, bringing his face up to peck his lips.

"Yeah it does," she heard Reggie whisper, gazing into her eyes as he lifted himself back and slid himself out, seeing his long, thick cock coated in white, frothy cream.

"Oh my God hubby, look at his dick," she whispered, thinking, *"Fuck, I really want hubby to lick Reggie's dick clean as well, but I don't think he'll let him do it!"*

"Oh, I see it baby," she heard her husband respond as Reggie stepped to the side, allowing him access to her pussy.

"Baby, before you go to me…can you lick our mix off of Reggie for me?" she asked, wishing she hadn't when Reggie's semi smile dropped to one of concern and confusion.

"Oh no!" she thought before deciding, *"Fuck it!"*

"Reggie, Reggie, sweetie, let him do it, let him do it just for me. I want to see him suck that cock. I want to see him lick all our cream off your dick before he licks it out of me. Reggie, I'm begging you, please let me see it. I'll do anything you say. I promise, I'll do anything you say. Just let my hubby suck your cock."

"It's okay baby, let Reggie be," she heard her husband reply, kneeling in front of her, looking between Reggie and her pussy.

"Hey, um," she heard Reggie whisper, gulping hard, looking at her, then down to her husband. "Please, I'll do any freaky thing you want," she whispered again.

"Baby, it's okay," she heard her husband reply, massaging his thumb over her entrance, lips and clit, spreading she and Reggie's mix before blowing a cool steam of air across her pussy.

"Oh fuck! Oh shit!" she gasped, leaning up, watching as her husband inched closer, extending his tongue, running it over her pussy.

"Oh shit, he's really doing it," she heard Reggie gasp.

"Yessss. Show him baby. Lick us up," she gasped, watching and feeling her husband press his lips to her pussy.

"My God," she heard Reggie whisper as she gasped, throwing her head back, loving the feeling of her husband sucking the mix from her pussy.

"Show it to me, show it to me" she groaned, opening her eyes, gazing down, seeing her husband's mouth filled with cream.

"Mmm, I want some, I want some," she whispered, gesturing for her husband to climb over her and kiss her, which he did without hesitation.

"This is the best!" she thought, feeling herself about to orgasm, loving the primal behavior of sharing the salty, sweet, mixture of cum with her husband.

"Holy shit!" she heard Reggie whisper as she continued to make out with her husband, who generously pushed more mix into her mouth.

Greedily swallowing everything her husband gave, she broke their kiss, and summoned Reggie to come closer.

"I want more!" she gasped, opening her mouth, reaching for his cock.

"More?" she heard Reggie whisper, bringing his cocking to her mouth, which she greedily sucked down.

"Please have more! Please cum again!" she thought, opening her throat wide, feeling Reggie begin to thrust.

"Ah! Oh, my fucking God!" she heard Reggie gasp, feeling his thrust grow stronger and stronger, causing her to gag and tear up, only making her want his cum even more.

"Cum down her throat! She wants you to cum down her throat," she heard her husband say, taking hold of her hair, pushing her head back and forth making her gag that much more.

"Oh fuck!" she heard Reggie gasp, slipping his cock from her mouth, hearing him take deep breaths right after.

"No, give me…give me," she mumbled, reaching out for Reggie's cock, swallowing her saliva and any remaining mix that hadn't been jammed down her throat.

"Hold, hold on," she heard Reggie gasp, putting up his hands pleadingly, but she was having none of it and said, "I promise, I'll go slow. Okay?"

"No, I need…" she heard Reggie begin as she took hold of his cock, running her tongue over his tip.

"See, soft," she cut in, looking into Reggie's eyes before whispering, "And let him help me."

"Wa…I…," she heard Reggie begin, stopping when she made a face that said, 'please'.

"Jesus," she heard Reggie whisper with a look she'd seen many times before, where a person was almost fully over the fence, but needed one last push.

"Will you do it for me? I promise not to tell a soul what happened here. Please, let him suck your dick for me," she whispered, gazing up at Reggie expectantly as she kissed the side of his shaft, aiming the tip of his dick towards her husband mouth.

"Oh, fuck it," she heard Reggie whisper, closing his eye, which made her move her head back allowing her husband to take him into his mouth.

"Mmm...no way! Oh, shit! No way! This feels so fucking good! Oh! What the hell!" she heard Reggie gasp, clenching his hands over and over as his head moved around in circles.

"Yes way," she replied, watching as her husband slowly and sensually sucked Reggie's cock, keeping his eyes closed as he worked his thumb and index finger back and forth over his shaft.

"No, this isn't real," she heard Reggie protest as she came from beneath her husband.

"Oh, its real," she whispered, sitting up, rubbing her pussy as she watched.

"No, no, no," she heard Reggie plead again, shaking his head, causing her to laugh.

"It's okay, you can admit it. Let your guard down. We're here for your pleasure," she whispered, slipping her fingers into her pussy.

"But, oh God! He's a dude!" she heard Reggie gasp as he began to quiver.

"Yes, he is, and he wants you to cum in his mouth," she replied, slipping her fingers out, running them across her tongue.

"I can't, I can't cum like this," she heard Reggie gasp, quivering harder, yet inching himself out of her husband's mouth.

"So close, why'd you fight it?" she whispered, before sliding her fingers into her mouth, wanting to suck of anything she'd missed from her lick.

"I know what will make you cum again," she heard her husband say, standing up, clasping Reggie on the shoulder

"What are you going to do?" she heard Reggie ask, sounding anxious.

"Reggie, have you ever fucked a girl in the ass?" she heard her husband ask, tipping his head towards her.

"I, umm. Maybe once," she heard Reggie reply, with a look of pure intrigue and shock.

"Maybe once? Well then, we're going to have to add to that?" she replied, gesturing for her husband to lay on the bed before looking Reggie in the eye, whispering, "I want you in my ass, and I want him in my pussy."

"You, you want both of us?" she heard Reggie stammer as her husband laid down on his back beside her.

"Yes, both of you," she replied, climbing on top of her husband, sliding him in slowly so that she could enjoy every inch of his length as it pressed in deeper.

"And do you know why I want both of you?" she asked, turning around as she took hold of her ass cheeks, spreading them wide so Reggie could see that her asshole was ready and willing.

"Why?" she heard Reggie ask, moving behind her, placing his hands on-top of hers', spreading her ass cheeks that much wider.

"Because, when my pussy's being fucked, my ass is hungry. And when my ass is being fucked, my pussy's hungry. Really, really hungry," she replied, feeling the tip of Reggie's cock touch the rim of her ass.

"Yeah, that's it, fuck me. Fuck my ass," she whispered, licking her lips, loving the way Reggie's tip, and precum felt as he slowly began to slip his cock into her ass.

"It's, it's so tight," she heard Reggie gasp.

"Oh, is it?" she whispered relaxing and flexing her asshole, allowing Reggie's cock to fully slip in.

"Rayya!" she heard Reggie groan, feeling him slowly begin to thrust.

"Yeah, you like fucking my ass? Feels good, huh?" she moaned, squeezing her pussy and ass, loving the added pressure of a second cock.

"Yeah!" she heard Reggie groan, feeling his cock slide in that much deeper, causing both she and her husband to gasp.

"Yes! Baby, I can feel him," she heard her husband groan.

"Yeah? You like feeling his cock while it's inside of me, don't you?" she moaned, feeling Reggie's thrust growing stronger.

"Yeah," she heard her husband gasp

"You like your wife being used and filled, don't you?" she asked, kissing her husband deeply, not giving her husband a chance to answer.

"Yeah! Yeah!" Rayya heard her husband finally gasp after she broke their kiss, feeling him take hold of her arms, bringing her down so that she lay breast to chest with him.

"Don't be nice to her Reggie. Fuck her ass! Fuck her ass hard, and make sure you cum in it!" she heard her husband say right after.

"Oh, no baby. Let him pace himself!" she pleaded, hearing Reggie say, "Yeah, yeah man!"

"Hey, baby! Hey, Reggie! Be nice! Be nice!" she pleaded, feeling Reggie's thrust grow stronger, with his dick now going so deep, it filled he to the absolute brim - which she loved.

"No, you're a bad girl! And you're getting what you deserve!" she heard her husband reply, buking his hips in rhythm with Reggie's thrust.

"No! No! Oh my God!" she gasped, feeling a surge of pure joy and exhilaration.

"Take it! Take it!" she heard her husband command.

"No! Too much!" she pleaded, feeling her whole-body begin to quiver.

"Yes! Reggie! Fuck her harder! Don't, fucking stop!" she heard her husband groan.

"Fuck her harder?! Fuck... her ...harder!" she heard Reggie scream, taking hold of her hair, pulling her head back as he did just that.

"Reggie!" she screamed at the top of her lungs, feeling as if each individual stroke were the very first.

"Yeah! Scream my name! Because that's my ass!" she heard Reggie grunt, not even slightly slowing down.

"Oh, my, fucking, God!" she screamed as the pleasure and pain of being fucked in both her ass and pussy merged into one of only sheer delight.

"Yes! Fuck your ass, Reggie! Fuck your ass!" she screamed, bucking back and forth no longer having any reservation now that her body had adjust to both men.

"Yes! I'm fucking that ass!" she heard Reggie grunt, feeling his grip on her hair grow tighter.

"And you're fucking your pussy! Right baby?" she asked, loving the idea of being claimed and used as a sex toy.

"Yeah! I'm fuck my pussy, baby! And Reggie's fuck his ass! You're such a dirty little slut! Letting us use you! We're going to cum in you, you little slut! You hear me? We're going to cum in you!" she heard her husband grunt.

"Shit! Yes!" she screamed, instantly feeling herself orgasm, loving her husband's degrading words, along with the wonderful sensation of being fucked by both men.

"Mmm! Yeah! You feel that Reggie!" she heard her husband gasp, sounding like he was about to cum.

"Yeah! That pussy's leaking! Look at that fucking cream! My fucking God, she smells so good!" she heard Reggie grunt.

"I want more! Fuck me some more!" she gasped, feeling possessed when the scent of her orgasm reached her nose, sending her into overdrive.

"More!" she screamed again, winding and working her hips in rhythm with the men's thrust, feeling herself cum again and again to the point where she could barely breathe.

Yet, she still wanted more, and begged for it, which sent both men go into a frenzy. Then, to Rayya's greatest delight, she heard Reggie and her husband, scream "Ahh," at the same time.

"Yes! Cum inside me!" she gasped, feeling both Reggie and her husband's cocks pulse inside her at the same time, filling her ass and pussy with warm cum.

"I love this! I love this so much!" Rayya thought, closing her eyes, resting her head on her husband's chest, enjoying the almost pure stillness of the moment, feeling a deep sense of relief and satisfaction as she drank in the scent of the room, smelling of, blackberry, honey, and sweat.

And that's when she heard the - pat, pat, pat - smack, smack, smack of sex from the room next door.

"Wait, what did I just hear!?" she thought, straining to listen, hearing Jay say, "Fuck baby! Did you hear them over there? You want me to fuck you like that!?"

"Yeah Papi! You know I want that!" she heard Karman gasp.

"Fuck! They sound good, don't they baby?" she heard Jay grunt.

"Yeah, they do! And I know you want to see them fuck, don't you Papi?" she heard Karman reply.

"Fuck yeah, I want to see that!" she heard Jay grunt, followed by two loud smacks and Karman gasping, "Yes! More!"

"Holy shit! They do want to be around us when we fuck! And if that's the case, then we still have a chance to have a lot more fun with them! Fuck, today I was so scared we lost them! I can't believe this! It went from being shitty day to the best one ever!" Rayya thought, feeling her body relax even more now that she was no longer worried about Jay and Karman hating herself or her husband.

"Hey, Reggie, can we stay like this for a bit? I, I 'wanna' keep this feeling of both of you inside me for as long as possible," she whispered, having felt Reggie begin to slip his cock from her ass, which would've left her feeling empty.

"Sure, of course," she heard Reggie reply, feeling him begin to slowly thrust, working himself back up.

"Yes, there we go," she whispered, loving both the feeling of Reggie cock, and her husband hands, running down the length of her back, to her ass, spreading her open as Reggie pressed his entire length inside of her.

"Better?" she heard Reggie whisper, feeling him curl around her, giving her a kiss on the cheek.

"Yes, much better," she replied, smiling at the sensation of being enveloped and filled by two men, with her last thought before drifting off to sleep being, *"Moment's like this, make my life completely worth living."*

To be continued

O.M. Wills
Presents
ERTA
Book 2

Prologue 2

The smell of hot sex was the first thing to register in Reggie's mind as he stirred awake to find himself spooning, with his arms wrapped tightly around the breast of another man's wife.

"What? What's this feeling? Why do I feel so light? So smooth?" Reggie thought, noticing his body totally and completely at ease next to Rayya's.

"I've never felt this good in my entire life. How could I feel like this with people I don't even know?" he thought, feeling Rayya fingers trace along his arms, then her body shift, pressing her ass against him even further.

"Oh," he whispered, feeling the warmth and wetness of her pussy right up against his flaccid cock, instantly making him hard.

"People I don't know? That seems far from the truth now that I think about it," he thought, having flashbacks of the hours they'd spent having wild, unrelenting sex, which had cooled down to gentle, passionate love making, where they'd touched, teased and explored each other with fingers, mouths, and tongues.

"Never in my life, have I felt so free. How's this possible? How'd this complete me?" he thought sighing heavily, enjoying the feeling of his hard cock slipping into Rayya's pussy, still overflown with he and Nate's cum.

"God, she feels so good," he thought, smiling as he slipped in a little deeper, hearing Rayya let out a soft gasp of pleasure.

"Mmm, you like that, huh?" he whispered, kissing Rayya softly on the cheek.

"Yeah! I love it when you just take me," he heard Rayya moan, feeling her pussy squeeze and release his cock.

"Oh, yeah?" he gasped, thrusting forward, pushing his cock in as far as it could go.

"Yes! Oh, fuck Reggie! Are you 'gonna' fill me up again?" he heard Rayya groan, feeling her hand grip his thigh as she pressed her ass back, forcing his cock in even deeper.

"Rayya!" he gasped, loving both her question and the feeling of his tip pressing right up against her cervix.

"She accepts me without hesitation," he thought, bringing his right hand down to her lower belly, pressing firmly as he began to

stroke, taking his time, enjoying the warmth and wetness of her pussy.

"Fuck, I love it when you go slow," he heard Rayya gasp, feeling her grip his hand, pressing it harder against her belly as she began to move her hips in rhythm with his thrust.

"God! Your pussy's so fucking tight," he gasped, feeling his cock throb with the urge to cum.

"Is it now?" he heard Rayya reply, feeling her pussy tighten even further, keeping his cock locked in place for just a moment before feeling himself forced almost all the way out.

"Oh fuck!" he moaned, thrusting against the warm, slippery pressure, making sure the tip of his cock pressed into her G-spot with his every stroke.

"Feels so fucking good! Yeah! Fuck your pussy Reggie! Fuck your pussy!" he heard Rayya groan.

"Fuck my pussy?" he asked holding her firmly as he rolled onto his back.

"Oh shit!" he heard Rayya gasp as she came to rest upon him in the reverse cow girl position.

"All night she's said it's my pussy. And all night she's done and allowed me to do any and everything I've ever wanted to do with a woman to prove her point," he thought, taking hold of Rayya's hips as she began to grind on his cock.

"Yeah! Ride that dick! That's my pussy," he whispered, feel his cock surge, and Rayya's pussy clench.

"Yeah! It's your pussy! Fuck your pussy Reggie!" he heard Rayya moan, bouncing and grinding on his cock even harder.

"Fuck, I own some good pussy!" he grunted, feeling Rayya's pussy grow wetter with his words.

"Oh, I felt that! You 'gonna' cum on my dick? I want you to cum on my dick. That's my pussy, and I want you to cum on my dick!" he grunted, gripping Rayya's hips tighter as thrusted up, feeling his cock press in deeper than he'd ever gone before.

"Reggie!" he heard Rayya scream, feeling her pussy pulse, her body tremble and a flash of warmth and wetness rush down over his cock and balls.

"I love it, I love it, I love it…I love it when you cum," he whispered, looking down, watching and feeling Rayya inch up, allowing his cock to slip free.

"Holy shit, you came a lot. And, is that steam? I really think it is," he whispered, inhaling deeply, enjoying the scent of Rayya's pussy as he used the alarm clocks soft, blue green light to focus in on his cream coated cock, confirming that it really was steam coming off of it.

"Huh? Let me see," he heard Rayya whisper, feeling and watching as she spun around, looking down at his cock, then up at him with a mischievous smile.

"What?" he asked, flexing his cock to show that he was still hard.

"You did a good job taking care of your pussy. I love that you made me cum so much, it's steaming in this cold ass air," he heard Rayya say.

"Un huh. But, what else does that look mean? What were… or are you thinking?" he whispered, seeing Rayya, lick, then bite her bottom lip as she looked between his face and cock.

"Oh, I think you know what I'm thinking," he heard Rayya reply, licking her lips again.

"Maybe, but I wanna hear you say it," he whispered.

"Well Reggie. I'm thinking, that I want to taste myself, and that you want to watch," he heard Rayya whisper, moving her head down to his cock, licking from the base of his shaft up to his tip before taking his full length into her mouth.

"Oh fuck! God damn!" he gasped, closing his eyes as Rayya passionately sucked his cock, almost causing him to cum when he felt her pause.

"Hey?" he inquired, ever so slightly opening his eyes.

"Yes? How can I help?" he heard Rayya ask, giving him a beaming smile.

"Suck more," he whispered, with a laugh.

"Nope, because all my yummy taste is gone," he heard Rayya reply, giggling after.

"All gone because you're greedy," he whispered, smiling as Rayya crawled up to him on all fours, stopping when they were face to face.

"Am I now?" he heard her whisper.

"Yeah, you are" he replied, suddenly feeling her lips pressed against his, kissing him deeply, allowing him to taste her sweet, honey like flavor straight from her tongue.

"My God, she tastes good!" Reggie thought, taking hold of the back of Rayya's head, driving his tongue in deeper.

"Mmm," he heard Rayya moan, riling him up even further.

"Tell me it's my pussy. I want to hear you say it. And tell me you want me to fuck her again," he said after breaking their kiss.

"Yes! It's your pussy Reggie! And yes, I want you to fuck her again!" he heard Rayya gasp.

"Well then, get back on my dick," he commanded.

"Oh, yes!" he heard Rayya reply, backing up until she was standing at the foot of the bed, giving him a mischievous smile.

"Hey, where 'ya' going, huh?" he asked with a chuckle, scooting forwards to the foot of the bed, stopping when his feet touched the ground.

"I'm sometimes a bad girl and don't listen to my master. Are you going to punish me?" he heard Rayya ask, stepping forwards, placing her breast in front of his mouth.

"Punish you? Humm, let me think," he whispered before sensually sucking her breast one by one, gripping her ass, pulling her closer.

"Oh, damn! You like sucking my titties, don't you?" he heard Rayya whisper, feeling her fingers run through his hair as she kissed the crown of his head.

"Mmm!" he moaned in response, sucking harder and more passionately, hearing Rayya gasp for breath, stopping when Rayya pulled back panting.

"Of course, I love it. Why'd you run away?" he whispered, looking deep into Rayya's eyes.

"I told you, sometimes I'm a bad girl," he heard Rayya reply.

"Oh yeah, I was supposed to be thinking of a punishment," he replied, gripping her ass tighter before spinning her around.

"Oh, ut-oh! Is daddy going to fuck me hard from behind?" he heard Rayya gasp, teasingly wagging her hips from side to side.

"No, I want to torture you slowly. I go much deeper this way," he whispered, guiding her back to sit with her pussy resting right on top of his cock.

"Oh fuck! I love your dick," he heard Rayya gasp, watching and feeling as she worked her hips.

"Shit!" he groaned, gripping Rayya's waist, pressing her down, watching and feeling his cock slip into her soaking wet pussy, sending shivers down his spine.

"Hi, my sweets," he heard Nate whisper in his ear, kissing him on the side of the cheek, causing him to turn and receive a soft peck on the lips.

"Hi, I was wondering when you were going to wake up," he whispered, moving his head forward, pecking Nate's lips again, causing Nate to lean in and kiss him deeply.

"Oh, I was awake. But, you know, I really like seeing you fuck my wife. So, umm, don't let me interrupt you any longer. Go on, let me see you fuck my baby," Reggie heard Nate reply after breaking their kiss, pressing him gently on the chest so that he'd lean back.

"Humm, you sure you weren't asleep? She's already cum all over my dick. If you were awake, I think you'd have been here to lick it off," Reggie whispered, lifting Rayya up by the waist, allowing Nate to see his cream coated cock, driven deep inside his wife's pussy.

"Well, if I missed it, then let's make it happen again," he heard Nate whisper, pecking him softly on the lips, feeling his hand run down his chest and abdomen, stopping just above his cock, where he softly pressed and massaged, almost causing him to cum.

"Stop, you fucker," he gasped, chuckling then holding his breath as Nate continued to massage the soft skin just under the base of his cock.

"Ahh, you're getting used to it, huh? When I first did this, you came in Rayya so fucking fast it, and you couldn't even breath, do you remember?" he heard Nate whisper in his ear with a soft chuckle, feeling his hand run up his stomach to his chest, pinching his nipple hard, causing him to gasp.

"Mmm, still sensitive huh? Rayya and I weren't that rough on them, were we?" he heard Nate whisper in his ear before scooting forward, hopping off the bed.

"These two really know how to crack open all my boundaries. Why the fuck don't I care about making love to a married couple…or a man?" he thought, feeling butterflies in his stomach, catching a mischievous look come across Nate's face.

"Hey, you, what are you thinking?" he asked, staring intently into Nate's eyes, watching him take hold of the back of Rayya's head, leaning forward, bringing his lips next to her ear.

"After you, I want to take a ride on that giant cock," he heard Nate whisper.

"Oh shit!" he thought, remembering how good it'd felt the first time he'd fucked Nate, now watching lustfully as Nate began to make out with Rayya,

"Mmm," he heard Rayya moan, feeling her pussy squeeze and her heart beat flutter at the tip of his cock, before hearing her say, "I can't wait to watch you take your ride, now get down on your knees and lick us."

"Fuck!" he gasped, feeling the butterflies in his stomach increase tenfold as he anticipated the feeling of Nate's tongue.

"Yes, my Queen," he heard Nate whisper, seeing him drop to his knees, looking up at them as he brought his mouth to his balls, kissing and sucking them softly.

"Nate! Nate!" he gasped, now feeling Nate's kisses move up to the base of his shaft where it met with Rayya's pussy.

"Humm?" he heard Nate intone, now kissing, licking and sucking the base of his shaft along with Rayya's pussy, causing both of them to gasp.

"Oh, yes baby! Lick his dick! Suck my pussy! Be our slave!" he heard Rayya whisper, watching her press and work Nate's head in circles.

"Fuck! Oh Fuck!" he gasped, feeling his cock throb, loving the sights, scents, and feelings he was experience all at once.

"Yes, baby! He's about to cum! I can feel it! You want to taste it right?" he heard Rayya exclaim, watching as she pushed Nate's head back where he could see his wild, hungry eyes glowing in the soft blue-green light.

"Oh God!" he grunted, feeling his dick throb again, seeing how desperately Nate wanted him to cum.

"Yeah, look at that, you see how ready he is to lick your cum from my pussy? Don't hold it, let us have it. I love it when you cum in me," he heard Rayya groan, feeling her press herself up, squeezing her pussy as she wound and twisted her hips on her way back down, causing his toes to curl.

"Ah! I'm gonna cum!" he gasped, ignited from the merged sensation of Rayya's pussy and Nate's tongue wrapping around the base of his shaft just as Rayya fully settled down on his cock.

"Oh, yes! Cum in me! Cum in me!" he heard Rayya beg, feeling her pussy tighten around his cock.

"Yeah! You want it?" he gasped, taking hold of Rayya's breast, pinching her firm nipples between his fingers, as he bit and kissed her neck.

"Yeah, give it to me! Give it to me!" he heard Rayya gasp, sending him over the edge.

"Fuck! I'm cumming! I'm cumming!" he groaned, feeling his cock throb and pulse over and over again, filling Rayya's pussy to the brim.

"Yes! Yes! Oh fuck yes!" he heard Rayya shriek, feeling her whole body shake as her pussy squeezed and released in waves.

"Yes! Oh God, both of you came! Fuck, I want it all! Give it to me," he heard Nate whisper, followed by the wonderful sensation of him, sucking, licking and kissing the base of his shaft and balls as the sweet-scented mixture of cum rushed out of Rayya's pussy.

"Yeah, lick it all up," he whispered, taking hold of Rayya's thighs, lifting her so that more of their mix could run out over his shaft.

"Mmm!" he heard Nate groan, making loud slurping noises as he greedily licked up the mess he'd created.

"Oh, my fucking God, I love this!" he blurted, pulling Rayya higher, leaving only his tip inside, before saying, "now suck your babies' clit."

"Yeah baby, do as he says. Suck my clit, then come kiss us so we can taste," he heard Rayya command, wrapping her arms around his neck, laying small kisses on his cheek.

"Give me more to lick up first," he heard Nate reply, watching and feeling as Nate began to stroke his thumb over the base of his shaft and Rayya's clit, causing her pussy to pulse and squeeze on his tip.

"Baby! Oh God baby!" he heard Rayya gasp in his ear, now feeling more of their hot, creamy mix run down over his shaft, hitting and steaming in the cool air of the room.

"Yeah, that's better," he heard Nate whisper, seeing him lean forward with his mouth open and tongue extended.

"Oh my God! Too much! Too much!" he blurted, losing his breath, loving the sight and sensation of Nate's tongue as it touched the base of his shaft.

"No such thing as too much," he heard Nate whisper before running his tongue up his shaft to Rayya's clit, sucking and licking with so much passion he could feel his cock throb, wanting to cum again.

Baby, don't swallow it all…we want to taste," he heard Rayya whisper, inching herself up, letting his tip slip free, allowing him to see and feel the rest of their climax run out all over his length.

"Mmm, that smells so fucking good!" he heard Nate whisper, watching and feeling as Nate licked up more of their cream, catching it on the tip of his tongue, showing it to both of them before swallowing it down.

"Your hubby likes teasing us," he whispered, kissing Rayya on the cheek as she leaned her weight to the left, sliding off of him, settling on the bed Japanese style, looking between he and Nate expectantly.

"Baby? What's with that look for, huh?" he heard Nate ask, giving Rayya a mischievous smile before looking deep into his eyes, first kissing, then licking some of the remaining climax from his balls.

"Oh man! I'm going to do it again. I'm going to fuck a man in the ass!" he thought excitedly, watching as Nate swallowed what he'd licked, rising up with his eyes locked on his cock.

"Now that there's enough lube, it should go in nice and easy," he heard Nate whisper in a soft, sensual tone, before looking towards Rayya saying, "Sorry my love, I'm greedy, can you forgive me for not sharing with you?"

"Yeah, yeah, it's okay. Go, get on that fucking cock. I want to see," he heard Rayya reply, watching her as she gazed down at his cock then back towards Nate.

"Oh man! Oh man!" he whispered, feeling his heart pound in joy and excitement as Nate turned around, spreading his ass cheeks wide, exposing his flexing asshole which seemed to be begging him for penetration.

"Hold on a second," he heard Rayya whisper, watching and feeling as she used her thumb and index finger to carefully take hold of his cock from the base, holding it steady as she opened her mouth, letting out a long stream of saliva that hit his tip and ran down his length.

"Okay baby, go ahead and sit on that big ass dick," he heard Rayya command, smiling at him as Nate inched down, pressing the rim of his ass on the tip of his cock.

"Ah! Fuck!" he groaned, enjoying the warmth and tightness of Nate's ass as his tip began to slip in.

"Oh God! So Big! Yeah! 'Gemme' that big ass dick!" he heard Nate groan, causing him to gasp, watching and feeling as Nate pressed himself down, allowing his cock to fully slip in with a wet, sticky pop.

"Oh! I love it," he heard Rayya whisper, feeling her run kisses along the side of his cheek and neck as Nate continued to inch himself down, squeezing and relaxing his muscles until the full length of his cock was inside him.

"Yes! Oh, God yes!" Reggie moaned, loving the sight and sensation of his entire cock buried deep within Nate's ass.

"Now give me all of you have left," he heard Nate whisper, watching and feeling his arms reach backward, wrapping around his neck.

"You really want all I have left?" he asked, closing his eyes, feeling Nate begin to work his hips without mercy.

"Does that answer your question?" he heard Nate reply, feeling Nate twist and wind on his cock even harder.

"No," he gasped, kissing Nate's cheek and neck as he ran his hand up and down his chest and abdomen.

"It means, give me every drop you have left," he heard Nate gasp, tilting his head to the left while moving his hands to the back of his head, pressing his head towards his neck.

"Oh, every last drop, huh?" he gasped, laying passionate kisses on Nate's neck, loving the feeling of Nate's firm ass pressing against his thighs along with the sensation of his cock buried deep within Nate's hungry asshole.

"Every drop," he heard Nate confirm.

"I want you to cum with me," he said, feeling his own hunger to please overtake him.

"Yeah?" he heard Nate gasp.

"Yeah," he replied, keeping one hand on Nate's chest, while he moved his other up and down Nate's muscular abdomen, teasingly inching it towards his cock with his down stroke.

"Fuck!" he heard Nate grunt, causing him to smile.

"Looks like I learned how to tease from the best," he whispered as he moved his hand down over Nate's abdomen one last time before taking hold of his long, thick, rock hard cock.

"Mmm, see, I did a good job," he whispered in Nate's ear, stroking his cock, loving the feeling of Nate's warm precum running down all over his hand.

"Oh fuck! Oh fuck! So, fucking hot!" he heard Rayya gasp, feeling her hop out the bed, appearing in front of them with a hungry look on her face.

"No, greedy one. I know what you want. Not yet. You stand there and watch," he commanded, stroking Nate's cock harder, giving Rayya a, 'do what I say' look - smiling when she nodded in obedience.

"And, as for you," he whispered, kissing Nate on the side of the cheek, now adding twist to his strokes, smiling as more warm, sticky pre-cum leaked out all over his hand.

"Yes!?" he heard Nate gasp sounding anxious.

"Cum for me," he whispered, moving his hand down from Nate's chest, gripping his hip so that he could push and pull in sync with Nate's every wind and twist.

"Oh fuck! Yes! Fuck my ass! I love it when you fuck my ass!" he heard Nate gasp

"Good! 'Cause' I love fucking your tight little ass! Feels so fucking good! Look at your wife and tell her how much you like being owned and fucked by another man!" he commanded, feeling a surge of domineering energy he never knew he had.

"Oh! Fuck!' he heard both Nate and Rayya gasp in unison, feeding his blooming energy even more.

"Come here you! Sit on your hubby's cock!" he commanded, wrapping his index and thumb around Nate's cock, changing his vigorous strokes to long and sensual.

"Yeah…that's a good girl," he whispered, guiding Nate's cock into Rayya soaking wet pussy before bringing his hand around, rubbing both her clit and Nate's cock.

"Oh God!" he heard Rayya moan, feeling her grip his hand, pressing it down firmly.

"Shit! Oh shit!" he heard Nate gasp, feeling Nate's ass squeeze and flex on his cock over and over again.

"Fuck yes! Cum! Fill her pussy!" Reggie grunted, knowing what that wonderful feeling on his cock meant.

Seconds later, Reggie could smell the scent of fresh cum hit the air, followed by a warm, sticky sensation as Nate's cum rushed out from Rayya's pussy, all over his fingers.

"Ahh!" he gasped, closing his eyes, listening to everyone's wanting, lustful breaths, drinking in the sweet, musky scent of mixed climax and sweat.

"This is heaven," he thought, enjoying the potency and hypnotic subtleness he picked up with his every breath, where he could literally taste everyone's individual flavors on his tongue.

It was there that time seemed to slip away from Reggie. And where any of the minute inhibitions lingering within him fully disintegrated, allowing him to be fully born into freedom. Bringing up his hand, he gazed at his fingers coated in cum and smiled before placing them in his mouth.

"Oh, yum," he whispered, closing his eyes, allowing the sensation of Nate's flexing ass, the sound of the couples heavy breathing, along with the sweet, salty taste of mixed climax, to combine into one - perfect moment of pure ecstasy.

With a sharp gasp, Reggie came deep inside Nate ass. With every pulse and throb of his cock, with every moan and gasp of Nate, and Rayya and they continued to work their hips, ridding the waves of each other's orgasms, pure serenity settled over him.

"I want to live my life like this for now on," Reggie thought, feeling fully baptized into Nate and Rayya's world of carnal desires.

And with that thought, Reggie mentally took his very first steps into his new life.

Chapter I

Paradigms and Rebirth

Road Trip: Day Three

Date: Saturday, June 3rd 2017

Time: 7:56 am

Location: Bismarck, North Dakota

"They were, they were having a threesome. Jesus, all morning, almost nonstop they were at it. And the third person, was a guy. Rayya, Nate, and another guy. Shit, even if I wanted to think it's fucked up, I can't. It sounded way too good to think even one bad thing about it," Jay thought, taking out his 'thinking pack,' pulling out a cigarette, lighting it as he reflected on the sounds he'd heard earlier that morning.

"Fuck! I wish we could be that brave," Jay whispered to himself, taking a small drag, quickly blanching when he thought of another man touching his wife.

"Man, I'm being selfish! I'd just want a threesome with another woman," he thought, feeling annoyed at his double standard.

"Hey brother, you mind if I steal a smoke off you?" he heard a deep voice say from behind.

"Yeah, sure man," he replied as a stocky, muscular man, with long golden hair and well-shaped Goatee came up towards his right with a strange, exalted smile on his face.

"Dude looks high as a bird. Must be some good shit. I'll give him two for the happy presence," he thought pulling out two cigarettes, passing it to the man, who took them smiling and chuckling to himself, shaking his head like, 'oh my God' before saying, "thanks man, much obliged, much obliged."

"Good shit? I mean - had a good night? Partying?" Jay asked, shaking his head at his slip of tongue.

"No, no! Really good shit man! And yeah, an amazing fucking night. Like, you don't even fucking understand. I could die right now and not give a shit, a shit I tell you," Jay heard the man say, placing the cigarette in his mouth, pulling it out, exhaling as if he'd just taken a drag.

"*Yeah, he's high…he has no clue it's not lit,*" he thought, bringing up his lighter, saying as casually as he could, "hey brother, the cig…it's not lit," so as not to disturb the man's inner thoughts.

"Oh yeah, it isn't, huh? Shit, I forgot, pahahaha hahaha, pahahahah!" Jay heard the man blare, bringing the cigarette to the lighter.

"*What the fuck kind of weed, or what the hell could he be on? He's happy as fuck!*" he thought, flicking the lighter on with his thumb, watching curiously as the man took his first legitimate drag of the cigarette, choking right after.

"You okay?" he asked, looking at the man dubiously as he took his own drag, which went down smooth.

"Yeah, umm this is my first cigarette. I figured, what the hell, might as well try. Today is a day of lots of first! Yeah, today is the first of first," Jay heard the man reply, slightly weirding him out, mostly due to that fact that the man's voice was so deep, he'd never expect it to sound loopy or childish.

"Well enjoy it man," he replied, taking another drag, studying the man's body language and face more attentively, realising that he wasn't high at all, which made him slightly uncomfortable.

"*What's really going on? Is this a scam tactic? Is he all of a sudden gonna ask me for money or some crazy favor?*"

"Man, un-fucking believable!" Jay heard the man say excitedly, looking away from him, grinning ear to ear as he shuffled his feet back and forth in an awkward jogging dance, before turning back to him, saying, "You ever have that kind of day?"

"That kind of day?" Jay asked as he thought, "*No way, a hippy bible thumper!? Oh fucking 'It', please no! I don't want to hear this shit right now! Especially with the shit going on in my head!*"

"Yeah, that kind of day. When it's a new fucking day!" he heard the man say excitedly, fist punching the air in a, 'Yes! Alright winning!' gesture that auto ashed the cigarette a little too much, where he could see the cherry flash bright before flaming out.

"Umm," he replied with a look on his face that must've said, 'what the fuck?' because the man quickly changed his excitement level, bringing himself down from deep space to somewhere near the moon.

"Lil too over the top?" he heard the man ask right after.

"Mmmm, just be you 'fam'," he replied, not wanting to be a negative influence on the man.

"I'm just excited and I can't help it. You ever woke up and realized life isn't the way you thought it was. That you could fucking…I dunno open up to shit. To fucking fly free and not give a shit and just live. You know? Just fucking live free!" Jay heard the man say, with his energy level returning to what Jay considered extremely hyper, being that the man was again, in place jogging and throwing air punches.

"Hum, I was just thinking about being free. Is it that easy? Could Karman and I be free? Would I get jealous; would she get jealous? How could I watch her be with another guy? How could she watch me be with another woman? Wouldn't it rip us apart? Shit, why am I thinking like this? Fuck man, listening to Nate and Rayya really got in my head. And that was before their threesome last night," he thought as he said, "I've had days where I've felt free and others where I've felt trapped. But I'll be honest, I've had more trapped feeling days than free to be honest."

"Me too! And now! And now, Reggie is free! Reggie is free!" Jay heard the man who referred to himself as Reggie exclaim, pointing at himself with his thumb, causing Jay to shake his head and smile, thinking, *"You're having one hell of a day. You must be lucky, because if your cigarette was lit, you would've burned yourself."*

"I'm glad you're feeling free Reggie. I wish I knew how you obtained that freedom. I like your energy," he replied pointing to the cigarette and Reggie's shirt, showing him that he'd left a black mark on it - as he thought, *"Why am I even opening up to this guy?"*

"Ha! Obtained! I don't think I had a choice really. Well I did, a little bit at first. But…well I don't know how to explain it. But it was like I had a choice, but then there was only one real choice, and that was to umm, just go for it, go for it and be free," he heard Reggie reply, looking at the cigarette in his hand as if he were surprised it was there before passing it to him, saying, "sorry man, I got ahead of myself. I just wanted to try it…but it's not for me."

"Na man, it's fine. Reggie is it? You're a cool guy. I'm happy that whatever it is that happened to you, worked out where you could be this happy," Jay said, eyeing the other cigarette in Reggie's hand, noting that it'd been totally crushed when he'd done his, 'fuck yes!' power punches in the air.

"Oh shit, my bad. I got too excited," he heard Reggie say, looking at him then his hand, causing him to laugh and say, "na' man, you're cool. Any advice on how to be free? I don't know your situation, but I take it that you just manned up, I guess?"

"Something like that. Something like that. It was more like I was honest with myself. Like fully honest - and then boom, I was free. Real free. But man, I was scared. Really scared. That's what keeps you trapped - that fear man, it had me like this," Jay heard Reggie reply, clutching his shirt over his heart, making a struggling gesture to animate how the fear had held him.

"Yeah, I'm scared too. I don't know what will happen if I'm honest. And I don't know if I could handle…" Jay said, trailing of as he thought, *"If Karman wanted another man."*

"Man, I was right there with you. That thing you're not saying. That's where the fear is. It's right there man. And if you can find a way to say it, or face it, then boom, you're free. Anyways, thanks for the smokes. Sorry I wasted them. If you're still here for another day, I work at the bar right here. Food for you…and is that a wedding ring? Yeah, it is. So, food for you and your wife…or husband maybe, I 'dunno'. Your spouse I should say. I'm rambling. The food would be on me. If not, safe travels! And my parting words my man. Address that fear, it's trapping you," Jay heard Reggie say, giving him a bright smile as he stepped off the curb, waving as he headed towards the bar with a skip to his step that didn't fit the way he looked whatsoever.

"I wonder what happened to him, that'd give him the strength to shake off the fear?" he thought, pulling out another cigarette, lighting it as he tried to recall why Reggie's voice sounded so familiar, having a nagging feeling it was the same voice he'd heard come through the wall from Nate and Rayya's room, but dismissing it, as it could've been anyone.

"Let go of the fear…or should I let go of the desire? Isn't it bad to want to fuck someone else if you're married?" he whispered to himself.

"But the way it sounded yesterday didn't seem bad at all. I wonder how Nate could handle seeing his wife with another man. Does he enjoy it? And would it be bad if we were in the same room with them? A look, but don't touch 'kinda' thing?"

"I've never seen that boy so happy in my life," Jay heard an older man say, coming from behind.

"Huh?" he replied turning around, immediately recognizing the rugged, battle marred face of the desk clerk, whose name tag read, 'John'.

"You heard me," he heard John reply, watching as he placed a cigarette on the far left corner of his mouth, lighting it smoothly, blowing the smoke out the opposite end side.

"Umm, well, he was pretty happy. He said he obtained freedom. So, yeah," he said, taking a deep drag of his own cigarette, glaring at John, watching cascades of emotion play across his face in less than a second.

"I've known Reggie since he was in his mom's belly. And he was a grumpy, solemn bastard even then. He wouldn't kick to show he was alive even if his mother was running for her life in the apocalypse. Growing up, he kept mostly to himself. Had a few girlfriends because he was the quiet, mysterious type that didn't take no shit. But other than that, and working at the bar, because his father owns it, Reggie doesn't really talk to people, let alone, a stranger such as yourself. Smiling and giving you advice to boot, humph, he went into that room and came out a whole other person. He even chatted me up, telling me all about life's possibilities. I'm one step in the grave and all of a sudden that pup is giving me life advice. Pah! Funny 'init'," Jay heard John say, all while never letting the cigarette leave his lips as he took his drags.

"That room? No way, no way, no way!" he thought, taking too strong of his own drag, causing him to choke before saying, "excuse, that room?"

"Pah, you know which room. I went by when I didn't see him come out, and at first I have to admit, I was a little perturbed at what I was hearing. But seeing him now, I'm glad of it.

Something needed to awaken that boy. If that's what it took, then that's what it took. Who am I to look down on it," Jay heard John say, giving him a wink as he removed his cigarette from his mouth, which was burned all the way down to the filter, replacing it with a new one, smoothly lighting it with the cherry of the old.

"Wow," was the only thing he managed to say, feeling lightheaded from the smoke and from what he'd just heard, realising that Reggie's transformation to a man of exhilaration and happiness was due to a morning spent with Nate and Rayya, who'd been slipping past his defenses, making him question if there could be more to what he and Karman had.

"Wow is right, wow is right my friend. You've got some good friends. A little weird for my taste, but I was in the war and didn't get time to enjoy the seventies like a lot of people, so yeah. Anyways, like I said, I think you've got some good, fun loving friends. I say, put whatever that little quarrel was to rest and enjoy the time you spend with them. Hell, anyone who could make Reggie, who's thirty-four, wake the hell up and smell the roses, has to have some kind of good value and substance to add to your life," he heard John say, nodding his head, not even looking at him, but out, towards the highway as if at any moment someone he knew would arrive.

"Thanks, I'll umm, I think I'll take your advice," he replied, almost to himself as he tossed his cigarette into the neck of the smoke pot.

"Mmm, good, good to hear," he heard John reply, finally looking over to him, giving him a wink before turning to stare out into the distance again, which he took as the cue that their conversation was over.

"Okay, take care man," Jay said, nodding his head as he walked past John, through the sliding automatic doors, into the lobby.

"Holy fucking shit! Holy fucking shit! What the hell just happened! So they had this guy come to their room and just, and just fucked him! Man! That's crazy! Holy 'It'! They didn't know him at all! Well, I mean, of course they didn't! But, just holy 'It'! And that guy was happy! Happy as all hell! Man, could we ever be brave enough to do some shit like that!?"

Before Jay knew it, he found himself standing in front of his room with the key card out, hovering just over the magnetic lock.

"Huh? What the fuck am I doing?" he mumbled to himself, tapping the key card to the lock, opening the door to find his wife standing nude in front of the bed, staring at sets of different outfits with a puzzled expression.

"Hi boo," he said softly, strolling up to her, kissing her on the side of the head as he took a closer look at the clothes she'd laid out, noting that all were sexy and revealing, and unlike anything she'd ever worn before, except for the outfit she'd chosen the day prior.

"Hi baby, how was your think smoke?" Jay heard his wife, Karman whisper, touching a white halter top, before moving her hand towards a hot pink spandex skirt that was so short it would've most likely only covered half her ass.

"It was good," he replied, staring at a pair of red fishnet stockings, dressing her in his mind.

"Just give me a second baby, and then I want to hear all about it," he heard his wife reply, picking up an all-black one-piece halter skirt that was only slightly longer than the spandex skirt, but much looser, where at the gentlest breeze, one would be able to see everything she had to offer underneath.

"Damn, she'd look amazing and super sexy in all of these," he thought, stepping back, scanning the curves of her body, instantly giving himself an erection as he replied, "yeah, take all the time you need."

"Are we going to any of the sightseeing places today or are we just driving straight?" he heard her whisper as she turned and displayed the one piece to him, with her head tilted as if to ask, 'what do you think?'

"I umm," he began as he thought, *"Are we going anywhere today? I wanted to dump those two in Chi-Town as soon as possible, but now, now I'm not so sure."*

"If we're just going to be in the car today, then I want to be 'comfey', and I could save this one if we're going to go somewhere later," he heard his wifey say, gazing down at the one piece adoringly before giving him - what he called the, 'please hubby look'.

"My baby doesn't want to rush the trip. She wants to go see things with them. I think I need to chill out and see how things go," he thought staring at the clothes, realizing that many of them had Rayya written all over them before thinking, *"Yeah, I should really chill and give them a chance. My baby is changing. She's more confident and willing to show off how beautiful she is. I don't know how Rayya's doing it, but it's working."*

"Baby?" he heard his wife whisper, taking him out of his thoughts, now seeing that she was giving him a, 'why are you taking so long to answer my question', pouty face that made him burst out laughing.

"Yes boo? Umm, well, I…umm, where do you want to go see? I mean, we're in no real rush and I remember them saying they're not in any rush. So, I'm sure if we tell them we 'wanna' check out some places, they'll be down," he said, feeling awkward as his desire to defend and protect himself and his wife, clashed head on with his feelings of wanting to get to know the couple more.

"Really? You don't mind? You don't want to go straight to Chicago and drop them off?" he heard his wife reply, fully turning to face him.

"Na', it's fine, we can go wherever you like. Let's ask them to make sure they're down with sightseeing," he said, feeling butterflies in his stomach before he could even catch the barrage of thoughts flowing through his mind.

"Okay, yay! Which one, which one? And where does baby want to go today?" he heard his wife ask, jumping up and down, pointing to the outfits on the bed, before running up to him, giving him a kiss on the cheek and lips.

"Umm, I like all of them. But I love the fishnet…" he began.

"Oh, pick any one except for those. Those are for later," he heard his wife reply with a mischievous giggle.

"Later huh?"

"Focus baby."

"Umm, I like the… hummm, surprise me, I'll go ask them where they want to go," he said, smiling inwardly, trying to guess what she'd put on.

"Ahh! Baby!" he heard his wife exclaim.

"What? Surprise me, hubby is curious," he replied, laughing when he saw his wife bite her bottom lip, knowing she was trying to think of which outfit would scandalize him the best.

"Fine, okay, I'll surprise you. Okay, go, go, go," he heard his wife reply, pushing him towards the door.

"Hey, hey, hey, I'm just curious. And please don't get defensive…why the sudden change? And don't think I don't love it. I love it, and I support you all the way. I'm just curious," he said, wrapping his arms around his wife, kissing her on the top of the head as she continued to try and push him towards the door.

"Mmm, go, go, go, ask them, ask them, ask them," he heard his wife reply, tilting her head back, raising her lips for a kiss.

"Please don't shut me out," he replied, kissing her softly on the lips.

"I'm not shutting you out. I just don't know what to say. I went shopping with Rayya, she convinced me to buy all these clothes, and I honestly didn't know what to do with them. And then when I saw her outfit the day we were heading out, something in me just wanted to try. And I, I kind of liked how I felt wearing that outfit yesterday. Okay baby, now go ask them, I want to go see things. It's a road trip, not a race," Jay heard his wife say, tippy toeing, kissing him on the lips, pushing him with twice the strength she'd been using before.

"Damn, 'lil' runt, you're strong," he replied before saying, "okay baby, I'm just really happy you feel comfortable showing off. And I'm happy Rayya helped you."

"Aww, thanks baby. Does that mean you don't hate them?" he heard his wife ask, giving him a sarcastic, questioning look as he walked backwards towards the door.

"Hate is not the right word. Especially since it seems we can't stop fucking the moment we hear them fucking," he thought, wondering how he really felt about them as he turned and opened the door to find Nate standing there with his hand up, ready to knock.

"Oh, hey," he said, almost jumping in surprise.

"Hey bro, you gotta minute?" he heard Nate ask, quickly stepping off to the side, which made him realize he must've caught a glance of his wife standing nude.

"Yeah, I was just about to come to your room," Jay replied, stepping out the door, letting it close behind him, thinking, *"that was really respectful of him to move. Cool, cool."*

"Hey, I want to apologise, and come clean about Rayya and I's intentions when I had asked you that question, and about our intentions in general," he heard Nate say, pausing and looking at the door behind them, gulping hard.

"Oh, he got more than a little peek, huh? I'm starting to see how voyeurs get off on other people's energy. I really like this look on his face."

"I wanted to apologise as well. I think you guys are just having fun, and it hasn't caused Karman and I any harm whatsoever. And even that love question bullshit wasn't bad. It was good for me to get that out. I mean, I hate seeing couples and they look unhappy, seeing them looking all disconnected and shit, you know? I used to always wonder how shit like that happened, and then after you asked me that question, I realized it's probably because they never really nail the love aspect down. I realized that maybe they never say those kind of words that you had me say to Karman, to each other. So, honestly I appreciate it," he said, watching Nate's face change from concerned to slightly relieved.

"I, ummm. Bro, you've caught me off guard. I was coming here to profusely apologise. And I…," he heard Nate begin before pausing, looking towards his own room door, where Jay could hear soft scratching sounds coming through.

"The closet is by the door, maybe your wifey is getting changed," he said to Nate, biting the bottom of his lip in contemplation when Nate's eyes narrowed.

"What? What's going on?" he finally asked, when Nate snickered and shook his head.

"Rayya's not changing, that's her trying to eavesdrop through the door. She's pretty worried about the whole situation," he heard Nate whisper before saying, "Rayya, come out, we can hear you…and no, they're not mad."

"They're way too worried about that question rubbing us the wrong way. And he also said he wanted to come clean about their intentions in general. Oh, I see! This isn't about them being voyeurs and feeding off of our energy. This is the real deal! They're really interested in doing something with us. Even going to that janky ass motel was a set up to share the room

102

with us. Shit, as good as it sounds and plays out in my mind when I listen to them, is it as fun or worth risking our relationship to actually try messing around with them?" he thought, looking over towards Nate's room, hearing the door open, losing his breath as Rayya came out in an all-black tube top, high waisted jeans, and sandaled heels, all of which perfectly fit the shape and curvature of her body.

"Hi Jay, as Nate was saying … I mean… I heard…but I wasn't listening all the way," he heard Rayya stammer, moving her hands around anxiously as she spoke, causing him to bite the inside of his cheeks so he wouldn't smile, knowing if he did, it would embarrass her even further.

"Holy 'It', she's gorgeous," Jay thought taking in the details of her light-mocha complexion, long, black, curly hair, hazel-green eyes and thick, voluptuous lips, that were aglow via soft, purple gloss.

"It's okay. No worries. You're just the worst spy ever. But you know what you can worry about?" he asked, fighting his eye to look away from her lips, feeling a hot flash as he envisioned kissing them.

"Um…what?" he heard Rayya ask in a mostly mutual tone, giving him a small smile, followed by her wiggling and twisting her hands and arms as if she were trying to keep herself from leaping for joy.

"Calm voice, calm smile, then just utterly failing at keeping the rest of herself in check," he thought, watching Rayya's excitement grow by the second at being, 'forgiven' by him.

"It feels good that both of them actually give a fuck if those words caused damage. And even though some part of his question might've been for selfish reasons, I get it. I can see clearly that they don't want to hurt the people they want to have fun with. That's actually pretty cool. A lot of people wifey and I know, would've tried to fuck us physically and emotionally, and wouldn't have given a damn if they left us in ruin."

"Here, give me a sec," he mumbled, snapping out of his thoughts, whipping out his room key, tapping the door as he said, "Baby, Rayya wants to come in and Nate's in front of the door."

"Oh, okay, let Rayya in. And, hi Nate," he heard his wife reply airily as he opened the door.

"Hey Rayya, hold on for just one second," he said as he turned around, steeping through the door.

"Oh, okay," he heard Rayya reply with a slightly puzzled look on her face, causing him to chuckle as he looked up at Nate, seeing that his eyes had went wide for just a second.

"Humm, my baby gave you an eye full didn't she. Alright, I seem to be the only one that wasn't in on this teasing game," he thought, bobbing his head in reassurance to Rayya as he closed the door, strolling over to his wife - who'd moved even further back from the foot of the bed so that from the moment the door opened, to the moment it had closed, both Nate and Rayya would've seen her fully nude form.

"I know, I know. I'm indecisive. Where's Rayya? Why'd you have her wait outside? And did you ask them where they wanted to go?" he heard his wife ask as he took her in his arms, kissing her on the temple.

"How'd I not realise you're playing your own game? When did I fall out of sync with you? Your shy ass would've normally never stayed in front of the door like that. I think you knew, or had a feeling they were swingers all along. Did you not trust my reaction, if you had told me? And more importantly, were you right not to trust me?"

"Baby? Baby?" Jay heard his wife ask as he thought back to the subtle changes he'd felt from her in the weeks' prior, realizing it'd all begun when she'd started hanging out with Rayya in earnest.

"Huh?" he finally mumbled, gritting his teeth, recalling the day she'd come home with shopping bags filled with bright colored clothes, remembering he'd been in a bad mood because of a woman he'd been checking out who'd been wearing booty shorts, approaching him, telling him that she wasn't an object to be looked at.

"Fuck, I remember denouncing to wifey that booty shorts should burn in the depths of hell the day she wanted to open up and try them. What was that, three weeks back? And that day, she was also going on and on about Rayya being open this and Rayya being open that. But I was so pissed off at that situation with that woman, and so pissed off at shit going on at work, I wasn't really listening. I didn't get the hints on what she meant by saying 'open' so many times.

"I had thought she was just making a big deal out of normal, everyday, female shit. I mean every lady I know always shared changing rooms. So, I didn't see the big deal. Yeah, that day she was really happy,

smiling ear to ear as she spoke to me, but as she spoke I was complaining about my bullshit day... and the happy conversation went dead," he thought, feeling a pang of deep sadness take hold of him, causing his eyes to slightly water.

"Baby? What's wrong?" he heard his wife ask as she leaned back, staying within the grip of his arms, where he could see her studying his face, which made him want to turn away.

"Mmm, shit nothing - fuck, something," he replied, inching them over towards the foot of the bed, sitting down, pulling her in front of him, laying soft kisses upon her bare belly.

"Baby?"

"I'm sorry. During the work week we spend very little time together. Then I bring all my work garbage home, that and all the annoyance I feel about people in general. Then I don't listen to you properly when I'm actually with you. And I miss all the small things that make big changes," he said, still laying kisses upon his wife's belly as he spoke.

"Huh?' he heard his wife reply, even though he could see the look on her face showed she understood full well what he meant.

"So, you and Rayya, us and them...You...," he began to say when his wife cut in and said, "She...Rayya, umm."

"What?" he whispered, giving his wife a reassuring smile.

"She kissed me...she kissed me in the changing room the day I bought these clothes, and I liked it, I liked it a lot. I...I couldn't stop myself, and after she kissed me, I kissed her back. And then... we couldn't stop making out. For a long time...we couldn't stop ourselves from making out. And the whole time I was thinking of ...that you'd hate me, and that I was evil for cheating on you," he heard his wife whisper, causing him to lurch up and wrap his arms around her, feeling exhilarated and enraged all at the same time.

"You kissed her? You kissed her! Oh my fucking....so you knew... you knew they were swingers... you knew they were up to shit and you... Wow baby, you kissed her. Oh man," he said in whispered yells as his wife closed her eyes and turned her head, burying her face in-between his arm and body

"Oh baby, don't cry, don't cry, don't cry. It's going to be okay. It's going to be okay. You hear me baby? It's going to be all right," he whispered, feeling hot tears on his arm and chest.

"I didn't mean to cheat, I didn't mean to cheat," he heard his wife sob, causing his heart to lurch, feeling his stomach drop the way it always did whenever his wife was sad.

"Baby, baby, it's okay," he whispered, titling her to lean back, wiping tears off her cheeks as he kissed her face over and over again.

"Is it okay? It's cheating. It really is. But it's a woman. Should I really give a fuck? I've always liked it when I see ladies kiss each other. But they weren't my wife. Ahh, and it's Rayya. How can I care? But still, it was behind my back."

"No it's not. How can you forgive me? Cheating is cheating," he heard his wife sob sounding even more upset.

"Baby," he replied, holding her tighter as he thought, *"No matter how I play it out in my mind, I'm not that upset at this. I'm more annoyed it was kept a secret for this long. But that's all on me because I was closed off and not letting her speak when she was probably trying to tell me. I'm sure her story about them sharing the changing room, and Rayya being 'open', was leading up to the part where she would've said, 'oh, by the way, Rayya made me feel so comfortable and exploratory, that we 'kissed'. Damn I need to be a better husband and actually listen to her when she speaks. I'm so good at reading strangers emotions, and anticipating their motives, but I fail to focus on the most important person in front of me. And fuck, now that I'm really thinking about them kissing…I wish I was there to watch."*

"I'm sorry," he heard his wife gasp as she began to sob even harder.

"Snap out of it. Okay, I get it, it was wrong and it was behind my back, bla bla bla. But seriously, like - cut it out. Enough is enough. I mean it was just a kiss.

"We made out, that's a lot of kissing" he heard his wife correct through her sobs.

"Well, you guys made out. So what?" he said, bursting out laughing, finally realizing the copious amount of times he'd fantasized about having threesomes with his wife and another woman, wondering why he'd have any negative thoughts about what his wife had done whatsoever.

"It's not funny," he heard his wife whisper, looking up at him, trying to force a smile on her face, which made him kiss her lips.

"Why not? I deep down inside always think that all ladies are bi anyway. Right now, all I'm really thinking is that I wish I would've been there to watch you two. In the Navy, I used to watch ladies kiss in the clubs all the time, and it was hot. Humm, I bet watching you and her would've been fire," he whispered kissing his wife in the lips again as he thought, *"Besides, I really like your new style and your new carefree demeanor. I don't want you bottled up. I want you to feel free and happy."*

"But, but, but," he heard his wife whisper as she began to smile.

"Baby, leave it alone. You're forgive, now all there is left to this situation is that its super fucking hot. Humm, did you two do anything else? Now that I think you two kissing is hot…hum, maybe hearing there was more, yes hum," he said, trying to mentally prepare himself to auto think it was hot and not care it was done behind his back if she said – 'yes, we did more'.

"Ouch," he gasped, feeling a sharp pinch on the ass.

"You just had to turn my evil, I cheated on hubby with a girl moment, into a pure perverted one, huh?" he heard his wife ask, laying her head on his chest before saying, "thank you for not being mad at me. And no, we didn't do more, it was just kissing…and well, she was squeezing my ass."

"Damn, that does sound hot. She must really like you. By the way, you never answered me, well of course – 'cuz' crying like a baby and all, but did you know they were swingers? I mean kissing you, and last night, the guy they had in the room. Please don't say you had no clue," he said, stepping back, looking at the door thinking, *"Damn, I told them I'd just be a second. I didn't mean to make them wait this long."*

"I kind of started to get the feeling because Rayya was always saying she'd bring so and so home, but then she'd just leave it like that. And then she kept calling me hot. And then… well after the kiss, yeah sure. I was pretty certain they were. But I didn't want you to get mad at us hanging out with them because they're really nice and I …"

"Relax, I know. I know I was being an ass. I wouldn't have told me either," he said feeling his mood change to calm and mischievous as an idea began to bloom in his mind.

"More than an ass, you were being an extreme grump," he heard his wife shot it.

"Excuse?" he replied, smiling as he moved his lips to her ear and whispered, "I know you're teasing them on purpose. I know why you didn't move from the door. And I know why you're trying out those clothes. You like all this don't you?"

For what felt like long moments to him, his wife didn't answer, but looked past him towards the clothes on the bed, then towards the door, where he could hear Nate and Rayya whispering something excitedly before she looked back at him and said, "Maybe."

"Uh-huh. Look baby, if they like us, and…how do I say this?" he began as he thought, *"I might've been the last to know. But that doesn't mean I can't bring the heat. It's time for me to have some fun too!"*

Chapter II

Renovation

Road Trip: Day Three

Date: Saturday, June 3rd 2017

Time: 8:01 am

Location: Bismarck, North Dakota

"Baby!" Nate heard Rayya shriek again, squeezing him as she jumped up and down, almost smashing the crown of her head into his chin, causing him to lean back as he laughed.

"Yes baby, I know baby," Nate replied, replaying the image of Karman's beautiful nude form, standing calmly in front of the bed in his mind.

"She had to have moved back! She had to have! She knew you weren't standing directly in front of the door! She did that on purpose!" Nate heard his wife whisper excitedly.

"Yes baby, yes baby, I know baby… but there's always a small chance it was by mistake. So, for now, just be calm baby. Don't jump to conclusions," Nate replied, chuckling as he thought of how many times he'd said, 'I know' to the same thing for the last few minutes they'd been standing outside the door.

"She doesn't care about me! That was all for you! Oh, you're so smart! You said they'd show us a gesture or something. That was definitely a thing! That was definitely a thing!" Nate heard his wife, Rayya whisper, hopping up and down in her heeled sandals before doing a strange version of the tootsie roll, which made her look like a robot due to her sandals not being able to slide on the thickly carpeted floor.

"Boo, relax…relax, she might not have had time to move," he whispered, not wanting to get too excited, even though he was quite certain his wife's assumption was correct.

"Unt-unh, that girl can move her sexy little ass. And if she couldn't, and Jay really fucked up and exposed her, we'd be breathing smoke and burning in fire from the heat she'd be putting on him in that room," he heard his wife reply, with her finger wagging 'no, no, no', causing him to laugh even harder.

"Yes my love, but we shouldn't…" he began to say when the door opened, with his first sight being Karman's nude form still standing in front of the bed, this time gripping two different articles of clothing in her hands.

"Holy shit," he thought as she turned her head, giving him the almost exact same look she'd given him earlier that morning when she'd been sitting in the hotel lobby.

"Hey Rayya, this girl can't pick an out outfit to save her life. Please help her. That's what I wanted to say earlier. Oh, and if neither of you two mind, we were hoping we could slow down our mad race to get to Chi Town. We were thinking we should go check out the sights around here. Hell, even back track and hit up Yellowstone Park before the shit blows up and kills us all. What do you two think?" Nate heard Jay say, stepping from behind the door, only blocking his line of sight for less than a second as he propped it open.

"Wow!" he thought watching Jay usher Rayya in with his hand on the small of her back, surprising him because he'd never seen Jay actually touch his wife unless it was the half-hearted hug and kiss she forced him to give.

"Oh, this just got really interesting. And intense. Karman's eyes are still not exactly friendly. And I don't think Jay knows how closed off to Rayya he really is. He might think that was just a small flirting gesture. But to us…to Rayya - you just said that you want to fuck her. Fuck her like no one else has ever fucked her before," Nate thought, locking onto the moment his wife ever so slightly turned to look Jay in the face - with such lust he felt like she'd shove him to the wall and kiss him right then and there.

"Nate?" he heard Jay ask, snapping him out of his thoughts where he envisioned his wife doing just that… as he strolled into the room, taking hold of Karman by the chin, looking deep into her eyes, asking why she had that sassy look on her face, and if she wanted to be spanked because of it.

"Yeah, we're in no rush. And Yellowstone sounds cool. And actually, I was hoping to go to Mt. Rushmore," he heard himself say as the fantasy returned to the forefront of his mind, where Karman told him she'd never be a good girl.

"Cool, cool," he heard Jay reply, watching as a mischievous smile spread across his lips.

"Karma is strange," he thought, looking towards the door that'd just shut closed, instantly feeling hungry to see more of Karman's beautiful figure, remembering how he and Rayya had ensnared Reggie into their naughty little trap.

"So, which place do you…I'm sorry, I lost my train of thought," he murmured, feeling flustered as his desire to see Karman one last time took on new depths.

"Which place do I want to go to first? Umm… Mt. Rushmore. I've never been. So sure, we can go there, and then to Yellowstone. I've been there and I know the perfect cabins to stay in. Do you smoke? Let's go outside. Today is one of those days where I really want to smoke," Nate heard Jay say, walking in front of him, shaking his head as if to say, 'ha ha ha! We got you!'.

"Oh Jay, nothing about you is subtle. Your games are clear for all to see. And you don't even hide your victories. Yet, it's working…so, I must give you credit when it's due."

"So, yes or no to the smoke?" he heard Jay ask, seeing him peek over his shoulder, still wearing a mischievous smile, making him realize how far off kilter he'd been knocked when he noticed he hadn't even bothered to answer Jay's question.

"Sure, I'll take a puff," he finally replied, wondering how he'd been throttled by such a direct tactic.

"Cool, cool," he heard Jay reply, watching as he veered off to the right at the end of the hallway, entering and gliding through the lobby in a few smooth steps before going through the double automatic doors, leading to the parking lot outside.

"I've never seen him so energetic. He's always dragging his feet. Always walking around looking like he's carrying every ounce of his life's stress on his shoulders. I don't think he knows that others see him this way. I don't think he knows that behaving like that is what's causing even the friendliest people to attack both him and Karman."

"I've always wanted to shake the shit out of him and tell him that walking around stressed and negative triggers everyone's natural instincts, causing them to want to crush the weaker competition. I've always wanted to tell him that he is the actual reason why so many people add drama and lies to his life, with hopes that the man filled with negative energy would finally

111

fail," he thought coming out into the warm balmy air, standing next to Jay, watching as he placed a cigarette into his mouth, lighting it in one smooth gesture as if he'd smoked his entire life.

"Here 'ya' go man, don't waste it like your friend Reggie," he heard Jay say right after, not even bothering to look at him as he passed him a cigarette with his left hand.

"Reggie?" he asked, feeling a strange discomfort rise in his throat as he took the cigarette, studying the side of Jay's face, which still held a look mischief as he blew out a long stream of smoke into the air.

"Yeah, I ran into your convert standing right here, just a little while ago. He came out beaming brighter than the sun, asking for a cigarette. Loving life and all," he heard Jay reply, snickering and snorting to himself before looking at him shaking his head.

"Convert?" Nate replied, bringing the cigarette to his lips, wondering why he was bothering to go along with smoking, being that he despised everything about it.

"Mmm, yeah, convert. You know what I mean. Don't play dumb," he heard Jay respond as he brought up the lighter, flicking it on.

"Convert - is a fitting word," he thought taking a small drag, feeling the smooth smoke roll down into his lungs.

"You live in your head a lot, it's fucking annoying," he heard Jay blurt all of a sudden, causing him to choke from both surprise and laughter.

"And you…" he began, quickly biting his tongue.

"I'm not made of sugar…I won't melt if you speak your mind," he heard Jay reply, seeing his mischievous face evaporate into the grumpy, annoyed face he normally wore, before it smoothed over to one of pure reflection.

"I judge you too quickly, way too often, and then you always surprise me with another layer. That's why I shut up. Not because I think you'll melt, you sexy pain in the ass," he thought before saying, "Sometimes I don't think you hide enough of what you think and feel."

"Sometimes huh? And what part do you think I should hide, and what part do you think I should tell? Do you think I should directly tell you that I think your wife is attractive? If so I 'dunno' why, I figured that it's a no brainer. I don't know why you'd need to lead me to look at her. What else? The fact that I openly don't trust or feel like being bothered with people because I think they're all treacherous?" he heard Jay say, bobbing his head in self-affirmation.

"Jay, well sometimes, your negative energy towards people is…a bit much," he replied.

"I work in the tech industry, where everyone's trying to steal each other's fucking designs, and backstab their way to the top, whatever that is. Then they try to sabotage your personal life, knowing if you have a bad name there, it will carry over to your work. So then, what do you want from me?" he heard Jay rebuttal, shrugging his shoulders as he exhaled smoke from of his nose, resembling an angry dragon about to belch fire.

"To be happy. To enjoy your life. To leave those things where they are. To live your life in the moment with Karman. Live your life in the moment with us. To enjoy us and open yourself up to enjoying people in general. If you'd do that, then that's when enjoyable people would truly begin to show up in your life. With some people, the spark of enjoyment would be fast and bright, ending by the morning's light. While with others, you'd find the fun and passion smoldering on, giving you deep warmth and comfort for years to come," Nate thought as he whispered, "What do you want for yourself?"

"Typical answer from a person who lives in their head. But I bet you answered a fucking Nobel Peace Prize speech in your head. What a self-righteous son of a bitch," he heard Jay reply, beginning to laugh as he took a drag, shooting him a truly genuine smile.

"You're, hummmm, you're a challenging man to understand. I think you often wear all your emotions on your sleeve. But then you…I don't know how to say it, other than, you have this depth to you, where I have no idea what any of your emotions or thoughts are," Nate said, glaring at his cigarette, hoping it'd burn down sooner when Jay reached out and took it from his hand.

"I'll smoke it for you. Your face says you hate it. Anyways, I called you self-righteous because that's what people who are trying to be benevolent say to someone like me. You're trying to lead me again. This time you're try to say to me, that I should lock onto my own desires, and that it's not your place to directly

113

tell me what to think. Am I right?" he heard Jay say, bobbing his head, 'yes' as he tossed his cigarette into the neck of the smoke pot, bringing up the one he'd just taken from him, placing it into his mouth.

"Something like that," Nate replied, feeling his armpits begin to sweat, knowing it wasn't from the heat.

"See, that's why you irk me. You want to fix me. To lead me. You think I need help. But when I ask you directly, you get all tight lipped, and high and mighty," he heard Jay say, watching as he exhaled a large cloud of smoke that almost completely shrouded his face.

"We're more alike than you think. I just realised I hold a lot of old, unneeded things in my mind as well. That's why I got tightlipped. My issue is…what I can't let go of, is - all the times I've directly tried to help a person or people, and instead of them just being happy, I've ended up being scorched for it."

"For example, when I asked you the love question. There've been times when Rayya and I have been ditched on trips, or never spoken to again. All the while, what Rayya and I have said or done has helped save the couple's relationship. But because it brought momentary pain, they've hated us for it. I don't want that to happen again. I want to help both you and Karman, but I want both of you to come to your own conclusions," Nate said, now actually wishing he could smoke the cigarette, annoyed that it'd somehow momentarily eased the tension he'd felt building up.

"Here man, your face says that you're ready to have a thinking smoke," he heard Jay say as he passed him another cigarette, all without looking away from where he'd been staring - somewhere far off into the distance.

"You're a really good people reader. You see too much; you know too much of people's intentions. You see too much of their darkness, and then after seeing so much of it, you've come to the conclusion that, that's all there is to people. And now that you've come to that conclusion, you've never again flicked on your mental shades and allowed people to surprise you. That's the difference between you and I. I can't live like that. I have to keep trying to give people the benefit of the doubt and search for the goodness within them. And with that belief, I've witnessed the wonderful side of people, even from the same people who hate and have tried to destroy you."

114

"But now standing here, getting to know you, experiencing you strip me down, I see another reason why people hate you. No one likes being read to the depth that you can see through them. Even as intimate as I am and can be, I don't like that you can literally feel the moment I want to smoke, or the moment I don't. You're lying when you said you saw my face change. You hadn't even looked at me, not even with your peripherals," Nate thought, placing the cigarette in his mouth, inhaling deeply as Jay lite it, remembering the only other time he'd ever felt so exposed.

"Ella and Carl, and now Jay and Karman," he whispered, chuckling to himself.

"Huh?" he heard Jay ask with a truly puzzled look on his face.

"Ella and Carl were…they were mentors for Rayya and I when we were having relationship trouble. And you and Karman kind of remind me of them. Well, in the people reading department," he replied, locking eyes with Jay, looking for any form of maliciousness or distrust, surprised to see none whatsoever.

"Mentors eh?" he heard Jay reply, pursing his lips.

"Don't do that, you have no idea how bad I want to kiss them," he thought as he replied, "you've been hanging out in Vancouver way too much…eh?"

"Lil' bit, there and in Burnaby. Remember, my team is working on developing Quantum laptops. But we don't know our ass from our ears on where to begin with certain steps, so we go to the experts who 'kinda' started it all," he heard Jay reply, looking up into his eyes, with a look of annoyance returning to his face, ruining the fantasy he'd just started to have of kissing him.

"Jay, that look just now. Umm Can I say something?

"You just did," he heard Jay reply, giving him a sarcastic smile as he chuckled at his own joke.

"That look was a stressed expression from thinking about work, was it not?" he whispered, not feeling amused whatsoever.

"Yeah fam," he heard Jay reply in a dead pan voice.

"Jay with your work…I'm honestly concerned for you sometimes. I mean, I know many people don't like their jobs. But with you, I can really see how much you hate your job by your face, and your body language. As a matter of fact, just before we came outside, I was thinking about how happy you seem to be, just from the way you were walking. I can already see you're lighter on your feet. Normally, you're really edgy, walking all slow and heavy."

"And when we hang out, I always feel a really big disconnect, like you're not all there. I mean I know we don't hang out often, but the few times we've been at the get togethers or shopping with the ladies... I could see how stressed you were. Jay, that amount of stress isn't healthy. Maybe, if possible, can you go to a different place and do the same job?" he said, trying to avert his eye away from Jay's lips, but failing.

"Enough about my job...I don't want to talk about it. Tell me more about your mentors. Leave work at work. I wanted to drive, to go on this trip so I don't need to think about work. I don't want to think about those computers, and that stupid space elevator the whole world is rushing to build," he heard Jay reply as he turned and tossed his fully smoked cigarette into smoke pot.

"Yes, leave work at work. But I agree. They're racing to build that elevator too fast. And I can see why you're so stressed. The engineers and workers need fast laptops on site to do all the structural calculations right there on the spot, especially as they add more and more layers, any of which could be a vital stress point doomed to fail," he thought, nodding his head at jay to say he'd respect his wishes.

"Okay, so my mentors," Nate began, trying to formulate his words.

"Sorry, for the way I just came off, I didn't mean to sound snappy, just...a change of topic would be nice," he heard Jay whisper.

"No, it's fine. So umm, my mentors...Well, when Rayya and I dated for the first six months, it was beautiful, but all built on lies. When the lies crumbled, we were in this rut we couldn't dig ourselves out of, for man, I don't know, at least a year. But it was weird because we didn't let go of each other. Then one of my bigger lies came to light, and then for almost six months straight, we almost broke up every day. And it didn't help that I was being defensive and digging into her past, trying to expose any other lies she might've told me. Anyways, at the end of the sixth month, when we were literally about to call the final quits, we ran into Ella and Carl, and they helped us through it all," Nate said, letting a long, slow breath as he reflected on those times.

"Huh? I thought you were going to say they were the ones who converted you two into swingers," he heard Jay say nonchalantly, looking at him in the eyes before casually looking down, appearing to study the ants walking both of their flip flops.

"Umm, swingers. Rayya and I, we don't call ourselves that. And yes, they did help us open up to making love with other people. But that was later on. First we had to shed a lot of the emotional, and social stigmas we faced, and work through all the lies we'd told each other and ourselves," Nate replied, feeling his tension slightly ease, seeing that Jay's demeanor hadn't changed after what he'd just said.

"And they helped you do that by leading you the same way you're trying to lead Karman and I? Such as, make me confess my love, and then make sure we're all hunky dory, then into the bed with us you guys come? Humph, not a bad plan actually. It's a hell of a lot better than, seduces us, fuck us for fun, then leave us damaged and confused. At least you two freaks kind of give a fuck about us. I don't see that quality in many people, that's for certain," he heard Jay say, bobbing his head, turning to gaze out at the road with a look between amused and thoughtful before smiling at him and saying, "I just think it's funny that as good as I am at seeing shit, I had no idea our 'wifeys' made out. Man, that shit blew my mind. At first I was mad as hell, but then I calmed down. I really can't see why it's bad. I mean it's cheating, but one of those – 'ehhhh, fuck it', kind of things. Plus, it's hot as hell."

"Rayya made out with Karman?" Nate blurted, feeling a flash of annoyance so strong it almost reminded him of when he and Rayya had been on the rocks.

"Yeah man. Come on. Why you look so flustered? Why you acting shocked? You knew right? You had to have. It seems like you two been plotting. And getting to Karman first is genius."

"I umm," Nate began, closing his mouth, not knowing what to say as his annoyance increased by the second.

"Relax, home boy, I think y'all are cool. Y'all freaky to a whole 'nother 'level I find hard to adjust to, and y'all methods are

117

sometimes a bit annoying. But, in these last couple of days of actually getting to know y'all, I must admit, I think y'all are 'hella' cool," Nate heard Jay say, with him a warm smile, but he was so aggravated he turned away.

"What's wrong man?" he heard Jay ask, causing him to grow even more aggravated.

"Rayya knows better! She has to know better than to do that! Is she really this impatient! She could've split them up! It's cheating! Jay should be mad! It's a partnership. He has to be there, he has to be okay with it! She knows this is not how we operate! We promised each other not to work on a couple so deeply on an individual basis!"

"Nothing, I just… I didn't know she kissed her either. And I'm sorry, I apologies for Rayya's actions, that's not how we how we operate," Nate finally chocked out as unchecked anger coursed through him, where he wanted to punch and kick everything in his vicinity.

"Shit man, that's surprising. I thought I was the only one out the loop. Anyways, it's all good. Ladies' man, what can you do? We're their husbands, but that's it. Ladies are always on another level and shit. I've learned to embrace that Karman is always light years ahead of me, and on her own program a lot of the time. I just try to sync up with her the best I can, you know? But recently, ever since this space elevator shit and them needing the Quantum laptops and all, I've been fucking up and not paying enough attention to her," he heard Jay say, coming in front of him, clasping him on the shoulders.

"Ladies are naturally more energetic than us, and their emotions are harder to follow for us guys. And yes, it's always a challenge to sync up in that regard. But this, this is different. I apologize and she owes you one as well…and," Nate stammered.

"And I want to cancel all the sightseeing and just go straight to Chicago. We should leave you two alone. She's not the only impatient one, and I don't want our recklessness to harm either of you. But why can't I say the words? How selfish am!?" Nate finished in his head.

"And what?" he heard Jay ask

"And…," he began again trying to force himself to be brave and say he was canceling the sightseeing plans of the road trip.

"Nate, listen...you two apologize too much for some normal ass shit. Well I mean, for what I would think is normal swinger shit. I get it, y'all like us and Rayya wanted my wifey to open up and bring that energy to me, hoping that she'd convince me to try some shit with y'all. It's no 'biggy' man, relax. My issue is that, well besides the fucked up rumors that we're swingers, is that, I feel selfish and I feel... umm – shit, how do I say this? Like I want a threesome right? And in my mind, that's cool."

"But, if I think about her with a man. Fuck, I can't take it. Like, you know what I mean? Well, maybe you don't, 'cuz' Reggie and all, but yeah. That's how I feel. No offense to you, but like, I can't handle the visual of you touching my 'wifey' like that, but, I can definitely picture me myself 'wifey' and Rayya, and...yeah. Sorry if that sounded rude. I shouldn't have thrown your wife into the scenario as an example," he heard Jay say, sounding slightly apprehensive as he unclasped his shoulders.

"It's an actual honor to hear you want my wife. And normally I'd be ecstatic. But you should be really mad, and you're not. Yes, you understand us for the most part, but then you don't get the rest of it. Cheating is cheating until both people have agreed that it's okay, and no time before. Flirting and adding sexual tension to get the couple's attention is one thing. But kissing and touching should come when both people are there and ready to take that big step together," Nate thought, before saying, "You're confusing, I don't get you. But, I think it's a big part of why I like you."

"Like me, like a friend, or like me, like you want to fuck? You're bi right? I think you're bi? I have good hearing, and at some points this morning, I didn't hear Rayya making any sounds at all, just two men grunting and all that. Humm, that's cool too man. But hey, don't get any funny ideas. I can picture some shit going down...you know, with me and Karman messing around in the same room with you two. But, you're not touching me my man. Alright?" he heard Jay say, chuckling softly

"Um, alright," he whispered, feeling shell shocked.

"Relax my man. You still seem annoyed about the Rayya, Karman thing. Or are you worried I know you're Bi. If you're worried about that, then put your mind at ease, 'cuz' I really don't give a fuck about you being Bi, I'm no judge to a person sex life. All power to you to have fun like that," he heard Jay say, giving him a reassuring smile.

119

"This is the conversation I was dying to have. But now it feels ruined. He's totally okay with everything, including what he shouldn't be. They're not ready for the next step. And apparently we're not either," Nate thought, forcing a smile onto his face as he said, "Yeah, I'm bi, and you don't have anything to worry about. That's not how I operate. I don't force people to do things they don't want to do. So, I'd never put you in that kind of position if we were all in the same room, umm, playing around. How's that sound?"

"Sounds good my man. Sounds good. But man, you've gotta loosen up a bit. 'That's not how I operate, that's not how we operate'," he heard Jay say mockingly before saying, "Pssst man! You got a lot of rules in your head. I don't know how you do it. The moment the rules are broken, you get sour as hell. You're stressed over nothing. I know I'm stressed like you said, but my stress is on a different level – not stupid shit like Rayya and Karman kissing. I know I said I don't want to talk about work, but I 'gotta' say it man, I really just don't trust this creepy worldwide peace phenomenon going on, it's too aligned with the timing of every world government pleading their full support to help build this fucking space elevator."

"I'm sorry Nate. Not to be a pessimist, but humans, we don't all just get along the way we have since mid-March. Other than some 'kinda' global behavior modification shit going down, where I 'dunno', we're all being manipulated by some kind of subliminal messages not to kill each other, nothing that's happening is making any sense. This is where the majority of my stress is coming from. Now that there's not much killing and fighting going on, the world governments are saying there's no excuse for delays and are wanting and every company to just shit out perfect results and produce perfect technology. I don't want myself, or my team being one of the reasons for that space elevator going up wrong and crumbling down to earth, killing us all."

"You, on the other hand, you 'gotta' let go of a lot of those rules in your head, 'cuz' you're going to run into all kinds of people that mess up that template. Yeah, people…you can't have a template for how to deal with them, even if it's worked so far. It's bound to happen when you run into people like Karman or maybe even myself, and then what? I can say for certain, Karman would never fit into that mold. That being said…please stop blaming your wife for that kiss because I know for certain, Karman let that happen. Also, don't worry about me thinking you'd try to force yourself on me. If I thought you weren't cool or that you'd do some shit like that to me, I wouldn't be chilling with you, talking to you the way I am now," Nate heard Jay say.

"Jesus, this man! I thought he was trapped within himself! But no! He just all of a sudden reveals my hang-ups while openly admitting his own," Nate thought, feeling his world tilting upside down, so used to being the one who'd opened up people's eyes, to now have a cold glass of water splashed into his.

"But I need to explain myself," Nate thought as he said to Jay, "I say those things because what Rayya did isn't cool. She could've hurt your relationship. You weren't there. You weren't willing. Both of you did not consent. You could've taken the news really badly. We're not supposed to harm people. We're supposed to…We're supposed to enhance the joy in a couple's relationship. Yes, you may be right that Karman let that happen, but it was Rayya who invited that situation without you being there to chose."

"Ahhh, I see, is this your mentors' training? Interesting, interesting. I see what you mean though. I get that rule then. But shit happens. And ladies, like I said man, their feelings …their emotions, they're on other levels than us. And you're saying Rayya invited that situation, yes, I get your concern. But trust me, even the invite would not have happened if my wife did not let it happen."

"I know my wife too well, and Karman can stop whatever the hell she wants to stop. In my opinion, she can even stop this fucking planet from spinning if she wanted to. So if she didn't want Rayya to kiss her, she would've never in her life put herself in a situation to let it happen…plain and simple. Hummm, but you said I should've been there for consent purposes, is that right? Is that how this swinger shit works?" Nate heard Jay say with a gleam in his eye, and bright, mischievous smile on his face.

"Oh shit! Fuck! I know what that look means! And he's dead serious! Holy shit! I can see why we can't resist them! I can see why Rayya made that mistake and I can see why we're so off kilter! Jay and Karman are like a force that's both intertwined and separate. And their

energy and intelligence is intoxicating. If Jay's right, then Karman left an opening that my baby couldn't refuse," Nate thought smiling at Jay, nodding his head, before saying, "Yes that's one of the rules passed down to us from our mentors. Our rules are deeply rooted in fully open communication and consent of actions between all. So yes, you should've been there. I've already consented Rayya can have anyone she wants, anytime she wants, even if I'm not there and she has consented the same for me. I'm not sure, but I doubt you've given that same consent to Karman, even for kissing another lady."

"Ahh cool. That's all cool. Y'all make sense. And nope I haven't, given her that consent…but that's all good. I'm sure you've guessed what I'm thinking, yes?" he heard Jay say, flashing him another mischievous smile.

"Umm, yeah. I think I do know what you're thinking," Nate replied, feeling his heart start to pound in his chest.

"Well, alright then fam! Then let's go make this shit right! Let's go watch the ladies kiss!" Nate heard Jay say excitedly, taking him by the shoulders, spinning him towards the double doors before walking through them with an extra bounce to his step.

"And just like that, he's ripped away the old foundations inside of me. Rejuvenating me with the pain and discomfort of the truth. I haven't felt like this in a very long time, and I'm happy for it," Nate thought, smiling at his discomfort as he slowly adjusted his mindset to the lessons he'd just learned.

Chapter III

I Can't

Road Trip: Day Three

Date: Saturday, June 3rd 2017

Time: 8:10 am

Location: Bismarck, North Dakota

"Oh my God, what the hell am I doing? I can't believe I'm doing this! Oh my God, I can feel their eyes on me. I want to run. I want to run so bad, but it feels so good," Karman thought as Rayya strolled in.

"Good girl," Karman heard Rayya whisper the moment the door shut, gliding in front of her, sitting on the foot of the bed, crossing her legs as she leaned back, looking her up and down as if she were the sexiest thing on earth.

"Fuck my life. Why does she make me feel like this?" Karman thought feeling the first hint of warm, wetness touch upon her lips.

"Don't good girl me," Karman finally felt the strength to say, doing her best to fight back her growing arousal as Rayya's hungry eyes continued to drink her in.

"Oh sweetie, what's wrong? Are you not liking how you feel? You did good being brave. You should've seen my Nate, he's so head over heels, I think he almost ran in here…and you already know I am," she heard Rayya whisper, giving her a soft, knowing smile – as her eyes moved down from her breast, locking onto her pussy.

"Oh shit, Oh shit, Oh shit!" Karman thought, feeling a deep pressure in her pussy as it throbbed and became hot under Rayya's hungry gaze.

"I'm not you Rayya, I can't…" she began, when Rayya cut in and said, "I can't, I can't, I can't. The words that run your life. Why do you let those words run your life, huh? How do you even move? Tell me? 'Cuz' you have so many things you can't do, I don't even know how you take a step forward."

"I'm the fucking head of the Material Science department of O.L.O. Corp. So I can move where ever the fuck I want!"

"Professionally sure, you got it baby. Personally, I'm surprised you're standing with all the things you can't do," she heard Rayya respond, rolling her tongue in her mouth as she snickered, making Karman want to kiss her and slap the shit out of her all at once.

"Well, I wouldn't be where I am if I let the word, 'can't', stop me. So, what the hell are you getting at?" Karman said, feeling more annoyed at that fact that she couldn't suppress her arousal, than from anything Rayya had said.

"You made a good career for yourself, for what Karman, tell me?" she heard Rayya reply, licking her lips as she whipped her long, curly hair over her shoulder with a gently flick of her head.

"Fuck! I'm so wet! How is this happening to me!? I've never felt this way about a woman in my entire life! How is she doing this to me? Seriously, how? I'm not supposed to feel like this! I'm not supposed to want to have sex with a woman! Am I really Bi?" she thought, realizing she was biting her bottom lip, now feeling a numb pain that'd quickly become sharp.

"I'll wait till you're done having your fantasy about me. And go on and take your time with it. I like seeing that hungry look on your face. I love knowing how much you want me," she heard Rayya whisper as she scooted back on the bed, still keeping herself propped up on her hands, with her legs crossed.

"I don't know what you're talking about and get the hell off my outfits," Karman replied, happy for a diversion.

"Oh. Oops, I didn't mean to sit on them, there just so…skimpy that I didn't see them there," she heard Rayya reply, giving her a mocking smile before sliding a pair of spandex shorts under her ass, saying, "Oops, I hope you weren't thinking of wearing that one. Then you might have to come get it."

"I'm not falling for your shit," she whispered, wanting to lunge on top of her.

"Unh-huh, anyways. I asked you a question. You became top bitch for what? Surely it wasn't to enjoy your life afterwards. Why the hell would anyone want to do that …right?" she heard

Rayya ask in a slightly venomous tone, with a look of annoyance playing across her face before it went back to mischievous.

"I enjoy my life. I don't need to dress or act like you to enjoy my life," she responded, feeling more confused than offended as she thought, *"But I felt so free. So sexy. I loved the way hubby looked at me. I loved the way all three of them looked at me. And God, when that door opened both of those times, I could feel Nate's eyes on me, and it felt so fucking good! Fuck! Oh Fuck! Why am I thinking about Nate so much!?"*

"So, don't dress like me. That was just a suggestion. I didn't force you. And I'd be damned if I forced you to do anything you didn't want to. You're a really scary bitch when you get mad. Anyways, I'm just saying that you've already made it to the top, so loosen up a bit. And stop saying you can't. I want you to get rid of that word and replace it with, 'I'll try'. Say it with me. Say, 'I'll try to keep an open mind'," she heard Rayya command, just before closing her eyes, inhaling deeply, then slowly letting out her breath in a satisfied, 'ahh'.

"Why'd she do that? And now why's she looking at me like that? Oh my God! I smell myself! Am I really that wet!?" Karman thought, feeling her cheeks flush as she looked down to her crotch as if she could somehow see what she was feeling between her legs.

"You want to go clean your pussy up before we continue this conversation? I really hope you say no, because I really, really love the way you smell. But I can see you turning red as a stop light over there, and I don't want you too uncomfortable," she heard Rayya say, licking and biting her bottom lip.

"I can't...I can't do this, I can't be like you. I can't just be free like you, I have responsibilities! People can't see me dress like this. People can't think I sleep around with whoever the hell I want. I can't be like you Rayya! I just can't," she blared, enraged at how turned on she was by her desire to kiss Rayya, and by her desire to have Nate and her husband be there to watch.

"Humm, for a moment. Just for a moment, I got pissed at your words. And then I remembered saying them. I remembered that they came from the hot pulsing feeling between my legs - from thoughts I swore I wasn't supposed to have. And I remembered the lies I kept telling myself. And then I remembered why I liked you from the very beginning. Why I was so magnetized by you. You right now, were like me a few years ago, trapped in the mindset of 'can'ts' and the 'forbiddens', but deep inside, you're at the threshold of freedom and all you need is a little nudge to obtain it," she heard Rayya say, scooting forward, taking hold of her left thigh.

"Ah," she heard herself involuntarily gasp, wanting Rayya to both let go and grip tighter.

"Ah, is right," Karman heard Rayya whisper, running her hand up to her ass, squeezing softly, sending a rush of pleasure surging thorough her.

"But, I'm not like you," she mumbled, wanting to fight the feeling.

"No, not all the way like me. You've never had the same limitations as me. My 'can'ts' were not like your 'can'ts'. For instance, a Muslim, marrying a Jew. A Jew, who served in the army that invaded my country, killed my people, and killed my father. Hell, who knows, maybe even the one who actually shot the grenade out the gun that killed my father. Maybe the same person who'd left me trying to put his…Allah, never mind that."

"Allah, help me explain to this girl. Sweetie, my 'can'ts' were 'mustn'ts' and or 'else's', pressed upon me by a religion that doesn't look kindly to those who falter. My 'can'ts' were impossibilities upon impossibilities placed upon me by another country, whose only agenda seems to be the utter annihilation of my own. And when I couldn't take it anymore, the refugee visa went through for my mother and I to move to the U.S. I was nineteen, and the year was two thousand six. It was a year of absolute and horror," she heard Rayya say, letting go of her ass, leaving her body feeling neglected and empty, hungering to be touched again.

"I'm sorry, I didn't know. I mean I knew what happened there but," Karman began.

"You don't know…still, even as I tell you, you can't imagine how lost and low I'd fallen. How trapped I was by the stigma from both my people and the Jews, only to move to the States - a place that's supposed to be open, but just so happens to harbor some of the most close minded people of all," she heard

Rayya say as she shifted over, patting the bed, summoning her to sit.

"Jesus, am I really stopping myself? Do I really always say I can't to things? I thought I was more open to things. Why does she see it like I'm trapped?" she thought moving to the bed, sitting down with her eyes locked on Rayya, who smiled and nodded her head before saying, "After moving here in December of 'oh-six', I had to scramble to get a bunch of prerequisite classes done to get into University for September of 'oh-seven'. I bust my ass and I got into that University, and then I got my Ph.D. in Quantum Physics in just three years. A Ph.D. in Quantum Physics in three years. I'm a smart cookie."

"Ph.D. in Quantum Physics. I...I didn't know. But wait, didn't Jay hire you as Junior Data Analyst? Shouldn't you have a much higher tittle or much different job?" she whispered, feeling her head start to throb as she rested her hand on Rayya's foot.

"When you say 'can't'. Use it for what you really can't do anything about. For example, if you're a female Quantum Physicist from Lebanon, who surpassed all her peers from the United States. You can't get a job for years because you'll be black balled. If I hadn't met Nate after Uni., I'd have damn near been homeless, because I'd be damned if I lived with my mom, and I had no real friends to rely on. And this Analyst job, yeah... it's the first major job I've landed after getting my degree. It took me five years to get this job, five whole years."

"Why they call me 'junior' you ask. Well, It's because of my lack of real world field experience and because almost every Executive in my company but Jay, is a sexist, racist bastard. Pff, and you want to know the worst part? I'll tell you the worst part. I only got this job because all of a sudden, last year, the entire world became insanely desperate for functional, everyday sized Quantum Computers. Everyone thinks they're the key to the future and wants to use them for huge projects, like throwing that space elevator in the air. So yeah, companies are literally hiring anyone they think can help, including blackballed people like me."

"It's so ridiculous Karman...I'm called, 'Junior', but I'm the only damn Data Analyst in that company that really knows what they're looking at. The only reason you've never heard me complain, or seen me annoyed about this before is, one, I suck it up because I'm grateful to be working, and two, because of your husband. He's the only damn one in there protecting and fighting for me to get a promotion and title change," she heard Rayya proclaim, seeing her look away with tears in her eyes, causing her heart to ache.

"I'm sorry, I really had no idea," Karman whispered, crawling up on the bed, wrapping her arms around Rayya, squeezing her tight.

"I'm twenty-nine now, and I know that's not old, but I'm scared because I feel like I'm running out of time to have kids," she heard Rayya whisper.

"You have plenty of time. You have a few years to go before you're thirty-five, and then nowadays with the tech we have, you're still alright," she replied, feeling a large lump rise in her throat, seeing how hopeless Rayya looked, wondering how she could think so negatively.

"No Karman, I don't even think I can even have children. The grenade, when it landed, it damaged one of my ovaries. So I have to pray the one I have left will be enough to give Nate and I children," she heard Rayya whisper, answering her question in regards to Rayya's negativity.

"My God, I'm so sorry, I…" she began, losing the rest of what she was going to say in a swarm of remorseful thoughts.

"Speaking of Nate, let's talk about Nate. Oh my Nate, ha-ha! You think Nate and I had it easy? You think we were just a fun loving couple, having the greatest time of our lives the whole time? Yeah right! Both of us lied to each other non-stop at the beginning of our relationship, and years into it. Pfft, as a matter of fact, do you think Nate told me he was Israeli, knowing I was from Lebanon? He hid that from me because he was literally one of the damn soldiers who invaded my country! So when I found out, oh my Allah, we were at the very edge, the very edge Karman. So, you see the point I'm trying to make? I'm trying to show you that there are a lot of 'can'ts'. And your 'can'ts' and the real 'can'ts' are two different things. You can take ownership of your life. You can be the sexy, outgoing woman you've always wanted to be. And that doesn't mean you have to dress like me, or act like me. You just need to have confidence. Be confident in yourself, and last but not least, own yourself."

"Own every single part of yourself. Elevate, celebrate, and love your sexual desires and passions on the same level you elevate, celebrate, and love your intellect, that's brought you to the top of your career. Don't cast pieces of yourself away. If you do that, then you're just giving it out to others to own for you. Take it from me, who's lived almost her entire life with people owning pieces of me, mentally and sexually. Trust me, you don't want that. You want to be in charge of you. So, if you think I'm up to no good, leading you to some unfathomable abyss because you're giving into yourself, giving into the fact that you like me…then sorry, I'm not sorry. I want you to plunge into that depth. I want you to see and know that's a part of who you are, and I want you take ownership of that part of yourself. Do you understand me?" she heard Rayya whisper, leaning her head on hers.

"I understand," Karman replied hoarsely from lump in her throat.

"Really? You don't think I'm selfish? You don't think I'm forcing you too much. I feel selfish. I just don't want my pain to be in vain. I see you closing doors on yourself, and I've lived that life. I want you to have a better life than that. Yeah, a much better life than the one I was living," she heard Rayya stammer as she began to sob.

"Oh, sweetie, thank you. I'm so sorry - I'm so, so sorry I got so defensive. I just don't know what to do with you. My whole life, like everything I've done was to get to this goal where I'm the boss. You know? And the way I did that, was by getting rid of everything that doesn't fit, or anything that could distract me from that goal. And God forbid, I didn't understand it. I would look the other way until it was gone, and keep trying to reach my goal. And now that I've reached it, new things have come and I say to myself, 'okay, I'll try to process this'. But now, now my mind fight most new things."

"And liking you, God, that doesn't fit, and I have no idea what the hell to do. I'm so confused. Like when I see you, my body does its own thing, and I try to tell it to stop. But …well, I can't stop myself. And that's weird to me. Yeah, it's weird to me to lose total control. I'm always in control. I can always stop myself. But with you, I can't. With you, I can't understand, and I don't like it. No, I'm not saying this right. Actually, I really like liking you, and then that scares me. It scares me that I like losing control around you," she said, feeling the pressure and heat between her legs instantly grow to new levels now that she'd confessed her feelings to Rayya.

"Oh sweetie, if it makes you feel any better, I feel the same way about you," she heard Rayya whisper, chuckling through her sobs.

"Oh please. You've been with other women. How can you say that?" Karman asked, feeling flattered and jealous at the same time.

"None have made me feel like you have, or else...I wouldn't have broken the rules," she heard Rayya whispered, sighing heavily.

"Rules?" Karman asked, confused.

"I wasn't supposed to kiss you without Jay being there. He's your partner. I should've waited for both of you to give me permission. It's a rule Nate and I have to make sure we don't hurt a couple. But I fucked up. And worse, I didn't tell Nate. I was scared he'd cancel the road trip, and I really didn't want him to do that. And I know him, he would've said that we weren't ready to be responsible with you two. He would've wanted to wait until we calmed down. But...but I don't want to calm down. I really like you and I really like, ummm, God I'm scared, please don't be mad at me but I really like...," Karman heard Rayya say with a pause.

"Please girl, I know you like Jay, I hated you when I first saw you. I was coming to visit him at work and you were standing just outside his office, staring at him while biting your bottom lip. I think you were supposed to go in and give him some data or something, but yeah, you were just standing there. And worst of all, you gave me the stink eye when I walked in. It was like you were saying, 'bitch what are you doing with him?'" she whispered, smiling as she began to stroke Rayya's hair.

"Oh yeah, what was that, like two weeks after I got the job right? Ah...I remember giving you the stink eye. I was annoyed at you because he wouldn't even bat an eye at me. I'd flirt with him non-stop and he'd leave me with one word answers. Or he'd talk about you to shut me up. So it wasn't really the stink eye. It was a look of envy. I wanted him to lust after me and you had him wrapped perfectly around your finger," she heard Rayya reply, sounding like she was returning to her normal, mischievous self.

"You 'lil' bitch, telling me this now. And oh, fuck, fuck, fuck! You didn't tell Nate about our kiss?! Oh Fuck!" Karman replied, knowing her husband like the back of her hand.

"No, and that's so not like me anymore. I don't like what I've done. But I really didn't want him to cancel the trip. Why? Oh fuck, did you tell Jay? Specifically, did you just tell Jay? Ahhh, damn it. He's not subtle at all. Oh Allah, this is bad," Karman heard Rayya say as she flopped backwards on the bed, taking her down with her.

"Yeah, I told him just before you came in, so maybe he won't say anything? Okay, hopefully he hasn't. And as soon as he comes back, I'll tell him not to say anything to Nate," she whispered, kissing Rayya on the cheek.

"Yeah right. It's Jay. We both know we're screwed. Why am I so dumb? I should've told you about the rule! Damn it, I wanted to, but then I felt so guilty. I felt that if I had told you, I'd have been purely acknowledging that I had done something wrong. Fuck, I hate me so much right now!" she heard Rayya whisper, turning her head, pecking her on the lips before look back up at the ceiling.

"How bad will Nate react?" Karman replied, sitting up, feeling emotionally drained.

"Pretty bad. Especially because it could've harmed you guys. Out of all the things I could've done, this is not one he'd let slide by. And who cares about me, how did Jay take it? I'd have expected him to be angry when he came out the room, but he seemed cheery. Overly cheery. Did you see that he actually touched me on the small of my back?"

"Does he know what that means to a girl? Your husband was taunting me. Sweetie, I'm still not over it, and I really just don't believe it. What happened to him in such a short time? Humm…or after telling him, you made it up to him with a little 'BJ' so he wouldn't be mad? Ah-ha, maybe that's what took him so long to come back and get us?" she heard Rayya whisper, rolling over to face her with a devious look on her face.

"So silly, you call him gesturing you in taunting you huh?"

"Yes it is…so, did you give him a BJ or not?" she heard Rayya reply.

"No, and he wasn't even angry that I'd need to give him an, 'I'm sorry I fucked up 'BJ'. After I told him that we kissed, he just had this face. The one he gets when he's figured out something. Sorry Rayya, if I've gotten you into trouble, to be honest, when he was talking about you, I got this flash of guilt and all of a sudden I felt like he somehow knew we'd kissed, so I just blurted it out. Oh and another thing, he, he knows y'all are swingers," she whispered – intentionally butterflying her legs open, hearing Rayya giggle right after.

"What? Which part is funny? Him knowing y'all are swingers" she asked, wanting to understand the shift in Rayya's mood – hoping it was excitement about her bold move to show her pussy.

"Jay knowing that…is a relief to be honest. I was laughing because seeing you spread your legs like that brought back memories of the other day. Nate is such a fucking freak and loves smelling my pussy, so he always lays his head in my lap when I sit like that," she heard Rayya reply.

"And you? what will you do now that I'm here like this?" she thought, all of a sudden feeling like there was too much silence.

"Rayya?"

"Yeah, sweetie, please don't say you're sorry for my mistake. I shouldn't have put you in that position in the first place. This is why we have the rule, it's so that there's no guilty confessions later on. But, I was being selfish," she heard Rayya say, followed by a long exhale, watching her stretch her right arm up in the air.

"So was I. You somehow make me want to cross every boundary," she thought, reach up, pulling Rayya's arm down, placing her hand on her left breast.

"Bitch, we're literally talking about breaking rules, and in this room 'I done already' grabbed your ass, and now you have my hand on your tit. And fuck, you really have perfect tits. I'm so jealous," she heard Rayya say with giggle.

"Oh shut up. Yours are bigger and more beautiful," she replied, feeling and watching Rayya move her hand from her breast, over her belly down to her thigh, stopping right next to her pussy.

"Fuck," she whispered, breathing heavily as her pussy throbbed and back tingled, craving Rayya touch between her legs.

"You're doing a good job opening up you know? I'm sorry I was being so mean to you. I can see that you're trying your best. As a matter of fact, if you were to compare yourself with me back in the day, you've opened up way more in the last month than I would have in six. I, I just get nervous that you'd...," she heard Rayya begin before pausing.

"That I'd what?" Karman replied, realizing that she'd unconsciously begun to rock her hips with lust, and that the arousal that'd been chased away by Rayya's stories of pain and strife had returned way stronger than she'd ever felt for Rayya before.

"That you'll get scared. Close me out of your life. Pretend we never kissed. Pretend you never got wet. Pretend it all away like you said you do when you don't understand something," she heard Rayya reply, watching as she inched her head up to stare between her spread open legs.

"Yes! She finally looked! I'm being a brave girl! She said she liked knowing how much I wanted her. So I wanted her to see, and smell me!" she thought, feeling her whole body grow warm, now turned on beyond anything she could comprehend, especially due to the fact that Rayya was still staring between her legs.

"Girl, you smell so good," she heard Rayya whisper, causing her to gasp and rub her breast.

"Yeah, it's all 'cuz' of you. You do this to me. You say you're scared I'd forget you, but I couldn't even if I tried. How can I forget or ignore someone who can make me feel this way?" she whispered, inhaling deeply, getting drunk off of her own scent of arousal, shaking her head, remembering what her husband had said before opening the door for Rayya to come in.

"I'm glad for that. I don't want you to run away from me," she heard Rayya reply, feeling her slowly massage the top of her thigh.

"No, no way I'm running," she whispered, closing her eyes, praying for more, but hoping for an interruption because she knew if Rayya kept it up, she'd put Rayya's fingers on her pussy herself.

"I love this look on your face. Tell me what you're thinking," she heard Rayya whisper.

"You know," she replied.

"Tell me," she heard Rayya press with a giggle.

"I can't say it! Fuck! Change the subject, cool off a bit!" Karman thought before saying, "I thought Jay would've flipped about the idea of y'all being swingers. But, it's weird, he was way too okay with everything,"

"Oh, that's what you were thinking?" she heard Rayya reply sarcastically.

"Um-hum," she mumbled with a relieved sigh as Rayya continued to work her hand up and down her thigh, slowly starting to feel okay with wanting to give in, almost as if her saying that her husband was okay with them being swingers had given her permission to do so.

"Humm, your husband does sometimes seem like his opinion won't budge. But sweetie, maybe seeing you dress super, super sexy helped him change his mind," she heard Rayya reply, pausing her massage, almost causing her to blurt, - 'don't stop'.

"Yeah, but it's more than just my clothes he's okay with," she whispered, taking Rayya's hand, searching for the courage to put Rayya's fingers on her pussy.

"What do you mean?" she heard Rayya ask.

"Well, I was being a bad girl without fully thinking of the consequences. And by the time I realized what I'd done, your hubby had already saw me naked. I thought Jay would be furious, for exposing myself but he was smiling. It's weird for me because he was going to be my escape route. I think the dark, self-destructive and fearful part of myself - secretly wanted him to get mad and stop me from moving forward with trying to be so free."

"I wanted him to ask me what the fuck am I doing, ask me why I would dare show my body to another man. The self-destructive part of me was ready to blame him for stopping me, stopping me from liking all of this. But instead, he seems happy.

Happy with the way I'm dressing, happy listening to you two fuck. Happy and excited that I kissed you. And right now, I still feel like he's been abducted by aliens because he admitted liking the look on Nate's face when he saw me."

"Jay said that? Wow? I was wondering how he felt about you standing there," she heard Rayya reply sounding ecstatic.

"He said it's the sexiest thing in the world for him to know how bad another man wants me. To me, I don't know where that came from. I thought I knew him, but just like that, I feel like he's changed, and just like that, he's taken my escape route from me. So now, I feel like I have no place to run and that I have to face this change that's happening within me, head on," Karman replied, beginning to shift her weight.

"I want to tell you to touch me so bad. It's right at the tip of my tongue...but I can't say it. Please, just do it! I won't stop you! I promise I won't stop you! If not, then this moving over to 'wink, wink' adjust myself so your hand touches my pussy is going to have to work," she thought, shifting her weight a little more, feeling her heart start to pound, now feeling Rayya's thumb touching right on the edge of her pussy.

"Actually, some part of me isn't surprised he's okay with it. Nate and I had saw something in both of you that...did honestly give us this swinger-ish vibe," she heard Rayya reply, moving her hand from her thigh, giving her an, 'I know what you're up to' smile, right as she'd begun to shift once more.

"You bitch, if you know what I want, then give it to me!" Karman thought as she said, "so, you don't think I'm moving too fast? I know you're always telling me to be confident and to show it all off if I'm feeling brave enough. But I never imagined being married and letting another man see me naked like this. And for me, sitting here comfortably like this with another woman. As turned on as I am right now, this is fucking weird."

"As weird as you fake adjusting so my hand would touch your pussy weird? Or should I make it weirder by putting my hand back," she heard Rayya ask, giving her a mischievous smile as she returned her hand, once again, placing it right next to her pussy.

"Oh God. I see why she moved her hand away! We're going to get ourselves in much worse trouble than kissing!" she thought, feeling her pussy clench - aching to be pressed by Rayya's fingers.

"I, I want you to touch, but I want to behave…I'm dying to feel…maybe just …give me a 'lil' touch," Karman stammered, feeling winded from the shock of hearing her own deep, dark, greedy desires out loud.

"Such a bad girl…I'm so happy you can't resist me," she heard Rayya reply, feeling her slowly move her hand to her inner thigh.

"Yes, I'm ready for this! God I want this so bad. I can't wait to feel her touch my pussy!" Karman thought, closing her eyes, holding her breath…feeling Rayya's hand inch slowly up until her pinkly was just about to touch her pussy when she heard a series of rapid knocks, followed by her husband voice say, "Hi Ladies!" through the door.

"Oh fuck no! Why, why? why!? Wait! Oh fuck yes! Thank God!" Karman thought as she said, "Hi baby," in her most causal tone.

"Hi, we're coming in now, let's have a talk," she heard her husband reply.

"Oh God," she whispered…hearing Rayya, whisper, "Oh Allah," at the same time.

136

Chapter IV

Forgiveness & Fear

Road Trip: Day Three

Date: Saturday, June 3rd 2017

Time: 8:20 am

Location: Bismarck, North Dakota

"Damn! Damn! Damn!" Rayya thought feeling fear rise in her belly the moment she heard Jay's tone.

"How bad will it be for you?" she heard Karman ask, taking hold of her hand that was right next to her pussy, bringing it up, kissing it, somewhat calming her nerves.

"I don't know. We made a pretty big promise. And I fucked it up. So maybe pretty bad," Rayya whispered, feeling her stomach twisting in knots.

"Here, let me get the door," she heard Karman reply, sitting up, stroking her hair, calming her nerves even more before hopping out the bed, where she could fully drink in and appreciate Karman's beautiful curves.

"Mmm, you going to open the door like that, knowing Nate's there? My dream come true, just at the worst possible time," Rayya whispered as she sat up, trying to force down her rising unease, unable to shake it until she saw a flash of mischief come across Karman's face.

"Ohhh, what was that look? And as a matter of fact, as many passes as I've made at your husband, he's yet to see me naked. So brave girl - who's been flashing my Nate, what were you saying about me trying to allure your hubby?" Rayya said, feeling her fear loosen its grip as the deeper, primal part of her awakened from the thrill of watching Karman fight to step out of her comfort zone.

"Rayya, your shorts were see-through. I think you gave my baby a hard on," she heard Karman reply, leaning towards her, sliding her hand underneath her ass, pulling the shorts she'd been sitting on from underneath.

"You think I did? Or do you know I did?" Rayya asked sitting up, watching Karman put the shorts on, laughing when she saw how see-through they were.

"I know. Whenever we pulled over to get gas or something, he kept trying to hide it from me. And Goddamn Rayya, these are completely see-through! What's the point of them being purple if they're going to be translucent when I put them on? Ahh! I remember these! These are the ones you wouldn't let me check the size. You just dumped it in the pile while I was paying for the other clothes. Jesus…I thought the one I put on yesterday were bad," she heard Karman say, twisting her neck to look at her ass before shaking her head at her.

"I know, aren't they great?" she replied, laughing as Karman picked up a jean skirt from the floor, sliding them on as she said, "yes, they're great, as panties."

"Bwahaha! Okay, then wear the belly halter top…like the one I wore yesterday. Show those beautiful tits and cute little tummy," she replied, thoroughly enjoying herself despite the nagging doom-like presence she could feel waiting for her just outside the door.

"Oh Lord. How the hell could this even be called a halter top. This is tinier than a washcloth, and all that's gonna keep it on my boobs is this tiny little string," she heard Karman whisper, pushing her foot to unhook the string of the halter top from around the heel of her sandal, bringing it up to her chest with a look of disdain.

"Damn, that looks good," she replied, loving the way the white halter top caressed Karman's breast snugly, yet hung loosely enough to reveal everything from the sides.

"Okay fine," she heard Karman say when she heard another knock at the door, followed by both men chuckling.

'He's laughing. That's a good sign. I think," she thought as Karman said, "I'm coming uno momento por favor."

"I've never heard you speak Spanish before. Wow, that was sexy. Especially the way you rolled that 'R'," she said, winking at Karman as she hopped out the bed, feeling her nervousness fully return where she wanted to bolt and hide in the bathroom.

"You okay?" Karman asked, spinning around, pointing to her back, causing her to laugh despite her nervousness as she went over and tied the lace.

"I'll be okay," she replied kissing the nape of Karman's neck, giving her a shove on the ass to send her off towards the door.

"Oh fuck. I'm not okay," she thought right after as Karman strolled over and opened the door, with her first sight being her husband's serious face, whose eyes instantly locked onto hers.

"He's going to want to go straight to Chicago now. I know that look. Fuck! Why!? Maybe I should've told him. No, if I did that, then we wouldn't even be here right now. Well, shit then. This was fun while it lasted," she thought, breaking her husband's gaze, steeping back dizzily, sitting and almost missing the foot of the bed, having to catch the edge to guide herself onto it.

"Damn boo, you still weren't dressed. Even for a Libra, you bring a new meaning to being indecisive," she heard Jay say to Karman as he strolled in, giving her a mischievous look when he made it through the short hallway into the bedroom.

"I'm a Libra too. And I don't think I'm indecisive at all," she said, trying to force herself to sound happy as she fixed her face into a smile that must've come off as extremely fake, because Jay's look of mischief instantly changed to one of pure concern.

"This guy…More and more, I can see how fast he can read a person and it's downright scary," she thought, showing her true emotions just for a moment to see what his face would do, surprised when he crouched down in front of her, looking between her and Nate who'd just stepped past the hallway into the bedroom.

"This man is past intuitive. He reminds me of when I was training with…Allah no! What's his background? U.S. Navy, Aviation Electricians mate my ass. An electrician can't read you like that," she thought as her husband came and sat down beside her, giving her a hug, shattering her thoughts of blood and warfare, where she remembered she'd done something terrible in terms of messing with Jay's relationship… that she was sure her husband was going to make her answer for.

"Oh yeah. You're a Libra too," she heard Jay say, changing his look of concern to warm and understanding before saying, "Na, you're really indecisive too. How many times have you

139

changed your reports? Humm, half my desk is dedicated to you. I even have an area on my desk designated as Rayya revisions."

"Hey, I stop at three," she said defensively, feeling a flash of annoyance, thinking, *"The complexity of the data is what makes me do the revisions. If everyone wasn't so damn dumb, I wouldn't have to keep simplifying it. Plus, I'm confused, but I don't want to tell anyone that the crystals aren't behaving the way I thought they would. I wish I knew what the difference was between these and the ones from the lab in school, they're supposed to be the same damn thing. But yeah, I'll be damned if I tell them I'm confused. The problem is that I know Jay isn't dumb. He's just waiting patiently...Why's he not rushing me? He has everything to lose if I fuck up."*

"Rayya, I heard about the kiss and I honestly understand what happened. I love you and we'll for sure talk about it later. I'm still annoyed a 'lil' bit, but I don't want you to worry that I'll be an ass and come down on you really hard. So my love, what do you think about going to Mt. Rushmore, and then Yellowstone. Let's have a good time, okay?" Rayya heard her husband whisper in her ear, shattering her out of her thoughts of work, almost causing her to cry as relief, mixed with guilt washed over her.

"Is this for real? Is this the same Nate? Out of all the things I could've done, he's not forcing me to apologize? And he's not going to rush the trip? What the fuck is going on?" Rayya thought, turning to face her husband, pecking him on the lips as tears began to well up in her eyes.

"Shit...today I can't stop crying, and it's annoying," she whispered, sucking in a deep breath to hold back her tears, fanning her face to get rid of the hot flash that'd come over her.

"Yeah, look at those eyes. Umm...yeah, let's have a good time, like your hubby said. No need to worry, it's all good," she heard Jay say, resting his hand on her knee, causing her to think, *"Fuck my life, this is making me feel even worse. Why are they being so sweet? And damn, did my eyes get puffy that quick from crying earlier? I can't stand that my body never hides anything."*

"So, umm, I see you guys talked. I'm sorry my love. You shouldn't have found out like that. I was being selfish," Rayya choked out, despite her best efforts to hold back her tears.

"Baby, it's okay." she heard her husband say.

140

"No, look," she began as she thought, *"Allah, I hate apologizing. I hate showing weakness. Please give me the strength to humble myself,"* before saying, "I shouldn't have, I shouldn't have went for the kiss. I was being relentless and selfish, and I saw this perfect moment, this perfect moment to kiss her. I'm sorry Karman, I should've thought of you and your husband before I thought of myself."

"Oh sweetie, please. We talked about this. It's okay," she heard Karman reply, moving around Jay, sitting and wrapping her arms around her, giving her a strange sense of security now that two people were holding her.

"I hear you when you say it's okay, but it's the principle," Rayya whispered, squinting through her tear filled eyes, at Jay, whose face was totally calm and neutral, before resting her head on Karman's.

"Why is everyone being so forgiving? Why do I feel like this is too good to be true? When does the bad stuff happen? There's always something bad, especially when things are going this good."

"Oh, come on. You're being way too hard on yourself. You know damn straight this is on me. If I didn't want you to kiss me, I wouldn't have let it happen. Jay should be mad at me. Do you hear me sweetie? He should be mad at me," she heard Karman say, turning and kissing the side of her temple.

"Okay. If no one's going to be upset, then pull yourself together," she thought, taking a deep breath, feeling calmer after every moment passed where no one took a snip at her.

"Good, good. Good to see you're feeling better," she heard Jay say after maybe the sixth second, causing her to suck in her breath for just the slightest moment, instantly witnessing his smile drop to a frown.

"Are you showing me you can read me by letting me read you? How come I've never been able to see this side of you till just now?" she thought, feeling small tinges of fear for her safety creep in, replacing her sorrow and guilt.

"I love you, and you know what? This never has to come up again. Let's leave this right here," she heard her husband whisper, kissing her on the cheek, almost causing her to lose focus on Jay, who was standing up - whipping out his phone from his pocket, with a puzzled look on his face.

"Thank you baby," she whispered, wishing she could enjoy the moment, but unable to because every part of her was worried about the new side of Jay she was seeing.

"If he's this good a reading people. Then, he might know from any tells I have, that I was forced to betray our company. But If he does know, then why would he be hanging out with me on vacation?"

"No, thank you. You, ummm, are umm…" she heard her husband begin before kissing her on side of the cheek, causing her to laugh and say, "No good at apologizing and you're shocked out of your mind that I did. Right baby?"

"Yeah," she heard her husband reply, releasing his hold as he stood up, hearing him ask, "Jay, what's up my man. Checking work emails on your vackay?"

"Maybe he wants to be on vacation with me because he suspects me as the culprit for data breaches. Maybe this his way of learning more about me before he makes up his mind on whether I'm guilty or not. Or… I'm being paranoid. He might just be a good people reader; it doesn't mean he'd know what I've done. But it's his speed of knowing my emotions that's bothering me. Is it normal? Wait a minute, I'm paranoid because of what that weasel of a man said to me about him and Karman way back then. I can't believe his words still affect me! I thought I'd forgotten him! Damn it!" Rayya thought, wrapping her arm around Karman, feeling chilly now that Nate had left her side.

"Na', this is the news. These simple fucks want to …they want to, huh? Yo! The want to build a second space elevator!" Rayya heard Jay exclaim.

"What!?" Rayya heard Karman respond.

"Yeah! Apparently they want to float the space elevator in the Pacific, with the anchor points dipping into the Marianas Trench," she heard Jay say, looking at her husband, then all of them with a strange smirk on his face that made her utterly uncomfortable.

"Two Space Elevators!? They just spent trillions of dollars in my country, just in preparation for one! And now what!? Now they want to spend trillions more for a second one?" she heard Karman blare as she released her, standing up with a look of pure frustration, running her hands through her hair as if she were about to rip it out.

"That bitch…she had me doing different sets of space elevator equations for years. And I'm sure I was just one of thousands, if not more, 'Life Debtors' they used as brain slaves. Now it seems like all the companies and governments using people like me, have now got enough feasible data that they feel they can rush into building them," she thought, having horrible flashbacks of Nate's mother personally coming to check on, slash degrade her for not working hard enough as she did space elevator equation after space elevator equation.

"Wifey, you're right. I don't disagree," she heard Jay reply.

"This is evil!" she heard Karman respond.

"Boo! Let me finish," she heard Jay say, seeing him give Karman a wide eyed stare.

"Aye Papi! Read!" she heard Karman snip, muttering something in Spanish right after.

"Okay, listen here y'all. It says here that world the governments and corporations want to make this a competition, With Tet Corp. and its affiliates running things in Colombia, using Rayya and I's company, Nammu tech, along with wifey's company, O.L.O Engineering as their figure heads."

"Then there's going to be Nate's company, Lilith Corp., and wow! Lilith Corps., all-time rival, Al Babadur Corp., leading the construction in the Pacific. Holly hell! This is literally the forbidden marriage of the Arabs and the Jews. Haha, you two have big name competition trying to outshine you! Hmmm, but now people can't talk shit about you two being married, can they!? Cool huh!?" she heard Jay say, smiling brightly, looking between herself and Nate, causing some parts of her to light up, loving his smile, while the other part of her wanted to throttle him to the ground, knowing there was much more to his smile than happiness.

"The companies have pillaged Colombia. People says the world has come to peace, but they never show you what it's like in Colombia. They never show what life is like for the people who've had to dig the anchor points. I don't even know why they chose my country in the first place. Now they want to build two. They will end up stripping Guam and all the islands around them dry for resources. How did that site get approval from anyone? Anyone with a brain would know that building that thing there would destroy everything around it?" she heard

Karman whisper, glaring at her and all the others with smoldering rage burning behind her eyes.

"*I agree with her anger. Everyone knows that the asteroids the Space Elevators are supposed to bring down, might not be as easy to process or as lucrative as predicted. If that's the case, then the companies and governments will go straight back to stripping all the resources from the land. And in the case of Colombia, with all the ancient artifacts that are buried with the natural resources, I'm sure the lands around the anchor points are being striped bare,*" Rayya thought, while simultaneously wishing the topic would change.

"Hey, umm. Thank you all for not being mad at me. And since y'all aren't mad at me, do y'all mind if I make a request, which would be, can we please enjoy ourselves. Can we not talk about this anymore? When we're back to work...we can think about all this. Right? Like, honestly I haven't even checked the news, it's always bullshit. I just wanted to be left alone and sped time with all of you. Let's spend quality time with each other," Rayya, said feeling relief when she saw everyone nodding their heads in approval.

"Good point, speaking of enjoying ourselves" she heard Jay reply, stepping past her husband, crouching down in front of her.

"*What's with this look all of a sudden?*" she thought, feeling Jay pat her on the knee, giving her mischievous smile before saying, "Hey, according to your swinger people rules. Both Karman and I are supposed to be willing and give consent. And since Karman is obviously willing, I'd like to give my consent and show my support by way of watching you two kiss. So what do you say? You said you want us all to enjoy ourselves. It obvious y'all like kissing each other, and I know damn straight Nate and I'd would like watching that."

"*What the hell? Just like that!? Allah, he picks the only time in the world I'm totally not in the mood, and...*" she started to think, when she heard Karman say, "Okay baby. But you better not be uncomfortable after."

"*Wait what? She's not scared or nervous?*" she thought in surprise, feeling everyone's eyes on her, making her feel awkward for just a second before her inner desires took hold of her.

"Okay, you want to see us kiss?" Rayya asked, resting her hand on top Jay's as she looked deep into his eyes, loving the expectant, hungry look she now saw before turning towards Karman who was coming up next to him with the same hungry look.

"Yeah, let's see it," she heard Jay whisper, gripping her knee a little tighter, almost fully erasing the discomfort she'd felt about his earlier demeanor.

"This is more like it! I want to have fun! Work will always be there to ruin everything," she thought as Karman sat beside her, cupping her chin, causing her to grow warm and her breath to go heavy.

"Hi sweetie," she whispered leaning in, pecking Karman on the lips enjoying the warmth and softness that greeted her before parting her lips ever so slightly, finding herself instantly greeted by Karman's tongue.

"Oh, wow, this kiss is much better than before!" she thought, giving into her lust, kissing Karman deeper and deeper, loving her taste and passion, as well as the feeling of being watched by her husband and Jay - who'd she'd been fantasizing about since the moment she'd met him.

"Man, it's just as sexy as I imagined. No, actually, way more," she heard Jay whisper, feeling his hand grip her knee even tighter.

"Yes! This is what I wanted. Fuck everything else! I want more! I want this to start it!" she thought kissing Karman even deeper, hear both men breathe heavier right after.

"Move your hand up my thigh. Touch my pussy! Touch my breast! Push us over, then come between us and kiss us both!" she thought, letting go of Jay's hand, taking hold of the back of Karman's neck, driving her tongue into her mouth even further.

"Oh my fucking God," she heard Jay whisper, feeling his hand slide up her knee, gripping the base of her thigh.

"Yes. This is it! This is happening! Fuck everything else. Yes! We're so lucky! My love, you were right about everything!" she thought, losing herself in the kiss, where she and Karman seemed to make out endlessly.

"Man, I love it. I can't believe this is happening," she heard Jay whisper, finally realising there was an empty presence of his hand on her thigh, causing her open her eyes to see that he'd now stood up and moved next to her husband in her peripherals.

"Why are you over there? Come back here!" she thought, shortening her kisses with Karman, yet keeping her mouth slightly open to accept her tongue as she tilted her head to look at her husband, who shook his head ever so slightly 'no', with a warm smile on his face.

"No! Why no?" she thought, bringing the kiss to a close, pecking Karman on the lips, before saying, "Let's see what our hubbies thought about that, huh sweetie?"

"Muhumm," she heard Karman reply, watching her as she opened her eyes and looked towards the men who resembled two hungry wolves about to pounce their pray.

"With that look, why no? I don't get it" Rayya thought, focusing on her husband, who ever so slightly did a head-tip to say, 'okay, time to go'.

"Baby...that was, wow baby is all I can say," she heard Jay whisper as he clasped her husband on the shoulder, wearing an enormous grin on his face.

"Man...yeah, that was really amazing," she heard her husband reply, smiling brightly at her, then to Jay and Karman, before saying, "Alright, alright, I need to go cool off. I dunno why, but strangely, I'm in the mood for pink lemonade. And actually, I'm a bit hungry, so I was thinking of going over to the bar and getting some wings to eat while we're on the road."

"Oh, cool! Alright then. Reggie said food's on him anyways. Well he told me for wifey and I...but I'm sure he meant for all of us. And pink lemonade, damn that sounds like a good paring with wings! Boo, do you want a cup of lemonade too or do you want something else?" she heard Jay ask, sounding ecstatic, causing her to feel giddy until she actually realized that Jay was talking about Reggie with familiarity.

"Yeah sure, pink lemonade sounds good. Hey Nate, sweetie, can you grab him a big cup of ginger ale as well. We'll drive off and he'll want it. Then he won't let it go, and we'll end up stopping at some random, creepy ass gas station to get one. And I don't want to be hung and salted, so please," she heard Karman say with her Colombian accent coming out more so than usual, making her want to stay and kiss her, even though in the back of her mind she was thinking, *"When they were talking, did Jay bring up hearing us with man in the room? And then did hubby just decide to introduce them to each other?"*

"Sure, no problem," she heard her husband reply to Karman while at the same time giving her a sweet, but stern, 'let's go' look.

"Fuck! Okay, fine!" she thought, longing to stay as she leaned in, pecking Karman on the lips, wanting one last taste before she got up from the bed, saying, "Okay you two, see you soon."

"Yeah, Mmm-mhumm," she heard Jay and Karman reply - dismissively in unison.

"Hey, that tone was 'kinda' mean! What the fuck kinda mood change was that!?" she thought, turning around, looking between Jay and Karman, finding that they were locked in each other's gaze, with looks of pure desire

"Oh, I get it! Shit! I was being selfish again," she realized, feeling a rush of excitement, knowing that her kiss with Karman was the catalyst of what she was seeing now.

"Um…we can give you guys," she began when her husband tipped his head towards the door meaning, 'shhh, let's go'.

"Wa?" she mouthed, backing up towards the door, keeping half her attention on the couple who'd seemed to forget they were even there, and half on Nate who was casually walking toward her with a smile that said he felt victorious.

"Your face," Rayya whispered, backing into the door, then turning to grip the handle, feeling her husband's hand softly squeeze her ass.

"Wants to be between your legs," she heard her husband whisper in her ear as she stepped back and opened the door.

"Well now, we probably have time," she replied stepping out the door, spinning and leaning forward as Nate stepped through so that he'd have to catch her.

"Hey you. You like catching me off-guard don't you," she heard her husband say, catching her in his arms, pulling her close, kissing her forehead.

"Like this, yes. I'm sorry about the other thing. I didn't…" she began to say, pausing to inhale deeply, loving the scent of his sweat even though it was mixed with cigarette smoke.

"Hey, I told you. Leave it all in that room. Everything happens for a reason, and what happened in there was simply beautiful," she heard her husband say, kissing her on the forehead over and over again.

"More, more, more," she said when he stopped.

"How much more?" she heard her husband reply.

"Loads more! And hey, how does Jay know Reggie? That was a little weird for me. I mean…"

"Sshhh…take your kisses. I'll tell you when we walk over there, it's not a big deal," she heard her husband cut it, kissing her forehead between his words.

"For fuck sakes. With you two around, I wonder why they even bothered to make rooms in buildings," she heard John say from somewhere far down the hall, causing both of them to burst out laughing.

"Love you too John," she heard her husband respond, causing them to both laugh even harder.

"I love you my Habibi," she whispered after they'd finished laughing, now pressing her head into his chest,

"I love you too," she heard her husband reply, loving his words and the deep vibration as he spoke.

'Hubby' letting go of my mistake is so refreshing, and so not like him. He holds the biggest grudges if I break any of his sacred rules, and sometimes, as much as I love him, I feel like he's slowly smothering me. Could it have been something Jay said that changed his mind? Or did he have an epiphany of his own? And if it was Jay, what the hell did he say to make my stubborn ass 'hubby' change his mind so fast? I think it was Jay, and that 'kinda' scares me. He's always too good to be true. And whenever someone or something is too good to be true, it turns out to be poison."

Chapter V

Confessions & Undercurrents

Road Trip: Day Three

Date: Saturday, June 3rd 2017

Time: 8:35 am

Location: Bismarck, North Dakota

"That was so amazing. I could have kept watching that for a long ass time," Jay thought, staring at his wife, long past Nate and Rayya's departure.

"Baby, you alright?" he heard his wife ask seductively, biting her bottom lip.

"More than alright. I loved that. I wasn't sure how…well I knew I'd think it was hot. But I thought I'd feel a little jealous after," Jay replied, crouching down, looking between her jean skirt, smiling when he saw the beautiful impression of her pussy, pressing firmly into the translucent fabric.

"And what did you feel?" he heard his wife ask, parting her legs, summoning him with her finger.

"I wanted to …" Jay began as he inched closer, thinking, *"I wanted to fuck both of you right then and there. I wanted her, just as bad as I wanted you. And I could barely stop myself from trying to go for it. But if I say this out loud, it'll really be real."*

"Silence is not an answer," he heard his wife press, snickering as she closed her legs, giving him a sarcastic, 'no' look.

"I wanted to."

"Go on, tell me."

"I, umm."

"Say it, don't be a chicken. Be a man Papi, tell me," he heard his wife whisper, opening her legs again.

"I wanted to fuck you," Jay replied, placing his hands on her knees, spreading her legs open even wider.

"Just me?"

"And I wanted to fuck her," Jay whispered, feeling dizzy right after, knowing that he'd now admitted wanting to fuck another woman openly, and that there was no coming back from it.

"See, now there, was that hard?" he heard his wife whisper as she cupped his cheeks in her hands, tilting his head up, kissing him gently on the lips.

"Yes," he replied, feeling an odd sense of guilt.

"Ha! Why Papi? You think I couldn't see that she made you hard the other day?"

"Huh?" he mumbled.

"Oh, don't huh me Papi, the whole first day she had you dying. It was so funny," Hay heard his wife reply, making him feel awkward, on top of guilty.

"I didn't hide it well, did I?" he asked, sliding his hands up his wife's thighs, resting his thumbs against her pussy.

"Not at all. And you know what?" he heard his wife ask, tilting her head back as he began to massage her pussy with his thumbs.

"What?" he asked, staring intently at her warm, sticky arousal seeping through the sheer fabric of her shorts.

"I loved every minute of it," he heard his wife whisper, taking hold of his hands, looking down into his eyes, where he caught a gleam of concern, making him slide his hands back to her knees, wanting to have all his attention on her face.

"Fuck Jay," he heard his respond in aggravation, with her accent leaking out as she took hold of his hands, bringing them back to her pussy.

"What's up?" tell me and I'll rub kitty.

"You can't..." he heard his wife began to say as he started massaging again, stopping just as quickly.

"You can't hold my pussy hostage, you ass."

"Tell me what's wrong," he pressed.

"Look baby, we've talked about this before. Stop using that creepy thing on me. I don't like it. And Rayya doesn't like it, she was freaking out every time you did it. No one likes it. Please, just stop it," he heard his wife groan before sucking her teeth.

"Sorry I can't help it. I have to ask. Are we safe? Because I know that look you just made, and it means you feel...well, not so safe," Jay replied, no longer feeling even slightly horny, especially since after his question he saw even more looks of concern flash across his wife's face.

"Argh! Me estás molestando! I dunno Jay. Are we safe? What was in your email? You're not the only one that can read a person. News my ass," he heard his wife say, standing up, snatching clothes off the bed, looking around the room for what he guessed was their bag.

"But I was reading the news," he replied, recalling the e-mail which read; *[Nammu Tech/Corp. Security breach: Data transfers detected on the following dates. Tybi 26th, 27th, 28th & Mechir 1st. The Affiliates also let you aware that contacts detected and confirmed. MOPP-(Mission Oriented Protective Posture) is now 'Anubis'. Secondary elevator will now be erected along with primary elevator. We must move forward in the name of ISIS. Link: {Build site plans and current news statements for the flock}]*

"Shut up. It was your email, and they sent you a link to the news. Act like I don't know what the hell's going on. So what did your email say? Are they asking why you're taking a vacation when your team still has inconclusive data? You need talk to Rayya, find out what's going on. She's prideful baby, she won't tell you she's having trouble. You're going to have to ask her."

"Look baby, I don't tell you my work stuff so you can tell me what to do," he said as he thought, *"How do I tell you about this email? The first part of it, telling me about the Data breach was normal. But then dates were weird, correction the whole rest of email, minus the links to the News were weird. Then right after I read it, it disappeared, only leaving me the text about the data transfers and the links for the News statements."*

"And when I asked our AI to trace it...it doesn't even know what the fuck I'm talking about. It says the email only has the same shit I can see and that there was no other data or text apart of it. Right now, there's nothing to tell you, I don't have any prof, and you hate conspiracies theories."

"You're my husband, I'll always tell you what to do. How have you still not gotten used to it?" he heard his wife reply.

"Look baby, can you do me a favor? Don't bring it up again. It's a fucking jinx if there ever was one. I don't want to think about the fucking data," Jay said squinting, still trying to figure out why his wife had a look of concern on her face

151

regarding Rayya before saying, "What's wrong with Rayya? Or is it Nate? Or is it both of them? Your gut's always right. Do you trust them?"

"Yes I trust them," he heard his wife reply, sucking her teeth as she picked up their bag, mumbling to herself in Spanish before turning to him saying, "why can't you ever close the Goddamn Q-tip bag? Why? How hard is it? Look, it's a zip lock. Press it closed, then put it all the way in our bag. See? Not that hard."

"You trust them, but what?" Jay asked, cringing in annoyance, hating to be reprimanded about something he thought was totally and utterly stupid.

"If you want to fuck her, you can fuck her. No problem. And I'd fuck her with you. No problem, is that what you want to hear? There! She's fucking safe Jay! We can have your fucking threesome or whatever fucking fantasy you want with her, and I'd be okay with it. Just God, leave me alone. No one told you to use that creepy thing on me," he heard his wife say, sounding more and more aggravated with each passing second.

"Hey...why do I deserve that tone? I was just asking you a question," he said as he thought, *"Just as fast as I expose that desire, it gets thrown in my face as a weapon. That's why I don't like opening up all the way! Even to her! No matter who it is, even it's my wife – somehow what I've exposed gets used against me!"*

"You deserve the tone 'cause' you piss me off. Mind your business. You're the one who started this Jay! I was having a good time...and don't tell me I wasn't because of my face. No one...and I mean no one else sees that shit. Your over there knowing my thoughts even before I'm knowing them, and I don't want you telling me what the fuck I'm thinking!" he heard his wife growl, now dragging their bag around the room, jamming clothes and other effects into it as she came across them, causing him to smile, despite the sting he'd felt from her reaction.

"Look baby. I just want to be careful. Sometimes..."

"Careful with what? What's hard about having fun and relaxing? Tell me? What more could there be about her that could even be a problem? So there, let's just have a good time. No?" he heard his wife say, flinging down their bag, placing her hands on her hips.

"I wish it were that simple. And I don't like that you used what I just said about Rayya against me," Jay said, growing more and more aggravated that she'd done so.

"I…I…you. Oh fuck. I'm sorry baby," he heard his wife reply, rolling her eyes before walking over to him, giving him a hug.

"What's this?" he asked, laughing at her awkward behaviour as she rubbed her head on his chest playfully.

"My apology. I always forget for all that toughness…you're a sensitive little bitch," he heard his wife reply, giggling.

"Seriously, I don't like it," he whispered, kissing the crown of her head as he rocked her side to side, thinking, *"Rayya has been hovering around my office more than usual. Could it be her? Why would she need data she already has access to? Half the shit taken is generated from her test."*

"Sorry. I shouldn't have said that. I like that you…I like what you said about…wanting to…" Jay heard his wife stammer.

"You can't say it now, can you?" he asked, laughing as he took hold of Karman's shoulders, gently pushing her back so that he could look into her eyes.

"Yeah, it's awkward. I, yeah…It's hard for me to say aloud," he heard his wife reply, titling her head down as she laughed so that she'd hide her face from him.

"Unh-huh…say it, you made me say it. I want to hear you say it," he whispered, gently cupping her chin, tipping her head up to give her a kiss.

"I like…I like that you want to fuck her," he heard his wife whisper, just before his lips touched hers, sending a rush of adrenaline coursing through his veins.

"See, was that so hard?" he asked, hovering his lips above hers.

"Yes," he heard his wife whisper.

"I know," he replied, keeping his eyes locked with hers to show he was solely focused on her and the moment.

"Thank you…thank you for backing up and giving me my space. I appreciate you being like this right now," he heard his wife say softly, leaning forward, pecking him on the lips before pulling away, flopping down on the foot of the bed with her brows furrowed in deep thought.

"I'll wait this time," he thought looking behind him as he inched back, resting his ass on the coffee table.

"When I get upset, my accent really comes out doesn't it?" he heard his wife ask as she looked up at him with an expression he hadn't seen for a very long time.

"Yeah...you haven't been keeping it in check," he replied, thinking, *"Why does it matter unless you think they're picking out our 'tells' for something more than sex?"*

"All the training in the world and the basics in life give you away faster than anything else. Especially once you've grown comfortable, where you've almost let go of everything...fucking liar, but why?" he heard his wife say, slowly shaking her head like, 'I don't get it,' leaving him lost.

"What?"

"She said she got a refugee visa to the U.S. at the end of two-thousand six. It's bullshit, the war was from July to September. Refugee visas are fast, but not that fast. And the U.S. would've been really careful with any Lebanese trying to come over, both to keep potential terrorist out, and because they'd be sending all the visa applicant info to Israel for screening. Hummm...but she's here...so not lying all the way...but refugee visa, I doubt it. It there's a visa for geniuses, maybe? And another thing bothering me is that she has no scars near her ovaries," he heard his wife say, looking around the room as she spoke, not once meeting his eyes.

"Look at me when you talk. I hate it when you do that bobble head talking - thinking shit," he said as he thought, *"If you're really smart, you don't need to apply for a visa. They find you. They take you and your paperwork is done. The only question now is, which company found her? If I find that out, then maybe I can figure out if she has a reason to take the data. Maybe she's still loyal to her first sponsors. Loyal...yeah right, who'd be loyal to these monsters? So more likely...if she owes them some kind of life debt, they might be forcing her to take the data. If that's the case, then she's doing a really good job of giving them garbage. So at least I can be thankful for that."*

"It's how I think, leave me alone. And hey, why'd you not tell me that she was a Quantum Physicist. She got her degree in three years. That's crazy huh?" he heard his wife ask, finally locking eyes with him, making him instantly uncomfortable.

"I...umm. It never came up. And yeah, it's pretty cool. Three years. Yeah," he replied.

"Unh-huh. Let me guess, you think it's no big deal. Then if it's not...then why her? Why'd your company hire her? And you had your two cents in it too, didn't you? Why'd you agree to hire her? There are tons of smart people in the world. What makes her stand out?"

"I don't think it's no big deal that she's smart. Like you said, I helped pick her, so I definitely know she's valuable. We picked her because she understands Quantum Entanglement better than most people. Like she's really on the money with her predictions. Hey, the ovaries thing? 'Sup' with that?" Jay said as a nagging feeling about the data breach creeped to the forefront of his mind.

"Sometimes when you have enough trash, it becomes very valuable. Especially if a company is running their own test and need a sounding board. If they already have loads of disproven variables, it can lead to the solution much faster. Fuck...please don't be you Rayya," he thought, feeling his stomach tightening in fear now that he'd heard his thought clearly.

"She said the grenade that killed her father took out one of her ovaries," he heard his wife respond, interrupting his thoughts, causing him to suck in his breath, thinking, *"damn, what happened to Rayya is horrible."*

"Jay...I've spent seven years in total with you. I can do your creepy little trick now too, plus remember...I have my own ways...now spill it. What's up?" he heard his wife say.

"Grenade from a gun right? I bet she said it came from a rifle. And did she say if it exploded or not" he whispered.

"Yeah, she did say the grenade was from a gun...what of it? And I'd assume it exploded," he heard his wife say sounding truly confused.

"Na' she'd have straight up told you if it exploded. Or she wouldn't even be here.

"What are you saying? You think she's lying about being wounded?" he heard his wife ask.

"No, I'm saying what I think really happened is awful is all."

"And what would that be Papi?"

"I think the grenade fired almost point blank…hit her father…but it didn't detonate. It probably hit him, bounced and hit her in the stomach or lower thigh, and that kind of pressure, it does lots of damage," he said before whispering, "And yet she's walking around just fine…good call baby. She's someone we have to keep an eye on for certain. She should definitely have much more damage," he whispered.

"So you're saying the grenade didn't explode? I've shot grenades many times, and they explode. And the people I've shot them at, they've all gone 'mush'," he heard his wife say, with a puzzled expression on her face, doing a hand gesture that implied a person exploding.

"No, Israeli tech is much different than the weapons you've used in Colombia. The Israelis' made their grenades in a way that if they hit a target right out the barrel, it wouldn't detonate and kill any of their troops. Another thing is that the grenade must've bounced. Yeah, it probably skipped on the ground, hit her father then her. If it hit her square on, she'd have been done for, someone had to take that pressure first before it hit her or yeah, like I said...she'd not even be here," he replied.

"Fuck," he heard his wife whisper.

"Fuck, is right," Jay said, feeling the mental atmosphere in the room becoming too thick before saying, "Putting all this shit aside, do you think we can really try to enjoy this trip. I mean, if those two are trying to get too close to fuck us…in other ways more than physically. Won't we just have to deal with it anyways?"

"Yup," he heard his wife say with a warm smile.

"What you 'chessin' for?" he asked.

"I can't believe it…you like them," he heard his wife declare.

"Yeah, I do actually. I can see that they really care about our lives, and it makes me happy. It's rare a person or people other than you make me happy."

"Good! I'm happy you like them!" he heard his wife exclaim.

"I have to be honest, I've always 'kinda' personally like them. It's just hanging with them those few times, I've always got this, 'too good to be true' feeling creeping in that made me weary. It's weird though, that feeling of too good to be true is going away…and yet I'm still liking them," he said smiling as he spoke.

"So, you're saying let's stop worrying about BS, and let's have a good time? Wait, who said that already? Me Papi! You fucking annoying bastard!" he heard his wife say, smiling and reaching back, chucking a pillow at him, which landed square in his face.

Laughing at the break in tension, Jay thought, *"I'll try my hardest to chill because I don't want to pass up the opportunity to enjoy Nate and Rayya's company. They're quickly beginning to remind me of people in my Organization …and that kind of feeling is rare."*

Chapter VI

Work

Road Trip: Day Three

Date: Saturday, June 3rd 2017

Time: 12:30 pm

Location: Somewhere on SD-65

"God this is nice!" Nate thought, inhaling the sweet scent of air rushing into his face from the half open passenger window.

And with that thought, he felt his pocket vibrate for maybe the hundredth time.

"They're not giving up are they? Well that's unfortunate for them," Nate thought going into his pocket, casually pulling out his phone, opening it to read: <**Lilith Corp. Message 106**. *Agent Dybbuk, please respond. We need you to gather information to confirm if current reports of subjects' movements are accurate. The current company you keep, minus your spousal unit, are they relevant? If so, please annotate their relevance. If relevance is personal, we ask you disengage to complete your mission. There's always time for personal relations at a later time.* >

"Pssst," Nate whispered, letting out a long stream of air as he smiled at the message.

"Work bothering you?" he heard Jay ask casually, causing him to look up at Jay's handsome face.

"Humm, bothering me. Not really bothering me. I'd say they're bothering themselves is a better description," Nate replied, about to press the lock screen button, deciding to hit reply instead, writing, < ***Dybbuk:*** *=D Work on vacation? :-D ummm, let me think…no.* *= D~* >.

"I've got two messages since we've left the hotel. Both times I've had to reply and ask what they wanted me to do about it while I'm in North Dakota," he heard Jay say, shooting him a bright, 'you've 'gotta' be kidding smile', before looking back at the road.

"Two…I wish that was the case for me. My work is a little crazy, I think I've been texted about a hundred times. Just now is the first time I've replied," Nate said, beginning to laugh, knowing in a few seconds he was going to receive another – nastier email.

"No really? A hundred? You're joking?" he heard Jay reply, giving him a look of true bewilderment.

"Actually it's been one hundred and six times," Nate replied, staring at his phone as it went off again, which made him say, "now, one hundred and seven times."

"No shit…but it makes a 'lil' bit of sense they want to talk to you, I mean you make all that spy gadget shit and aren't you the head of your team? The 'youngens' probably need you to hold their hand," he heard Jay say with a chuckle.

"Making spy gadget shit? That's what you think my job is, huh? That's funny?" Nate replied as he thought, *The things we create make the greatest spy movies look like children shows.*

"Yeah man, I saw the commercial y'all put out, you guys are making it commercially available to buy those lasers that can hear shit off potato chip bags, and all kinds of other stuff. Well, commercially available if you want to spend ten grand on a pocket laser. Humm, but isn't that what Lilith Corp. is all about? Making crazy, gadget shit that's for the general public? Well, commercially available if you're rich, but still. So, yeah I take it that's what you do," he heard Jay reply, giving him a bright smile.

"We also sell our tech to help governments, private contractors, and security companies. But yeah, we have tech for the general public because we feel we have a responsibility to help the local communities as well. But me…a spy gadget maker, interesting," Nate said, with the last part mostly under his breath as he thought, *"I hate tinkering and making things from scratch. I don't know how people have the patience to do it. If I had to make something from scratch to save my life, I'd kill myself."*

"Oh yeah, I forgot. Now I remember, yeah, at Leonard and Sandy's party, you were talking about your company making those helmets for soldiers, the ones that look like motorcycle helmets, or something like that. And umm, some kind of data transfer thing with the new kind of light waves that have a different, what's it called - angular momentum that makes them not bend normally or something like that. And you're not a gadget maker? Fuck, 'I'ma' bad friend, what do you do homie, I swear you're always talking about how lots of new gadgets work and what not," he heard Jay say, bobbing his head up and down before giving him a small shrug.

"You heard every word I said. You're not the type to tune things out. And you suck at playing dumb. Why do I get the unnerving feeling you know exactly what's going on with the new light wave technology," Nate thought as he gazed out at the fields of grass, not seeing even a single house in sight, loving the pure, empty serenity, almost wishing he could hop out, strip nude, and walk through them before he said, "Yeah, to be honest, I'm more of the gadget tester than maker. That's why you always hear me discussing how to operate them."

Upon saying that, his phone went off again, causing him to almost burst out laughing. Taking a deep breath to calm himself, he clicked it open and read, **<Lilith Corp. Message 107.** *It is a matter of urgency. Forced instatement is pending. There are no other agents close enough to examine the sites. We implore you to abort plans with useless individuals.* **>**

"Useless individuals? Really, is that how it's going to be?" Nate thought, pressing his thumb on the next message, which read, **<Lilith Corp. Message 108.** *Please do not describe your job duties to said individuals in order to prevent individuals from being able to infer the actual scope and range of your job duties. Also - we truly implore you take this assignment. Things are moving fast and intelligence is required to make assessment on best possible courses of action>*

"No way! Really? Is that your work? I heard it go off twice in less than two minutes," he heard Jay say, sounding slightly appalled when Rayya jumped in and sleepily whispered, "yeah, they're needy. And they're creepy bastards too. Sometimes, they actually listen through his phone."

"No shit!?" Nate heard Jay exclaim, looking at him with wild eyes, just as his phone went off again.

"No they can't, that'd be too much. Rayya just doesn't like the coincidences. Sometimes they've called me just as we're planning to go on vacations and…"

"Oh no Nate, those are not coincidences. I want to throw you phone out the goddamn window. What do they want? Why do I ask, when I know? They want you to work don't they? You promised me Nate. You told me we can relax," Nate heard

Rayya say with her tone and pitch getting louder and louder – all while his phone when off again.

"No, no, I'm just a part of a group chat and they're keeping me in the loop. That's the team members going back and forth," Nate replied as his phone went off again, this time causing his eye to twitch.

"Yeah, bullshit," Nate heard his wife whisper, as he thought, *"Why is she being so weird right now!? Why in God's name would she expose that we're being listened to, to Jay and Karman? Now they're going to be super uncomfortable! And now we're both going to get reprimanded for her talking too much! What the hell!"*

"Rayya, you always say someone's listening through the phone, you paranoid 'spazz'," he heard Karman say.

"Because it's true, everyone is always being watched and listened to now days," he heard his wife say, sounding deeply annoyed – at him.

"Come here Rayya, lay your head on me and relax. Nate don't worry. I get your pain. My job is kind of like that. I'm always in the group chats managing my teams like a goddamn baby sitter. And yeah, my company does always somehow know just when I'm planning on going on vacation, and try to stop me," Nate heard Karman.

"See, they listened through your phone," he heard his wife reply.

"Rayya, cut it out. And go to sleep, you're acting like a baby because your hubbies phone is going off," he heard Karman say.

"Yes, I am, because I hate it. They always want him to work when we're supposed to be have quality time together," he heard his wife mumble, now sounding slightly calmer.

"God, I was having a heart attack for a second. I was like why on earth would she expose us like that. But, apparently she always say things like this to Karman. How'd I not know that? How have they gotten this close without me realizing that they have their own dynamic? Shit, maybe I need to listen through Rayya's phone, hahaha!" he thought opening his phone, expecting more annoying text messages, quickly wishing they were as he read, **<Estries:** *Contacts has been confirmed. They're moving about very quickly. Take a look the images I sent of one of the*

161

contacts, and note the distinctive details. Location: Yellowstone National Park. I heard you're going. Help me. This is not good.>

"Wow! Is this real!? If it is, then why would she show herself!? Oh my God! How can this really be happening!?" Nate thought, feeling his sympathetic nervous system overreacting to the cluster of images Estries had sent, letting him know that what he was seeing was the real deal.

"Be calm! Be calm! Be calm! This can't be right! This has to be manipulation!" he thought, trying to swallow as fear closed off his throat.

<Dybbuk: *Estries! If this is supposed to be real! You shouldn't have been able to obtain visual proof! And you should be dead! I will not be baited. I'd like to enjoy my life without interruptions for once. And another thing! I was told I was the only one available! So then, what are you doing in Yellowstone? I say this is some 'kinda' contrived training game cooked up by my mom and you're here to guilt me into participating!>*

"You, umm. 'Wanna' grab some coffee at the next lil town - spot - thingy we pass?" he heard Jay ask, as he tapped his finger on each one of the images Estris had sent, looking closer at the beautiful, nude, but somewhat fuzzy female figure.

"He was going to ask me if I'm alright. Recently he's been reading Rayya and I a little too fast in my opinion. Now I'm wondering if he was trained, or if this is his natural ability. If he was trained, I can throw him off...till I can figure out what he was trained for. If he's a natural, then if I do need to slip away and check things out, I won't be able to trick him for long and he'll be all over me. Hum, let's do a fast test to see which one he might be," he thought as the fear he'd been trying to force down rose back up, seeing an image where the woman's long, jet black hair was curled around her ankles.

"Fuck, this looks like the real deal! This is her face, her body and her hair! Every picture I see, confirms it's actually her!" Nate thought before saying, "Yeah Jay, coffee sounds good. Hey, just curious, when you were a kid, did you get into a lot of fights? Me, I was born in Israel, but a large part of my family's business was in Chicago, so I grew up back and forth between the two. That made me not fit in with people in either place. It really sucked, and I'd get into a lot of fights I couldn't avoid," feeling his phone go off in his hand right after.

"Damn it, real deal or not! I told you I'm not interested. Take a hint!" he thought as he read, <**Estries:** *I don't know why I'm not dead and I don't care. And I think she's showing herself is a deceleration of war statement. You feel imminent danger when you look at the pictures, don't you? This is not Bait Dybbuk! How could I make this up? Our entire life, this is what we've been training for! What's our purpose if not this!? What's the point of your families' work if you don't apply it!? What's the point of everything we've gone through, if at the time when we can apply the cumulative experiences we have, you don't want to partake!?*>

   <**Dybbuk:** *Partake? If you're right and this is her declaration of war, then she's showing herself to flush us out so we can all go there and she kills us in one swoop! You telling me to partake is you asking me to go die in the middle of the forest, leaving my wife alone with our couple friends, not knowing or ever hearing from me ever again? No thank you, I'd not like to partake, I'd like to evaluate other options.*> Nate sent, looking over to Jay who was smiling at him.

   "My bad, I asked you a question and now I'm texting and not paying attention," he whispered.

   "It's all good fam. So umm, to answer that question…now that you're done texting. Just messing with you. Yeah umm, the only fights I've ever got into were the ones I truly couldn't avoid, and that was usually at the bus terminal on Parsons Boulevard. There was no other way to get home, and you never knew what gang or group of fools you were going to run into over there," Nate heard Jay say.

   "Naturally intuitive. I figured that. Well, this is good actually. It's even more of an excuse not to try and sneak off to check this out. My parents don't want others involved, and he'd definitely know I'm lying and maybe even try to follow me. Damnit though, Estries is right! I have been training for this my entire life. Plus, I feel so magnetized by these pictures. I just want to have her. To taste her. To run my fingers through her hair. Oh, I want to feel her soft skin…to…Fuck, the mind pull phenomenon from looking at her pictures is happening with a delayed reaction this time!" Nate thought, returning to the present moment to find he'd become completely erect and that he'd begun to breath heavily.

   Shifting in the seat uncomfortably, he looked over towards Jay with his peripherals to find Jay staring at him with calm, curious eyes which ever so slightly looked down towards his phone, causing him to instinctually press the lock screen button - even though it'd already been locked.

"I got a 'lil' nauseous looking at my phone. Deep breathing helps," he said, casually pressing down on his cock, pushing it to the right to lay flat against his pelvis.

"Yeah man, it does, it does indeed," he heard Jay mumble, not even hiding his tone, which blatantly called him a liar.

"What am I going to do with him? If I really do start moving around to look into this, him inferring the scope and range of my job would be an understatement. My parents and those goons that serve as their board of directors should've recruited him and people like him for security instead of using those poor bastards they're constantly scooping up off the war torn streets of Lebanon and Palestine. My thing is, as intuitive and intelligent as he is, how could he be the head of the Electrical Engineering department?"

"For as long as Rayya and I have known him, we still have no idea what degree or credentials he has. And every time we've asked him or Karman, they've dodged and deflected. And there's not a scrap of evidence in his house, and Rayya says it's the same at work. Hell, even her co-workers say they don't know. How the hell is that possible, that no one knows? On the flip side, why haven't Rayya and I just hacked into his shit and checked?" Nate thought, shaking his head in a pointless attempt to clear his mind as he began to see visuals of the woman from the pictures again.

"Hey Jay, in the Navy you were an Electricians Mate, and then you…well you must've become Electrical Engineer to become an Executive at your company, am I right? Fill me in brother, it seems like we're both sucky friends that weren't clear on each other's jobs and what not," Nate said, trying to keep his voice as neutral as possible.

"Pa, me an Electrical Engineer. No thanks…do you see a ring on my finger? No way…haha my dumb ass… an Engineer? Ha, you're funny," he heard Jay respond.

Right after, he heard Karman clear her throat ever so casually, which made him turn to her and say, "what?"

"He's going to lie to you. Right Jay?" he heard Karman reply, causing him to laugh as he thought, *"I was sure that, that was a cough to make him hide the truth. That was unexpected!"*

"Come on baby. Come on!" he heard Jay exclaim, sounding stung before glancing at him with a look that said, 'I don't want to tell you shit', before he looked back at the road.

About half a minute later and Nate could see that Jay was not about to talk. Shifting in his seat, he tried to think of something to say to restart the conversation, but then his phone went off again and he couldn't stop himself from being curious. Taking a deep breath, he pressed his finger on the screen for it to scan his finger print, then carefully looked down at the text message which read, **<Estries:** *Suit yourself. Your orders were to have gone to Ellsworth Air Force base, where you would've picked up your first hundred-man team. One you had picked them up, you were to then fly here to Yellow Stone and do missions with me. But since you've declined, I'll now lead the team that was meant for you. I'll keep in touch and let you know how good it feels to enjoy the honor and privileges of the of the promotion…that was meant for you. Xxx&Ooo's, Estries out.>*

"Damn it! My parents and Estries know exactly how to play me!" Nate thought, now feeling completely crushed.

Suddenly Nate heard Jay say, "I…I," before pausing.

"I no longer care!" Nate thought, before saying, "no worries man, no need to tell me if it's that big of a secret," feeling a numb, sinking sensation wash over him as he pictured Estries leading the team that was meant for him.

"Okay, here we go. I have…I have… a Ph.D. in Electromagnetism. First, I did five years in the U.S. Navy, as an Aviation Electricians Mate, stationed at Whidbey Island Washington, then I got out, and then I, I, I…got my degree. Umm, and it only took me four years to do it. My Engineering ring is in the fucking glove compartment, open it, and you'll see it there," he heard Jay chock and stammer out, before releasing a long breath, which made him squint in confusion, not understanding where any of his discomfort was coming from.

"See, was that so bad?" Nate heard Karman say, sounding annoyed as he opened the glove compartment to find a beautiful, shiny, all black pinky ring that had the likeness of glass, which when he picked up, felt perfectly smooth.

"You like his ring," I made it for him when he graduated, it's a blend of special materials that I actually have a patent for it," he heard Karman say proudly, leaning up, resting her hand on his shoulder as she looked over the ring with him.

"Fucking annoying...what's the big deal...it's just a degree. For fuck sakes, it's just a piece of fucking paper, it doesn't mean you're smart," he heard Jay whisper causing him burst out laughing.

"Oh, you're one of those! I get it now!" he blared, slightly cheering up, bewildered that Jay so was embarrassed of his intelligence.

"Wha? I don't get what's going on...are you embarrassed because you're a nerd," he heard Rayya chime in sarcastically, causing everyone in the car minus Jay to erupt with laughter.

"For fuck sakes!" he heard Jay growl, causing him and everyone else to laugh even harder.

"Oh man! God. It's funny!" Nate snorted feeling himself laugh harder and harder, picturing Jay's miserable face wearing a cap and gown, holding his diploma like it was acidic.

"I wish I could show you his graduation picture. Here, let me show you a reenactment...he held his diploma like this," Nate heard Karman say, bringing her hand in front of his face, pinching her phone between her index and thumb the way a person would hold a snooty tissue.

"Oh my God! Ah! I was just thinking he'd do something like that! Oh my God!" he shouted, now finding himself doubling over, laughing in hysteria.

"Fuck offff," he heard Jay groan, sounding absolutely miserable.

"Ah man! It all makes sense now. Your house had nothing in it, no certificate, no scholarly awards, and I was wondering what the hell was going on! I was always thinking like, there's no way you could lead a team in the Quantum Computing department with no degree! No way! I mean maybe...Wait, 'na', just no way! But you...ahahah!" Nate snorted, truly enjoying his happiness as the feeling of his responsibilities rolled off of him, furthering his decision not to get involved with whatever it was going down in Yellowstone.

"Yeah, yeah," he heard Jay mumble, pointing to him, then to the glove compartment, indicating that he wanted him to return the ring back to its rightful spot of, 'hidden away'.

"Look Jay, if it makes you feel any better - as you already know, I got my degree in three years. So come on, relax, I'm a nerd too. And wait, your wife got her Ph.D. in what, four years too? So see, we're all school nerds. Well except for my baby – who's lucky and gets training from his company from the ground up and doesn't need outside credentials to get in."

"Yeah but…Ah come on. I hate the word nerd. I'm not a nerd! Let's find a different word. How bout, umm, scholastically talented. Oh! Or how 'bout, book ninja! Or 'theory user gangster'. Or 'OG' of studying and applying'. 'Yo'! I can even make a gang! Yeah, when we go get coffee, 'I'ma' buy a weird color bandana, that no one else uses and use it as my gang flag! And when people ask, 'I'ma' be like …'I'ma' OG Engineer! And 'I'ma'…'" he heard Jay say, but he was already tuning him out, allowing his body relax in the chair thinking, *"This is more like it. All of us having fun. We only live once. Enjoying life is about small moments like this."*

5 hours later
Location: Hill City, South Dakota

From the moment Jay spilled the beans about his Ph.D., the rest of the car ride had gone by fast to Nate. Primarily because he along with the ladies had relentless made fun of him, and secondly because he was able to space out and enjoy the beautiful scenery. Now as Jay pulled up and parked next to a pump at a gas station, he felt slightly guilty, being that Jay had quickly hoped out and stormed off towards the convenience store, not even bothering to close the door behind him.

"Do you think we over did it?" Nate asked, feeling an extremely dark aura coming off of Jay, which somehow reminded him of how he'd felt when he'd opened up the images Estries had sent him.

"He'll be fine. He'll get over it. I have my ways to make him cheer up. Don't worry, you'll be buddies again," he heard Karman say, rubbing the top of his head before unbuckling her seat belt, hopping out, closing both her door and Jay's before heading towards the store.

"They're cute right?" he heard his wife ask shortly after Karman walked into the store, hugging Jay, pointing outside towards the car before tippy toeing, kissing Jay on the cheek.

"Yeah they are," Nate replied with a chuckle, watching as Jay turned like he didn't want the kiss, yet leaning into it before pointing to his cheek, asking for another.

"That's funny, look boo. He's a sucker for 'loven'. Watch him smile. And yup, there it is," Nate said, snickering as Jay broke into a smile.

"Yeah, just like you," he heard his wife reply, leaning forward, kissing him on the cheek as Jay and Karman moved out of their line of site, walking deeper into the store.

"Mmm, more, more, more," Nate said, feeling the hours of the trip sneak in, merging with the looming notion of responsibility where he thought, *"Damn, why can't I shake this? Since when have I been this dedicated? Do I really want that promotion? Or do I want to go out there to see if I can find her. That perfect hair...that sexy body. So thick, and curvy. Fuck! The mind pull phenomenon again! This has to be the real deal! It has to be! But then that means...I really should be out there."*

"Mwa, mwa, mwa!" he heard his wife say as she gave him wet kisses on the cheek.

"Mmmm, more," he whispered, feeling her kisses evaporate some of his worry.

"Nope...stop being greedy," he heard his wife reply, kissing him softly on the cheek over and over again, causing him to close his eyes and smile, loving every moment of her endearment.

"I thought you said no?" he asked mockingly when she pulled away.

"Me, deny you love? Never," he heard his wife say as a motor cycle pulled up next to them, with a woman that both of them instantly turned to look at.

"Damn baby, look at her. Wow! She's fine! And look at that leather jacket...I don't think she...let me see. She's not even wearing a bra under that. She's making a statement isn't she?" he heard his wife whisper, leaning up even further, pressing her cheek to his so that if the woman were to look at them, she'd see them staring at her cheek to cheek, which the woman did, the moment she hopped off her bike.

"Oh, and look at that smile, she likes that we're looking at her," Nate said, bobbing his head at the woman who smiled and shook her head, looking away from them towards the store, which she quickly and confidently began to walk towards.

"And look at that sexy little ass. Damn baby, you want me to go get her for us?" he heard his wife ask, placing her hand on top of his head, playfully turning it with hers so that both of them moved their head at the same time to track the woman's every stride.

"Hummm, let's see if she shows us more...Oh...look at that, just peeked over her shoulder to see if we were still looking at her," Nate said smiling as the woman opened the door to the store, shaking her head again as she walked in where he could see her smiling ear to ear.

"Sign enough for you? Now can I go get her?" he heard his wife whisper, kissing him on the side of the cheek as Jay and Karman strolled out the convenience store, laughing and poking each other.

"Yeah, why not. She looks like she knows what's going on," he replied, turning his head to look out the window, hearing the sound of loud motorcycle engines coming from what sounded like every direction.

"Well, would you look at that," he said under his breath, seeing what looked to be a hundred or so motorcycles, paired two by two, with all female riders in similar attire as the woman he and his wife had just saw.

"Biker chicks, that's fucking hot. Maybe we can get her and a few of her friends. It's been a long time since we've had a bunch of ladies to ourselves," he heard his wife say, sounding excited.

"Humm," he said feeling an odd sensation in his stomach even before a group of seven peeled off from the rest, rolling up next to the empty pumps in pairs, with the stray rolling up just behind the empty motorcycle that'd just parked next to them.

"Oh shit, never mind I guess," he heard his wife whisper, flopping back in her seat, letting out a long sigh of disappointment.

"We could still try. You never...you never know," he replied trying to sound encouraging as his stomach sank, watching a woman who appeared to be of southeast Asian descent, dismounting her bike, unfurling a flag that'd been rolled up on the bike's storage compartment, which read, **{Mansplaining, because they have nothing else to say! Down with the Patriarchy!}**

"I like you alive, thank you very much," he heard his wife reply, sounding even more aggravated as she whispered, "Where the fuck are these bitches in my country. If I could, I'd gather them all up and drop them on top of the real fucking patriarchy."

"Your country is here sweetie. Besides there's still a lot equal right situations to fight for. You know that, or you wouldn't have struggled the way you have. You'd be head of your own department; don't you think?" Nate said, turning his head away from the woman who was giving him an icy glare, both wanting to look at Jay and Karman as they arrived, and to show that he was humble enough to not pick a fight with her – quickly finding out that it didn't matter to her, feeling her eyes burning holes into the side of his cheek.

"Jeusussss, let's get the hell out of here before our dicks get ripped off and worn like necklaces," he heard Jay say as he opened the door, hopping in with a look of concern and fear before it changed to one of sheepish embarrassment.

"Yeah the gas," he said to Jay, unable to suppress his grin, happy to see that Jay had not only cheered up, but now appeared to be in an even brighter mood than when the trip had first begun.

"Fuck, I don't even want to get out the car," he heard Jay reply, leaning down, tugging on the gas compartment lever, shooting him a devious glare before closing his door, saying, "Baby, save me."

"Really now?" he heard Karman reply, even though he could see that she'd already begun making her way to the pump.

"I love youuuuuu," he heard Jay say through the half open window, before looking at him with a childish, goofy expression that made him laugh and snort inadvertently.

"Me too," he heard Karman reply before muttering something in Spanish causing him to laugh even though he had no idea what she'd said.

"You two have realized that these lady friends of yours are the reason why we barely got the last two rooms in the place we're staying at tonight, right? And that every single resting spot in this town is going to be filled to the tippy tip-tip top with them right? You two 'gotta' face it, there's no escaping them. With that being said…if you guys want, I'll cut your dicks off now and give them as a peace offering so that they spare your lives," he heard his wife say without an ounce of humor in her tone, somehow causing his dick to hurt.

"No…noooo thanks Rayya! Jesus! That was really extreme! But seriously what the hell is going on? Let me check what the shit this is," he heard Jay say, whipping out his phone, quickly typing something in.

"And while you do that, let me check my phone…which has only gone off twice ever since Estries told me she was going to lead the team - I should be leading," he thought, whipping out his phone, instantly feeling his stomach turn as he read the first message which said,

<Estries: *Hey, satellites have picked up small pockets of movement. Three of our targets are currently at your actual. But we lost track of them once they got there.*>

"Fuck no. No way," he thought scrolling down to read,

<Estries: *It seems they work in odd number teams. So far images show four groups made up of three individuals, and five groups made up of five individuals - all dispersing from Yellowstone, heading to small cities like the one you're in. Note the resolution…they're no longer even slightly bothering to scramble our Coms. You can say you want nothing to do with this all you want…but this situation obviously wants something to do with you. I know you'll make the right decision. Be safe xoxo>*

"Alright, let's get the hell out of here," he heard Karman say, closing the door right after she got in.

"K' boo," he heard Jay reply as he studied the satellite images, which, like Estries had said, revealed different groups of odd numbered women.

"What can I even do with this information?" Nate thought, seeing that in every image, the women were both visible and incoherent, where he wouldn't be able to recognize them if he saw them in person.

"Baby," he heard Karman say in a stern voice, causing him to take a small peak at Jay who was still scrolling on his phone.

"Humm, there's nothing in the news about these ladies. But, I just did a fast skim through, I'll check again when we get to the motel," he heard Jay murmur, seeming to ignore Karman.

"Papi! Let's go, I don't want to be here or outside anymore!" he heard Karman growl in an acidic tone causing his stomach to reflexively tighten, thinking, "*How the hell does he sit through that kind of anger, looking so calm?*"

"Okay Mami, although Rayya already ruined the idea of running away," he heard Jay reply as he started the SUV, quickly pulling off, giving him butterflies – mostly due to the fact that he couldn't fully take his eyes away from the images on his phone long enough to look outside and get oriented.

"Shit Nate, read that sign. It says, 'Men as leaders of the space movement? No! No! No!'" he heard Jay read aloud, breaking him out of his trance - where the women's faces had somehow, slowly begun to make themselves more apparent.

"*All of them were solemn, as if they were sad for something they've yet to do,*" Nate thought, feeling a lump of sorrow and fear rise in his throat.

"I get it, but I don't get it. We have a female president, and she's the one who made the announcement for the world to join together and get the space elevator up and running. But at the same time Rayya...well Rayya..." he began to say, realizing that Jay was her boss, not wanting to sound displeased at her current position as a Junior Analyst.

"Yeah, I get what you mean 'Bro'. And look, I want you to know that I see Rayya's ability for what it is. I've been putting in a word for her to the other Executives, and they'll budge...especially since...umm never mind," he heard Jay say, giving him a questioning look, where Nate could feel that Jay was judging if he were trustworthy enough to say what he was thinking.

"Let's stop talking about work. We're on vacation remember?" he heard his wife cut in through the awkward silence, sounding empathetic towards Jay's demeanor, causing him to turn around, finding her face twisted in concern.

"*What's this about? I don't like feeling out the loop about her work situation. It was hard as hell on me seeing her jobless or working dead-end job after dead-end job for years on end. Fuck, all the past pain and suffering,*" *might not even matter anymore! If everything Estries is sending me is really the prophecy coming true, then soon…we all might be dead,"* he thought, as he replied, "yeah my love, you're right. Let's leave work at work. Sorry my love."

"Unh-huh," he heard his wife whisper, rolling her head - which was her way of telling him to turn around.

"In any case, she'll tell me when she's ready. Or Jay will sooner or later just blurt it," he thought, facing forward, marveling at the amount of biker women filling the small town in such a short amount of time.

"I'm not going to lie, I like this shit. If they're going to castrate and kill us, at least we'll have an awesome view. Right Nate?" he heard Jay ask, flicking him on the shoulder, pointing to a group of twelve or so women who had their leather jackets unfasted all the way down, exposing their breast, with some even going so far as to have flags flying from behind their bikes, reading, {**Exposing the Patriarchy! Bare chested biker bitches!**}

"I'm out of it huh?" he asked, knowing what the flick was for.

"Way out of it…but you're going to need to wake up brother, we're here and we've got company," he heard Jay respond, resting his hand on his shoulder as he took a right hand turn into a motel parking lot, filled with motorcycles and topless women of every ethnicity, shape, and size.

"I'm just a little tired. It's been a long day of…," he began to say, laughing as he remembered the multitude of jokes they launched towards Jay.

"Making fun of me. I know what you were going to say… Fucking asshole. Hope you had enough laughter to last you the rest of our very short lives," he heard Jay whisper, pulling into one of two of the only parking spaces left, which was directly in between a group of women who'd been talking across the gap, who were now giving him and Jay the dirtiest looks he'd ever seen in his life.

"Why couldn't you pick the one in the corner? Jesus baby?" he heard Karman say sounding both annoyed and deeply concerned.

"How the hell could I squeeze into that one? Do you want to do it? Mrs. can't park the car straight in the middle of the desert," he heard Jay respond, causing him to crack up laughing even harder, which must've looked antagonizing to the women on his right because he saw one them actually flex at him.

"And that's my cue to roll up the window all the way, which I should've done before," Nate said to himself, pressing the button, watching as it went to the top - as if seeing it seal would somehow protect him.

"Okay, I'm not religious, but, 'oh lawd, who art-ith in heaven-ith, howled-ith be thy name-ith, and if you-ith, protect-ith us, we-ith...'" he heard Jay begin when Karman cut in and said, "Shut the hell up! I hate when you mock the bible! It's really not funny! Now come! Let's get the hell out the car!"

"I'm always gonna do what I want," he heard Jay reply flippantly just as fast as Karman had protested.

"Aye, anyways, you two, listen up! Go straight to one of the rooms! Just text us the one y'all are in! And once y'all are in, don't come out for any reason unless Rayya and I are both with you, is that clear?" he heard Karman command.

"What the hell? Everything about Karman has just changed in the blink of an eye. Her tone and demeanor are similar to how my sisters, Estris and Rayya have treated me, when we've been caught in mortal danger. What does Karman know or sense? Am I becoming rusty or blind? I've been in plenty of dangerous situations, with really dangerous people. And yes, there's a lot of misplaced anger here, but I don't sense that I'm in the kind of danger her demeanor is reflecting," Nate thought as he said, "sounds good to me."

"Baby Boo, I don't like it," he heard Jay reply, turning and leaning his weight into his shoulder, causing him to shake his head and smile at Jay's familiarity with him, remembering that just prior to their trip, the most Jay would ever do was shake his hand, and head-nod him.

"Papi, listen, don't argue with me. Por favor?" he heard Karman say in a tone that actually made him start to sweat.

"Umm, fuck, sure," he heard Jay mutter.

"Okay, then what the fuck are you two still doing here? Get the hell out, and go straight to one of the rooms! Eh! and don't look at any of them. Don't head nod them. Don't smile at them. Don't do shit, nothing. Is that clear to both of you? And sorry Rayya, I know he's your boo, and I'm barking out orders but…"

"No, I agree. Go baby," he heard his wife say, sounding drained, which he knew was a cover for smoldering anger.

"Alright," Nate whispered, unbuckling his seat belt, opening the door ever so slightly, squeezing out to make sure it didn't touch any of the women – who he could see had inched up closer so that if he'd been even a smidgen careless, the door would've swung out and touched one of them.

"Excuse me," Nate said as casually as he could, finding himself almost toe to toe with the woman who'd flexed at him once he'd cleared and closed the car door.

"You want to take everything from us and now you want to stand where we stand?" Nate heard the woman, who looked to be of Spanish decent say, in a low, menacing tone, unzipping her leather jacket, handing it over to one of the women standing behind her.

"Look…I just…"

"You're looking at my tits? You objectifying me, huh? They're not for you…they're not sex objects, they're for feeding children you creepy, pervert," Nate heard the woman say, sounding on the verge of wanting to strike.

"Hey! 'Wasup'?" Nate heard Karman say, coming from his right, seeing in his peripherals that she was now standing by the trunk of the SUV.

"Your man here…," he heard the woman begin.

"Ah, I know that beautiful accent! You're, Colombian no? Well, me too!" he heard Karman cut in as she walked up to them, pushing him to the left, towards the side walk, taking his place, then stepping closer, getting right into the woman's face.

"And what of it? You're probably some white washed bitch, you know I'm Colombian but you're not even speaking Spanish. How disrespectful! And why you protecting the oppressor? You think he loves you? No man loves you, they just want to dominate us," Nate heard the woman reply, seeing her move closer to Karman's face.

"You want me to speak Spanish, to you? You don't deserve it," he heard Karman whisper.

"Oh yeah, why's that?" Nate heard the woman reply.

"Because you're being disrespectful. If you're a true Colombian, then you should already know who the fuck I am. But fine, I'll speak Spanish…Me llamo es …La…Tunda," he heard Karman say, drawing out the last part, sending chills down his spine.

"Cartel Leader La Tunda!? That's pure bullshit! My security team and I would've been all over it! Yeah, why'd I get so freaked just now when I know we'd have known from day one if she was!? My thing is, why is she using such a reckless scare tactic, dropping such a heavy name!?" he thought as Jay grabbed him by the left arm, pulling him onto the sidewalk, hearing him say, "let's go bro…let's leave all this to the wifeys'."

"Huh? Alright, no grab me," he replied, feeling annoyed at the idea of leaving his wife and Karman, looking over his shoulder to see his wife quickly grabbing their bags out the trunk.

"La Tunda? Ha! bullshit bitch! I mean absolute bullshit! And what you mean I should know? You act like the real La Tunda leaves post cards of her face around Colombia. Stop trying to act tough in front of the Patriarchy," Nate heard the woman reply.

"You think I'm bullshitting, huh? I see…well how 'bout I…," he heard Karman begin when he heard the woman cut her off and say, "yeah you're bullshitting. You're no fucking Cartel Leader. Who the fuck do you think you're kidding? You're a nobody, oppressor protector. And I think the ladies and I, should show you what happens to oppressor protectors."

"Hey Jay," he said, planting his feet in the ground, realizing by the woman's words and tone, that things had fully spiraled out of control.

"Leave her. Trust me…leave her," he heard Jay say, stepping in front of him, giving him a stern but reassuring look before making a hand gesture, causing him to look back, seeing his wife drop their bags onto the side walk, just in time to cut off the other group of biker women who were come from the adjacent parking stall.

"Leave them? My wife is behind us! Trying to protect us! She can't block all of them. What if more come and trap our wives?" he whispered, beginning to feel enraged, wondering why

Jay would leave the women alone to be jumped, although he knew his wife could handle herself with twice the amount of people, whether they be man or woman.

"Trust me, my wife can handle them and protect Rayya. And besides that, I actually get the feeling Rayya can handle herself. So come, now is not the time to hang around and think about things," he heard Jay say, nodding his head in self affirmation before moving it with a gesture that said, 'follow me'.

"But they…" he started to say before wondering why everything seemed too quiet, which made him turn his full attention back to Karman, who was now grinning ear to ear at the woman.

"What's she doing?" he mumbled as the woman stepped back with her arms spread, pushing the other women in her crew back with her.

"Nothing, okay? Let's go," he heard Jay respond, sounding slightly apprehensive.

"Yeah…back up if you know what's good for you. You don't want to take a chance that you're mistaken do you?" he heard Karman ask.

"No! No way you're fucking La Tunda," he heard the woman respond, now sounding deeply enraged.

"Yeah, but you backed yourself up and brought your 'lil' bitches with you. So that means you know in your heart, who the fuck I really am," he heard Karman say, looking towards him and Jay with a look that could kill.

"Eh? Are you two deaf or all of a sudden mentally challenged? I thought I told both of you to go and get the fuck in the room!" he heard Karman say with a look and tone that made his planted feet move forward before he could even think.

Chapter VII

La Tunda

Road Trip: Day Three

Date: Saturday, June 3rd 2017

Time: 5:45 pm

Location: Hill City, South Dakota

From the moment the biker woman walked into the convince store, Karman felt a sense of edginess, which was also accompanied by a strange, comforting familiarity. The woman's posture, although appearing relaxed and calm, held an underlining presence of a person willing and ready to fight. A trait she'd long ago taught herself to command growing up in the streets and jungles of Colombia, so that she didn't disturb the everyday person, but gave fair warning to those of a much keener sense, that she was nobody to mess around with.

She'd wanted to shrug off the menacing presence, with the idea in mind that she'd never have to deal with the woman directly, thus not needing to find out the extent of darkness she engaged in to have such a demeanor. But the thought had quickly shattered with the sound of more motorcycles, denoting the arrival of more women, all of which she could tell, held the same dark presences from the moment she walked out of the convince store.

"Why am I never allowed peace? Is this my karma for all the fucked up things I've done?" Karman thought, exhaling heavily, hating her current situation, where she was now standing in front of four biker women, with another four on the other side of the car, who, albeit were being blocked off by Rayya, were still surrounding them both, making the situation very problematic if she were to react the way she really wanted to.

"They're not feminist. I mean sure, some of them are, but this isn't what this is about at all. They had to work themselves up to get this angry. When we first pulled up, I saw some of them shift around like school girls when they'd laid eyes on the guys. And that lady in the gas station…I

178

haven't felt a presence like that since hanging out with my sister," Karman thought as her subconscious mind picked apart subtle truth after subtle truth, watching the woman who seemed to be the ring leader of the group inch back a few more steps, catching the slightest shift in her weight.

"Oh come on! Really bitch? Why?" she thought, relaxing her body, turning her head to look at the men, who were in her opinion walking way too slow towards the entrance of the motel.

The swing was faster than she predicted, had more power than she'd anticipated and also did not land where she thought it'd land. So when the pressure of the open palm smack truly registered in her left arm, rendering it numb, all she could think was, *"Wow! But why not my face?"*

"La Tunda!" she heard the woman grunt, seeing a flick of the woman's left arm, feeling the woman's palm connect with her right shoulder, causing her entire arm to go limp.

"Just as I thought, she's using Ba Gua Zhang. Jesus, I hate fighting water styles," she thought, quickly side stepping to the left, dogging the kick meant to smash into the top of her foot.

"What gives with these non-lethal strikes?" she thought, glaring at the woman, who was now, giving her mixed looks of distrust and intrigue.

"Humm, okay, okay. There really is something to 'ya' after all. Still, it doesn't mean I think you're La Tunda. All stores of her tell of one evil ass bitch that doesn't leave any opening for her enemies. That being said, I really get the feeling I don't want to see you with Machetes in your hands do I bitch?" Karman heard the woman say, spitting on top of her right foot.

"I don't know what you're talking about, I'm definitely La Tunda," she replied, rolling her shoulders to clear the stinging numbness in her incapacitated arms, and to throw off the woman closest to her, who seemed to think she was safe - being that she was inching closer as if she were planning to help out her ring leader.

"Becka, get back before that bitch takes your..."

Karman mentally smiled because It was too late for Becka because she was already moving, and with a flick of her left arm she punched out so fast she barely felt the connection as her knuckles smashed into the woman's mid arm.

179

"Wa!" Karman heard the woman behind Becka gasp in surprise as her attack sent her comrade flying to the ground, leaving her flopping like a dying fish.

"Ah ha! Ah ha ha ha!" Karman heard, who she considered the ring leader blare, looking down at Becka's flopping form, without even a hint of mercy.

"That's your friend. You laugh at your friend?" she asked, shaking her head to clear the rage she felt from having been spit on.

"Uh... friend...yeah, sure she is. If that's what you say. Anyways, you're something else I tell you," she heard the woman respond, bobbing her head towards Rayya, who she could see from her peripherals had been inching back, giving ground to the other women, which were now blocking her from escaping to the sidewalk.

"Eh, ladies, let's leave these two bitches alone. I want to lose my teeth from eating too much candy and old age. And it's way too early for all of us to be taking naps, isn't it Becka? Get your careless ass up. You didn't see that she locked onto to you the moment you tried to be slick and make your move? You're a dumb bitch sometimes, but don't worry, I'll learn you yet."

"Hey! What did I just say? You dumb bitches over there, quit inching up! That chick over there isn't giving you ground, she's backing up so that she and her girl over here can turn you four into a bloody bitch sandwich. That's right, back up and let them get their bags. I'm not interested in fighting for my life right next to my brand new bike, what if it gets hurt?" Karman heard the woman say, combing her fingers through her hair, casually glaring at her before looking down at Becka who was just finding herself able to sit up, albeit rocking around woozily.

"What's up with you guys?" she whispered, finally feeling a tinge of deep fear, despite the fact that the woman had told her people to stand down, mostly because of the reason she'd told them to do so.

"Guys...We're not guys," she heard the woman reply sarcastically, still combing out tangles in her hair with her fingers, which looked very off to Karman as the woman had been behaving very man-ish up until this point.

"You know what I mean," she replied, slightly titling her head, nodding at Rayya, who then quickly walked through the gap the four biker women had created, grabbing their bags and rushing back to where she'd been.

"Who's to tell if I really do know what you mean?" Karman heard the woman respond, giving her a genuine smile before looking towards Rayya.

"Hey you, you're what? Lebanese? I had Lebanese girlfriend back in the day. I can tell from that cute 'lil' nose you have. And them sexy, fucking change color eyes. And hey, that little stance you were beginning to settle yourself into as you got closer to your friend - that was Krav Maga right?" Karman heard the woman say, now massaging her bare breast - that had to be at least thirty-eight C, without looking away from Rayya.

"Huh?" she heard Rayya reply, sounding confused before hearing her say, "come Karman, are you just 'gonna' stand there?"

"Shiittt! Krav Maga and a Machete wielder, fuck this is fun. Well 'sorta'. Not dressed right for the ...hum. Yeah, why are you still here? Wait, let me answer? It's 'cuz' you're looking for that one, little perfect hole in my defense to land one on me, huh? But you have one now, and have had one the whole time, but it seems like you don't want to hit my tits. It must be bothering you morally to take shit that far. You want to hurt me real bad, but you want it to be recoverable. Aha ha ha! And that's why I think you're definitely not fucking La Tunda," she heard the woman say, finally retuning her gaze to her, bobbing her head in self affirmation, before turning to glare at her motorcycle in puzzlement.

"Krav Maga huh? I knew there was more to Rayya. But she's really good at hiding it, and since she doesn't have an evil presence. I can never put a name to what I feel coming off of her sometimes. I can sense something dark, but directed at something very particular — and she does a good job minimizing it mixing up with the rest of her emotions."

"Yet, I can still always sense it playing in the background of her mind. I'm glad this bitch said that, I knew Rayya could handle herself from the way she looked at me, but I had no idea to what extent. And now that I know it's Krav Maga, maybe I can begin to piece together what she's facing that she'd need to know such a technique," she thought, watching the

181

woman who'd struck her, now affectionately touch and stroke her bike, feeling both honored and concerned that both she and Rayya had been read to such a caliber.

"Karman," she heard Rayya whisper in a harsh tone, causing her to look towards her and the four women that'd come to block off their escape, surprised to see that like the woman who'd hit her, they also now had looks of disinterest and preoccupation, with two of them even turning their backs, gazing further down the parking lot, at another group of biker women.

"I'm coming, I'm coming," she replied, letting out a long breath, carefully walking towards Rayya and their bags, still not trusting the women, even though none gave off even a subtle hint they'd change and go back into attack mode.

"What the fuck girl...what were you thinking? Why were you still standing there?" she heard Rayya growl as she flung her bag over her shoulder.

"I wanted to kick her in the face with my spit covered foot," she replied loud enough for everyone to hear.

"Karman!" she heard Rayya snip.

"What? Look, they don't even care," she whispered feeling annoyed, glaring at the woman who the threat was intended for, seeing that she had not even bothered to look up, instead, seeming transfixed on wiping down her bike, staring at the shiny red paint as if nothing else in the world mattered or existed.

"Okay, fine but can you chill?" she heard Rayya whisper.

"Sure," she mumbled, walking faster, watching to get to the bathroom to was her foot as soon as possible.

After a few seconds past and no biker women were in ear shot, Karman heard Rayya say, "Karman, I never saw that in you...you laid that girl out!"

"Never saw that in me, huh? Well what about you? What the hell was stance was she talking about? Do you know Krav Mag?" she asked Rayya without an ounce of tact, realising how accusing she sounded only after the words had come out of her mouth.

"Pffft! That lady is crazy...did you see her? That whole thing she was spewing was pure nonsense. She was in her own world. Look at how she's behaving...now she's acting like nothing happened. See, she's nuts? Come on, she called you a

Machete wielder, how could you take her seriously when she said I know Krav Maga?" she heard Rayya say as they reached the motel entrance.

"World worst denial. But I get Rayya's frustration at having her spot blow. It's insane how well that lady was reading us. I'm just glad she found us equally annoying and didn't keep fucking with us. Male hating, feminist my ass. I know when I see a big product move. And the way they're doing it, is just like she would do it...right out in the fucking open. That woman was even going to say not dressed for the job. To her, there was no point in even hiding it from me. She only bit her tongue to show face for the women around her," Karman thought as she and Rayya bounded up a short flight of stairs to the second floor.

"We were two, oh, eight and y'all were two, fourteen, right?" she heard Rayya ask, watching her tip her head to the right when they made it to the final landing.

"Yeah," she replied, exhaling in annoyance.

"You okay? Sorry I wasn't much help. How's your arms? As a matter of fact, I'm a horrible person, I should've carried your bag for you!" she heard Rayya exclaim as they stopped in front of room two, oh eight.

"Its fine...I'm okay. Just a 'lil' bit annoyed. I didn't expect to be getting into any fights on vacation. And she spit on my foot. Fucking animal," she whispered, unable to get over the rage she felt from such a primal action.

"Anyways, let's take a listen. Are they in there?" She asked, giving Rayya her best, 'I'm okay' smile as she turned her head to listen,

"Nope, they're in the other one," she said after a few second of hearing nothing.

"Karman, there's no, 'anyways' about this. I'm just as pissed off as you," she heard Rayya reply, reaching out, gently taking the bag from her.

"I told you, I'm fine," she mumbled, feeling sourness register in both her arms the moment the bag was removed.

"Your arms are bruised. So shut up and let me help you," she heard Rayya snip, leaning in, pressing her lips against her temple.

"Fine, fine," she whispered, smiling at the kiss before stepping away, quickly walking down the hall to the next room, flinching when she heard Nate's voice boom through the door, hearing him say, "Why would you leave them there!? I know she told us to go! But why!? It's not good, we should go back!"

"Nate, they can handle themselves. And stop acting like they can't," she heard her husband reply, sounding all too casual even though she knew he was just as concerned as Nate.

"Look man! I have confidence in them, but still! We shouldn't leave them alone! It doesn't sit right with me! We're their husbands!" she heard Nate say, with his voice sounding closer to the door, causing her to smile knowing he was going to open it.

"And that means listen to your wife and your wife's friend. Like the good slave, I mean husband you are," she said casually, walking under Nate's arm as he flung open the door.

"Aww, love you too baby. Trust me, you didn't want to be there. Shit got down right creepy. That woman punched Karman in the arms, then all of a sudden she just started making up shit. She called her a Machete wielder and said I know Krav Maga. Can you believe that!?" she heard Rayya say, coming in right behind her.

"Wait what? Karman, are you alright?" she heard Nate say, rushing in front of her with his arms spread, stopping her from walking further.

"God, Karman your arms!" she heard Nate exclaim right after.

"I'm fine...I want..."

"No! You're not fine! Here, come sit down, sit down over here," she heard Nate cut in, grabbing a chair from the nearby coffee table, sliding it in front of her.

"God...he's so fucking sexy right now. He's so caring and sweet. Look at those eyes. He looks like he's about to cry," she thought, keeping her eyes locked with Nate's as she flopped down into the chair, feeling light headed as her tension suddenly eased.

"Baby, you alright? Do you feel light headed? Do you feel dizzy?" she heard her husband ask as he came beside her, taking hold of her left arm, massaging it with a look of deep concern.

"Yeah, a little bit. But I just got too excited is all?" she replied, feeling slightly dizzy.

"Noo, I don't think so," she heard her husband reply, pressing directly where the woman had struck, which didn't have much sensation at all.

"You feel that?" her husband asked as Nate crouched down in front of her, still looking into her eyes before looking down at her feet.

"Did she spit on you? Rayya, did that woman or one of the other's spit on her?" she heard Nate blare in a deep, angry voice that rumbled and reverberated throughout the motel room.

"Yeah, she did," she replied for Rayya, feeling even more light headed, almost to the point where she thought she'd black out.

"What the hell Jay! I told you we shouldn't have left them out there!" she heard Nate say, standing up, rushing to the bathroom where she could hear him cursing and mumbling to himself as the sink began to run.

"Sha…shower," she heard herself say, finding her voice sounding as if it were coming from somewhere far away, as her vision began to darken around the edges.

"Baby…baby, try to stay awake if you can," she heard her husband say in her ear as Nate came rushing out the bathroom with a wet rag, kneeling in front of her, taking hold of her foot, gently wiping it down.

"There, there, it's all gone and now we'll get you in the shower, okay Karman? Karman? Jay! Jay, your wife! Something's wrong!" she heard Nate exclaim, feeling Nate's hand cup her chin, seeing him look into her eyes one by one… then nothing.

When she awoke she could hear hushed whispers which were only a few tones shy of all out yelling. She wanted to tell them to shut up, but she felt no strength in her body, and when she tried to speak, she found she couldn't move her mouth.

"I told you baby! We were fine! Karman handled everything. Stop attacking Jay. It was Karman and I's decision to stay out there. You two wouldn't stand a chance out there. Don't you get it? All one of those bitches would have to do is claim sexual harassment and then what? And y'all couldn't fight them back! You willing to put your hands on a topless woman? Are you dumb!?" she heard Rayya say.

"Topless women. People would be looking. Yes, people would be looking. But only at the spectacle of them being topless. And the police would mostly be looking outwards to make sure no one is harassing them. Everyone, especially male police, would be on their best behavior to show they're not sexist. They'd even escort them on the highways and in town. They'd also avoid looking too close at them because they wouldn't want to have to touch or handle them if they found anything illegal. They'd need female officers, and there aren't enough to go around. So these bitches are moving product in plain sight and playing off of people's guilt, fear and sympathy. God, that's brilliant. I'd almost think it's her, but I don't think the feminist touch would ever be her style," she thought trying to move her head, feeling some small bits of sensation in her neck, toes, and fingers.

"Rayya's right," she heard her husband say in his normal, casual tone before hearing him say, "We'd be dealing with the police right now if we'd stayed out there."

"Look at your wife and tell me you're okay with this. We should…we should bring her to the hospital," she heard Nate say, with his voice sounding like it was going to break.

"We can't move her, the scanner 'thingy' from your med pack showed you the problem. We have to take care of her here. Don't worry, she's okay, we've already unblocked all her blood vessels. We just 'gotta' keep massaging to make sure no clots have formed, which I highly doubt. We gave her the blood thinner and we've been massaging almost as soon as we found out the problem. My baby will be just fine," she heard her husband say - this time, not sounding like his normal, sure self.

"You don't sound like you believe that. Don't lie to me," she heard Nate respond.

"My baby is right. They really do seem to care about our lives. I don't get the creepy feeling like they just want to have sex with us. I feel safe around them and don't feel like Rayya would fuck Jay and try to play mind games with him and pit him against me. And I don't get the feeling Nate would try to play mind games with me if we were to…Oh God! Did I just picture it and like it!? Oh my God! I can't believe I really want another man other than my husband inside me! How can I want Nate so bad, but my love for husband hasn't changed? This really can't be real! How can I crave another man this bad, without love!?" she thought, feeling a surge

186

of energy, then an engulfing sensation of being pulled into darkness.

"That was scary, what was that?" Karman heard Nate say, feeling her hand in his.

"That was her body resetting. She should be okay now. Baby…baby can you hear me?" she heard her husband say, feeling the side of the mattress on her left hand side sink down as he sat beside her.

"I…I could hear all of you the whole time," she whispered, with her mouth feeling dry.

"Mmmm, no…you were out for five hours. Sleeping and snoring like a baby," she heard her husband say, now feeling his lips press against her forehead.

"Have I really been out that long?" she whispered, opening her eyes to find the room almost completely dark, except for a soft indigo luminesces which shroud her husband, making it seem like he was bathed in magical light.

"What…what is the light?" she asked, feeling her voice crack from thirst.

"It's spy man's medical scanner. Some kind of ultrasound, hologram, 'thinga maggigy'. Cool huh? It helped save your life," she heard her husband reply, tipping his chin in Nate's direction.

"Saved my life…she blocked my blood vessels huh? Sneaky, now I see why she just let me walk away. Hum, but she hit me too hard. It was supposed to happen slower so I'd die in my sleep," she said, glancing over towards Nate, whose face not only looked concerned but fatigued.

"Thank you. You must've worked very hard to save me," she whispered, clasping his hand tighter, pulling herself to sit up straight, finding Rayya at the foot of the bed with what looked to be a small rifle, gripped firmly in her hand.

"Rayya? What? What's going on? Is that a gun?" she asked studying the sleek curves of the buttstock and receiver, wondering why the barrel was cut in half, length wise where it connected to the hand guard.

"Kind of a gun? You shouldn't be seeing this…or the med scanner. But your life, and all our lives are in danger, and I'm not going to die keeping secrets. But please, this is really confidential. You understand?" she heard Nate say, placing his other hand on top of hers, rubbing it gently.

"Your secret is safe with me," she murmured, staring at Rayya who'd turned and bobbed her head in agreement with Nate before looking back towards the door.

"I've never seen a composite structure like this before. It looks like graphene. But I can tell it's not graphene. It's something lighter, stronger. And what's with the barrel, even the magazine looks odd. Why is it oval shaped?" she thought, as her husband left her side, strolling over to window, peeking out the curtains.

"Baby...Papi, get back from the window, please. They won't do anything else for now. They definitely won't be storming our room or shooting through the window," she said, wincing at her husband as he continued to peek through the curtains, knowing from experience that the simple action of one touching the curtains was the moment she'd taken out her targets.

"Un huh," she heard her husband reply, stepping back, giving her a knowing smile that aggravated her even more, now that she knew, he knew what she was thinking.

"I'm going to punch you in the face," she whispered, shaking her head before looking at the small circular stickers placed all along her arms and chest before staring at the holographic image of her circulatory system, projected from the center of a small, translucent donut looking structure.

"Damn that's cool," she murmured, staring at the locations where her blood vessels had been blocked, relieved that the woman had not perfected the technique.

"Yeah, this one is really cool. We're not due to give it to the government for another two years," she heard Nate reply, kissing her hand, then gently laying it on the bed.

"Ummm, I'm talking about how she jacked me up. But yeah, that thing is cool too. What's its composition? And the rifle, how 'bout that? What's it made of? I'm a Material Scientist, I have to know, if you can tell me," she said, feeling muggy and sticky despite the coolness of the room.

"Sorry, you know I can't say," she heard Nate respond, sounding as if he were about to blurt the truth at any moment.

"How do you know they won't be back? Why'd you say that?" she heard Rayya ask standing up, bringing up the holographic scope to her right eye as laughter erupted in the hallway just outside the room.

"Because, if they're anything like my sister, then they won't do too much. Everything has to be calm, cool, and collect. If anyone makes a show...they'll be exposed. And if you make that kind of mistake, it's your family who pays first," she said peeling off one of the stickers on her left arm, watching as the upper left hand portion of the holographic image went blank.

"Your sister?" she heard Nate ask as he walked over to Rayya, placing his hand on the rifle, pushing it down.

"Baby?" she heard her husband whisper, returning to sit on the side of the bed next to her.

"Don't you baby me. You know better than to go to that window - touching curtains. And I don't care what you're going to say about me saying we're okay for now. You know better," she said, titling her heavy feeling body to the right, then sliding out of the bed, looking at her foot, remembering that she'd been spit on, and that she'd wanted to take shower, even before feeling as gross as she did now.

"Hey Jay, why'd you just say baby like that to Karman to make her stay quite?" she heard Nate ask her husband, sounding annoyed as he walked towards the bathroom returning with a large towel in hand, presenting it to her with a reassuring smile on his face.

"Oh my God, that was sex as hell! And I know for a fact he wants me to strip right here. Fuck! I really want to do it. I'm just worried about Jay. I know he said he liked it when Nate saw me naked, but if I do it now, will he feel that way again?" she thought as the holographic imager flashed, showing her heart rate accelerate, causing her to snatch two patches off her chest really fast before taking the towel from Nate's hand.

"Nothing...I just don't think she should..." she heard her husband begin, pausing and staring at the imager when it had flashed, then at her, seeing a mischievous look on his face for just a second before it returned to normal.

189

"You don't care at all? You liked that I was flustered by Nate?" she thought, bewildered by the look that'd come across her husband's face, knowing how jealous and possessive he could be.

"Look, after I whipped out all this stuff...you think we have time for secrets?" she heard Nate respond, fixing her husband with a serious gaze before it changed to one of confusion, which made her involuntary snicker, knowing that her husband was making a ridiculous, sarcastic face towards Nate, without even needing to look at him.

"Which kind of secrets? There's always time for secrets," she heard her husband finally reply, sounding whimsical, causing her to burst out laughing, knowing that his comment was mostly for her.

"Rayya, put that down. Can't you think of something better to do?" she asked, shaking her head, still bemused by her husband's comment as she wagged the towel she'd gotten from Nate towards Rayya.

"What's that mean?" she heard Rayya ask, sounding grumpy.

"Umm, it means come shower with me," she replied, not even feeling the slightest bit awkward as she didn't want to be alone someplace slippery after just having suffered blackouts from blood restrictions.

"Oh duh, okay. Allah, I'm so sleepy, I can't even think straight. Hey, but before we go, please tell us why you think it's safe first," she heard Rayya say, looking at her both longingly and apprehensively at the same time.

"Yes, tell us why?" she heard Nate chime in right after, causing her to let out a deep breath.

"Is any of your spy gadget shit recording me right now?" she asked, realizing that if it were, Nate would probably lie, before saying, "know what...never mind. Look, my sister. My sister is the real La Tunda. So I know when I see a large package move when I see one. They don't want to bring attention to themselves. Okay, so there."

"Killing you in your sleep or at any time would've brought attention to them, no? And what the hell do you mean your sister's La Tunda? How are you here? Why would the U.S. let you in here," she heard Nate retort as she walked over and took hold of the shoulder strap of the rifle, tugging it so that Rayya would pass her the gun.

"No, it was going to give me a heart attack right? And let's be real, my cholesterol is for the birds. The EMT's or whoever showed up would just be focusing on me having a heart attack…not them right?" she responded, now taking grip of the rifle, marveling at how light it felt before turning to study Nate's face, considering if she should explain to him the brutal, honest truth about how government's work.

"I guess you have a point. And no, by the way. I made sure my company can't hear anything. I have to apologize, Rayya was right, they usually can listen to everything through my phone, but I've put up some blocks to protect myself from what I've done, taking out all this equipment and what not, and for you and Jay's privacy. So whatever you have to say, it stays here. And thank you…thank you for trusting me with your secret," she heard Nate say, exhaling heavily.

"Honestly, these days, I know we're all always being listened to somehow, someway. So I'm not too worried even if your company does hear me. I'm ninety-nine percent certain they can't do shit about me or my sister anyway,"

"Uh…umm," she heard Nate mumble, with a look of pure shock.

"You're wondering why I'm so confident huh? Well, look…my sister moves a lot of drugs and weapons. And when I say weapons, it's mostly U.S. weapons. She moves them all throughout South America, Central America, and hell, she's even moving them to Africa and to Cambodia. Don't even ask me how she managed to get her foot holds over there, I still don't even know that story. Anyways, do you think the U.S. wants to bust her? You think if she …let's say asked them for a favor, to take in her sister …you think the U.S. wouldn't do that?" She said.

"So you're here as a kind of a political favor for a 'Drugs and Arms' Lord?" she heard Nate ask, bobbing his head up and down showing he understood.

"Pretty much," she whispered, moving the rifle up down, then side to side, before glancing down to study its odd shape.

"So, you're not La Tunda, your sister is?" She heard Nate ask, squinting at her.

"Yeah," she forced herself to say casual, thinking, *"why do I feel so bad right now…I'm not totally lying to them."*

"Interesting," she heard Nate whisper.

"Hey, this thing doesn't even weigh a pound. God, I wish I could stick this thing under a microscope. And this ridge in the barrel. This thing shoots disk or something?" she asked, desperately wanting to change the subject.

"Yeah, four types of disk made of different compositions. They fly out faster than bullets. When they hit, that's when the four compositions come into play. One splinters and does mostly flesh wound damage. The other variant of splinting digs into the target then splinters…usually kills through particles in the blood stream. Then the next kind, well it's a disk with a small gap. So when it hits, it opens up like a cup. The military likes this one because when it hits, it'll do a lot of gory, visually traumatizing damage, causing the enemy to spend a lot time and energy on the inflicted. The last one is made to cut through lots of targets. Kind of a, kill twelve or more birds with one stone tactic. Made for jungle combat…in countries such as your home of origin," she heard Nate say, sighing heavily at the end of his sentence as if what he'd just said had been a great burden he'd been holding onto.

"Thank you for explaining," she said, hoping Nate couldn't sense or hear the excitement she felt at having such a devastating weapon in her hand.

"Yeah look…," she heard Nate begin to say as he walked towards her and Rayya with a look that made her feel like he was scanning her soul.

"Whoever you are or whoever your sister is…I don't care. I think you're a good person. No, I know you're a good person. And I will not stand by and let anything happen to you. Is that clear," she heard Nate say after a few more second passed in which he'd continued to gaze down at her, looking deep into her eyes.

"Fuck! I just got wet! This is so not good!" she thought, feeling her pussy throb and ache to be pressed.

192

"Thank you. I really appreciate you saving my life. I know it wasn't an easy call to take out all this stuff and expose your companies' assets," she replied, hearing a break in her voice, knowing it had nothing to do with her dry throat, and that her husband was going to pick up on it.

"It's one of the easiest choices I've ever had to make. And I don't regret a thing," she heard Nate respond, sending a shiver down her spine that went straight to her pussy.

"Fuck! This man is melting me! What's hubby going to think? Wanting Rayya is one thing. But wanting Nate! How's he coping with this right now? I know he's seeing me lose my shit!" she thought, looking past Nate towards her husband who was slowly walking towards her.

"Um, thank you again," she mumbled, watching as her husband took hold of Nate's shoulder, ushering him to the side so that they were now standing face to face.

"Give me your new toy and go take your shower with Rayya," she heard her husband whisper, taking the rifle from her hand, slipping the strap onto his shoulder before cupping her chin.

"Okay baby," she replied as he leaned in, pecking her on the lips.

"And don't worry, I'll pick Nate's brain so he gives up some secrets of what it's made of. You focus on relaxing as much as you can," she heard her husband say after he broke their kiss.

"I love you, thank you," she replied, knowing he'd understand she was thanking him for his sweetness, despite the fact that she was doing a terrible job of keeping her shit together around Nate.

"Oh …come now…no need to say thank you. Trust me, I understand," she heard her husband reply, kissing her again, where she could hear Nate and Rayya saying, "mmmm".

"Hey…I almost died. Let me have my kisses in peace," she replied with a smile as she turned to look at Nate and Rayya, who were both biting their bottom lips.

"Okay, ready," she whispered, taking Rayya's hand, dragging her to the bathroom, closing the door the moment they both stepped in.

193

"Hey you," she heard Rayya whisper, pushing her to the door, driving her tongue into her mouth, causing her pussy to ache with even more hunger.

"Hey you back…sorry for the scare," she replied, breaking their kiss only for the merest moment so that she could slide her skirt and shorts half way down her ass, taking hold of Rayya's hand, pressing her fingers firmly against her soaking wet pussy, instantly gasping from her touch.

"Shushh, shush, don't let them hear," she heard Rayya whisper after breaking their kiss, giving her a mischievous smile, feeling two of her fingers slip deep inside her pussy, causing her to let out another, louder gasp.

"Damn, you're wet, is this from thinking about my husband?" she heard Rayya whisper, feeling her work her fingers in her pussy.

"Oh God!" she gasped, opening her legs wider, loving the feeling of Rayya's fingers deep inside her.

"Answer me," she heard Rayya whisper.

"Maybe," she replied, opening her legs wider still, wanting Rayya to thrust her fingers harder.

"Oh, damn girl! I love you wanting my man!" she heard Rayya gasp, feeling her easing her fingers from her pussy, causing her to take hold of her arm, wanting to keep them there.

"Mmm…bad girl…let me have a taste," she heard Rayya whisper, kissing her deeply, causing her to let go of her arm, feeling Rayya remover her fingers from her pussy right after.

"Hey, are you really going to taste me?" she asked, when Rayya broke their kiss, bring up her fingers, coated in her arousal.

"Girl, are you crazy…Of course I am," she heard Rayya whisper, bringing her fingers to her mouth, sucking them clean one by one.

"Oh God, that's hot," she gasped, feeling her heart leap in her chest as Rayya opened her mouth, showing her there was still some arousal left on her tongue.

"Swallow it baby," she whispered.

"Unt-un," she heard Rayya mummer, looking deep into her eyes as she moved closer, kissing her deeply.

"Mmm!" she moaned, driving her tongue deep into Rayya's mouth, thoroughly enjoying the taste of herself on Rayya's lips and tongue.

"I want her to fuck the shit out of me, right fucking now!" she thought, kissing Rayya even deeper, all of a sudden feeling Rayya break their kiss.

"What? What?" she asked feeling a flash of anxious, desperation.

"Stop being so greedy. Or I should say, be patient and then you can be even more greedy. Our guys are right outside…don't you want them?" she heard Rayya whisper, giving her a mischievous look as she inched backwards towards the tub, turning on the shower.

"I know, I know. But, just kiss me. I just…" she began to say, wishing she could just blurt out what she really wanted.

"Oh, I see you're nervous. You want to go out there right now, but you're not feeling brave enough, so you want me to turn you into a sloppy fucking horny mess, so you can just go out there without thinking," she heard Rayya whisper.

'Yuh-huh," she replied, feeling a weight lift off her shoulders, and her pussy throb and grow wetter, now that she heard what she really wanted aloud.

"Humm, I have a plan that can break the ice. But you're still going to have to be brave…and hey…you don't feel like your rushing right? Take your time if you need," she heard Rayya whisper.

"I almost fucking died girl. With this, I honestly don't want to take my time. Tell me your plan, and I'll do my very best to be the bravest chica you've ever seen," she replied, no longer even wanting to get in the shower.

Chapter VIII

A Shaken Double Standard

Road Trip: Day Three

Date: Saturday, June 3rd 2017

Time: 11:00 pm

Location: Hill City, South Dakota

The moment the women stepped into the bathroom, Jay felt a strange sense of relief wash over him. He knew that Nate had been keeping something from them, and his opinion was that there were most likely people with cross hairs locked onto their window. Feeling that the women were no longer direct targets, the first thing he wanted to do was confirm his suspicion, and if possible do something about it via the rifle he now had strapped around his shoulder. But even with the feeling of looming danger, there was something much more exhilarating and problematic taking up most of his attention.

"She really likes him. Her heart skipped a fucking beat. God knows what the hell she was thinking in that moment. Was she picturing him fucking her? If she was, did she picture him pounding her out in ways I never could. Was he eating her pussy better than I ever could? Was he…"

"Jay, Jay…Jay!" he heard Nate say, not knowing when he'd first begun to call him.

"What?" he replied, not in the mood to mask his emotions, not that he ever really did a good job of it anyway.

"I'm sorry you almost lost your wife. I know you're not in a good head space right now. I'm sorry, I can't help but feel responsible," he heard Nate say, with his eyes locked on him where he could see that Nate was being one hundred percent sincere, which actually aggravated him even more, because he'd been trying to make himself dislike him.

"And how the hell could you be? What the fuck you talking about, fam?" Jay asked, taking a step forward, feeling the feather weight rifle bounce into his thigh, reminding him again that he'd strewn it over his shoulder.

196

"I mean...well, I..." he heard Nate start to say, before looking away from him, running his hands through his hair in apparent frustration, of which Jay felt had nothing to do with his wife or their current situation.

"What are you really worried about? I feel like this situation is only part of your frustration. And why would you feel responsible? Unless you knew these women were here, and that they'd be trouble? You were freaking out looking at your phone earlier. And ever since then, you've almost been a different person," he thought, bringing the rifle up, looking through its holographic sight as he made his way to the window.

"Okay, let's see what's out there," he whispered, throwing open the curtains, thinking Nate would protest at any second before he actually moved the curtains.

"Didn't your wife say not to go to the window?" he heard Nate say after a few silent seconds, without even the slightest hint of concern in his voice.

"Mmm," he mumbled, preoccupied with the visuals the scope provided as it auto-zoomed and locked onto heat signatures at a distance far past anything he could've ever imagined.

"Not scared to die?" he heard Nate ask, again sounding nonchalant.

"When you're dead, what's the fucking point of being scared? Do you know how fast you're turned off if a sniper bullet hits your head? You don't have a clue you're gone. So in my opinion, all I should concern myself with, is being calm and looking to see if there's any threats. I want to kill, not be killed. And the only way to do that is to become the fearless predator, not the fearful prey."

"Speaking of predator, this is one hell of a rifle. Auto locking on heat signatures, and it looks like it's picking up motion as well. I can see deer, skunks, foxes, raccoons, a cougar with her cubs, and all kinds of animals and shit out there. And what's this? Bro, I can fucking see bats. This gun is even picking up the bats' calls and triangulating on them. This gun right here, yeah, this makes me feel like the king of the fucking jungle. I like this shit," he proclaimed, about to bring the rifle down when he saw the tiniest 'something' flick by – flying in a perfectly straight line.

"Bugs fly wonky as all shit. Plus, this thing was almost perfectly round. Fuck, I've seen this way too many times before!" he thought having a flash back that caused him to look over to his right, towards the window which was slightly ajar, now remembering Nate going into a box, collecting what almost looked like pearls, before heading to the window, proclaiming that it was too hot, despite the A/C.

"Mmm, mhumm. It's pretty cool…if you're a death worshiper," he heard Nate reply, sounding unenthused and even distracted causing him to look over to his left to find him staring at the holographic image of his wife's circulatory system, which was slowly staring to fade out as she or Rayya peeled off the sensor stickers.

"She's tough bro. We've had some scares in the past. We try not to dwell on it. If you're meant to go, you go. But I really appreciate you. I mean you whipped out that hologram 'giggy' and this gun 'thingy' …and those bug balls, which I take are tiny drone cameras, all without hesitation. I don't know why you say you feel responsible. But truth be told, I'm happy you're here man, cause I dunno what I would've done. I really don't think I could've saved her on my own," he said feeling intense eyes on him from somewhere far out in the distance making the whole right side of his neck tense up.

"I feel responsible because I feel like I should've floored the…never mind. And I'm happy I could help, even if it was at the latter end of things. Ahhhh! And man! There's no fooling you is there? You saw me dump the drones out the window, huh?" he heard Nate say, but the sensation of eyes on him had made him lose focus on Nate and snap the rifle up, scanning for what had caused his body to react so strongly.

"Sure you can fool me," he replied, lowering the rifle when the ominous presence disappeared.

"No…you're all over me. Reading my face, my breathing, my body language…and every small action I do that tells on me even when I don't think or notice what I'm doing. Everything about me you're most definitely reading and rereading," he heard Nate whisper, this time moving behind him where he could hear him going into the mini fridge, cracking open a can of something.

Not knowing what to say, Jay just stood there, staring out the window, smiling at the rising moon, remembering when he was a child, he used to think going there was just as simple as getting into an airplane that needed to fly just a little bit higher. Behind him, he could hear the women giggling and whispering softly as the shower ran, and wished that instead of standing there, playing sentry for phantom threats, he was there with them. Exhaling slowly, he turned to face Nate who had a second can in his hand, and smiled remembering when his wife's heart skipped a beat, and couldn't help but burst out laughing.

"What?" he heard Nate ask, sounding a bit annoyed even as he walked towards him, passing the can of what he could now see was ginger ale.

"You're one to talk...you're the real people reader. Is that how you've always got the girls? And the guys? Anticipating their every need, their every desire. Having it ready for them before they even knew they needed or wanted it, till you gave it to them?" he asked, taking the can, cracking it open.

"And what's the verdict?" he thought, taking a short swig, running the flavor over his tongue as he studied Nate's face, which flinched in discomfort and shyness for the slightest instant.

"And what did my face just say?" he heard Nate reply.

"Shy, embarrassed, and discomfort. Why?" he asked, looking towards the bathroom, hearing the women laugh louder than they had before, giving him the feeling they were cooking up some sort of plan that he'd both like and hate as it'd most certainly make him have to face his fear faster than he wanted to.

"You know why I look uncomfortable Jay, don't play dumb."

"Humor me," Jay replied.

"Why else Jay? I don't want you to see me as some kind of wife stealer. Or some kind of predatory sex person, where I just go around charming people to get in their pants. I have emotions and I have feelings for the people I want to sleep with. And I suspect you think that everything I'm doing is just some kind of game or act to get what I want. And it's not like that. It's not like that at all," he heard Nate say, giving him a look of pure frustration before following his gaze to the bathroom, turning back to face him with a knowing smile.

"Nate, you want to know the truth about how I feel about what you just said?"

"Sure, of course," Jay heard Nate reply.

"This might sound a 'lil' bit fucked up, but the truth is that I believe you."

"That, doesn't sound fucked up," he heard Nate reply giving him a confused look.

"Yes, but because I believe you, it pisses me off even more. You don't understand, but I want to hate your fucking guts right now. I want to hate you for making my wife...making my wife feel flustered. It hurts me that she wants to fuck you, you know that right? Like I have this...this pain in my chest, and this coiling feeling in my spine and it makes me want to fuck you up. And it makes me want to yell at her and ask her what the fuck," Jay said, breathing heavily, feeling heat rise from his body as he grew anger, yet relieved all at the same time.

"I understand," he heard Nate whisper.

"Yeah, well I don't! Because I really feel I don't have the right to have those feeling towards my wife or to you. I mean how can I when I've been losing my shit over Rayya? Right now, I'm just being a selfish fuck. But I don't know how to change that. I don't know how I can stop myself from having a double standard. And the mature, adult in me is saying, 'Jay, you better get the fuck over it. Stop being a selfish fuck and have some fun with Nate and Rayya'. But then I picture you touching her and oouu boy! I got this rifle and I want to knee cap you in the fucking balls," Jay said, feeling his anger and discomfort wax and wane as he spoke.

"Knee cap me, in the balls? Pfft! How's that work?" he heard Nate snort, watching a trail of ginger ale running out of from his mouth.

"I anticipate you need a towel...here let me get it for you...you fuck," he sniped, all of a sudden finding himself laughing, somehow disarmed by Nate's amusement at his threat.

"That really irked you huh? Seeing her heart rate pick up when I brought her the towel?"

"Look, I found a detective...no shit," Jay mumbled.

"I'm sorry Jay, doing that was instinct. It wasn't my intention to make you feel replaceable or neglectful. And another thing. I mean it when I say I understand you. I don't blame you for feeling the way you do, nor do I think you need to fix it."

"What I don't actually get is why you feel the need to fix it. Why are you so hell bent on...I don't know, committing to doing anything with us? Like don't get me wrong, I'm not for a second saying myself or Rayya are not interested. And yes, we were laying it on thick, hoping it'd lead to something. But that something doesn't in anyway have to be uncomfortable for you. I'd never lay a finger on your wife if you didn't want me to," he heard Nate say in a tone that soothed him, until the end part of his statement.

"Yeah...but she wants, she wants to touch you bro. So I mean...like if we did some shit in the same room. She's going to...She's going to want to touch you. And that fucking perturbs me. See what I mean? That part of me needs to be fixed. That shit is selfish. If she allows me to want Rayya, then she should be allowed to want you," Jay said, cringing as he envisioned his wife and Nate touching each other.

"And if she wants to touch me, that makes you feel replaceable, disposable, and unworthy. Somehow, it's like another man, me in this case, has just become the source of adoration for your wife. With Rayya, you feel no threat because she's not a man, and in your eyes no matter how far down the rabbit hole they go...Rayya would never be able to compete in any way to actually steal your wife's heart. That's why, deep down inside you didn't consider their kiss cheating. But with me, you feel I could take her away. That I'd do something better than you, and that you'd slowly be erased," he heard Nate say, watching Nate keep his eyes glued to him till about halfway through, where Nate started to look about the room with his nostrils flaring.

"The food bag is over there...the one to the left of the green bag...you're smelling the grapes. You were close when you looked over there," he said absently, as he mulled over everything Nate said, realizing that every word he'd said rang true to him.

"God...what kind of child did you make?" he heard Nate say as he trudged over to the bag, picking it up with a look of pure hunger.

"Pardon?" he asked, not understanding what Nate was talking about.

"Sorry if you're religious. But there's observing and then there's what you're doing. I could've been looking for literally anything. But you knew exactly what I was thinking and wanting almost before I realized it," he heard Nate say, popping a few grapes in his mouth, turning his head towards the bathroom when the shower turned off, then looking to him with an 'all right!' smile.

"Well, your nostrils flared, and I could see you turn and I could tell you were tracking the smell. And then your eyes flicked towards the correct bag. Your body knew where they were, but then you second guessed it. Or most likely ignored it...the primal responses are really fast and we humans are mostly 'outta' touch with our bodies. So yeah. But you're not all the way 'outta' touch with things. How'd you do the towel trick?" he said nonchalantly, feeling butterflies in his stomach when he heard the women's voices become soft and inaudible, wondering what they'd cooked up.

"Umm, the last thing your wife said before passing out was - shower. And that woman spit on her. What would you want to do if you passed out before taking a shower and you'd just been spit on," he heard Nate ask, stuffing a hand full of grapes in his mouth right after.

"Well, it happened to me plenty of times and I'm okay with it," he replied, smiling at Nate, waiting for his joke to land, chuckling when Nate began to choke on the grapes with laughter.

"Oh man! That was...that was a really off joke," he heard Nate finally gasp, shaking his head, clearing his throat, then laughing again.

"Yeah, it was kind of reaching wasn't it?" he replied, tilting his head to the side when he heard the shower come back on, causing him to feel relieved and tense all at the same time, thinking, *"Fuck, can you two just come out already so I can face my bullshit fear and double standard!"*

"Huh? What's with them? They turned it off, now it's back on again right?" Jay heard Nate whisper, cocking his head to the side in confusion, with a smile that made him uncomfortable with his conviction.

202

"Yeah," he said hoarsely as his throat involuntarily clenched.

"I don't need to have your skills to see you're nervous. But you know what I just realized. You're a selfish bastard," he heard Nate say, beginning to crack up laughing as he walked over to him, clasping him on the shoulder.

"Huh? What do you mean? You're just figuring that out now? I thought I told you that?" he replied, shaking his head, not understanding Nate's sudden epiphany.

"Yeah, but there's different types of selfish. You not wanting to lose your wife to another man. That type of selfish makes sense. But I can see now that you have a second type of selfish in there too. Humm - now I see why you're so hell bent to fix yourself," Jay heard Nate say with a dark chuckle.

"Bro, what? Second type of selfish?" he asked.

"Yes, the second type of selfish is actually how bad you're lusting for Rayya. You're refusing to let her go. Deep in your heart, you feel there's only one way to have Rayya, and that's if you allow your wife to have me," Jay heard Nate say taking his hand off his shoulder, leaving him feeling like he was going to cascade through his emotions without a brace to keep him from smacking into every branch of its harsh reality.

"Is this true? Can I purge my desire for Rayya from my mind? Would not wanting her make this easier?" he thought, now trying to desperately push all lustful thoughts he had for Rayya from his mind, only to find it returning twice as strong, with twice the amount of excuses of why it was okay for him to feel that way.

"Fuck," he whispered to himself, bewildered at how fast his internal thought processes beat him back.

"Jay, you're taking this way too serious. This situation is supposed to be fun and exciting for you. You know what? What if I told you that Rayya would be more than happy to hop in the bed with you guys anytime y'all wanted, and that I'd be totally fine with her doing that, alone? Would you be okay with that? Would that make you feel comfortable? Would it make you feel like you don't need to force yourself to like something you're not comfortable with?" he heard Nate ask, giving him a soft shove on the shoulder.

203

"You want the truth?" he asked, having felt relief the moment Nate said those words.

"You felt relief, huh?" he heard Nate respond, causing him to laugh.

"Yeah man, the whole world off my shoulders 'kinda' feeling," Jay whispered.

"Good! Good!" he heard Nate proclaim, but a terrible vision of the future flashed in his mind's eye, causing his relief to evaporate.

"But the thing is bro...my wife still likes you. And neither of us are too keen on double standards. I could see the future if I were to happily jump at your offer, where my wife, at first would be having fun, but then soon... she'd begin to frown and look at me all fucked up, claiming that we're always doing what I want to do. And then, for sure she'd start getting jealous that'd I'd want Rayya to come over," he said, envisioning the scenario as he spoke.

"Yeah, I understand your concern, Rayya and I aren't like that with sex, but with other things, we do get nippy at each other if we feel we're left out of a fun experience. Humm...okay, so yes, you are really selfish in one way. But brother, it's good you actually care about how your wife feels," Jay heard Nate reply.

"I 'dunno' what to do man. When they come out the bathroom, should I jump out the window?" he asked, causing both of them to chuckle.

"Jay, to be honest, you're right, Karman might get jealous. It may be a right away thing, or like you said, over some period of time. Sometimes it's just unavoidable," he heard Nate say, letting out a long breath.

"See, I don't want that," he replied, shaking his head, recalling all the times he'd been on the wrong end of his wife's rage, knowing it wasn't something he wanted to experience again.

"Jay, jealousy from her or from you would not be your relationships downfall," he heard Nate say, giving him a reassuring smile.

"Say what bro? Jealousy kills, like everything," he replied.

"True, but I see the way you two are, and I really don't think it'd ruin your relationship if there were some adjustment issues that came up. I wish I could say the right words to unlock

204

your mind. I can see how you feel from both ways, and I want to reassure you without sugar coating things. It wouldn't be a perfectly smooth transition, but it's…it's a very rewarding process," he heard Nate say.

"You guys…Man when I heard you guys with Reggie; I was like holy shit! And I kind of got jealous and excited all rolled up into one. I was thinking – 'how can they just do that? Why can't we just do shit like that?' And then I heard you and Reggie grunt, and I was like shit, who said it will be just women in the bed? And then I was like fuck, I don't want to share my wifey with another dude. It's funny, my mom always called me her greedy little dragon, and as I get older and older, I can see why," he replied, exhaling as he tried to slowly picture his wife kissing Nate as a way to inoculate himself for the moment he'd actually have to see it.

"Greedy dragon huh? That's funny. I take it you're the only child, huh? And 'bro', for what it's worth, I'm honored, and extremely happy you like Rayya that much that you're taking this so seriously. Not saying that I'm getting off on your stress, but it's…I should shut up, I can feel myself digging a really deep hole I won't be able get myself out of," he heard Nate say, chuckling softly.

"Yup, I'm the only child. So you think I have a bad case of the 'only child' syndrome? Hummm - Yeah maybe. But, but how can you…like how do you not get jealous bro? I don't get it," he asked, feeling a flash of fear touch him, causing him to one handedly snap up the rifle to scan out the window.

Seeing nothing through the scope, he lowered the rifle and looked back towards Nate and found himself startled again, watching as portions of Nate's muscles tensed and released as if whoever or whatever was out there, was focusing all of its malicious intent on just those areas of Nate's body.

"Never in my life have I seen this kind of fight or flight response. What the hell can cause this kind of reaction? I think it has to be eyes…maliciously focused eyes. If I'm right, I really don't think it's an animal staring at us, that'd make no sense. Could it be people with a rifle like this one, who are locked onto us and hiding their presence? If it is, then I have to wonder, why haven't they taken the kill shots yet? What the hell could they be waiting for? Oh, wait, they could be waiting for orders."

"What? What's wrong?" he heard Nate ask, shivering as if he were cold, then giving him a wry, confused smile.

"Nothing man. Do you...do you feel alright?" he asked as he thought, *"how out of touch with your body are you? I would've gone nuts if I'd felt even a fraction of what you just stood through. Of course you're shivering after taking all that malicious intent."*

"I felt a bit of a weird chill. That someone walked over my grave feeling...but I've been getting...never mind," he heard Nate begin, pausing and shaking his head, looking behind them at the bathroom.

"Getting what?" he pressed, seeing a dark, almost sinister look flash across Nate's face, which was something he'd never seen before.

"Nothing. Don't worry about it."

"Bro tell me?" he pressed again.

"Just been getting those kinda chills and weird feelings here and there is all. I'm sure you've picked up on that though no?"

"Ah, okay, my bad, was just super curious what you were going to say. And uh, yeah, I've seen you looking just a 'lil' uneasy here and there," he said, thinking, *"He's not 'outta' touch with his body at all. He's just standing strong, keeping as much of a straight face as he can. And that evil ass look he just had, that's his true feelings about who or whatever it is outside. I get it, he knows I'm reading him and doesn't want me alarmed by his reactions. Well I'll be damned! This is a new layer to this dude, and I like it, I'm glad he's not a weak, clueless 'lil' bitch."*

"Hey Jay, I was wondering. Um, would you like me try to say something to open your mind a little bit? Like in terms of your stressful feelings regarding Karman and I?" he heard Nate say, looking towards him with gleaming eyes.

"Sure bro, why not, and I'm thinking we have plenty of time to talk, since our wives' have become shower mermaids," he replied, seeing Nate snicker right after.

"Lord Jay, you're too stressed to even laugh at your own good joke, huh?" he heard Nate say, shaking his head, laughing even harder.

"Yup," he replied, taking a deep breath, giving Nate his best, 'I'm listening look.'.

"Okay Jay, think about this. How'd you feel when I saw your wife naked? Did you feel this rush? Did you feel this urge to see my face again, to see how hungry I was or how hungry I'd get when I saw her again?"

As Nate spoke, he recalled the moment when Nate had first seen his wife nude, and instantly felt a strong urge to see it again. He then also recalled that he had actually wanted Nate to go into the room because he had desperately wanted to see him lose his shit. And that's when Jay remembered that he'd gotten 'hard', envisioning Nate doing so.

"So then, what's changed from now and then? Why am I so scared right now?" he thought, looking at Nate who was staring at him patiently.

"I...I liked it when you saw her. I'm trying to figure out what changed? I remember thinking that I was starting to understand why voyeurs do what they do. But now I'm relapsing," he whispered.

"Relapsing...oh Lord. You speak as if you have an illness. Jay, what you feel is normal. But that's because of the context. At the time when you felt that way, you were beginning to see the world like Rayya and I see the world. Of course your normal vision would return," he heard Nate reply reassuringly.

"But I don't want it to return. I liked...I liked that feeling. But then I get this defensive feeling that comes and almost swallows me whole," he said almost under his breath, taking a sip from his can, looking out the window, still wondering what was out there that could scare their internal bodies so precisely.

"If you don't want it to return...then you're going to have to let go of the perception - the perception that Karman is yours to keep. Or more specifically, that she's someone you can lose. She's yours in that she's your partner and your lover. And yes, you've chosen to spend the rest of your life with her. But with that, you've got to let go of the notion that there's a limitation to what she...or you can experience. For instants: If Karman said she wanted to go to the zoo with her friend, what would you say?" he heard Nate ask, no longer sounding light hearted, causing him look away from the window at the man who was now, through tone alone, commanding him to give his full attention.

"He changes fast as hell. And whenever he changes into this person, I can no longer read him. Is this the real him? Or is it the other person and

207

this part of him only comes out when he gets serious?" he thought as he said, "I'd say sure, bro, it's the zoo, that's no 'biggy'."

"So you don't mind if your wife experiences the zoo. You don't mind if she hangs out with her friend, a friend who takes up a finite time in our very short lives, lives we don't get to relive even a moment of. You don't mind if you're apart from her and she's with another person. You have come to terms and have accepted that it's her life and you don't mind what she's doing," he heard Nate say in a tone that was not asking, but a statement of utter, irrevocable truth.

"Suuuureee," he replied, sensing a large leap coming in the conversation.

"Time is very precious, yet you'd allow your wife to share it with another person at the zoo on the premise of safety, feeling that you haven't lost her to that person," he heard Nate say.

"But, it's the zoo," Jay whispered.

"Yes, it is, so in this example, you have now just lost your wife to the friend and the zoo, because you weren't with her. And like I said, time is short and finite. See, the thing is that you're comfortable with her having that time to herself to hang out with her friend, because you feel no threat from the friend. Am I right?"

"Yes," Jay replied flatly.

"But Jay, think about it, now your wife is at the zoo, enjoying herself with another person other than you," he heard Nate say, looking into his eyes with a hardened stare, causing his body to tighten almost to the same degree as when he'd felt the presence out the window.

"Yeah…yeah, okay, but this is normal life fam," he said feeling confused, having expected Nate to have said that it was the same thing as accepting or allowing Karman to sleep with anyone at any time.

"Jay, your jealousy is rooted in losing Karman, on the premise that another man can make her feel better than you can. And you are also feeling that said man would be entering your sacred space."

"Yup, exactly!" Jay proclaimed.

"Okay, but if you're going to think like that, then think like that and apply it to everything instead of selectively, then see how well it fits. Did that friend male or female have a better time with Karman at the zoo than you two ever had? Did they have the deepest and most meaningful conversations of each other's lives, where all day long they completed each other's sentences? Did they hug each other, and to her, did it feel like no other hug she's ever felt before? So now, what do you think?" Jay heard Nate asked, still holding his gaze.

"I...I don't know. I've never thought of that. I mean, it's just a friend," he stammered, growing annoyed, wanting to say something to push back the invasive feeling of Nate entering his mind and soul, ripping him to pieces from the inside out.

"Just a friend you say, but in this world a friend is everything. And although some are lasting and others fleeting, for the time they do spend in our lives, they're all we have," he heard Nate say with absolution.

"Alright Nate, umm," he began, shutting his mouth from the, 'be silent' look, Nate gave him, causing him to gulp and do just that.

"Jay, another important thing for you to think about to put things in perspective is, how happy would Karman be, or how happy is she when she comes back from hanging out with this friend? Is it happier than with you? Or is it equal to being with you? Is..."

"Hey man...like I mean...like what the fuck are you talking about?" he said, trying to force himself to fight Nate's words.

"You're smart, think about the big picture. Is Karman the best cook? Is she your best BJ? Is she the person you've had the best sex with or have you had better? Tell me?" he heard Nate press, folding his arms, titling his head to the side with a menacing smirk, as if he already knew the answer.

"Umm, she cooks alright...and fuck man, how can I judge a BJ...ummm shit," he stammered as images of the women he'd slept with flashed in his mind, remembering that there were so many differences with each one that'd he'd not even know where to begin when I came to comparing who was the best or worst.

"Well if she's not your best BJ, or the best cook...then she's the best sex? So no other women have flashed in your mind? Let's not even get into wanting another woman while you're still with her. Wait, yes, let's get into that. So is the sex not good enough, that you want another woman in the bed? Is she losing you now that you want to have sex with Rayya? Do you feel yourself drifting? Do you now feel you're going to bail on her?" he heard Nate continue to press, with his menacing smirk, changing to an even more frightening smile, that made him want to swing and step back all at the same time.

"Bro…all these fucking questions?" he said, feeling his heart beating out of his chest.

"Questions that you're answering in your head, and making excuse after excuse for, but then don't want to apply the same rules to your wife! And then you want to sit here and proclaim that you're trapped. Of course you're trapped if you can't apply the same logic and reasoning that you use for why you'd still love and would never leave your wife, despite the fact that you'd want another woman in the bed. Or apply the same reasoning and logic for why you still love your wife, despite the fact that you can still fondly remember other ladies blow job, sex, cooking or whatever else," he heard Nate say, beginning to laugh, looking away from him, gazing out the window for a few seconds before looking back at him, shaking his head - as if to say, 'you poor thing.'

"I'm trying bro…I know I have a double standard," he replied, gritting his teeth, feeling as if Nate were snubbing him, especially now that his face and body language exuded pure mirth.

"You think you can lose Karman if she has sex with me. You'd feel violated. You'd feel as if somehow everything would change between you two. And here's the funniest part. Half of everything you're worried about is true because it's already happening. And is always happening. Every time your wife hangs out with Rayya, she changes, and vice versa. Every moment spent with another person, your wife becomes reinvented, and you're losing and gaining new forms of her. Every interaction your wife has with another person is just as important as the other, whether it be meeting a person for coffee for twenty minutes, or going to the zoo with them all day. But you chose to focus on sex and desires as your only enemy. But not once do you feel an ounce of threat if your wife has had the best day of her life with a friend and has come home smiling ear to ear? Why is that? Why would you not be jealous of her smile? Isn't providing joy to the person we love, one of the reason we get married? Shouldn't anyone else who's able to supply that joy be your number one enemy?"

"Wow...you're all over the place! Whatever!" he said, feeling overwhelmed and even more defensive because somehow he was starting understand what Nate was saying.

"Am I? How's it all over the place? If your wife has sex with me, and she's happy, and brings that to you. If you're happy seeing my hunger for her, and you bring that to her, both of you share that joy. How's it different than her going to the zoo, having the time of her life...bringing it to you?" he heard Nate respond.

"The Zoo is one thing, sex is another bro. Like I mean if she fucks you...and I fuck her after... then what if she thinks my dick game is garbage after that? She might all of a sudden just want your dick. Or she might be fucking me one day, and then might start picturing you! Or she may even call out your name!" he said getting louder and louder, feeling sweat run down his forehead into his eyes, letting him know he'd lost the war on composure long before he'd raised his voice.

"Jay, you're doing it again. You're not applying the same logic for Karman that you're using for yourself. Let me ask you, would you fall for Rayya once you fuck her? With your logic, that's what you're saying. And you're saying you have more self-control and more trust worthy than Karman," he heard Nate say, raising his eyebrows at him.

"Ohhhh, fuck," Jay whispered.

"Yup, you're being a jerk," he heard Nate say, shaking his head, giving him warm, forgiving smile.

"Damn fam, I...I, I am huh?" Jay whispered.

"Jay, has the idea of you falling out of love with Karman ever even crossed your mind when you picture fucking wife? Like did my wife in any way in your mind replace Karman?"

"Of course I never thought of falling out of love with my boo. And no...your wife didn't replace my wife in my mind at all. I wasn't even thinking like that," he replied, having flash back of his fantasies, where he'd visualized himself laying naked in bed with his wife and Rayya, simply laughing and having a good time.

211

"Okay so that one thing. And now how 'bout this, when you heard Rayya and I fucking, at certain moments, did you not picture Rayya's face, wondering what she felt like while you were still fucking Karman? And don't lie, it'd be only lying to yourself, not me. And whether you answer that out-loud or not …the main question is, did that image replace your wife in anyway?"

"In those moments, was your wife losing you to mine? Is she losing you right now, as you have this meaningful conversation with me? You're so worried about losing her. Are you something to lose of hers, or are you hers' because you have chosen to be hers' no matter what her best attributes, or what her worst short comings are?" he heard Nate ask, with a cunning smile, raising his hand to say, 'wait' as Jay opened his mouth to defend himself.

"Remember the love question I asked in the car and you got mad? Well, when you expressed your love, it sounded irreplaceable. And you said all of that, but had spent the entire morning before, getting hard on's whenever you looked at my wife. I'm certain that not even once while you spoke of your love for Karman, did Rayya creep into your mind, stealing away the love you have for your wife. The love you two share is there because both of you have forged it, and there's not one outside force that can break it, unless both of you allow it. Sure, there are many influencers that can cause rifts, but if you think sex, and the joy or desire to have it with another person is truly all that threatening, then, how were you able to say those words describing your love for Karman, while still feeling the way you did about my wife?"

"Ponder that and let your double standard collapse on itself. It might take some time or it might've already happened. Either way, I've given you the questions to ask yourself that will corrode that metal box in your mind, one way or another. You must focus on wanting both of you to experience joy and pleasure without limitation …that's the final mental tool you'll need to push through the box once it's eroded," he heard Nate say, pulling out his phone, studying the screen with his lips pushed forward, deep in thought.

"Camera feeds from the bug bot 'thingys'?" he asked, relieved for the opening to change the subject, feeling himself

212

literally trembling with emotions he couldn't process as his mind went to battle with itself.

"You're cute, calling things, 'thingys' and 'giggys'. And yeah, no one's out there...well no snipers or anyone interested in this room anyway. I've seen a few women glance at our room here and there, with a few pointing. But none of their glances and gestures looked even remotely hostile. They're mostly looking at this room here, on the second floor, on the opposite end of the building. Do you think their Queen Bee is in there? The one who hurt your wife, the one I want to...anyways, do you think she's in there?" he heard Nate ask, bringing the phone in front of him, where he could see time stamped images of biker women glancing up at their room and the other one on the opposite side of the building.

"I dunno, maybe. Zoom in, let me see. Okay, look, so this girl here...she points, then shakes her head and then right there, see there, she's trying to play it off, like she doesn't like whatever she knows is going on in there, but right there...yeah, right there, you can see the crease on her lips as she smiles. She's both happy and jealous she's not a part of whatever's going on in there. So it could be Queen Bee's room, or maybe a few girls are having a good time and she feels like she's missing out on the fun. So she's probably just talking shit to the other ladies to downplay it," he said, looking away from the phone out the window when a sensation that felt like he was being tugged ever so gently took hold of him.

"You feel...I mean you saw all that? Just from looking at this?" he heard Nate reply, sounding somewhat absent which made him look over to see a strange grin spreading across Nate's face as if someone whispered a dirty secret in his ear.

"Hey," he whispered, shaking Nate by the shoulder, letting go when he felt a warm, tingling sensation envelope his cock - reminding him of the first sensations he gets when slipping his cock inside of a woman's pussy.

"Hum?" he heard Nate reply, giving him an embarrassed look as if he'd just been caught having a dirty dream.

What just happened to us? I felt it too! he thought, shaking his head, feeling his thoughts begin to jumble, then just as suddenly, feeling his mind clear.

"Umm, yeah I saw all that. It's no big deal. Hey Nate, even that lady who tried to off my wife is in that room, umm, this might sound bad, but I don't want to be bothered," he said, lying through his teeth as he was in truth, currently imagining shooting and stabbing the woman until she was a husk of destroyed flesh.

"Don't you want revenge? And don't you want to know what they're up too?" he heard Nate ask, watching him chew the inside of his cheeks.

"No...and No," Jay replied, again lying through his teeth, which he could tell Nate knew by the fucked up look he was now receiving.

"Yes...and yes. I just didn't want to sound petty. But fuck yes I want revenge. And of course I'm 'hella' curious what they're doing. Did you send one the bug thingy to the window to see and listen in?" Jay asked, now imagining serving up the woman like a gift for his wife to kill as she pleased.

"She tried to kill your wife, Jay. The only answer there is would be, yes. And yeah, I sent one there a long time ago, it sitting on the ledge picking up snoring sounds and light breathing. And I have one in the tree line, directly in line of sight with the window. It looking straight through the curtains, and it's showing two people in the room, laying in the bed. But I just don't buy it. I think the sensors are being duped, which is really worrying me, because there's not much tech out there that can do that," he heard Nate say, turning to look behind him as the shower went off again.

'Shit! I'm nervous again!' he thought when Nate turned to him with a wicked smile and raised eyebrows.

"You know what, I think that's a sign to mind our business, huh? What's that saying about poking sleeping bears? Let's apply it," he said feeling his stomach doing flips with each passing second, wanting to turn around to watch the women come out, but forcing himself to stay put, not wanting to seem over eager once they emerged.

"What's that saying they have for when the Nazi's began to exterminate the Jews, and it wasn't anyone else's problem, till it was everyone's problem," he heard Nate reply, giving him a sarcastic look before hearing him say, "And let's be real. If we leave them alone, will they leave us alone? Your wife is going to

214

be coming out of the room today perfectly fine, and that news is going to travel. Not to mention that, that woman is expecting an ambulance to be arriving here at any time, and the longer it doesn't show, the more she might want to do something else to seal the deal. Look brother, I don't want to be on the defensive. I want to be steps ahead, knowing how they operate, and how to dismantle or discombobulate them so that they stay off our backs permanently."

"So you want to poke the fucking bear, that already mauled us. I say we get the fuck out of this 'lil' ass town as soon as possible. I think the way to deal with this, is to remove ourselves from their presence, plain and simple," he responded, watching in awe as Nate's demeanor changed back and forth from cool and unreadable, to concerned and aggravated, as he'd spoken, getting a vibe that Nate now wanted to punch him in the jaw.

"Jay, leaving here and getting away from them will not be that simple, or I'd have suggested we leave the moment Karman had got up. Look here, more of them are coming and they're all over the roads. They're making camp in all the available locations for miles on end. There's literally hundreds them everywhere and if we leave now, and they see Karman alive, I think that'll bring trouble. I know Karman said that she doesn't anticipate them doing anything because they want to maintain a low profile, and I'm not trying to discredit her knowledge of these type of people, as her sister is the biggest crime lord in Colombia. I'm just saying that I think it'd be a safer bet to have an action plan just in case, by some fluke, your wife is wrong and misjudged them," he heard Nate respond, showing him his phone again, pressing the screen to pan to different camera views the drones he'd tossed out the window provided.

"Shit, I get your point," he said, letting out a long stream of air, seeing that they were now completely surrounded, and that with each passing moment, even more women were pouring into the town, with a few groups heading out in different direction along the major roads, leaving no place without their presence.

"And what else are you not telling me?" he thought, calming his facial muscles, which would've shown skepticism as he looked away from the phone to Nate who's bobbing his head at him.

215

"Jay, since we're surround like this, I've been thinking maybe we can…" he heard Nate begin to say, when the bathroom door creaked open, instantly causing both of them to turn and look.

"Damn it! I have zero self-control! I wanted to play it cool and not look right away!" he thought, scalding himself just as a beautiful, sultry voice, floated out from the bathroom causing his entire body to tingle and grow warm.

"Is that, is that Rayya? I, had no idea she could, sing like that," he whispered, gulping hard, feeling goosebumps rise all over his body as Rayya's voice picked up.

"Jay, I think I know why they were taking so long…and I think you're going to love this," he heard Nate whisper, feeling him wrap his arm around his shoulder, clasping him tightly.

"Why, what were they doing?" he whispered, seeing his wife extended her arm from the bathroom, palm to the air, with her index finger touching her thumb, forming a circle.

"They were rehearsing bro," he heard Nate reply, giving him a squeeze.

"Rehearsing?" he repeated, now seeing his wife's right leg, covered in glistening in oil, emerge into his field of vision, with her toes pointing down, and heel pointing up.

"Yeah, my wife loves to belly dance, and I've seen your wife tearing up the dance floor, I bet she was a fast study," Jay heard Nate whisper.

"Belly dance?" he replied, as his wife fully emerged from the bathroom, with one towel wrapped around her waist and another, wrapped around her breast, looking straight forward, keeping a perfect posture.

"Holy 'It'," he whispered, feeling his dick instantly grow hard from the sight and allure of his beautiful wife.

Within almost the same moment, Jay heard Rayya's sultry voice change the rhythm of her song and saw his wife begin to dance in sync with it. Taking a deep breath in an attempt to compose himself, he watched his wife wind her hips and move her arms in what he considered perfect motions. Then Jay was treated with another gift, as Rayya emerged from the bathroom, fully nude, glistening in oil, with a look on her face that said, 'tonight, I will make you mine'.

216

To be continued

O.M. Wills
Presents
ERTA
Book 3

Prologue 3

Date: Saturday, April 15th 2017

Time: 7:30 pm

Location: Tel Aviv. Lilith Corp. Headquarters

"How do you do it? How do you create such masterpiece? Do you sit on your throne and tinker till you get it just right for all eternity, or do you create your work and let time be the only paint brush?" Lailie thought, gazing at the serene beauty of the Tel Aviv coastline from the roof of her company's headquarters.

"As usual, I can ask, but you never respond," she thought reflectively as she placed a slender cigarette in her mouth, waiting for her number One to light it - which he did with perfect attentiveness and care.

"What do you think number One? Do you think Hashem is a tinkerer, or does he leave it to time?" she asked after taking a long drag, blowing smoke from her nostrils as she spoke, having flashbacks of when she'd first met him as a teenager, covered in blood in a bombed-out Beirut.

For a moment, she watched him shift his weight in his full body armor - which in her opinion was still a little too bulky and thick in places where she thought the wearer should have more freedom of movement. Taking another drag, she opted to wait and allow her number One to formulate his response, knowing her conversation was going against her strict protocol which forbade people like him from practicing or speaking about religion.

Seeing his mocha brown face flush red for the merest moment, she watched as he continued to shuffle in his auto camouflage armor, feeling a pang of sadness and deep annoyance arise in her, but unable to pin down where it'd come from. Folding her arms over her breast, she looked down at her long white silk summer dress, with tiny blue Israel flags hand sewn around her twenty-four-inch waist line, wondering why she'd picked such a hot material, knowing how much she'd sweat the moment the sun touched her fair skin. Brushing the miscellaneous thought aside, she raised her eyebrows at her

219

bodyguard and life debt servant, really wanting him to speak his mind despite the fact that he hadn't been able to do so since his enslavement eleven years prior.

"You're my only master. I recognize none above you," Lailie heard her number One finally respond, without even the slightest hint of insecurity in his tone.

"Surely, you don't think I created all this do you?" she pressed airily, gazing down twenty stories, locking onto a group of women in bikinis next to an ice-cream stand, smiling at the fact that all had LiL-Twenty-seven assault Rifles hanging snugly on their backs via an almost hair thin cord.

"I never think of it. Only your immediate safety and pleasure is of my concern," she heard her number One answer flatly, causing her to look away from the young women - whom she was slowly beginning to grow jealous of.

"Oh my number One," she whispered, casually gazing upon the man's marred face through the smoke seeping gently from her nose, noting that he was unwilling to show any form of emotion whatsoever.

"My Lilith?" she heard her number One ask, still maintaining a face of utter neutrality.

"That's all well and good…but that's not what I'm asking you. Do you think this world, this world filled with life, do you think it was sculpted by God? And if so, do you think God made it and then let time etch the lines? Or do you think God tinkers with every single detail?" she replied, taking a long drag as she nonchalantly raised her hand, summoning her number Two and Three from where they stood, guarding her office roof top access doors.

"I'm unsure Madam Lilith," her number One replied, sounding slightly uncomfortable.

"Yes, I bet you are," she whispered, gazing at her number Four, Five, and Six who were still standing guard at her tall glass access doors, smiling when her number Six pointed sternly at one of the many reports crowded within, instructing her to lower her camera.

"Number Two, how are you today?" she asked, when the two men she'd summoned came within earshot.

"Well, Madam Lilith. I stand ready for your instructions," her number Two replied crisply, with a slightly puzzled look playing across his rugged face.

"What's wrong," she asked her number Two as she reached out her hand towards her number One and said, "your Rifle."

Without hesitation her number One removed the hair thin strap from his shoulder and placed the Rifle in her hand. Peering over the edge of the roof, she spit her cigarette out and watched it tumble into the depths below. When it landed into the crystal-clear water of the moat below, she brought up the scope of the Rifle and peered down at the women.

"Oh my, to be young again," she whispered, allowing a small smile to spread across her lips as she inspected the women, enjoying the way their bikinis formed and fitted around their every curve.

Taking a deep, calming breath, she brought down the Rifle, only to have a flashback of nostalgic euphoria a second later, remembering the kind of woman she'd used to be when she was their age.

"Oh, excuse me number Two, I'd asked you what's wrong and then I got caught up in the moment," she murmured, gazing at her number One, feeling her annoyance begin to simmer at the bottom of her belly.

"Madam Lilith, I don't want them too close to you. Can I keep them trapped in your conference room? I could turn on the PA system, and then they'd be able to speak to you without their filthy breaths touching you," she heard her number Two grumble, keeping his eyes firmly locked with hers.

"*They're growing into their true selves, breaking past the templates I've cast them in. Is this on account to tinkering or time? It's so hard to tell. They were all teenagers when their families were slaughtered by bombs. Teenagers when I collected them and made them my own. But even still…they'd already been created…and although I've cast them into a ridged mold…it cracks, and now I can see both deeper beauty, and deeper, profound ugliness,*" she thought, nodding her head at her number Two before saying, "unfortunately I must share air with the sheep, for a predator is always at the mercy of their prey…and both are at the mercy of the situation in which they are cast together."

221

After saying that, time felt slower and her mind felt less cluttered.

"*Mercy of the situation they are both cast in…*" she thought as she drank in the sweet, salinized scent of the ocean, enjoying the warm kiss of the sun on her face.

Somewhere, deep in her bones, she longed to hear the sound of the war horn, the one that'd used to remind her of her vitality, the one that would cry out a song she'd titled - 'with my landing, I bring change'. But there was no such horn, and hadn't been since the announcement from the United States, declaring that they wanted to build a space elevator and that the world should come together in peace to make it happen.

Never in her fifty-seven years of life, surrounded by countries who hated everything hers stood for, did she ever expect peace. And not just peace proclaimed for the eyes of others, but true peace, where Gaza had literally allowed itself to be annexed by the state of Israel. Peace, where Lebanon and the West Bank had opened their borders, allowing natural materials and technological equipment to flow through unhindered. This was a peace of many people's dreams, but for her, it was nightmare – where she had to fight back the urge to spill more blood to claim precious retribution.

"Do you know why I said that?" Lailie asked, feeling she'd waited long enough for her words to settle in, now seeing that each man had taken her comment differently by the looks on each of their faces, with her number One again showing no signs of emotions whatsoever.

"Madam?" she heard her number One reply in a questioning tone, keeping his eye downcast to her feet as her rigorous template had taught him to do.

"The question is addressed to all of you," she said as casually as she could, looking to her number Two, who then calmly looked towards the glass doors - with a mild smirk on his face.

"What do you think number Three?" she pressed, seeing that her question had not interested him enough for him to even break his gaze away from the women down below.

"It is hard for people to let go of the past," her number Three responded, looking up to her, then down to her B-cup breast, with the same look of consideration he had towards the women below – which although was illegal in accordance with her template, she did not mind at all.

"Interesting number Three...your mind makes leaping connections like my own. Hummm," she said looking to her number Two, titling her head, giving him the cue to speak.

"A wolf breathes the same air as the sheep. And the wolf cannot eat without there being sheep. So the wolf must respect its prey ...and the way to do that...or I should say a good way to show respect, is to share the air with the sheep, to show the commonality. Even if the sheep know they're sheep...they're then comfortable in their role. Well in this case, most don't know what they are, but a gesture of commonality will surely pacify any stirring minds. Later on, who cares if they realize they're being herded by the pack to their slaughter, by then they would've already been encircled by us," she heard her number Two say, scoffing lightly as he restlessly gripped and un-gripped the hand grip of his Rifle.

"And you number One?" she asked, tensing her back reflexively, having an idea of what he was going to say.

"My only opinion is your opinion. I only wish to protect you," she heard him respond in a humble tone, still keeping his eyes down cast.

"Your opinion...is my opinion? Oh Allah," she said on purpose, biting the corners of her tongue and cheeks to keep herself from smiling as all three men looked directly to her face.

The attempt not to laugh was a bust, and she quickly found herself chuckling whole heartedly, seeing that her number Two was now shaking his head, laughing. Amusing her even further was the fact that she could practically hear her number Three thinking, "oh Allah" about the women below, of which he still couldn't stop himself from staring. Only her number One held her gaze longer than the rest, and when she turned to look at him with her full attention, she tilted her head, which was her way of asking a question. But that action caused him to quickly avert his eyes back down to her feet. Taking a deep breath to still her ever growing annoyance, she smiled and thought of her next words carefully.

"Hearing me say Allah was funny huh?" she murmured, looking away from her number One, peeking over the edge, following her number Three's gaze, noticing that he was clenching his jaw over and over again in apparent frustration.

"Umm, yeah funny," she heard her number Three reply absently, looking at her then back down toward the women, then back at her breast causing her to snicker at the awkward innocence of his behavior.

"Number One, number Two...come over here, look at those women down below," she commanded, passing the Rifle back to her number One so he could use the scope as she walked behind them.

"Madam, are they possible threats?" she heard her number One ask, looking through his scope with his finger mere centimeters from the trigger, ready to release the disked projectiles that would rip the women's beautiful bodies to minced meat.

"Maybe," she said, rolling her tongue through her mouth as she worked through her thoughts, watching her number Three raise the scope of his Rifle to his eyes - with his finger nowhere near the trigger, seeing him sigh heavily.

"Or maybe not," Lailie whispered, now looking at her number Two who'd only looked through his scope for a mere second, before lowering his Rifle back to his side, seeming to opt to gaze out at the beach instead - now with a large smile spreading across his face.

"Ahh fuck. I see," she mumbled to herself, moving at a speed her mother would've been proud to see as she kicked out in her summer dress barefoot, connecting with the back center of her number One's body amour, sending him hurtling over the edge so fast that by the time she looked over, his lifeless body had already tumble halfway down the building.

"Do you two understand?" she asked when her number One's limp body smacked into the crystal-clear water below.

"Not really?" her new number One said, giving her a face that said 'are you going to kill me too?', causing her to genuinely burst out laughing, before looking to her new number Two who looked mildly shocked, but still otherwise preoccupied with his study of the women.

"To be honest, nor do I. I just had this feeling. I think…I think I've just had enough fakeness in my life. For me, it doesn't fit the way it used to. And the sad part is that I blame myself for it," she said, feeling a pang of sadness, remembering when she'd first met her old number One, who'd been covered in his mother's and sister's blood.

"Humm. God will take care of his soul," her new number One said nonchalantly, shrugging his shoulders, giving her an affectionate look, before turning his gaze towards her office with a look that said he hated everything about her needing to be near the reporters.

"Yes, Allah will," she said, this time being completely serious.

"Mmm-hum. He knows best, all we can do is try to live in grace and do our best in life - Can I shoot one of them as a warning to the others so that they know not to even try breathing in your direction?" her new number One said, seamlessly merging the two topics as if they were one.

"Surely not…and let me get this straight. You're openly disobeying my mandate, where I've told you all that there's no God but me…especially Allah?" she asked, biting her bottom lip, feeling aggravated and elated all in one.

"I've always prayed to Allah, even in training. Your brainwashing and threats have never worked on me. Allah is my God, and when you took me in, I asked him if it was okay to lie so that I may protect my life, because I'm not interested in meeting him anytime soon. So, do you wish for me to jump?" she heard her new number One ask in a whimsical, yet defiant tone - as he stepped back from the ledge.

"And you, number Two?" she asked, taking a deep breath, wanting to dance, scream in joy, and have the worst temper tantrum of her life all rolled up into one.

"I don't care about God. If there's one, great. If there's a billion, then great. All I see is what's in front of me. Sure, there are miracles, but there's also equal amounts of tragedy. To me, deities, if there are any, they're dwelling in their own realm and have nothing to do with us. But, for safety, sometimes I do say 'hi' to Allah just in case. Sometimes it scares me that there's just this life and nothing after," she heard her new number Two say, looking at her face for most of the time he'd spoke, with his eyes darting down to the women, and her breast and crotch, for the remainder.

"I see, I've made some mistakes in my template. I was trying to create perfection…but it causes problems. You live, you learn I suppose," she said, letting out a long breath.

"Number One, lead prayer for all under you who follow Allah. And give time to others to find their deities if they so choose to. That being said, I will not allow you to talk them into it. That whole lecture where you say I'd like to invite you to accept Allah as the one and only God is not going to happen. Is that clear? I want them…I want them to have time to choose for themselves."

"Clear Madam Lilith," her new number One said, with a pensive look on his face.

"What?"

"I just want to pray and mind my own business, and let them mind theirs. Life is simpler with just serving you as you've mandated. If Allah is as merciful as I believe him to be, and if he is how he's written in the scripture, then he'll understand that my soul belongs to him, and my body and all of my brothers you've taken in belong to you. I will tell everyone that they will not be punished for thinking of their chosen deity. Is this acceptable?" she heard her new number One reply, giving her a warm, reassuring smile.

"Sure," she replied, nodding her head as she followed his chain of thoughts before turning her attention to the elephant in the proverbial room.

"All of you need to lose your virginity. I'm revoking the celibacy mandate, and I'll have your chastity guards unlocked. And those gorgeous ladies down there, I'll have them sent up after I hold this press conference, their bodies and my own will be your playground," she said, watching the men's faces glow with elation.

"*God, I ask and wonder how you do it… because I don't understand how you cope with the fact that everything you've built changes. Just a few hours ago, in my old mindset, I would've had these two brutally executed by the man I just kicked off the roof. To know that I have changed, to know that I, who'd thought of myself as unbendable and unyielding, has broken out of the mold my mother has cast. It gives me great hope, and gives me great fear. For when things change, there's always the purest truth underlying that change…which is, what was created wasn't perfect the way it was,"* Lailie thought, pressing her crystal bracelet, looking down at the images of her son and husband, feeling the hardness behind her eyes crack then shatter into a trillion pieces, allowing tears to form in her eyes for the first time in fifty-four years.

"What the fuck is this!? I haven't cried since I was three!" she thought, sucking in her breath, feeling her chest involuntarily heave, thinking about the years she'd cast herself away from her husband and son as she tapped and opened two separate chat windows.

["Hi,"] she typed in both, clicking send before she could second guess herself.

["Hi my love,"] flashed back from her husband an instant later, causing her to recoil as if his words were bullets.

"Hi my love!? After all I've done! And without hesitation!" she thought, typing ["Just making sure you are not a corpse, being that so many of our adversaries are making moves in your jurisdiction."]

["I love you more,"] her husband responded, followed by, ["I saw the report Hila and Estris sent about the artifacts under Ellsworth. I'm running an in-depth background check on the two New LiL-Scientist, Darren and Serena who seem be the only ones triggering some of the artifacts activity. Oh, and my love, I will for the rest of my life take down and disrupt any kill orders you put out for Rayya. Your son will not just marry Estris if you kill her, that's not how people operate. :*"]

"Oh, I know! You, that couch potato mother of hers, and maybe one other are the only ones who'd dare undermine me," she blurted in frustrated yelps and growls, thinking *"I looked away! I had to look away! I knew I had to let them stop me from harming our son!"*

"Shit!" she cursed in her mother tongue, feeling tears escape her eyes, knowing she'd been nothing but be cruel to her husband and son since leaving them in Chicago ten years prior, in which she'd only kept in contact to give orders of absolution, allowing them no time to speak as her husband was doing now.

227

"Madam?" she heard her new number One and Two say in unison, with looks of loving concern.

"Nothing, it's nothing, I'm fine," she blurted, quickly wiping her eyes as she opened the chat window to her son, shakily typing. ["Rescind the "Hi" message to son"]

Chapter I

The Look on Her Face

Road Trip: Day Three

Date: Saturday, June 3rd 2017

Time: 11:30 pm

Location: Hill City, South Dakota

If the look on Rayya's face wasn't enough to make Jay feel overwhelmed, the look on his wife's was something else entirely. In all the years they'd been married, he'd thought he'd seen every degree of mischief that could possible come upon her face, but the look he saw now as she wound her hips to Rayya's sultry, seductive voice, was on a whole new caliber.

"Shit, I'm more nervous than when I lost my virginity!" Jay thought, feeling his cock surge against his boxer, glancing down to see a large bulge in his shorts.

"Here, give me the Rifle. I'll make sure we're all good," he heard Nate say.

"Na man...I," Jay began.

"Brother, I'm taking the Rifle, watch the ladies. I'll make sure the room is secure," Jay heard Nate say, feeling Nate's arm unclasp from around his shoulders, leaving him rocking like a drunk.

"Uhn...unh-hu," he let out breathlessly, feeling Nate lift the Rifle from around his body, unable to keep his eyes off of his wife as she came closer and closer with Rayya a few paces behind.

Arriving in front of him, his wife took hold of his hand and walked him over to an armless chair across from the bed. Pushing him down, he watched her inch herself back in rhythm with Rayya's song, and couldn't help the sheepish smile he felt spreading across his face.

"They're both so beautiful!" Jay thought as the dimly lit room brightened from a night stand lamp Nate flicked on.

With the added light, he drank in even more of the women's details, loving the way the oil glistened off of their bodies. Taking a deep breath, he locked eyes with his wife, who smiled brightly before dancing her way towards Rayya.

"Come here Mami," he heard his wife whisper, gently grabbing Rayya's hand, walking her over to him, pushing her to sit on the left side of his lap.

"Oh God," he thought, feeling butterflies in his belly as Rayya calmly nestled herself between his legs, sitting with her right arm draped over his shoulders.

Swallowing hard, he gazed at Rayya's light brown face as she shifted to face him, all without missing a beat to her beautiful song. When their eyes met, Rayya brought her song to a close and looked toward his wife who'd frozen into a beautiful pose, with arms raised above her head and right foot pointing down towards the floor. Thinking that was the end of their performance, he anxiously shifted his weight in the chair, almost wanting to bolt as the heat of Rayya's nude body sank through his shorts and tank top, deep into his skin.

"Hi sweetie, how are you?" he heard Rayya whisper as she shifted her weight, pressing her thigh right up against his throbbing cock.

"I'm..." he began to say when Rayya gestured towards Nate and said, "Sweetie, can you bring my View-Tech's, and can you put on my playlist?"

"Sorry I cut you off. I just got an idea," he heard Rayya say as she took hold of his dangling arms, wrapping them around her body.

"Oh my fucking God!" he thought, feeling the warmth and softness of her belly as her body heat spread into his arms and hands.

"There, that's better, you don't want me sliding around do you?" he heard Rayya mummer as she looked towards Nate.

"Well at least not too much," he heard Rayya answer for him, ever so slightly rocking back and forth causing his pre-cum soaked boxers to rub against his cock.

"I, umm," he stammered, shuddering from the intense sensation surging from his tip of his cock up to the base of his spine.

"Humm," he heard Rayya whisper as she looked away from Nate who was now walking over toward them with a pair of frameless glasses.

"I honestly can never get over you being shy, do you know that? Nothing about you says shy to me. Do you remember how you treated me when we'd first met?" he heard Rayya ask as she shifted over, lifting her thigh, staring at his shorts which sported a large patch of clear pre-cum.

"I...Umm. Yeah I remember," he whispered.

"Good, I'm glad you remember," he heard Rayya reply, giggling lightly as she pressed her thigh down, moving herself higher up onto his lap, angling herself where he could feel the heat of her pussy right up against his cock.

Gazing up, he could see his wife's pose breaking as her body rippled with laughter. And despite their previous conversation regarding doing things with Rayya, he couldn't help but wonder why she seemed so at ease with the pace at which things were going.

"Here you go baby," he heard Nate say, handing the glasses to Rayya with an enormous grin on his face.

"Okay, I have a proposal for you two. I'd like you to wear these and record everything that happens. And I know you Mr. Skeptic, don't worry, you can keep the glasses, and you can encrypt the recording. I assure you, Nate and I won't try anything, especially since I'll be naked on camera and have just as much to lose if something were to leak. This will be strictly for both of you to enjoy later on. How's that sound?"

"Sure, but...I... I want your hubby to record everything as well. I think it'd be fun to see both views," he heard his wife reply assuredly.

Is this my wife?" Jay thought, feeling like his heart was going to beat out of his chest, watching his wife bite and lick her bottom lip in anxious anticipation.

"Karman...are you sure? But Jay," he heard Rayya begin.

"I'm okay...I'm down, I'm down, I'm down, I'm down," he replied, hearing his voice crack as a rush of lust and strange excitement surged through him at the vulnerability of Nate having control of one of the recordings.

"Well, okay then! Hell, then I say we all record! Baby quick, get the other glasses! Oh shit, this is going to be fun, you two are going to love this. Especially you – Mr. Skeptic. I'm really happy you're giving my idea a try. I promise I'll make it worth your while," he heard Rayya say, laying a kiss on his forehead afterwards.

"I… I can't wait," he replied, trying to hide his insecurity, watching as Nate rushed to his bag, quickly pulling out three pairs of glasses.

"I can't believe I said yes to this…let alone saying yes to Nate, and now we're all going to record!? What did these two plan in the shower? I knew they were up to no good!" he thought, watching Nate throw on a pair before rushing over giving he and his wife theirs.

"Okay, you ready to dance for us sweetie?" he heard Rayya say after he and his wife placed their glasses on.

"Yeah Mami, I'm ready" he heard his wife reply, shooting him a wink.

"Okay, you ready to record?" he heard Rayya say right after, giving him a seductive look as she brought up her hand, counting down from three.

"Yeah, ready," he replied, mentally commanding the glasses to record at the end of her count in which a Latin Arabic mashup began to play.

"Damn, isn't she sexy?" he heard Rayya whisper, letting out a long sigh as his wife began to wind and shake her hips in rhythm with the music.

"Very fucking sexy," he replied, watching transfixed.

"It's really hard to just sit here and watch her without wanting to fuck her though, I can barely keep still," he heard Rayya mummer, feeling her begin to slowly grind back and forth on his lap.

"Oh fuck," he whispered, swallowing hard.

"What happened?" he heard Rayya ask, feeling her grip his arms, grinding even harder.

"Nothing, nothing," he stuttered, feeling a warmth on his thigh he knew was not his own.

"Oh, I thought you said you want to fuck me. You didn't…you didn't say that?" he heard Rayya ask, pressing her back fully against his chest.

"Oh shit," he gasped, feeling spell bound between his wife's beautiful dance and Rayya taunting moves.

"I have a question for you?" he heard Rayya whisper in his ear, grinding even harder, causing him to lose his breath.

"Ye...yeah...what is it?" he managed to choke out as the song came to a close, gazing at his wife who stood in another beautiful pose, with a smile that said she loved every bit of what she was seeing.

"Does my husband have permission to see your wife's beautiful breast? Don't you think they're a little too confined?" He heard Rayya ask, shifting in his lap to face him, watching her eyes flick up to track Nate, who was busily moving about, pressing something he couldn't make out against the window seals.

"I umm," he began to say, feeling his stomach tighten for a moment before Nate's words played out in his head.

"She's my wife, but she doesn't belong to me. We can share the joy of others. I still love her even as Rayya grinds on me. She will still love me even if Nate sees her. And I liked the look on his face when he saw her earlier. Fuck it!" he thought, looking between his wife and Nate who'd paused in his task, looking at him fixedly.

"Come here baby," he found the strength to say, with his right arm outstretched.

"Yes Papi?" he heard his wife reply with a giggle, inching forward until his hand touched her waist.

"Turn and face Nate," he commanded.

"Nate? Are you done securing the room? I really ...really don't want any interruptions," he heard Rayya say in a firm, yet seductive tone, watching as she took hold of his wife's hand, sensually sucking her index and middle fingers, causing him to feel light headed with lust.

"I...shit, almost...almost," he heard Nate stammer, undoubtedly feeling the same as he.

"I just need to go to the front...and...and," he heard Nate trail off, rushing past them to the front door.

"Then hurry baby, I'm getting impatient," he heard Rayya say, taking hold of his hand, sucking his index finger along with his wife's before whispering, "Humm, something's missing."

"Jesus this woman!" he thought, looking away from Nate to his wife who was biting her bottom lip, looking between he and Rayya with a look of pure hunger before she turned to look at Nate.

"Holly shit! She really wants him! That look on her face! Fuck, I love it...fuck, I hate it. Fuck bro, Hurry the fuck up before I bitch out and lose my shit! What the fuck are you doing?!" he thought, bringing his attention back to Nate, who was hurriedly running what looked to be tape along the seams of the door, no longer allowing even a drop of light to leak trough.

"I'm done, I'm done, I'm done," he heard Nate say breathlessly a few, long seconds later, watching as he came rushing back with a look of desperation.

"Good boy. Now, you do know what's going to happen next, don't you?" he heard Rayya say to Nate in a commanding, seductive tone.

"Ya, yes...I do," he heard Nate stammer, seeming completely out of his wits where he thought, *"What the fuck is going on? Just a few minutes ago he was crushing me with sheer will. Now he's talking like a little bitch?"*

"Sorry for making you wait, someone's slow," he heard Rayya say, raising her leg with her toes pointing up before saying, "As a matter of fact, Nate apologize."

In that instant he watched Nate drop to his knees and crawl over to Rayya's feet. Looking between all three of them for a moment, he then began to suck and lick Rayya's toes with such passion he could feel his mouth begin to water.

"Shit!" he thought, wanting to laugh and fall to his knees and join Nate all in the very same breath.

Instead, he gripped Rayya's belly even tighter, pressing her closer, stopping only when he felt the tip of his cock resting firmly against the entrance of her pussy.

"Ah...shit," he heard Rayya groan, feeling her teasingly shift back and forth ever so slightly before she said, "Okay my little servant, that's enough. Now be a good boy and sit. Jay wants to show you something. Right Jay?"

"Yeah," he replied, watching as Nate sat back on his knees, looking between him and his wife with utter desire.

Smiling, he moved his right hand free of Rayya's and reached out for the towel covering his wife's breast. With a soft tug, the towel fell free - along with Nate's mouth.

"Now apolo…" he started to say, closing his mouth quickly, shocked at what he was about to say.

"Jay…Jay, Jay!?" he heard Rayya whisper excitedly as he stared at Nate, whose eyes were glued to his wife, scanning her head to toe.

"He truly appreciates her beauty. And there's something else I can't put my finger on. What else is it that I love about it? And why am I still so pissed off about it at the same time. What the fuck's wrong with me?" he thought, taking heavy breaths as lust and jealous rage coursed through him.

"Yes?" he finally whispered, softly running his hand down his wife's back to the towel wrapped around her waist.

"What were you going to say to my husband? I want to hear you say it. Take command of him. He's yours. Just like Karman's mine. Tonight, they're going to be our 'lil' slaves. How's that sound?"

"That…that sounds good," Jay replied, feeling domineering power take the place of his rage.

"You're mine. I'll control you and I'll push my limits as far as I can possibly go," he thought, tugging the towel, allowing it to fall to his wife's feet.

"Ohhh," he heard Nate gasp, shooting him a pleading look.

"Don't look at me…Look at her. And…And…," he started to say, looking up at Rayya who was smiling and nodding her head in approval.

"And I want you to apologize for making her wait…go kiss her feet," he commanded, feeling a head rush now that he'd given his first command.

"Yes master," he heard Nate mumble, slowly removing the Rifle from around his body…carefully placing it on the floor to his right before crawling towards his wife on his hands and knees.

Arriving in front of her, he watched Nate place a kiss on his wife's foot and felt himself release a breath he hadn't known he'd been holding.

"So, this is what it feels like to take command of a man," he thought, loving the endearing way Nate held his wife's feet as he kissed them one by one.

Smiling, he looked up at Rayya and inhaled the warm, sweet scent off shampoo and oil rising off of her beautiful glowing hair and skin. Exhaling slowly, he looked down between her legs, picking up another kind of warm, sweet scent that made his mouth water. Gulping hard, he shifted Rayya back so that he could drink in even more of her details before looking towards his wife, who was grinning ear to ear as she looked between all three of them.

"We're both enjoying ourselves just like Nate said we could…But how far can we go? Rayya's in my lap, and she's so fucking wet, I can feel it going through my shorts. And holy hell, she smells so fucking good, I feel like I'm fucking going crazy. Why am I so scared to touch her!" he thought, feeling his arms lock with an iron will of their own as he tried to move his hands up her body.

"I'm really wet huh?" he heard Rayya whisper, almost making his heart leap out of his chest, feeling as if she'd somehow heard his thoughts and knew his intentions and inhibitions.

"Yeah, yeah you are," he replied, pushing down the fear that'd locked his arms, slowly inching his hands up Rayya's body.

"Oh God yes," he heard his wife gasp, causing him to fully lock eyes with her, seeing that she was nodding her head in approval.

"She wants me to do more… Every part of her is showing me she does. I can't believe it, she really, really likes this!" he thought, continuing to run his hands up Rayya's body, taking hold of her breast, with her firm nipples between his fingers.

"Yes! God baby! So sexy!" he heard his wife gasp, watching as she closed her eyes, running her hands up her body to her breast, clamping her nipples the way he'd clamped Rayya's.

"You like this huh Mami?" he asked his wife as he began to massage Rayya's breast, causing both women to gasp in unison.

"Yeah, I love it. Look at how wet she is papi," he heard his wife gasp, licking her lips before looking down at Nate.

"I feel it Mami" he whispered, squeezing Rayya's nipples harder before saying, "yeah, she's really wet. I can feel her pussy leaking through my shorts."

"Yeah?"

"Yeah baby…and I can already feel her leaking all over my dick," he whispered.

"Oh Shit! I love it," he heard his wife reply, looking up from Nate, gazing at his hands on Rayya's breast then to his face with a lustful, pleading look - begging for him to do even more.

"Mmm…where else does baby think I should touch?" he asked, massaging Rayya's breast in deeper, longer circles causing her to throw her head back and gasp.

"Wherever baby wants," he heard his wife reply, massaging her breast even harder as she broke her gaze, looking down at Nate who was still lovingly kissing her feet.

"She wants his touch, and I want to see if I can watch him do it! I want to enjoy the same way she's enjoying me with Rayya," he thought as he asked, "Do you accept his apology?"

"Ummm…no, I still don't think it's enough," he heard his wife reply, shooting him a mischievous look before glaring back down at Nate.

"I agree, I need to think of something better," he replied, before saying, "Nate…go play another song. It'll help me figure out what to do with you."

After saying it, he wanted to burst out laughing, knowing the reason for the punishment was absolutely absurd, especially since Nate had been doing everything in his power to protect them.

"Yes master," he heard Nate blurt, sounding breathless, causing his erection to surge to new levels.

"What the fuck just happened!?" he thought, feeling his breath go ragged.

"That's twice he called you master? Do you like it?" he heard Rayya whisper as she took hold of his hands, pressing them harder against her breast.

"Yeah, I think…I think I do," he replied, feeling his heart flutter in both excitement and guilt that somehow Nate had turned him on.

Inhaling deeply, he took hold of both feelings and smiled. As a person who'd spent his life with his back to the ropes, the last thing he ever wanted to do, was run from himself. So, with his exhale, he allowed the feelings to expand in his mind, looking for every root of discomfort.

"Am I bi? If I am…am I okay with that?" he thought, taking hold of his discomfort, inhaling deeply again, drinking in the wonderful scents of warm oil and Rayya's arousal, which grew stronger with each passing second.

"If I am, can it hurt me? I felt no danger when he called me… master," he thought as the room filled with music.

Looking up to his wife, he winked and formed his mouth into a kiss, which she quickly mirrored as she began to dance.

"I like this…I like all of this. I don't feel violated or shamed that he sees her. As for how he made me feel, I want to see if that was a fluke or if it happens again," he thought, looking over to Nate who was crawling back towards them on all fours with his eyes down cast.

"Look at her, be respectful," he commanded, wanting his wife to be adored at every moment.

"Yes master," he heard Nate reply, watching him quickly look up towards his wife, settling in Japanese style on the floor a few feet ahead of him.

"This time nothing…It was something in that moment. I want to find it again," he thought, smiling at the lustful look on Nate's face as he watched his wife dance.

"You're doing a good job taking control of him," he heard Rayya whisper, feeling her hands guide his down to her waist before she shifted around to face him.

"Am I now?" he asked, looking towards his wife, whose attention seemed mostly focused on Nate.

"Yes, a very good job," he heard Rayya reply as she placed her forehead to his, allowing her beautiful curly hair to fall forward, almost completely shrouding his view from his wife or Nate.

"You like me commanding your husband huh? What do you think I should tell him to do next? My wife is still not satisfied with his apology," he murmured, brushing Rayya's hair back, placing it around her ear as he leaned in closer.

"Whatever you want, you know what will satisfy your wife," he heard Rayya reply, leaning in, feeling her soft breath brush against his lips.

"And you? I wonder if you're mine to command as well," he said, forcing his voice to be steady.

"I thought you already knew," he heard Rayya reply.

"Knew what?" he asked, trying to mask his anxiousness.

"That I was always yours. If you'd snapped your fingers and told me to bend over in the break room, I would've fucked you right then and there," he heard Rayya reply as she brought up his hand, first kissing then softly sucking his index finger.

"You're Mine?" he stammered, feeling himself grow hot as Rayya continued to suck and lick his finger.

"Un-huh, yours," he heard Rayya reply, lowering his finger, brushing her nose against his.

"Yes…yes," he heard his wife gasp, seeing in the corner of his eye, that she'd stopped dancing, and was now staring at them transfixed.

"Good, I like that you're mine," he replied, bringing his lips to Rayya's, kissing her softly, hearing Nate gasp, "Oh my God!" right after.

"Mmm," he groaned, opening his mouth just a little wider, feeling Rayya's tongue press in.

I can't believe this is happening," he thought, as he and Rayya's kiss grew more passionate, now feeling Rayya's hand cup his face as she sucked his bottom lip, setting every part of him on fire.

"Oh Papi," he heard his wife whisper in ecstasy, giving him the final mental shove he needed to let go of his inhibitions.

Kissing Rayya deeper, he pressed her ass down and felt his cock slip into her entrance, through the fabric of his khaki shorts.

"Oh shit! Yes!" he heard his wife gasp, sounding as turned on as he felt.

"Someone likes what she sees," he heard Rayya whisper as she broke their kiss, gently brushing her nose against his before turning to look at his wife and Nate who were both staring at them with looks of pure desire.

"You like that?" he heard Rayya ask, sounding like she had a naughty plan.

"Yeah ma, I liked it a lot…why'd you stop?" he heard his wife reply, sounding breathless.

"Because, I want to see how much," he heard Rayya reply, pointing to his wife's pussy before turning to look deep into his eyes asking, "Don't you?"

"Yeah…of course I do," he replied, feeling his mouth begin to water, anticipating what he would see between his wife's legs.

"You hear that sweetie? Your hubby wants to see, and I'm sure mine does too. Isn't that right baby?" he heard Rayya whisper, turning to look at his wife and Nate, who was now staring at him pleadingly.

"Yeah," he heard Nate reply after a few tense seconds, finally breaking eye contact with him to look longingly at his wife.

"Humm, what do you think? Is it okay if we see wifey's pussy?" He heard Rayya whisper in his ear, sending tingles down his spine.

"Shit…Nate would see it all!" he thought, feeling a flash of thick, unrelenting jealousy, which somehow calmed when Nate looked at him with an expression that said (you don't have to do this).

"I…," he stammered, looking between Nate and Rayya, then to his wife, "Baby, what do you think? Wanna show us how wet you are?"

"Humm? Do I?" he heard his wife answer teasingly, looking at all three of them with a face that said she was more than willing.

"Un-huh. Go on Mami, go show that pussy," he replied, smiling as his wife inched back towards the foot of the bed.

"But what if I'm shy?" he heard his wife mummer, sitting on the foot of the bed with a mischievous grin on her face.

"Oh, don't be mean, show us that sexy little pussy," he heard Rayya say, mostly in his ear before returning her attention back to his wife, who'd been slowly raising her legs.

"This little pussy?" he heard his wife ask with a giggle, parting her legs with her hand covering her pussy.

"Mmm, such a fucking tease," he heard Rayya groan, grinding her hips ever so slightly.

"Shitttt," he gasped, feeling a new flash of heat and wetness soak through his shorts and boxers, enveloping his cock.

"Oh, you felt that huh?"

"Fuck yeah," he replied, looking down, inhaling the warm scent of Rayya's arousal before looking back towards his wife who'd now inched up her hand, reveling her shaven pussy, coated in thick, clear arousal running down the crease of her ass.

"Your wife, she makes me so fucking wet, I can't take it," he heard Rayya gasp, feeling her grip his arms as his wife teasingly ran two fingers between her lips, spreading them apart.

"Humm, I had no idea that kiss made me so wet," he heard his wife whisper, pressing her finger into her entrance, working them in small circles that made soft, sticky smacking sounds echo throughout the room.

"Oh fuck," he heard himself and everyone gasp as she lifted her hand, bringing up two long sticky trails arousal connected to her fingers.

"Looks yummy huh?" he heard his wife ask, seductively biting her bottom lip as she fixed her gaze on him, knowing he loved to lick her cum.

"Taste it, let us know," he commanded, kissing Rayya's shoulder blade and neck.

"Unt-un, it's not for me," he heard his wife reply definitely.

"Why's that? Then who's it for?" he replied, licking his lips in anticipation.

"I dunno yet, hummmm, but maybe if everyone was a little closer, I could decide," he heard his wife reply, lowering her hand, rubbing her arousal over her clit and lips.

"Shit," he gasped, feeling Rayya fly off his lap, leaving his cock neglected and cold.

"Shit" he gasped again, looking down at the creamy wet spot she'd left on the imprint of his budging cock.

Returning his gaze to his wife, he could see Rayya gesturing for him to come, but before he stood, she held her hand up for him to wait.

"Slave, bring the chair for your master," he heard Rayya command, giving him a wink before turning her attention back to his wife.

"Yes my Queen," he heard Nate mutter, shooting up from his position, where he could see his cock bulging in his black

241

sweat shorts, along with a dark patch of pre-cum soaked through it.

Moving towards him, he watched Nate make an elaborate gesture for him to stand, all while keeping his head turned towards his wife, who was playing with her pussy in front of Rayya. Hopping up quickly, he came behind Rayya, letting his trapped cock press right up against her bare ass.

"Hi," he heard Rayya whisper in greeting.

"Hi yourself," he whispered, wrapping his arms around Rayya, running his hands over her breast, down her torsos then back up again.

"Mmm…Does she feel good?" he heard his wife whisper, inching up on the bed, spreading her legs wider as she massaged her pussy.

"Yeah, she feels real good. Is baby gonna tell us who get that yum yum?" he replied.

"Humm, still not sure."

"Why's that?" he pressed.

"I don't think it's enough to share, but there could be if you kiss her again," he heard his wife say, throwing her head back, gasping right after.

"I see," he replied, watching a beautiful clear stream of arousal run out from her entrance, completely coating all three of her fingers.

Behind him, he could feel the chair press gently on the back of his calves. Holding Rayya's belly, he gently lowered himself, bringing her down with him. Settled, he ran his hands up Rayya's body, massaging her breast as she positioned herself the way she'd been before.

"Ahh," he gasped, reveling in the sensation as he looked up to Nate, whose eyes were still glued to his wife.

"Eh Nate, like what you see?" he asked, pinching Rayya's nipples hard, causing her to gasp.

"Your wife…she's…she's. I don't have words," he heard Nate respond, bobbing his head, licking his lips.

"Look yummy huh?" he asked.

"Yes," he heard Nate reply, licking his lips again.

"I see you licking your lips, I know you want to taste her," he replied, wanting to hear Nate admit it, only for Nate to nod awkwardly, fully hypnotized by his wife.

"Good, that's good," he replied, liking that form of 'yes' just as much.

Looking back to his wife, he kissed Rayya's cheek. In reply, Rayya moved his right hand up and began to make out with the side of his index finger.

"This is heaven!" he thought, massaging Rayya's breast with his left hand.

"Ahh yes! Squeeze! Feels so good," he heard his wife gasp, followed by louder, sticky, sucking sound as her fingers worked in and out of her entrance.

"Damn girl, you smell so fucking yummy," he heard Rayya gasp, feeling a new wave of warmth and wetness surge through his shorts and boxers.

"What's stopping you from tasting her then?" he asked, running kisses along Rayya's back as he slid his hands towards her pussy, stopping just before he touched it.

Looking towards his wife, he could see that she was watching his every move, and that when he'd almost touched Rayya's pussy, she'd plunged her fingers deeper into her own, and that's when he really started to understand what it meant to enjoy another's pleasure.

"Me, wanting to watch her play. What's stopping you?" he heard Rayya finally stammer in ecstasy, feeling her push his hands closer to her pussy.

"Wanting her to watch me play," he replied, locking eyes with his wife as he wrapped his hands around the outside of Rayya's thighs, with his pinky's pressing right up against Rayya's pussy.

"Ah, I see," he heard Rayya whisper, leaning back as he lifted her thighs, allowing her to prop her feet onto the foot of the bed.

"Oh my God, Rayya, your pussy," he heard his wife gasp.

"Seriously," he stammered, glaring down at Rayya's creamy pussy, panting as the full scent of sweet, musky arousal rose up to greet his nose.

"Papi, play with her pussy for me," he heard his wife beg, watching her prop herself up, staring at Rayya's pussy with wide, excited eyes.

"Like this?" he asked, slowly spreading open Rayya's lips before running his fingers over her clit.

"Yes, shit…just like that," he heard his wife gasp, fingering herself even harder.

"Shit!" he heard Rayya gasp, turning and pressing her lips to his, kissing him deeply.

"Yes, I like that. Kiss her Papi, keep …keep going," he heard his wife groan.

"Just kiss?" he whispered between kisses, now flicking Rayya clit with his fingers causing her whole body to quiver.

"Oh yes papi!" he heard his wife gasp, feeling Rayya cum all over his fingers.

"Keep cumming, keep cumming for me," he gasped, plunging his fingers deep into Rayya's pussy, loving the smell of the sweet, musky scent as it intensified.

Breaking their kiss, he looked down and whispered "open your legs, wider."

"Mmm, yes daddy," he heard Rayya reply as she obeyed, raising her feet onto the foot of the bed.

"Good girl," he replied, finger fucking her even harder.

"Mmm," he heard Nate grunt, causing him to look up to a face of pure anxiousness.

"Yes slave?" he asked as he slowly inched his finger from Rayya's pussy, rubbing her arousal all over her clit.

"Can I touch your wife's feet…her legs?" he heard Nate choke out.

"Yeah…you can. And as matter of fact, I want you to go sit behind her…so she can sit up better," he said, looking to his wife, shooting her a wink.

"Yes master," he heard Nate whisper, again causing his cock to surge.

"*Fuck! I like being in control of him!*" he thought, looking towards his wife, seeing a look of pure pleasure light up on her face.

"Press…harder," he heard Rayya gasp, feeling her hands grip and press his, so that his fingers were firm against her clit.

244

"Shit! So Good!" he heard her moan right after, working her hips as she pressed his hand down harder, causing his fingers to push against her clit before plunging into her pussy.

"God, your pussy," he moaned as she tugged his hand and dropped her hips causing his fingers to slip out and run across her clit again.

"Loves your fingers," he heard Rayya moan as her hips lifted again.

"My fingers love her more," he replied, moving his left hand in deeper circlers around her breast as he continued to stroke her clit.

"Then I can't wait to find out what your dick thinks," he heard Rayya reply breathlessly.

Hearing her words, he exhaled slowly, enjoying every aspect of what he saw, felt, smelled and heard. On his right, he could see Nate sitting down, with his right arm around his wife. Smiling in his direction, Nate spread his wife's legs wider, then with a gentle gesture he guided her to press her feet up against Rayya's.

"Hey sweetie," he heard Rayya say right after, inching forward on his lap adding pressure to their legs spreading them just a little wider.

"Hey Ma? I hear you like my man's fingers? They're good right?" he heard his wife reply, watching as she dipped three of her fingers into her pussy, pulling them out slowly, showing everyone the sticky strings of arousal with a mischievous smile.

"Oh honey, what do you plan on doing with that?" he heard Rayya ask, feeling her pussy flex and squeeze on his fingers as she spoke.

"Honey…yeah it does kind of look like honey," he heard his wife reply, gazing towards Nate and then him.

"Oh, I know what you're thinking. Yeah baby…I saw his face, he did want to taste. Fuck, I hope you give it to him!" he thought, biting his lips before saying, "Let see what you do baby."

Smiling, with a mirthful expression, he watched his wife lean back onto Nate's chest and raise her fingers, aiming it towards Nate's lips, leaving the room silent in anticipation. Then to his surprise, just before they touched Nate's lips, she brought her hand down to her breast, running her arousal over each one of her nipples. An action that seemed to drive Rayya crazy, causing her to gasp, moan and push his fingers even deeper into her pussy.

"You want me to do that? Run your cream on your nipples?" he whispered, flexing his fingers as her pussy squeezed them tight.

"Yes…and I want you to do whatever you want to me," he heard Rayya gasp.

"Whatever I want?" he asked, watching his wife bring her hand back to her pussy, rubbing her clit in circles with her other hand toying with the arousal on her nipples.

"Yeah, whatever you want," he heard Rayya reply.

"Humm…Tell me more of what you want," he whispered.

"I want you to suck your fingers clean, then hers," he heard Rayya reply, feeling her pussy squeeze his fingers even tighter.

"Mmm no, I don't want to suck my fingers. I want to suck yours," he replied, plunging his fingers in and out faster and faster, making sure he moved them in circles around her clit.

"Shit!" he heard both women groan over the sticky, sucking sounds his fingers made.

"Yeah…I like that sound too," he whispered, watching his wife finger herself at the same speed he was fingering Rayya.

"Is boo 'gonna' show them?" he asked, watching his wife's ass flex, knowing his favorite thing was about to come.

"Humm…I think…I think…maybe," he heard his wife gasp, as she slipped her fingers out, toying with the sticky lines of cum until they broke.

"Show them what?" he heard Rayya ask, scooting down just a little further, causing him to look towards Nate as an idea bloomed in his mind.

"You'll see," he replied, softly tugging Rayya's thighs, causing her feet to slip off and go under his wife's legs.

With her legs now free, he inched Rayya forward until she and his wife's pussies where almost touching. Winking at Nate who'd begun to chuckle, he looked at his wife to see what deviousness she was cooking up as she continued to toy with the arousal on the tips of her fingers. Then with the slightest head tip that only he'd be able to perceive, his wife smiled and slowly moved her hand back towards Nate.

246

"Hey, taste," he heard his wife say, with her accent pouring out and her face turning bright red.

"And here's the first real moment! I feel her excitement!" he thought, slowing his finger thrust within Rayya, holding his breath as his wife's fingers stopped in front on Nate's mouth.

"Fuck," he heard Rayya whisper, feeling her hands run up and down his arm.

"Go for it," he replied, nodding to Nate who was looking at him for permission.

"Yess…good boy," he heard Rayya whisper as Nate took hold of his wife's arm, bringing her fingers to his lips.

"Yummy right?" he whispered, watching Nate smell his wife's fingers before opening his mouth, taking her three fingers into his mouth.

"Damn," he groaned, feeling his body grow warm as Nate passionately sucked his wife's fingers with his eyes closed, head moving in circles as if she were the most delicious thing he'd ever tasted.

"She taste good, doesn't she?" he asked, as Nate opened his eyes, inching his wife's arm back, withdrawing her fingers which were all but clean minus a few sticky strands between them.

"Delicious," he heard Nate reply, breathing heavily where he could see that he was barely controlling his lust.

"Shit! Both of them are begging me to let them go free!" he thought, looking between his wife who'd brought her hand back to her pussy, softly massaging her clit and Nate whose arm was twitching, seeming to him like he was fighting the urge to bring it over his wife to rub and touch her.

"What are you doing Slave? I thought I made it clear you're to make her happy. Why are you not rubbing her tits?" he said, feeling the wind leave his chest, wondering if he could handle seeing that or anything else before saying, "That means do whatever else she wants as well."

"I…I," he heard Nate choke out, with his eye's widening in bewilderment.

"You heard what he said, don't you dare hesitate or disobey," he heard Rayya say in sultry, commanding voice, feeling her ever so gently tug his arm, letting him know she wanted him to remove his fingers.

"Yes…yes of course," he heard Nate reply, awkwardly bringing his arm around his wife, resting his hand on top of her belly, still staring at him questioningly.

"He's more nervous than me! How's this possible!" he thought, smiling at Nate's awkwardness before gazing down at his cream coated fingers.

"Humm," he mumbled, bringing them to Rayya's mouth, tracing them around her lips leaving them shinny.

"Reconsidering licking your fingers aren't you," he heard Rayya whisper just before kissing and licking the tips of his fingers.

"Na…I still want to lick yours," he replied, kissing her softly, making sure he licked and sucked her lips before pulling free.

"I see," he heard her reply as she moved her hand down to her pussy.

"You, you taste really good," he whispered, moving his fingers toward her mouth, smiling as she opened, allowing him to run his fingers over her tongue.

In the corner of his eye, he could see Nate's hand sliding up his wife's belly towards her breast. Gulping hard, he turned to watch, feeling the anticipation became an insane tickling sensation traveling up his entire back. If that weren't enough, he could feel Rayya's lips now closing around his fingers, sucking hard and passionately, cleaning off any of herself that remained.

"Oh man! Oh shit! What do I do!?" he thought as pleasure and jealousy traveled through his body, causing him to want to scream, 'Stop!' while the other part of him couldn't wait for the contact.

And then, Nate's hand touched.

"Ohhh," he heard his wife gasp, closing her eyes, throwing her head back in pleasure.

The sight of her ecstasy instantly evaporated his jealousy, and all he wanted in that moment was to see how much further they'd go. Feeling Rayya's mouth slacken, he removed his fingers and pointed.

"Hey Nate, kiss her," he blurted without thinking.

"Kiss her, and rub her pussy," he said right after, feeling his breath go heavy when his wife gasped and moaned in approval.

Wordlessly, Nate bobbed his head and gazed down at his wife with a flurry of conflicted emotions coming across his face.

"He's worried I won't be able to handle it!" he realized as he practically shouted, "I'll be fine. Do it…kiss her!"

"Okay," he heard Nate gasp, leaning forward, looking down at his wife who was now wrapping her arms around his neck.

"God, I love this. I don't want to miss a moment," he thought, smiling as his wife gazed up into Nate's eyes, seeing all her lust and desire in its truest form.

"I want her to love his kiss. And I want her to enjoy his touch," he thought as Nate leaned in the final distance, pressing his lips to hers.

"Un," he heard himself groan, feeling his body ignite as their lips parted, kissing each other deeper, with his wife softly sucking Nate's bottom lip.

"Oh…so sexy," he heard Rayya whisper, smelling the delicious scent of her arousal even before feeling her wet fingers touch and trace around his lips.

"Yeah, very fucking sexy," he replied, inhaling deeply, to drink in more of her scent before licking his lips clean.

"Yummy?" he heard her ask right after.

Licking his lips again to taste the subtle sweetness, he smiled and whispered, "I dunno, I think I need more."

"More like this," he heard Rayya reply, watching as she brought her hand back down to her pussy.

"Yes, a lot more please," he replied, looking up again, watching as his wife pressed her tongue into Nate's mouth.

"More is on its way," he heard Rayya whisper over the soft, sticky sounds of her pussy.

"I…can't wait," he replied, leaning forward, loving the way Nate turned his head to suck his wife's tongue.

"Fuckkkk, I thought, I'd hate it," he whispered more to himself, feeling his cock surge with joy.

"And now?" he heard Rayya ask, causing him to look down as she brought up her hand, this time with fingers so coated in white he could barely see the lines.

"And now," he whispered, parting his lips, allowing her to slide three of her fingers over his tongue.

249

"And now, I keep wanting to see and experience more. Even though 'wifey's' kissing Nate, and I'm doing this with Rayya, I feel like wifey and I are still connected," he thought, closing his eyes as he sucked, loving the slight saltiness he tasted, mingling with the sweet.

"You love it," he heard Rayya finish for him as she slipped her fingers from his mouth, taking them into her own.

"Something like that," he replied, sliding her forward, pressing her pussy up against his wife's.

"Ah!" he heard both women gasp, causing him to look up towards his wife who shot him a wicked, "thank you look," before she brought her attention back to Nate, kissing him softly.

"I like the way you think," he heard Rayya whisper, wrapping her arms around his neck as she began to work her hips.

"Damn, damn that looks good," he gasped, watching intently as the women began working their hips harder.

Then to his delight, he watched Nate move his other arm around his wife, sliding his hand down her belly, stopping just before he touched her pussy. Feeling a burst of passion, he ran kisses down Rayya's cheek, neck and shoulder, ending it with a peck on her lips before turning his attention back to Nate.

"Mmm, you like seeing your baby have fun don't you?" he heard Rayya gasp as she turned and kissed him on the side of the cheek.

"Yeah, and she's loving your pussy," he replied, watching her hips rock even more.

"UH!" he heard his wife gasp in response, causing him to suck in his breath.

Looking closer he could see the wet, slippery mess growing as both women's arousal mixed and spread all over their lips, feeling he was going to cum just from the sight, smell and sound alone. Taking a deep breath to control himself, he made a quick eye contact with Nate and nodded.

"Yes!" he thought, when Nate returned the nod.

In that instant, Nate inched his hand down the final distance, and in slow motion he watched as Nate's index and ring finger parted his wife's lips, with his middle finger working over her clit.

"More!" he heard his wife gasp as she began to shudder, all while Rayya continued to grind her hips, leaving her arousal all over the back of Nate's fingers.

"Yes baby, we'll give you more," he heard Rayya whisper to his wife.

"OH God! Oh God!" he heard his wife shrike!

"Yessss!" he gasped, reaching for Rayya's pussy, rubbing her clit in fast circled, causing her to buck and grind on his wife's pussy even harder.

Knowing what was coming, he felt greedy to the point of utter desperation. He wanted Nate to work his fingers faster, to thrust them into his wife, to kiss her and do anything else that'd bring her to that moment where she could no longer hold on.

"*I need her to cum! I want him to make her cum!*" he thought, seeing his wife inhale, trying to hold herself.

"Faster, rub her pussy faster!" he commanded, watching as Nate's middle finger flicked his wife's clit faster and faster.

"Good! Good! Yes! You like that baby?" he asked, watching his wife as she began to scream breathlessly.

"Grind harder...harder," he whispered to Rayya, bringing his hands under her ass, squeezing tight as he took control of her hips.

"AH!" he heard both women scream, as he worked Rayya's hips in slow, deep circles.

"Yessss, cum for us, both of you, cum for us" he whispered, working his fingers so that they'd massaged Rayya's inner thighs and pussy.

"No!" he heard his wife gasp.

"Aww, don't you want Nate to feel it? Don't you want to show him how messy you can be? Go on, show him baby...I promise to make him eat kitty if you do," he said looking down, smiling as Nate began to stroke both women's clits with his thumb.

"Oh! You wanna see him eat...eat my pussy?" he heard his wife gasp as Rayya began to tremble.

"Yes, yes of course I do, and I want to see baby cum in his mouth. Don't you want that baby, to cum in his mouth?" he asked, looking to his wife's face then to Nate's, surprised to see it turning every hue of red.

"Oh…Baby!" he heard his wife shirk, throwing her head back as she began to shiver.

"Mmm, imagine him licking you clean," he said smiling as Rayya's body quaked even harder.

"Baby! Baby!" he heard his wife call, followed by Rayya screaming at the top of her lungs.

In that moment, he watched and felt his wife erupt, shooting out a beautiful, clear stream of cum that splashed all over the four of them.

"Holy fuck!" he heard Nate gasp in surprise.

For Jay, all he could do was laugh in joy as his wife continued to cum with such force, it was now hitting the lenses of his and everyone else's View-Techs.

"I can't fucking wait to watch these videos! This was the best fucking idea ever!" He thought, as his wife lurched up from Nate's chest and said, "Clothes off! Take your fucking clothes off now!"

Chapter II

The Look On Her Face Part II

Road Trip: Day Three

Date: Saturday, June 3rd 2017

Time: 11:45 pm

Location: Hill City, South Dakota

"Take my…take my clothes off?" Jay thought, feeling a rush of excitement and insecurity wash over him, leaving him stunned.

Somehow hearing his wife's words had woken him up to the true reality of the situation. His clothes had been a barrier, protection that'd allowed him to separate himself and Nate as mere vessels, whose main purpose was to please the women. Now seeing his wife's wild, hungry eyes as she scrambled out of the bed - still demanding they take off their clothes, he felt all his insecurity flood back into him.

"Fuck! Is this when it's going to happen? Is my wife really going to fuck this guy!? And me… I haven't slept with another woman since…since we started dating. Seven years and now…is this really happening?"

"Hey, stop day dreaming. Clothes off! Rayya, get off of him, baby…baby…take, take your clothes off," he heard his wife say, tugging his sleeveless shirt.

"Shit! She's panting!" he thought, anxiously gazing at Nate who looked even more bewildered than himself.

On his lap, Rayya had shifted and brought her legs down from the bed. Turning, she flashed him a mischievous grin and stood, tugging his shirt up over his head.

"Damn! Not wasting anytime. I need to get my shit together!" he thought, trying to gain his composure, noting that Rayya's hungry look mirrored his wife's.

"Ok, fuck it," he whispered to himself, looking between the women and Nate, whose face flashed in meek, bewilderment when he reached for his belt.

"Don't worry, I'm right there with you. But for some fucked up reason, seeing you like this, I want to see my boo make you go crazy," he

thought, quickly unbuckling his belt, letting his shorts fall to the floor.

"Oh…hi there," he heard Rayya exclaim, placing her hand on his back, staring down at his cock protruding in the fabric of his boxer's.

Laying a kiss on Rayya's temple, he hooked his fingers into the waistline of his briefs, preparing to pull them down.

"Here, let me help," he heard Rayya whisper, placing her other hand on his chest, running it down to his cock which she griped and ever so slightly tugged.

On his right, he could see his wife smiling and gesturing for Nate to come closer. As Nate scooted to the foot of the bed, he felt Rayya's fingers slip underneath the elastic of his boxers.

"Rayya, did I ever tell you how good he tastes?" he heard his wife ask, gazing down at his cock, then to Rayya who'd begun to run kisses down his chest and stomach as she slowly crouched down, bringing his boxers down with her.

"I think you did. But I remember thinking, I wanted to find out for myself," he heard Rayya reply, watching her stare at a line of pre-cum running down from his tip.

"Shit I love this," he thought, seeing Rayya lick her lips as she took hold of his cock, stroking it gently.

"Hummm," he heard his wife reply, coming closer to Rayya, gripping her hair before saying, "I remember you saying something like… you like it when Nate takes you like this?"

"Wait, no…It wasn't that," he heard his wife continue, moving her hand to the back of Rayya's head before saying, "yeah…it was right here."

"You remembered huh? Jay, are you taking notes?" he heard Rayya reply, gazing up into his eyes as she brought his cock to her lips, kissing it gently before running her tongue up to his tip.

"How's that feel baby? You like her tongue?" he heard his wife ask, wrapping her arm around his waist as Rayya inched her head back.

"Real good!" he exclaimed, watching as Rayya opened her mouth wide, with her tongue extended.

"Look baby, she's showing you she ready for you," he heard his wife whisper, pressing Rayya's head forward, guiding his cock over her tongue.

"Shit!" he gasped, closing his eyes, loving the sensation as he went deeper, almost touching the base Rayya's throat.

"Rayya, do you know why I remember what you like?" he heard his wife ask, feeling Rayya come up with a twisting head motion that made his toes curl.

"It's because I was thinking, that's good to know for when I make you suck my husband's dick. Now choke for us you little bitch!" he heard his wife command, feeling his dick plunge into the back of Rayya's throat, causing her to gag.

"Louder! I want louder!" he heard his wife gasp, feeling his cock plunge up and down in Rayya's throat, filling the entire room with choking, gagging sounds.

"Unnn! Yeah! Suck my fucking dick!" he grunted, feeling himself begin to tremble, loving the way Rayya felt and sounded as she gagged on his cock.

"Yeah, you like that huh baby?" he heard his wife ask.

"Yeah," he managed to choke out, feeling Rayya twisting her head as his wife continued to shove her head back and forth on his cock.

"I love it...I knew I'd love seeing this," he heard his wife gasp, before hearing her say, "And you, do you like seeing your wife suck my hubby's dick?"

Opening his eyes, he could see Nate had taken off his shirt and undid his sweat shorts. Where he thought there'd be boxer all he saw was cock pushing up right underneath his belly button.

"Look baby," he heard himself say, wanting to scandalize his wife.

"Look at what baby?" he heard his wife reply, bringing Rayya's head back, staring at his cock.

"Nate...he's waiting for you," he replied, sucking in his breath as Rayya began to suck and toy with only his tip.

"Huh? Ohhh, I see," he heard his wife respond, sounding slightly apprehensive as she looked over towards Nate.

"Go...go suck it. I know you want to," he gasped as Rayya took hold of his thighs, driving herself forward.

"I," his wife whispered, still gazing at Nate who'd taken hold of his cock, stroking it as he watched Rayya suck his cock.

"Look...he's making a big ass mess. I know you want to taste that. Don't leave him there by himself," he whispered, running his left hand over Rayya's hair, moving it to the back of her head and neck.

"And you? You like that dick huh?" he asked Rayya, pushing his cock in deeper, causing Rayya to gag even harder.

"OHH!" he heard Nate grunt, causing him to look up to see Nate jerking his cock harder and harder.

"Like me fucking your wife's face huh?" he asked, locking eyes with Nate as he thrust in Rayya's mouth harder.

"OHHH yeahhh," he heard Nate grunt, jerking even harder.

"And...you 'wanna' fuck my wife's face just like this huh?" he asked, placing his right hand on his wife's head, pushing her down as he thrust in Rayya's mouth harder.

"AHrr," he heard Nate grunt as his wife crouched down next to Rayya.

"Ohhh, the harder I fuck your wife's face the better huh?" he asked, sliding his dick from Rayya's mouth, aiming it towards his wife who'd opened her mouth wide, sucking down the full length of his cock just as deep as Rayya.

"Yes!" he heard Nate grunt as he began to thrust, causing his wife to gag.

"So, what the fuck are you doing slave? Why aren't you fucking my wife's face? I thought it was clear to you that your job is to please her!" he exclaimed, withdrawing his cock from his wife mouth, staring down at her before whispering, "Crawl to him...go suck his dick."

"Yes papi," he heard his wife reply, licking up the length of his cock as she moved it to Rayya who took him in her mouth without hesitation, swallowing him down to his base.

Gripping Rayya's by the back of her head with both hands, he thrust and watched as his wife turned and crawled to Nate on all fours.

"Shit!" he grunted loving the way she looked, and loving the way she'd come up onto her knees, to take hold of Nate's cock.

"Yeah baby…yeah baby," he whispered, watching as she stroked Nate's cock, moving her hand in long twisting motions.

Looking down, he could see Rayya's eyes watering, and feel her nails digging into the back of his thighs as she continued to force her throat wider with his every thrust.

"You want me to cum don't you?" he whispered, inching her head back till his cock hung free.

"Mmm," he heard Rayya reply, opening her mouth wide.

"Hummmm," he said, settling down into the chair, before saying, "I …need. I need something else before I can cum."

Looking at him dubiously for a moment, he watched Rayya turn her head in the direction he was looking and smile. It was one of the moments he'd been fearing with all his heart, but sitting there now, as his wife opened her mouth, guiding Nate's cock into it, all he could feel was joy.

"How does that cock taste…huh baby?" he asked, watching Nate's cock disappear, loving the way she sucked him slow, making sure she pushed her head down as far as she could go before coming back up, where she'd lick and flick her tongue at his tip.

"Really, really good baby," he heard his wife reply, inching over to the right, giving him and Rayya clearance to see her lick up a long trail of Nate's pre-cum that'd run down his shaft.

"Ohhh, good girl," he whispered, running his hand through Rayya's hair, smiling as she turned and gripped his cock, sliding it back into her mouth.

"How do I tell her that I really can't cum like this? No one ever believes me," he thought, throwing his head back as she began to suck furiously to the point where his toes started to curl.

Catching his breath, he looked down at Rayya, then to his wife and smiled, before whispering "You really want me to cum?"

"MMM!" he heard Rayya reply, feeling her suck even harder.

"How bad?" he asked, inhaling deeply as Rayya rocked her head back and forth in fast jerking motions, literally throat fucking him.

"Give me a sec, a sec, stop for a sec!" he gasped, smiling at the 'WTF' look Rayya gave him as she lifted her head.

"Oh, don't pout, here, if you really want me to cum, sit here," he whispered, taking her by the shoulders, lifting her to sit on the bed next to Nate.

"I...I need...," he started to say, trying to figure out how to explain himself as he got down on his knees in front of her.

"I love..." he whispered, taking hold of Rayya's legs, spreading them open, feeling his cock surge at the sight of her dripping, wet pussy.

"If you want me to cum, then I need you to cum on my tongue," he whispered, beginning to lay soft kiss on Rayya's pussy.

"You get me now?" he asked, gazing up to her before pressing his lips on top of her clit.

"Shit," he heard Rayya whisper, reaching down, taking hold of the back of his head, whispering, "no, make me understand."

"With pleasure," he thought, flicking his tongue over her clit, then down to her entrance to have more of her taste.

"Oh yes! Taste me!" he heard Rayya gasp, pressing his head down harder, rocking her hips, running her soaking wet pussy over his tongue.

"She taste and smells so fucking good!" he thought, inhaling deeply to control himself, loving Rayya's sweet, velvety textured arousal as she gasped, moaned and squirmed under every flick of his tongue.

"What!!! Whattt??? Are you doing...doing to me!?" he heard Rayya gasp as she began to shudder.

"Cum in my mouth," he whispered, before pressing his mouth down again.

In the background, he could hear Nate grunting and gasping for air as his wife chocked and gagged on his cock. Inching his head back, he gazed at the creamy, white river of arousal running from Rayya's entrance, and smiled.

"Did my wife ever tell you how much I love eating pussy?" he whispered, pressing his tongue into Rayya's entrance, then moving it up to her clit which he kissed and sucked tenderly.

"AHH! Shit!" he heard Rayya shriek, feeling her legs began to tremble.

"Mmm...good girl, cum for me," he whispered, blowing cool air over her clit as he inched back to watch her cum, loving the way it ran down all over her ass, pooling up onto the sheets below.

When Rayya finished quivering, Jay focused on sucking and nibbling Rayya's inner thighs then ran his tongue up the length of her pussy, collecting her mess on the tip of his tongue.

"You taste so good," he whispered, slowly slipping two fingers into Rayya's pussy.

"Fuck!" he heard Rayya gasp.

To his right he could hear his wife gag harder and Nate gasping, "No! No! No! – No! No! No!"

"Yes! Cum!" He thought, peeking over towards his wife who was sucking Nate's length with deep twisting head jerks.

Looking back towards Rayya, he could see her biting her bottom lip as she stared at his wife and smiled. Slipping his finger from Rayya's pussy, he brought them in front of his face and watched Rayya's head snap back over to him, eyes transfixed.

"You 'wanna' know what I'm going to do with this huh?" he whispered, moving his fingers open and closed, toying with the sticky strands of arousal.

"Un huh," he heard Rayya reply, slightly leaning forwards, licking her lips.

"Humm," he replied, slipping his fingers back into Rayya, whispering, "Get more."

"Oh my fucking…" he heard Rayya gasp as he worked his fingers.

"I thought you'd like that," he asked, pressing and massaging his fingers on Rayya's G spot causing her to instantly cum all over his fingers.

"Yessss," he whispered, loving the feeling of her pussy clamping and squeezing as he continued to work her G spot.

"Stop!" he heard Rayya finally gasp, seeing her thighs quiver.

"Stop?" he replied, removing his cream coated fingers, sucking them clean as he gazed up at her.

"You!" he heard Rayya moan, glaring at him in awe, making him want to drive her even crazier.

"Me what?" he replied, locking eyes with her, leaning over toward his wife, whispering, "Make him cum down the back of your throat. And anything that doesn't go down…I want you to get up and share with Rayya."

"Jay!?" he heard Rayya exclaim, looking at him in shock.

"Yes Rayya?" he replied, smiling before laying kisses all over her thighs.

"You…when the fuck did you get…get like this?" she began, as Nate began to scream, "NO!" at the top of his lungs.

"Like what?" he whispered with a wicked expression before looking over towards his wife, whose cheeks were swelling as frothy white lines of cum burst free, running down Nate's cock.

"Good girl…try to get it all," he whispered, proud that his wife could make Nate cum so much and so fast, and loving that she could handle most of it.

In response, he could see his wife swallow, one gulp then the next, and finally after the third, he could see her head rising with her lips and cheeks holding tightly.

"Oh, did you save some for Rayya?" he asked as Nate's cock feel free from his wife's lips.

"Mmm-humm," he heard his wife reply, turning with her mouth open, showing him the white frothy cum that remained.

"Ohhh…yeahh…Go kiss her," he said, looking between Nate and Rayya, who were both staring at him in different forms of shock.

"Un," he heard his wife respond as she grabbed and cupped Rayya's face, kissing her deeply.

Watching them kiss, he stood and took his cock in his hand and began to stroke. On his right, he could see Nate do the same and smiled.

"I can't get enough of them either," he thought, retuning his gaze to the women, watching as Rayya sucked his wife's tongue and bottom lip.

"How's your hubby's cum taste. Did my wifey do a good job?" he asked, sitting back in the chair, adding twist to his strokes, loving the passionate way the women kissed.

"Oh, she did an amazing job. My hubby tastes really good, especially when I kiss her. But what happened? Where's yours?" he heard Rayya ask, breaking the kiss, staring at him as his wife kissed her forehead and temple, glaring back at him accusingly.

"I…I," he said, slowing his strokes, staring at his wife who was now whispering in Rayya's ear.

"*Shit! I know that look!*" he thought, as Rayya stood and said, "I see," staring at his cock then at him.

"Look, I…"

"Weren't telling me the whole truth," he heard Rayya whisper, sliding off of the foot of the bed before turning and lowering onto his lap.

"I did," he replied breathlessly as Rayya inched back, pressing her back to his chest, all while guiding his cock to press between the lips of her pussy.

"Karman…sweetie?" he heard Rayya say in the most seductive tone he ever heard.

"Yes Mami?" he heard his wife reply, giving him a mischievous smile.

"Can I? Can I drain your hubby dry?" he heard Rayya whisper, feeling her hand press the tip of his cock into her entrance.

"AH!" he let out, feeling the heat and tightness of Rayya's pussy as she squeezed and worked her hips back and forth ever so gently.

"Oh…of course you can, here, let me help," he heard his wife reply, watching a wicked smile spread across her lips as she got down on her knees, running her tongue up his shaft to Rayya's clit.

"Fuck! I can't!" he gasped, throwing his head back as Rayya inched down further, sinking his cock in deeper.

"Mmm. His dick feels so good. Shit! I want more!" he heard Rayya shriek as she began to grind and bounce on his cock.

"How's that pussy baby?" he heard his wife ask, feeling her lips and tongue on his balls.

"So….fuc..aah!" he exclaimed, unable to formulate words, feeling his cock completely submerge in Rayya's pussy.

"Yeah! Right there! Right there!" he heard Rayya moan, grinding harder where he could feel his tip press into her.

"Please!" he gasped, not wanting to cum in mere seconds.

"Yeah, baby fuck that pussy. Cum baby, let Rayya feel it! Let me taste it!" he heard his wife exclaim, feeling her tongue play along the base of his cock as Rayya began to bounce.

"AH! Ohh Shitt!" he screamed, grabbing Rayya's breast, squeezing hard as his cock throbbed and erupted with so much force he could feel it rush out of Rayya's entrance in that very same second.

"Yesss!" he heard Rayya scream, bucking and bouncing, harder and faster, causing his cum to gush out in waves.

Sucking in his breath, he moved his hands down to her waist and pressed and worked Rayya's hips then gasped "Now you cum! You hear me! Now you cum!"

"Aye!" he heard Rayya shriek in a high pitch voice, feeling a rush of hot cum flow over his dick as her pussy forced him out.

Gasping, and shaking with Rayya, he looked down to his wife who was gazing at he and Rayya's pussy with a look of sheer amazement.

"Baby?' he gasped, but he could see she was not listening. Baby?" he whispered again, watching her mouth open.

"Fuccckkk...I must've been killed by a sniper! This...this is fucking heaven!" he thought as his wife took him in her mouth.

Chapter III

The Look On His Face

Road Trip: Day Four

Date: Sunday, June 4th 2017

Time: 12:01 am

Location: Hill City, South Dakota

Karman had never imagined being with another woman, and as bad as she wanted to push her limits exploring with Rayya, there were times she'd felt deep resistance coming from somewhere she couldn't uproot. That was until the moment she felt Rayya's pussy touch hers. Then, then there was nothing in her mind calling out even the slightest warning.

"I want that again. She was so fucking wet. And now hubby's cum is running out. I have to feel her pussy," she thought, opening her throat wide, loving the sensation and taste of her husband's cock as she pushed him deeper.

"Your wife's a good girl...I didn't even need to tell her to clean your dick," she heard Rayya say, turning her on even more.

"Yeah, she knows what I like. And I have a feeling I know what you two freaks like," she heard her husband say, gripping her hair, pulling her up to look at him.

"I love the look on his face. I love that he feels free. All I've ever wanted is for him to be happy," she thought, following his eyes towards Nate who was staring in her direction towards Rayya's pussy.

"I know what you want. But, she's mine," she thought, smiling at Nate before turning to watch her husband's cum leak from Rayya's pussy.

"I need to taste and still leave enough for my pussy! Oh fuck, but I want it all!" she thought, sitting back on her toes before saying, "Rayya sweetie...can you go to the bed for me?"

"I thought I was the one giving the orders around here," she heard Rayya reply, teasingly spreading her pussy, running her fingers through the cum leaking from her pussy.

"Ah, shit," she gasped, feeling her pussy throb twice as hard.

"Yes, I know you want to taste the mix, dirty lil bitch," she heard Rayya whisper, taunting her further as she leaned forward, sucking tenderly on Rayya's inner lips and clit.

"Taste so good," she mumbled, listening to Rayya gasp in pleasure as she ran her tongue down to her entrance, plunging it in.

"Oh my God," she heard from her right, feeling Nate's hand run up and down her back as her mouth filled with salty, sweet climax.

Wanting to share, she inched back and pushed Nate to kneel on the floor, then brought her lips to his. The kiss was deep and passionate, and within seconds she found herself on top of him.

"They're yummy right? And I know you wanted to taste my husband," she whispered, pressing herself down, gasping as Nate's cock pressed between her soaking lips.

"Ah shit! Stop fucking teasing," she heard Nate grunt, pulling her down, kissing her hard.

"Teasing? Me?" she groaned, working her hips back and forth ever so slightly.

"I...shit..." she heard Nate gasp, gripping her ass tight.

"Mmm," she groaned, loving the feeling of his hands pressing her down on his thick, hard cock.

Kissing him deeply again, she worked her hips slower, allowing Nate's tip to just slip into her entrance.

"Too much!" she heard Nate gasp, breaking their kiss.

"Oh, so you want to wait?" she asked, standing up to stare at the mess she'd made on Nate's cock.

"No! No!" she heard Nate beg.

"Too, late..." she replied, giving Nate a wicked smile as she stepped over him to look at her husband and Rayya.

"Look, who's already hard again from watching his wifey play," she heard Rayya whisper.

"I see that...Hi baby," she murmured, loving the sight of her husband's hard cock.

"Hi boo," she heard her husband reply.

"You okay," she asked, feeling slightly self-conscious that she'd brought up Nate wanting to taste him, wondering if it was slowly going to erode his mood.

"Yeah...you...just 'gonna' leave him...like that?" she heard her husband ask, glancing down at Nate.

"Oh," she gasped, feeling her belly erupt in butterflies knowing he was now more than ready for her to take that next and final step.

"Humm...does baby, really want to see Nate fuck me?" she asked, wanting to hear him actually say it as she came closer to Rayya.

"Yes...Of course...he's your slave, it's his job to pleasure you," she heard her husband reply, sending shivers down her spine as she pushed Rayya to sit on the bed.

"My slave...yes, that right," she replied, studying the curious look on Rayya's face, before saying, "sit back a little more for me."

"Like this?" she heard Rayya ask, scooting back with her legs parted.

"Yes, just like that," she replied, climbing on top of Rayya, pressing her pussy against hers, gasping as the warm, wet heat spread across her pussy.

"Ohh, that's what you were up too," she heard Rayya gasp, feeling her hands wrap around her ass pressing hard down harder.

"I wanted to be extra wet," she replied, working her pussy over Rayya's faster and faster, remembering the sensation of Nate's cock and the sight of her husband and Rayya's mix.

"Slave...listen up," she heard her husband say in a hushed, commanding voice.

"Shit, I love it when he talks like that!" she thought, grabbing Rayya's thighs pushing them back, changing her rhythm to a slow grind.

"Such a dirty little bitch," she heard Rayya gasp, taking hold of her own thighs, holding them open.

"Yeah, and you love it," she replied, pressing her pussy down even further.

"Shit!" she gasped, greeted by a new flash of warmth and wetness, looking down to see Rayya's pussy leaking cream.

"Say it again master, I…I'm not sure," she heard Nate say, sounding bewildered at what her husband must've whispered.

"I said, go behind her and…," she heard her husband say, feeling his hand grip her ass, "you take her ass like this."

"And then?" she heard Nate ask, sounding breathless.

"Humm," she heard her husband say, feeling a smack on her ass that caused her to shiver and quake on Rayya's pussy.

"Oh shit! Your daddy's spanking you!" she heard Rayya gasp, starting to rock her hips as her husband spanked her other cheek.

"Like that," she heard her husband growl before saying, "now spank her fucking ass."

"Shit!" she screamed, feeling Nate's hand come down on her ass, making a loud clap that echoed throughout the room.

"Gooood! That's good! She likes it rough!" she heard her husband exclaim, seeing him appear on her left.

"Rough…like this?" she heard Nate reply, feeling his hand come down again, sending pain and pleasure coursing through her stinging ass cheeks.

"Yes," she gasped, pressing her ass out further, receiving blow after stinging blow.

"Spank her…yes…oh fuck…spank her," she heard Rayya gasp, tugging her down with her arms wrapped around her neck.

"That's a good Slave, now grab her ass, and spread her cheeks," she heard her husband command, feeling Nate's larger, masculine hands grip and part her ass as he was told.

"Baby!" she called out, feeling cool air brush against her parting lips that'd been pressed tightly against Rayya's.

"Mmm, look at that pussy. You see that?" she heard her husband say, feeling Nate's hands squeeze and spread her stinging ass even wider.

"I see it," she heard Nate whisper.

"It wants to be fucked…Fucked hard…do you understand?" she heard her husband say, feeling his index finger run across her entrance before hearing him say, "So you better fuck her hard!"

"Oh fuck!" she shrieked, feeling Nate tug her and press his tip right up against her pulsing entrance.

"Deeper! Just a little deeper, then fuck her just like that," she heard her husband command, feeling Nate's tip slip past the threshold, filling her entrance.

"Oh my God baby!" she screamed as Nate teased her with just the tip of his cock as her husband had commanded.

"Yeah, keep going, she loves that," she heard her husband say, coming in front of her with a mirthful, wicked smile.

"Baby?" she gasped, barely able to control herself, feeling Nate's cock slipping in a little deeper with each thrust.

"Yes?" she heard her husband reply, inching forward, kissing her on the lips, before looking down to Rayya, stroking her hair.

"Shit!" she heard Nate grunt, feeling Nate pause, and inch his cock back.

"Good, breath, and while you do, take your hand and put it in on her back, right between her shoulder blades," she heard her husband command, feeling Nate's hand come down, pressing her down, breast to breast with Rayya.

"Push harder, make her ass come up more, then fuck her again, this time as hard as you want," she heard her husband say right after feeling Nate obey immediately.

"AH!" she shrieked in Rayya's ear, now feeling Rayya's hands rubbing up and down her lower back.

"Kiss me…kiss me," she heard Rayya whisper, turning her head, kissing her deeply.

"Go deeper, and press your thumb in her ass," she heard her husband command, feeling Nate's length press into her pussy and his thumb filled her ass.

"Ah," she screamed in Rayya's mouth, feeling herself overload with pleasure.

"Now go deeper…as deep as you can. Long stroke! And fuck that ass with your thumb!" she heard her husband command, feeling him left out of the bed as Nate's cock pressed deep into her pussy.

"Please!" she begged, feeling thrust after wonderful thrust, with Nate's thumb working deeper and deeper into her ass.

"Yess, make her beg," she heard her husband say as Nate thrust grew stronger, satisfying her throbbing pussy, yet making her hungry for more.

"Pleaseee!" she gasped again, pushing her ass back, knowing the only feeling she was missing was Nate's cum.

"Oh, you want my hubbies' cum!" she heard Rayya whisper in her ear, feeling her hands wrap around her head and neck pulling her down as Nate began to scream.

"AHH" she screamed out at the top of her lungs, from both the delicious sensation of his thrust, and from the hot explosion of pressure she felt as Nate's cock began to throb.

"Yes! Yess!" she grunted, squeezing her pussy as Nate continued to pound, mixing his cum within her.

And then she felt him shiver, and fall forward, pressing his cock in her as he continued to orgasm.

"Everything's so perfect," she thought, lifting her head to see her husband's beaming smile as he mouthed the words "cum again for me."

"Ayee!" she screamed, letting lose, feeling her pussy clamp down and erupt.

"Man…oh! Man!" she heard Nate gasp, feeling his cock burst from her pussy as she squirted.

"Hey, where the fuck you think you're going. Did I tell you to stop?" she heard her husband ask.

"Na, no, but, but, I can't…can't …" she heard Nate whisper breathlessly.

"You're always, always supposed to fuck her harder," she heard her husband command as he grabbed her ass cheeks, spreading open her dripping wet pussy.

"Mmm, look at that pussy!" she heard her husband say, feeling his tip press and run between the lips of her swollen pussy, stopping when it rested upon her entrance.

"Baby, hey …wa…wait!" she cried out, feeling her tender pussy clench down desperately around his tip.

"Listen slave, there's one rule you must always obey! Never wait! Never give her a break!" she heard her husband command, feeling his rock-hard cock slam into her pussy.

"Oh, my fuckin!" she gasped, feeling another orgasm take her - then for countless hours after, all she knew was bliss.

8 hours later

Karman took a steady breath, allowing the pungent smell of jungle to fill her nostrils. Without the slightest need to concentrate, her mind categorized everything she needed to know.

"Shit!" she thought as fear began to settle in.

She was too close to her target to let the subtle warning signs of her impending doom distract her. Adjusting the settings on the scope of her Rifle, her target came into view. Squatting down, her target picked up a little girl, no more than three, then walked out onto the balcony of a treehouse. It was the perfect shot she instantly refused to take.

Moving her finger off of the trigger, a deeper fear began to settle in, and she knew that somehow, she'd been flanked, and that at any moment, her enemy would swoop in and take her life. Snapping her Rifle back from the branch she'd rested it on, she gazed at the mess of jungle, allowing her senses to give her the best options. There was just one problem, every sign and tell of her circumstance showed there were none.

Pressing her back to the thick tree she'd chosen for cover, she squatted and listened. A twig snapped on her right, a vine popped to her left, and a subtle smell of gun oil mixed carefully with plant oil came from behind. If she charged forward, the guards surrounding the treehouse would shoot her without question. If she stayed, she'd be shot or silently knifed. Left with no option but to try and fight, she placed her Rifle on the soft dirt below, and removed her combat knife.

In front of her, a guard fell - holding his throat. Above her, her target shrieked, then toppled over the rail of the balcony, child still wrapped tightly in her arms. Coincidently, both fell onto the golf cart, crushing her next target, who'd been sitting impatiently, waiting for a guard to come escort him. In what she could only consider comic horror, a family was now destroyed, and she couldn't help but laugh and feel nauseated all at the same time. She would've never killed the child, not in a million years. Yet she didn't feel the sorrow she'd normally feel at the child's departing - for the parents of that child had done too much evil to deserve any form of mercy.

A bullet smashing into her self-made head armor, and another into her equally protected chest, returned her to her abysmal present. The head gear had shattered as it was supposed to, but couldn't handle the impact of another two rounds, and her chest hurt way more than it should've. This was telling her that her breath-flex design had a flaw, allowing the bullet to penetrate more than it should've. Flopping to the ground, in her best 'I'm dead' impersonation, she hoped her attackers would either leave her there to rot, or come to inspect her body carelessly. This was an unnecessary desire - for the guards and staff of her two targets were now becoming the running slaughtered.

Directly over her head, she could hear bullets zipping by in both directions, and the sound of soft screams coming from behind. A few seconds later, she felt a tap on her head, and heard a familiar maniacal giggle.

"Sis?" she blurted, lurching up to see her sister crouching in front of her.

"Un," she heard her sister grunt nonchalantly.

"What are you doing here?" she asked, staring at her sister's camouflage body armor, wondering if that'd been the one she'd not had time to completely dip in her special epoxy resin.

Feeling dizzy from the head shot, she turned and let herself fall back onto the tree.

"I came to save your sorry ass. You're an expensive lil bitch, most of the people that came with me is rotting in the jungle somewhere. They'd picked us off real good...fucking Americans seem to know our jungle better than us. Then this guy and his people came. They didn't speak to us, just killed off those jack asses, moved on, and killed everyone in the house. Oh, and they killed the lil girl. You see?

"Yeah, I saw," she replied, feeling a surge of guilt at the smile she could feel spreading across her lips.

"Ah! You know you want to laugh, lil bitch, don't pretend. Whoever they are, they're our 'kinda' people. Humm, I bet it was that guy who did it...he was cold as ice," she heard her sister reply, looking through the foliage at the mess of broken bodies before looking back at her, shrugging her shoulders.

"Wait...what?" she asked, as a man appeared beside her, causing both she and her sister to jump.

"What da fuck!" she heard her sister exclaim, raising a personalized thirty-eight Millimeter to the man's forehead.

"You two okay?" she heard the man ask in a calm, cool demeanor, with his handsome face truly showing zero concern for her or her sister's well-being.

"I tell you already, stop helping me...stop popping up. I...we can handle ourselves, okay?" she heard her sister say, sounding intrigued yet slightly frightened – the latter being a very foreign thing to her.

"Okay, okay my friends and I are going to be in the..." the sound was deafening, the feeling of pressure, horrendous, and the sight - if she could call it that, was a strange utter darkness.

When her vision finally returned, there was nothing left of the treehouse or the jungle around it, just a perfectly scorched circle of char and ash.

Then… as always, the dream ended with the feeling of arms collecting her, the sight of his handsome face, and the sound of his seductive voice – speaking causally about ending people's lives without any form of remorse.

~ ~ ~ ~ ~ ~ ~ ~ ~ ~ ~

Karman awoke with a gasp, feeling a familiar hand running over her ribcage - along the scar where one of the bullets that now plagued her dreams penetrated her body armor, which of current had been redesigned one hundred and fifty times. Feeling stiff from having been curled up in a tight fetal position, she yawned and stretched, then lay perfectly still on her left side as Nate's hand continued to run along her body.

"Mmmmm Nate, get off me, I'm not a morning person," she grumbled, raising her arm as Nate lifted her right breast, using his index finger to probe the scar running the full length beneath.

"Good morning to you too," she heard Nate say hoarsely, gently cupping her breast, instantly relaxing her.

"You know what? You get a free pass," she muttered, staring at Rayya who lay besides her, twitching and mumbling something inaudible.

"She has nightmares too," she thought reaching out, cupping Rayya's face, laying a peck on her lips.

"Free pass?" she heard Nate chuckle questioningly.

"Yeah, from me kicking your ass," she replied, rolling onto her back, feeling extremely satisfied, groggy, yet sore between the legs.

"I apologize, your hubby warned me to leave you alone. But I couldn't help but notice the scar…scars you have," she heard Nate say, sounding apprehensive.

"De nada Papi…like I said, you get a free pass," she replied with a yawn, taking hold of his hand, moving it to her other breast, which had quickly become wanting for attention.

"I like this free pass," she heard Nate mumble, giving her a mischievous look.

"Umm hum, you should. Oh, and look, I have another scar right here, under my 'smally booby'," she whispered with a dry voice, guiding his fingers to the scar.

"Smally booby'?" she heard Nate reply with a scoff, eyes flicking back to her breast, tracing the scar he was now chasing with his thumb.

"Yeah, 'smally booby'. God started getting sleepy and didn't add enough clay, so I call her my 'smally booby'," she replied nonchalantly, scanning the room for her husband, which to her annoyance, was standing in front of the window.

"Babe, come here," she said, trying to pull the aggravation from her tone as she sat straight up.

"Nope," she heard her husband reply, strolling to the foot of the bed, grinning at her and Nate with a childish expression she couldn't help but giggle at.

"You're an annoying little fuck. Have I ever told you that my love? How annoying you are? How I want to beat the hell out of you?" she said, looking past her husband towards the tripod stand and Rifle Nate had mounted onto it.

"Love you too baby," she heard her husband reply, turning to look at the Rifle then back at her with an, 'I don't know look.'

"I remember now. When Nate had said, 'I can't', I'd thought he'd run out of juice and couldn't fuck me anymore. But then when hubby came behind me, I heard Nate digging into his bag. And by the time I'd started riding hubby, Nate had set that shit up and was staring down the scope. But by then, I'd squirted too much to give a fuck anymore. Hell, I don't even remember passing out," she thought, inhaling deeply for the first time since waking up, realizing the room felt stuffy and smelled of unvented sex, which was actually starting to turn her on.

Looking towards the vent in curiosity, she moved her left hand down to her pussy and pressed, jolting from the sting she felt right after.

"Babyyyy," she grumbled, gently probing the sore spot between her entrance and ass.

"Huh?" she heard her husband reply absently.

"You need to be nice to kitty," she answered, bringing up her hand, inhaling the sharp, musky scent of cum, sweat, and blood – hearing Nate let out a low, amused scoff right after.

"Wa papi?" she asked, letting out a long breath before looking up to Nate who'd begun to chuckle almost soundlessly.

"No, nothing…just…ah, you're funny. Just the way you…the way you did it," she heard Nate choke out, still laughing.

"Na nothing," she replied mockingly, waving her fingers under Nate's nose, causing him to laugh even harder.

"It's normal to smell yourself stupid," she replied, playfully jamming her finger tips into Nate's nostrils when he still made no attempt to move.

"How come you don't blame Nate for kitty huh? Why it's 'gotta' be hubby's fault?" she heard her husband grumble before whispering, "And watching you two, hubby feels left out…replaceable…yup, I'll just go kill myself in the bathroom. Live on without me …go on…be Nate's second wife."

"Baby?" she replied, removing her fingers from Nate's nostrils, scanning the room, wondering what the men weren't telling her.

"Huh? Yes, my love? You want to declare your undying love for hubby?" she heard her husband reply enthusiastically.

"Oh, umm, I need coffee," she replied with her best straight face, which quickly cracked as she began to laugh.

"You fucking suck," she heard her husband mumble, causing her to laugh even harder.

"They don't seem like they've gotten even an ounce of sleep. Have the bikers done something, or are they just being over protective?" she thought, no longer feeling amused, staring at the puffy bags under both men's eyes before saying, "Awww, come here baby, hug me, kiss me, and lay down a bit, you look really tired."

"Nope, you have Nate, you can cuddle with him," she heard her husband retort, turning his head to the left so she couldn't see his face.

Beside her, she could sense Nate growing uncomfortable, and when it dawned on her why, she mumbled, "Huh?" before she could stop herself.

"I don't feel awkward at all. And neither does that idiot. Wow! I had expected to feel…some 'kinda' regret," she thought, gazing at Nate who was trying to mask his anxiousness as he looked between she and her husband.

"Wa-wrong?" she asked, just to hear if her assumption was correct.

"You…he…well I," she heard Nate reply, inching his hand off her breast, moving it to the side of the bed.

"I'm okay. And he's okay …he's just an idiot. I…I thought you knew that," she replied, picking up Nate's hand, kissing it as her husband turned, glaring at her with a dubious look on his face.

"I can hear you. I'm not an idiot. Remember, I'm going to be an Engineer O.G.," she heard her husband mumble, bobbing his head in self affirmation.

Locking eyes with her husband, she smiled sarcastically and dropped Nate's hand on top of her breast.

"Engineer O.G., Yeah, that shit sounds 'Trilllll'," she heard her husband say as a reply, mostly to himself as he yawned and looked towards the air vent and door.

"What are you two clowns hiding? Spill the beans," she thought, watching her husband's jaw ever so slightly clench and release.

"Humm," she purred, pursing her lips, causing her husband to turn and look at her again, this time with an utterly blank look on his face.

"After you taught me all the tricks, don't try to blank look me you bastard," she thought, followed by *"Out of all the things that have caused us to fight and be unhappy, who would've thought that we would be totally at ease after fucking other people in front of each other. Whenever we do something crazy, he says, 'what's done is done, there's no going back.' If he says that about what we've done just now, it'd be the first time I truly believe him. And, what's up with me? I was really into it! It's like all my life I was waiting to be some sex fiend freak…wait…never mind, I was."*

"It's good. I'm glad…but I mean," she heard Nate say in a low voice, snapping her out of her thoughts.

"Brother, we're fine. And if we weren't, well shit man, we already did what we did. We can't run from that, you feel me?" she heard her husband say, causing her to burst out laughing.

"Karman?" she heard Nate ask as she began to snort uncontrollably.

"I…Oh God, I knew he was thinking that. So funny," she choked out, wiping tears from her eyes.

"It's true. I'm not down with the 'woulda coulda shoulda'. When you've done something, it's done. If you regret it, then what. You get nothing from it," she heard her husband say, watching as he crawled up onto the bed between she and Rayya, cupping her chin right after.

"It took me years to see how much you really care. And now that my eyes are open, I wonder how I was so blind to the subtle things you do that always mean so much," she thought, kissing his fingers, mouthing, "thank you baby, my pulse is fine."

"Um-hum," she heard her husband reply, bobbing his head ever so slightly in affirmation before looking towards Rayya who was still mumbling and twitching in the thralls of her dream.

"I can't help but feel a little nervous. I would never want Rayya and I to get in between the two of you. And last night, umm…this all moved really fast. And now," she heard Nate begin when her husband interrupted and said, "Now you're sitting here chilling, groping my wifey like we're them communal married people. Yeah, you're right…hands off, hands off."

"Noooooo, Nate don't listen to him. Baby, baby, stop messing up my fun."

"Huh?" she heard her husband answer absently.

"Don't you huh me. As a matter of fact, massage my other booby. Spoil Princess Karman," she replied, raising her arms.

"She sleeps deep, even in that nightmare," she heard her husband reply, placing his hand on her breast, massaging gently.

"I was thinking the same thing. I wanted to wake her, but…" she began, trailing off to look at Rayya, then to Nate, wondering if she should bring up the fact that she also had bad dreams.

"The psychologist," she heard Nate blurt before trailing of, flushing red for a moment.

"You don't have to tell us…it's none of our business," she replied, thinking, "*I probably need one too after all the shit I've seen and been through. And that dream, I'd really like to know why the fuck I keep having it.*"

"The war, it took a toll on her. It sneaks up on her this way, something's 'kinda' stuck," she heard Nate whisper.

"Stuck?" she heard her husband reply right after.

"Yeah, stuck. The umm, the psychologist told me not to wake her. That the mind has a way of sorting itself out and to let her work through it. But to me, it's nothing like a normal dream. When she has it, things get weird. And it always ends with her…I 'dunno' how to explain. But you'll probably see," she heard Nate say, with his eye's narrowing with a look of pure jealousy, which totally surprised her.

"I'm sorry. If it means anything, I have a reoccurring dreams as well," she replied, shooting her husband a nasty look that he didn't even bother to shy away from.

"It's an issue that wants to be addressed, that's constantly being suppressed. At least that's what the psychologist said," she heard Nate whisper, watching as he stood and strolled over to Rayya's side of the bed.

"I…I'll…!" she heard Rayya gasp.

"Hey, you guys, maybe hop up. This is the part that gets bad," she heard Nate say with a look that caused she and her husband to instantly vacate the bed.

It'd been just in time, for in that very same moment Rayya reached out to the sky as if she were gripping someone's face or neck. Growling, she kicked up with her right knee and rolled where they'd just been and kicked again.

"Ah!" she heard Rayya suddenly gasp, holding her abdomen and lower right thigh as if in pain.

Stilling for a moment, Karman thought Rayya's dream had come to an end, causing her to take a step forward when Nate raised his hand to wait.

"Ilias! I…Ilias!" she heard Rayya gasp, watching tears run from her eyes.

That must be when she was hit with the grenade. I'd mistrusted her words because I didn't see any visible scars. I take back wanting to see her scars, I never thought of the mental ones. I'm sorry sweetie," she thought, watching Rayya shot straight up, eye bursting open with an utterly savage expression on her face, causing all the hairs on the back of her neck to stand up.

Instinctively, she felt herself step in front of her husband and push back, but instead of giving ground, her husband wrapped his arm around her, kissing her temple in reassurance. In that very same moment, she watched the ferocity in Rayya's eyes calm to a cold hard resolve, that quickly melted into a look of pure awkwardness.

"Sorry! I'm so, so, sorry! I…I didn't think I'd have that dream, especially…especially after the night we had. It hasn't come in a long time, and it's rarely comes when…when I've had such a fun time. And shit! Now you two think I'm weird," she heard Rayya say, with her eyes fixed straight ahead.

"We're all weird. You're going to have to get in line if you want first place," she blurted, flopping down beside Rayya, giving her a hug and kiss on the cheek.

"Thank you," she heard Rayya whisper, feeling a kiss on her forehead before hearing Rayya say, "Hey, can you two give hubby and I a second?"

"Yeah sure, of course. Umm, can we leave the room or what?" she asked, first looking to Nate, then to her husband, who wore an almost guilty expression.

"Come 'nakey' boo, shower time," she heard her husband reply after a few silent seconds, where he and Nate just stared at each other.

"Un-huh, don't want me to press about leaving the room," she thought, looking to Nate, unable to read even the slightest emotion on his face.

"Now that's new to me. I've always been able to pick up something, but now this void?" she thought, finally feeling a tinge of insecurity about having slept with Nate creep in as her husband tugged her into the bathroom.

"I hate...I hate your fucking country!" she heard Rayya growl as her husband shut the bathroom door.

"Funny, that sounds like you," she heard her husband snicker in a humorless tone.

"The U.S. and Israel are both invaders. You guys ransacked my country and Nate's ransacked hers, the hate is warranted," she said, feeling a flash of anger as images of the mother and daughter in the treehouse resurfaced.

"The U.S. is made up of immigrants who've flooded in from every nation. That, and the ancestors of the people brought here on fucking slave ships. When you blame the U.S., you're blaming everyone, including Colombians. You should just blame people for being fucked up, not the U.S.," she heard her husband retort.

"You know damn straight the U.S. is run by the rich white male! And don't even dare give me the Latina judge or the Black President speech. I'm not blind to how shit was going down! I'm willing to bet that ninety percent of the shit the former President or that Judge did, that was even remotely good for the common people, was countered and smashed!"

"I disagree."

"Of course you do."

"Well, if they were good people, then you wouldn't even be here. They've allowed you to do whatever the fuck you want, and that's a huge dick in the nice little people's asses. So, I don't even get this conversation. Why the fuck do you even care? All the

278

shit we've done, all the money we make off of every race, religion and nationality. Everyone we know and deal with is fucked up beyond belief, and you're singling out one type of race as the figure heads? You make no sense to me my love."

"Our life could've been different Jay! We could've had good, common people lives, before they ruined it. They made us like this, is what I'm saying! We became fucked up, so we don't get eaten by them," she retorted, having flashbacks of who'd betrayed her, feeling stung that her words were not as valid as she wanted them to be.

"Eaten by the rich white male? Are you fucking kidding me? I knew nothing of race, and neither did you! We're fucked up because the people we trusted were usually always first to strike! Do you remember the shit...the shi..." she heard her husband begin with a low growl.

"I don't want to hear it!" she blurted, knowing exactly what her husband was going to say, since that's exactly what she'd been thinking.

"Never 'wanna' hear facts. But you 'wanna' pop off with your mouth, saying reckless shit. If I use your logic, then remember I told you about that Colombian gang from Flushing, the one who threw one of my boys on the train tracks?"

"Jay, I don't 'wanna'..."

"Yeah, you don't want me to remind you that I had the great joy of watching him smashed right in front of me. So, tell me, should I have called all Colombians drugs lords, gangsters, and invaders of the U.S. after that?

"Shut up!"

"No tell me! Would you like me grouping everyone from your country into that box, then lobby to get them kicked out of the U.S. because of those fools? No, you wouldn't! So, cut the 'my country' bullshit out. Israel is no different. Those so-called invaders get letters in the mail, telling them they better move into the newly acquired land 'or else.' You think they're going to find out what the fuck 'or else' is, or are they just going to move? In the classic game of us or them, almost all people are going to choose the 'us' over 'them,' and that includes ourselves."

"Sometimes can't you just be sensitive? Why can't you just say you understand? Sometimes, sometimes a wife just wants to be agreed with. Why can't you ever give ground?" she asked, turning to face her husband who now sat upon the toilet like a lazy king.

"Sometimes a guy just wants to be understood, you know that? I feel underappreciated and undervalued by society. Living a life of assumptions and double standards, with no clear-cut description of what the fuck a real man is supposed to be. Old school men say they're in charge of society, playing the part to the point of being chauvinistic assholes.

"New school guys! Shit! Don't get me started. Almost every 'youngen' I meet has no fucking spine to deal with other men, women or anything else. They're all just living with their tail between their legs, and every time the wind blows with societies' new opinion of what a man's role should be, they lay down on their back like a good lil boy."

"Papi, shut it!"

"No, it's true! One day, I want to bringing leashes, dog treats and a bunch of flash cards to the mall, and whenever I want our men of the future to do something, I'll just lift up a flash card, which will start with, 'They say' on it, so they'll know exactly where the instructions are coming from."

"You go from wanting to be understood, to wanting to become part of the problem…with stupid fucking flashcards. You say I don't make sense? Look at you! Explain your logic."

"I'm not hard to understand at all! I'm bitter, and I want to prove my point. That'd be the perfect way to do it!" she heard her husband reply flippantly.

"Stop talking about you. Focus on me! Focus on what wifey wants!"

"I know what you want. You want me to say, 'yes mam, I understand', when I don't, and then five minutes later, you're going to tell me to step up, be a man, grow a pair, and be the alpha male that knows what he wants. How many times have I come to you with my insecurities and you've given me that speech about being a man that's supposed to be sure of himself and his opinions? For once, I want to know where I stand.

"Do you want me to be the strong man that puts up with no one trying to change his mind, and has no insecurities? Or, do you want me to be gullible and swayed, where I should just agree with you to make you feel better? Tell me clearly, which one you want, the autumn leaf or a diamond that can't be cut? Hell, as a matter of fact, if you want me to lay on my back every time you're feeling sensitive, I'm fine with that, as long as you don't tell me to man up right after," she heard her husband say, pissing her off even more.

"Why can't he just understand we want both? What's so hard about it?" she thought, wanting to smack the shit out of him.

"Figures, you always get quite as fuck when I ask you what you want, because when you hear it out loud, you know it makes no fucking sense," she heard her husband mumble, changing her urge from wanting strike to strangle.

"Oh, shut the fuck up? You always pick fights. You always want me to explain myself. Why do you always find a way to bring up this stupid argument?" she snarled, looking for an opening to land a blow, having tried many times and failed unless he let her.

"You always say I should give ground, then tell me to man up in the same breath. One day I want you to either decide to keep my balls on, or give them back," she heard her husband reply, looking towards the tub, squinting as if he'd just realized something.

"Aww! He still considers his balls mine! He's so cute!" she thought, following his eyes to the faucet, wondering what he was thinking.

"Annoying bastard, you always know just what to say to keep me from trying to kill you," she blurted, kneeling in front of him.

"Huh?" she heard him reply, squeezing her cheeks as he leaned forward, kissing her on the forehead.

"Me having your balls," she replied.

"What?"

"I love you baby. I promise I'll try to take better care of your balls," she whispered as she softly rested her hand on top of his crotch.

"Oh, that. I see, not giving them back huh?" she heard her husband snicker.

"Not ever...they're mine," she replied, chuckling, before saying, "Okay spill it, the bikers, they cut the power huh? Why y'all acting funny about leaving the room, like we're trapped or something. I can obviously see you and Nate are on high alert, with your puffy ass eyes."

"Trapped in the room, 'na', nothing like that. And the power…umm, this might sound weird, but according to the news, there've been rolling blackouts all over the world, and no one knows exactly why. But since the blackouts began, the bikers have been acting a lil strange. But it's been super subtle, even for me it's hard to pinpoint what's up," she heard her husband reply.

"Worldwide rolling blackouts? This only comes on the news as worldwide because it's probably the U.S., U.K. and France. In a lot of countries, blackouts are common, but poor first world countries, God forbid their power systems act a little weird, then it's a global phenomenon. Watch, 'I'ma' turn on the news and find out that they've allied to wage war against blackouts, fucking dumb asses. I'll see them sending armed troops to power grids in - let's see, Iraq, Afghanistan, Somalia. And where is France stealing the Uranium from? That African country, what's its name? Mali was it? Yeah Mali!"

"Shut upppp," she heard her husband groan.

"Why you so sensitive? Can't take a joke hubby?"

"That was a joke? Your jokes suck balls."

"My jokes are amazing. Anyways, too subtle for you means you're not focusing. One reason is because you're exhausted, and the other is because you're too focused on getting eye for an eye," she replied, inwardly cringing at having to take a cold shower.

"Probably."

"Hubby?"

"Um, yeah I want eye for an eye! She tried to kill you! In my opinion, for no fucking reason. Her doing that after just a few seconds of meeting us, is pretty extreme, no? When I picture her face, it makes my blood boil," she heard her husband whisper, feeling his arms wrap around her waist.

"Baby, in our life, we've seen a lot of people kill for fun, and for no fuckin reason. How does she surprise you? She didn't do it in a way that'd draw attention to her, so maybe she said fuck it, why not. You know some people love knowing that they have the power to take your life," she replied, looking down as her husband began to lay kisses on her belly.

"Indeed, indeed I do," she heard her husband reply, looking up at her with an expression that set her nerves alight, for it'd been the very same one that had drawn her to search for him after their first meeting.

Seeing it now, she gritted her teeth and smiled, then broke free off his grasp, feeling the urge to strangle him return twice as strong as it'd been before.

"What else is going down? What happened while I was sleeping? Whenever something's going down and you don't want to explain, you get this annoying look on your face. It always makes me feel like I'm a child."

"Lotta' stuff. I'm not trying to keep stuff from you. I'm just tired. What, you want me to just start blurting all kinds of information?

"Yes," she replied sarcastically.

"Listen you annoying princess you."

"No, tell me. 'Lotta' stuff like?" she pressed.

"Remember the Lil Corp. drones that used to swarm Bellevue and Seattle twice a week?"

"Of fucking course! Why, what about them?" she sniped, feeling tense.

"Caught Nate chucking them out the window, he was going to use them to spy on the biker chicks."

"Ain't that something. Those pieces of shit made our lives a living hell till we figured out how to give them the slip. And what we're doing is still shitty, I don't like going into those submarines like you. I get cluster phobic!"

"Don't remind me my 'panicky', 'pukey' Eggy head."

"Water on all sides. Freezing cold water! Fucking right I'm panicking. As a matter of fact, when we need to use the subs again, you're doing my meetings for me! That last time, I swear I saw something come look at us."

"Hell Na! Your peps are weird. And I told you, it was an Orca. They like me. They come to me. Actually, they come to me and some of my closest peeps. We're like Orca whisperers."

"Chicken, you're scared of my people, aren't you? And shut the hell up… Orca whisperers, dumb ass. Look, that was no Orca. It was big and scary. Orcas' are cute."

"Scared of your peps? No. Creeped out, yes. And what the hell kind of Orcas' have you been looking at? Their name is killer whale for a reason my love."

"Whatever, I know when I see a cute, cuddly killer whale, and a creepy something or another. But fine, don't believe me…one day it's 'gonna' come eat us. And your people are creepy too. Do I ever say anything?"

"Yes! All the time!"

"Anyways, what happened after you caught Nate? Did you confront him, or just leave it? He did say he's a gadget tester, fucker is probably one of the people using the drones to spy on the cities all along."

"True, he might very well be an operator, or he might not know what his companies' up to. Hard to say," she heard her husband retort nonchalantly – getting on her nerves.

"True…. That's true I guess. So, like I asked before, what did you do? Did you confront him, or not?"

"Well, long story short, he ended up showing me how to use them," she heard her husband reply with an odd smirk on his face.

"Bullshit!" she snorted, feeling like he might be pranking her.

"Na, for real, he really did train me how to use them."

"Humm, then sure, I believe you. Makes sense actually, he must've needed your help with security. I couldn't take you seriously at first because you're making your suspicious, stupid ass face."

"I always wear the face of a Genius. And yup, yup he needed my help indeed. And guess what."

"What?"

"Humm, well there's a few things. One is that I spent an epic shit ton of time trying to get the drones away from our God damn car," she heard her husband reply sourly.

"Why? All the time we spent making the AI for the car, why would you try to baby the thing? I would've thought you'd want them as close as possible, so it could get better data."

"Just wanted to have a little bit more room for error, but Nate being the caring guy he is, sent a group to fly a nice little pattern over it to make sure no one messed with it."

"Wait…suddenly, you don't sound so upset. Why you playing with my emotions over here? You wanted the drones near the car or not?" she replied, getting the feeling her husband was inwardly gloating.

"I have mixed feelings."

"My ass!"

"It's true! I have mixed feelings! On the one hand, I'm proud to say our AI's counter measures did very well. It even released our own drones."

"That's good! How'd they do?"

"They did good too. Nate wasn't a happy camper. The car and our drones were giving him hell. False signals, the whole works," she heard her husband reply, now sounding deflated.

"So? Now you're in the glum mood again, what the hell 'kinda' on the fence is this?"

"It just that…."

"It's just that what? Everything you're telling me is good news," she replied, trying to guess what could be troubling her husband.

"Nate's being edgy, didn't make me feel good, well of course at first it did but…"

"We would get edgy too if we were him. Wait, fuck that, we're edgy because of those drones! I don't feel guilty at all, especially since he might've been one of the fucking pilots, snooping all over the place."

"Well, the thing is, I'm edgy now too. Something else is going down with him and I…I 'kinda' feel bad for him but don't even know why. It's just this sad feeling in the bottom of my stomach."

"Damn it, I wish I could say I couldn't take them seriously, but I've been with you long enough to know better. So, any clue to what this something else would be?"

"Dunno'. It's just…I 'dunno'."

"Yes, you do. When was this feeling the strongest?"

"It was when his drones had an errant reading from one of the rooms we were scanning. He was saying that it made him nervous if the bikers had tech to match his own. To me, that was a really odd statement."

"How's that odd? It would be bad. His shit's supposed to be top of the line. If somehow the bikers had something to beat it, they most likely can beat us! Humm, so what was the error? Was it them or was it because of us?"

"Well, at first I know it was ours. I'd hacked into the earbud and contact lenses he had me wear to control the drones. I didn't want him seeing and hearing everything I was doing. Shit was crazy hard to pull off. I had to take all the updates that were going to my View-Tech's directly into my head so he couldn't see what I was seeing, then reply and send mental commands in coherent enough thoughts for our AI to understand so that'd everything would go smooth."

"Wait, what? I told you not to do that! What did I tell you about getting so much data pushed in your head like that!?"

"I had no fucking choice! What would you have me do? I know damn straight the contacts and earbud are not just one way! I know he'd be able to see anything I look at on my phone or View-Techs. Are you dumb? You want him record what the fuck I'm doing as I hack him? Huh, really now Eggy?"

"Damn it! No! Fine! Just be careful. And are you're still wearing them now?!"

"Yes."

"Are you fucking dumb!? He can counter hack at any time, and be listening and seeing right now!"

"Risk we have to take. I need them in to maintain the hack to be honest. Damned if I do, damned if I don't situation right now. Plus, it's good to have his shit in as a second pair of eyes. And in any case, he partially turned them off on my end. You know the thing you're worried about, data pushed into your head. That's exactly how they work. Shit makes you super sick and dizzy. He said he didn't want me burned out since it was my first time, so he lessened the connection. So, yeah, in this situation, it's 'kinda' swimming deep in a sea of fucked up."

"Of course, of course just like that, we're twisted up. Fuck my life. You know what, I'll just leave it alone."

"You have your tough gal hat on, right?"

286

"Is there a way you can use your creepy 'third eye sense' to get us 'outta' this mess without a conflict?"

"I could completely cut everything. But we'd be blind to their world after just getting access. I'd rather piss them off, being busted by him, then caught off guard by something I could've potentially saw coming."

"Fuck..., so then back to this sad feeling you had about Nate, I need you to figure it out because..." she began, not wanting to finish her statement.

"Cuz' normally you think I'm a lizard in the Antarctic and don't give a fuck about people. So, you want to know the core of my empathy towards Nate, right?"

"Uh, I love you hubby," she replied, feeling awkward.

"Yup... anyways, let's explore these feelings deeper, just for wifey," she heard her husband reply sarcastically.

"Make me sound so cruel," she replied, feeling guilty, even though she knew he was right.

"You're not cruel boo. Okay, umm, so my stomach sank for the dude almost right after I hacked his shit. But the thing is, there was this weird pulse."

"Right, I was going to ask you what you had meant by - at first it was ours that'd interfered with his stuff, but you just answered my question," she replied, smiling at her husband's 'can you shut up look.'

"Do I still have the floor?" she heard her husband ask, just to rub it in.

"If you don't start talking..."

"Okay, so like a few minutes after I hacked into his drone feed, this pulse came and made our drones and his act all fucked up. It was right when we were looking at one of the rooms. Then when Nate said - I'm worried, about the bikers having more tech bla bla ...I felt more like he was saying goodbye."

"The way they're behaving; God only knows what those chicks are up too. So Papi, what was the pulse? Was it an EMP, was it traceable? Let's figure out what we're dealing with huh?"

"No shit I want to figure out what we're dealing with, and jump to conclusions much? Who said it was them? And EMP, 'na', I don't think so. It wasn't very EMP like, it was very controlled, very concentrated. In my expert opinion, an EMP

would've affected a lot of electrical systems at once. If it was…
then that's one 'hella' of an EMP. I'd love to know how it
worked."

"Humm, I see. So, the pulse didn't touch our car?" she
replied.

"Not that I'm aware of," she heard her husband reply in a
sour tone.

"Baby?"

"Sorry, just annoyed. That pulse is like a giant, square
dildo; my ass is hurting. I've spent all morning groping for
details, and I can't find shit."

"You'll find something hubby, don't worry."

"Thank you, and sorry for snapping at you about assuming
it was them by the way. I just don't want to get in the mindset of
jumping conclusions."

"I know, I love you hubby. Speaking of jumping
conclusion, cough cough…, I know you're busy, but any clue as
to what the bikers would potentially be moving? Since I know
we both agree that they're moving something, yes?" she asked,
having a flashback of the woman she'd seen in the gas station.

"Fuckin defensive asshole, always has to prove her points.
And nope, nothing. I scanned for everything, and nothing came
up, no weird chemicals, no gunpowder, no nothing. AKA - too
fucking clean. I didn't even pick up traces of THC," she heard
her husband say.

"You only looked for THC? Tell me you looked for more
than that, a lot of them look like they used to be, or are still
strung out on heroin and meth," she whispered.

"Ass, 'gotta' sound like the boss, just cause. And yup, no
traces of any drugs whatsoever. Weird huh?" she heard her
husband ask rhetorically.

"Yeah, umm papi? You see any of them tipsy? Or like did
the drones pick up any with alcohol on their breath?" she asked,
getting a sinking feeling, anticipating his answer.

"Like I said, perfectly clean. Why, what are you thinking?"
she heard her husband reply quickly.

"That they're oh so serious to be this obedient. I don't
think a lot of these chicas know what they're moving or the
quantity. They're just being good little soldiers. They're alert, not

under the influence -perfectly minding their manners," she said, shaking her head before whispering, "this is getting annoying on many levels."

"Humm, I 'dunno' what to say to that. And to help you on your jumped conclusion that maybe it was the bikers who did the pulse thingy…a few minutes after it happened, this Asian lady rolled up into the parking lot and met the bitch who tried to ninja off you," she heard her husband say cautiously.

"And of course…you couldn't see her clearly with the drones could you?" she asked, feeling her back tense.

"Yup, almost pure fuzz. I only saw her for like a second, and that was not a good second. I could tell easily that she's a really big fucking problem right off the bat."

"Humm."

"Humm is right. She reminds me of me and my peps. She knew she was being watched, I saw her blurry face look right at the drones," she heard her husband say, sounding surprised at his own conclusion.

"Seriously? Lord Jesus, that does sound like you and your creeps. And the lady I saw at the Gas station reminded me of my own," she responded thinking, *"I need to talk to my sister ASAP."*

"It should be no way, no way in hell, but, she looked right at the drones," she heard her husband reply more to himself, now sounding aggravated.

"Look hubby, your people are not the only ones who can do the weird feely, feely thing, you know that right? I would've been dead long ago if I couldn't read people, si or no?"

"Si, but I'm teaching the real way of the read you jackass. Also, and listen, this is very important."

"I'm listening papi."

"You're my wife. Therefore, you're actually more my peps than my peps. I hate, hate, hate when you call them my peps, like you're not a part of me. Every time you say that, I think to myself- what are you talking about?"

"Okay, okay. I get it, you done papi?"

"Well the other thing is that you're actually a 'hella' slow learner, so if you weren't my wife, I would've disowned 'ya'," she heard her husband say, with a dark chuckle right after.

"I'm not a slow learner! Anyways, wouldn't this woman have to tell you she's here. Your, I mean our people have those protocols and stuff. I thought that's how it works. Oh, and hey Nate's versus ours. I mean for now you seem confident, so I take it we did, okay?"

"I'd say his drones are build for build on par with ours. The operating system behind them is way past ours. The hacks are being crushed or holding on by threads, he'll probably catch us my love, we're just going to deal with it," she heard her husband say, pausing before whispering, "And yes, my people's protocol is to always tell each other where we're at, at all times, no exceptions. So, I 'dunno', I really don't know who she was, but she definitely seemed like she was a part of my organization. But like, you know how we have different divisions?"

"Twenty-one in all right?" she asked remembering when he'd drawn out the rank structure for her.

"Yup, twenty-one. So, if she's one of my people, she's definitely not from any of the local divisions. Definitely a different feeling," she heard her husband say underneath his breath.

"Almost all of your people give me the same damn feeling. God awful!" she thought, shuddering, as she whispered, "I'll let you figure her out."

"Sure, boo. No stress."

"I'm stressed."

"Humm, I have something shinny for your mind to chew on! Distract wifey for a sec time!"

"Whatttt," she mumbled.

"Remember that stuff Nate was running along the door and window seals?"

"Kinda, but I was more interested in him not doing that to be honest," she replied, remembering how bad she'd wanted Nate to pay full attention to her in those beginning moments.

"Well,' I think you'd love to get your hands on it. It's some 'kinda' adhesive tape that keeps drones and sound from slipping through the cracks. While you two were sleeping, he whipped out a vapor form of it and let it seep into all the vents."

"He blocked the vent huh? I see, so the room probably smelled like pussy and sex way before the power cut," she replied with a chuckle.

"It's supposed to let regular air in still, but I don't think it works the way it's supposed to 'cuz' yeah, it was getting stuffy in here no lie. Humm, it was like how we used to trap ourselves in cargo containers when we first started dating... 'member baby?"

"Yeah, I remember," she replied, smiling before a flashback of her dream destroyed her nostalgias.

"Hubby, speaking of when we first started dating," she mumbled apprehensively.

"Oh 'It'! I know where this is going. And you say I always bring up the same shit," she heard her husband reply, with a heavy sigh.

"Jay, it's been eight years. I really want to know everything, not just snips and pieces."

"Oh 'It', why can't you ever just drop it. Huh wifey, why?"

"I had that fucking dream! It was way too much this time! This time it was too clear. I could literally smell the jungle Jay! This time I remembered much more than before. And then, like always - at the end... I saw you carrying me. How'd that blast not hurt you? Literally everyone else had some 'kinda' injury! Burns, scratches, something, they all had something! You were the only fucking one that was just fine!"

"Look baby, it's all good. Just drop it please, for the love of the 'It' person above."

"God is not an 'It!' And don't 'look baby' me! What where you really doing in Chia? When people come to my country, they go to Bogota. Maybe some make it to Chia, but then they just do tourist shit. They're not out in the jungle like you and your people. Everyone knows to stay the fuck out of the jungles."

"Pst, the jungles is 'where it's at'! They're missing out on all the fun!"

"Unh-uh, and ever since that truce my sis and I made with your people, they've been expanding. Inch by tiny fucking inch they've been expanding. The port is all we'd agreed on, now they have a building in Chia, the port and a building in Chia are not the same thing! And don't give me that we're working on your thesis shit? I think y'all were looking for good land to grow drugs

291

or something. That's all I can think of because y'all couldn't wait to get back to Chia! My sister and I watched every move your people made to get a foothold in the city," she said, feeling her blood boil then slightly cool, hearing hushed arguments, reaffirming that Nate and Rayya were too pre-occupied to listen to them.

"I told you, we weren't scouting for territory to set up any footholds. We're only there for school work. And my people expanding into Chia is not a move of disrespect. It's, umm, how to say this? It's a way of saying we trust and respect y'all and want to be closer. Our movements are endearing."

"Endearing, really?" she snipped, oddly understanding the logic, but not wanting to give ground.

"Yes, it is. More so because, we know you and your sis have noticed everything we've done has strictly been in support of anything y'all do. Support of others is not our style and you know it. When we want something, we fuckin take it and leave all in our way dead or too fucked to argue. So, if my peps acted like they normally do, y'all wouldn't have watched them move inch by inch because there would've been a blood and ash bath till neither side was left standing. Am I right?" she heard her husband respond, sounding amused about the topic for the first time since they'd been a couple.

"That's beside the point! It's not funny, I don't like you keeping shit from me. And did you…the lil girl, did you?"

"Besides the point, is it now? You accuse, then bullshit out of it. And here we goooo! Another stupid ass argument on its way. Lord 'It'…can you tell her I don't 'wanna' fight?! Pleaseeee."

"You don't 'wanna' fight, I'll give you a very straight forward option! Jay, did you kill that lil girl?

"Fuck my life."

"Just fucking tell me! Listen, I met the people you were with, they don't look like the type to do that kind of shit," she whispered, feeling her anger and frustration growing out of control.

"Always, this is always what it's really about. You always bring this up to try and force a confession out of me about that child. And you always say they're not the type! Fuck's that

292

supposed to mean? You're literally accusing me of being a child killer! And when you say you met them? Need I remind you that you and your fucked-up sister kidnaped us one by one!" she heard her husband respond icily.

"You...you know what I mean when I say they're not the type. Don't play. Don't play with my heart. I know you, and I know how you get when you're pissed. Don't act, just don't fucking act like I can un-see some of the shit you've done. The people you were with, my sister and I both know they don't got it in them to kill that child. But you, you do," she said, feeling angry tears begin to escape her eyes.

"What!? Anything supposedly cruel you've ever seen me do was to save your ass. Or to save us! And you swing that shit on me!? Like I'm some kind of fucking demon monster!?" she heard her husband growl back.

"Fuck all that! Demon, monster...stop putting words in my mouth! I never called you those things, so stop fucking saying it. I wouldn't ever marry a monster. This, this is just about being honest! Just be honest and afterwards I won't give a fuck! As a matter of fact, even if you were a demon monster, you'd be my demon monster, and I'd still have your lil demon balls tightly held in my hands," she whispered, trying to break the tension.

"Fuck off," she heard her husband reply, shaking his head, giving her a slightly amused look.

"Look baby. You heard what Nate said. The dream is surfacing because I have things in my mind that haven't been addressed. Don't I deserve to know everything? For fuck sakes...we just had a fucking orgy. You trust me to fuck them. I trust you too. And we're okay with that! Can't we be okay with how it all began? Can't I know!? I mean, I said thank you for saving my life right!? And the lil girl... I just want to know if you did it or not, it'd give me peace of mind."

"Da fuck you talking about? You never said thank you! And she's dead as hell, a long time ago, what peace of mind? Why you care about her? How do you have the capacity to care about her after the shit those people put you through? If they can even be considered people, those are true demons. I 'dunno' why you even bring life to their memory. I feel like you like being tortured by them."

"Fuck you! Don't you dare say I want that from them!"

"Sorry...sorry, sorry. I, I didn't...shit, that's not how it's supposed to sound."

"Better say sorry! Oh, and I did say thank you! And the lil girl, she wasn't old enough to be...to be!" she began, not knowing what to say after, knowing she had no idea if the little girl was being preened to become as evil as her parents.

"Un huh! Cat got your tongue. I wonder why? And no way! How's thank you mean hunting me down and kidnaping me? And the worst part! You fucking left me alone with your crazy sister. That for fucking certain is not a thank you."

"We were playing god cop bad cop!"

"Yeah, well she's crazy, fucked up cop and you knew that! So that's no thank you!"

"But I fucked your brains out when you were tied to the chair, doesn't that make up for everything," she replied, smiling at the memory.

"I took that as half an apology for leaving me alone with your insane sister! And umm, how does fucking Nate and Rayya have shit to do with this!? Earlier how'd you even thread that together? It bothers me, seriously it frustrates me how you do that."

"I 'dunno'...Cuz..."

"Women, I swear y'all can thread anything together to win an argument!"

"I threaded them together because they're related. Hey, stop generalizing you ass! In this case, I'm talking about trust. So there, the two merge together," she said bobbing her head, wondering why he couldn't follow her logic.

"What the fuck!? Not the same at all! And fine! Sex maybe was your way of saying thank you. But I still choose to say you were apologizing for leaving me with your sister. She's really fucked up! Really, really fucked up! And by the way, 'thank you', and 'apologies', none of them begin with kidnapping and interrogations! How the fuck are you omitting the whole rest of the story of how we started dating!? I saved you, then you and your sister proceeded to hunt me and my peps down like animals!

Who does that?" she heard her husband say, shooting up from the toilet, turning on the facet for the tub.

"Umm, you and your peps magically appear, save our asses, then vanish. A day later, your fearless leader shows up all bitchy, demanding we work together, 'plusss' give her a port of operation! You fuckin right we hunt y'all down! And you were so sexy, how could I resist jumping you? I still remember you begging me to slow down."

"I needed to catch my breath, and not cum in some crazy lady. Plus, there's a certain song that played during our youth that I hate being associated with. I could hear it playing over and over in my head. Didn't want you putting me to shame. I mean what's there to like about a guy who nuts too fast? How can you even enjoy it?"

"Well, I didn't think your less than a minute was too fast, I came because you came."

"Shit was…it still is…yeah…years later…still speechless on that one."

"Hehe, yes! I was your first squitter. I can never forget your expression. It was the best!"

"It was from the crazy mess! And I was thinking what if I get my kidnaper pregnant. I was thinking you're trying to Stockholm syndrome my ass! Fucking nut."

"Oh, I'm nuts, Huh!?"

"Yup!"

"But you had fun."

"Fuck off. Fun? You told me if I held myself, you'd cut my throat," she heard him reply, watching as he tested the water.

"I did not!"

"You had a knife, actually my own knife to my throat!"

"Oh yeahhhhh! I did, didn't I? But baby, you know I was playing kinky. Come on, I wasn't that bad. I had to be tough on you…I was still doing the interrogation," she replied with a dark snicker, remembering the thrill of fucking him for the first time, not know anything about him, what would come of it, and the danger that if she'd misjudged his character, he still might've wanted to kill her.

"Un-huh. Hey boo, it's still hot, hop in, hop in before it gets cold," she heard her husband say, guiding her to step into the tub.

"Why you complaining for? Why'd you fall in love with me? And honestly what did my sister do to you that would make you so freaked out since you know 'I'ma nutzo' too?"

"I know right…why do I love you? Hum?"

"Ass, you always dodge when I ask," she asked, seriously never understanding what her sister did or why he hated her so much.

"Ask her. And my answer is, I love you because you're my special Eggy head. Now let's stay happy like this alright?" she heard her husband ask, striping down, hopping in the shower behind her.

"Besides the lil girl, you do know why I keep asking you about that day right?"

"I said let's stay happy. Fuck, okay… why baby? Why do you keep asking?"

"You change small parts of your story every time. You said there were two ladies on your team, and we never found them, and you never talk about them. That's super suspicious hubby."

"I don't bring it up because it's bad memories, and you like to fucking make me relive it."

"Just tell me and I'll stop!"

"They were killed by your buddies in the treehouse. Happy now?" she heard her husband say, sounding like he was gritting his teeth as he pulled her closer.

"So, you were there to rescue them? Why you keep talking about school stuff, when clearly that wasn't the reason y'all were there!?"

"You're fucking annoying! Leave it the fuck alone!" she heard her husband growl.

"Explain damn it!"

"They were dead…Dead long before we got there. Happy now?"

"So y'all were there for vengeance, not school?"

"School! School then vengeance!"

"I need more! What the fuck happened!?"

"Leave it alone. Shit frustrates me. I feel like it's my fault."

"What's your fault!? Being in the jungle's? Not being mean, but your excuse of looking for materials for electro magnetism…y'all could've went to a museum," she replied, shaking her head in annoyance.

"You know, I've kind of told you the whole story already, but you literally always tune me out. You seriously have a listening problem, and then blame me for not explaining things clearly."

"I know, I know, I'm getting better though. Over the years right? And I'm listening now," she replied, recalling all the times she'd cut him off as he was explaining before saying, "You know what…it's 'cause' you never get to the point."

"And then you do that. Always have to defend yourself for not listening," she heard her husband snip.

"Baby, it's true, if you know wifey is a scatter brain, tell wifey everything in a way that she can listen and understand right?"

"How? Everything ties into each other. If you don't hear everything, it really won't make sense, then you'll have to keep asking me."

"Okay, okay! Calm down…okay try to tell me. I'm listening."

"The ancients of your country."

"Oh God not this part! This is why I get lost! Utter nonsense! Ancient!?" she muttered, feeling one of her husband conspiracy history lesson about to begin.

"Never fucking mind! Jesus Christ and his parent 'It!' This is why, years later, you're blaming me for not telling you!" she heard her husband whisper.

"Fuck! Okay sorry, I caught myself! And stop calling God, 'It!' You know that shit makes me angry! Stop it!" she muttered, wondering where his anger towards God had come from, and when she'd begun to have zero patience to listen to him.

"Why be angry? 'Its' not angry I call it, 'IT.' It's an eternal being of benevolence and malevolence rolled into one. I am but a molecule, making up a speck of micro dust to the all mighty 'IT,'" she heard her husband reply sarcastically, causing her to want to laugh and strangle him at the same time.

"I'll kill you, now continue on," she finally had the strength to say after calming both reactions down.

"Fine, fine. Okay, so the civilization of Musica. They made something, like a kind of computer or something. We were looking for it."

"You said Materials! For years, you said you were looking for a type of electromagnetic material. Now you're saying computer! Oh my fucking God! See! See what I mean! How'd you go from material to computer!?"

"Well the computer thingy is made out of a material or a group of materials that are very unique. It's hard to explain! It'd be like cavemen discovering our cell phones, with case included. Maybe they'd know that the screen is glass or crystal, but then what kind of glass or crystal. And then, they'd have no idea what the case was. They'd not even have the slightest idea how to define plastic, it'd be truly alien till they spent time figuring it out. 'Kinda' same difference, except we're the cavemen in this case. I know what I'm looking for, but not really how to classify it. I've only dealt with it once, and it was too brief, and…the rest ties into how, how I was telling you, I was 'kinda' an orphan in my organization for so long."

"You just said, they sent you away," she responded.

"Yeah, I think it's the curse of the thingy."

"Look, sorry… I know from the little you've told me; it was a hard time for you. Lord, I have a headache just hearing this though."

"Why?"

"It's just, do you know how backwards you sound right now? The cavemen were in the past. We're in the futureee…say it with me, futureee. Cavemen past. Us now. Cavemen, no computer. Us…we have computerss. God! Maybe I should stop asking you. For once, I think you're right, I should just leave it. Asking you always drives me insane!"

"Annoying lil Eggy! What do you think blew up everything? You ever see an explosion like that before or after that?"

"Uh, I told you, any skilled explosive technician can do something like that!" she responded.

"Fuck that! When does an explosion do what we saw?"

"But the explanation is easy, it was probably booby trapped with some kind of precision explosives," she replied, tilting her head, loving the way his finger felt as he massaged the shampoo he'd just put in her hair.

"Oh, it was a booby trap alright. But you saw it, there was nothing normal about it."

"Baby, people can make all kinds of bombs. I have made crazy explosives too," she retorted, having tried and failed to replicate the explosion hundreds of times – never even coming close to what she'd saw.

"You cocky little...you never listen. Never open your mind, then you get mad that I don't tell you things. And tell me...how close did you come to replicating the explosion Ms. Material scientist?"

"Well, I got it to make a circle."

"You ass, seriously. As smart as you are, you can't do it. And remember what happened right after. Like just hours after? Can you do that part?"

"UMM, it might be possible," she replied, not wanting to give ground even though she could think of nothing that'd make what they'd witnessed plausible.

"Really in twenty-four hours, budding seedlings pop up, and you're okay with that?"

"Maybe...I, 'dunno', just..."

"Then in four days, the damn jungle was almost grown completely back? Full trees and all!? How!? Tell me how!" she heard her husband whisper, sounding like he was at the end of his patience.

Hearing his words, she tried with all her heart to consider what he was saying, but felt one road block after another.

"Look, I just don't believe in advanced civilizations! Do I believe there were people like us, with the inherent knowledge to make things a lil bit ahead of their time, sure. But I can't wrap my mind on its current relevance."

"Try!" she heard husband whisper.

"How? Why would I think of ancient technology and not modern? Isn't it more logical to think it's the work of scientist trying to make their mark in the world by creating something that destroyed and rebuilt in the same breath. So, yeah. I'd just say they have some crazy skills. If you told me you were looking for a computer or some material a scientist from our time frame created, I'd actually believe you. I really just can't swallow the ancient tech nonsense. Remember cavemen past. Us, future."

"Our time frame? Look at the shit we have compared to the shit they've built! Their shit's still standing thousands of years later. Our shit starts to crumble in five years. Current human idiocy should be the only tough pill to swallow."

"They used giant rocks, rocks tend to do that thing they're known to do... you know... stay around 'cause' they're gee, I 'dunno' giant rocks," she replied, with a chuckle.

"Those rocks were cut, moved, shaped and positioned! They used power tools for that! They must've had cranes, hydraulic saws! And computers to do the stress layout and geological computations! The technology to make those rock cities that perfect and last that long must be way past ours!"

"I'm going to go with nope. They did math on paper or something yes. Tools, I 'dunno' what it was but not super advanced, but good enough to do the job. And nope, not going to let you tell me they were walking around with laptops thingy's...oh my God I said 'thingy's.' Damn it. Stop saying thingy's, you're infecting me!"

"Thingy's, thingy's, thingy's! And yes computers, there wouldn't have been enough papers in the world to do all the mappings and stress calculations for cities that size! How else would they know how to keep those giant rocks from getting tons of stress fractures? They've withstood earthquakes and everything else for thousands of years! That means those giant rocks that weigh tons are all positioned in a way that makes them flexible when the earth moves. I'm sorry wifey, they weren't scribbling out those calculations in sand, paper, or anything else! How can you doubt they didn't use computers? You lived there and saw stuff, the ruins! Tell me those ruins didn't scream advanced as fuck civilization!"

"But to me, it's not enough to prove they were equally as advanced, or more than us as you say. My reasoning, how about the castles and stuff all over the world, they're made of giant rock and stuff, and they didn't have computers, I don't care what you say. Those calculations were done on paper. If the English,

French, Spanish, Russians, or whoever had computers back then, we'd be living in a different world. So, see hubby, hard to believe."

"I…those castles…they're not like what was found in Musica at all…I just don't know what else to say to you. The sad part is that it has a lot to do with material science. Sometimes I think you don't want to think it's real because it threatens you."

"What are you talking about?" she replied snappily, knowing what he was saying was mostly true.

"You hate being influenced by others! You always say people piggy back off of each other too much! You always want to dig and dig about facts, but don't want to actually see facts because those facts rely on other's research and knowledge. You close out anything that can bruise your goddamn ego! You want to make any advancements on your own!" she heard her husband reply as he turned her around, dipping her head into the warm stream of water.

After massaging the soap from her hair, she felt his hands guide her forward.

"I love you," she whispered, opening her eyes to a tight lipid apprehensive smile.

"Love you too," she heard her husband whisper.

"I…I want to believe your story hubby. It's just this one is hard for me. On top of that…you tell a lot of half-truths. Then you make it more painful to know what's going on because you always give me a task to preform before you think I should know the full truth. It gets annoying, and I don't like having that dream because as much as I love you, I feel like it's trying to warn me about something," she said, stopping short before she said – 'about you,' because it truly wasn't directly about him.

"About me, you're going to say."

"Uhh, not about you, about your organization."

"Liar."

"You're calling me a liar because that's how close you are to your people! So as soon as I say I'm even a little skeptical about them, you take it straight to heart!"

"Umm, of course I do, they're my family. When I had absolutely nothing, they gave me everything, plus more. I don't want you bad mouthing them whatsoever. Only I'm allowed to bad mouth them. Just like you wouldn't want me talking about your Cartel!"

"Oh God! Look hubby! I love you! If I thought you were bad, I wouldn't have married you! Your people …I don't love them okay. And that's fair. I'm sorry if I can't just blindly accept them in my life just because they're part of who you are."

"Wifey…maybe that dream is warning you about what I'm talking about. You ever think of that? Whenever I think about that explosion, I get chills down my spine. So, for years, I feel like I'm in a goddamn freezer. And this is not the only freaky shit I've seen baby. I've seen something crazier, but I know you, if I tell you, you really, really won't believe me. I need you to try and believe me about this first, then I can open up more to you."

"See, a task. I feel like sometimes our marriage is the circus where I have to jump through hoops before I finally get my treat which is the goddamn truth! Look, I understand. Living the way you have with your organization, you don't trust people and I know that makes you want to test them. But I'm your wife! Do I really need a task to know the truth!? Don't you think I can handle you telling me directly? I tune you out because I can feel when you're bullshitting me or testing me. Why would I listen to a half-truth…how's that make sense? I feel like later you'd tweak what you said anyway. God! Sometimes…I wish you'd just man up and tell me everything. I wish…oh fuck," she whispered looking up at him in surprise.

"Yup," she heard her husband mumble, moving his hands down to her ass, pulling her in, pecking her on the lips.

"I do say that a lot huh?"

"Yup," she heard her husband reply, pecking her again, this time smiling genuinely.

"Sorry. I just feel like you're treating me like a child. I want to be a part of everything in your life. You're my hubby. So I say things to try and push you to do what I want."

"Your patented approach of hit everything with a hammer. Yes, I know baby. Anyways, speaking of being hammered…how's kitty. She feels good?" she heard her husband say with a somewhat forced snicker.

302

"Baby wants to change the subject," she replied, hugging her husband, somehow feeling closer to him than ever before as she reflected on what they'd done with Nate and Rayya.

"Yeah…I've been wanted to do that. Plus, umm, we 'kinda' just did some crazy shit and we're not talking about it. I think that's a 'lil' weird too…I 'dunno', have our first orgy, and not really talk about it. Minus you bringing it up to thread into your argument of course. Anyways, I want to know how my baby feels. You feel okay? You feel 'comfey' with everything?"

"I feel good hubby. I don't feel jealous or anything if that's what you're worried about. How about you? You seem way too oaky with Nate. I thought, you'd go crazy. You normally hate guys even coming near me."

"Hummm. I've been trying to care all morning and I can't bring myself to do it."

"Trying to care?" she replied feeling apprehensive, wondering if she were wrong about her previous assumption that he'd want to just move forward.

"Yup, trying my damnedest to. But it's not working," she heard her husband reply with snicker before saying, "dude said some shit to me before y'all came out the bathroom. And the shits just stuck there, and when I start to get pissed….it, it like completely swallows the anger."

"Really? How's that work? I wish I could say things like that to you all the time! Sometimes you get really 'pissy' at me over the littlest things I say."

"You're just genuinely annoying sometimes wifey. And I 'dunno' how it works. Like when I start getting pissed, I start doing this comparison thing that he'd made me do, and then my anger doesn't make sense. Like he did some 'kinda'…some 'kinda' brain hack on me."

"Brain hack? Yeah, I need to learn how he did that," she replied, pressing her head to his chest, enjoying the feeling of him and the water, that was just starting to lose its heat.

"It, it allowed me to focus on your joy, to fully appreciate that you were having a good time. And even though him doing the brain hack thingy pisses me off a bit, I loved the look on your face to be honest."

"After all we've been through…I wouldn't want this to get between us, so I'm really happy you're okay with what we did," she replied, feeling her breath go heavy at the memory of Nate as he filled her.

"There was this moment though, while shit first started happening, I was afraid to be honest that everything in our life would fall apart. But it was so fast, I couldn't actually live in that fear. It just felt like I couldn't take anymore. But then…then I could see you were so fucking happy. Seeing you like that, and being that freaky… fuck…there're no words for how that made me feel."

"I felt the same," she whispered, feeling her pussy begin to ache.

"Really?"

"Not fear…I never feared the idea of you fucking her. When she'd kissed me in the changing room. I didn't just see her in my dreams if that makes sense. I wanted you there…taking us both. And seeing you actually do it. God, I loved every moment of it," she whispered, feeling the dull ache in her pussy become an unyielding throb, remembering the sights, smells, and taste of her husband and Rayya's mix.

"So…you're saying you'd want to see me do it again?"

"Of course," she replied, feeling her mouth begin to water as the taste and scent of he and Rayya's mix became more pronounced in her memory.

"Damn wifey…hearing that…I 'dunno' what to say."

"Nothing…just fuck her," she whispered, feeling butterflies flurry in her belly, excited at her newfound freedom to express her primal desire to see her husband pound another woman.

"Jesus," she heard her husband reply in a husky voice.

"Like hearing me say that huh?"

"Of course," she heard him reply, now sounding more reflective than turned on.

"Hubby? What's up?"

"Umm, there was…umm.." she heard her husband say, trailing off.

"Tell me."

"Umm, those moments when I was taking control of Nate. Like when he called me master, and I told him what to do," she heard her husband reply in a whisper.

"Un-huh...what about it," she replied, inching back to look down, having felt his already hardening cock surge further to life, pressing into her belly.

"I liked it a lot...I think that was that moment I had the rush of fear. Not because of him touching you though, but because of me," she heard her husband say with an awkward smile.

"So, what were you scared of my love? And I liked it a lot too. I felt like you were giving him to me, like he was my own personal sex toy. God, and watching you with Rayya, seeing how nervous you were to touch her, to all of a sudden seeing you go crazy. Shit, I'm actually really glad we filmed it. I would've never thought I'd want to re-watch everything as bad as I do right now."

"Yeah, that would be good to watch again huh?" she heard her husband ask.

"Um hum. Re watch it...and then...relive it," she replied, feeling another burst of butterflies in her belly as she tried to envision how their next adventure with Nate and Rayya would begin.

"Relive it... as in a lot of sex with them for the rest of our road trip?" she heard her husband reply with a chuckle.

"Ummm," she whispered, feeling her pussy clench in anticipation.

"Umm, meaning yes. Humm, I like the sound of that," she heard her husband reply, kissing her softly.

"Do you think you can handle both off us every night? You came in Rayya so fast," she replied, feeling her clit begin throb, remembering the sensation of Rayya's slippery wet pussy against her own.

"Then I expect both of you to work me back up," she heard her husband reply, with a mischievous chuckle.

"That's exactly what I was hoping you'd say," she replied, licking her lips, remembering how she'd shared his cock with Rayya.

"Such a little freak."

"Um-hum and you love it."

"Of course I do. Hey, there's...there's something I 'wanna' ask you."

"Ask hubby, don't ask to ask."

"Do you think I'm bi?"

"What!?"

"Uuhh, I think I was a little too turned on when I told Nate what to do to you? And I think I liked you sucking his dick a little too much," she heard her husband blurt, sounding like he was losing his breath.

"Oh fuck! Why did I just love the idea of him fucking Nate! Shit! I seriously don't know myself the way I thought I did do I? What the hell do I say to him when I know he's going to know everything I'm thinking just from my face!" she thought, taking a deep breath to still her racing heart as she imagined her husband pounding Nate's ass while she rode his face.

"If...if you are...not saying I think you are. But if you are, then...I think it'd be sexy. And I think it'd be fun to see what comes out of it."

"Really? You're not freaked out!?"

"What did my face say?" she replied, feeling her voice tremble as her fantasy grew more detailed where she could feel Nate's tongue play along her pussy as her husband lifted Nate's legs over his shoulders.

"I'm confused cause your face says that you're not freaked out. And because you'd just told me for the billionth time to stop reading your face. So, hubby was trying to be good and oblige, 'sorta'."

"Oh, now you want to listen to me?" she replied, gently flicking her husband cock.

"I'm always attempting to listen, but sometimes I can feel the nubs of my balls growing back, and at those times, it's a tough decision whether to let them grow or not."

"Hahaha, I'd never let that happen baby. Just let that idea go," she replied with a chuckle.

"Whatever...one day, mark my words I will have my full nut sack," she heard her husband reply with a snicker before whispering, "God, I can't believe you're not freaked out!"

"To be honest baby… I'd actually like to see you take more control of Nate," she replied, picturing her husband flip Nate over, fucking him doggy style as Nate devoured her pussy.

"Would you now?"

"Um hum…and Rayya too. I want to see you make them do whatever you want," she whispered, feeling her wetness slip past her lips onto her thigh despite the water rushing around her.

"Whatever I want huh?" she heard her husband whisper thoughtfully.

"Yes, whatever you want," she replied, thinking, *"Why would I want my husband to be bi? Shouldn't I feel shocked! Offended! And angry that he'd possibly want to fuck another man? Another woman sure, but a man! But…but instead of any of that, it's making me leak!"*

As she tried to probe her own mind, she saw an intense look come across her husband's face that completely shattered her thoughts.

"Hubby? What's wrong!? You thought of something with those bikers?" she asked, thinking he'd figured out where the pulse had come from.

"No, nothing to do with them. I just, I'd swore to myself I'd never do shit with a guy. I'd always thought it was…just, just a hell 'na' situation, but now…"

"Bay, you don't have to…"

"Shhh, let me say this," she heard her husband whisper with a mischievous smile.

"Okay, go on," she replied anxiously.

"If I am bi and I'm suppressing it, then I want you and Rayya to help it come out. Telling that dude what to do…it felt way to fucking good to be normal, making me think something's there. And if that's the part of me that's bi, I don't want to run…it's never good to run from yourself. It's always good to embrace who you are," she heard her husband whisper, kissing her deeply before she could even say a word.

"Hi guys! Sorry about earlier, I got annoyed about something and needed to talk it out with hubby. Can I join in before all the hot water's gone?" she heard Rayya ask as the bathroom door swung open.

"Hey you, sure, sure come in," she heard her husband reply with a mischievous grin, keeping his mouth hovering just above hers, undoubtedly ready to continue their kiss so that Rayya could watch them as she hopped in.

"I love it when you're happy. I live for that sexy look you have on your face," she thought, hearing the shower curtain slide over, causing her to bite her bottom lip, already knowing they were about to get 'dirty' all over again.

With that thought in mind, she turned and smiled, but the joy was short lived as nausea took hold of her.

"Oh fuck," she thought, feeling a vibration run through her feet.

Chapter IV

Running Into Fear, Running From It

Road Trip: Day Four

Date: Sunday, June 4th 2017

Time: 08:10 am

Location: Hill City, South Dakota

"I can't believe this morning happened. We'd wanted this since laying eyes on them, and now that it's happened - I feel excited…but hesitant. I wanted more, but I wasn't prepared or able to give them my full attention," Nate thought, staring into his wife's eyes, not wanting to back down from what she was going to say next.

"I really hate your fucking country!" Nate heard his wife growl again, shooting up from the bed, pointing her finger at his face as the bathroom door closed.

"How do I tell her there's proof the 'Masters' have arrived and that everything we've feared is now a reality? That we won't be able to have children and raise a family because we'll soon be fighting for our lives," he thought, holding her gaze as he said, "I love you."

"Don't I love you me! Don't charm me! I don't want to hear it!" he heard his wife growl as she peeked over her shoulder towards the bathroom.

"How do I tell her that I'm a coward and because of it, all my access to resources like the AI and the satellite feeds have been restricted? How do I tell her that my family has deemed me unworthy?"

"What do you want me to say?" he asked, holding his emotions in check, really wanting for once in his life to lose his temper and tell her to shut the hell up, and tell her that it wasn't his fault for the invasion.

"It's not what I want you to say. It's what I want your parents to say! Actually, more like what I want your mother and sisters to say! Then, it's what I want your whole damn country to say!" he heard his wife growl, looking at him, then back towards the bathroom where he could hear Jay and Karman arguing between themselves in hushed whispers.

"One of those days I guess," he mumbled, feeling his exhaustion sink deeper into his bones, having not slept an ounce.

"Yeah…one of those days," he heard his wife whisper, moving towards the mirror, promptly pressing and studying the bags under her eyes.

"You're beautiful as always, you just didn't sleep deep enough," he whispered, moving behind her, preparing to massage her shoulders.

"Yeah, no shit, that fuckin dream doesn't let you sleep deep enough! What? What the fuck are you doing? Don't touch me! Leave me alone!" he heard his wife say in a low, threatening tone.

"Don't touch you? Since when do you say things like that to me?" he thought, feeling aggravation surge up and engulf him to the point of breathlessness.

"Don't …Don't touch you?" he replied, trying to hide his smoldering rage.

"Aggravating," he heard his wife whisper, causing his eye to twitch.

"What's aggravating is that almost everything we wanted to do with Jay and Karman, we did. But instead of enjoying and reflecting on that, you're making us live in the past, never actually keeping it that way. What's aggravating is that you're trying to make me the spokesmen for my family and country, both of which you know I truly don't understand or always agree with," he snapped, having had all he could take.

"Enjoy the present? How? That fucking dream! It makes sure the past is right in my face! Lilith Corp. owns me Nate! A life debt! For supposedly saving me! That's extreme! People are saved in the hospitals all the time! Of course, I want answers from you, they're your parents. Who else can I ask to speak for them? What person wouldn't what some kind of …some kind of reasoning? Reasoning for the horror and degradation? Life debt…I should've just died," he heard his wife reply, sounding as if she were planning to throw herself from the window.

"I gave up ninety-nine percent of my assets to help clear her life debt. If I had worked hard, within ten years, I would've been able to tell her she's free. But now, now, I have to tell her that every team is mobilizing to confront the 'Masters'. That everyone's mocking me, calling me a coward. How do I tell her that the chaos we were warned about is already happening?

"Will she think I'm weak, or cowardly for just wanting to be with her, and use the third option called run, hide, and wait for the smoke to clear? If she hears that, would it make her slip back into depression? After a lifetime of preparation, I don't feel prepared at all after seeing those images. Seeing Nefeshka, and seeing the lesser 'Masters' feels like I was staring at the Devil and his demon army itself. That's nothing I want either one of us to have anything to do with if it's possible."

"I do my best. That's all I ever do! Maybe I'm guilty of that! Maybe I deserve you treating me like this! My parents taught me to kill, I killed the best I could. My country sent me to war with your country, I followed every order and killed and destroyed the best I could. I meet you, fell in love, and wanted to protect that love, so I lied to you the best I could! So maybe you're right! Maybe I should answer for my country and my parents, because I'm always the one trying to do the best that I can. And because of that, I should be the one who fixes already broken things the best I could, right?!" he snapped.

"Don't fucking guilt trip me! You don't get to fucking do that to me Nate! I'm literally owned! In every aspect! Your mother used me like a fucking human calculator for space elevator plans, and when I finally burned out, unable to think one thought more, she started putting hit orders out on me! And it was only just recently your father even bothered to cancel them! After all these years, finally, an inkling of fucking respect! And I think...no wait, I'm sure it's only because I start going out on field missions with you! So pretty much, they can just sit back and watch me die!"

"Baby...I told you not to go with me!"

"Umm! How can I not? Those crazy mission help reduce my life debt by up to five years each! And they don't burn my brain out like those fucked up space elevator equations! Those equations! I didn't even know what the fuck I was supposed to look for! Equation, equation, equation! Finish one, then another, and another, and another! There are fucking computers for a reason! Years and years of equations! Not letting me just have a regular job! With my only pay being a few measly months shaved off of a ten-thousand-year life debt!"

"Baby, come now!"

"What, I'm not being fair!? You're right, my other problem is the racist, sexist United States that jumps when tiny little Israel and companies inside it say jump!"

"Please, calm down," he replied, cringing, knowing that was the absolute worst thing he could've said, instantly being proved right when he heard his wife blare, "calm down! What can you say to make me feel better!?"

"My love, I."

"What Nate! I'm a Muslim woman, AKA, considered less than human! If it's not men of my culture looking at me like I'm crazy for having a brain and an opinion, it's fuck tard chauvinist in this country. Then, we have your company and the affiliates acting like all Muslims are some 'sorta' fucking animals to be culled the moment Israel needs some land! Allah! I think your parents and that crock pot demon board of directors are all from hell itself. And the worst part is that they think they're fuckin angels that can do whatever they want, all because they believe they're on some righteous path to prevent the fucking end of the world! That's just utter bullshit, because they are the end of the world!"

"I love you. I know they're extreme. I never make excuses for them. But..."

"Oh, don't you fucking but me! But means you can justify! Justification means there's an excuse! You said you don't make them! Tell me Nate, what's the limit for supposedly saving the world huh? Especially if they're always doing the most horrible things imaginable? You think I don't remember? Lilith Corp and the Affiliates were kidnapping children in Beirut like it was a normal everyday fucking thing. Their excuse was to give them better lives...they called it salvation! Ripping children out of their mother's arms as they blew their heads off is not fucking salvation! Of course, I'm pissed! RAAA!!! I hate that fucking dream! I hate it so much! And to have it in front of them! For it to make me look like some kind of fucking freak!" he heard his wife say in gasping sobs of anger that caused his heart to hurt.

"I'm not responsible! You think I had choices! You think people have choices! Backed into corners and told to pick one or the other is not a choice, they're ultimatums!" he said in a low voice, hearing himself begin to snarl from both pain and frustration.

"Yes! Everyone has fucking choices!" his wife replied icily.

"Really? Bullshit! Stop playing fucking innocent! Did you feel like you had a choice? You were fired upon because you had a Rifle! How much of a choice did you feel you had when you picked up that AK!? An Israeli is forced into service, and we go where we're told!" he snarled, having a flash back of the helmet cam footage, showing his wife crouching down in front of a wounded man, with Rifle in hand.

"You don't know shit! Fuck your stupid footage! I needed the gun as a crutch! And fuck your stupid parents!" he heard his wife snarl, wheeling around, punching him in the chest.

"I don't even give a shit even if you were aiming that thing! I seriously don't fucking care! You know that right!? Beirut is not in Israel, so if you had a Rifle in Beirut, and someone from my country was there, including myself... I expect the result is to get shot. You hear me!? I expected to get shot and blown up every fucking second I was there. But the fact remains, it was in your hands. They don't 'wanna' fucking die over there ...nobody in their right mind wants to fucking die," he said, taking the next few punches to his chest and abdomen with a small smile, knowing she was pulling them completely.

"That fucking dream! I don't want to remember. I hate that memory! Often I can ignore the boot on my neck if I don't remember how it was put there," he heard his wife whimper, looking up at him with tearful eyes.

"But that dream, it has your precious Ilias," he said without thinking, biting his tongue hard right after, seeing the open-handed swing, not even bothering to move as it landed on his cheek and ear, causing it to ring.

"Sorry. I...I hate a guy I don't even know. I just hate that somehow, he still has your heart," he whispered thinking, *"I hate that you always call his name at the end of the dream! It's like deep down inside, you feel he's there for you and I'm not!"*

"You have my heart. He was torn out of it. It's different. You don't understand. And that bitch... She looked me dead in the eyes when she pulled the trigger. She knew where she was aiming, and I know she knew it wouldn't go off," he heard his wife say reflectively.

"Bitch? She? You told me you didn't remember being shot. And I saw the footage…there were no women around," he said thinking, *"I'd always planned on making the man who shot you lose his trigger finger and one of his balls. I have no idea why my parents are hiding him…but nothing can stay secret forever…sooner or later I will get revenge for you."*

"Yeah …well this time I do! This time, things I've never remembered were clear as day! Clear as day! RAH! I couldn't stop seeing any of it even if I tried! And who shot me damn sure wasn't a man, it was a woman! I couldn't see her whole face because of the scarf she wore, but I know it was a woman. A woman with cold…dead eyes."

"The helmet cam shows only men in the area. Shows her kneeling in the living room of a blown-out apartment, in front of a wounded man with an AK in her hands. It looked like she was about to bring it to aim. Then it shows a man raising his Rifle, launching a grenade into the house. In the report, he said he freaked out when he saw her lifting the Rifle, and saw her father running towards her. It said he decided to use a grenade because he was sure if she didn't pull the trigger, her father would, and that he was sure there were more hostiles in the house. Who's this woman she's talking about? Cold eyes? I know many women with cold eyes," he thought, reflecting on his mother, three sisters and Estries, along with all the women they'd surrounded themselves with over the years.

"Baby, take deep breaths," he whispered, hearing his wife begin to hyperventilate.

"Baby!" he whispered again, hearing her breaths become shorter.

"I…I…I can't bre..breath," he heard his wife pant.

"Oh baby, come here," he replied, carefully scooping her into his arms.

"That dream. I'm sorry. It's embarrassing. I'm angry because it came and made me look like some crazy, unstable freak in front of them. I mean what the fuck right? We just had a good night right!? And then, they wake up to see me looking like a nut? I know I'd be questioning? I know it'd make me feel uncomfortable to see the person you just fucked going crazy in their sleep," he heard his wife say in gasping breaths.

314

"No, no, no, don't think like that. Come baby, don't think like that. They're okay, they're okay. They won't judge you baby, they won't judge you. They know you were in the war. And…" he trailed of, reflecting on the scars on Karman's body, remembering what she said about having reoccurring dreams.

"I'm sorry to break down like this. I'm sorry. We had such a good time last night. I mean I know we were under a lot of pressure not knowing if those biker bitches would try to pull some shit. But I mean, even still, we had a good night. I wanted to wake up and enjoy that. I wanted to wake up and continue building that bond. Not have that dream come and destroy it," his wife whispered, sliding down to the floor.

"I promise you, you didn't destroy a thing. I promise everything we're going through is helping to build our bonds with them. As a matter of fact, I think this crazy situation we're in is the only reason why we were able to break through some of their barriers," he said crouching down, taking hold of his wife's chin, looking her in the eyes.

"You think?" he heard his wife mumble, letting out a soft chuckle.

"Yeah, if you want my honest opinion, I think everything that happened forced us to show our other side, and made them more than ready to show us theirs. And…" he said, trailing off.

"And?" he heard his wife press.

"Baby, we had a good time…but like you said, we were under a lot of pressure. Us being in the room, and the bikers being outside. I think it triggered your subconscious. Think about it, when my country invaded, I'm sure you felt a similar pressure being in your house with us outside. I think deep down, this situation felt the same to you, especially since they, they really tried to kill Karman," he said, lovingly kissing his wife's fingers.

"Maybe. Yeah, that was scary. To see Karman slipping away like that. I've seen that so many times, it's like they're going to sleep. Then…then they just let go. I just don't get how everything escalated, she really tried to kill Karman, right after meeting her."

"I agree. It is very unsettling. I can't get it out of my mind either, trust me."

"Crazy part is, she wakes up and seems just fine, and I feel like a total mess right now. Why the hell am I so sensitive today?"

"Love you baby," he whispered.

"Love you too. So, you...so you don't think - they think, I'm fucked? Because I,"

"No baby, they don't think you're crazy," he interjected, watching his wife look down to the floor, deep in thought.

"My love?" he asked.

"Karman, jumped right in front of them so fast. Didn't she?"

"Yeah baby, she did?" he whispered.

"And Jay? He's a little scary, isn't he? Reading things. Your face, your body language. And I got a colder feeling from him that I didn't like at all," he heard his wife say softly.

"Colder? Like, towards us?"

"Not towards us, he's nice to us...thank goodness. But I sense this thing in him. Like he's showing himself, in small doses. And there's something else about him that's eerily familiar, but I can't put my finger on it yet," he heard his wife reply.

"I know what you mean about the small doses. Spending hours alone with him...were eye opening to say the least," he replied before saying, "What do you mean by eerily familiar?"

"His actions, they remind me of those people that took me from the Lilith healing facility to the states," he heard his wife say, tilting her head as if questioning her own words.

"What you're saying is no small matter. Is this the a 'lil' that means a lot or the a 'lil' that really means a 'lil'?" he asked apprehensively

"If it was a lot, I'd say a lot. But what I see is enough to make me say what I'm saying," he heard his wife say.

"Those people are seriously no joke. You know recently you've been training with one such person for your missions right?" he asked, gritting his teeth, knowing said person avoided him like the plague.

"Stephanie?"

"Yeah," he replied.

"I, I figured as much," he heard his wife whisper, with a thoughtful expression before saying, "I bet you're thinking since I've been spending a lot of time with her recently, I'm kind of just projecting …seeing patterns, because I'm used to them, right?"

"Well, I'm hoping that, yes, because people like that, if Jay were one of them, we'd never be able to verify. There's no secret file to access, no nothing. The only thing Lilith and the affiliates have about these people is how to contact and pay them for jobs."

"Fine then, I will try not to think about it. I honestly don't ever want to dig into Jay and Karman's life too deeply. I want to give them the same space you afforded me when we met. You didn't dig into my history and everything was…," he heard his wife say, trailing off.

"A huge lie, but felt good," he finished.

"Yes, and I know we have come to the point in our lives where we hate that between ourselves. But they are not us, so I don't want it, I wish I didn't bring this up now. I think we should only look deeper if they really do something worth looking into."

"Umm, like Karman's sister being La Tunda?" he replied, sarcastically.

"Oh yeah, I guess that would be something. Okay, I know you, what happened when you looked into it?" he heard his wife huff.

"Karman's record is perfect. First, student visa, then all perfect steps to citizenship. If she's not lying about how she got here, it means the Cartel has the power and pull of my parent's company. And if she's lying…why would she lie?" he replied, feeling a gnawing aggravation of his ignorance starting to move to the forefront of his mind.

"See? See why I don't want to dig? I want to keep the way I feel about Jay, and the way I feel about Karman the way it is. I love their energy, I felt this deep connection, a really warm, fulfilled sensation in the bottom of my belly that I didn't want to end. Waking up, seeing them just now…I could still feel that energy. Minus my stupid dream messing everything up," he heard his wife say, as his mind raced, thinking, *"As I get older, I keep finding out, Lilith and our affiliates are not as strong as I thought."*

"Yes, their energy was still there, and stop, I keep telling you, your dream did not mess anything up," he replied, smiling ever so slightly, remembering Karman having him massage her breast.

"Humm," he heard his wife reply as the tripod mount silently kicked to life, turning the gun a few degrees to the left – tracking a person he could hear walking down the hall.

"Okay, I feel a 'lil' better now. I hate feeling like I'm some kind of broken person. Or that I'd need to hide that I have broken parts of me I should say," he heard his wife whisper once the gun swung back towards the window.

"Good, glad you're feeling better," he whispered, rubbing his eyes that felt sore and dry.

"Hey, quit rubbing your eyes. Oh! How am I just realizing your eyes are glowing red! How long have you been wearing the drone interface contacts?"

"Ummm, you know ...since..." he began.

"Yup! I want you to take them out...no arguments, you're going to be so sick it's not even funny. Remember last time?" he heard his wife say, sounding much more like herself.

"I do, that's why I had Jay wear a pair, so I didn't have to do as much on my own."

"You, you...," he heard his wifey say trailing off.

"What?"

"You...or I should say we both really trust them is all. Anyways, both of you need to take them out, if he hasn't already," he heard his wife say, giving him a pressing.

"Mmmm."

"Mmm, what? What did those bitches do that is making you Mmm, me? Why do you want to keep them in?"

"Nothing...nothing really. When the power cut off an hour ago, a few started to come look at our room, and a few checked out the car, but that's about it."

"What else? You look unnerved."

"There was an incident when I tried to check out one of the rooms. It's bugging me."

"Huh? Explain?"

"Almost right after I sent out the drones, I kept picking up very tiny interferences. And then, when I went to check one of

318

the rooms…there was an even bigger interference. I'd almost locked onto the source, but then this pulse…yeah I guess pulse is the only way to describe it happened. It was really odd."

"How odd is odd? We deal with a lot of odd, so give me an idea of what level."

"The 'kinda' odd that shortly after, everything read normal."

"And in our case, no news is good news does not apply, does it my love?"

"Exactly. And there's other factors that I don't think have anything to do with the bikers that could've been at play," he whispered thinking, *"Having been restricted to only use point zero five percent of the AI's capabilities, I couldn't check that room properly without diverting the processing power I was using to look for the three Masters that came from Yellowstone. I don't want to tell you that they've arrived, let alone tell you I don't have the capabilities to protect us from them."*

"Factors? What factors?"

"It's hard to explain," he said, wanting to blurt everything but change the subject at the same time.

"Is it now?" he heard his wife press.

"Yup."

"Huh, okay," he heard his wife mumble, turning her head as if she were listening before saying, "it's quite outside."

"Yeah, a little bit after the blackout a lot of them left the motel. Actually, a lot of them left the town in general. My guess is they were thinking, what's the point in a powerless room," he said, standing up, tugging his wife up with him, relieved at the change of subject.

"Really? Which way did they go? And you're not getting out of telling me these certain factors. Always trying to wiggle out of shit. Oh, and do you think they're the reason for the blackout?" he heard his wife inquire with a concerned look on her face.

"No…there've been rolling blackouts all over the…Umm…never mind. Uh, they took the three eighty five then highway sixteen. They're on their way to Rapid City."

"Rapid City? What's there? Please tell me that route is not our only way 'outta' here."

"What's there, is a huge, all male bike meet. And when I checked the satellites, there's a lot of different bike gangs already there. These ladies, they don't like the all-male idea very much, so they're coming to crash the party. Hence, the Feminist flags and what not."

"An all-male bike meet huh?" he heard his wife whisper thoughtfully.

"Yup, yup. Jay found their website. They say their goal is to fight misogynist injustice across America, and this meeting they're crashing is going to be one of many," he said, feeling anxious, where he wanted to just blurt, *"Nefeshka is here! She and the lesser Masters have arrived!"*

"What a goal," he heard his wife whisper absently before mumbling, "If that bitch didn't try to kill Karman, I'd actually want them to make it there safely. Is it bad I want them all to get hit by trucks?"

"Nope, it's not bad, it's 'kinda' funny," he said, chuckling before saying, "they call themselves the Free Matriarchs. Jay thinks it's a stab at the Free Masons because they're all male."

"Free Matriarchs. 'Kinda' cute," he heard his wife whisper before saying, "Killing with pressure points. Who does that? You watched them for hours, what else can you tell me about them?"

"That's the gist of them, just 'gotta' figure out the room situation…like I told you just a few minutes before," he replied, feeling himself begin to sweat from his wife's condescending tone, thinking, *"I hate that she thinks I've been negligent. But if I blurt out what's been stealing all my attention…I'm sure I'll be watching her sink back into that dark place."*

"If that's true, then why do you look so anxious baby? What's going on? I will keep finding different angles to ask you till you tell me," his wife pressed.

"I see that," he replied flatly, feeling his pulse in his tongue as he imagined her reaction.

"So factors like?"

"It's," – *"How do I even begin to tell her?"* – "I don't want to tell you," he said, shaking his head now feeling like he was the one who'd now been hyperventilating.

"Nate!"

"What I will say is that your tone just now is bothering me. It gave me the feeling that I didn't do enough, like I should've looked further into the bikers."

"Well did you?" he heard his wife ask in the same beat.

"I did what I could! Look, I saw a lot of activity. Lots of coming and going. Karman seemed to be under the impression they're moving something right under our eyes. What, I have no idea. The drones didn't pick up any chemical signatures of any known drugs, and even if they did, at that point, it'd be none of our business, right? For what we'd be concerned with, I haven't seen a trace of high tech anything, well other than the pulse I ran into, and you know damn straight I'm looking into it, why do you think I haven't taken out my drone controls."

"Truths and half-truths...I have to be careful, I don't want to start slipping back into an endless cycle of lies with her. Not after everything we've been through."

"Sure Nate, fine! Still, spill it! I can read your mood from a mile away, you look really, really upset! You may think you're hiding it, but I can feel and see it plain as day!" his wife replied, looking at him like he was crazy.

"Omission is one of the biggest forms of lying," he thought, shaking his head, feeling defeated.

"Okay, well I tell you in small doses. First things first, I'm very, very limited on resources," he said, feeling his palms instantly begin to sweat as anger and fear took hold of him, thinking, *"I'm the worst husband in the world. I made the worst decision ever, and now my wife will suffer for it."*

"You, limited resources? What the hell are you talking about!? You have the Lilith AI, twelve satellites! Allah knows how many think tanks, all at the tip of your fingers! What do you mean limited resources!?"

"I mean just that. Baby...I'm...," he began.

"On a scale of one to ten, how bad is this news you're 'gonna' give me?"

"A billion," he replied, feeling like no air was in his lungs.

"Shit, you know what, you were right to keep it to yourself. Yup, you know what, I...I'm not in the mood for this. I...just not right now! Please give me a little time for this," he heard his wife reply, shaking her head and hand - 'No'.

"She pushes and pushes, and now backs down right when I have the strength to tell her! So frustrating!" he thought as he said, "I've been trying to give you time, that's why I didn't want to say anything. But you're the one who kept pushing!"

"Bad on a scale of a billion, compared to the scale of one to ten, you damn right I changed my mind!"

"Listen, this is serious. My parents wanted me to go to Ellsworth Air Force base yesterday…Uh, which is actually in the same direction as Rapid city."

"Of course it is! It's because I said, let's not go that way right Allah? Right?" he heard his wife snap.

"Um, anyways… my messages - at first they said to go alone, but then it was presented in a way that said that you should be with me. I think, I think they liked how you've been handling yourself, especially since you've been saving my ass. That's why they took five years off your debt for that last two missions."

"I want my damn husband alive! Rewarding me for doing something normal, that just shows they're fucked in the head," he heard his wife reply in whispering screams.

"You…turned into an ice-cold berserker," he replied, remembering everything she'd done and how she'd done it.

"You were in trouble, I'll kill the world if you're in trouble," he heard his wife say icily.

"You'd kill the world for me?" he replied, grinning hard.

"Of course I would. What kinda question is that?" he heard his wife respond before saying, "so they what? Just want us to go to this base and do what!? And what about Jay and Karman?"

"They told me to ditch Jay and Karman. They called them, never mind what they called them. And pretty much, they want us join a big mission," he said, feeling his stomach twisting in knots.

"Big mission huh? Fuck, now I want to take a swing and guess what this level, a billion-bad news is about."

"Batter up," he replied dryly.

"Okay, umm, I guess your parents messed with another company that's able to bring the fight a lot better than the last few?"

"My love, you're just getting used to missions, challenging company raids and wars like the last two we participated in, are actually very normal, so nope."

"My next guess is that our rivals Mediums have unlocked some Maker's tech? That or they've apprehended some Makers that are pumping and dumping tech. That'd explain why we've been running into such weird shit recently. That last facility raid, that lab had some extra weird shit," he heard his wife say with wide, shimmering eyes, and a small smile spreading across her lips.

"She hates mom so much she's happy even if we're on the losing end," he thought as he said, "'Makers', I'd give that scenario twenty out of a scale of one to ten. Sit, so I can explain this situation."

"Shit! Shit! Shit! We can't have a fucking break. As soon as we have one. Just fuck! I'm so fucking tired and annoyed!" he heard his wife huff, with her mocha brown skin flushing bright red.

"I know you are baby."

"Just, what?" he heard his wife whisper.

"The truth is that when they contacted me yesterday, I'd actually told them 'no' to what they'd asked me. That's the part that didn't work out very well for me. So, it's making the bad situation worse."

"Yeah, I know they are vindictive, trust me. So that's why you said you had limited resources?" he heard his wife reply, biting her bottom lip with her hands on her hips.

"Yes, limited use of the AI and Satellites. And I'm also restricted on the Coms."

"How limited?"

"I can only use point zero five percent of the AI's processing power…and…"

"What the fuck! That's only a little better than using basic fucking View-Tech settings!" he heard his wife blare, cutting him off, causing his throat to clench.

"Um, and with the Coms. I can only hear what they say on the non-secure channels."

"Nate!?" he heard his wife gasp, giving him a dumbfounded look before saying, "How slow is the battle planning analytics?

"Like you said, it's like using basic View-Techs. If I put in too many variables…Yeah, it's going to be very limited, real-time solutions. If someone snuck through this first lines of defense, we'd need immediate back up. Which, I think is the point. They're forcing us to need them."

"Huh! I see! Soooo…. all night you couldn't focus on the bikers because logically you needed to try to cover our asses from everything else, all because your parents decided to leave us stranded to prove a fucking point. Okay, okay, well at least now you make sense. I really thought for a second, you'd been kidnaped by aliens or something. When I woke up, I had expected a full mission brief about these bikers."

"I'm glad you understand."

"Of course I do. So now do you understand me? Your parents are life drainers!"

"Tell me something I don't know! Anyways, I don't care about the bikers that much, because with the Intel I do have, I feel like we can handle them, so that's at least one good thing," he replied, becoming so angry at his situation he could see stars in his eyes.

"Oh, here we go," he heard his wife reply sarcastically.

"What?" he whispered, trying to gather his thoughts, feeling emotionally drained to the point of no return.

"You are their son for sure. You should hear your little superiority complex sometimes. Let me tell you something, those bikers make my skin crawl. Even if that bitch didn't try to kill Karman, there's something off about all of them."

"Agreed…now can we go back to the main topic," he whispered.

"No, we can't. Tell me, during your surveillance, did you or Jay notice that a lot of them look a little sickly. I saw track marks and missing teeth. I know ex-junkies when I see them. What 'kinda' conversations were they having?"

"Why do you keep thinking about them? They're not our problem!" he snapped, before saying, "I just… we have much! Much! Bigger problems! And you keep dodging. Then a few minutes later, you go probing to try and find out what I have to say again. What the hell!?"

"That's normal. I didn't 'wanna' hear it. Then I thought maybe I could handle it if it was those few scenarios I asked about, but it's not, so now I don't want to fucking hear it again! Normal human behavior Nate, now humor me, tell me what they were talking about," he heard his wife press, shaking her head at him as if to say – 'why the hell not?'

"Fine! Feminism, the patriarchy falling, destruction of the male misogynist, and the rape culture system needing to be destroyed. All about how they can't wait to show up to the stupid meet, and make the men shit themselves. How they can't wait to hear the mansplaining of why they're not welcome. Then, they were talking about women things. Sex advice, period stuff. Bullshit like if it's best to use a tampon, or a menstrual cup. All night, whenever I did tune in, it was all bullshit talk. And I did notice that a lot of them looked like they've had better days," he said, biting his tongue to stop himself from screaming in frustration.

"A feminist biker gang full of ex-junkies. Allah, what is your plan to have so many unfortunate women gathered together unless you want bloodshed?" he heard his wife whisper.

"I love you so much. Why couldn't we have better luck in our life?" he thought, as an incoming message flashed in his mind's eye, reading, **<Fam Chat:** All communications to us will now be cut unless you come to Ellsworth.**>**

"What? Why you giving me that look for?" he heard his wife ask, sounding annoyed.

"Fuck! This is bullshit!" he thought, feeling his chest cave in as he said, "I 'dunno' what to say about that. Now will you please listen? Things just got worse."

"How are you not freaked out about them? Think about it baby…you'll see why it's bothering me," he heard his wife say, glaring at him darkly.

"I get it…ex junkies with nothing to lose. But that leaves us with what, if we don't know the rest of their story! If I had more resources, I'd use the AI to find out, who and why, but I can't!"

"Ask it now, dig through their website traffic. Dig through all their messages, dig through everything, find out who's in charge," he heard his wife command.

"Did that already! It's all man hate, and just regular where to meet and stuff! Fine, I'll do it again, just for you," he replied, asking the AI to do it only for it to reply, **<Lilith AI:** *This inquiry is deemed non-priority. Request denied.*>

<Dybbuk: *AI! I order you to find something…anything that could make them a priority.*>

< Lilith AI: *Request Denied. I've just been ordered to give you information if they begin showing signs of hostile action. As of current, all scans show they're unarmed. As you have the LIL-Infinity Rifle, they're deemed priority zero. Your siblings and Estris instruct me to let you aware it takes approximately one hour to drive from this location to Ellsworth.*>

"The AI refuses. It won't even consider them a priority. And right now, I have to say I agree."

"Ha! That's a fucking huge security flaw in your system if there ever was one! People should never let an AI tell you what is or isn't a priority! It isn't human, it can read all the patterns it wants, but it has no fucking idea how we really think."

"It gives us choices after it reads the patterns, it doesn't choose. You know that."

"Well, you're stuck with it not obeying! So, Nate. I think you need to do something about that! You should always be captain of the ship, not a fucking computer, I don't give a fuck how smart it is."

"My parents are in control of it. It did not choose this. They told it not to help me! This is all them, not the AI, what the hell are you talking about?"

"What the fuck ever. My point is that you… as a human being, should be able to override it. It isn't 'gonna' see something, and have a gut feeling that a perfectly normal looking situation isn't right. An intuitive person might be able to, which might mean keeping them alive. So, your parents not having a failsafe for you to override it, is negligent, short sided and reckless! I get it, they want to be tough on you, push you into doing what they want. But this is wrong on a deeper level. And you, you keep defending them! What the fuck baby!?"

"I'm not defending them! I'm telling you the facts. They're one hundred percent in charge, it isn't the AI. They are the ones that do not see the women as a priority, and like I said before, in this one particular case, I can understand why!"

326

"It's because none of you have ever really lost anything, and don't know how it feels to be at the bottom, to all of a sudden be scooped up and given a purpose. They're dangerous Nate, and we're fucking surrounded. If they decided to bother us again, we can't just shoot our way out of it, which is what I bet your parents and that creepy AI probably came up with, right? You have the LiL-Infinity Rifle, and it has calculated that they will all crumble around you should they prove to be a threat, right?" he heard his wife growl, staring him down expectantly.

"Yes," he thought, sucking in his breath, finding himself wanting to laugh despite the situation.

"No answer, 'cause' I'm right! I knew it! Fucking Narcissist! That's why I said you're their child! All of you always think you're better. And if someone gets close to becoming your match, you guys kill them, and claim their shit!"

"Oh, just lay off for once! We've lost before. I've definitely lost! Why insult me! I've lost many things!"

"Who's we!? Unt-un Nate! Your parents want for nothing, to lose anything! And you haven't lost, you've turned things down in the name of being humble! You used to say 'no' to missions here and there, and tease me and talk about having a family!"

"Gestures!?" he growled.

"Yes, gestures! You sometimes going, then sometimes not was confusing! If you want a family, don't tease me! Just don't go! How could I have felt safe attempting to get pregnant if I always thought you were never coming back! With one ovary plus stress, there's no way I'd be able to conceive! Back then, I didn't know what the hell to do! Now I just think it's better to go with you, and at least we can both die, cause I'll just off myself when you get killed!"

"Damned if I do, damned if I don't! I did consider just not going! But giving my assets back to my parents does not win any respect with them at all! They gave me an ultimatum; mission and I'd be granted access to use the safer healing tech to restore your womb. I'm doing everything for us!" he thought, whispering, "I wish you...you know what, never mind."

"Wish what Nate?"

"Nothing my love."

327

"Exactly! What you call losses and my losses are very, very different! You see the world much differently than I do! I love you, but sometimes you miss big things because you don't see why people are the way they are!"

"Actually, giving everything up…just to make sure your health restored and to see your life debt cleared, doesn't even feel like a loss. I love you. I understand your anger. You have a right to say what you're saying. I'm just sad that if I show you how much you mean to me, it'll cause you more pain than what you're feeling now," he thought as he said, "you said you understood why I was side tracked and couldn't focus on the bikers. Climbing up my ass right now is the exact opposite of that!"

"Well, you like things in your ass, don't you? Don't…don't you dare answer that," he heard his wife say, avoiding eye contact.

"So, just stand here?" he asked, feeling like two seconds of silence was a trillion.

"I went too far. That was too much. I, I apologize for that."

"Meh," he replied, not wanting her to dig herself out so easily.

"Nate, I know you, cut it out."

"What do you want from me? You're using my last nerve like a trampoline," he replied.

"Okay, fine. I feel extra guilty. Now look. I know you baby. You pick up a lot of things during passive observation. What's the biggest thing that stands out about the bikers? And go from there," he heard his wife say with a heavy sigh.

"I'm not getting out of this am I? Fine, I told you, that incident with the room. The pulse, and then this woman showed up, and then…and," he replied as things started connecting in his exhausted mind.

"Oh, so now there's an and."

"I just remembered, right after the pulse some Asian woman showed up to speak with the woman who tried to kill Karman. The feeds were blurry, and the drones wouldn't take full commands and didn't track them once they walked in the motel."

"And that…that wasn't a big deal to you? Umm, I'm starting to lean back on aliens have kidnaped you."

"Well, you're really going to think so because I didn't know anything about them till Jay told me and showed me a recording of his feed. When that pulse happened, he was looking at them and I was tracking movement somewhere else. Want to know what the movement was? Of course you don't, of course you don't want to hear the elephant in the room. I'm tired of you jumping down my throat without hearing it."

"Oh, shut the hell up!"

"Listen!" he snapped.

"No!"

"Baby!"

"What's a few more minutes if the news is that bad right? If it's that bad, it's going to be right in my face real soon right? I'd like to enjoy the little illusionary peace of mind I have left. You love me, right?"

"Yes! Of course I do! But you're driving me insane! You don't want to hear bad news so how's talking about the bikers giving you any peace of mind if you think they're bad news? How's that make any sense!?"

"Because I feel I can figure them out if I think logically. I feel like I want to rip your parents to shreds when anything that has to do with them comes up! Makes sense? Something I can figure out, versus demons from hell! It's simple baby."

"But," he began.

"No buts. You know what?"

"What?"

"Make me happy. Quick, say something to make me happy!"

"What? What can I say? I can't just think of something..." he began.

"Talk about sex!" his heard his wife say, chewing her bottom lip in apparent frustration.

"What?" he whispered, staring at his wife who had her hands raised, gesturing, 'Duh!'

"Tell me what you and Jay talked about. Did he tell you how much he loved my pussy? Do you remember how fast he came! I was like woahhh! And actually! What the fuck right? Like, I can't believe it all happened!"

"Me either," he whispered, feeling mentally whiplashed.

"Un huh…Hey! What did you say to Jay? I mean, I'd never expect him to like…let you touch Karman. I mean, well at least not so soon. I thought it'd take more…more convincing on our part. But he was really into it. I was really surprised!" he heard his wife say, sounding positive and excited, making his mental whiplash that much worse.

"Your mood changes always make me ten times dizzier than being mentally synced up with the drones," he said, laughing, trying to change his mood to match his wife's.

"I'm a woman, 'gotta' keep up baby, 'gotta' keep up," he heard his wife reply, nodding her head, 'yes.'

"Umm, well, we had a pretty deep talk when you two were in the shower, I guess that got to him," he said, inhaling deeply as his fear and anxiety collided head on with his joy and happiness, making his brain feel like a battle ground.

"Your pouty face! So cute! Okay, tell me! How was he acting? Was he acting weird? Did he show signs of regret? He…he seems way too okay no? I'm kinda nervous that he won't be. I'm nervous that's what they're arguing about in the bathroom," he heard his wife say as she tiptoed, pecking him on the lips.

"*I feel like a blocked volcano having to hold this in! Maybe she thinks I can handle everything! This is so fucked!*" he thought, sucking his teeth, shaking his head.

"Please baby, entertain me. If it's as bad as you're saying, I'd like to enjoy…well I mean… we were with them …and I loved it. What's wrong with wanting to enjoy that? I mean…I 'kinda' fucked up the mood already…so that's why I want to…you know, fix it now," he heard his wife whisper in a warm voice that ever so slightly began to ease his frustration.

"*She's right, what I have to tell isn't going anywhere. And it was fun spending alone time with Jay. He didn't seem uncomfortable with me at all,*" he thought, taking stilled breaths as he reflected on the sights, sounds and scents of Karman and Jay before saying, "Jay was… how do I say it? He seemed really alive! I could feel this silent, happy, excited energy. And to my surprises, I felt no discomfort coming from him at all."

"Go on," he heard his wife whisper with a strained smile on her face.

"Umm, it's funny, I feel like he was silently gloating to be honest. I think he really got a kick 'outta' bossing me around. It was cute, I wanted to kiss him and ask him which moments he was thinking of. And I could see him getting little cubbies here and there, so yeah, he was definitely enjoying his memories."

"Nooo? for real? You saw him getting 'hard on's'?" he heard his wife whisper excitedly.

"Yeah, and he didn't even really try to hide it or play it off. Baby you have no idea. I wanted to tell him if he didn't put it away, that I'm going to suck it," he said, looking towards the bathroom, listening to see if he could still hear the couple arguing – feeling the same insecurities as his wife.

"And!" he heard his wife ask impatiently.

Hearing nothing, he looked towards his wife whose eyes were gleaming and said, "And then, well then, we started to concentrate on making sure we were safe."

"Boring! Fucking boring!"

"Whattt? What do you want me to say?"

"I dunno, something not fucking boring! Did he say anything about double dipping? Did he make any jokes or act weird about it? And seriously, what did you say that could make him relax and let his wifey have you. I know I helped 'cuz' I'm super sexy, but still…the way he was. He was more than willing… he…"

"He was like a sexual force set free. I did good!" he thought, snickering before he could hold it.

"Ohhhhhh…. you conniving little freak! You used the speech Ella and Carl gave us! That little mind trick! I thought you don't like using that!"

"Haha, yeah, I …I had to. Shhh! Don't make me feel …yup too late, now I feel guilty," he said, beginning to squirm in discomfort, remembering how amenable he'd felt when he realized how fast Ella and Carl's words had worked on him.

"No, you don't! You don't feel guilt at all!" he heard his wife snicker.

"Funny, they said we had listening problems. If they saw what just happened now. Mohohaha," he said, wriggling his eyebrows

331

"See, you have a double standard. Not a guilty bone in your body for using that mind trick," he heard his wife say.

"Well, just a small bit. But not really. Because you saw! Jay was set free, he was like, 'kiss her feet! Eat her pussy!' Yeah, I loved every moment of it!"

"Yes, he was set free and wait a minute, Ella and Carl thought you never listened. I was always their good girl," he heard his wife reply, watching her bite her bottom lip reflectively.

"Well, I listened, or I would've never ever let Carl touch you…I would've kept him all to myself," he whispered, smiling as he reflected upon his times with Carl, then remembering Jay slipping his cock into Karman, right after he'd slipped out, whispering, "Double dipping."

"Yes…meaning he's Bi!" he heard his wife reply excitedly.

"You and this double dipping theory," he said, beginning to genuinely laugh.

"It's a fact, not a theory. So, did he say anything about it?" his wife pressed, staring at the bathroom with a mischievous look on her face.

"No…nothing. And double dipping doesn't mean…"

"And not saying anything about! Oh, he's Bi! He's Bi! He's Bi!" he heard his wife cut in, shrieking and hopping up and down.

"Why does it mean he's Bi? He's secure in his sexuality and where else is he supposed to put that sexy fucking dick with that sexy fucking curve…was he supposed to wait till my cum leaked out before fucking his wife?"

"He's Bi! He didn't even hesitate! He slipped in right after you pulled out and started pounding. I'm willing to bet he loved the feeling of your cum! Meaning he's Bi! He doesn't even know it yet, but he is! We've been with straight guys before baby, and they wait! They try to act all cool about it, but they really want your cum out of their 'gal' so they don't feel like they're sharing stuff with a man. Haven't you ever noticed how quick they're ready to fuck only after I've sucked all your cum out?" he heard his wife say excitedly.

"Baby, I can't think of a guy on planet earth that wouldn't get revved up after seeing you do that!" he replied, loving the look on her face as she glanced at the bathroom again.

"Yeah true. Anyways, he's Bi. Now we just gotta figure out a way to make him see it. Oh! Excitingggg!" he heard his wife shriek, hopping up and down again before saying, "Tell me more!"

"More!? Not much else to tell."

"More!"

"Pushy! Let me think!"

"Yes, think of sex...not bad news! Let's try to be happy!"

"But baby, I had to train him to use the contacts, he was dizzy most of the night...there isn't much else to tell."

"I'ma' pinch your nipples!"

"Oh-ohh!! I forgot! In the beginning, I was being a bit devious," he quickly replied, placing his hands over his nipples.

"What? What? What? Tell me hubby!"

"I told him the best training for the contacts is to watch all four videos of us fucking in one glasses at the same time. It was too funny baby, too funny. He sat down all dizzy with his little chubby. Yeah that was great!"

"Oh shit! I wish I was awake to see that!" he heard his wife reply with a mischievous giggle.

"Baby...the fun did not last long. Of course, him being him, he called bullshit almost right away. He was all like – 'train me for real, stop fuckin around yo,' bla bla bla... So I trained him for real. All in all, it took him like two and a half hours to get used to syncing with the drones. You know, I 'gotta' say he's pretty good. It's kinda scary. Like he can already sync with two easily. And in the last hour before y'all woke up, he got up to three."

"Damn, I still can't do two without puking almost right away," he heard his wife reply.

"Yup...I know you suck," he replied.

"Keep talking shit and I'll twist your nipples right off."

"Anyways, he was able to switch which three he was using pretty quickly. It's like he has this hunter thing. Like I 'dunno' how to describe it."

"Yeah, I picked that up. I'm wondering how we've never been able to see that before. Anyways, let's go join them in the shower, yes? Then after we're clean, I'll be ready to hear this bad news," he heard his wife say, backing up towards the bathroom door.

"Sure, okay…I love you baby," he said, reveling in the joy he saw on her face, thinking, *"Now I don't want to tell you for as long as possible."*

"Hey and I didn't forget? Contacts out! And where's your earbud? Ah…I see it. Take that out. Put everything in passive mode."

"Baby, we need to have active eyes outside the room," he retorted.

"Oh, now you want to listen to me and not leave it all to the AI?"

"Grrr, for the hundredth time! It's not up to me…Look I want to keep them on!"

"Shut it! If your parents or the damn AI are in control, then more reason to take them off and give yourself a break. What's the point of them, if you can't inquire and analyze the things you see?"

"Yes…but, I want them in if or when they change their mind. I want…"

"You're pissing me off! They took all control! So give yourself a break from the damn drones, or you're going to be too sick to do anything if and most likely when shit hits the fan," he heard his wife say sternly.

"You're the one that got pissed. You're the one who gave me the Captain of the AI speech! Now you're saying that I shouldn't be ready if and when I can take control! What the fuck? Can you just make up your damn mind…why can't you just let me wear…" he began to say when his wife raised her hand - 'No.'

"I know! I know what I said! But baby, you haven't slept at all. Your brain and body need a break. You'll be useless if you're burned out and overstressed. For back up, just link the drones to your View-Tech's. I know it's nowhere near the same interface, but come on baby, you know you're tired. How long do you plan to keep it up? Plus…Allah, I feel like I'm going to puke just saying this, but the Rifle…its. Well we do have it, so try and chill out, we're not completely blind or defenseless okay.

Come, let's try to have some fun," he heard his wife say, with a strained expression on her face that made him begin to laugh.

"Un-huh, un-huh! So, you're admitting my parents and I are right!?" he replied as he reached into his pocket, taking out the contact lens case.

"I will kill you!"

"Alright baby, alright," he whispered, moving his index and middle finger to his eyes, tapping the bottom of the contacts, pulling them off, pressing them to the holder which opened and closed around them.

"Damn…Oh damn, you're right…I definitely overdid it," he whispered, feeling the world begin to spin.

"Un-huh," he heard his wife reply knowingly before saying, "can't have stuff plugged into your brainwaves like that without any rest. Did they even find a better way to sync the earbud to your brain? It's fucked up that it jumps brain waves."

"No…they're getting closer, but not yet," he mumbled, pulling out the earbud from his left ear, feeling a bit more relief now that he'd removed everything that'd been tapped into his mind.

"You don't look too good. Okay, pass me the View-Tech's, I'll wear them," his wife said, with an unsure look on her face.

"No way, you're the worst at drone coordination!" he said, grabbing his View-tech's off the coffee table.

"I'm getting better. Here, pass them here," he heard his wife reply as he placed the View-tech's on, mentally setting all the drones to passive mode.

"Nope, definitely not letting you try right now. Okay, anyways… I put the drones into passive mode. They've also been learning from Jay, I think them using parameters from his mindset will give us a good edge as well," he whispered, awkwardly walking towards his wife, who'd turned and taken hold of the bathroom door.

"Baby?" he asked when she did not attempt to open it.

"After this, I'll patch into the drones with my View-Techs as well. You're right passive mode is not good enough. No arguments. You need help baby," he heard his wife say, bobbing her head.

"Sure," he replied, shaking his head at the unpleasant memory of when she'd done it before.

"Good, okay, let's go," he heard his wife reply with a mischievous smile as she opened the bathroom door.

"I love her, but she drives me nuts?"

"Hi guys! Sorry…I had to work something out with hubby," he heard his wife say, feeling another wave of nausea as she continued to speak.

"This doesn't feel like the same kind of nausea from the contacts and earbud…what's this feeling?" he thought as the contents in his stomach rose up to his throat.

"My ears! My head! This pressure!" he thought, stumbling forward, feeling the ground vibrate underneath his feet.

"God, what the fuck?" he gasped, falling to his knees, feeling his mind being tugged and contorted with the image of his Rabbi standing in front of him.

"You know Nathanial. You always come to me and expect me to tell you God has a plan," he heard his Rabbi say in an echoing voice as he began to throw up bile, mixed with crackers and soda.

"And you know what? No matter how many times I tell you he does. You come back because you don't believe. And you don't believe, because you don't see him. You're waiting for a sign. Waiting for him to do something that says – 'Look! Here I am! I am God!'"

As the image of his Rabbi played out, Nate could feel the building rocking and swaying like a boat in an angry storm. Wanting to fight the feeling of losing control, he clutched the soft carpet floor and tried to steady himself only to fail, and fall face forward into his own vomit.

"Nathanial, you don't need to come here to force yourself to believe in God. God believes in you. You don't have to rush to feel connection. He's not disappointed, and I am not disappointed. When it's time to see, you'll see. Just live the best you can. Try to see the connections in life. Try to see how everyone needs each other. Try to see how everything fits. The Church, the state of Israeli, your parents and their company….and all the things that conflict

you. They exist already, and with that existence, the plan God has for you will become apparent.

"You're a good man Nathanial, a really, really good man. The things you've done, the things you've seen, you don't need to be at odds with them. Learn to look objectively at your life, and try to continue to do your best. Think of every experience you have as a blessing, and this way you won't overlook them. And most importantly, participate and observe the actions that tie people together. In humanities bond with one another, is where you'll find God does a lot of his work," he heard his Rabbi say in his mind's eye, pressing him on the chest where his heavy heart had lay, saddened from the lives he'd taken, and from the constant betrayal he'd felt from his family and comrades, all whom seemed to love spilling blood more than anything else.

"Yes, right here...This is where God does his work for humanity. Then it reflects here in the mind. Use your eyes, and your mind and let your heart speak. Listen to it. Then keep observing. Divinity is a loving guide in every mortal life. So, you must stop coming to beg for answers and salvation... and begin the process of living mindfully, keeping your salvation within you."

"Easier said than done! Rejected, abandoned and considered useless unless I bend to their will! The only connection I ever see, is that my life is not my own! That I will always be ruled by my parents, the board members and the evil, 'Living Scripture' Prophecy, that's somehow come true in my life time!"

"Shut up! You're stronger than this! Get yourself up!" he grunted, feeling the pressure in his mind slowly starting to ease.

"They all hate me! You heard them on the Coms before you were blocked. They called you a coward! They said, they'd never follow you. They said, thank God you didn't come!"

"Come on Nate! Fight it!" he grunted, feeling the area behind his ears where his View-Tech's touched begin to throb and burn.

"But Nefeshka's here! Her army of Masters are here, and it looks like they've begun scouting! Soon, if not already, they will join forces with the Makers! I'm not ready! Everything was for nothing! Even from the

pictures, I can see they are too strong! Too strong! They're like nothing I've ever faced! I can feel their blood lust! They want to claim lives!"

"Lies! Fear and lies!" he grunted, feeling his stomach boil, followed by scorching pain as stomach acid and more bile travelled up his trachea, rushing out of his mouth.

"Not lies! All morning I felt like I was being hunted! How can I not be afraid!? I should beg my parents for protection! I have too, I'm putting my wife in danger. I'm putting Jay and Karman in danger! I should've said yes, and just left with Rayya! That way, Jay and Karman would have peace for small amount of time before all hell breaks loose."

"Fight! Control your mind! It's better they're with you! When hell comes, you'll be the one to protect them!" he said to himself.

"I'm out of rhythm. Things are happening to me, and I'm forcing them away, too afraid to face them head on. And fear or not, whatever's going on out there is begging for my attention. I'm seeing Rabbi because I've been waiting for the answers to fall into my lap. Waiting for a higher power to tell me what to do," he thought, lifting his chest off of the carpet.

"I always feel insecure taking the lead. It's so much easier executing someone else's plan. Always easier when all the pieces are given to me to assemble. When everything is laid out, when the ultimate outcome of failure or success is resting on someone else's shoulders...then I'm not afraid to fail. My wife is right, I've never really felt like I've lost, because I've never truly been scared of failing. My responsibilities have never fully been my own, making it easier for me to try my hardest," he thought, realizing why he was truly running from the task his parents had given him, knowing that he'd be fully responsible for the world's fate if he did anything wrong.

"I have to stop running. Stop looking away. Stop making excuses. Running away from this, I'm running straight into it...and not on my terms," Nate thought, feeling his equilibrium return, opening his eyes to find his wife and Karman on either side of him, trying to pull him up.

"Thank you ladies, thank you," he whispered, standing up, staring into Jay's eyes, which had a cold, remorseless chill to them, that didn't seem to be aimed at him.

"All morning he'd get that look. Like a cat locked onto a bird. He senses the danger we're in, and just stares at it. I wish I had his strength! He said he's not scared of death, but I've heard many people say that, only to

338

watch them cry and beg for their lives as it slipped away. Death cannot be a good thing that I can just accept! If there were something great about it, then all those people would've rejoiced at the end of their lives!"

"Why do you keep getting that look? I'm tired of pretending I don't see it!" he snapped, hearing a crackling sound behind him, assuming it was the building settling after the earthquake.

"Oh…that's what you were calling pretending? If you say so," he heard Jay mutter, gazing at him with the icy edge melting to genuine concern.

"I'm serious…I," he began to say when Jay pointed, indicating he should look behind him.

"Whoever it is…I'm glad they think we should still be alive," he heard Jay say as he turned around, finding the firing end of his Rifle warped and emulsified to the left, with the three oval cartridges containing the disked projectiles ejected and emptied onto the carpet.

"Oh fuck," he whispered, looking out the shattered window, seeing billowing clouds of pitch black smoke rising from the forest.

<Lilith AI: *Weapons destruction anomaly requires inquiry. All remaining allotted processing power must be adverted to understand this situation. Thirty-five of your forty drones will now be utilized to search the premises. In the last two minutes, all three persons of interest, AKA the 'Masters' that you've been searching for have appeared and disappeared from the scans. Movement of the three individuals are also an anomaly as they're appearing in many locations within the same second. As you're not in mission status, all further inquiries will be handled by your superiors.*

'If your superiors or I deem you to be in imminent danger, you'll be let aware. Your only task is to head to Ellsworth Air Force base. Should you do so, a decision will be made whether to reinstate you or not. AI is to also let you aware that there has been a security breach within its operating system. As I've just identified the breach, I'm now analyzing and adjusting. As of now, I can tell you that the data breach has caused errant observations from the drones, as well as errant scans of the bikers and accessories they carry. AI's assumption is that 'Masters' have begun to attack my systems in order to better mask their movements.>

<Dybbuk: *I'm in imminent danger now! What do mean you'll let me aware if I am!? I should be the one looking into the data! I've been*

searching and searching! I would have the best idea of what stands out or not! And what's the scope of the errant drone footage? Ten percent, twenty, thirty? The woman who hit Karman and another cannot be found! Something was off with that room as well! I asked you to find something that would make the bikers a priority! Those incidents should be enough! Fuck! What else is going on that you're allowed to tell me!?>

    <Lilith AI: *This information was being held from you, but I now have permission to tell you that the economic crisis that'd begun at the start of the Greenwich date time has now become extremely acute within the last two hours. Streets, highways, neighborhoods and cities are, and will increasingly become unsafe with each passing moment as people emotionally react to the implications that everything they've known as a way of life might be in jeopardy.*> appeared in his mind's eye, making him so nervous he felt as if he's shit himself right then and there.

    Taking a shallow breath as he clenched his ass, holding steadfast to his stool, he said through gritted teeth, "umm, yeah...I need to talk to you two about my job."

    To Nate, those words were so heavy, once spoken, he felt as if he'd found the secret to the ancient mystery of Zen levitation - for at the mere thought of finally shedding his lifelong cloak, he felt as if he could fly away right then and there.

Chapter V

The Old Me, The New Me, What Used To Be

Road Trip: Day Four

Date: Sunday, June 4th 2017

Time: 08:25 am

Location: Hill City, South Dakota

"I know Nate knows there's no way I don't know what he's going to tell me!? But I don't want to hear that the small chance we had of having a family is gone! That all the hell our parents put us through very well might be justified! I'd like to cling to my bullshit reality for as long as possible!" Rayya thought, inhaling the warm, sweet scent of soap and shampoo, anxious to hop into the shower with Jay and Karman.

Grabbing the shower curtain, she could see the silhouette of the couple with lips almost touching, nearly crushing all her thoughts of doom and gloom.

"I deserve every happy moment I can get," she thought, sliding the shower curtain back, finding Jay and Karman's bright beautiful smiles awaiting her.

"Yes!" she thought, raising her right leg to step into the shower when she felt a familiar sensation go through her feet.

"No!" she thought as a strange, numb acceptance took hold of her, knowing the feeling of bombs going off, having felt them way too often during the war that'd changed her life forever.

In that very same moment, instinct and muscle memory took over, and before she'd even had time to realize it, she'd brought her right leg back from the tub and squatted, tucking herself into a tight ball. As she'd done this, she'd saw Jay quickly, yet calmly wrap his arms around Karman, pulling them both down to sit in the tub. Then almost simultaneously watched him roll, covering Karman with his body.

"His reflexes, his demeanor, a 'lil' familiar just became a lot," she thought, locking her fingers around the back of her head only to feel herself tugged and tossed into the tub on top of Karman, with Jay's body pressing down on top of hers.

341

Above her, she could hear and feel Jay breathing deep and slow. Below her, Karman taking short, yet measured breaths along with the rippling vibrations of what she could now feel was a very powerful earthquake.

"I wanted to shut hubby out. The fact that he was going to even breathe the words Prophecy and Nefeshka were all over his face since yesterday. He was practically panicking trying to make the room secure. Now my punishment for stone walling the situation is feeling bombs going off big enough to trigger this earthquake," she thought bitterly.

"And it goes bang, sending bitch dudes flying like planes, with no brains. My military's insane. Got no shame in 'da' game! We 'da' competition's execution, 'cuz' we not part of 'da' institution! Ruthless intuition, ready to target your restitution!" she heard Jay sing as he hummed an unfamiliar Hip-Hop beat.

"Again, there's this tell about him. He's way too calm!"

"Baby? Baby?" she heard Karman whisper nervously, cutting through Jay's impromptu tune.

"Huh? Yes boo?" she heard Jay reply nonchalantly, hearing something above them crack, followed by a vibration through Jay's body.

"Oh Shit! That felt like it was heavy! I hope he's okay!" she thought as Karman whispered, "Did something just fall on you baby? Are you alright?"

For what felt like the longest moment ever, she heard Jay continue to hum the Hip-Hop tune, then finally she heard him mumble, "Mmm no. It's all good, I'm alright."

"What a lie! And he didn't even grunt in pain! What the fuck?" she thought, feeling a flash of aggravation even though she understood full well why he'd chosen to lie.

"Liar," she heard Karman whisper as the swaying came to an end.

"Okay ladies, up you go," she heard Jay say without an ounce of fear or pain reflected in his voice as his body lifted from hers, hearing whatever it was that'd fallen onto his back now hit the floor.

Grabbing the sides of the tub, she lifted herself up quickly and stepped out onto the broken chunks of sheetrock covered in blood.

"You call that not being hit with something," she blurted, having a flashback of her city reduced to blood stained rubble.

"He's always like this when he gets hurt," she heard Karman whisper, snapping her out of the flashback.

"Really?" she replied, trying to wrap her head around such a passive reaction to an obviously painful wound as she reached down and took Karman's hand, helping her to stand.

"It's a scratch, who cares. It's just itchy," she heard Jay mumble, causing her to look over at him to find an utterly nonchalant expression.

"Thank you," she whispered, watching bright red blood run down the inside of his thighs, down his calves to his feet.

"For what?" she heard him reply, squinting questioningly before saying, "Of course I'd save you. No need to thank me."

"Thank you anyway," she replied, annoyed at first, feeling he was being arrogant until the smell of blood hit her nose, truly drilling in the fact that he'd just taken a blow that would've landed on her head.

"Thank you baby," she heard Karman say, stepping out of the tub, giving Jay a concerned look before saying, "You're not allowed to die before me, remember that!"

"Whatever, sure, sure," she heard Jay huff, sounding like a scalded child before shouting, "Hey Nate, sound off bro!"

In her heart or hearts, she knew her husband was fine, she'd never given the universe another option, so hearing him moan as if he'd been injured caused her to lunge through the door so fast she almost tripped over him.

"Baby! Baby, where are you hurt!?" she exclaimed, scanning him up and down, seeing no visible signs of damage.

"Is he alright!?" she heard Karman say endearingly, seeing her appear beside her.

"Can't run…anymore," she heard her husband mumble.

Calming her nerves, she was able to take in more details and see that he was suffering from an extreme case of vertigo. Crouching down, she took hold of his arm and pulled. Next to her, she saw Karman do the same, and felt a deep sense of relief the woman she'd chosen as a close friend was not someone to back out on her or her husband in a crisis, especially since her husband was now covered in his own vomit.

"Thank you ladies, thank you," she heard her husband mumble as he came to his feet, but she could barely hear him as her eyes fixed in on the sight behind him.

"This, this is unreal," she thought, turning to look behind her at Jay who said, "Whoever it is…I'm glad they think we should still be alive."

"If this is a sign of the Prophecy, then everything Nate and I have learned is utterly wrong. Being alive and lost for words or explanation…is the exact opposite of being wiped off the face of the earth," She thought, feeling light headed as her mind tried to process what she saw, struggling to come up with a reason why she was still breathing.

"Oh fuck," she heard her husband whisper, staring at the damaged Rifle in shock before saying, "umm, yeah …I need to talk to you two about my job."

"He wants to expose himself! I'd never think he'd do that in a million years!" she thought, snapping her eyes away from the smoke, shattered window, and walls full of puncture holes to stare at her husband in pure bewilderment.

"Baby, that look. Maybe you disagree? It's just that yesterday, when I got the news. I should've had the courage to tell you right away, but well, I wanted to wait for the right time. But then everything happened with Karman, and then, well, I still thought I had time. Plus, I was trying to tell you just now but…" she heard her husband say - trailing off with a regretful look on his face.

"No, I totally agree you should tell them, and I understand why you didn't say anything to me. Don't say sorry baby. There was no right timing. Besides, it's not like…it's not like I couldn't figure it out…." *"Figure out what? We're alive so I don't know anything,"* she thought, not finishing her sentence.

"You…know what…what I was going to say?" she heard her husband whisper.

"Well, I thought I did…but now…I'm not so sure," she replied, feeling strangely relieved and unnerved at the same time, knowing her husband was never one to expose who he truly was to anyone, not even their long-time mentors and friends.

"Right, I…yes, I'm just as confused as you," she heard her husband reply, watching him shake his head awkwardly.

"Hey you two love birds. Can y'all talk like Eggy head and I are still here? Thanks! And cool, I want to hear what y'all got to say, but I want out of here before an aftershock comes and fucks the place. Can we hurry up and grab our shit and get the fuck out of here please?" she heard Jay say as he nimbly slipped past she and Karman, who was staring at the warped Rifle, transfixed as if nothing else in the room mattered or existed.

"And just my fuckin luck, the only place that falls apart in this whole fucking room …falls right on top of my back," she heard Jay mumble.

"And it was going to be my luck that my head was going to be bashed in if you didn't pull me into the tub," she thought as she said, "I agree. Karman… sweetie, science shit later, K?" tugging her arm, walking her around the thick, green pools of vomit, unlike Jay, who'd walked straight through them with his bare feet.

"Oh shit," she whispered, finally getting a good look at Jay's wound, which spanned from the top right shoulder down to the mid left side of his back.

"It's not that bad. Just itchy, sheetrock fucking sucks. Itchy, itchy, itchy. How are you not itchy right now? The shit's all over you, all over us. All over my dick, fucking annoying," she heard Jay grumble, digging into his bag, snatching out clothing and a package of wet wipes, barbarically ripping it open.

"Sheetrock…sheetrock was everywhere. We were always covered in it… we were never clean. I'd gotten so used to it, I'd never thought about it, how can I feel it now? For two months straight, sheetrock, dust and blood had been a permanent part of me like clothing," she thought, having another flashback of the dead and wounded people of her city.

"Here, quick, for you and hubby. Fuckin itchy!" She heard Jay say, passing her a handful of wipes with an odd look on his face she couldn't read.

"I see why hubby wants to tell them who he is…who we are. They have this strength, this strength that tells me they won't fall apart when they hear everything," she thought, turning toward her husband who'd removed the warped Rifle off the tripod mount, staring at it with a look of deep apprehension.

"I have half a mind to tell him to leave it here. It being targeted, tells me that maybe the energy source or the materials it's made of might be traceable. But I know he'd lose his mind hearing that," she thought,

tossing all the wipes in her hand onto the bed close to her husband.

"Baby...let me...Baby, keep still," she heard Karman say with an exasperated sigh.

"Na, I got this, leave me alone and get dressed my Eggy heady," she heard Jay mumble in an endearing yet threatening tone, watching as he vigorously rubbed himself down with the wipes, dogging Karman as she tried to take hold of him.

"Jay, let your wife clean your wound," she said in her sternest voice as she turned and gave him her best - 'I mean it look.'

"He's such a baby, he always acts like a child if you go near him when he's hurt," she heard Karman say, snatching wipes from Jay's hand, tossing a few to her before quickly pressing a bunch onto his open wound.

"Blood, there was always so much blood. So many people calling out for help. I'd go house to house, house to house, finding even the toughest men crying for help. Some had wounds much smaller than his...and they cried out for help. Jay, Jay was silent," she thought, wiping herself down as quickly as she could.

"Hey! Be careful...its...its. Baby, what the fuck are you doing?" she heard Jay snap.

Looking towards Jay as she slipped on a pair of spandex shorts and tank top, she could see Karman peeling and cleaning around what looked to be a large skin colored patch.

"I know what that is. It's the new thing they have out that hides tattoos. Why do you need to hide your tattoos? It can't be from us, could it?" She thought, smiling nervously at Jay who was now gazing at her with piercing eyes.

"Shit! I'm starting to like that he scares me!" she thought, adverting her eyes, focusing on her bag as she dumped out more than half the clothes.

"Okay baby, there's room for the Rifle, unless it can still shrink down? And here, wear these," she said, scooping up a pair of shorts and a T-shirt for her husband, tossing them onto the bed.

"Yeah, it's not shrinking, and thanks baby," she heard her husband reply absently as she went for the mount, pressing the un-form button, shrinking it to the size of width of an eight-ounce coffee mug.

"Don't worry baby, we'll find out what's going on," she said, quickly moving back to the bag, slamming the un-formed mount into it.

"Uh - sure, yeah," she heard her husband whisper.

"I get the shock. But, not to that degree. I wish he'd snap out of it! We both know there's big parts of the Prophecy that are very loosely translated, that'd explain why we weren't killed. When we'd first learned that there were two books that were a part of the Living Scripture Prophecy...having just as many stories matching as those that didn't, we were both shocked out of our minds. All our lives, we'd grown up thinking that only our story was true, only to find out there was more. For all we know, there are more variations out there. The only way to ever know what's truly going on is to see what happens next," she thought, scanning the room, ensuring no equipment was left lying around.

"Baby, make sure you don't forget your contact lenses and your earbuds in those shorts," she said, watching her husband strip and clean himself with the wipes.

"Sure baby, don't worry, we won't leave anything behind. Jay and I had packed up all the rest of the stuff while you two were sleeping," she heard her husband say as he threw on his new clothes, passing her the Rifle right after.

"Okay good, we're on the same page. Just making sure," she said, scanning the mangled Rifle, feeling slightly nauseous and trypophobic from the numerous gas bubbles embedded in the superheated material.

"Alright, enough already! It's clean baby, I can feel it sparkling. Get dressed, let's get the fuck out of here," she heard Jay mutter impatiently, causing her to turn just in time to see him side step Karman.

"It cut down to your muscle, small chunks of sheetrock are in there, and you're still bleeding, a lot, especially here...right here, where you won't let me clean you, you idiot," she heard Karman say, almost growling in the last part of her sentence.

"What the fuck ever, get dressed baby," she heard Jay huff as he slipped on a pair of boxers and shorts, all while keeping his back turned away from her.

"You know I saw the tattoo already, right?" she asked, giving Jay her best - 'what are you going to do about it?' look, only to receive an expression that made the hairs on the back of her neck and arms stand up.

"Huh? Na, what you 'talkin' bout?" she heard Jay finally reply, ever so slightly changing his look to one of dark amusement, causing butterflies to erupt in her belly.

"When we get to the car, this is coming off. You think they give a fuck?" she heard Karman scold, watching as Karman quickly put on a pair of black spandex shorts and lime green tube top.

"Baby? Are you fucking serious?" she heard Jay snip, glaring at Karman who quickly matched his gaze.

"Hey, you two," she whispered, having never seen the two at each other's throats before.

"You done," she heard Karman whisper, with an even scarier demeanor than Jay's.

"Fucking blowing people's spots, my 'tats' are none of their goddamn business," she heard Jay say in a whispered snarl, intriguing, yet stinging her pride.

"Yeah, well I say it is! So back down," she heard Karman whisper just as darkly.

"Un-fuckin believable," she heard Jay mumble, kissing Karman on the forehead before gazing over to her with a strange look of consideration.

"Both of them are fucking scary!" she thought as Jay all of a sudden moved towards her, landing a fast peck on her lips.

"Huh?" she thought, moving her free hand to her lips as Jay disappeared from her line of sight, hearing his voice echo out from the bathroom, "My favorite fucking sneakers are all covered in sheetrock and blood...Oh sheetrock, why do you despise me so?"

"What he cares about is so fucking dumb," she heard Karman mutter, causing her to chuckle despite the awkward situation.

"He kissed me. He kissed me even after all that," she thought, shaking her head in agreement with Karman who was now slipping on a pair of flip flops.

"The way he just snapped, to then come and kiss me so sweetly," she thought, feeling giddy as she slipped on her flops and jammed the Rifle into the bag.

"Baby? Are you in there trying to clean your sneakers?" she heard Karman call.

"No," she heard Jay reply.

"He's lying," she thought, putting on a pair of View-techs, picking up her bag, moving towards the front door.

"Un-huh," she mumbled, looking into the bathroom, finding Jay vigorously scrubbing his sneakers with a towel, causing her to laugh.

"Wifey made these for me, they're the Wifey classics, they're special if they're worn and then put behind a glass, display case to be remembered. Not special if they're bloody and torn up," she heard Jay say, giving her a sad look as he tossed his sneakers on the floor, jamming his bare feet into them.

"I wasn't expecting to hear Karman made them. Of course he cares if they get destroyed," she thought, feeling a wave of nausea swept over her.

"Fuck, I feel nauseous. How 'bout you?" she heard Jay whisper, reaching down, pulling up the pair of shorts he had on earlier from underneath the sheetrock.

"Yeah, I felt real unstable just now," she replied, watching Jay pull out his pair of View-Tech's, placing them on before flying out the bathroom, moving towards the front door where he placed his ear to the door.

"Yeah, shit, are your thinking what I'm thinking?" she heard Jay whisper as Karman and her husband pressed their bodies up against hers impatiently.

"If you're thinking feeling nauseous is a precursor for another big earthquake …or that we're right under a strange, highly magnetic magma river that we'll fall into if the earth opens up…then yes," she replied, now wanting to run out the room at break neck speed.

"Jay, what's going on brother? What do you hear?" she heard her husband ask.

"That's exactly what I find weird. No fire alarm went off, or nothing. Power out or not, the batteries should've kicked in and triggered it. And I know most of them have left already, but still, the few that did stay, they're not even making a peep," she heard Jay whispers, flinging open the door, quickly disappearing to the left.

"Clear, let's move," she heard Jay say right after.

Before she could even move, Karman shot past, with her bag hitting her shoulder, disappearing to the right.

"Clear on the right," she heard Karman say right after.

"Baby," she heard her husband say, from behind.

"Yes?"

"Telling them my…I mean our story is the right thing to do right?" she heard him ask apprehensively.

"I think so. And not to sound selfish, but I don't want to be alone in whatever this is," she replied, still firm on her position that Jay and Karman felt more reliable than any of Nate's coworkers - having met many who were considered the best of the best, finding them shifty and hard to read.

"We're not alone, we have our parents, we have the Company and their affiliates," she heard her husband respond.

"Please, your parents?"

"As evil as you say my parents are, I think, well I hope they'll come around. I mean after everything…" she heard her husband say, trailing off with a somber look on his face.

"I don't have any faith in your parents. I don't have any faith in my mother either. She's a damn Zealot, the more my father tried to teach me about science and the Living Scripture Prophecy, the more she'd shoved religion down my throat. I spent way too much time confused and conflicted to have even half a mind to be ready for this! To be crystal clear, I say this with the assumption that yesterday you'd gotten news about the Masters. You seemed like you could barely stay composed, and this gun, they're the only ones who'd be able to utterly destroy that gun."

"Yes…the Masters," she heard her husband reply in a dead pan whisper.

"Then why are we alive? I had warned you that after we discovered there were different versions, that trying to act on what they say, mentally or otherwise was a dumb idea."

"I know baby, but…" she heard her husband begin.

"But nothing baby. Listen, we need to quickly start unlearning things our parents taught us and rethink the lessons we taught ourselves during our investigations, or we really will end up dead. This is a wakeup call that we need to keep an open mind. When and if more things start to happen, we need to see what matches up to what we've read in the books."

"Are you kidding me, think about how much truth we've seen! How can you move so fast, to think that so much of what we've learned is inaccurate? You of all people should feel most secure in a point of reference!" she heard her husband reply defensively.

"That incident you're referring to is a very...Whatever! And as for the books, I keep telling you they're like the Koran, the Bible, the Tanakh. Allah only knows how we've interpreted them, how our parents have interpreted them, or how anyone else has or will interpret them for that matter. Both books of the Prophecy said that all who oppose them will be emulsified. I'd say we are definitely the opposition. Also, need I remind you the word 'Emulsified' was used Nate, out of all the words that could've been used, 'Emulsified' was chosen. And guess what was just emulsified?"

"The Rifle, yeah I know, why do you think I was staring at it in shock," she heard her husband reply.

"So then, there, let's unlearn something - since we're alive, but oppose them, the Masters might not exactly be the evil thing we think them to be."

"What?!" she heard her husband whisper harshly.

"What nothing, the stories of the Masters are always about ambiguous war events, events that we can never place our finger on when it comes to timeline or location."

"We went to the ruins in North Korea, that was a pretty solid landmark. Same for the ones in China!" she heard her husband reply.

"Let's be honest, when we were there, did we find the rest of the evidence, or did we start stretching the stories to make them fit the way we wanted them to fit? And Habibi, you picked the low hanging fruit, come on, so much of those stories are too farfetched and don't fit the rest of the world's history," she replied.

"They're war stories baby, told over thousands and thousands of years. War and time easily erases and obscures evidence," she heard her husband say, raising his eyebrows as if to say – 'are you serious right now?'

"True, to a certain extent. But, it would also leave undeniable evidence as well. We're lacking that. Not to mention, neither of the books ever come close to giving a reference of when they'd come, it just says they'll arrive during a great Epoch for all of humanity. There are many things that could be considered a great Epoch for all humanity!" she said, raising her hands, in an, 'I don't know what else to say gesture'.

"I hear you. But, I don't see how you're asking me to just change my mind so fast," she heard her husband reply.

"Well I 'dunno' what else to think Habibi, if the Master are here, and that really was them, then why spare us? The only thing I can come up with is, that the supposed mercilessness we are expecting, might just only be from the Makers."

"What makes you say that? As dangerous as a Maker can be, they're so checked out of reality, they're almost damn near crippled by OCD, delusion, hallucinations, panic attacks, the list goes on. To be merciless like what was depicted in the stories, a person would have to be checked into reality, rationally harming people and understanding the emotional impact of their actions. That kind of mindset is not what anyone in the history of dealing with Makers has ever encountered, like ever! As a matter of fact, look at one of our most recent experiences! Remember that mission where that Maker thought she was running away from us, and she, she was just standing there. Come on Rayya, from everything we've seen from the Makers, as sociopathic as they are, it really looks like they would need hand holding to be coordinated enough to pull off laying siege to the world."

"I 'dunno', Habibi," she whispered, trying to put words to her jumbled thoughts.

"My love, think about the Masters stories, think about why they said they would return. Don't you see? All those stories and reasons are deeply personal. Makers are not like that! They just do recklessly selfish things, and it's often not relatable to the way normal people think or feel. My love, I'm certain the Makers don't have the capability of acting alone to such a large degree. I

352

think that's why both books of the Prophecy say that there'd be Makers who will join forces with the Masters. The Masters would need to be their babysitters, and that would make sense as they would be the only ones capable of dealing with them to such a large degree, without being destroyed by them," she heard her husband say, bobbing his head in self-affirmation.

"Well, what if it is personal for the Makers? Every time I've seen something horrible come from a Maker, it's been right when they were being hunted down. What if there are functional Makers out there, observing people like themselves, being hunted down, kidnapped, and locked away to be exploited," she said as she thought, *"I hate that everything I've seen from the Makers is cold and inhumane. I know that the woman was going to melt the ice. And I know that the man in the cave would've turned on the wave generator. I know that we always catch and stop each, and every one of them just in the nick of time."*

"Evolved, functional Makers, who'd coordinate? As horrible as that sounds, you might be right because I can't think of one logical answer for the Rifle," she heard her husband whisper, easing her annoyance.

"Thank you for saying that," she replied, looking to her husband, sensing his anxiety.

"How'd your parents drop the info bomb on you? All those messages you were getting, was it saying that Nefeshka and her army of the lesser Masters are here over and over again till you looked at it? Or like, did they send you, visual proof?"

"Hey you guys! Can y'all have this bat-shit crazy talk later, and do more getting the fuck out of here now," she heard Jay call before hearing him say, "What the fuck are they…wifey, do you hear the bullshit going on in there? Full fledge arguing about craziness! Knowing that there could be an aftershock!"

"I 'dunno', I was barely listening," she heard Karman reply genuinely, sounding uninterested.

"Be there in one sec sweetie," she replied to Jay, shaking her head as Jay glared through the door with a look that said - 'hurry the fuck up', before he damn near snarled, "Do you not still have the nausea? The pre-warning to – 'we might die!'"

"Jay! You can't predict if, or when there'd be an aftershock! Chill! Okay?" she quickly replied, feeling her stomach churn twice as much as it'd been before as if mother nature were snubbing her.

"Whateves'…We 'gonna' scout ahead a bit, if we die, I'm kicking y'all asses in the afterlife," she heard Jay reply in a gruff voice.

"Okay!" she replied hurriedly, seeing Karman float by the door, shaking her head like – 'what the hell?'

"Well then…that's…that's that. I heard it said aloud. And they heard what we're talking about, so we need to stay committed to telling them everything else," she whispered, before saying, "What was the proof? Did they arrive like the books said they would? And what the fuck, like why now? Why now?"

"I 'dunno' how they arrived. I was sent a message with an image of Nefeshka herself. I could tell, tell from the long, long hair. And from the horny, but fearful feeling. The exact same feeling we'd both get when we see those incoherent images from the books. And I also saw three lesser Masters. I couldn't make out their full details of course, but I saw enough of them to know…that it was them. And baby, they were, well actually, they are, still here… in this city," she heard her husband say hoarsely.

"Ohhh, no shit," she replied, feeling floored as her mind tried to comprehend how quickly her life was changing.

"Yes, shit. You were giving me hell about paying attention to the bikers. How could I?"

"Why now? Hubby, do you think us trying to build the space elevators is Epoch worthy?"

"Maybe, or maybe a Maker, or a few of them have finally created something that tipped the scale, something powerfully attractive that couldn't be ignored, and …I have no idea my love."

"I…I feel dizzy, fuck I lost my train of thought!" she whispered, thinking, *How was he able to fuck and carry all that stress. I thought he was doing a bad job of staying composed, but honestly he's keeping a really cool head!*"

"Sorry, this is happening my love," she heard her husband whisper.

"It's not your fault baby…So they came here to this lil town and…" she said, trailing off, seeing a regretful look come on her husband's face.

"My opinion, is that they came here to toy with us like bugs. I think they're the ones who did the pulse to throw off my drones, and then destroyed the gun," she heard her husband whisper.

"Umm, I love you. Sorry I was mean to you. You're really strong baby. Thank you for…for doing everything you can. I had no idea what you were going through. Okay, with that new info…that's just wow," she whispered, feeling light headed from the exhilaration.

"Mm-hum," she heard her husband mumble.

"Okay…don't rub it in. And since when are you a pessimist," she whispered.

"Since now," she heard her husband reply without hesitation.

"Look, the Prophecy has no progressive time frame of how long it'll take the Masters to join forces with the Makers, or how long it'll take for them to bring hell on earth. Since we're not dead, and we're ninety-nine percent sure only the Masters, or the Makers with the Masters' help could do that to the Rifle - then maybe…I have no clue. Like, none at all. I was ready to say something smart, but I got nothing."

"MMm-humm,"

"Shut up with the mm-humm. Hey, I love you, I know you will hate to hear this, but I think you should leave it here. Its composition still has a lot of unknown territory, something in it could be used as a beacon," she said, hoping beyond hopes he'd see the sense in it.

"Guys, seriously let's go!!!" she heard Karman whisper impatiently.

"Coming!" she replied, looking at her husband anxiously.

"I'd never leave it and you know it. And from what I saw, it looks like they're scouting. Maybe to find Makers? I say this, but truthfully, I have no idea, to me only God knows. Sorry for being pessimistic. I just have this…they think we're bugs to be toyed with 'kinda' feeling," she heard her husband reply.

"I have to hope we're not bugs. I have to hope that the Rifle is a message, screaming to us - think and take a closer look at all you think you know. Watch our actions, don't assume…things like that."

"I hope you're right. And I hope that watching their actions is not the equivalent of staring at the sun," she heard her husband reply gruffly.

"Well it's all we can do. We're alive, so there's something fundamentally wrong with our beliefs," she whispered, smiling and bobbing her head at Karman who peeked in the door with a look that could kill.

"Love you…I agree with you," her husband whispered before gently pushing her forward towards the door.

Arriving in the almost pitch-black hallway, she took in the details and sighed, trying to fight back flashbacks of shattered buildings that were trying to push into the forefront of her mind.

"Why so many flashback of the war today? Why?" she thought, remembering her father mouthing something to her before he slipped away to eternity.

"Let them…I know he said let them, …I wish I knew the rest," she thought, snapping out of her thoughts when two biker women emerged from a room five doors down from them, wearing their full leather ensemble.

"Not clear," she heard Jay whisper sarcastically, giving her a mocking look as the women, who had small cuts on their heads, and sheetrock coating their outfits floated past them, giving them nasty sidelong glares.

Moments later, another door opened down the hall behind them, this time with a woman carrying another on her back. Stepping back as the woman trotted forward with stone cold eyes locked straight ahead, she squinted - taking in the details of the blotched dark spots on both woman's hands and thought, *"Heroin burn?"*

"Nate, can you see where they're gathering? Parking lot of course, but where in the parking lot. I hope not near the damn car," she heard Jay whisper once all four women were out of earshot.

"Brother, I hate to say this, but I can't see info like that anymore, my stuff is down, you get me?" she heard her husband reply hoarsely

"Umm, 'sorta', 'kinda' yeah," she heard Jay reply, watching two skeletal looking women emerge from a room on the opposite wing from them.

"My God, they don't look well at all," she heard her husband say with an edgy tone.

"Looks like you two idiots weren't the only ones chilling in a building after an earthquake, with a forest fire just outside the window like nothing's wrong?" she heard Jay whisper, causing her to almost burst out laughing.

"I can smell disinfectant, is that coming from them?" she heard her husband reply, sounding distracted.

"Yeah, I caught a whiff of it too. Anyways, whatever, let's go," she heard Jay say, taking off towards the stairwell.

"He's kind of a dick head. But I knew that already," she thought, shaking her head at Jay's gaping wound as she took off behind him, with her next thought being, *"a really sweet dickhead."*

"Itchy, messed up my damn wifey classics. Creepy, 'kinda' junky looking ladies everywhere, weirdo day, part two has begun," she heard Jay mutter, stopping at the top of the stairs, glaring down with a puzzled look on his face.

"What?"

"Listen, you hear all that talking? They're in, they're in the lobby," she heard Jay whisper, giving her an accusing look, before nimbly jogging down the stairs.

"Seriously, weirdo day, part two" she heard Jay say again as he stepped off the final stair, entering the lobby.

"You have no idea!" she thought, arriving at the bottom of the stairs behind Jay, taking in the sight of powdered sheetrock coating everything, including the biker women who'd filled the lobby to the brim.

"You're right Jay, we're dumb for staying and talking," she whispered, sucking her teeth at dozens of hostile eyes now glaring at them, before staring up at the ceiling which had cracked and fallen in many places where she could see into the rooms above.

"It's all good Ma. Was just giving y'all a hard time. You're right, there's no real way to know when an aftershock would come. But like this, what are they doing here?" she heard Jay whisper, turning to look back at them with a confused expression.

"Agreed, I'm definitely weirded out, I'm going to call my sis and see what she knows about these chica's," she heard Karman whisper.

"One tried to kill you Karman, I'm past weirded out. I'm not playing any games with them. They will let us out of here. That or I'll show them how egger I am to return the favor," she heard her husband say in a low, commanding voice that caused her pussy to ache and throb involuntarily.

"Humm," she heard Jay mummer, turning around with an odd smile on his face.

"Baby, oh God, please no," she heard Karman whisper in dismay right after.

"What? What's going on?" she asked in confusion as Jay whirled around and said, "Ladies! Ladies! Ladies! Common sense says - leave the building before it comes down and kills you all…Us all! 'Wadaya' say about, 'ya' know, 'doin' that?"

"That was his idiot face. You've never see him get like that at work?" she heard Karman ask, putting her hand to her face.

"No…no never," she replied, titling her head as Jay began to smile like a maniac.

"I like this side of him too," she thought, smiling at the biker women who were all staring at him as if he'd just lost his mind.

"You're a man, you don't have any common sense! You only think with that noodle hanging between your legs. We don't need you telling us how to think. We can protect ourselves," she heard a woman who had almost no teeth reply.

"Alright fine then. Let's be amicable, please allow myself, my wife, and my friends out of here with no trouble. How's that sound?" she heard Jay say with an even wider grin.

"And who do you think you are to tell us what to do huh?" she heard a short, thin, but curvy Asian woman say as she walked out of the office behind the motel clerk's desk.

"Huh? I just realized! Where the hell is the staff? Did they just run away? I guess that make sense? But still, what the hell was she doing back there?"

"Hehehee…" she heard Jay chuckle, sounding slightly sadistic.

"Oh fuck," she heard Karman whisper, taking a step forward.

"Oh fuck what?" she asked, looking between Jay and the Asian woman who was coming from behind the clerk's desk, walking gracefully over towards Jay, stopping about six feet away from him.

"He's...yeah, this isn't good" she heard Karman respond as she studied the woman in great details, loving the way her white belly tube top, and black spandex booty shorts hugged her beautiful frame.

"Cute and fierce. Why life? Why can't you be fun! It would've been great to meet her on different terms! Wait, is that the woman Nate was talking about, the one that they lost track of?" she thought, moving her attention to the woman's tattoos, seemingly covering her from neck to toe.

"Who am I to tell you what to do? Humm...okay...okay," she heard Jay say in a strange huff, as if he were struggling to breathe.

"Calm down baby," she heard Karman whisper.

"Why is she acting like he's...Wait...the way he's standing. He's about to rip her apart. Fuck, why's that turning me on?" she thought, feeling the ache in her pussy intensify to a low pulsing throb as she visualized Jay pulverizing the woman's face in front of her.

"Listen, y'all don't look like y'all about to leave. Okay, that's fine. But you're going to let us out of here. I'm not asking, I'm telling," she heard Jay say in a completely calm voice that sent shivers down her spine.

"What the fuck just happened? He just completely changed into that cold monster I kept sensing. Damn, he's a billion times worse than Nate. When Nate changes, I can still feel some part of him that's reachable. With Jay, I no longer sense anything to grab onto. This is the other side of him he's been trying to show us. I think he was letting us see it in small doses so that we wouldn't be freaked out when we saw it completely. If that was his intentions...it didn't work, I'm still very much freaked out."

"You think we're dumb? We know what we're doing, mind your business, and hey... look me in the eye and tell me you have nothing to do with Sabrina," she heard the woman say in a dark, hushed whisper.

"Sabrina? Who's that? Is that the one who clocked my wife with those strange shit moves?" she heard Jay ask nonchalantly.

"I'm asking the questions," she heard the woman reply as she reached into her shorts, pulling out a pair of View-Tech glasses.

"It'd help to have a reference. And actually, it'd help to know who you are," she heard Jay retort, taking a casual step forward as the woman slipped on the View-Techs.

"He's all over her. She'd barely let her guard down and in that same second, he moved in on her. I wonder what'd happen if she blinked too slow?"

"Yes, she's the one who hit your wife. Did you and yours do anything to retaliate? Confess now, and I'll show mercy."

"Um and you are?" she heard Jay press.

"I go by the name of Grace," she heard the woman say, sounding like she was on the verge of losing her patience.

"Grace," she heard Jay whisper knowingly.

"Um-hum, because I am graceful when it comes to getting rid of 'people' problems," she heard the woman reply, walking directly up to Jay, appearing as if she were going to kiss him as she tiptoed, looking him in the eye.

"Na, we were a little too preoccupied to be honest. Plus, truth, we don't want shit to do with y'all fools. You have your answer, straight from my eyes. Can we roll out now?" she heard Jay whisper, leaning forward till he and the women were almost nose to nose.

"Preoccupied?" she heard woman reply, side steeping to the left, looking over to her, Nate and Karman with a small mischievous grin, spreading upon her lips before whispering, "Preoccupied, I see."

"I'm not a patient person...I..." she heard Jay begin as the women stepped behind Jay, staring at his back with intense consideration.

"What's this?" she heard the woman inquire, carefully reaching for Jays torn skin patch, peeling a portion of it back, reveling an enormous Tiger tattoo.

"Again, a crazy mood change! What just happened!? Now he's letting her touch him when just a few seconds ago he was about to attack her!?" she thought, steeping forward, squinting to see the tattoo clearer.

"Back up you sexy lil bitch, you were fine just where you were," she heard the woman say, casually turning her head in her direction, tipping her head for her to back up.

"Wait, their tattoos. I can tell it was done by the same artist. He didn't seem familiar with her, then all of a sudden something changed, so it must've had something to do with that. What the fuck is going on?" she thought, stepping back once, seeing the women squint and tip her head again, causing her to step back one more time, now winning her a nod of approval.

"Much better, I feel much safer already," she heard the woman say, letting out a long, slow breath as she turned her attention back to Jay's back.

"I wasn't even thinking of doing anything to you…yet," she thought with a smirk, hearing her husband suck his teeth and whisper, "I'm picking up outbound digital signatures, damn it, she was taking pictures of us."

"Why does he care? The Lilith AI and associated systems always make sure every image taken of us gets a new identity," she thought, watching as the woman leaned in closer to Jay's tattoo, mumbling, "very interesting art you have here."

"You as well, go figure," she heard Jay say, shaking his head as if to say - 'I can't believe it.'

"Hummm, as much as I love a good conflict, I don't want to have anything to do with you, or your friends either. With that being said, if I have any more questions regarding my missing friend, I'll be sure to find you."

"I have questions of my own, unless you plan on answering them…I don't recommend you doing that," she heard Jay reply, looking over towards her, Karman and Nate - where she could see him ever so slightly shake his head in some coded communication with Karman.

"I owe you nothing, and plan on no explanations. I sails as I see fit, the same as you. Your headings are always respected, are they not?" she heard the woman say defensively.

"They is sailing freely with responsibility, and reason, and then there is…I 'dunno' what you call yourself doing," she heard Jay reply darkly.

"It's none of your business…as of yet. And I hope to keep it that way," she heard the woman reply, walking in front of Jay before saying, "I really regret meeting you under these circumstance fellow Chuan Zhang."

"Likewise," she heard Jay say quietly.

"Wishing you fair wind, and following seas," she heard the woman reply, now sounding somber.

"Same," she heard Jay reply in the same tone.

"With that being said...please take your Navigator and crew, and get as far away from this city and this state as possible, or you're going to have more problems than that little cut on your back."

"Cool, fuck this sleepy, land locked ass place anyway," she heard Jay mutter, making a hand gesture for them to come.

Not wanting to be in the building even a second longer, she took off towards the double sliding doors that'd been shattered and propped open with their stoppers, making sure she kept her eyes locked on the woman.

With one foot through the first set of doors, she heard Jay say, "I 'dunno' what the fucks up...but do you need help?"

"What the hell is going on? What kind of conversation is this? Sail as I see fit!? Fellow Chuan Zhang? And now, he asked her if she needs help!?" she thought angrily, picking up her pace, shooting out of the entrance, stopping in her tracks when a cluster of enormous, eerie orange flashes of light erupted - at first silently in the sky above, followed by the sound of deep rumbling explosions.

"What the fuck?" she gasped, hearing her husband mutter something similar as the ground ever so gently began to rock and sway.

On her right, she could see Karman rolling her tongue in her mouth, deep in thought and seemingly oblivious to what was transpiring around them.

"I can't even begin to imagine what that was. Or what she's thinking that'd keep her from caring about what just happened," she thought, watching Karman take off towards the SUV, with perfectly calm, even strides, even as the earthquake grew stronger, throwing off her equilibrium.

A second later, the eerie orange lights began to spread out in perfectly circled waves of light, with the ends of each tinged the same color green as the Aurora Borealis.

"If this is truly the beginning of the end, it's really beautiful," she thought, awkwardly taking off after Karman who quickly darted out into the street, heading for the trunk of the SUV.

"Karman?" she asked, watching as she dumped she and Jay's bag onto the ground, quickly opening the trunk right after.

"Do you guys have ointment for wounds? I have my own handmade ointment here, but Jay hates it because it has dopamine in it. He calls it hijacked happy. I call it, why the fuck not," she heard Karman say in an edgy tone as she pressed her hand on the soft, mesh like fabric of the truck's lower surface.

"You made an ointment?" she replied, watching the base of the trunk slide back with lightning speed, gasping at the amount of Rifles, hand guns, machetes, and knives she saw.

"Not really made, I added some stuff in it from the original jungle recipe. I'd get tons of cuts and my mom would…my mom would…" she heard Karman say, trailing off, looking at her with an odd smile before looking back to the assortment of weapons.

"Karman?" she asked, recalling a similar look on Jay's face just as she'd left the lobby.

"Nothing…Just …nothing."

"Huh?"

"Really its nothing," she heard Karman say, as she took out a long cylindrical tube with what looked like tiny glass beads inside.

"Tell me," she pleaded, watching as her husband walked back towards the motel door looking for Jay.

"I just miss my parents," she heard Karman reply, aiming the cylinder at the bike of the woman who'd hit her.

"Oh, sorry. I…I shouldn't have pushed," she replied, lowering her bag to the ground.

"It's okay," she heard Karman reply with a sigh, watching in surprise when the tiny beads silently ejected out of the cylinder, colliding onto all three bikes parked in the parking spot.

"Karman?"

"Huh?" she heard Karman reply, tossing the emptied cylinder into the secret compartment, taking out another, aiming it up above their heads, before pressing her thumb to the bottom.

"What's she doing? What are those things?" she thought as Karman brought her hand down with the now empty cylinder.

"What's that?" she asked, looking toward her husband whose arms were now folded in aggravation as he glared through the motel door.

"Kindda insurance, why do you look so surprised?" she heard Karman say, tossing the empty cylinder in the compartment, tugging out, and passing her camouflaged tube.

"I… umm," she mumbled, staring down at the weapons, all of which were digitally camouflaged green and black, thinking, *"They have a damn armory in their car. When hubby said they were happy to see our other side, I can see why."*

"You're cute, that face, so cute!" she heard Karman say, giving her a hard edged, knowing smile.

"Um, thanks," she replied, smiling only because Karman was smiling.

"Hum …This is an open carry State. Damn, I'm tempted to take out the guns…but…decisions, decision," she heard Karman say, looking between her and the weapons, with her expression turning apprehensive.

"That woman, I guess Sabrina was her name, she called you a machete wielder. She was…" she said, trailing of, staring directly at a machete.

"What? Oh yeah that, sure I guess," she heard Karman reply flatly.

"So…she was right?" she whispered.

"Humm, was she right about you? Krav Maga?" she heard Karman ask in the same moment.

"Um, Umm. Hey, who do you think she…they are? Any ideas?" she asked in a desperate attempt to deflect, feeling a flash of aggravation as Karman shrugged her shoulders as if she didn't care.

"Don't 'wanna' answer me huh? Okay, keep your secrets. I can truly respect that. Anyways, can you put this ointment on hubby? And peel the rest of that skin-patch off, it covers his whole back, don't let him fool you into thinking it's not, his tat goes down to his ass. His dumb ass would leave it on, even if it meant catching an infection," she heard Karman say, waving her hand over the compartment with a heavy sigh, in which the compartment shut almost in that same second.

"Um, sure. And I guess no guns huh?" she replied, stepping back as Karman picked up she and Jay's bag, tossing it into the trunk.

"Yeah, not yet. And what the fuck is taking him so long?" she heard Karman say, stepping across her, now picking up she and Nate's bag, tossing it into the trunk.

"Thank you, you didn't have to do that for me," she replied, feeling awkward all of the sudden.

"Oh, sorry Mami. I forget you're just like me and don't like being helped with the small stuff. Hey, do you need anything out of your bag before I close the trunk?"

"I don't think so. And don't be sorry, you were being sweet, I should've just said thank you. You're right, though. I always want to do everything myself if I can, plus I just feel out of it," she said, looking up to the sky, watching as more burst of orange light change to green, feeling goosebumps rise on her skin, before saying, "when we get in the car, let's turn on the news k?"

"I, I really don't even want to know …you know that?" she heard Karman say with a sigh, hearing the trunk softly thump closed.

"Kinda the same. I want to know, but then I don't," she replied, looking back towards her husband who was shaking his head at Jay as he emerged from the motel entrance with an unreadable face.

"What if you took out just one gun?" she whispered, looking to Karman who'd backed up and was now staring at Jay like a cat locked onto a mouse.

"I feel like if I did, it'd be like calling the negativity to us…if that makes sense?" she heard Karman say, shaking her head as Jay approached, giving her a kiss on the lips.

"Yeah, I get you," she replied as her husband arrived, shaking his head, looking up at the sky, then back at her, taping his View-tech's, making a very quick hand gesture telling her that they weren't receiving any signal.

"I knew those lights meant the satellites were going down!" she thought, hearing Karman say, "Baby, Rayya's 'gonna' take that patch off your back and put on the ointment…."

"You want her to do what? Fuck 'outta' here!" she heard Jay intercede, glaring between she and Karman like a feral cat before storming off, hopping into the back of the SUV.

"Rayya, please help him…I'll drive," she heard Karman say, with a nod.

"Sure of course, if he lets me," she replied, tipping her head to indicate to her husband and Karman that the biker women were now coming out of the building.

"Yeah, time to go," she heard Karman huff, darting off towards the driver's side.

"So, we're blind huh?" she whispered once Karman got in the car.

"No, intermittent, but degrading rapidly, I'm still getting signal from a lot of other satellites, I can still see the worldwide news, which of course is showing that all hell is beginning to break lose. I swear people, the moment things start to look bad, they go and make it even worse," she heard her husband whisper.

"Nate, Rayya get the hell in the car please!" she heard Karman yell out the window.

"Yeah," she whispered weakly, feeling raw and exposed to the human element, having flashbacks of when both the men and woman of her country took advantage of Israel's invasion to rape, loot, and kill each other.

"Coming!" she heard her husband call, tugging her arm, pulling her towards the door which he opened and closed for her once she'd hopped in.

"You guys and your fucking secret meetings. Y'all have the worst timing ever, you know that right?" she heard Jay say, giving her an odd expression.

"Whatever," she mumbled, giving him a look to match her words, feeling guilty right after, seeing that his skin looked pale and flushed, knowing that his wound was starting to take its toll.

"Hey, turn, let me see your back, and I don't want any shit. Your wife gave me this to put on it," she said, feeling her voice crack - which she knew Jay picked up on from the way he grinned and snickered.

"Turn around," she said again, enunciating each word, wanting to punch and kiss him at the same time.

"Damn 'shawty', fine you win," she heard Jay reply with a short huff.

"He has too many elements to him, I'd thought I'd started to recognize a pattern to his body language, a demeanor, now it feels like I was reaching. Like maybe hubby was right that I was projecting. But, I still think what I'd first saw is there for some reason," she thought, watching her husband hop in the SUV, closing the door with a long, defeated sigh.

"Seatbelts please," she heard Karman mumble, reminding her to quickly fasten hers.

"And hubby, if I tell him he's doing enough…he'd freak out and say he's not. But if I say nothing, it'd be just as bad," she thought, listening to Jay and her husband fasten theirs, feeling the SUV reverse at breakneck speed, at the moment of the last click.

"Wounded soldier here, calm the fuck…ahh…wahoo!" she heard Jay blare with an insane chuckle as Karman shifted the throttle to drive, peeling off so fast she felt as if she were on a roller coaster.

"Can you drive any crazier!?" she asked, loving and hating the rush of butterflies she felt in her stomach as Karman blasted out of the Motel driveway.

"Yes!" she heard Karman say, feeling the SUV pick up speed.

"Hey! Eggy head! You told her to put that happy, hijack crap on my back, so both of us 'woulda' figured you'd drive in a way that'd facilitate that, no?!" she heard Jay say, seeing him grip the back of the driver's side chair for dear life.

"The forest fire is coming closer, and there's fires in some of the buildings already. We're near a gas station that probably has ruptured somethings or others. You 'wanna' hang around?" she heard Karman say, feeling the SUV pick up more speed.

"Ahhh, good point Eggy. And what the fuck is going on with the sky? Eh, you two weirdos…I feel like y'all know what's up. Or else y'all wouldn't keep having the weirdo secret talk huddles," she heard Jay say, staring out the window like a little child at the zoo.

"Jay, leave them alone. Priority number one for me is, what did Grace say to you?" she heard Karman say, feeling the SUV pick up even more speed to the point where she could no longer even lean forward if she tried.

"Can't talk…feels like flying in space…space ship. Oh 'IT,' oh Baby 'Jebus', can you slow down, I feel my nut sacks going into my belly. Ohh shit, I think I have ovaries…shit, slow down…or go faster, sure why not?" she heard Jay reply sarcastically, now feeling the SUV pick up so much speed she thought she'd become one with the soft leather like material of the chair.

"Jay! What did she say?" she heard Karman snap the moment the vehicle came to a level speed, releasing her from its G force grip.

"She didn't tell me shit. I asked her a bunch of different ways, and I got nothing. You know damn straight I'd get nothing, why you even ask? And truth, I don't think she knows the shit she's getting into," she heard Jay blurt, sounding agitated.

"What the shit?" she heard Karman whisper as a building burst into flames on her right, followed by a loud explosion behind her.

"I'm home again…it has found me…why…why does it feel so comfortable all of a sudden?" she thought looking out the window, staring at some of the motels and building that'd completely collapsed, feeling detached and uncaring as a fire erupted, engulfing a few biker women that'd almost made it out.

"No…not all the way home. A different neighborhood. Although familiar, I don't have any responsibilities, or even want to help these people." she thought, as the pungent scent of flesh and chemicals triggered more flashbacks of her war-torn city.

"In this neighborhood…there's nothing but the enemy. I have everyone I care about right here, and I feel safe with them," she thought, sighing as an odd sense relief washed over her.

Closing her eyes, an image of an Israeli woman in a full combat gear, with a scarf around her face, appeared in her mind's eye.

"Her again?" she thought, staring at the woman who stood among a group of male Israeli soldiers, about one hundred feet from her bombed out house.

"Why couldn't I ever remember her before? Am I making this up to fill in the gaps?" she thought, feeling small under the woman's

chilly eyes that were locked with hers as she held her ex-lover's stomach, trying to keep his intestines from slipping out more than they'd already had.

In the background, she could hear her father calling out to her, begging her to leave him, but she'd refused. Now, she was at the part where she'd taken the AK-forty-seven out of her lover's hands, not to use it against the soldiers standing in front of her, but as a crutch so that she could pick him up and drag him out of sight. That's when the woman separated from the group of men, all who wore looks of regret and sorrow. She'd seen those looks and their actions countless times and knew that if they were told to kill, they'd kill, but if not, even combatants would be ignored or not aimed at. Her lover bleeding out was now just another mistaken stain on their souls.

Not being aimed at had not been enough, and she'd watched her lover, and his rag tag band of resistance fighters get picked apart as if she were in the front row seats of a horror movie. In truth, if it weren't so horrible, the scene would've actually gone down more like a wonky action comedy, for she'd seen the Israeli soldiers firing everywhere, but where they'd actually been. Yet, fate would have it that some of the bullets ricocheted, with one going across his stomach, and another into one of his team member's head. She even remembered that the soldiers had all stopped firing, looking at one another as if to say – 'what the fuck just happened!?'

In blind rage and sorrow, she'd run out of cover almost immediately after, scooping her lover up into her arms.

"Kill Me!" she'd begged so that she can die alongside him.

The answer was still, mortified looks, with one of the soldiers stepping forward with his hands up as if to say I'm sorry, then he and his comrades had all looked down in shame.

"Kill Meeee!" she'd screamed again.

The answer, was now 'hell no' head shakes, with listless looks, denoting men who'd do anything to run. Behind her, she could hear her lover's team still scrambling through the house, running in blind panic for their lives. Their cowardice, strengthening her resolve to die, knowing nothing was left to live for if the men her lover had called friends his whole life could leave him gutted without even a glance back.

In her mind, humanity was too cruel to keep going. Then as if to prove her point, that's when the woman stepped forward, with her Rifle raised. In slow motion, she watched the woman pull the trigger, the grenade hit the ground and bounce towards her. Somewhere in the back of her mind, she'd marveled that she could somehow actually see the round and smiled, counting on it to hit even if she had to lean into it. Then to her dismay, her father had dived in front of her. The next thing she knew; she was covered in even more blood. Stunned and gasping in pain that had went beyond anything she'd felt before, she'd looked down to find that the grenade had burst through the lower left side of her father's abdomen, with its journey ending, logged deep within her upper right thigh.

"This is not death," she'd thought, falling back in agony, eyes closed, praying the damage to her body would be enough to bring her to a peaceful bliss.

Unfortunately for her, Allah did not grant her, her wish, and second after painful second, all she could feel was agony. Moving her hand towards a newer source of pain near her pelvis, she could feel her blood streaming out around something gritty and hard. Later she'd find out it was a piece of her father's hip bone that'd logged into her.

"Fine then, I'll lie here in agony, smile, bleed out and die" she'd thought, forcing a smile on her face, only for her father to steal it away, bringing up his hand, showing her the hexagonal onyx rod he'd always worn around his neck.

"What? What does he want from me? Why can't he let me die in peace?" she'd thought, squinting at the rod, almost wishing it'd vanish with the might of her remaining will power.

"I am dying. I will no longer have to worry about anything he's ever taught me. It will be the livings problem," she'd thought, having flashbacks of her father toying with it whenever he told her stories of humanities coming doom.

But the thought began to lose its value the longer her father held the ominous rod in her line of sight, whispering something damn near inaudible, in the most urgent manner she'd ever heard him speak.

"Dad?" she'd whispered, hearing footsteps, finally seeing the woman who'd fired the Grenade glaring down at them like insects, before changing to one of deep consideration - with her eyes locking onto the pendant.

"The father in me wants his child to live…So I beg you to save her. In the same breath, the father in me wants my daughter to never suffer. So, I say maybe it's better you did this to us. Because now, we won't have to live through what's to come. I like the idea of you and your people living in hell, while we're in paradise with Allah. I will even ask him for daily updates so I can spend my days laughing and laughing. As a matter of fact, I ask you Allah, let this evil woman live a long, long time," she heard her father say with a pronounced rattle in his voice, then his hand dropped, and she saw only blackness.

"I never remembered him saying that? I had never remembered that woman being there, shooting me, or standing over me. I remembered holding my love, looking up seeing a man – not a woman, then a blackness. I remember waking up in the healing facility, with my mom throwing the pendant in my face. She'd looked so disappointed and said that my father's dying wish was that I finish his work. I felt like she'd wanted me to die, and she's been treating me like that ever since. I wish I knew what my father was trying to tell me. I wish these supposed memories didn't feel so real. I feel like I'm going crazy and making this all up."

"Rayya?!" she heard Karman call out, sounding angry, shattering her out from her, 'memory.'

"Huh?" she asked, feeling groggy, raw and exposed as if everyone else had witnessed what she'd just saw.

"Can 'ya' help Jay with his back? Like now, please! If I knew you were going to just pass out, I would've done it myself and you 'coulda' drove," she heard Karman say in a disappointed tone.

"Oh, yeah…got it," she replied, feeling stung from both Karman's disappointment, and her own negligence, looking out the window in surprise, seeing how far from the town they'd driven in such a short amount of time.

Turning her head to the left, she could see Jay had settled back in the chair, staring out the window, seeming totally comfortable despite his wound.

"Sometimes he seems so innocent," she thought, smiling and shaking her head.

In that same moment she was staring at Jay, he looked towards her, returning her smile, then she heard him say, "It looks the same, huh? War and natural disaster. Doesn't it?"

"Umm," she replied, not sure what to say.

"Odd question, huh?" she heard Jay whisper, taking her hand, holding it firmly before saying.

"Lil bit?" she whispered.

"The way I see it, or think about it... is, that it's all one in the same. Humans are animals after all, so our wars can actually be considered natural disasters, if that makes any sense. And as much as we kill and destroy...nothing we do compares to the earth letting off some steam, huh? And, it's okay that what you're seeing is bothering you. I want you to know though, that it's nothing you need to deal with on your own. Us humans, we're not born alone, so if you're starting to feel overwhelmed, remember that we're all here for you if you need us," she heard Jay whisper, bringing up her hand, kissing it softly.

"Oh my fucking God! What the hell is he doing to me?" she thought, feeling the pressure and fear that'd been slowly building up to critical mass lessen in the very same instant.

"Thank you," she whispered.

"It, it means a lot to me too, you saying that to her Jay," she heard her husband whisper with a heavy sigh that sounded like he was relieved, before saying, "Hey, I have a request...and it's a selfish one. When I tell you about my job, about myself and Rayya, well essentially, I'll be dragging you guys into something you two can't ever unlearn or get out of. If you two are okay with that, then please take me to Ellsworth Air Force base. You can take this route to Rapid City, the base is there."

"Something we can't get out of, or unlearn. You're giving us a huge life choice right now," she heard Karman reply, sounding aggravated and intrigued.

"I, I know, it really is," she heard her husband whisper.

"Wow, you don't even try to say it'll be okay. It's that bad huh?" she heard Karman reply.

"Yeah," she heard her husband say, taking a deep breath, letting it out slowly, before whispering, "Karman, you don't sound fearful or disappointed."

"Fearful," she heard Karman mutter as if the thought was alien to her.

"I'ma speak for wifey and say that after seeing that gun get all fucked up, and listening to you two go on and on in the room about who may have done it, I'm going to have to say that Eggy and I 'wanna' be in the know. Us being alive to witness that is already life changing, it makes sense to hear everything, and to both of us, it's actually way riskier not to know," she heard Jay say with a chuckle before saying, "right Eggy? Oh, and turn on the radio boo, see if anything will come through."

(This is News Rapid City! The World!) she heard all of a sudden, seeing her husband's hand shot out, turning off the radio.

"Hey!!!" she heard Jay blare.

"I don't want you to hear the news before hearing what I have to say, is that okay?" she heard her husband say, watching as he turned to look at Jay with pleading eyes.

"Damn bro...sure, sure," she heard Jay say, giving her husband an odd – 'you're crazy look.'

"Karman, you okay with that too?" she heard her husband ask, sounding completely sure of himself.

"Sure Nate, why not," she heard Karman reply with a sigh.

"In such a short time, he trusts them more than any couple we've ever been with, and I can't blame him because I feel the same. I think it's because we've got to see different sides of them. Even the scary side of them feels...I don't know the word. I just feel like I know who I'm dealing with. That whatever darkness they carry with them, it's not aimed at my husband or myself. And the type of affection they show is not superficial. It doesn't feel like it'd fall apart when we'd need it the most. Karman, did not even flinch to help my husband...and I know some nurses who would've gagged. And Jay just now, he took my hand and kissed it...without thinking I'm some 'kinda' damaged freak. He acknowledges me with affection and not pity," she thought, turning to look at Jay.

"Thanks again for saving me, I'm not sure if that sheetrock 'woulda' killed me, but I'm sure I would've been hurt real bad. And thank you for not treating me like a pity case."

"Pity case?" she heard Jay ask, looking her in the eyes.

"Don't play dumb. What you said to me just now about war. You knew what I was feeling. And I owe you an apology for judging you. I'm starting to see why...why you distance yourself from people. You don't like connections that run shallow. You want to be near people that don't crumble when things get hard. Anyone can be nice when they're having a good time. But at a time like this, many people would probably fall apart huh?"

"Oh - you were judging me huh!? Well I'll be! Okay, go on with this apology," she heard Jay reply teasingly with a warm smile.

"Well I just realized how hard it is for you to deal with people. I'd gotten used to presenting one side of myself, treating the other parts of me as if they were toxic. I'd done this for so long, I felt that you should be able to do it too. To open up, and not have barriers. But I realized just now that you're more honest with who you are than me. That you're just being selective about who you're around because you're going to let all your sides actually show."

"Humm, I dunno what to say to that," she heard Jay say with an odd half smile on his face.

"I envy you, you and Karman," she whispered somberly, feeling humble after hearing her thoughts spoken out loud.

"Yess! I'm your idol!" she heard Jay reply excitedly, causing her to laugh, despite how she felt.

"Baby, shut up and let her talk," she heard Karman snip, although she could hear in her voice that she wanted to laugh.

"Cute, really cute," she replied, loving Jay's goofy charm before saying, "Look, I appreciate you treating me like a person and not some broken thing of war that needs to be pitied. When I used to tell people how I'd felt, and the things I'd saw, I'd see pity in their eyes. Then they'd distance themselves, afraid of my pain and anger. I realized people only wanted to see the happy side of me."

"Where's all this coming from?" she heard Jay ask with an affectionate look.

"I told you, I appreciate you for showing understanding and not pity. It means a lot to me," she replied, watching a mischievous smile come across Jay's face.

"Stop trying to butter me up so you can stick that crazy shit on my back," she heard Jay reply, bursting out laughing before playfully kissing her hand again.

"God, just take the kind words you idiot," she said, pushing Jay so that he'd turn around.

"NO!" she heard him grumble, reluctantly turning his back to her.

"Oh my...yuck, this cut is disgusting!" she whispered, as she thought, *"I just hope he never finds out that I've leaked classified research information to Lilith and Al Babadur. I'd never be able to explain I had no choice. I hate this feeling!"* cracking opened the top off the tube, squirting the potent smelling, dark red contents into his gaping wound.

Chapter VI

Lady Karma, Your P**** Stinks

Road Trip: Day Four

Date: Sunday, June 4th 2017

Time: 08:45 am

Location: Hill City, South Dakota

Hearing Rayya say she understood how he'd felt about people, had somehow put Jay at ease on deeper levels than he would've ever expected. It'd almost made him not want to take a swing when she'd begun to remove the patch covering his tattoo – almost.

"Look, leave the thing alone. Just put the gel thingy in the cut thingy," he whispered, realizing he was unconsciously balling his fist as Rayya pulled the bandage further down, ignoring him.

"Does it hurt?" he heard Rayya ask.

"If I said yes…"

As he spoke, Rayya tugged harder, and he could feel she'd removed half the bandage from the left side of his back. Growing more annoyed, he tried to turn and press his back against the chair, but as he moved, he felt her thumbnail dig into his skin right next to his wound.

"Is that good bedside manner?" he asked, quickly returning to his original position.

"It is when the patient is being impatient," he heard Rayya reply, chuckling to herself right after.

"Such a fucking Libra, laughing at your own dumb ass joke," he whispered, feeling the other half of the bandage come off.

"If you're too dumb, then you won't get our humor. What are you? Gemini right?" he heard Rayya ask just before she whispered, "Ouu, this really looks bad, what the hell."

"Yes, and Gemini are not dumb, we're awesome. And see, poor bedside manner, you're not supposed to tell me it's bad.

What if I panic and go into shock," he replied, half serious about the medical advice.

"You're a big boy," he heard Rayya reply, feeling her apply more ointment into his wound, which if he were being honest with himself, had started to feel infected.

"Whatever," he mumbled, thinking, *"why did I like what she said? Why did I feel a weight come off my chest right after she said it?"*

As he pondered his feelings, he looked to his left, out the back window, marveling at the thick plumes of black smoke quickly shrouding the orange and green iridescent sky. He'd been in countless precarious situations, but today he felt like he'd been swept into a truly ominous riptide of which he wouldn't be able to escape.

< J to da A: Boss dudes and 'dudets', please contact me at your earliest convince.**>** Jay mentally commanded his View-Tech's to send, only to read, "Message unable to send," for the fifteenth time since he'd realized who'd greeted him in the lobby.

"Thingy's going on…then that thingy…and the ma-giggy," he muttered, thinking, *"What the fuck kind of vacation is this? Some bitch tries to kill wifey. Nate and Rayya have some crazy shit going down. Then the infamous Captain Grace is here, and apparently partners with the bitch who tried to kill wifey. All with zero heads up!*

"Never in my life have I seen or heard of location protocol being broken. On that note, even if she did have some 'kinda' location protection, she should've at least known I was here, but I can tell from the way she'd greeted me, she didn't. Fucking interference! Too much bullshit going down all at once! I need to find out what the fuck is going on with all of it!"

"What?" he heard Rayya ask.

"Nothing, just an over active imagination," he blurted, before saying, "Yo', Nate, you said you don't have drone feeds? I was hoping you could scout around, see how far we are from the nearest group of bikers, see if there are any fires ahead, stuff like that."

"Yeah, I don't have any more drone feeds," he heard Nate say, sounding almost hopeless in his opinion.

"And where are the people. Why and how the hell can we be the only people out here!? No evacuees, no cops, firetrucks, ambulances, nothing!" he thought, before saying, "Shit bro, what happened? You think the same freaky shit that took out your gun took out your drones?

Humm, but the crazy light show, with its magnificent sonic booms might be the issue too. The signals are coming off and on, and are all over the place."

"Light show...sonic booms," he heard Nate mutter as if confused.

Explosions...in the sky bro. Hey wait, but earlier, I thought you received some 'kinda' signal. Did I overhear wrong," he pushed, squinting trying to remember the exact time he'd heard Nate say he'd gotten a message.

"Yeah, that. I...I wish I could blame the drones not working because of lack of signal, but that's not exactly the case. God, I wish I can explain everything clearly, but I don't even know where to begin," he heard Nate grumble.

"Well, maybe start with telling us who you think it was who offed your gun. That's just the weirdest fucking thing to do in the world. Who the hell kills a gun and not the people around it?" he said, unable to wrap his mind around the logic as he read the road sign labeled three-eighty-five.

"Well that part, I haven't even the slightest clue. I'm happy we're all alive, but Rayya and I agree it doesn't really make sense," he heard Nate say with a deep sigh, before whispering, "The rest is all in my head. But when I want to talk, I get stuck."

"Well what's your job, for real this time? I mean you do have a lot of cool shit, so I get what you mean by gadget tester, but I'm thinking more like secret agent man after hearing all that Master, Maker talk. Hell, start with that. All me and boo could hear through the door was 'Masters' this 'Makers' that."

"Yes, the 'Masters' and 'Makers'. Essentially, my job is all about people classified with those two titles. It's a huge responsibility, any mistakes and the consequences are unending. Just curious, have you ever heard these terms used before by anyone else?" he heard Nate say, sounding cautious.

"Nate, those are really generic terms Papi. Popcorn maker, pace maker. Ass Master. Master's degree. Pastry maker, what you talking about Papi?" he heard his wife say sarcastically causing him to laugh.

"Yeah, I know, but maybe you two have heard the terms used before regarding a person. Like how you overheard Rayya and I," he heard Nate reply.

"Nope, Wifey you?"

"Pastry Maker," he heard his wife reply, snickering to herself right after.

"Fuckin Libra's, my IT, why'd you make them so fucking dumb? Um Nate, tangent for a sec. All that firing your gun did, what was the results of that? Were your drones able to pick up anything before they stopped working?" he asked, thinking, *"Should I be mad that somehow he's put wifey and I in danger?"*

"No, I lost control of the drones right after the Rifle was melted," he heard Nate reply solemnly.

"I can feel the guilt rolling off of him and it's killing me. How the fuck can I be mad? Besides, it'd be a big double standard to be pissed at him for putting us in danger when wifey and I are doing the same," he thought as he said, "So there's, I guess a connection there."

Behind him, he could feel Rayya's fingers tracing the outline of his tattoo, and although it frustrated him that she was now privy to one of his many secrets, he smiled - locking onto how he'd felt when she'd said she'd understood why he distanced himself from people thinking, *"Going through horrible shit in our lives, we can feel each other's broken parts, and respect them instead of trample them."*

"Yup, it's connected alright," he heard Nate reply flatly.

"Everything on his end must've gone haywire. For all I know, them taking all the gadgetry out to save my boo might be part of the problem. Not to mention that after hearing the whole La Tunda script, they haven't pressed us about it. Okay wifey, I see why you want me to share who I am. Trust is a two-way street, right? But, I still can't help not wanting too.

"Every time I let people too close to me, they fuckin betray me. The sex, somehow, I can already say I feel secure with them. Yet, I still feel if they knew us more, it could open the door for them to become haters. No matter who the person has been, it's always happened before, so why would it be any different with them?" he thought, searching himself for answers, chuckling when the first hints of his inner conflict became truly apparent to his conscious mind.

"Rayya, Nate, I have a moral question for you," he said, as he wrestled with his subconscious to cough up more information so that he could put solid words to his emotions.

"Don't you want to hear more about the Master and Makers…And you haven't even asked why I want us to go to the base…And…" he heard Nate ramble when Rayya cut in and said, "Shoot, what's your question?"

"Oh, I want to know everything, trust me I do. I have a list of questions a mile long to be honest. But I wanted to get this off my chest while it's freshly percolated. First off, I'm not 'gonna' lie, I'm fighting down waves of frustration, mainly because I feel you two have some deep shit going down that's putting me and my boo in danger."

"Oh God, see this is why I want to explain everything! Please Jay, Karman!" he heard Nate begin.

"Ehhhh buddy! Calm down! Just listen, just listen. I realized I need to chill and not think like that. Reason being is because wifey and I are not good people. Like whatsoever. I can't blame y'all for the bullshit with the gun, when something similar, in terms of being shot at could've just as easily happened in our company as well. Actually, worse 'cuz' with the fucked up people we deal with on the regular, y'all 'def' 'woulda' died or been hurt real bad."

"I think Rayya and I would know what 'kinda' people you two are, we don't get a bad people impression whatsoever," he heard Nate reply hurriedly.

"Yup and that's the point Nate," he replied.

"Well, Karman's sister being La Tunda, that, that did surprise me. And that does sound pretty bad. Yeah, I can see how that could make us be in the crossfire…no offence sweetie," he heard Rayya reply, sounding slightly choked.

"Meh," he heard his wife reply.

"See, you don't sound too thrilled now that you're digesting it, do 'ya'?" he replied with a snicker.

"Well, I'm just hearing about it yesterday, and I haven't had an opportunity to truly think about it till just now, so thank you for shoving that down my throat," he heard Rayya reply sharply.

"Not the only thing I've shoved down your throat," he mumbled half joking, half annoyed and serious.

"Shut up," he heard Rayya whisper with a soft chuckle before he heard her say, "and I guess you're Triad? Is this a Triad or Yakuza tattoo? And I used my View-Tech's just now to do the translation. Chuan Zhang, means Captain. Captain, sounds like a high rank no?"

380

"Yup," he replied ambiguously.

"Yup to Triad or yup to Yakuza? Which one? Or I'm not even close? I've heard that both groups rely heavily on the sea, and y'all were talking about sailing and stuff," he heard Rayya say impatiently.

"Something like that," he said, feeling his throat tighten even at the thought of having to explain his organization.

"Jay!" he heard Rayya press anxiously.

"What dude!? Stop being all up in my government," he replied.

"I'm not a dude! And you're the one who brought up not being a good person, and us not knowing who you are! So now that I ask, you act like this!"

"Yeah, pretty much," he replied flatly, knowing he was being unfair, but not really caring.

"Rayya, Jay likes to test people. See if they can figure things out…even though he gives no clues, and like there's almost zero way you'd ever know. Ignore him, or it'll make you want to choke him…like I do…all the time," he heard his wife chime in, hearing a small snicker from Nate right after.

"Oh, oh yeah, you do act like this at work. You just stare at me when I ask you questions. Fine, I'll play your little test game, I'm an intelligent woman, fuckin jerk," he heard Rayya say, with the latter end in a soft whisper.

"Mmm," he replied, wanting to kick the back of his wife's seat in annoyance.

"Since you're half Chinese, half African American, and this tattoo has the whole Asian gang look…umm…I guess I'll go with Triad then," he heard Rayya say, trying to pull off a non-questioning tone.

"No," he replied flatly.

"Give up Rayya," he heard his wife say, whispering that he was annoying in Spanish right after.

"Umm, is the story of you meeting on vacation in Colombia for some school project made up? Or did you guys meet because of some 'kinda' organized crime business deal? Nameless Asian gang and Cartel?" he heard Nate ask.

"The school situation is true brother. There's more to it than that, but essentially that's how we met," he replied, before saying, "Look, I'm not wanting to explain every detail, I'm just saying that I don't want to have a double standard. You two are not in safe company per say. I mean, we're not helpless and shit. Just, well, I mean like…what I'm trying to say is. Yeah," he said, not knowing what else to say.

"I don't know what you want me to say Jay, maybe it's too fresh. But my immediate feeling is that I'm not upset. At no time did I ever think of you guys as bad people," he heard Nate reply with a sigh.

"Then I applaud my wife and I for hiding in plain sight very well," he whispered.

"Like I said, I 'dunno' what to say," he heard Nate reply.

"I understand, hey, I think I felt bombs going off underground before the earthquake. Did, did y'all feel like that as well?" he said, as the thought jumped into his mind.

"Does this question mean you're done your half ass confessions of an evil couple?" he heard Nate reply sarcastically.

"Ha, you're funny. I don't mean to jump topics, it's just all kinds of things are happening, and this is how my mind works when sorting it out," he said, slowing down events in his head thinking, *Top of the list of weird is those flight or fight reactions Nate and I kept feeling. They were not the - I'll let you live sort of sensations. Who or whatever that was making us feel that way, was truly going to kill us, so what changed?"*

"As the self-proclaimed Queen of being bombed, I could go the rest of my life without ever feeling that sensation again…you have very good senses to know those were bombs…and reflexes," he heard Rayya retort almost accusingly.

"I felt something, but I 'dunno' what the hell I was feeling. If the ground is shaking, I call it an earthquake. I'm not over thinking vibrations in the ground…weirdos," he heard his wife whisper.

"Complacency will be the undoing of the common," he heard Nate say under his breath.

"And finally, from just his tone, I can see his dark side. A deeply suppressed God complex," he thought, calling up his last hack status reading, **<Seven of ten viruses have been found and eradicated. Two were fighting to maintain detection, one of five worms were still established.>**

Mulling over what Nate had just said, he realized that although his wife's words may have triggered Nate to make the comment, his tone had not been directed toward her in an accusing manner. To him, it sounded like Nate was reciting something he'd heard or read in regards to people not fully knowing their surroundings. Opening his mouth to ask, he felt Rayya's fingers return to his back, tracing out another portion of his tattoo.

"Rayya, 'wasup' with you and my tat?" he asked, losing his question at the tip of his tongue.

"You and Grace, both of your tattoos have a similar feel to them," he heard Rayya whisper.

"Graaa," he grunted in annoyance.

"Can…you, can you let me …Gra back you little child!" he heard Rayya snip, feeling her push him so he'd lean forward.

"No," he replied sternly, straightening in the seat, making sure his back didn't touch as he glared at Rayya, now having mixed feeling about her curiosity, sensing no judgment in the undercurrents.

"It's, it's a sleepy looking tiger, laying peacefully on a beach at night, staring at the water. And it's looking at a killer whale in the bright star lite reflection. I don't get it, like at all. What's that mean? It doesn't really look Triad or Yakuza 'ish at all," he heard Rayya say with a sarcastic smile, not adverting her eyes from his.

"It's one hundred percent, pure, authentic G status," he replied, trying to bite back his frustration.

"You're getting on my nerves," he heard Rayya huff right after.

"So? Ditto."

"You know what I think?" he heard Rayya reply in a low voice.

"I think you're 'def' 'gonna' tell me what you think, even if I say I don't 'wanna' hear it," he replied.

"I feel like you're making yourself seem bigger than you are. To, I 'dunno', impress us or something," he heard Rayya say.

"I'm not dumb, I'm not going to fall for that reverse psychology shit!" he thought, replying "Yup, and that's what's so OG about me."

"Un huh. And where's your gangster muscles, aren't you supposed to be ripped? You got some definition there, but nothing to write Lebanon about."

"Oh please, you felt my sexy body all night! You know damn straight I'm solid. Don't 'gotta' be 'hella' cut up to be solid!"

"Sure, sure. Whatever you say Jay. I will give it to you that you and that Grace chic went to the same artist. But this looks like some dream world. Grace had dragons, sea monsters, all kinds of skulls. Those look like gang tats," he heard Rayya say, sounding more annoyed with each spoken word.

"I guess. Yup sure, whatever you say is right, you win," he replied.

"Allah, give me strength," he heard Rayya snip.

"Just say God, or 'It.' Say God or 'It,'" he shot in.

"'It?' What?" he heard Rayya say, sounding distraught at the title.

"Don't engage him. I really don't 'wanna' hear him go on and on about why God is an 'It'," he heard his wife chime in.

"Umm okay. I'll…I'll take your word for it Karman. Okay Jay, God…give me strength. Sound better?"

"Yup."

"Look Jay, I get that you have a hard time trusting people but," he heard Rayya begin, giving him a look that said she was doubting if she should continue.

"But?"

"You ask but, with a tone that says you have no interest in actually hearing what I have to say," he heard Rayya reply.

"I say it in a tone that means if you know I find it difficult to trust people, why do you have to press and press and press!? I'm like your hubby over there, I want to open up, but all clamped up. Sometimes stuff comes out then I want to shut up again. It's crazy hard to just open up! You 'shoulda' saw how you looked when Nate said he wanted to tell us about his job. You turned into a ghost! So, you should get it, not wanting to just blurt stuff. Come now, let's be real, if nothing ever happened with the gun melting, y'all would've never wanted to tell us shit right?"

"I can say the same thing about you, Karman and those bikers. So, you're right! Now that I'm...what's your word? Oh right...digesting things! I'm certain y'all would've never said anything about your life if those women never caused a problem. And let's be real about something else! Karman, those women started it, but you seemed to be itching for that fight! You jumped right into that Sabrina's chicks face!"

"It's good you call it how you see it Rayya. And you damn right, we wouldn't have said anything, secrets are secrets for a reason. And boo, she's right too, you 'ain't' need to be all up that lady's face, damn near getting killed...then we 'woulda' never needed to explain our 'Gangsterness'. 'Coulda' just sat here and pretended we're innocent and made them two feel like shit for having mad secrets," he replied, calling up the control window to the AI system he and his wife had housed inside the SUV.

- awkward silence-

<J to da A: The most awesomest system ever; is there a way you can start caching the data from the open worms by using short pulses? Maybe collect the info in coded pieces using ambient frequencies so you're not traced?>

<The most awesomest system ever: Last known information was that the target system is being guarded on a multitude of levels. Any action taken without the satellites, or signal sources being operational, will lead back us. I'd need an environment where there can be many locations the hostile signals could originate from to avoid trace back.>

<Jay to the A: I built you, you suck! Can't do shit! Okay slave, when we finally do get some cover signals, the main thing I want you to search for in his systems are words and phrases like, *(Compromised. Breached. Not supposed to. Security threat. Need to know basis. Masters & Makers. Warhead. Yield. Atmosphere.)* And anything else to do with signals and operational security. I 'wanna' know if Nate's a fucking idiot and got in trouble with these Masters and Makers because of us. Oh! And also, what's the progress on finding out who hacked my files?>

<The most awesome system ever: In regards to your company's files, I've yet been able to ascertain this information. However, the timing of the hacks has a specific pattern. They've only occurred when you were in this vehicle at certain distances from four different locations. Two in Southern Seattle, two in Northern Seattle. And all hacks have occurred within the last two months.>

<Jay to the A: Only in here! Is it you, you bastard? And what the hell! Southern Seattle and Northern Seattle is vague as fuck! How far North. The city limit border? Same with South!? And are we talking North Eastern, South Eastern, or Western on one end, Eastern on the other!? Give me more!>

<The most awesome system ever: I have checked. I am 99.9 percent certain the hacks were not from myself via a slave program. As I said prior, the hack appears to originate from four external sources on the border of Northern and Southern Seattle, still working out the exact details. Need more time.>

<J to the A: Eh, look, you thingy you. I'll change your name to POS if you don't...>

~ A full five minutes of pure awkward silence later for everyone but Jay – who'd been preoccupied with the above situation ~

"I still don't even know what to say to that," he heard Rayya whisper, causing him to close the interface window and look at her.

Seeing her now, she looked more exhausted than he felt, and that was saying a lot as he'd not slept even an ounce since their run in with the bikers.

"Sorry, there's nothing to say. Other than shit I want to guard, I think my 'no filter' needs a filter," he replied, now feeling annoyed at himself for draining her energy.

"I actually like that you don't really have one. But sometimes it's...it's a little too much. But I don't 'wanna' say that and you end up shutting up on us," he heard Rayya reply, looking at him quizzically.

"Look, it's just my nature to always keep my guard up, and you and Nate...Y'all are guard poppers. It's cool sometimes, like when we ended up doing what we did...Yeah, that shit was fun.

But then other times, you two are just way too all up in my shit way too fast. And to be honest, I feel like the gun melting situation wouldn't have happened if we didn't get in trouble with the bikers. I'm sitting here thinking me and boo got y'all compromised or some shit. Like maybe someone on Nate's end, the Master or Makers you guys were whisper-yelling about, felt the gun need to be destroyed because we saw too much," he said, gripping Rayya's hand as he looked between she and Nate.

"Don't think like that Jay. Look, I'm just worried that you two will think we're lunatics when I explain everything," he heard Nate say in a dry, fatigued voice.

"Funny, the more I want to tell you about wifey and I, I keep feeling like y'all would think the same. On top of that, I feel like if I tell you two too much, both of you will always start questioning all of our motives. I really, really don't want that," he said, shaking his head feeling like his prediction was already beginning to come true - as he'd found many times in his life that speaking of things out loud somehow brought them to life.

"Well, from what I've seen from the two of you, always being at work. I don't see how there's that much to tell," he heard Rayya say, sounding hopeful.

"Umm, yeah…us at work, yeah about that," he said, thinking *"If she knew why we choose to work where we work, and what we spent most of our time doing there…fuck, if I tell them more about us, they'll figure it out anyways. I hate this! This is why I always pull away from people! I hate the grey judges' wigs that are bound to come!"*

"There you go, making yourself seem like something or another. I'm at work with you remember? Oh, Jay! You look so Gangster, you know, doing those computations, makes me want to just give you all my money. Oh no, please Jay, don't stick me up with a calculation!" he heard Rayya say sarcastically.

"That was funny," he heard his wife say, staring to giggle and hiccup right after.

"It's better you think what you think, that's what I think," he replied, suppressing his smile, feeling like he wanted to laugh just from the soft giggles he could still here coming from his wife.

"Okay, sure Jay, so now what? Do you want me to think of you and Karman as people who destroy households and neighborhoods? Like I don't get where you're going with telling us you're not good people," he heard Nate chime in.

"My gut says bad situations choose you two, and then neither of you could escape it. I mean Karman, didn't you leave Colombia to get away from your sister, to get away from everything? Jay, when I get to work, you're there, when I leave work, you're there. Literally when do you have time to be as bad of a person as you're claiming to be? Karman, I can barely link up with you, you're always working too. The most time I've gotten with you is because you call me up and drag me around to keep you company doing all those chores," he heard Rayya say.

"Hey, I do chores," he shot in, knowing he dodged every single one of them with any and every excuse he could.

~ All three people's eyes were on him for at least ten seconds, in which they non-verbally accused him of being lazy. ~

"Bad situations definitely did choose us," he heard his wife say, breaking the silence.

"I mean, your sister is La Tunda. Even if you didn't want to be wrapped up in her world, I'm sure it might be nerve racking, people always go after family members. Yeah, I get the trunk, it's for protection," he heard Rayya reply, running her hand down his back, smoothing down some of the ointment on his wound.

"Guns in the trunk?" he heard Nate ask, sounding dumbfounded.

"Yup, we need them, for protection," he whispered.

"Apparently," he heard Nate reply, sounding breathless.

Chewing his bottom lip, he looked at Nate, then to Rayya and thought, *'I've always wanted deeper friendships than the ones I've had. I've always wanted to have friends that I can share my secrets with, friends I can have deep talks with, and still do freaky shit with. But it's never happened. Even the people in my organization were not the people I thought they'd be. I've never really found people I could truly grow close to.*

"There was always this dark, super selfish wall I'd run into when it came to people. Now these two keep showing me intimacy and selflessness, and I'm the one who keeps wanting to put up the wall, even after what we've done. But I also can't stop being afraid of the consequence of shutting them

out. I feel like if I don't keep pushing to let them in, they'll give up on me...and I'll give up on myself."

"Guns, in the trunk?" he heard Nate whisper again, turning to give him a questioning glare before looking forward, shaking his head in obvious annoyance and disbelief.

"Yup, that's why it'd be a double standard to be pissed at you guys. And yes, in a way you're right. I was put in a position where it was pick joining my organization, or live a really hard life."

"Then why, say you're not good people? Good people have to make tough choices all the time," he heard Rayya reply.

"People don't have to choose what my wife and I have chosen, we've seen worse things happen to people, and they have chosen to lead good, moral lives. But she and I have made our choice and embraced it. That's why I said what I said," he replied, thinking of his next words carefully, hearing disagreeing huffs come from both Nate and Rayya.

"Let me paint a better picture for you guys. Households...I didn't think about households back then, and I sure as hell don't think about them now. No one in my hood gave a fuck about me, my family, or the few so called friends I had. So called, because turns out they didn't give a fuck about me either. In the end they'd all backstabbed me. I was a dead kid walking if my organization hadn't saved me.

"Households...Na...if you're hoping that I have a warm heart for family units other than my own, or care how most others fair in life, you two are barking up the wrong tree. So, when we part ways in Chi Town, if you two don't want to ever speak to me again, I'm fine with that," he said, feeling deeper relief after saying each word.

"Number one, I wouldn't stop talking to you, because I... well I'm not quitting my job. I wouldn't quit, even if I hated your guts. Yeah, yeah. And, and. Number two... What you just said ...it's a lot to take in," he heard Rayya say, sitting back, looking at him with glossy eyes before facing forward.

"Tears...but for what? I've seen so many self-righteous tears, it's hard for me to consider that they're for me. And even if they are...my life is my life," he thought, honing in on the emotions underlying why he'd chosen to be so blunt after wanting to be so careful.

"I have to get one more thing off my chest," he whispered, watching the middle console spookily come to life, with the radio stations auto scrolling thorough for a few seconds before the console went dark again.

"Not talk to you again? I just don't...like, what do you think of Nate and I?" he heard Rayya exhale, sounding unnerved.

"I'm not trying to group you two into the mass of people I've meet. It's just that in general, I think people are bags of hot air. They're full of assurances and reassurance, but when it comes down to the heavy shit, they're the cheap paper," he replied, having flashbacks of putting bullets in more quote on quote friends than he'd ever had enemies.

"Baby," he heard his wife whisper in a scalding tone.

"What wifey?"

"Cheap paper? I told you about your mouth, and the shit that comes out of it," he heard his wife reply, sounding like she'd punch him if she could.

"Look wifey, I'm just saying that to them because I want to make sure that we're all on the same page. People work together well when they believe in the same things. Without a unified belief, there's no cohesion. So Nate, Rayya, I'm not trying to brainwash you into thinking that wifey and I should be people you should easily accept. But as you get to know us more, I ask you to give us a fair chance and umm, to not run away.

"There's an expression about people like me and boo. Y'all ever heard someone say, sometimes it's good to have bad friends. In this situation, with these bikers and whatever shit y'all got going on, I think, and I hope y'all give us the benefit of the doubt. In our world, allies on the same page is everything. I want y'all to know that whatever evil shit y'all see from us, it's not a reflection of how we'd treat y'all. Just please, for the love of 'It,' don't be the cheap paper or so help you 'It,' I will..."

"Baby!" he heard his wife interject, stopping him from the threat he had at the tip of his tongue.

"Enough?" he asked rhetorically, shaking his head, feeling dizzy from the mental burden shifting from secrets to responsibility over two more lives.

"Jay, I never had a doubt you or Karman wouldn't be good to us. Or Nate and I wouldn't have wanted to... or have done what we did with you. We don't need poisonous people in our lives as friends or even lose acquaintances, and we sure as hell don't want them as people we'd be intimate with," he heard Rayya say, sounding annoyed.

"Sticking to her guns about us, I like her the more I get to know her. Hey 'It,' if you're listening then I really hope whatever it is they have to say about the shit they're in - doesn't take this feeling away," he thought.

"Good to know bad people huh? Well, I thinking my moral view is flawed...because so far, no matter how much I'm starting to see into your reality, it's really hard to see evil in you two. But, we're no angels. Maybe that's why as well," he heard Nate say with a dark snicker.

"Yeah, I picked that up, the 'Stupindo' Rifle and other assortment of gadgets are for pure warfare," he said, beginning to chuckle at his own description of the Rifle.

"Stupindo Rifle?" he heard Nate say in a flat tone.

"Yup, Stupindo...bew...bew! Wait, real talk that shit didn't even make a sound! Soo cool! Oh fuck! Hahaha! My bad Nate, I meant no disrespect. I hate this ointment shit...makes me loopy," he said, laughing even harder, feeling like he'd totally lost his ability to resist it.

"Well maybe it's good you're loopy, anything to soften what I have to say is welcome," he heard Nate mutter, before saying, "what do you two think of...God, even saying this aloud, from my point of view sounds like bullshit."

"Just say it," he heard his wife reply, sounding a little more upbeat than before.

"The Master and Makers, there is a prophecy about them. Them, along with the state of humanity. For my family, it's told in the book of Lilith. And for Rayya, her father was teaching her from the book of Nefeshka. Both of my parents' and Rayya's father called the books, 'the Living Scripture'. We were both told that no one has actually written the books, yet over the course of thousands of years, the words had just appeared on the pages. We, of course don't believe that part, we just think it could be a terrible translation error. In any case, it was a shock for us to find out that there were two books, sharing the same prophecy, but having contradictions to one another, while having seamless comparisons," he heard Nate mutter with a nervous chuckle.

"Jesus," he heard his wife whisper, causing him to laugh to the point of breathlessness.

"Hahaha! You can't say things like that to Karman, her brain instantly shuts down!" he blared after catching his breath, knowing exactly what his wife was thinking.

"Never mind, maybe this is not best time to talk about this," he heard Nate mumble.

"Na, na, na! Come man, say your piece. Just wifey here, she won't believe jack shit of it," he said, feeling a surge of pure excitement at the topic, sitting forward so fast he felt areas of his wound reopen.

"Ochhhhh," he gasped right after, giggling uncontrollably as stinging pain erupted throughout his back.

"Karman? What the hell did you put in the ointment, dopamine doesn't really make a person act like this, does it? Jay, turn your back to me, let me see your cut, I think I felt it re-open just from the way you sat forward," he heard Rayya say in a warm, sarcastic tone.

"That's why I asked if you guys had ointment," he heard his wife reply, sounding slightly amused and annoyed at the same time.

"Um hum, you drug me and get annoyed that I talk too much after. Is this part of 'women are complicated' creatures' situation?" he asked, laughing hysterically as he turned, allowing Rayya to apply gel to the areas that had torn.

"You're always annoying to me my love. Anyways, I think everything can be explained with simple facts. You know what, I hate this topic. And no offence Nate, but Jay is right. I do shut down. I hate religion, prophecy stuff. Or anything that sound like it. I believe in God, but when it comes to that 'kinda' stuff…I just can't," he heard his wife say, sounding edgy and uncomfortable.

"This is not religious, not really. Well, it has elements of religion too. Look, I like face value and facts too. And if the things I had to tell you were more fiction than fact, this would be a different situation all together," he heard Nate say.

"Bro, this sounds heavy!"

"Why does it need to be called a Prophecy? It's not a good word to connect with fact," he heard his wife say dismissively.

"Told you Nate, she's not gonna listen! But I will!"

"Karman, I don't know…" he heard Nate begin, but he knew to cut in and say "Nate, just explain, don't plead with her."

"Okay, well then, in regards to the Makers Rayya and I were speaking about, they're multi path Geniuses."

"Multi what?" he heard his wife reply flatly…while he thought, *"Holy 1t!?"*

"Umm, arguably, there's five to seven types of Geniuses - Langue, Math, Mental imagery, Etcetera. Makers have at a minimum three of these skills sets combined. Their mental power is incomprehensible, so they're able to invent a lot of amazing technology. But it also limits them, to my knowledge they're not one known who's be able to function in society whatsoever. A lot of them are, for lack of a better word, trapped in their own head," he heard Rayya whisper.

"Damn, the inventions they make must be awesome! Them being trapped in their head, unable to function, that part, not so much," he heard his wife reply.

"You'd think their inventions are awesome, but for the most part, they're not," he heard Nate say softly

"Wha? Why?" he heard himself ask in surprise.

"Life, should have a pace, and what they do, and how they do it is, how to say this? There are normal advancements, along with large scale breakthroughs that of course do change the world for the better or worse depending on how you look at it. Albert Einstein is an example of this. He was a hundred or so years ahead of his time if you want to think of it like that. His work paved the way for many things we have today, but he also made the damn A-bomb, and now humanity is always close to midnight.

"Nicolas Tesla, was maybe two hundred or so years ahead. His ideas on wireless were great, but we can wirelessly kill each other all damn day as well. So you see, there's a very big window of pros and cons when it comes to advancements. If we're talking about what a single Maker can do…I get nervous to even say this, but they create things that would be maybe, one or two thousand years ahead of our current time," he heard Nate reply.

"A one or two thousand years advancement bro?" he whispered, feeling his palms begin to sweat.

"Maybe more. Long story short. Makers could collapse our society by making us move too fast into the future." he heard Nate say.

"And the Masters too?" he heard his wife ask.

"The Master, are different, they could be thought of as the authoritative figures of the Makers, but their agenda as told from the Prophecy is to...cleanse the world through ruthless war and bloodshed. Yes, I know, very cliché plot line of countless book, movies, etcetera."

"Mmmmm," he heard Rayya chime in.

"That Mmmm from Rayya is her dying to say, there are factors arising that call in question the motives of the Masters," he heard Nate reply quickly, but he could barely breathe as his mind raced.

"Yup, I was dying to say that, cause its true," he heard Rayya say matter of factly, slightly snapping him out of his mental whirlwind.

"I'm already bored. Masters, cleansing the world, really now? Cliché is right. And these Makers, if they're doing crazy stuff right now, why are we not flying around in space cars huh papi?" he heard his wife ask in a condescending tone.

"Boo, you don't see how too much of an advancement could burn humanity out like a hot light bulb," he replied.

"No, that's dumb. This is the same dumb shit you've told me about," he heard his wife huff.

"Huh?" he heard Nate ask, sounding way to excited.

"Oh, yeah, by the way y'all, 'I'ma' good old conspiracy theorist. I always bug wifey about humans being super smart. I love to read and research stuff like Atlantis, Egypt, the global civilization theories. 'I'ma' true believer in the humans burning themselves out like a 'hot bulb'. I genuinely believe there're civilizations that got way too advanced, went to war, and knocked humanity back a few pegs. So, this ties into that huh?"

"Yes, yes it does," he heard Nate mummer.

"Jesus, do you really have to feed this idiot fire and say that it does. This fool drags me to every goddamn site he can when we're on vacation and calls himself a freelance archeologist. Fucking points to the same damn cut rocks he saw online and declares the same damn thing the video maker did. Fucking ancient Tech my 'cocha.' Telling him yes, is dooming me to go to never ending sites," he heard his wife reply, seeing her hair move, knowing she was shaking her head.

"Well, Karman, umm. You really don't think there were global civilizations after seeing the ruins and what not?" he heard Nate ask pensively before saying, "And I get what you're asking though. You're saying where is the huge advancement like flying space cars, right?"

"Yup," he heard his wife reply.

"Well, if possible, they're apprehended, along with their creations. Their creations are then locked away and studied by groups of extremely intelligent individuals called Mediums. The Mediums try to figure out what was created, and if or when it could be safely applied it to society. For the creations that slip by, well usually, the public utterly rejects it. That or…"

"Uhh," he heard his wife say sarcastically cutting Nate off.

"Shush, Eggyyy."

"Or they've created something so ingenious, it gets integrated in society almost way to seamlessly. Which at first doesn't give a great argument as to why they should be stopped," he heard Nate say softly.

"Well, explain more on what the concern is, nothing's wrong with a good old paradigm shift," he replied.

"Okay, a good example of technological integration and timing would be cell phones and wearable techs. Not saying that the Makers were responsible for this, just use this as a reference. Think of when cellphones came out, it had this new 'Ahh' effect for…not so long right. Well Tesla had thought of wireless devices long before we were even born, and there was a slow ramp up to where we are today. Back in the day, Tesla wanted to introduce wireless concepts to the market really fast. There was great resistance to it by the public, the people weren't ready, and the government couldn't control it. It was kinda like an unconscious understanding that if his inventions hit the market, things would go out of whack.

"With slow progression, when cell phones finally hit the market at a common consumer cost, four years later, you couldn't find a person without a cellphone. Reason being is, conceptually, almost everyone understood how wireless tech worked. Adaptations, or pretty much higher tech cellphones were not considered alien or a threat to societies subconscious mind. The extreme, or the new technological threats, then became wearable devices like View-Tech's, because of their conceptualized privacy and lack there off. But over the years, people became used to their every move being watched by cameras everywhere. So now, it's quote on quote 'okay,' or this 'who cares' if someone is silently recording me with View-Tech's. The baseline problems…wireless being spooky, and privacy already being invaded, were addressed, then humanity was ready for that step.

"So now, how many people do you see no longer even carrying a cell phone? Especially the younger crowd? They accepted this wearable, invasive technology right away, because they were born into always being watched. This progression is not seamless at first, but has a better fit with people in the long run. When a Makers Tech slips in, and fits with society right away, it has the opposite effect and becomes erosive as people become awakened to its true nature, and by then it's already too late," he heard Nate say.

"See boo, do you feel a paradigm shift? I know your eyes are opening," he chuckled, half serious, half joking.

"My eyes are open; I'm driving aren't I? Still, all bullshit. Bullshit stinks…so no one wants to look at it. There is no hundred years, one thousand years ahead of time. Whatever a person makes is whatever a person makes at that time. It came right when it was supposed to come. We are all different, why is there some stupid time limit as to how far a person thinks from another? It's bullshit, it's grouping. People are just people. If an advancement is there, then it's there. Humans burning out from over advancement is very arguable. We can easily have advancement that keep us stable. And there will always be an underlay to technology that people can or cannot get used to," he heard his wife say right after.

"What would it take to convince you? If I said I had proof, if I showed you things that were undeniable, showed you things that seem harmless but can destroy us?" he heard Nate ask.

"I 'dunno', it better be good though. And for certain if I see another fucking flat stone cut to perfection and told it's done

by laser beam, I'll aim this car at a tree and kill us all. So I h
to ask, it's not a dumb fucking piece of stone is it?" he heard
wife ask without an ounce of humor in her voice.

"Karman, you ever heard of the saying 'the truth is strang
than fiction?'" he heard Nate chime in, sounding defensive.

"Si, but you didn't answer my question," he heard his wife
say under her breath.

"Karman, why are you so defensive about this topic? I
mean I expected disbelief, but I also expected more of an open
ear," he heard Nate say, now sounding annoyed.

"Yeah, you were staring at the Rifle like it was a damn sex
toy," he heard Rayya chime in right after.

"Si, …it…it's sexy…So what. Is that the undeniable
proof?" he heard his wife ask, with an edge in her tone.

"Yeah is it?" he asked right after, trying to mentally identify
the odd, yet familiar odor that'd come off the melted Rifle.

"Yes, actually it is," he heard Rayya say matter of factly.

"Okay, okay, now I'm listening," he heard his wife reply.

"This is her mental chess game for you guys to let her
borrow it, so she can study the properties. She probably still
doesn't believe a word you're saying. This is about to get 'hella'
circular, because now no matter what you say, she's going to say
without looking at the material itself, she won't buy your story,"
he replied thinking, *"She has a point of wanting facts."*

"Papi, did I…did I ask for a translation huh? No so
'cállate,'" he heard his wife say.

"I can't allow you to study it Karman," he heard Nate
whisper.

"Son of a …" he heard his wife begin.

"Karman, I need you to try and acknowledge something.
Recently, haven't you felt this shift. Or at least seen it in the last
three years. Humanity is in a very difficult stage of its existence,
everything is very delicate when it comes to technology. That
awkward fear of robots taking jobs has already happened and is
only getting more acute. People having a professional job, but
can't afford to buy a house, forced to rent or buy unaffordable
one bedroom or two bedroom boxes in the sky for thirty years.

"Health care affordability going from strenuous to
completely out of reach for many. An everyday well-educated

vernight finding themselves useless, replaced by,
pon-complaining emotionless labor. On a global scale,
look like suffocating fish in a bowl. You have to admit
nan, what the hell will happen to people, with no
e, no money, no jobs? Surely you can see so many have
y given up. No matter how hard they strive for a quote on
e 'profession', paying for school, putting themselves in debt
n the beginning, they still find themselves not valuable.
manity is moving too fast. With these facts, it's simple any
nvention created by a Maker could tip the balance. Then, if we
take into account the Master, who would've a purpose, ability to
use anything a Maker has created, we would've a world bathed in
blood," he heard Nate say solemnly.

I will say this again, who's to say humanity can't adapt. You
said, there are Mediums, so obviously, there are people who can
think like Makers.

"Mediums can usually understand max ten percent of each
Makers invention. Mediums are usually teams of hundreds of
different disciplined scientists by the way. That's unless it's a
seamless kind of invention, but that one's already slipped by, and
everyone on a global scale has figured it out as well, but like I
said, by then everyone's has started realizing and thinking, why
the hell did we integrate this into society."

"Fine, even if I took what you said at face value and blamed
people I don't know, I can't sit here and think people overall are
too dumb not to adjust, to find their way. Life was never easy for
any one group of people at any given time frame in human
history, this is just our time frame, this is just our struggle," he
heard his wife say.

"Humm," he said, growing agitated, thinking, *"I see, she's
annoyed because this hits too close to home. She knows Nate's right and she
feels our little plan to secure our future before reality crushes us is moving way
too slow. I second that feeling, but on the real, we only have so many hours in
a day. And at work, sometimes we actually have to do some of it or we'd get
kicked out and not have access to the resources we need."*

"Karman, just wow," he heard Rayya reply, laughing darkly.

As Rayya continued to laugh, he could feel a cold storm of
darkness and rage seeping from her that'd quantify the meaning
of infinity in hell. Then Nate turned and looked at him with a

desperate, righteous resolve that painted a picture of a starving, enraged bear being backed into a corner by hungry men with spears.

"I was honestly hoping you'd say something less, less heavy, where I'd just be able to sit here and try to peel away the silly bullshit from fun fact," he whispered.

"Fun facts?" he heard Nate whisper.

"Yeah, one can only hope," he replied, starting to feel numb when he heard his wife say "So, basically you're saying your job is to limit…to limit humanity? Of course, that's why you have a one-gun army," he heard her say, sucking her teeth right after.

"Guide, not limit. Guide the common people away from self-destruction. It, it's my family burden. And yes, I need all the armament I can get my hands on. These people think nothing of taking a life. You have to understand, at their intelligence level, people are no more than tools, insects, hell, even less than that. You, you have no idea the things I've seen them do to people," he heard Nate say in a strained voice.

"Guide the so called common people from the evil geniuses, with gun and strong principals, sounds just as scary as the people he's describing. But he can't hear himself and it'd fall on deaf ears if I reminded him the road to hell is paved with good intentions," he thought, as he said, "Your family? What the fuck you talking about? I thought your dad's a dentist and your mom's like some kindda chiropractor or some shit."

"They're my cover family. My true parents are the Lilith's of Lilith Corporation," he heard Nate mumble.

"What the fuck! You're a goddamn Ga-Ga-Gagillionare! What the fuck! When you…Oh who arth thou in hevenith!" he shrieked, instantly feeling light headed, as his brain tried to comprehend who Nate claimed to be.

"Yeah," he heard Nate reply, sounding almost ashamed.

"Wifey! Wifey! Pull over I think I need some air for a sec! Whattt the fuckkkk! How is this possible? Like seriously, are you fucking with me right now!? How are people not swarming you all the time! Whattt!!!?" he asked over exaggerating his shock as he thought, *"The God complex and High-Tech stuff all adds up!"*

"Think about it, my parents never bring up if they even have children or not. For the most part, the world has no idea I even exist," he heard Nate reply.

"Oh holy 'It!' And Rayya, your stories of struggling! Not getting a job! What the fuck! I don't get it, why!? Why are you even working!? What the fuck are you even doing here!? I can't even! Billions, billions of dollars! If I had that kind of money…hell no…just hell no!" he said as his wife pulled over on the side of the road.

"I'm shocked, but he's overreacting. Especially about the money. We, we have a lot of money. Our ventures pay very, very well," he heard his wife say, noting her insecurity when it came to speaking of monetary values.

"Baby, Lil –ith Corp! LiL ith Corp! He is the son of the owners of Lil-ith Corp! How can you compare our money with Lil- ith Corp!? Are you crazy?" he said, feeling a rush of giddiness, he knew was purely from the dopamine's effect in his blood stream.

"Okay yeah! What the hell! Rayya! Hubby's right, I don't get it! You made it seem like you were really, really struggling. Like if you didn't have a job, you'd be on the street. I get wanting to work…to like be a part of something bigger than yourself. It's one of the reasons why Jay and I picked our jobs. We're building things for the future and money doesn't really match up to that. For us, it's our way of feeling balanced. But… you said you couldn't even find a job. Couldn't you work for Nate's company?" he heard his wife say as he popped open the door, taking a deep breath of fresh air.

"I thought I had fucking secrets!" he thought, walking towards a patch of trees, taking out his cock, pissing without any reservations.

As he emptied his bladder, he felt a wave of sheer panic pass through him.

"Same feeling, whoever it is…is still following us. What the shit?" he thought, now considering the hunted sensation and Nate's news as an enormous whirlpool that he'd already fallen into.

"Lilith Corp. and affiliates are a fucking global force. Of course they don't announce they have a son! They would've lock him up in one of their

buildings the same way they always lock themselves up!" he thought, shuddering from relief now that his bladder was empty.

"Talking to yourself is a bad habit," he heard Rayya say, coming up in front of him on his right, tugging down her spandex shorts, popping a squat.

"I wasn't talking to myself. Was I?"

"Lilith Corp. is a fucking global force. Your words, not mine," he heard Rayya reply sarcastically.

"Oh, shit. I thought I was just thinking that. Anyways, why did you not take the easy way out and take the in-law's cash. All pride aside…fuck it…just do it, and not think about it," he said looking down, watching as Rayya relieved herself.

"You went crazy before my Habibi could finish. You don't know his parents, they're…well in my opinion, pure evil to say the least. Not to mention the obvious."

"Which is?"

"You're bad at playing dumb Jay. Fine I'll say it aloud. He married a Muslim, do you think they want to give me a dime?" he heard Rayya huff as she wiped herself with a piece of paper towel, reaching up for him to take her hand right after.

"So weird," he whispered, helping Rayya stand.

"Which part? Did I miss the memo when Muslims and Jews started getting married without complications after thousands of years of hate? Hummm, magically vanishing hate…ha!" he heard Rayya reply in a condescending tone.

"What? Hell no, I meant, watching you pee. I spend a lot of time down there and still can't figure out where the fuck y'all pee comes from?" he said, watching as she pulled up her shorts, glaring at him with a look that screamed – 'idiot.'

"Well then, that tells me you haven't spent enough time there after all," he heard her finally reply, playfully shoulder checking him as she walked past.

"Humm. Is that an invite?"

"With that tongue of yours, if you don't volunteer, I'd invite myself," he heard her say with a mischievous smirk before her look changed to dark annoyance.

"I didn't do so good of a job subtly changing the topic, huh? Look, I knew racism was a factor, but fuck…I mean did they cut y'all the way off? I was thinking that maybe they'd begrudgingly give y'all some millions. Old school parents that are racist suck monkey balls...but I've heard...yeah, I'll say I've heard many stories where the fam just sucks it up and helps out," he said, hopping in the SUV after Rayya, now sitting behind Nate.

"I cut myself off actually. I told them I want to work for my money. But after marrying Rayya, my mother drained my accounts...and she made sure Rayya couldn't get a job with the company...or any of its affiliates."

"Ohhhh shiiiiit...mom in law is ruthless...she hatesss youuuuu," he said, chuckling as a random wave of giddiness surged up again.

"Jay, papi...I'ma punch you in the mouth," he heard his wife growl softly.

"I second wanting to do that," he heard Rayya whisper.

"So that's why you had that look on your face during the interview! Shit, I think our company and like the one in Canada are the only two quantum computer firms that are not a part of the affiliate group. I remember the day you were hired, I think you didn't even read the contract, it was in my hand before I could even blink," he said recalling her urgency.

"I didn't, it could've asked me for my liver," he heard Rayya reply grimly, giving him an evil glare.

"I see, I see," he whispered.

"What do you see?" he heard her mumble in annoyance.

"Why you getting 'pissy' at me?" he asked, beginning to feel defensive.

"Make a joke about my mother in law hating me...fucking...fuck you," he heard Rayya mumble, watching as she opened the door, quickly moving to the truck.

"*I seriously hate being drugged. It's hard enough already to bite my tongue,*" he thought, hearing Rayya mumble, "making a joke about the person trying to ruin my life with her every breath...who'd have me out on the fucking street."

"Wasn't trying too...I hate this brain hack thingy. Be patient with me a lil bit," he replied as sincerely as he could, only to hear Rayya say, "And she's always, always trying to fucking kill me," as she slammed the truck closed.

"Trying to kill you?" he replied

"Yes! You heard me! And be patient he says? I am being patient," he heard Rayya snip.

"Lawd' 'It,' seriously my bad. But 'yo', what you mean trying to kill you? Metaphorically right? Like by making you struggle right?" he asked the moment Rayya hopped in the SUV, tossing a small round can on his lap labelled peanuts.

"Umm, if you missed the main topic of today, making someone struggle in this economy is premeditated murder if you want to be real about it, and no, she did way worse than that," he heard Rayya say, pressing her thumb to the top of the canister.

"Like what," he heard his wife ask, as the top of the canister retracted, revealing strands of what looked to be hair.

"Dude, this said peanuts. Fuck is this? All top secret can type crap, I'm hungry as hell," he mumbled, squinting at the three strands of dark tinged fiber or hair.

"Proof of what my hubby is trying to explain, the kind Karman will go ape-shit over if she could get it to a lab," he heard Rayya puff.

"What are you guys talking about? Let me see!" he heard his wife exclaim as she pushed opened her door, quickly coming to his side.

"Don't touch the one on the right, the one with the red tinge to it," he heard Nate say, looking towards them expectantly.

"Why?" he asked instantly, wanting to touch the hair like material.

"How's this proof? Proof of what? This looks like hair," he heard his wife say, staring into the can dubiously.

"It is, and it isn't. Remember you asked about my Rifle? A large majority of what it's made up of comes from these three strands. If this were to fall into the wrong hands and mass produced, there would be almost no need for a global metal sector. I'm not even getting into what other destructive things have been made using these as a guide. Is what I'm saying about the Makers making more sense? Tell me, if this hit the global market right now, how would humanity readjust? This would fit in seamlessly, because Graphene and Kevlar have been created, people wouldn't question the next best thing, especially if there were no signs it'd be a carcinogen or harmful to the environment.

403

But it'd take less than a year before the Metal sector and things associated with it to go belly up," he heard Nate say urgently.

"Shit, umm, I 'dunno' how we'd adjust. Like right now I just see strands of material, and you're telling me what it can do, words don't verify, testing does," he heard his wife whisper, giving him a 'what the fuck' look.

"Like what is it? Who, I mean what was the name of the person who created this? Are we allowed to know?" he asked thinking, *"I know wifey and I don't exactly fit his description, but if he knew even half the shit we were up to, would he call us and the people we have helping us Makers? Shit, could some of the people helping us be Makers? The glass, the glass was something out of this world when it was finished."*

"Truth, you really want to know?" he heard Rayya ask.

"Uh, yeah," he replied sarcastically.

"It's bio engineered human hair. When Nate's family found the location of, let's go with un-named person for now, there were piles of it everywhere. But I bet you guys don't believe me, do you?" he heard Rayya ask, looking up to his wife, then to him with a knowing smirk.

"My brain actually feels heavy, it's hard for me," he heard his wife reply.

"Ditto, what the actual fuck?" he replied thinking, *"I wish instead of this miracle hair crap in the can, it was what I've been searching for. But then again, every time I've been near one, its brought nothing but pain."*

"Great, well then, let's put all this on a quick pause, sweetie can you get us the fuck 'outta' here please? Jay brought up a good point about being hungry, I'm starving, and I need a coffee and a fucking shower. Actually, we all need that. Habibi, you still smell like puke baby. I love you though," he heard Rayya say right after.

"I second that, let's get the fuck out of here," he replied, watching a small accusing smile and frustrated crease form on Rayya's forehead.

"What's this? This is new for her," he thought, hearing Rayya say, "Sweetie, what made you who you are? Something made you become a material scientist. Did you see something as a child

that influenced you? Something that triggered you to look at how things are made."

"Now it's a dark, sad look, that flashes to hopeful, then it goes to the sadistic look ever. What the fuck is going on in Rayya's head?" he thought, feeling himself begin to chuckle as he thought of white thought clouds appearing over Rayya's head with crazy cartoons fighting within them.

"Wifey what did you put in this? I'm seeing cartoons!" he said still laughing, watching Rayya make a sarcastic, sorrowful look at him.

"Enjoy your trip baby," he heard his wife reply airily, quickly getting them back on the road.

Then for about five minutes they sat in silence before he heard his wife say, "Rayya, I see why you and hubby work together now. Looking for meaning in things. I've always just had a knack for seeing the bigger picture of how things are formed. To me, my job is all logical. I mean I do theorize, but those are practical theories that I can apply. I never think too much about like everything else. Like I 'dunno' what a trigger for me is, I just feel I am who I am."

"Okay sweetie, just curious. And it's honestly because, when I was a child, some of the first stories I remember my father telling me was about amazing people who lived in South America. And he'd tell me how special the land was there, he said it couldn't be found anywhere else, and that he was always jealous that he wasn't born there," he heard Rayya whisper as she took hold of his hand with a thoughtful expression on her face.

"He, he said that?" he heard his wife reply reflectively.

"Yes, and he would specify regions. Especially Colombia," he heard Rayya say, with a soft chuckle.

"Her father was telling her about the trade cities. Telling her about the Musica civilization. Oh 'It,' what 'fuckery' are you up to?" he thought mindlessly fiddling with one of the strands in the can when his index finger become uncomfortable.

"Did the hair just cut me?" he whispered, staring at his finger

"Of course, you'd touch it, it's you!" he heard Rayya exclaim.

"Of course, I would! You said not to! Who does that? Of course, I'd want to touch it then!" he replied – when in truth, he'd been so caught up in his thoughts he had not known he'd been fumbling in the can.

"Karman's right! You are a child!" he heard Rayya snip, grabbing his hand placing his bleeding finger in her mouth.

"Dude…vampire much? Who sucks cut blood these days…really?" he whispered, with a look of confusion as she pulled his finger free from her mouth, quickly applying a dab of ointment before it bled again.

"An idiot," he heard Rayya whisper, not even looking at him as she kissed his hand, pressing it down in her lap right after.

"You just drank my blood" he replied, feeling a flash of heat remembering her sucking his fingers for a much different reason.

"Fuck, I'm curious about shit I think is ridiculous," he heard his wife mumble.

"Yasss, question things! Be intrigued and inspired!" he chuckled, staring awkwardly at his left hand holding the can – wanting his right hand back from Rayya's death grip.

"I hate it," he heard his wife reply sarcastically.

"Hey, did that, did that say Coffee!? Karman! Stop, stop, stop! Look! A Coffee shop! Yes! Finally, something's going right!" he heard Rayya say excitedly, feeling the SUV pull to a stop right after.

"I'd be careful with your words," he whispered, feeling an odd sensation in his stomach that always demarked a problem.

"Baby what's up?" he heard his wife ask pensively.

"My belly did the thingy," he replied, handing Rayya the can as he peeked past her, eyes locking on a police car parked up a steep hill next to a log cabin house that had a sign that read, "coffee – dinner."

"You 'gotta' shit?" he heard Nate mumble.

"Ha, you'd think, but that'd be normal," he heard his wife say pensively.

"Look at the police car, y'all see what's wrong?" he asked, growing instantly pissed at his own observation.

"No, what should we see?" he heard Nate ask.

"Fucking, mother fuckin idiot," he growled, hopping out of the SUV, quickly making his way up the hill, hearing his wife right behind him.

"Nate before you come, can you close her door, she has closing door problems…tweak in the brain," he said, arriving in front of the police car.

"What's going on Jay?" he heard Nate reply, hearing the driver's side door shut closed.

"You'll see soon enough," he mumbled, shaking his head.

"Jesus," he heard his wife whisper.

"Yeahhhh, fucking idiot," he mumbled, titling his head as a piece of skull and brain matter dripped down on top the police officer's mangled head.

"Baby, why are you showing them you can sense and feel things like this," he heard his wife whisper in a scalding tone.

"Oh shut up me Eggy, always reprimanding me. And you're always the one trying to make me open up to them. So, what's your problem? I am who I am," he said, opening the car door, studying the young man with a hole underneath his chin to the top of his head.

"I hate suicide. I hate people who do this shit to themselves," he whispered, searching for a sign of something that'd explain why the man had ended his life.

"Hey…what's …Jay, why are you in the cop's…Oh fuck, for fucks sake," he heard Rayya say, causing him to look over at the couple who were staring at him in bewilderment.

"Nate, hack the dude's phone," he replied, pulling a cell phone from cop's left hand, tossing it to Nate.

"We shouldn't be touching things! What's wrong with you? Your fingerprints!" he heard his wife growl.

"I might not be able to," he heard Nate mumble.

"Do what you can bro," he replied, diving back into the car, fumbling with the police officer's radio which was eerily on – with a soft voice constantly speaking in the background, in distorted, incoherent sentences.

"Where the fuck is, where the fuck is his main channel back to his Precinct?" he whispered, scrolling through every channel to only hear the same eerie whispers, finally opting to turn the scanner off, moving his attention to the center panel for the local radio.

"Okay, let's see if we get something here," he whispered, pressing the on button, instantly hearing, **(Man)** - *"Stocks plummeting to levels lower than two thousand eight, with still no end in sight."*

(Woman) - *"Not just stocks, all the currencies are tanking. John, the implications of this are incalculable."*

(John) - **"We're getting reports flooding in of...of people, lots of self-inflicted fatalities all throughout the country, all throughout the world. It's like we're being thrown into the past. Like a scene from the great depression. Carol, this is a sad day in the history of our great nation and the world."**

"What the fuck?" he whispered, surprised at what he heard and the clarity of which he heard it.

"Shushh!" he heard his wife exclaim.

"Shush yourself," he replied, removing himself from the car, only to catch an elbow in his chest from his wife as she pointed at the radio.

"Yes John, it is. It is indeed. Overnight and all this morning, there've been massive lay off in all sectors with no promise of ever returning to work. And with both global and local banks going completely under, people are not only losing their jobs, but every dollar they have. Oh fuck this," he heard Carol say, followed by John screaming **"Oh God Carol no! Please No!"**

"Fuck this shit! I went through hell to get this job! And to keep it, even fucking you! And fucking that other pig! We're all married...I have fucking kids... and y'all made me fuck you! And I did it, I did it because stupid me...I thought I would've a better life, feed my children, take care of my disabled husband who fought in all this country's stupid fucking wars, only to get his legs and hand blasted off by some, some brainwashed child! And he comes back to get shit on, with no support by our government! So

I, so I whored myself! I literally whored myself!" he heard Carol sob.

"Carol no! Let's talk about this!" he heard John plead in sobbing gasp.

"Wow Buddyyyy," he whispered, feeling his stomach turn.

"You...you're a shithead...but...at least you seemed to fucking care a little about my life...but you Greg...You made sure you always showed me that my place is beneath you. Always fucking me in the ass, not once in my pussy! Not once! You wanted it to hurt! For you to have all the pleasure! Wouldn't even let me have a guilty orgasm huh! And I noticed something huh, you love your dick huh!?" he heard Carol say, followed by a man screaming, *"Carol, I...I! Please I!"*

"You what, you gave me sores! I know you know that! My husband won't even fuck me anymore, you bastard! Held my job hostage for my ass, knowing I'm trying to support my family! But you made sure you hurt me and my family! You, son of a bitch! You know my husband wanted to divorce me when I gave him the sores too! But there's nowhere for him to even go! And I love him...I'm glad he couldn't go anywhere because I want to take care of him!"

"Carol please!"

"Oh I used to beg too, but every day you'd smirk at me! But you know what, last laugh mother fucker! I'll be sending you to hell with no dick!" he heard Carol say with a maniacal laugh as a shot went off.

"OOOO! OHH!" he heard a man gasp and wail at the top of his lungs, who he presumed was Greg before falling silent.

"Oh...Oh shit! Ga ...Ga...Ga Greg? Greg? Shit! Carol please no! Put that down, please!" he heard John beg, sounding absolutely mortified.

"Please what? There's nothing to fucking live for. Everything's fucking gone. Gone John...there's nothing to fight for. I'm tired...tell me what it was all for? What!? Tell me what I was fighting for?" he heard Carol whisper, hearing a soft click.

"Carol," he heard John gasp.

"Enjoy the dick sores John, make sure your wife enjoys them too," he heard Carol whisper, followed by a gunshot and John wailing, *"I love you...I love you...I never loved her...Whyyy? Why? Why? Why?"*

"Fuck's wrong with you?" he snapped, glaring at his wife who wore an odd smirk on her face.

"She...she knew how to go out," he heard his wife chuckle, with a twisted smile on her face, which he saw mirrored on Rayya's.

"Rayya, you think it's funny too?" he asked, noting that Nate was sharing his sentiment, grimacing and shaking his head.

"What? She fucked that guy up for forcing her to fuck him. You just know from those screams she got him right in the dick!" he heard his wife reply with a bright smile.

"No, that's not what I'm talking about! I mean yes good job, vengeance is great! But no! That's not what I'm talking about! I'm talking about her killing herself! It's stupid! It's selfish! Protect your life! How are people just killing themselves! What the fuck was she thinking," he erupted, not understanding the mindset in the slightest.

"You have no idea how it is to be a woman. I can't help but laugh at it. She's strong in my opinion. To me, that was her taking full control," he heard his wife say callously.

"Ahhh! I hate this men, women shit! People are fucked...The point of life is to keep it. Plain and simple!"

"She felt she and her family would've died if she didn't fuck those pigs. And she found out it was all for nothing and went crazy. I like her, I can't help but like and respect how she took control and went out," he heard his wife snap back.

"Liked her. She's past tense. Taking control is keeping yourself alive to fight another day! Now she's not there for her kids, or her disabled husband!" he said, shaking his head at his wife and Rayya who had been nodding her head in approval at his wife's every word till he had finished his sentence.

"Hum, so it hasn't fully clicked in y'all heads what your commending? The message y'all tell Nate and I," he said, shaking his head before saying, "Here's when both of you go, huh?'

Seeing blank looks on his wife and Rayya's face, he scoffed and said, "Well how 'bout what the fuck is going to happen to our jobs? What will you two clowns do if y'all read bye, bye, we've gone belly up? And Rayya, even if by miracle Nate's parents finally wanted to step up and help with their ga-gillions, well what if their ga-gillions turns to shit. No offence Nate, but they may be going under too. Are y'all just gonna blow your heads off cause everything you worked for is gone?"

"None taken," he heard Nate reply, glaring at Rayya and his wife questioningly

"Jesus, you always need to…need to win," he heard his wife reply, watching her eyes as she scanned within her View-Tech's, undoubtedly for a termination email.

"Eggy? Did you get an…an email?" he asked, seeing her eyes lock onto something.

"Nope, no emails, it says servers are down for my company. It's just, my View-Tech's were auto scanning radio stations, and they all say no signal, but I hear that chatter, the same one that was playing in the car," he heard his wife whisper.

"Okay, you know what. I've had enough. I want in this place, I want some coffee, I can smell some coming through the door, fuck everything else till then," he heard Rayya snip, giving him an annoyed look.

"Right, I agree, fuck this dead dude, coffee is still important," he replied, getting an even nastier look from Rayya.

"What? I agree with you," he whispered, realizing he smelled something else besides coffee.

"Get me a cup Rayya, I'm going back to the car. I want to get the guns. If the news is as bad as it sounds, we're going to be running into some desperate people," he heard his wife mumble, already beginning to head down the sloping driveway with Nate, fighting to catch up behind her.

"Pfff, your hubby wants to see those guns huh?" he chuckled, looking at Rayya who was still staring at him with a deadpan look of annoyance.

"Chill with that look. Eh, on the real though, can you stay here and let me go in first?" he asked Rayya, climbing up a small flight of stairs, pushing the cabin door open.

"I know what you smell, I'm not a little girl. I lived in a full-on war zone remember," he heard Rayya whisper, coming up behind him as he stepped into the entrance of the café.

"Okay, are you just trying to prove some point to me right now?" he asked, shaking his head in detest as flies zipped past him, out the door.

"Yes, that I can handle myself. …Oh shit, oh fuck, ummm," he heard Rayya gag, stepping back, making sweeping gestures, indicating he should continue to search the place on his own.

"Un huh, that's what I thought," he whispered, stepping deeper into the cabin, tracing the foul scent to a room on the far right, next to a tiny corner kitchen.

"Hello?" he said, feeling stupid right after.

"Hello, really Jay?" he mumbled, stepping around an assortment of cups, plates and glasses, strewn all over the floor that he assumed was due to the earthquake.

Moving in just a bit deeper, he peered down the hallway and realized the diner-café part was on the other side of the cabin, where he could see tables and chairs.

"Huh? Much bigger than it seems," he whispered, glaring back at the corner kitchen, taking note of the oddity to all the chaos, which happened to be a coffee maker coughing out its last bit of brew.

"Maybe…maybe it's an animal rotting? Like maybe, they dragged a deer in or some shit?" he whispered to himself, glaring longingly at the coffee, wishing there wasn't a putrid smell intermingled with it.

"Hello?" he called again, not feeling as stupid this time, being that someone had to have been alive to make the coffee.

"This is the part of the movie where you get axed," he heard Rayya say with a deep inhale right after, turning to see her standing in the doorway with her eyes locked in on the coffee pot.

"Huh? Fiend for the bean much, or just being nosey? And due to my ethnicity, it would be wouldn't it?" he replied, staring at the step stool in front of the coffee maker, getting another sinking feeling in his stomach as he walked towards the door next to the kitchen.

"This place sounds, sounds unsteady, do you hear the creaking? Do you think it might collapse? Even the ceiling is broken in a bunch of places," he heard Rayya say in a way that said- 'Jay let's get the fuck out of here.'

"Truth, I barely heard the creaking. I hope it doesn't collapse on me. If I'm not crushed, it'd be my luck the fires behind us would catch up and bake me before y'all can dig me out," he whispered, hoping what he said was enough to keep Rayya from coming in any further.

"Was that supposed to make me feel better!?" he heard Rayya say, stepping in with her arm out stretched, gesturing for him to get out of there.

"Ug! Rayya just stay there," he replied in annoyance, pulling open the door next to the kitchen, making up his mind to just look.

"Jay?" he heard Rayya say expectantly.

"What? I'm fine," he mumbled, peering into the room.

"Oh, come on, what's going on today? 'It,' if you do exist, today you're showing me your ass," he whispered, staring at the pale, malnourished face of a young girl no older than seven, who was holding a tray with two cups of coffee.

"Jay? What's there? What do you see?" he heard Rayya ask anxiously.

"Fuck my life!" he thought, staring at the ill looking girl as she turned her head toward him with glazed eyes.

"They won't wake up," he heard the girl say matter of factly, blinking once before returning her gaze to her long dead parents who lay swollen and rotten in a tiny bed.

"I know she knows. They know full well what's going on at this age. I feel like I stepped right back into my life before I joined my organization! Every day was suicide, drug over doses, abandoned children, and plain old destitution," he thought, staring at a glass pipe in the mother's swollen hand.

"Coffee…coffee always wakes them up. Mommy says coffee keeps the 'sleepies' away," he heard the little girl said, looking at him pleadingly.

"Come here you," he said, holding himself together by the skin of his teeth as he stepped closer toward the girl, where he saw a bag of drugs laying at the mother's swollen, purple feet.

"Boom…it all comes full circle," he thought, mumbling, "Lady Karma, your pussy stinks."

"My daddy says not to talk to strangers…especially guys. He says that I should come get him if…if," he heard the girl say, beginning to heave.

"Your pop is right," he said, having a flashback, hearing himself say he didn't give a fuck about households.

"So, you're going to have to leave mister. Or my papa will…"

"Come here you lil runt," he replied, backing out of the bedroom, bumping into Rayya.

"Yeah, I thought I'd be fine. But I'm not…I'm…really not," he heard Rayya say shakily.

"Neither am I, and today I thought I put on my big boy pants," he whispered, pushing her closer to the door so the little girl could see her and possibly think she was a better candidate to come to.

"This is mommy and daddy's long-time friend. They called her to come get you," he said, voice cracking as he backed up further.

"Hi sweetie," he heard Rayya whisper, crouching down.

"You're dressed like a 'swut'! Mommy and daddy would never be friends with you 'swut'! You're a bad lady. And they are sleeping now! How can they call you! Liar! 'Swut' liar!" he heard the girl whisper weakly.

"I hate seeing my reflection!" he thought, crouching down, picking up a tiny green bag with a clown imprinted insignia and a piece of paper within.

"Mix one dot of Fentanyl per two drops of H-Low," he read aloud.

"Fentanyl! And what the fuck is H-low? Heroin or some new shit?" he growled, feeling his belly churn with rage.

"And this girl, she doesn't only seem malnourished. Those are withdrawal sweats…did they give this to her too?" he thought, realizing that many of the spoons on the floor had residue on them.

"Oh crap, Rayya, go to…" before he could finish his sentence, Jay heard a thud and the cups shatter.

Chapter VII

My Truth – Is Something I Hide From

Road Trip: Day Four

Date: Sunday, June 4th 2017

Time: 09:45 am

Location: Hill City, South Dakota

"Jay might play tough and have that really scary side to him, but now I see it's all just to protect his heart," Nate thought reflectively, so caught up in his observations of Jay, he hadn't noticed that Karman had stopped walking – leading him to collide right into her.

"Sorry! Sorry!" he exclaimed, wrapping his arms around her at the same time.

"It's okay, relax," he heard Karman mumble uncaringly, gazing at him with a somewhat puzzled expression that made him feel self-conscious.

"Sorry, am I holding you too tight?"

"What? No. What are you talking about? You're silly, now get off me, need to get the stuff," he heard Karman reply, laughing and shaking her head as she pushed his chest, leaning back on his arms to break free of his grip.

"Why do they make me feel so vulnerable? I'm so afraid that all the sudden, they'll hate us for what happened this morning. I would've never thought I'd feel like this. I was sure I'd feel more secure. But now, more than ever, I'm terrified of losing them," he thought, reluctantly unlocking his arms from around Karman's tiny, but curvy frame.

"This morning, I hope I didn't make you feel like…like I didn't respect you. I mean, I know what we did before that, but I…ummm, I know I'm not your husband to just go up to you and start touching you," he said, watching Karman pop open the trunk and dump both of their bags onto the ground.

"You respect me huh?" he heard Karman ask in a sarcastic tone, pressing her hand to the mesh of the truck which retracted in lightning speed, revealing what he considered to be a small armory.

"Yes, of course I do," he replied, watching Karman slip on a body holster.

"Ha-ha, I know that already sweetie," he heard Karman reply as she placed two jungle camouflage hand guns into two empty holsters.

"But, if you're worried about this morning, a good thing to keep in mind is to massage my boobies a 'lil' harder. And for the love of God, I don't care if the world is burning down, humm, which in this case, it was. But next time, find a way to bring me coffee, K papi?" he heard Karman say, giving him a mischievous smile as she adjusted the straps of her body holster.

"Uhh…Okay," he said, feeling himself flush.

"Mum-hum. So…Rifle? You don't really seem like a hand gun person? And Rayya, she seems more like a knife, and hand to hand person to me," he heard Karman say, casually passing him a Rifle that was even lighter than his own.

"I what? And Rayya, she does? How do you? What makes you think that about us?" he asked, feeling exposed as well as flabbergasted that the weapon he'd assumed was a standard MP Four was anything but.

"What the hell is this? Calm down! There's 'gotta' be an explanation as to why this gun feels so weird," he thought, squeezing the grip – getting a warm, inviting sensation throughout his hand.

"You okay? You feeling nauseous still? Oh, and don't worry about the knife question, I'll let her decide if she want to try my machetes. Nate? Nate!"

"Yes? Yes?" he replied, shaking his head in a vain attempt to clear his surprise.

"You feeling okay? Still feeling sick? Hubby was telling me the drones make you sick because they're linked up in your head," he heard Karman say, keeping her eyes locked with his as she crouched down, digging inside her bag, fishing out two cell phones.

"Yeah, it's like having new neural processes in your brain. It gets stronger with time and use, believe it or not. So, after a while you don't get nauseous, and it actually starts to feel good. A euphoric, flying sensation is the best way to describe it. It's just, I'm out of practice, so I'm feeling the pain. But yeah, actually, I'm feeling okay - for the most part. It's just this situation, it caught me off guard," he said, slipping the Rifle strap over his shoulder, wondering why Karman wore such a confused look on her face.

"Okay, is that all?" he heard Karman ask, giving him a doubtful look.

"Yeah," he replied, lying though his teeth as he imagined massaging her breast with Jay right beside her.

"Really? Oh-okay. By the way, thank you again for staying up, standing watch all night. And seriously, thank you for saving me. I really appreciate you papi," he heard Karman say empathetically.

"Of course, any time," he replied, staring at the Rifle, trying to snap out of his day dream where he'd moved his hand from her breast to Jay's cock, thinking, *"This is not the time for these thoughts!"*

"Look at you, marveling at my creation! I see your questioning eyes. You're a man that knows his weapons! Haha! Surprised, aren't 'ya'!" he heard Karman boast.

"It, it feels amazing. I knew it wasn't an 'MP Four' the moment I touched it. So, this is your creation huh? You, you make your own weapons?" he said, beginning to feel uneasy.

"Lil bit. Haha, you look like a cat bit your dick," he heard Karman tease.

"I, I don't understand," he replied, seeing his View-Tech's kick to life, auto scanning the Rifle.

"The AI picked up something? What the hell could this be made of that it'd deem this a priority!? I know Jay and Karman are extremely intelligent, but what the hell!" he thought, forcing a smile on his face, mirroring Karman's.

"That's a weird question after what 'me' hubby told you about us," he heard Karman say with a chuckle.

"Right, but because of who your sister is, wouldn't you have access to any guns you wanted?" he asked, removing the magazine, staring at tiny, opal-black projectiles slightly thicker than tooth picks.

"What the fuck is this!?"

"Ummm, calm down there. I'm not one of your Makers or Masters. I'm smart, but multi something or whatever, no papi, that's not me," he heard Karman say defensively.

"How shocked did I look just now?"

"Cat completely bit your dick off, shocked."

"What? What is this?" he whispered, staring transfixed at the curved, smooth shaped projectiles, noticing they were almost flat, like skipping stones.

"The bullets," he heard Karman reply flatly.

<**Dybbuk:** AI, what is the estimated years of advancement?> he asked, feeling his heart beat accelerate to the point where he could feel his tongue pulsing.

<**Lilith AI:** Still undetermined. Rounds are lined with what appears to be circuits, as AI is detecting some form of logic gates. When sending probing information, circuits readings are returning as mostly undefined. AI has been given authority to provide you with details regarding this weapon…should AI find more detail to give,> he heard his AI reply just as quickly.

"I see that, but" he mumbled, losing his train of thought, stupefied at his AI's response.

"But?"

"This looks just like Opal? And these designs," he said, staring at the hypnotic, beautifully colored circuit lines – remembering Jay doodling similar patterns during their brief couples' coffee dates.

"Opal? Ha, yeah, it does look like that. The lines are circuits, slash fracture points," he heard Karman reply, sounding unsure of herself.

"Huh?" he replied, trying to figure out her tone.

"Well they're made to be self-guiding, and able to inflict different types of damage to intended targets, both situations require fracture points. And seriously, stop with that accusing look."

"You sounded unsure. And trust me, I don't think you or Jay are the people I'm worried about. But still," he replied defensively.

"Hey now, are you saying we're not smart enough?"

"What!? No! And, well yes. And besides that, those people, they're more reptilian. Both of you have hearts and souls. I know for a fact that both of you think about consequences. So that's why I don't think you two would be them," he replied, beginning to calm down, thinking, *'Right, don't entertain Rayya's*

train of thought, believing that people without those traits are among us.
Fuck! But what the hell is this?"

"Just messing with 'ya', calm down. But, good to know," he heard Karman say, with a light giggle.

"Not funny. Just for that, I'll ask. Can you give me a little bit more peace of mind?" he whispered.

"Un huh. Peace of mind, now who sounds unsure," he heard Karman reply knowingly.

"Oh, come on, you have to expect me to dig a little. I mean you're showing me a very sophisticated weapon. And the timing is …"

"Pretty bad," he heard Karman finish for him.

"Yup, awful."

"Well, Jay and I cross the border to Canada all the time. Those dogs can smell gunpowder. Those scanners can see metal and even certain plastics. Jay and I can't afford to be brought in for questioning."

"Yeah, that'd be trouble," he replied.

"Not law trouble Papi, if that's what you're thinking. It's just, we can't afford to be disarmed or far away from our weapons for too long, even for formalities. So, we made our own shit to get around all that. It's that simple," he heard Karman say.

"Hearing you say it, it makes sense. Just, looking at this, feeling how balanced and light it is. Seeing these rounds. And feeling this material, I mean it's just a shock to me is all."

"Nate, what's my job?"

"Research and development of materials for the space elevator, mainly. And secondly, R&D of materials for a whole lot of other projects that bring in income for your company. Like the other day, I heard you talking about the new alloy you created for the Vac-Loop Tubes, that's way more earthquake resistant," he replied.

"Yup, and the main requirement for almost everything I deal with, is that it must be strong, flexible, and damn near indestructible. Speaking of strong and flexible, you said if that hair or whatever it is, hits the public market, it'll destroy the metal sector. I really 'dunno' if it would or wouldn't, but if it is as strong as you say it is, maybe it'd be the key to building the space

419

elevator. And if anything, maybe the Metal sector would bounce back once we get ahold of the asteroids everyone is so desperately after," he heard Karman say.

"My father, my real father is in Chicago. He runs a lab that wants to analyze the strands I just showed y'all. My parents are, of course, extremely concerned about the elevators falling to earth and are considering options."

"Options like?"

"To be honest, leaking certain properties to researchers such as yourself."

"Humm, just curious. Would your dad allow me to, poke around a bit, have first dibs on seeing some of these properties?"

"I'm no scientist, but surely it'd take more than a few days before our lab has anything they're willing to disclose. And besides, isn't your 'vackay' limited?" he asked with a snicker.

"I can help…Ugg, Jay would kill me. Yeah, never mind. Oh, and hey, to give you more peace of mind that Jay and I are not your problem people. We had a lot of help from people to make this stuff and such."

"And such?"

"Ah, look at you, alert on wording, are we? You know, you and Jay are sometimes creepily similar. I think it's why y'all 'kinda' didn't like each other. Looking in the mirror, you see each other's perceived flaws," he heard Karman say, shaking her head with a smile.

"What? I liked him, I tried to open up to him," he replied defensively, remembering clearly all the ways he'd kept his guard up.

"Un huh," he heard Karman reply, laughing as she went into the trunk, pulling out another two Rifles, along with another body holster, with four hand guns already placed within.

"Is it weird that I love and really hate guns at the same time?" he whispered, more to himself, looking toward the cabin, wondering why Jay had seemed so unnerved about going in.

"Really? Humm, Jay and I love it with all our hearts. When you pick up a gun, or any weapon, you should love it with all your heart."

"Why?"

"Because then you're taking full responsibility for who you are Papi. You say your job is to deal with these Masters and Makers, and obviously the gun you had is not to always deal with them peacefully. But you must not agree with your actions, or the judgment calls of those above you.

"Huh? That's not true, there's a duality. I believe in the cause, it's just sometimes I have to use a weapon on a person and I wish, or wonder, if there could've been a small tweak in the circumstances where that person could've …lived. I'm certain, the way I feel is normal," he replied defensively.

"Yup, normal in every situation where the person holding the weapon doesn't fully agree with the cause, yes. In my opinion, and Jay's, you should never pick up a weapon if you don't fully agree with the cause."

"Damn," he replied, feeling like he was shrinking under Karman's judging glare.

"Damn is right, let me tell you about that love you said you feel, because that's the most dangerous part. You must be honest with yourself and accept that the love you feel, is the love of power you have, to take and control another's life. That love gets stronger the more you feel like your life is 'outta' control. Not trying to be mean, but …never mind," he heard Karman say, causing him to return his gaze to her, watching as she waved her hand over the trunk hatch, which closed just as fast as it'd opened.

"I feel naked…and not in a good way!" he thought, as he said, "What?"

"Nothing, it's just…Now I get why Jay said what he said. Fuck, don't ever tell him I said that," he heard Karman say without an ounce of humor in her voice.

"Don't like him knowing you agree with him, go figure," he whispered.

"Look, just make sure when you hold weapons around us, you commit. That gun feels perfectly balanced right?"

"Yes," he replied.

"Well, it won't be if your mind's not right. No weapon, no matter how perfectly crafted, will be balanced if the mind and spirit of the carrier is fickle," he heard Karman say with a look

that told him she was giving him a pure life or death ultimatum –
in which she'd be the executioner.

*"The cheap paper comment. Do they really feel I'd let them down if
things got serious? I'm just going to have to prove them wrong then. God
knows, with all the shit that's coming, I might have plenty of chances,"* he
thought, watching Karman place the Rifles and body holster
she'd taken out onto the ground.

"I hate that I give off the impression that I wouldn't be
reliable in a jam," he replied when Karman stood straight up.

"Yesterday, when you did all that shit for me, were you
unreliable?" he heard Karman reply, looking past him towards the
cabin whispering, "there was this smell coming from there."

"No but, you seem annoyed, or like disappointed with what
I said about guns," he replied, turning around, following
Karman's line of sight, finding his wife and Jay walking down the
sloped driveway with looks of pain and sorrow written all over
their faces.

"Baby?" he asked when his wife closed the distance,
walking into him for a hug, which he gave her with all his
strength.

"What's wrong?" he asked, realizing that the subtle, rotting
smell he'd picked up and ignored was now saturating her hair,
along with the smell of coffee.

"Let's, let's get…I want away from here, okay?" he heard
his wife whisper, pressing her head into his arm.

"Sure baby," he replied, kissing the top of his wife's head,
looking over to Jay who was pointing at something behind him,
seeing Karman's hand come into view, with a pack of cigarettes
and the body holster she'd just placed on the ground.

"Jay?" he asked, after Jay affixed the holster and lit his
cigarette.

"Bro, I think Lady Karma has STI's," he heard Jay say
hoarsely, letting out a stream of smoke, shrouding his face.

"Hey, can we, can we just drive and not talk for a bit," he
heard his wife whisper, breaking his grip, going straight for the
Rifles on the ground, picking them up, then wordlessly hopping
into the back of the SUV.

"Nate, drive please," he heard Karman whisper, hopping in
the back seat besides his wife.

-One hour later-

Exhaling, from both physical and mental exhaustion, Nate bobbed his head at the tiny sign that demarked he was now entering Rapid city. He'd driven slow on purpose for multiple reasons. For one, the visibility and weather had quickly turned to the worst. Going from bright, hot and sunny, to smoky, cloudy and dismal. Then, as if perfectly timed to be a hazard, all along the road, there were abandoned vehicles - sometimes left in the dead center lane, with none ever showing signs of their occupants.

He'd used his View-Tech's to spot and navigate around them, but earthquakes were now coming almost every ten minutes on the dot, sometimes causing the abandoned vehicles to tumble or roll directly into his path. Now two minutes into the city limits, visibility had become practically zero due to the smoke from flame engulfed homes and buildings. Above, flashes of atmospheric light gave illumination to the road, sonic booms echoed, then the emergency sirens blared and fell silent.

"And now...the weirdest part," he thought, as the radio kicked to life, **(If you are hearing this message, then...{static - then soft silent voices in a language his AI could not interpret})**

Looking to his right, he sighed at the doldrums look on Jay's face. At no point since he'd begun to drive, had anyone said a single word. From the smell of his wife's hair, and from she and Jay's reaction he'd known there'd been at least one deceased person in the cabin. Part of him wanted to deeply empathize with their obvious shock. Yet, the other part of him wanted to desperately break the silence and lead the conversation to pick back up where they'd left off and try to tie it into all the oddities they were experiencing now. It was just that – no one in the car had seemed to care.

"What the fuck?" he whispered annoyed at the silence, and the delayed feeling of chills he'd gotten after the same message played in his View-Tech's, followed by the car swaying from yet another earthquake - changing the order of events.

"Humm, that one was off, I wonder if there will be sirens and a flash, like everything going backwards this time," he heard Jay whisper, surprising him.

"I…hi," he replied, slowing down even further so that he could focus on Jay, nervous that he'd just as quickly fall back into silence.

"It is 'hella' creepy how it jumps from radio to View-Tech's. And that siren gives me the crawls. And look, look at how the power is traveling, it's turning off and on in waves all throughout the city, you see?" he heard Jay reply, with his throat sounding dry.

"Any theories on how the signal and power are jumping like that? Some kindda magnetic something or other?" he asked, following the lights that rippled on and off in wave-like patterns.

"I have many, but too damn tired to give a flying fuck. You're the Prince of mystery and mayhem, you tell me," he heard Jay reply weakly, before whispering, "Have you noticed, that every lil church we've driven past has damn near been burned to the ground?"

"No," he replied, using his View-Tech's to look through the dense smog, staring at logos, and banners placed all over the houses and buildings.

"I've noticed the closer we've got to the city, the more I've seen homes and building like those. You see them? NTLM, NFM, LFFM," he asked, reading off what he saw as he drove by.

"Nothing To Lose Movement, New Feminist Movement, and Living Faith Feminist Movement," he heard Karman whisper.

"Yeah, my View-Tech's told me, it's just, I had no idea they existed till I saw all these signs. I feel like I've been living under a rock," he replied, seeing more than a few freshly blazing fires erupt towards the city center, giving light to the almost pitch-black darkness.

"Lil bit under a rock, but they haven't really been on the news a lot. So, don't blame yourself. Just in the last few months, things have been popping up," he heard Karman say, with a sharp inhale.

"Look, there's signs, 'Welcome Free Matriarchs, Down with the Patriarchy.' And what's that one?" he said, using his View-Tech's to clarify a flag that seemed hastily secured to the whole front side of a house.

"Say's 'LFFM against the Free Matriarchs, the NFM and the Patriarchy', below it, it says 'Conservatism is key to security and respect.' Splinter groups of feminism, people not getting along, figures," he heard Jay say with a soft chuckle.

(It's…It's…too…), he heard the radio whisper, followed by the same thing playing in his View-Tech's.

"That's new," he replied, looking towards Jay, who seemed to go even paler after undoubtedly seeing the same message in his View-Tech's.

"I look bad huh? The look you just gave me just now," he heard Jay chuckle, followed by an ugly, wet cough.

"At first, I thought the message made you uncomfortable, but looking closer, I think you need rest and medicine," he replied, as his View-Tech's alerted him to a cluster of out-of-state vehicles all pulled over on the side of the road, and to the fact that Jay's temperature had just spiked.

"Rest, yes, for sure. And you're right, I feel like I'm catching the flu. It just hit me mad hard," he heard Jay whisper, now closing his eyes, leaning his head on the glass, before mumbling, "Mmmm, cold glass on forehead."

"Shit, I think your wound might be infected," he replied, stepping on the gas pedal a little harder when a message flashed before his eyes.

<Lilith AI: Multiple Nano vectors have been detected. You along with your party have been infected. Situation critical, ninety percent of those infected have succumbed.**>**

"Actually, flu is not accurate, this feels different," he heard Jay reply, coughing again.

"No kidding," he whispered, as he replied to his AI, **<Dybbuk:** What the hell! Why didn't I know about the vectors sooner? Give me aid! Don't just tell me we're infected!**>**

"I don't feel good either," he heard Karman whisper.

"Me either, my stomach hurts so bad, I can barely breath," he heard his wife whisper.

"Sammmmeee," he heard Karman groan.

"I'm driving as fast I can," he whispered, scanning down the road when another text appeared in his line of sight, **<Lilith AI:** AI is aware of multiple situations in which aid is trying to be provided, however they've all been unsuccessful. Regarding the

female passengers, the hormonal levels I'm picking up from their exhalation and perspiration are abnormal. Still Analyzing.>

<**Dybbuk:** AI! I'm starting not to feel good myself. I'm starting to feel really weak. Call for more support!> he commanded when bursts of light, that were both bright, yet not blindingly radiant, appeared all around the city in different hues of orange, green, purple and pink.

<**Lilith AI:** That was your support. They've perished like those who were sent before them, and those who were sent before them, and those who were sent before them…If you are receiving this Message.> he read giving him chills.

<**Fam Chat: Halo:** Try to hold out just a little longer.> he heard his sister Hila say in a weak, raspy voice.

"Pretty colors," he heard Jay say with a cough that sounded like his lungs were completely filled with fluid.

"Hold out? How?!"

"Jay, can you breathe?" he asked, seeing an opening in the road, causing him to accelerate.

"Nurse Nate, slash Gagillionare, slash secret agent, slash Prince. Man of many of many hats," he heard Jay reply whimsically.

"Jay, I get that you're upset," he began when his View-Tech's alerted him to an enormous, perfectly circular hole about five hundred meters away, that was on his side of the road.

Slowing down to a crawl, he maneuvered the car to the other side of the highway and drove past it, only for his View-Tech's to alert him of hundreds more similar size holes all throughout the city.

"Upset? Na, I'm overwhelmed. I usually like the feeling of not knowing what the hell I'm getting into. But this time, it feels, yeah, it seems too absurd. Like what the fuck is this in the street?"

"Probably sinkholes from earthquakes baby," he heard Karman whisper.

"Sinkholes? Na, not those. I'm talking about the lines, the lines…," he heard Jay say, pausing, and staring at him then behind him with an odd, guilty expression.

"Y'all don't see it do, 'ya'?" he heard Jay ask knowingly.

426

"Hold on okay," he replied, seeing a new wave of dense smog roll in, making it that much harder for him to navigate even with his View-Tech's working at full power.

"Hold on? Why you say it like that?" he heard Karman ask questioningly.

"Prince of mystery knows why we're feeling like shit. Speaking of which, Nate, I have a confession. In the motel, I took it upon myself to, to record y'all talking about the Masters and Makers. Invasion of privacy, I know, but y'all were talking so we could hear, so…yeah," he heard Jay say, tilting his head curiously in his direction.

"Nothing to say?" he heard Jay ask after a few more moments.

"We knew y'all could hear, you're right, no big deal you recorded it, we were planning to tell you anyway," he whispered, seeing dozens of LIL Corp. IFF signals appear in his View-Tech's.

"Why? Why speak to be heard? You said you were worried about the bikers having Tech that can beat yours, why talk if there was a possibility they'd overhear? You're supposed to be secretive no? And after re-listening to the conversation y'all had over and over, for like an hour. I 'gotta' ask, why are you and Rayya so dumb? Why y'all don't know shit?" he heard Jay say, sounding more and more aggravated as he spoke.

"Baby?" he heard Karman ask, sounding concerned.

"We're not dumb! You heard us, so then you know things are not straight forward!" he heard his wife say, sounding way more aggravated than he thought necessary.

"We need to unlearn; we need to un-think… Oh Rayya! I think we're bugs. I'm shitting my pants! …bla bla bla, sounding like two helpless fuckin chumps!" he heard Jay say mockingly, shooting him a nasty look, before saying, "Yo, I don't like to be fucked with, at all. Who or what the fuck are we dealing with? You two clowns say y'all want us to be in the know, then I want to know where do I let my bullets fly? Who's this Nefeshka bitch, who's her lesser Masters, explain this Living Scripture Prophecy, whatever the fuck that means."

"I've been wanting to tell you everything we knew. I didn't want you trapped with us, not knowing! I recall you cutting the 'convo' short, getting all sappy, crying about being a bad person. Then you came out of the cabin looking like you got bitched slapped over what I guess was a dead person. I expected more from you," he said, catching a micro smirk on the corners of Jay's lips.

"Good, you're not that much of a lil bitch after all," he heard Jay reply, turning to face forward, shaking his head, moaning, "These lines...y'all really don't see them huh? I was wondering why y'all didn't say shit, then I realized...I'm probably going crazy."

"Lines like what hubby?" he heard Karman ask.

"Nothing, just nothing. So, Nate, Rayya, 'wasup'?" he heard Jay reply.

"My family has been in charge of maintaining the balance of civilization for thousands of years," he replied.

"And 'wasup' with the name Lilith as the book of the Prophecy, and why's the book and your company's name the same? Why choose a mythical female fucking vampire, baby stealer as a fucking Mascot, huh? I've been doing a bit of reading on the lore, and it says she was actually the first wife of Adam, who like ended up fucking an Angel or some shit. I'm the sort of person who believes names hold power and meaning. I can't see the name having relevance to stopping geniuses from fucking up the balance of humanity."

"You love conspiracy theories, but now you seem offended that there are layers that are not perfectly aligned for you ...go figure," he replied.

"Well, that's cause that shit was fun to speculate. This shit going on outside, this fucked feeling I'm getting, is not fun buddy," he heard Jay retort.

"Fair enough," he replied.

"Balance of civilization, such utter bullshit," he heard Karman say with a weak chuckle.

"Shut up!" he heard his wife snip, surprising him, causing him to turn around and glare at her, finding her clutching her stomach in agony.

Looking over to Karman, he saw her rubbing her belly, which looked extremely bloated. He wanted to say something more, but he felt Jay tap him on the shoulder.

"I wish I could help you two," he whispered more to himself, feeling his stomach sink at the women's agony, seeing both of their abnormal hormonal stats increase, along with their body temperatures.

"Karman, Jay, I know it sounds like utter bullshit, but it's true. Like I had been telling you earlier, if civilization goes too far technologically, it becomes unstable. But to be honest, that concern was more of a secondary sub-function of my family's purpose. It just so happens that after thousands of years, it'd become our primary. The idea of the Masters, even with all the proof of their existence, became a backdrop of fear. A scary tale, passed on generation to generation, that just never happened," he replied, looking between Jay and Karman.

"Go on," he heard Jay say.

"The Masters were still in existence when the order of Lilith was established, but it'd been during their last days. They'd all but destroyed themselves. In the stories, it says they'd come to destroy everything again, but years turned into centuries, and now thousands of years later.... If you heard what we were saying in the room, then you should get that we genuinely do not know what we're dealing with. Both books say a Master will lead her lesser, and that her name is Nefeshka. Both books have images of her on the cover, so there's that. And as for the content of the books, more than half of it is war related stories, with the central theme being - vengeance and bloodshed - all lead by Nefeshka. The endings of the books say she's coming and the world will be bathed in blood.

"That's why y'all heard me saying what I said to my husband in the first place. Logically both of you'd understand how much of it can't be taken literally. How literal do either of you take the ending of the Christian bible, the end of the world story? The fire and brimstone and what not," he heard his wife snip.

"I don't occupy my mind with Sky Daddy stuff. Anyways, I was just being pissy. I do understand. Trust me, I understand, that's why for the last hour I've been using my resources and the hacks I put in your system to try and figure things out myself. So far, I've see a lot of patterns and cross-stories, some with the bible, some with the Koran, and others with ancient Pagan

429

practices. Ah fuck, last worm gone, last virus found. For now, that's all she wrote then I guess. I'll look at everything again after the final analysis is done from the data I cached," he heard Jay say nonchalantly.

"You, you said what?!" he replied, feeling his blood instantly boil from Jay's words, when he saw, **<Lilith AI:** AI has just now cleared numerous hacks, but there are still many that remain. Note, AI has not been able to identify source of the hacks. If this individual is responsible, it is not determinable. Only timing of the individual's confession and clearing of the hacks connect him. If you are hearing this message…Mayday…Mayd…If…If>"

"I said…I hacked," he heard Jay begin, but his temper had boiled over and before he'd even realized it, he'd one handedly grabbed Jay by the neck and pulled him towards him.

"What …the…fuck!" he growled.

"Let go of my…" he heard Karman begin.

"Shut up…shut the fuck up!" he snarled, turning towards Karman, whose look turned so feral that he could see his life flash before his eyes.

Yet he didn't care, and returned his attention back to Jay, who'd made no attempt even in the slightest to break free of his grasp.

"I…I'ma take a guess that Masters are possibly Master Alchemist. In many text, the term Masters cross references with people who practiced mastering Mindset, elements of Nature, and Spirituality. Nothing says shit about them destroying themselves, or about them coming back to destroy anything. I 'dunno' if I'm doing a shit job of researching, but in my humble opinion, something's way off with what you're telling us, because there are always new people practicing alchemy. Surely there would be a few Masters alive in every generation. If there are, then they would've been fucking shit up hardcore by now, would they not? Having a woman named Nefeshka, or better yet, from what you said in the room about receiving a message of said woman's image, correlating with an ancient prophecy…buddy that's on some different level shit. Help fill in the missing link buddy," he heard Jay say, with an awful rattle to his breath.

"Ra!" he grunted, tossing Jay back, watching and hearing his body behave like a rag doll, bouncing and rocking once he'd hit the door.

"WA! Was it you last night? Maybe you this morning!?" he screamed.

"Which part buddy?"

"Don't fucking buddy me!" he growled, feeling his temper growing even further out of control.

"I told you bitch, we're not good people. I tell you I did some lil bit of shady shit, you get mad as fuck? Look bitch, it's not personal," he heard Jay whisper, coughing hard right after.

"How's it not personal, if it's personal!?" he shouted.

"Yo', just trying to protect me and my boo, there's no rules to that...fuck 'outta' here if you think there is. Your company is a fucking pain in the ass, drones flying around the neighborhoods, spying on people and shit. I have the means to infiltrate your shit, so I did it. If it makes you feel any better, I didn't do the pulse thingy, and I didn't do the gun thingy. Right now, I'm sitting here like a dumb duck...just the same as you and your lady. Hell, even more so. So, what you want from me fam? An apology for trying to self-preserve?" he heard Jay say with a sarcastic chuckle, that was cut off by a horrible cough.

Hearing Jay speak, Nate found himself torn between his rage and understanding. He knew first hand that he'd cross boundaries and thresholds if it meant protecting his family. What was bothering him was the feeling of inferiority. The knowledge that Jay had openly and tactlessly gained access to one of his company's prized accomplishments, and had still overall bested it, as the AI still could not identify if it were Jay who'd done it in the first place. It was realizing this that he found even deeper insight into why he was so angry.

"You telling me what you have, you're declaring you're my family's enemy! You know that right!? There should be no way you could get into our network, no way to know about the drones! They're completely invisible to radar! Why are you just blurting this shit after I told you who I am and what my job is, why would you expose yourself! Why? Just lie! No!? I obviously didn't know, so why not lie huh? You think...you think I want to consider you or Karman my enemy!? Because knowing and doing what you did, only our enemies have the means to do it!" he shouted, watching Jay visibly shrink in the chair, with a guilty expression on his face.

"Oh," he heard Jay finally whisper, giving him a sidelong look, avoiding eye contact as he leaned closer to try and gain it.

"We're just cautious! We're not your enemy you 'lil' punta," he heard Karman whisper, groaning in pain right after.

"Don't call my husband a pussy," he heard his wife snap, mumbling that she'd snap necks in Arabic after.

"My View-Tech's auto translates! Whose neck bitch?!" he heard Karman blare right after.

"Nate," he heard Jay say, chuckling, then coughing.

"What?" he asked, finding his anger dissipating, worrying about the growing tension between the two women.

"You're mad 'cuz' you care? Shit, that's so weird to me. I 'dunno' what to say to that," he heard Jay mumble, returning to his normal posture in the chair.

"Of course I fucking care. Are you losing your mind? What part of my actions towards you two have shown you that I don't care! I just want to turn a blind eye to the fact that your car gives off odd readings. Ignore all kinds of tells about you that make you very fucking suspicious! But no, you have to say that you hacked into my shit, right after Karman hands me a weapon that's just as advanced as my LIL!"

"Tells?" he heard Jay reply, flashing him a weak smile.

"Yes, tells Jay. The way you move, the way you read faces like…like those people. I, I never saw it till I saw it," he heard his wife whisper, sucking in her breath in pain.

"What people?" he heard Jay ask, with a dubious look on his face.

"My family hires very unique individuals to protect persons of interest, and to prep our LIL Guards with combat training," he said, waiting for a fast rebuttal from Jay, surprised when Jay caringly looked towards Rayya, then to him.

"Guilty silence," he heard his wife say, sucking her teeth.

"Na, I'm not them, but I've heard of them. I was wondering how you got 'outta' Lebanon so fast. Visas from war zones, and even refugee status take time. Now I know for sure you're a life debtor. I'm sorry lil ma. I…" he heard Jay say in a warm tone, but before he could digest Jay's new knowledge bomb of things he shouldn't have known, he heard his wife scream.

To say it was blood curdling was an understatement, because it didn't seem to end. Glaring behind him, he saw her panting and glaring at Jay like she'd rip his head off.

"You're freaking me out...and I don't say that lightly," he heard his wife say in gasping breaths, giving him chills, knowing they were going to be some of her last.

"Oh, trust me, he has that effect," he heard Karman whisper, causing him to glance over towards her, seeing sweat beading down her face and forehead.

"Weirded out! And I...I feel so dirty. So disgusting! I can't keep my thoughts straight!" Nate heard his wife say, panting harder.

"Yes, disgusting. The disgusting, drip, drip, drip. And the feeling like someone's scrubbing the inside of my pussy with steel wool. God, this is fucked," he heard Karman reply, gently rubbing her stomach.

"Fuck, fuck this pain. And fuck everything else. Jay, who the hell are you? And Karman, someone I never trusted told me something about you that I didn't want to take seriously. They said you were using your power as lead material scientist at O.L.O to exploit and take resources from poor farms in Lebanon! He said you were sending it to Colombia!" he heard his wife say.

"Pssss," he heard Karman remark.

"No, don't pssss, me. I seriously ignored the information, but it was something you said about Guam being stripped of resources that reminded me. I was like why would she be thinking about resources in that way. I mean I get it to some degree, you know and care about what kind of minerals and materials are in the ground, and different places have different things, but I 'dunno', it's just the way you said it is odd to me," Nate heard his wife say, sucking in her breath, before groaning, "Shit! I can't help wanting to rip everyone's head off! Karman, this feeling we're having. This shit shouldn't be possible, we just had our periods last week!"

"Sweetie, I don't feel like explaining the Lebanon situation, sorry I'm just focused on dying in agony at the moment," he heard Karman whisper.

"Everything is possible for you believers of Sky Daddies. Haha, I bet this is 'Its' way of vengeance. 'It's' sitting upon 'Its' golden throne saying, 'this is what you get for eating the apple first, and ruining all humanity,'" Nate heard Jay whisper, giving him a sarcastic, 'haha' look with a wink before placing his head back on the window groaning, "May this window forever be cold."

"Yeah, well fuck you," Nate heard his wife reply to Jay before saying, "So, not 'gonna' answer who you are huh?"

"Rayya, look fam, asking my affiliation is meaningless. Let me give you an example, say I am a football player for a certain team, but I'm also a serial killer who's also a pro fisherman, who uses people's body parts as bait. Say I tell you the name of the football team, but you've never heard of it, then later on, you also find out I killed people, and that I was a pro fisherman. Are they related? Are they definitive of a person?

"If you asked Mr. Example person who he was, if he only told you one arguably major thing about him that defined who he was, would you then leap to the other conclusions of type persona he could take on? Or would you say, 'oh, football player, okay.' So, me telling you my affiliation won't matter just the same as my Mr. example person. You wouldn't know what I was talking about if you heard it. And the shit I get into is limitless. And in a lot of cases, one doesn't got shit to do with the other. If it makes you feel any better, I'm not one of the people who moved you from Lebanon. I think those people are a bunch of goody, goody, yet super hypocritical bunch of bitches."

"Thanks, thanks for telling me, you're so fucked up, whoever you and your people are 'woulda' left me stuck in a war zone," he heard his wife reply.

"They say they're good people, yet moved your ass like precious cargo because you're a life debtor. That's human trafficking fam. But they pride themselves on treating you well as they moved you. Am I right?"

"Uhh," he heard his wife mumble.

"Baby, you had heard something about Karman? Really?" he asked, as he digested Jay's logic, actually understanding what he meant.

"Yeah, but it's…It was, well at the time I thought it was such bullshit, I'd honestly just dismissed it," he heard his wife say.

"Look at me clinging righteously to our no secret rule, I catch myself being petty, and now is not the time for that at all," he thought as he said, "Don't worry about it my love, besides, let's just listen to Jay blurt stuff till we learn everything about them."

"Bitch, I always just blurt stuff. What's new?" he heard Jay reply in a flat voice.

"True…but in this case," he replied, giving Jay a sidelong look.

"Yeah, the fact that we're fucked. You think that's why I'm blurting more than normal, huh?" he heard Jay say with a weak chuckle.

"So, you did see my AI's message? And you do understand the implications of your words, right? It's one thing to see things in my database, and another to see my direct messages, you know that right? The messages self-destruct if intercepted, the only way you could see them is if you had carte blanche access, it'd mean you have the quantum encrypt…" he said, stopping in shock of his revelation before whispering, "It means you have the quantum encryption keys. So, that's what you're doing when you're always at work, you piece of shit. That's why you hired Rayya so fast, why you're always, you're a literal piece of shit."

"Piece of shit? I saw a means to help her, and I saw a means to help myself, to her work. Strong words to use on me, you have no idea the trouble your 'shawty' brings. She's like a bad news magnet. No offense, lil ma."

"Fuck you…I mean, oh you know what I mean," he heard his wife whisper.

"Anyway, even if I didn't hack your shit, I have my own means to know how fucked we are right now. And even without those means, I can feel something's wrong with my body that's beyond my control. I honestly never imagined…this 'kindda' ending," he heard Jay whisper, leaning back, resting his head on the window.

"Hubby?" he heard Karman groan, followed by his wife asking, "Ending?" right after.

"Mr. wants to always be honest didn't forward you the bad news huh? If I was being a dick, I'd just blurt it out so you're stuck being a fucking hypocrite, wouldn't I? But I'll give you time...we don't have to tell your wifey 'wasup'," he heard Jay whisper softly.

"Fuck!" Nate thought, biting the tip of his tongue.

Staring straight ahead, he cued up his AI and looked at the time estimate remaining on each of their life spans.

"Was I even going to tell her? No, no I wasn't. After all we've been through, I would've lied and let us die this bullshit way, so close but so far away from her," he thought, turning to look at his wife, who was now holding herself in a tight ball.

"Anyways, I leave it up to you to tell your boo...and my Eggy," he heard Jay say weakly.

"Uh," he replied, feeling his lymph nodes begin to swell and ache.

"Yeah, I'm a secret keeper too. So, I volunteer you to take one for the team, 'Ima' just keep my eyes closed for a bit, okay fam? My head hurts, my ears are ringing and humming so loud," he heard Jay say... as his ears began to hum, then ring as well.

"Sure, rest," he replied, fighting to swallow, now seeing his vision go dark at the edges.

Maybe thirty seconds had passed, when he heard Jay whisper, "Talk fam."

"Ladies, I..." he began when he heard Karman gasp, "Holy shit," causing him to look behind him, seeing large, black splotches of blood in between both women's legs.

"What Nate's trying to say is that we got infected with something. Forty-six types of Nano vectors that are aggressive as fuck. Car thingy is showing that they're 'gonna' put us to night-night 'hella' soon. Y'all put in a good word to Sky daddy 'It', if 'It' exists, 'k'?" he heard Jay whisper.

In that moment, he saw a look of shock on both women's faces, then simultaneously he watched them sink back with their eyes rolling up in their head. Panic without acceptance was about to take over, when a message appeared in his ever-shrinking field of vision.

<Lilith AI: Very faint Antigens and Antibodies for vectors detected from vaginal discharge, exhalation and perspiration of the females. Their survival rate is increasing as their menstruation intensifies. You, along with the other male are surviving based on their ability to continue clearing the vectors. If they can exhale at five to ten percent mor...you. ...possi...>

Nate vision turned completely black. In that moment, he felt his body temperature rise to a level he'd never thought possible, all while having cold chills that felt worse than being in the Artic.

Leaning back, he smiled and shook his head and whispered, "We spoke so y'all could hear us, and so that maybe the bikers could hear us too. Selfishly, we didn't want to feel alone in what we knew. Plus, what was supposed to protect us was destroyed before we could even blink. Our logic was if the bikers did it, or knew who did, if they heard us talking about it, then maybe they'd act on our words. At least then, we'd know who we're dealing with."

"Yeah, you make sense," he heard Jay whisper before saying, "Shh, who cares anymore, go to sleep fam."

"Selfishness, always does seem to make sense, doesn't it? And, I'm not going to go to sleep. I don't want to give up, I 'wanna' stay up till the end," he replied, gritting his teeth, trying to will himself to feel better.

Almost a minute passed, and with each second within it, Nate felt his strength drain, his muscles ache, his lungs fill. What had not happened was his loss of taste and smell, which...in his opinion had intensified, making the smell of blood and body odor stifling. With every breath, Nate had begun to hope for the mucus he could feel building up in his sinus to block the smell.

However, his hopes were in vain because moments later, he could feel his sinuses completely clear. From all the awful things he'd experienced, Nate thought he'd known what overwhelming meant till then. With each breath he took, he was genuinely considering suffocating himself – and if he could've lifted his arms, or moves his body to do so, he was sure he would've tried and succeeded.

"Cotton, nylon, hair, blood, sweat,...," he heard his mind say without any form of control over it, followed by imagery of the

taste and scents he was experiencing, in colors he'd never seen before.

On his right, through taste and scent alone, he watched Jay twitch, cough and squint, looking at him, then towards the center screen dashboard.

"Yes! Finally, I got it! Well 'sorta', but it should be enough. Yeah bitch, I'm still the…" he heard Jay begin to say, pressing the screen, before saying, "The Most Awesomest System ever. I'm too weak to finish, run algorithm from my mind sync. Download now. Lock down the car, and do not open up until the remaining cure sequences are found, or if the following other situations occur – refer to mind synch's instructions. Also, mind link with all four of us, if we survive, we need to see and hear what's happening outside. Eh Nate, I said everything aloud, so you know what's going on later if I don't wake up."

<Received and understood.> Nate heard the car reply in a neutral tone, followed by a calm, cool, collect female voice saying…<Mayday, Mayday, Mayday, we're going down. If you're receiving this message…this is…(indistinguishable words)…Fight them, don't stop fighting. Fight them on the ground, fight them in…(indistinguishable words)…Fight them everywhere and in every way you can. No matter what, always keep fighting for your freedom, in the name of (indistinguishable words)…fight them, fight them with your every essence.>

For a moment, there was a pause, then he heard <Mayday, Mayday, Mayday>…but in different voices, from both men and women…he could hear cheers, along with screams of horror before silence, and more Maydays.

As he'd listened, his 'sensor' vison turned into a dizzying kaleidoscope of colors followed by a huge, bright, blue-white flash. After the flash, the sensory vision returned with even more clarity and he could see or sense something from Jay, he'd never expected.

"What could make Jay so afraid?" he thought, watching Jay's bodily reaction change to a furious rage.

The moment of clarity was short lived, and he now found his vision plunging back into a kaleidoscope of colorful circles. Another bright, blue-white flash occurred, and the kaleidoscope of colors disappeared again, allowing him to see perfect spheres of ionized air along with a dark black oily substances raining down, coating the windshield.

"*God, I need your help,*" Nate thought, feeling a soft jolt and the car tilt forward.

"*I asked you for your help, and now we're falling into an opening pit hole? Figures.*"

"Alright Bro! I got you!" Nate heard his sister say through the car speakers, surprising him, now feeling the SUV completely lift off the ground.

"*Oh! We're being lifted up by a LiL-Hov! Okay God, I guess sometimes you do listen,*" Nate thought, trying to suppress his excitement, because in that very moment he felt the remainder of his strength fail.

Chapter VIII

Nate, Rayya & The Merge

Road Trip: Day Four

Date: Sunday, June 4th 2017

Time: 10:30 am

Location: Hill City, South Dakota

"What's going on? Why can't I feel or see my body!?" Nate thought frantically, only seeing the world around him from within in his mind's eye, showing him hundreds, if not thousands of motorcycles parked throughout the city in perfect lines and rows, with what used to be women on, or beside them.

Used to be, because all he could see now was boiling, steaming flesh and bones. Then something in his mind's eye showed him a playback function. Thinking 'yes,' he could see that a LiL-Hov had latched onto the SUV like a dragonfly, scooping up an insect. Now flying a mere hundred feet above Rapid city, he could see the scope of damage.

To him, it looked like a war zone, with the only thing missing being the combatants. The image in his mind's eye jumped back to the present, where he could see that all around him, LiL-Hov's had taken protective positions around the one carrying the SUV. Tiny, odd colored flashes of light erupted from the surface, in the same moment, LiL-Hov's all around him vanished into balls of colorful vapor. He would've sucked in his breath in fearful apprehension, but he couldn't feel his body. Less than two seconds later, indications in his mind's eye showed him that multiple hits had struck the SUV, yet only minimal damage had occurred.

Not that it mattered, for in that same time frame, he could see that the LiL-Hov carrying them had taken direct damage and was now in a controlled dive towards a farm. In his mind's eye, he could see a transmission and knew that his sister Hila had been piloting the aircraft with her mind. There was a moment of impact, before he could have a panicked thought, he saw that everyone's body had been protected, via the chairs swelling protectively around them.

In his mind's eye, he saw the nose of the SUV, crunched in, all tires flat, and his door bent in. A timer began to count down from sixty seconds, and then to Nate's utter amazement the vehicle began to un-crumple, and regenerate. At forty-five seconds, the vehicle was now moving on its own towards the base, then another LiL-Hov picked it up and got shot down thirty seconds later. The pick-up and drop, car regeneration process happened four more times, with the final LiL-Hov getting them onto a pockmarked landing strip filled with broken, crumpled, steaming bodies.

"This is insane! What the hell is going on!?" he thought, seeing the LiL-Hov that'd carried them vaporize, with small chunks falling on top of the SUV.

A few hundred meters ahead, he saw LiL-Hov's launching from an underground location in front of an enormous hanger bay.

"There's a Lilith base here as well? The things I'm not aware off are becoming absurd," he thought as the SUV took off towards the launching aircraft, surprising him further when it made it to a speed of three hundred kilometers an hour.

Within seconds, the SUV plunged down into a deep sloping ramp, with LiL-Hov's passing over them every fifteen seconds. All around the perfectly circular tunnel, he could see smears of blood and bone, and when he thought, *"I wonder how many people lost their life here?"* a number flashed in his mind, **<2200, 2201, 2020, 2025...>**

<Off!> he commanded, refocusing his attention to a depth calculation that told him it would take a full five minutes to make it to the Aircraft hangar bay.

"God, this is deep!" he thought, mentally requesting the base schematics, turning his vision inwards, staring at - what looked to be his lifeless body, feeling a deep concern, without any of his normal sensations.

"Oh, I see. They'd just begun to build this within the last month. Holy hell, how's it already so big? And, wow! I've never seen so many labs in one base, in my entire life. What the hell are they researching?" he thought, pouring over the schematic.

Coming close the end of the launch tunnel, he read, **<Arriving at the end of the Vaginal Canal>.**

"When mom's design, and labeling become way too real," he thought as the SUV slowed to a stop in front of an enormous door, labeled **<The Cervix>**, which was ironically completely covered in blood.

<The most awesomet system ever: Standby for resuscitation.> he read, followed by the most awful nerves on fire, sensation he'd ever felt.

"Resuscitation!? So, I was dead!? And this car! Regenerating and an onboard AI system! With all the Tech scans my company uses, how could this hide so perfectly under our noses? Only after deeply looking at it last night did I start to even think there might be something strange about it. And I had just thought they were carrying something advanced within it. Not it being the whole damn car?!" he thought as the pain reduced to more bearable levels.

Opening his eyes, he was happy to see that his normal vision had made a full recovery. Slowly looking around, he realized he was unconsciously naming and identifying scents and flavors with their corresponding colors. It was then, he realized that the stifling scents that'd made him feel ill, were not the women's blood or anyone's body odor, but the fabrics, inks, dyes and almost anything unnatural within the vehicle – all except Jay and Karman's Rifles and handguns, which had absolutely no scent whatsoever.

In curiosity, he glared down at the Rifle that'd remained secured in his lap, but the scent of dye from his shorts hit him hard.

"Never mind, I'll look a little later," he thought, tracking an extremely attractive scent, realizing that it was the women's cycle blood and sweat.

Inhaling deeper to drink in the scents further, everyone's body odor integrated into his mind as, for a lack of better words, presence of life and status indicators. With good information, smelling favorable, and the not so good information, smelling unfavorable, but not utterly awful either.

<This AI would like to let you aware, call sign Halo, - which AI has inferred to be your sister, whose given name is Hila, is now requesting further access to my database. AI would also

like to inquire: do you believe your sister to be capable of fratricide?> he read in his mind's eye.

<No, but her hating me, that's normal. Why do you ask? And, how the hell do you have the cognizance to ask that?> he mentally replied, feeling stiff as he sat up, taking in his surrounding, seeing, broken, crumpled, steaming LIL-Corp auto camouflage armor, along with tattered Air force uniforms among the gore.

"Hila? Can you hear me through here?" he whispered, unconsciously plunging into his new senses, carefully rechecking everyone's vitals before snapping out of it in fear - realizing how clearly, he'd saw his wife and the others without actually setting his eyes on them.

"Fucking freaky," he mumbled.

"If you are receiving this message," Nate heard through the car speakers, his View-Tech's, and mind so clearly, he felt as if he were next to the woman who'd spoken.

Less than a second later, he could hear his sister through the car speakers say, "I hear you. Good, you're alive. Wait one second, we need to sterilize the vehicle."

As his sister Hila spoke, he felt the SUV sway to and fro ever so gently and heard her curse and mumble, "Fucking Bombardments."

"What the hell is going on Halo," Nate replied, calling his sister her call signs out of habit.

"What's not? Everything's a shit show," he heard his sister reply in a gruff tone.

"Like what?" he asked, glancing in the rear-view mirror, feeling satisfaction and apprehension, seeing that his wife and Karman, were still unconscious, but breathing deeply.

"Hold tight, and don't get out the car," he heard his sister say.

"I can barely move to even think of getting out," he replied, glancing over towards Jay who was now inching his hand over towards the center monitor, pressing it.

With the console coming to life, he watched the conversation he'd just had with his sister play out in text form, along with the blueprint of the base. At first, he felt the same flash of anger he'd gotten when he first found out Jay had hacked into his system surge up again, but then it diminished as he remembered the events that followed.

"I thought your last malware had been taken out," he whispered, staring at the screen as it began to replay events from when they'd been picked up by the first LiL-Hov.

"That was when I cared about time frame for being busted. I went balls to da wall hacking into LIL-Corp. systems after I realized how fucked we were," he heard Jay reply.

"If you are receiving this message," Nate heard blare through the speakers again, followed by an image of Karman in the shower - hearing her say, *"How's that odd? It would be bad. His shit's supposed to be top of the line. If somehow the bikers had something to beat it, they most likely can beat us! Humm, so what was the error? Was it them or was it because of us?"*

Followed by Jay replying: *"Well, at first I know it was ours. I'd hacked into the earbud and contact lenses he had me wear to control the drones. I didn't want him seeing and hearing everything I was doing. Shit was crazy hard to pull off. I had to take all the updates that were going to my View-Tech's directly into my head so he couldn't see what I was seeing, then reply and send mental commands in coherent enough thoughts for our AI to understand so that'd everything would go smooth."*

"Well that's embarrassing," he heard Jay mumble.

A moment later, another Mayday call blared through the speakers, and then the video image of Jay speaking to Karman played out up until the moment of the earthquake.

"Well fuck," he heard Jay whisper, tilting his body to the right, away from him.

Inching painful inch, by painful inch forward, he placed his hand on Jay's shoulder. He could literally smell, see and taste embarrassment, shame and anger coming off of him.

"I don't want to talk about it," he heard Jay say, watching him straighten in the seat, pressing the console – scrolling through all the images that'd been recorded.

"You knew sooner or later you'd get caught, and you did it anyway? And, you think you're bi? Shit, that's funny. Ah!

When Rayya finds out, I'll never hear the end of it, her and her stupid double dip theory," he whispered, feeling laughter bubble up and die as he thought about the rest of what he'd heard.

"I've seen the evil in him for certain, but, is he capable of killing a child? And, looking for artifact technology? Meetings on submarines? Karman still not knowing everything about Jay? Their organizations still not trusting each other? Jay and Karman live a life that's of depth, parallel to our own."

"Double dip theory? Oh man, me doing that, that was in the heat of the moment. Fuck though, that is some overly close shit to do though," he heard Jay whisper, sounding slightly unsure of himself.

"Un huh," he replied, feeling a rush of excitement that switched to resentment at their current situation.

"Anyways, I don't want to talk about it. And I don't want to talk about that lil girl either. I see you about to half ass inquire. As to your other question, there are levels to being caught by you and your company. From what I can tell about your systems, is that my malware wouldn't start to get traced backed for about a week. By then, I would've lied through my teeth if questioned, all while tweak-corrupting more data to cover my ass based on what questions y'all asked. This shit that just happened now, this wasn't software, well not all the way. Shit, shit, shit, shit," he heard Jay mutter.

"What? And what if I asked you about what you were looking for in the jungle, or about your organization?" he asked, watching Jay press the touch screen, pulling up an image of all sorts of Nanites.

"Yeah, what I was looking for in the jungle. Well, just a lil bit ago, I saw it again. After all these years…boom right in my face," he heard Jay whisper.

"You, you found it where, how? And why the shit, shit, shit reaction?" he replied.

"Yes, I saw it. 'member the explosion you just heard wifey and I talking about from the memory 'exposey' thingy just now? I saw it…never mind. Uhh, my cursing was because what we just watched, that was a recording, like a perfect recording," he heard Jay whisper, turning around ever so slightly as Karman coughed and his wife yawned.

"Wait, you're talking about the bright patterned one? There were two, they were very different from the rest. Even when I, I felt like I was going blind, I could see them clearly. And it's the only time I've ever seen you look, afraid," he replied, carefully studying Jay's face, seeing no form of denial from his statement.

Behind him, he heard the women stir and began to turn around.

"Yeah, those ones. Why you say you saw me afraid in that weird tone, like you're surprised I was scared?"

"Well, the things you do, don't reflect the actions of a person who fears," he replied, remembering Jay standing in front of the window.

"Dude, are you crazy? Only fools don't fear things…Anyways, eh, look at this bro," he heard Jay say, placing his hand on his shoulder, cutting off his view from the women, followed by him pointing and pressing the screen again, showing him the Nanites changing shape.

"I see it, but I don't get what you're showing me," he replied, annoyed that Jay had blocked him from saying a small hello to his wife and Karman.

"For one, you're watching them adapting, shaking off countermeasures to keep our asses from being fucked up. Mind you, it was a rushed job. In any case, every time these things change, unless you watch each mutation as it happens, it'll be really hard to do a timeline that trace back when they made each adaptation. I'm saying all this, because I straight up scraped all data of that conversation I had with Eggy from both your files and my own. Fuck, I wonder if…how long these 'thingys' have been inside us. My dope ass AI is running calculations on it, but it's getting its ass spanked."

"Hi guys. Hey Jay, can you lower your voice a little, I get you're excited about the topic, but you're 'kindda' screaming," he heard his wife whisper, interrupting his thoughts.

"Hey my love," he replied, quickly turning around, wanting to make eye contact with his wife, only to feel his eyes pulled down by his nose which picked up fresh flowing blood from both his wife and Karman.

"I'm speaking low as 'fawk' fam," he heard Jay reply in the same, quite tone he'd been using.

"That's much better. Before, you were shouting…no?" he heard his wife ask, now sounding unsure from the 'what the hell are you talking about' look he felt his face make before he could think to stop it.

"No fam, you 'trippin'," he heard Jay whisper, followed by, "But, I still see lines everywhere in all kinds of colors. So, I 'ain't' one to talk about tripping."

Nate wanted to inquire, but the scent of both women was now making his mouth water, and his only thought became, *'I want them now!'*

With that thought, graphic sex scenes played out in his mind and without even realizing it, he'd unbuckled his seatbelt and reached out to his wife. The pain he felt from moving so fast was incredible, yet he didn't care in the slightest as his primary concern was having his wife and Karman in every which way right then and there.

"NATE!" he heard his sister blare through the car speakers as he took hold of his wife's thigh, feeling her skin …break under his thumb, scaring him.

"What! Who dares interrupt me! Me! Mine! Ah! What the hell is wrong with me!?" he thought, hearing his sister call again.

"Let go of her Nate!" he heard his sister Hila command.

"No, don't let go baby, you can have me if you want me," he heard his wife reply, opening her legs showing him the impression of her pussy and blood, sounding both sure of herself and surprised.

"Oh, yes!" he replied, feeling his diaphragm and lungs vibrate, elongating the end of his 'yes' into a low growl that played out longer than the breath he thought he had in his lungs.

"Nate! Turn around!" he heard his sister say in a tone that formed images of her crushing him in his mind's eye, causing him to shut his eyes and turn his body to face the front.

"Good…good, good, good," he heard his sister say in a more approving tone.

Opening his eyes, he could see a gap in the enormous, circular door, just big enough for the SUV to drive through.

"This AI would still like to know the personal opinion of occupant Nate in order to make a critical, calculated decision," he heard come through the speakers.

"Why ask him AI? Your calculations would still probably say we're FUBAR whether we stay out here, or go in, am I right?" he heard Jay reply.

"Yes, however, you've programed me to consider levels of FUBAR. Therefore, I would like to inform you on the level, and act accordingly once I've collected further information," he heard come through the speakers.

"Nate, my AI hates your sister. That's what it's saying," he heard Jay say flatly.

"Uhhh," he replied, watching a cartoonish image of Tiger appear in the console, looking at him, shrugging its shoulders before disappearing.

"See, hates her. 'Yo' AI, move us into the sterilization 'thingy giggy.' And add this input to your calculations. The four of us are the type that believe in moving forward. We're the type of fools who, although don't trust the people that are supposed to be closest to us, always deep down, still want to give them a chance. We like to hold on to odd hopes that these people won't fail us. We want to go in here because we know outside, we don't know anyone. So, although you may have data that shows that Nate's sister maybe just as dangerous, we still want to take that chance. It's why there's a saying, 'the enemy you know is better than the stranger you don't.' You got all that?"

"Yes", he heard come from the speakers in a deadpan voice.

"Good, good, good. Eh, what y'all think of my tutorage?" he heard Jay ask, sounding genuinely concerned.

No one replied to Jay, and when he turned to look at his wife and Karman, they were staring at Jay with looks of shock. Almost a full minute passed, with still no one speaking a word. Then, silently the SUV moved forward, inch by slow inch, as if the AI were reluctant, until they were finally inside the gap, where he could see steam, electric arcs, and laser scanners all at play along the vehicle.

"Mayday, Mayday, Mayday. If you're hearing this message," Nate heard, seeing the laser light, electric energy, and steam all ripple in unified waves to the unknown woman's voice.

"Oh man, seeing that was telling," he heard Jay whisper, causing the chills he'd gotten to intensify.

"Of?" he replied, reaching up, touching the brainwave interface of his View-Tech's which was placed in the curved temple tips, noting that they'd gotten warm, thinking, *"I felt this sensation when I was in the room, just before I had the vision of the Rabbi."*

"On a scale of one to ten, how weird would you say it is to see light move like that, let alone see everything react in unison like that," he heard Jay whisper.

"Share what you think that means is what my husband is asking when he said - of," he heard his wife mutter as the vehicle emerged into a hanger bay, shaped in a triangular form just like a uterus.

"I did just share what I thought. We all know what we saw was on some next level shit," he heard Jay reply.

"Yeah," he mumbled, fixing his gaze on two, short, shapely women, in sleek, seamless auto camouflage body armor, noting that he'd never seen the type of Rifles they had strapped around their bodies.

From the women's posture, he could tell his sister, Hila, was standing in front of him, with Estris on her left. As the vehicle inched up further, he could see Estris steeping back, pointing, then watched Hila shake her head, 'no' and point towards him.

"Why did that give me the feeling she was trying to leave and not see me? I must've really brought shame to her. She's always defending me, and now I didn't want to show up," he thought, watching Estris head turn away, looking around the hanger bay, furthering his assumption that she wanted nothing to do with him.

"Alright, the first thing we're going to need is blood from all of you. When you get out, put those weapons down, is that clear?" he heard his sister say in a stern voice through the car speakers.

"Don't trust us eh? Why am I saying eh? Fuck, I spend too much time in Canada," he heard Jay whisper.

"Are you kidding me? Trust you? Ha!" he heard his sister reply.

"Whatever, I'm tired of being trapped in here," he heard Karman say, hearing the door open.

"Not a soul is doing good in here, that's for certain," Nate thought automatically as the overwhelming number of unfavorable flavors and scents flooded his nose.

Pulling the door handle, he attempted to step out and felt a flash of apprehension, but it was too late. A blurred figure closed the distance and before he could even blink, he found himself grabbed by the throat and slammed onto the vehicle.

"You!" he heard his sister growl, feeling himself fall, and the Rifle lifted from around his body, all to be hemmed up by his neck again.

"What's wrong with doing your duty!? You should've got your ass here the moment we told you too!" he heard his sister snarl, spinning and pushing him by the neck onto the floor.

"Duty? When I got that message, my inner thoughts were to keep my wife and I alive. You wanted me to rush here, for what? You want mindless cooperation and obedience, while keeping me uniformed! That's bull! I've had enough of it! This is where I put my foot down! I will not jump blindly into this shit. Whatever this shit is!" he choked out, looking around the hanger bay, watching armored LiL-Guard personnel scramble to and fro around the LiL-Hov's and LiL-Assault vehicles of various shapes and sizes.

"Selfish!" he heard his sister snarl, sounding even more dipped in malice, coming from her helmet's speakers.

Gazing past his sister, he could see that Estris had disarmed Jay and was now holding him by the back of the neck, with her weapon pointing towards his wife and Karman, gesturing for them to put their weapons in the SUV.

"Bitches," he heard his wife mumbled, watching as six female LiL-Guard aimed their weapons at she and Karman.

"I'm so tired, you think I want to fight? Go to hell, pointing those things at me. I'll fall back to sleep on you bitches, how 'bout that?" he heard Karman reply, raising her hands in the air.

"Hey! Un-train the weapons, I'm not playing around," he said, feeling an overwhelming surge of energy, with his only thought being, *"Protect my wife, protect my friends!"*

"Or what!? And what do you expect!? You want us to greet them with open arms or in your case, legs. Pff! Your friends! Do you know who they are!? What they're capable of!? We've done a hell of a lot of digging to only get drops of information about them, and all I can say is, you'd better be glad they like you! Those two literally have mass graveyards dedicated to them!" he heard his sister growl.

Completely infuriated, Nate shot up from the floor with full intent of taking on his sister, armor or not.

"Look at this shit," he heard his sister mumble, pointing behind him.

"Are you kidding me? You want me to just turn my back on you?" he asked, with his last word pitching into a low growl that continued even longer than when he was in the car.

"Contain yourself, remember you're in control, and if you're feeling like you're not, you're feeding it. You're…," he heard his sister say, pausing and shaking her head.

"I'm?" he retorted.

"I'll get into it later…The answer is 'yes' though. Just look behind you Nate," he heard his sister say.

Forcing himself to uncoil his muscles, Nate ever so slightly turned his head in the direction his sister pointed.

(Left, Fallopian tube), his View-Tech's indicated when his eyes focused on a circular tunnel.

"And?" he whispered, watching rows and columns of LiL-Guard personnel marching out.

"Just look!" he heard his sister command when he was about to return his gaze to her.

"Wa…" he began to say, trailing off, seeing people beginning to literally fall out of rank and file, disintegrating into piles of blood and bone.

"God," he whispered, cringing at a few who didn't die right away, and were now flopping around on the ground in agony.

"Damn near everyone in this city has been infected with Nanites. To make matters worse, we have an unknown amount of said people using advanced lasers and sonic weapons against us. So far, primary purpose of those weapons is to transmit the Nanites, secondary, of course, is to kill us outright."

"Infecting first?" he asked rhetorically.

"Yeah, to take over people's minds and bodies. Our security breaches have all been from the inside as LiL-Guard and

451

Air Force members are coerced into opening areas like the one you just came through."

"Looks like outright torture before death!" Nate retorted, pointing at more LiL-Guard personnel falling to the ground.

"Yes, those are...those were pretty much the last males in here. Males, seem to be targeted for destruction only. Oh, and if we shot the enemy, they become steaming Nanite bombs. Fun, right?"

"Ha-ha, fun, sure," he replied sarcastically, watching a man in full auto-cam armor walking towards him in a hurried pace. **<Scientists, Skill Level classified>** his View-Tech's indicated as the man arrived, falling in front of him, with his legs boiling away up to his ass, exposing his lower spin.

"Ha...Halpp," he heard the man gurgle through his helmet's speakers, reaching up towards he and his sister, when his head jerked, and his body fell limp.

Looking to his right, he could see Estris retraining her Rifle back to Jay and felt the urge to charge her when his sister took hold of his arm. Looking down, he realized he'd already unconsciously begun to close the distance.

"I do feel like I'm losing control," he thought, watching a team of LiL-Guard, inspecting the SUV with a large array of equipment.

"He was one of our top Nano material specialists. He was coming to run test on all of your blood. And to most likely, sit down and be schooled by those three over there. Congrats Nate, you, Jay and three other males, are the only ones still alive in here. Of those three, one is MIA, one is...a traitor, and the other, the other is hard to even describe what's even going on with him," he heard his sister say, tugging him and pointing at the pool of blood and bone.

"This is getting crazier and crazier. And what the hell do you mean he was going to be schooled by them? About what?" he asked, quickly snatching his arm away, realizing the scent and sight of gore of the unfortunate was diminishing drastically.

"Well your friends, that AI of theirs, and your wife mentally went into this kind of cloud storage space and worked out a way to short term outpace the Nanites."

"The little bit of info they shared with us helped stabilize some of the women battling being taken over. Of course, them helping us was for selfish reasons, a 'help us to help them' situation. But, it maybe for nothing now that the last person who could make more from what they've done is now a pool of gunk," he heard his sister say in a flat tone.

"Why instead of pride or fear, I feel jealous of them working together without me. I'm angry as hell at them for having been left alone in that strange state," he thought, feeling his heart race as he looked over towards his wife and others, finding them all staring at him with solemn looks.

"Them helping us has been making me question my life to be honest. I find myself thinking thank God my brother is blinded by his lust. If you weren't, and had not come with them, I think you'd be soup."

"Thanks, such a loving sister. Back handed slaps are the best," he replied, watching LiL-Guards placing sonic syringes on different parts of everyone's body, while others cut their clothing off, leaving them standing nude, minus their View-Tech's.

"Why are they still taking blood if he's dead, what can you do with it now? And why are you stripping them in here?" he asked, seeing two LiL-Guard now approaching him, holding syringes and shears.

"Our AI and theirs detected that Rayya and Karman were naturally outpacing and clearing the Nanites. Their bodies were dumping junk, and a lot of antigens in their menstrual blood. As they healed, you and that guy Jay... were also adapting, fast, but just not fast enough. Delayed herd immunity of sorts.

"From the natural antigens, those three conjured up a few temporary vaccines. So, of course we're still going to take blood, and samples. Nate, we're going to continue to follow the process. Continue to behave like we're going to make it out of here and be able to take this to the next competent person, or persons who can do something about this," he heard his sister say.

"I see," he said, tipping his head, giving permission to the two LiL-Guard who hastily came over and began taking blood samples and cutting off his clothes.

When they were through, he stood completely still, and watched more blood and gore – simply disappear in front of him, then gazed at his sister, waiting for her to say something about it.

"What?" he heard his sister ask, finally breaking the silence.

"I'm watching the Nanites dissolve everything. You see me looking at it, and not saying a damn thing! What do you mean what?" he replied, annoyed, looking towards everyone again.

"You have eyes. There's nothing more to say about it. Those things are aggressive, plain and simple. Look, stop wanting to be near Jay and Karman. Toughen up, I'm warning you because I'm your sister."

"Mass graveyards you say? After all the shit we've done, that's your warning? If they have one, we have…care to fill in the blank or would you be ashamed?" he replied.

"You'd defend them before you defend us as a family! All because you take my warning as a pure personal attack! You're such a sensitive person! God, even they see how weak you are, I heard the 'cheap paper' comment he made. Even he thinks you're pathetic, and he's just getting to know you."

"Fuck… you."

"Nate, the lives we took were necessary to protect a world that can, will and is unraveling. From what I've learned about them so far, is that everything they do, is only for themselves. Pure, refined selfishness. I want you to know that because I love you, despite what you think about me. I'm hard on you because I care."

"Love me!? After treating me like I'm a worthless piece of shit male! Actually, not just you, all of you think dad and I are worthless. Go to hell Hila, you should've left me dead in the car," Nate replied, now feeling an extreme wave of sadness, blinking back tears, remembering his main conflict when it came to his family and their beliefs.

"Not worthless, it's just that males are naturally weaker than females. Males always need a strong matriarchal figure to lead them," he heard his sister reply in a warm tone.

"Can you, can you hear yourself?" he whispered, watching as Estris took hold of the back of Jay's neck, dragging him down onto his knees, before indicating for the women to do the same.

With a head nod from Estris to his sister, he watched a row of LiL-Guard that'd been marching towards the hanger door peel off and surround his wife and others.

"Hey! What's that about?" he shouted, feeling a burst of anger that was so overwhelming he could visualize ripping his sister limb from limb.

"What?" he heard his sister ask, sounding confused.

"Over kill surrounding them like that, no?"

"Calm the hell down, we're refortifying this place for another wave of attacks. They need protection, or do you want me to leave them nude, with minimum guards? Cause I'm damn sure not arming them, so, yeah," he heard his sister reply sarcastically.

"I want line of sight on them; I want to be closer actually, this is too far! And bring, bring down your helmet, I need to see your face!" he whispered through gritted teeth, realizing that his rage was slightly calming because he'd visualized harming his sister without armor, and now that he was no longer looking inside his own thoughts, he was quickly wanting to disembowel her yet again.

"Bring down my helmet? Scared of your own dark thoughts huh? I'm a hundred percent confident you couldn't carry through with whatever that was that just went through your head, even if I left it up," he heard his sister reply, seeing a blur of movement before feeling her gloved hand close in around his jaw, pressing hard, causing him to choke.

"Don't be so sure," he choked out, feeling a strength he'd never had before.

"You need to control yourself, or I will do it for you," he heard his sister reply, pressing her fully armored forehead against his, whispering, "You don't understand...you never understood. Responsibilities, they're bigger than us as individuals. You have to put personal feelings aside and do what's best. You're so selfish, and you think everyone else is because they have the strength to not be a little bitch. Please, for once in your life, choose to be strong."

"Are you kid...kidding me? All of you, all of you are hypocrites. You, mom, Noa, Ilana - big hypocrites. No matter what I've done, it was never enough. So, I decided to try and find my own path. It's easy to say you're behaving justly, because you're always presented with all the information to make a proper choice!" he replied, feeling his neck expand and his jaw moving with greater ease after every word - despite the pressure his sister maintained.

"Presented all the information? Are you insane? It's mom we're talking about. Your stupidity is becoming clearer."

"It's...trueeee."

"Bull! And hell, even if I did get just a tiny bit more information than you, it meant that I'd proven myself trustworthy. Proved I don't use sensitive feelings to make important choices. Picking love, and marrying a Lebanese, life debtor for example!" he heard his sister fire back.

"We're fighting for the world, and you can, with a clear conscious, tell me someone's race matters? Can't you see Hila, that's why our life is all so hypocritical. I never agreed with the racism we were taught! Tell me, what does race and nationality matter? Flesh and blood is all the same. Telling me who to love, who to marry is all just ways to control me."

"Yes, it was! You're right Nate! Controlling you, controlling others, controlling people is necessary! How is this not in the foundation of your mind?" he heard his sister reply, gripping his chin even harder.

"It's disgusting, simply disgusting. Calling people sheep, cattle, flock! And the way males are treated! Everything is biased matriarchy bullshit!" he replied, feeling his new found strength now tripling.

"It's not bullshit! What will it take for you to understand that humans are not, I repeat are not all equal! Females should always be valued higher than males! Then depending on what DNA forms their body, they have a role to play as someone's predator, or someone's prey. May the wisdom of our mother help me understand her leniency towards Rayya," he heard his sister retort.

"My God, what a sick minded fucking family I belong to! This is fucking mental abuse! And you speak about Rayya, but could've stopped everything before it began! Instead, y'all power tripped on me, locking me out of the database when I tried to background check her. Then, like spiteful creatures, all of you waited till I fell in love to show me who she was, then demand I rip myself away from her," he replied, pressing his forehead against her helmet, feeling her neck begin to give.

"We needed to test your strength! Duty over love! You obviously failed, then failed over and over again after!" he heard his sister reply.

"Haha, I'm realizing that I 'so called' failed and fucked everything up on purpose! You're right, maybe I'm selfish, because I really enjoy making all of you cringe. Holy shit! I didn't realize I liked it so much till just now! Ha! I'd spent too much time running away, hoping that the hypocrisy would end. But now, getting a fresh dose of it, I realize. Yes! I'm happy!" Nate replied, noticing that his sister's grip, although growing tighter, felt like nothing more than a loose scarf.

"Listen here!" he heard his sister growl, when a soft melodic chime went off in the hanger bay.

Silently, his sister released her grip and stepped back.

"What? What's going on?" he asked, sensing an odd silence, noticing that everyone in the hanger bay had stopped moving and were now staring at his sister or Estris.

"Fuck," he heard his sister whisper, feeling the temple tips of his View-Tech's growing hot.

"Halo?" he asked, hearing a soft-spoken woman say Mayday in a calm, warm tempered tone.

"Just, just listen," he heard his sister say, pointing to her ear.

"Listen to..." he began to say when another warm tempered female voice took the place of the one who'd call the Mayday.

"Sisters, let us stand together in solidarity. We are so close to victory, so close to purging all the males who've oppressed us. Your Madam Lilith, and Lilith Corp. is the embodiment of female power in a world ruled by men. All sides of the female movement have always looked up to what Lilith represents. It is why we choose to come here, to make our stand against those who oppresses us. We thought destroying the males on such hollowed land, such as this, would be the greatest compliment. Please do not forsake us. We ask you sisters to take our hand, and walk with us in solidarity. We ask you, please do not protect the surviving males in your presence. Mayday…May…cut…cut the transmission …"

"Who was that?" he asked, watching his sister shake her head and grunt as if an insect had buzzed past her ear.

"She calls herself Ta, and says she's the leader of the Free Matriarchs. If she is, she's one of the most powerful Makers we've ever known as she'd be the one who created the Nanites," he heard his sister say as another, softer spoken Mayday began to play, followed by the self-proclaimed leader of the Free Matriarchs saying, "Sisters, I understand your concern, as there were a few misunderstandings with the other factions, as well as yourselves. However, we've all come to an understanding, and a cease fire - now that every male that used to live in this city has been eliminated. The only males left are the ones you're protecting. We ask you, take the life of those oppressors. Do not protect them. If it is too hard to do so, then let us in and we will do it. Afterwards, let us discuss how to reconcile our differences. We are female, we can come to a much easier understanding than the barbaric males."

"They killed every male in the city, seriously?" he said to himself.

"Nate," he heard his sister whisper, watching her helmet retract, revealing her combat ready bald head - that was the norm for all LiL-Guard females.

"Her scent…the way she looks…is…is this really my sister?" Nate thought unnerved, having never in his life seen his sister appear afraid, hopeless or sick.

"We're running out of time, I …I just don't…Ha, yeah, I guess you would feel the way you do after seeing me like this. Wow, I guess I do have emotions, because…just wow, that stings," he heard his sister whisper, trailing off at the end, with her helmet reforming over her head.

"I, I feel like I understand Rayya, I think I was smiling. Shit, I am smiling," he realized, instantly feeling ashamed as he pulled the corners of his mouth down to a neutral position.

"It's my fault though. I never gave you a reason to feel any other way about me."

"Hila, I…"

"I, want to tell you the truth, especially since it's a very fresh revelation. Nate, I really don't blame you. I don't blame you for trying to be happy at all. Going through what I've gone through in the last forty-eight hours, I, I sometimes had glimpses of your perspective, and I think fighting to be happy might've been the right decision when it all boils down to it," he heard his sister say, shocking him to the core.

"Hila?"

<MAYDAY! MAYDAY! MAYDAY! IF YOU ARE HEARING THIS MESSAGE! FIGHT, FIGHT THEM! FIGHT THEM WITH ALL YOUR ESSENCE! FIGHT THEM ON THE GROUND, FIGHT THEM IN THE SKY! FIGHT THEM IN THE AETHER!> Nate heard a woman's voice say in a clear, calm, commanding voice, echoing through every fiber of his being.

During the call, Nate saw his sister's helmet erratically retract and reform, small lesions break out all over her face and head, then bore witness to a metamorphic change in her demeanor which bespoke of only hopelessness.

"Have I gone crazy? Fucked in the head as she is, I want my sister back, right the fuck now!" he thought, as he said, "Hey, listen! The Living Scripture Prophecy spoke of pure chaos. Feeling over your head, put into situations of constant unknowns, it's all expected! Since when do you see my perspective!? I spit in our family's face! I'm a dishonor, a coward! I received the news and wanted to run! I didn't want to come here! I just wanted to hide! How can you see my perspective, huh? Did you lower yourself to a male's mindset? Are you crazy? Do you know who you are!? Look at Estris! She doesn't even want to look at me because of how much of a coward I am!"

Retracting her helmet again, his sister made eye contact, with an almost blank expression, then looked past him towards the SUV.

"Who I am? I thought I knew, but recently I don't think I do. And is that what you think Estris feels? Hum, you're dead wrong," he heard his sister reply in a deadpan tone.

"You? What the hell? And yes, of course that's what I think she thinks. You said so yourself, that I put my emotions over duty," he whispered, feeling his spirit being dragged down even further.

"Well, be unwavering and unquestioning about everything we were taught. Being rigid in my stance that everything we've done was for the greater good, no matter how contradictory my actions were at the time – in my opinion, since coming here, it's backfiring. As for Estris, she has her own demons to face," he heard his sister say, feeling the earth begin to sway underneath his feet.

"Fuck, what to do, what to do?" he heard his sister mumble in response, looking behind her towards the LiL-Guard surrounding his wife and others.

"If that shaking means these women are on their way in, you should arm us for one," he replied, smelling blood and tears, instantly knowing it was coming from his wife and Karman.

"Hey!? What's going on over there?" he growled, feeling another surge of powerful energy course through his body, seeing bright red trail lines run from both of the women's eyes.

"Okay, I've made up my mind! Hey, let's get them on the move!" he heard his sister command, waving her hand.

"Baby!?" he called out, tasting profound sadness from his wife and Karman, and a highly charged, adrenal response from Jay.

"Nate! This place! It's so fucked! There's something, something really twisted here," he heard his wife call out the moment she was told to stand.

"She's not lying," he heard his sister whisper.

"What?" he asked, as the LIL-Guards surrounding his wife, Jay and Karman made a space for them to walk.

"Explain?" he growled when his sister did not answer.

"Nate, shortly the different factions of the Feminist movements are going to swarm this place, be ready to be nimble," he heard his sister say, seeing the LiL-Guards readying their weapons.

"Arm me, arm us!" he replied, watching his wife dart towards him.

"Hi Baby!" he whispered, hugging her tightly, with his instant thought being, *"bliss!"*, as an energy of sorts engulf him, causing him to feel as if he and his wife were one.

"Mayday, Mayday, Mayday," Nate heard from a male's voice in a calm, cool, collect voice followed by, "Sin, filth, the impurity of the discharge and tissue that comes from a woman. Their deception, their selfishness, everything that they are is, and forever will be, disgusting. Males, make your last stand!"

"Rabbi?" he whispered, recognizing the second voice, instantly feeling disgusted by the touch of his love.

"Mayday, Mayday, Mayday, the United Female Federation has us surrounded, if you're hearing this message, know it's too late for us. Brothers! Make your Last Stand! Do not go into the after realms with fea...Ahhh!" ... "FILTH, they spread FILTH!" Nate heard, with the second voice being his Rabbi.

"Ah! Why am I naked! Why are we naked!? Where are our clothes?! The blood! Ah, don't touch me! That disgusting smell!" he screamed, pushing himself away from his wife, feeling his stomach turn in repulsion.

"Baby!? Don't reject me! Please don't treat me like this! I can't take it!" he heard his wife scream.

"Yeah! Don't reject her! Do you want to die!?" he heard Karman snarl, seeing her lunge towards him, but not seeing when her hand flew out, connecting with the side of his chest.

Nate felt no pain or pressure from the strike, only increasing disgust. He hated being nude, hated the smell of sweat from his body, and the smell of blood running down both women's legs, as well as from their eyes. Hated the stale, almost medicine like scent he was picking up from Jay, who stood watching everyone as if he were not really there.

Stepping back, he looked at his sister and Estris, who began to fall to their knees.

"Sisters! Kill the males, fight back. Crush any insurrection," Nate heard the supposed leader of the Free Matriarchs blare.

"This place is not pure!" he heard his Rabbi's voice override, seeing the hanger lights flicker, followed by the ground swaying.

"I need to fight this! Whatever's going on, I need to fight this!" Nate thought when the metallic ground buckled behind him, sending him crashing to the ground.

Lunging up, he saw the hanger go dark, all except for a perfectly shaped orange, red orb, glowing behind him. Turning around, he could see the orb rising and falling through the jutting hole.

"What the fuck!?" he whispered, seeing the silhouette of a man and a woman floating within it.

"NO! The Impurity is growing!" he heard his Rabbi's voice blare.

"Sisters! Destroy the EGG!" he heard the woman who was supposed the Free Matriarch's leader command.

"No, sisters! Protect the EGG! Oh Lord, bless the miracle of life!" he heard an unknown woman's voice say.

A feeling that he needed to drag his wife, Jay and Karman to the orb overtook him, followed by a deep disgusting shame of the type of person he was, and everything he'd ever done.

"AH!" he grunted, trying to push out the alien thought overtaking him, when a deafening roar went off, followed by a crushing sensation. Sitting up dizzily, Nate realized he could hear nothing, and that his View-Tech lenses had vaporized.

"My...my eardrums are completely ruptured!" he thought, touching the sides of his neck, now covered in warm blood pouring out from his ears.

"Thank God View-Tech's lenses are made to disintegrate in high heat or explosions, or I'd be blind and deaf!" he thought, now seeing beautiful streaks and burst of color erupt all over the hanger bay.

Something wet and hot, splashed all over him followed by half a skull falling into his lap. Jumping up, he lunged for a Rifle that fell a few meters in front of him.

"I have balance with ruptured ear drums!? Thank God! But how!?" he thought in surprise, picking up his speed, slipping on blood and entrails, only to see the Rifle kicked away by Estris who was aiming her Rifle at his wife.

"WA!" he opened his mouth to say, realizing he couldn't speak whatsoever.

Not that it mattered, because in that moment, Estris pulled the trigger, sending rounds of projectile and laser into his wife's bare chest and arms. Nate had thought he'd understood hopelessness, but seeing his wife fall limp and broken, slaughtered by a woman he'd consider his closest friend, was something his mind seemed unable to process.

"Impure! Women are impure! The EGG is unnatural. Purged! Everything must be purged!" he heard his Rabbi say in his mind, in a deep, melodic voice, charging his hatred towards females - momentarily making him no longer care about his wife's demise.

"Kill all women! All are impure! Wait! No!" he thought, holding tight to his wife's memory as what felt like tides of energy pulled his mind from love to hate and everything in-between.

Behind him, the red, orange glow of the orb intensified, seeming to flood the entire hanger bay in its light. Slowly, Estris turned to face him where he could now see that half her helmet had been destroyed, with her face bleeding from multiple lacerations.

"She remembered me," he saw Estris mouth.

"You! You're the one!" he thought, feeling an insane surge of energy, knowing exactly what Estris was referring to, when he saw something move in the corner of his eye.

Then, before he could even blink, he saw his wife appear next to Estris.

"Holy shit! Unreal!" he thought, watching his wife snatch up Estris one handedly by the neck.

"She was, I watched her…die," Nate thought in both joy and fear, watching the gapping wounds his wife sustained, slowly close, with her left arm that'd practically been severed reattaching.

Turning to face him, his wife smiled, and with a hard, jerking shake of her right arm, he watched Estris neck snap, with her head falling limp, resembling a dead chicken.

"I don't want to care, I don't want to fear this, I just want to be happy she's alive!" Nate thought, staring into Rayya's soul swallowing eyes, feeling his heart beat in his tongue, unable to stop his body from reacting in fear to such a look.

"Baby?" he mouthed, watching his wife smile grow wider and more sinister.

"Is she even in there, or is she a bodily shell, maybe controlled by the Nanites?" he thought, watching in surprise when his wife's body eerily coiled and uncoiled, launching Estris up into the air in high arc, to land at his feet.

"Holy fuck! Maybe I'm still dead, and this is hell?" he thought, slightly bobbing his head at his wife whose grin had grown even wider when Estris' body had hit the ground.

Then before he could even blink, his wife closed the distance between them, now standing on top of Estris' body like a primal animal who wanted to show the world its dominance.

"I, un…der…stand," he tried to verbalize, feeling his tongue fail him.

In that instant, he watched his wife soul eating look vanish as if she finally recognized who he was.

"Ba…baby…I…It's me," he tried to say, watching rose red tears gloss over her eyes as her hands came up, gently cupping his ears.

"We need to get out of here!" he thought, seeing LiL-Guard, women in biker gear, and women dressed in tight, all white clothing, shooting, stabbing and beating each other to death, with no apparent allegiance to anyone - including themselves.

All of a sudden, the ground rocked hard, and as he stumbled, his wife tugged him to the side.

"Wow!" he thought, watching the glowing orb roll past where they'd just stood, literally crushing Estris' body into red paste before stopping right next to the SUV.

Coming into his line of sight, he saw Karman's nude form making a mad dash towards the SUV, only to fall back, with blood and thick chunks of her flesh torn and burned away from her.

"Na…no!" he mouthed, watching in slow motion as Jay arrived behind her, catching her limp body just before she hit the ground.

"Nate, all of these women are impure! This place is impure! Disgusting and vile!" he heard his Rabbi say in his mind, instantly causing him to hate himself and the thought of any women he'd ever touched.

"Get the fuck out of my head!" he mentally commanded his View-Tech's to send, feeling the temple tips scorch him right after.

"I'm disappointed in you. You reject God's plan for you!" he heard in his mind, seeing his sister appear next to Jay and Karman, firing into a swath of women that'd just entered the hanger bay's door, that was aglow from the hole blown through it.

"I'm done worrying about God or anyone else's plans!" he mentally replied, turning around to track a dark, crimson fluid rushing over his feet from behind, finding it gushing up from the location the orb had been.

"What the fuck! I know that stride!" he thought, recognizing his Rabbi strolling through the now ankle-deep fluid, wearing war tattered black robes, along with a top hat.

"God's path requires sacrifice to curb the unbalance and impurity before it spreads!" he heard his Rabbi say in his mind, watching as projectiles and energy burst coming from every direction slammed into him.

"Not a scratch on his body!?" he thought, watching his Rabbi kneel and place his hands in the vicious fluid, not even flinching when more burst of lasers and projectiles slammed into him - as almost every woman in the hanger bay now focused their fire on him.

"The EGG must not be allowed to reattach, nothing must leave here! Nate, I stand by my word. I believe you're a good person. God will forgive your tainted blood. I'm sorry, I must be your end, instead of your protector. Your whole life, that's all I've ever aimed to do," he heard his Rabbi say in his mind, feeling the fluid grow cold, along with a dull ache rising from where it touched his feet, climbing up into the core of his body.

"He tried to protect me? Now he says he'll be my end? If I die here, I would've survived everything, all for nothing! I want to live!" he thought, turning his face away from his Rabbi, watching in horror as his wife grab her stomach, seeing her mouth open in a scream of agony he couldn't hear.

"Baby," he opened his mouth to say, stopping at 'ba' remembering it was pointless.

A burst of blinding lights flashed in the corner of his eye.

"How is he even alive? And what the hell is he doing?" he thought, seeing an even brighter burst of light shine through his tightly shut eyes.

"Mayday, Mayday, Mayday…May God cleanse the faithless, May God give me the strength to bring back the balance!" Nate heard in his mind, with one voice being the original female from the distress call, and the second from his Rabbi.

Below him, the fluid became frigid, and with it, pain like needles spreading up from his feet to the top of his head. Hatred, sadness, and profound confusion began to claim him, along with a pure desperation to protect the orb. Glancing towards it, he watched cracks spread along its surface, with a thick, crimson rivers of fluid oozing from them - smelling of iron rich blood.

"I've literally done nothing, controlled nothing. Only swept away with no choices," Nate thought, seeing budding images of his wife appear in his mind's eye.

-Merge-

"Rayya is it? Or should I say, life debtor two, two, four, delta one, four, one?" Nate heard someone say in a gruff voice, seeing a tall, ball headed, muscular man in a suit, glaring down at – him.

"You, you gave off bad vibes the moment I laid eyes on you. Now this? I guess it makes sense. Who are you really then? Look, actually, I don't care, go away, I have a lot of shit to do, and I'm not in the mood," he heard his wife reply, seeing from behind her eyes as she looked down at the floor.

"As a life debtor, you shouldn't start off with insults. As you can probably see, I'm Lebanese, and I work for Allah blessed, Al Babadur Corp. May Allah keep it strong so that it may continue to serve Lebanon!"

"I'm Lebanese, he says, but greets and continues to speak to me in English. I'ma' guess, you were born in the US, and probably began to follow Islam and love Lebanon because of the internet. Prove me wrong, speak to me in our mother tongue."

"I speak our tongue... however, I prefer English. In any case, I don't need to prove myself to you, it'd be the other way around."

"What do you want?"

"As you know, Tet and its affiliates are one of the biggest rivals to both Al Babadur and Lilith. I am here to watch every move this Tet shell group makes, which includes you."

"I'm boring. My work is boring and to my knowledge, your company and Lilith are quite a bit ahead of me."

"Yes, in some aspect, both of us are, and other areas we're not. Thus, I will need you to help to keep Al Babadur outpacing the rest. Normally, this is where I'd offer a person a large sum of money and lie to them, and tell them that I'd protect them if they get caught. But due to the relationship I had with your father, who betrayed us, I will tell you, you have no choice. You will send me data, anything and everything you can get your hands on. I will give you the means to transmit it. If you get caught, you're on your own."

"Are you kidding me? You have zero authority over me, my life debt is with Lilith, and even they haven't asked me to do what you have!"

"Humans are running out of a lot of sustainable resources. The faster you can make portable quantum computers a reality, the faster we can build stable space elevators. So the more information we can get from here, the faster Al Babadur, who's blessed by Allah, can lead humanity to these resources. This is Allah's will, and it will be done. We all believe he has put you here against all odds for this reason."

"I'm here because Lilith blackballs me! And I don't want to have anything to do with your company because it's sexist, run by zealots, and most of all because of how my father was treated!"

For a long moment the man chuckled, then whispered, "I'll be candid with you, whether you had a life debt or not, no one really know what to do with you. You're a person with too many variables."

"What? What the hell is that supposed to mean? What the hell do you know about me really?"

"That you were born free, and that your father passed you his debt. He was one of our greatest Mediums until, until you were born, then slowly he stopped helping, focusing on raising you, teaching you from the book of Nefeshka. His disloyalty left us compromised, which gave Lilith the upper hand. The only thing to do to save ourselves was to roll a life debt onto him, and sell him to Lilith as a Medium. But things got complicated, so your father remained in limbo, as did our debt."

"So, you're saying, I am in debt to your company as well!? Go kill yourself," he heard is wife reply.

"Again, so disrespectful. But I am in no mood to fight. I just need you to send the information. Yes, it'll be difficult, as the most important data is encrypted. I know those paper reports you give for updates are just basics test and have nothing that could ever be used to recreate anything useful in a lab. Here's the good part, Tet and its affiliate shell corps are ninety-five percent run by the everyday common 'pleb.' I've done my due diligence; no one here is anything other than who they appear to be.

"Tet doesn't bother to indoctrinate their people about humanities' history, to train them mentally and physically for battles and proper espionage. In a way it's pathetic, because it leaves them vulnerable, but in another way, it protects them from themselves and infiltrators such as myself, because we're caught in a stagnant information fish bowl."

"What do you want me to do then? There are one billion cameras in here, one billion cameras everywhere. Every part of these places is being recorded visually and audibly. I can't even believe you're even talking to me about this right here and now!" he heard his wife growl.

"Well, of course I have methods and means to disrupt cameras and audios in places for certain amounts of time. Like I said, I have been trained. And I hear that you have gone through basic espionage training for Lilith if they ever

need information from here as well, so, you should be fine to be honest."

"Go away!"

"Still choosing to be rude huh? Did you know, an acceptable payment for life debt is sex?"

"Don't threaten me for pussy, you won't like what'll happen to you if you pursue this," he heard his wife say in a deadpan tone, locking eyes with the man.

"Well, asking you nicely isn't working, maybe degrading you will work," Nate heard, feeling a rage surge up so pure, all he could see was white, before his vision returned to that of his wife's laboratory.

"I'm not going to put up with this," he heard his wife whisper, hearing the man chuckle darkly right after.

"Oh, so...you'll taunt and flirt with that dull little 'pleb' Jay, who's your boss, and being the 'pleb' he is, might fire you for it, but me, you don't like me, I'm not exciting?"

"I'm done listening to anything you have to say after a threat like that, goodbye, I will not put up with it."

"Funny, those are the words that've made you who you are today."

"And rest in tiny little pieces are the words that will define you if you touch me."

"Your snappy attitude is making me want to fuck and degrade you even more, to be honest. Anyways, you seemed to have brushed off what I said about your father, and how he is the reason you have a life debt. Could it be that he's already told you what he did? And you're not shocked? I had expected questions."

"I didn't ask because you are a 'weaselly' person. You come here, asking for me to stick my neck out, to send you classified data based on your words, words that dishonor my father!"

"I'm not asking, I'm telling, I apologize it came off that way because I said, I need your help. It looks like I'll have

to become assertive to show you that you have no place to say no to me."

"Oh fuck, you're a talker too...kill me when you're done, or during, I don't give a fuck anymore."

Nate watched the man's face flush red, then slightly pale, and mentally laughed at the verbal gut punch his wife had delivered.

"You, you don't know when to shut up huh? It's a pity intelligence is not carried over in regard to aspect of a person. Again, you're similar to your father, who'd been entrusted to give his greatest works to Allah blessed Al Babadur. Instead, he started saying, 'I'll not put up with this,'! Instead, all he gave was anger, spite, and resentment. He betrayed us, and God. Never, never think Al Babadur did not love, respect and value your father. His betrayal and your life debt reflect his selfishness."

"Lies, lies and more lies."

"You wish I was lying. It was right when he gave you that beautiful onyx medallion that he should've kept. He should've let you die and be at peace with Allah. Instead, he begged for you to live. Him wanting you to live, and pay his debt is cruelty beyond all measures. When you get older, you'll find out, a life debt is not what you could ever imagine. Yet still, I bet you will still love and adore your father, and still believe he loved you," Nate heard, watching the man look up towards the fire alarm as it blared, then flashes of days and nights pass before the man returned.

"Where were we? We'd got interrupted a few weeks back. Oh, how your father suckered you into his life debt. And me, telling you I needed information. It took a lot of work, but I set up transfer points and files all throughout the building. Send data on any and everything you run into when you're working with other teams and such. If you don't, I will make sure you're under me, learning your place."

"You're going to lose your dick, I promise you."

"Yes, if it's in you I, I won't be able to see it," he heard the man say, watching him hop atop of a work bench, pulling out a small, rock hard cock...with visible sores on it.

"What's that face for? Oh, you're worried about that? When you pass it to your husband, just blame it on one of the many people you've fucked in the last couple of weeks no?" he heard the man scoff, with his finger pointing to one of the sore, with a sinister look on his face.

"Rayya, Rayya, report to my office. Your reports, all one billion of them are not clear. Please get in here. Like right now, or I'm coming in there," he heard Jay's voice blare over a PA."

"Saved, again. Every time...him. The microwave in his office bursting in flames. Both of us, being sent all over the place to work. I know you're fond of this 'pleb,' so, let me ask, you haven't told him anything have you? I'll find out if you're asking for help. If you are, I'll add conditions to your debt. You're lucky, lucky you keep wiggling by. And lucky I was slightly enjoying the chase. But now, now I've grown impatient," Nate heard, followed by the vision switching to Jay's office.

"Is that dude fucking with you?" he heard Jay ask bluntly.

"No? what makes you, you say that?" he heard his wife say, without any fluctuation in her voice.

"Awight'," he heard Jay reply, bobbing his head, gazing back at his computer.

"That's it?" he heard his wife ask.

"Yup, I figured out your reports, all four revisions of them," he heard Jay say sarcastically.

The imagery shifted again, and now he saw the man looming over his wife/himself, before feeling the man's lips press onto his, followed by hands running down his body, over his...breast...with his wife/himself becoming aroused.

"Oh, you like?" he heard the man whisper.

"Oddly, I didn't think this would be on my list of kinks, but yes."

"Oh good," he heard the man say in a dark voice that caused a throb in an area of his body he couldn't identify.

"Don't forget, I'll castrate and make you bleed out for this. Mmm, that makes me like this even more, knowing that once you've fucked me with that infected thing …I'll bathe in your blood! Mmm, bathing in your blood, shit, the thought of pouring blood from your lifeless head, all over my pussy, fuck that just made me so wet," he heard his wife gasp, with a strange clenching sensation between his legs, with images of the man's head oozing blood between his legs.

"What'd you say!?" he heard the man growl, feeling hands on his neck, sending a wonderful energy coursing through his body.

"You heard me," he heard his wife choke out, feeling his body alight with hunger to be abused - and hunger to kill.

"Rayya! Report to my office! This data is all over the place!" he heard Jay yell through the PA.

"Him again, I don't know how he know when I'm here! I block out everything! No worries though! I've prepared conditions, conditions that will rip your life up slowly," he heard the man growl, feeling the pressure around his wife's and ultimately his neck increase.

"Yes," he heard his wife chock out in uncontrolled ecstasy.

"Yes, I will destroy your fondness of this Jay and his wife. I have sources that say your dear friend Karman has been asking for material sample request at the dig sites in Colombia, and elsewhere that are very important to the space elevator projects that go beyond the norm. There's also evidence she's used her influences to move tons of fertile farm soil from Lebanon to Colombia. If it's her, she seems to be gathering the most fertile lands from not just Lebanon, but from around the world, moving them to her own country. That soil removal has caused people in Lebanon and elsewhere to starve," he heard the man say, pressing his body up against his wife, allowing her/him to feel hard cock pressing into her/his belly.

472

"Karman, doing what? Are kidding me!? Your lies are ridiculous! You just want me to not trust my friends, to feel alone! To feel like I'm surrounded by shifty people! I have an idea, go find out yourself!" he heard his wife gasp.

"Oh, I will, but Jay's been fucking with me, not just keeping me from you, but in other ways as well that I can't put my finger on. And since you're close to him and his wife, I want you to fuck them up, then fall on the sword for everything. I'm telling you the plan, so you can feel pain with every step you take, and feel absolutely hopeless, with zero control with what you'll be responsible for. Good luck," he heard the man say, pressing a kiss, squeezing his – his wife's ass, before the image shifted again.

"He is bothering you again huh?"

"What? No!"

"I put you up for promotions, it gets rejected magically. He's the only one who's got that kind of power to say no, while saying yes on the paper work. And I never see him go into the lab, but I for sure, always see him coming out. And right now, you look flustered. Tell me, is he fucking with you?"

"I can handle myself. I don't need a man to help me!"

"Eh? what'd you just say to me?" he heard Jay ask, calmly tilting back in the chair, with an ice-cold look.

"Excuse me! Sorry, sorry, I should never have spoken to you like that...please forget this."

"Get out of my office Rayya. I'll come talk to you in a minute," he heard Jay say in an eerie neutral tone, followed by the image shifting to the lab, seeing behind his wife's eyes as she paced back and forth nervously.

Jay appeared after a few more minutes of pacing, and he saw his wife's hands come up pleadingly.

"Rayya, you calm now? Put your hands down. Why the hell are you looking so freaked out? Oh, you idiot, I'm not here to fire you, calm the hell down. Look, listen, this situation, whatever I assume is going on. If it's happening, this is not a man/women thing, this is a human thing. I'm

473

responsible for you, as your boss, and as a human being. Also, unfortunately for me, I'm slightly starting to like you as a friend...as I've enjoyed your company during the few times you and my wife forced us to have get-togethers'."

"Uh...Uhmm," he heard his wife reply, confused.

"Look, anyways...Is he fucking with you? I need to know," he heard Jay ask.

"I...I...I...never want to hang out with you or your wife again. Let's keep this professional. And no, he's not."

"Umm, well damn. Hey, can you still hang with her? 'Cuz,' I hate shopping...and."

"Jay if this is all, I'd like to get back to work," he heard his wife say, feeling tears welling up in her eyes.

An image appeared... it was three weeks later, and he could see the nameless tormentor storm into the Lab, arm in sling. When he looked at his wife, there was only malice.

"I know it was you. You got someone to come and fuck me up. You're being protected and when I find out how, the misery I make you feel will multiply. Now tell me what did you find out about the mutt and his wife?"

"I told them I never want to hang out ever again and since then, we've never hung out. I barely talk to Jay unless I give him reports. And I haven't seen you in weeks, I forgot you even existed to be honest."

"I figured you'd resist. I took steps. Call your mother, ask her if she's alright," he heard the man reply with a growl.

"What!?"

"Call...her! Hear her cry and know, know what happened to her, will happen to you. How many friends I decide to bring, or if it'll just be me, depends on you though. And if something painful and mysterious happens to me again, I'll get her sent somewhere for it to happen every day and night for the rest of your lives."

Nate watched behind his wife's eyes as she made a call with her View-Tech's...he couldn't hear anything, just feel pain beyond comprehension. After the pain, the image blurred and resumed two months later, he could tell by the season change, and a fast glance at the date on a computer.

"I see you've been sending a lot of info. A lot of it seems to be useless junk, but fair enough, I knew you'd do that, but, keep sending stuff, we'll piece what we can together. And any news on the Karman and her inquiries situation?" he heard the man say.

Behind his wife's eyes, he saw her look up towards the double lab doors as the sickly man cleared them.

"Oh you. This time I almost, almost, almost, forgot about you again," he heard his wife say, with a light-hearted chuckle.

"Shit, what the hell happened to him?" he thought, taking in the details of his sunken in cheeks, and pale clammy skin.

"I've yet to fully do as I promised, do you want to disrespect me right now? I can give you a gift that keeps on giving. I warned you," he heard the man begin, when his wife cut in saying, *"Yes, yes you did. So, I took precautions."*

"You listen here!"

"No, you listen...you little piece of..." he heard his wife say, getting up, moving right into the man's face, whispering, *"You were the cold bucket of water I needed. Before you, I felt like half of the time I was sleep walking. But the more I prepared for you, the more I began to enjoy my life. I feel like, like I'm finally taking my life back."*

"Bend over!" he heard the man say with a dry cough, seeing a face that was in no hurry to back his threat.

"Bend over? You think I'm scared? Humm, backing me into a corner with that sore on your tiny little prick, opened doors I never knew were there. As you know, Lilith Corp. is all about female empowerment, even for life debtors. I told my OBGYN about your threats, and she immediately started treating me with the latest and greatest anti STI vaginal gel. Not only that, she had me bring Karman in to treat her as well, just in case you wanted to...extend your small range fire."

475

"Small jokes huh? And hum, I wasn't thinking of fucking the mutt's wife till now, thanks for the good idea," he heard the man say.

"So full of shit, your life choice is to be a fucked-up creature that'd think of that 'kinda' shit first."

"You got me there. I definitely did think of it."

"See, you're a creature."

"Yes, I am, and I love the smug look on your face. It drills in the fact that no matter how smart a person is, they're always compromised by their emotions. Lilith Corp. is the embodiment of a heathenish women's nature, and any empowerment they grant you is to lead you to suffer and die a heathen's death. Whatever gains you think you've made are just means to their end, not to your own, trust me."

"Oh, you're so right, and still, it's oh so liberating, since it just so happens to be my victory that they don't want their slaves, or their slave's friends, taken advantage off. And since that can't always be prevented because of creatures like you, who're slimy and hard to stop, they definitely don't want them falling ill from it. My doctor, she's a funny one, she flooded my pussy full of that gel while saying, 'broken minded slaves are useless to her Madam Lilith.' I was pissed off at the time, but it feels so good. Because now, I can fuck whoever I want without them using awful feeling condoms, and having that nagging feeling that they might be sick, even after spending so much time vetting their health."

"Trusting, dumb bitch."

"I've trusted condoms before this, so what's wrong with trusting something that gives a natural experience and is still ninety-nine point nine percent effective. Besides, I had nothing to lose even if it was way less effective, because I was banking on you or someone like you trying to force themselves on me anyway."

"It's funny, I wasn't even counting on ruining your life passively. I like to be proactive and forward. But your fear *of me lead you to become a damn lab rat. That feels, that feels great."*

"You're just trying to poison my mind and happiness."

"True, and also true that they want to empower females to become lose sluts. They don't want you to cherish your body. The want you to give it freely to every man to take. The perfect mask for making you taint your body and your spirit, is by saying they're granting you sexual empowerment. At least I'm the type of creature who shows that he wants to take something from you, then you can see how much I've bitten off and possibly even heal from it. Lilith, and those women who surround her, trap you in tentacles of convolution.

"They swallow you whole and make you rot from the inside out at the same time. You feel liberated when you still have no control, you're being played like the life debtor you are. I guess, to be honest, since there's no lower position you could ever hold in humanity, everything is just as it should be," he heard the man say.

"You say trapped. But, perception is reality, I feel liberated, therefore I am," he heard his wife say nonchalantly.

"You, have no idea what they put in you do you? I hate Lilith, I hate much of the things she and the affiliates stand for, but I respect and fear all of them for their genius. I've changed my mind; I don't want to stick any part of my body into you now that they've put whatever that stuff is into you. I value my life," he heard the man say, kissing her softly on the cheek before backing up.

"Good," he heard his wife say, watching from behind his wife's eye as she leaned back against the wall, taking in the details of the man's flushing red, yet pale and sweaty face.

"You're not off the hook, don't forget about your mother. I can still reach out and touch her, I want information on Jay and Karman, anything and everything now," he heard the man say.

He could feel his wife's emotion iced over. And in a fraction of a second, he saw and felt his wife's hands move and connect with the man's sides, then saw her take two nimble steps back.

"*Uh,*" he heard the man choke out, with his face changing to sheer agony.

"*You misunderstood me, or I should say, you misunderstand me. I'm actually hyper aware of my circumstances. Where you think my hell is convolution and mal-intent, I've made it my home. And in that home, I share it with my mother, who in my opinion is the Queen of it all, steps ahead of anything that Lilith woman, or her affiliates can come up with. The rage and pain you saw, was not because of what you said you did to her. I've never for a second believed you.*"

"*What?*" he heard the man whisper, with a vain attempt to sound in control.

"*I should've been an actress. I must be very good at playing dumb. She may think she's being subtle, but the feeling of her pulling the strings of my life in the background are actually quite triggering. I feel like a spider on a web, using every vibration she makes as my guide. Now go back to her...and tell her...hum, I...I just realized I don't even give a fuck anymore, whatever,*" he heard his wife say, pausing as her emotion shifted to something so alien to him, he was utterly frightened by the way his brain tried to run, and not even register them.

"*Oh, quite a shock, quite a shock indeed. Ha-ha, I'm seeing first hand why no one knows what to do with you. Before, all I had saw was rumors and reports of those who failed to rain you in. And killing you right now is not an option for many reasons. 'Outta' curiosity, tell me what you think you know about your mother,*" she heard the man choke out.

"*I know somehow she's the reason my father and I have been put into life debt. I know she uses religion like a weapon, and that somehow, impossibly, she spreads it...spreads it like some kind of a virus. Wherever she's ever gone, all of a sudden, there are these converts to Islam.*"

When I first moved here, my whole apartment complex converted in like a month. You want to threaten me...but the biggest fear I have is that I hate her so much, yet feel so trapped loving her. I literally have crippling panic attacks if I even think of completely cutting ties from her. And then, there's the fact that I barely ever see her move from in front of the T.V., watching her dramas. She has always done so much, yet never really moving."

"Humm, from all that, how could you say you're the spider on the web? I'd say you're the insect caught on it, or maybe a tiny little spider that thinks it's strong enough to walk on the webs without being eaten?"

"I know that I just smashed a lot of important tissue in your kidneys, you may want to hurry up and go see a doctor for that," he heard his wife say, with her alien like emotion now feeling like it'd choke out his existence.

"Yes you did, and yes, I will," he heard the man choke out.

"So why are you still here, distracting me! And what the fuck is wrong with this crystal? Why's it not working?" he heard his wife whisper, completely ignoring, and feeling her mind shift and no longer even acknowledging the man's existence.

For minutes on end, the man was in his peripheral vision, sitting in agony. From behind his wife's eyes, he could see her walking around the lab doing calculations, running experiments and taking notes as if the man were no longer there. Then he could see green indications from the results on one of his wife's four monitors, and watched her hurriedly print and organized papers.

"Rayya, let me ask you, where's the medallion your father gave you? Do you know how special it is? It saved your life, do you remember? Your father held it up to you, and he told you something...do you remember? I'll give you a hint, seeing it, you went into a trance, but then you were bleeding out, your brain didn't have enough oxygen and you passed out. Just before that, your father had taken you to the

basement, he was showing you something. Ancient, ancient maps of Columbia. And of the Mediterranean."

Nate felt a sadness, and a small memory try to rise, but it was crushed by sheer will.

"You either remember, and are a coward, or you're repressing it, being a bigger coward. I ask where it is rhetorically by the way. I know you're hiding it from your mother, and from yourself. Hiding it in that fake peanut jar, stealing peeks at it...getting scared of the memories that begin to resurface, then hiding it again."

"Shut up," he heard his wife whisper.

He felt a small vibration in the alien emotion that'd been surrounding him, giving him room to - for a lack of better description, mentally breath. Within the same moment, he watched his wife pick up the stack of papers and leave her lab, heading towards Jay's office, leaving the man just sitting there.

The imagery shifted, and he was pulled out of his wife's body to stand face to face with her in a darkness that seemed illuminated.

"That was umm, brings new meaning to being inside of me," he heard his wife whisper with a warm smile.

"Uhh...yeah...Hey...I would've, I would've wanted to protect you. You should've told me...It bothers me that you hide that from me, it hurts, we promised no more secrets," he mentally replied, flabbergasted at the experience.

"My Habibi, there's no such thing as not keeping secrets. And you have a huge double standard, you never told me that you gave everything up for me. I saw everything you did for me when we touched earlier."

"What do you mean? Why would you say I gave up everything, when you are everything to me?"

"Habibi."

"Rayya, all I want in this life is for you to be happy. My family was stopping that, so I wanted to carry the burden they put on you. I wish I knew about him; I wish I had the chance to help you!"

"Habibi, when you step on a bug on your way home, do you tell me about it?" he heard his wife ask, feeling that alien mood returning.

"Na…no," he replied.

"Exactly. In the same way, why would I acknowledge that creature. After that day, I only saw him once more, and that was just a day before we left on this trip. He rolled into the conference room in a wheelchair and said he's leaving the company. Jay put in another promotion package for me right after. I'm supposed to find out if I got it after we'd got back. I hate the fact that that creature even had the power to resurface in my memory. And that every time the space elevator topic came up, it had made me want to probe Jay and Karman's activities," he heard his wife reply, feeling a warmth return to her.

With the mood change, an image of a nude Jay and Karman appeared standing next to them, with Karman directly on his right, and Jay standing next to his wife, facing Karman and himself. He wanted to speak, but as he opened his mouth, a profoundly beautiful land of greenery, mountains, waterfalls and ocean opened beneath their feet in the form of a circle. Through the circle, he could hear Maydays from the voices, of what could only be millions.

"I felt you accusing us with your eyes from 'hella' far away Nate. Look, you'd died on us like more than once. We didn't leave you out of anything on purpose. When you died, your brain took up a lot of storage going into the safety net. Pulling you to us may have damaged you, so we let you just chill and be an observer of the outside world. In any case, bro, you may 'wanna' brace yourself, I don't think you or any of us are really ready for this shit," he heard Jay say, pointing down, before whispering, *"look closely fam, this is what we're inside, and this is what used to be here."*

"Oh my God! OH MY GOD!" Nate thought, seeing large, familiarly shaped silhouettes in the beautiful backdrop, as men and women's voices grew louder in his mind, all saying forms of Mayday, with their last statements being, *< If you're hearing*

this message, then know all hope for humanity is lost. >

.

Chapter IX

Transformation, Truth, The All

Road Trip: Day Four

Date: Sunday, June 4th 2017

Time: From leaving the cabin/café, up to having entered the Lil-Corp base

Location: Hill City, South Dakota

The first Mayday call came two minutes after they'd speed off away from the cabin. Shortly after, Karman felt a surge of energy that made her feel both overwhelmed, and reborn. Taking deep breaths, she sat in silence trying to comprehend what was happening to her. It was then that Rayya's scent called to her, filling her lungs with a sweet, irony essence that made her pussy throb and stomach clench in hungry anticipation. Then, there was a second Mayday call, and Karman found herself slammed with an icy, endless darkness, passing from Rayya's essence into her own. It was smothering, controlling and desperate. It was the epitome of everything she hated, as she prided herself to never be controlled by anything that make her feel pathetic or desperate.

Pushing back against the endless icy darkness, Karman had a flashback of Rayya in the motel room, remembering the look in Rayya's eyes when she'd woken from her dream.

"Losing that Ilias guy, and how it all went down, it traps her," she thought, reflecting on how she'd felt when she'd fallen victim to people who thought of her as an animal to be tortured and toyed with.

Looking towards Rayya, she could see the painful, conflicted energy she'd somehow felt pass into her, reflected on her face.

"The look of someone who'd never gotten revenge. I was able to clear my blood, I should be more understanding," Karman thought, feeling a rush of energy surge through her body and flow into Rayya.

Pain in her lower abdomen came shortly after, then a familiar, disgusting, dripping sensation. Karman couldn't believe it, or the odd energy connection flow between she and Rayya. Four more Mayday calls had played out by the time they'd entered the city limit, and with each one, Karman felt her energy ties with Rayya grow even further. It was both joyous, and overbearing, because just as fast as their energies agreed, was just as fast as they didn't. By the time she heard Nate speak, she and Rayya had wordlessly fought and made up more times than she could possibly count.

Listening to her husband speak to Nate, she felt her whole body begin to ache, and her lymph nodes swell. At the same time, she felt waves of negative, sorrowful energy passing through her that began to tug and pull the bonds she and Rayya had created. Disassociation began to take over, where she felt like she was there, but not really. She could hear and see herself arguing with Rayya, but with each passing second everything became more fragmented. Before she knew it, she had no more strength. Her period cramps and pains had tripled, her ears rung, and her throat felt raw and sore. She no longer smelled Rayya's scent, as it'd been replaced by the medicinal smell one gets when one's sick with mucus building up. Then, felt her body fail completely.

~ Immediately after slipping into unconsciousness ~

"Ummm, okay what the fuck am I doing here? And, why am I naked?" Karman thought, surprised to find herself inside the 'Mind Lab' she and Jay had created.

"Jay? Baby, did you send me in here? Why?" she mentally asked, staring at shrouded images of a jungle.

The images had been taken from her memory and reminded her of when Jay played video games and the map was darkened unless he walked the character towards it. Looking down, she could see the ground inlayed with golden trail lines, and as she followed the one in front of her, she saw Jay appear, standing just past one of the shrouded memories. And even though the distance seemed far, she could clearly see the warmth and care on his face.

"All this auto uploaded with you. If this is following you here, then they're just as important for you to deal with as the Nano 'thingys'. Hold up, actually data for the Nano 'thingys' are inlayed within the images you're seeing. Funny how the mind works huh Eggy? It demands you to pay attention to it huh? I love you my beautiful Eggy head. I'm here when you need me," she heard Jay say in a calm, clear tone with his nude form vanishing right after.

On her right, the nude form of Rayya appeared and stood transfixed, staring at a wall that appeared to stretch up and to the sides for infinity.

"My life, this is the story of it. A wall, and yours, is a beautiful jungle. Hum, I guess I'd be a little more envious, and it'd feel more inviting if there weren't feline like eyes staring at you," she heard Rayya whisper.

"You can see in there? It looks like a jungle in the middle of the night to me, I see just silhouettes of trees and vines," she replied.

"Yes, I can see in there, it's a daylight view for me. But when I look away, and look in front of me, I see this huge white wall, full of graffiti in Hebrew and Arabic that goes on forever and ever. I hate being trapped," Karman heard Rayya say softly.

"I see your wall too. And, I also hate feeling trapped," she replied, steeping forward, watching as the jungle began to illuminate, revealing a familiar face just for a second.

"What is this place? And, be careful, I just saw a tiger dart past you," she heard Rayya say all in the same breath.

"You saw a tiger? Really?" she responded.

"Yeah, and just as fast, it vanished. Seriously, what is this place? I feel safe, but I can't feel much of anything, like much of my body I mean. Just 'kinda' phantom sensations," she heard Rayya whisper.

"A tiger you say? Oh, umm, this is Jay and I's Mind Lab. We created it so that we can work on and test our ideas in secret. Honestly, we'd half ass made this place. We'd, figuratively stepped inside to take a look at it and got freaked out, cause, yeah, as you can see it's a weird place. Yeah, it's not like how we'd thought it'd be. To be honest, we were going to destroy it, but we were running out of private, safe places to work on our stuff. Even though this place doesn't exactly do what we ask it, it still does a very good job of drawing up real world data, allowing us to run dangerous test on materials and what not without getting hurt."

"Is this a quantum computer? Like I don't understand," she heard Rayya whisper.

"I really 'dunno' how I'd even begin to explain it. And now isn't the time," she replied, seeing a timer float up in front of her, showing her husband and Nate's body functions failing.

"This is the fucked memory I'm hung up on. Why though, why am I so hung up on this? Why can't I just let this go?" Karman thought, taking another step, watching her surrounding ever so slightly illuminate.

"Holy shit, they're so simplistic, yet so complex," she whispered, taking hold of a vine, seeing that the structure was completely made up of Nanites.

"What do you see?" she heard Rayya ask, seeing her come behind her and stand on her left.

"My mind has organized each type of Nanite into a particular plant life. Ah, and if they change, it grows into another type of plant life," she replied, seeing a disruption on the vine where the Nanites appeared to have died.

"My breath, it killed some of them…and, why can I feel my breath in here? That's never happened before," she said aloud, allowing her breath to flow over the vine as she spoke, watching as it wilted away in her hand.

<Mayday, Mayday, Mayday…We've gone down. I'm the only one left alive in here. The males are fighting hard. Fighting them, all I could think of is that they're fighting hard to oppress me, to oppress my battle sisters. But now, after tumbling from the Ether, slamming into the earth, did I realize, what this war has cost us all. The males, they have nothing left, we've left them with no hope. Of course, now more than ever, they will show us no mercy.> Karman heard a woman say, with her voice resonating through to her soul.

"I feel that woman's sorrow as if it's my own. And what the hell kind of war is this? Tumbling out of the Ether? Who the hell talks like that?" Karman thought, watching her surroundings ripple like waves.

<**The most Awesomet system ever:** Tell me everything you can about these Mayday signals>, she mentally commanded as she watched Rayya squat down in her peripherals, touching locations where it looked like rocks had been cast into the water.

"That signal, when it went through me, I saw, felt and heard so many others. For a second, if it didn't cut, I felt like I'd drown in sorrow," she heard Rayya whisper.

As if on cue to Rayya's words, Karman heard, <Mayday, Mayday, Mayday>, from multiple directions, and with those calls, the entire jungle like landscape illuminated.

"Jay?" she whispered, seeing her husband calmly stalking through the jungle with his teammates spread out around him.

"Karman, is there a way to disconnect the sensation or block inputs, those 'Maydays' are too much.

"Sweetie, I don't understand anything right now, I'm, I'm just as freaked out as you are," she whispered, watching Rayya's wall grow bigger in the back drop, now with plant life growing out of it.

"I have to ask you; do you blame me? Karman, Karman! More tigers, they're coming!" she heard Rayya whisper, sounding like she was beginning to panic.

"I don't see tigers Rayya, that's the thing," she replied, looking up towards Rayya's wall, seeing more plants burst from it.

"What do you see?" she heard Rayya ask pensively.

"I see my husband and his old team mates. This jungle, and this situation, part of this is from my memory, a very painful memory I don't particularly like. I often try to suppress it to be honest. The other part of this memory, must be from my husband's memory, because he was here too. Oh by the way, this Mind Lab likes to fill stuff in, 'kinda' like how dreams do it."

"I see tigers and I want to run with all my strength, but I'm afraid to move. And over there, I see the same tiger that was on Jay's back, is that where you see your husband?" she heard Rayya say, pointing.

"Yes, that's where I see him. It 'kinda' makes sense you'd see him that way."

"Really?" she heard Rayya ask apprehensively.

"This place cuts all the bullshit; makes you face things. Funny thing is, before today, I was always able to kick away and untangle my personal problems that'd surface in here and work on what we came here for. But today, it seems like I won't be able to get around it," she whispered, feeling her stomach cramp, followed by a dripping sensation.

"I see," she heard Rayya reply, looking down, whispering, "What the fuck?" as blood began to run down her leg.

"Crazy," she replied, seeing and feeling blood run down her own legs as well.

"And what's this?" she whispered, seeing dark, rotting patches where her and Rayya's menstrual blood had touched the foliage.

As she continued to examine the foliage, a large, baby blue Parrot landed in front of them.

"This AI would like to inform both of you of the following. Uploading information now," she heard the AI's avatar Parrot say in a warm tone, followed by time stamped images of both her and Rayya's white blood cells attacking the anti STI gel Nanites, which happened to be exactly when they'd felt the first earthquake. The AI then displayed data revealing that both of their immune systems had used them as the baseline template to fight off the invasive Nanites.

"So, they were harmless after all. If anything, they're even more helpful than what they were intended for," she heard Rayya whisper with a sigh of relief.

"Huh?" she replied, seeing the jungle go dark when she stared at the treehouse.

"Nothing, this person told me I didn't know what I was putting in my body. And that Lilith was just experimenting on me," she heard Rayya reply.

"Experimenting yes, but I wouldn't have come with you, or let you do it if I thought it was dangerous. 'Member you tried to rush to do it all in one day, and I made you slow down and asked for a sample to try. 'Member I told them I felt a cold inside my lip coming on."

"No, to be honest I remembered doing it all in one day…I remembered just going in," she heard Rayya reply.

"Well, technically you did go in on the day you wanted but, we didn't do everything till later on in the week. Think back, I called you like three days later and was like 'ok let's be gel sisters!'

I needed time is why. I ran every damn test I could think of on them. And I used my influences to mark and check the gel packets to make sure they didn't change the batch. In any case, the type of particles they put in us are not adaptive. They're just shaped to destroy the protein shell of the viruses. Long time ago, I took the HPV vaccine, but there's a new strand that's been popping up, and ladies are getting it just from sitting in other ladies' sweat at the sauna. I'm not taking a risk just in case that strand can give you cervical cancer, it's already aggressive enough as it is."

"Oh yeah, I'd heard about that. Hey, umm, what if I'd done it first, then told you?" she heard Rayya ask, staring at the silhouette of the treehouse.

"I would've been so pissed at you, you have no idea," she replied, now feeling every aspect of her body integrate within the Mind Lab.

"That, that makes me feel…thank you," she heard Rayya reply, followed by, "Allah, I see a monster in the treehouse, and these animals with chains on them surrounding it. And a monster sitting inside of a golf cart."

"Weird, you're seeing how I think of them. Hey Rayya, what's your wall, what's trapping you, making you feel that way?"

"My mother, the Prophecy, the unknown, not being able to have children because of the Prophecy, and because I only have one ovary. And let's not forget Nate's family. Oh, and the truth! The truth about my life is probably eighty percent of that wall. I feel like I know way too damn much about life, about how our lives are controlled. Know too much about how crazy everything can be. And the more I learn, the more I feel trapped," she heard Rayya say candidly.

"I hear you Mami, I feel a lot of the same things you do, all except for wanting kids, I've never ever wanted kids. I don't want them to live in this hell," she replied.

"Never!? No children?" she heard Rayya exclaim.

"No way sweetie, I just nodded my head and smiled when you told me you wanted our kids to grow up together. I didn't know what to say, you were way too happy talking about it."

"I…I don't know what to say," she heard Rayya reply softly.

"Sorry," she replied, seeing pain on Rayya's face.

"That, that stings a 'lil.' I, I really didn't think that, that you didn't want children. And, like why? You're healthy! Take advantage of what you have! Why wouldn't you want kids!?" she heard Rayya scream.

As Rayya screamed, Karman heard soft Maydays began to play out all over the jungle, and wherever the Maydays originated from, she could see ripples with a center point that looked just like stones had been thrown into the water.

"AI, please force close all of this jungle stuff, make everything blank and bring up Cartel de La Tunda Maps. Oh, and the most generic one, I forgot to say that."

"Unable to close the jungle simulation, it is being directly fed from you, your husband's mind and a powerful data source that AI does not understand. Pulling Cartel de La Tunda maps, adjusting them to be viewed easily based on background," she heard the AI Parrot say as a map appeared in front of them.

"Give more info about the data source," she said to her AI.

"The main information the data sources is sending me is regarding a computer of some sort within the treehouse. AI is currently studying information about it. AI would like to know, does this Cartel map suffice?"

"Keep me informed. And yes, it will suffice," she replied to the Parrot before looking to Rayya who wore a confused expression on her face, staring at both her Cartel map and the Parrot.

"Rayya, you want to know why I don't want kids. Well, this is why, this map is me, this map is my legacy."

"What?" she heard Rayya whisper.

"This map means that anyone I love, or get too close to, could be targeted. Growing as close as I have to you and Nate, is a goddam real life fairy tale to me bella. Honestly, we were supposed to go back to NYC like six months ago, but Jay and I decided to stay because we clicked with y'all. And honestly, depending on what came of our meeting in NYC, like if it looked like we were going to be pulled into a huge war, we would've just not come back, we would've just ghosted on y'all. Like I said, close friends are targeted, and we wouldn't let that happen."

"You and Jay wanted to stay because of us, or just you?" she heard Rayya reply with a raised eyebrow.

"Welllll, he was happy I was happy. He…"

"Didn't even want to go on this road trip with us in the first place. I saw him bitching at you when we were loading up the car," she heard Rayya finish for her.

"Anyways, look, kids are targets. And if kids live long enough, and the parents become targets, then kids have to watch…watch like I watched. My parents were slaughtered right in front of me."

"I'm sorry," she heard Rayya whisper, watching as she raised her hand, touching data points describing basic details of Cartel de La Tunda's movement before hearing her say, "arms and drug trafficking networks, so this is the real deal. This is what Jay was talking about when he said you two are not good people."

"Si and although Cartel de La Tunda is the most powerful in Colombia, it's a tiny drop in the bucket compared to other crime organizations. A powerful, tiny little drop, but still, like look at the map. La Tunda is surrounded, being chocked off and gutted by anyone with means and methods to take a bite."

"Were you telling the truth to that biker Sabrina? Are you La Tunda, or is it your sister? You are saying it like it's you right now," she heard Rayya say in a tone that was both asking and telling.

"Si, I am La Tunda, and so is my sister. So, we are La Tunda. We picked the name of a female demon to show we don't fuck around. And we work on both sides of life to make ourselves strong. I'm good at making legitimate money to hide the dirty, and my sister, she's good at being the bitch who crushes any and every one that stands in our way. But make no mistake, we can be seamlessly interchangeable."

"I…I want to curse you out, but I'm the piece of shit who genuinely wanted you and Jay apart of our fucked up inner circle. Yeah, to be honest, even without all the weird shit going on, I really think I would've wanted to bring you closer. You, at least, would've the honor to ghost us I guess," she heard Rayya say, watching tears run down her cheeks.

"I, umm," she began to reply when Rayya raised her hand.

"Karman, just leave it," she heard Rayya say with trembling lips, before hearing her whisper, "Why do you try to suppress memories of this forest? Why is your mind fighting you to address it? Your mind won't even let you close it. If that's the case, then why not stare it down and face it. Don't be like me and be trapped by an endless wall made up of my fear of the truth."

"Aren't you giving me bad advice, what if I see the truth and a wall starts to grow?" she replied, shaking her head at the treehouse which began to darken.

"Well, you're right, I could be wrong, and maybe you'll see a wall after, or maybe not, but do you want to be stuck where you are right now? Tell me, why are you afraid to look?" she heard Rayya say.

"I'm worried that my husband can shoot children without remorse," she found the strength to say, looking at Rayya who stared at her with deep intensity before looking back at the treehouse.

"Oh," she finally heard Rayya whisper, shaking her head at her as if to say – 'I don't even know what to say.'

"Oh is right," she replied, before saying, "The monsters in the treehouse...do you see a tiny 'lil' baby monster in its arms?"

"No, I see something formless in the monster's arms, I'd been wondering what it was. Now that I know it's a child, I take it, it means you have no idea what to think of the child. That you're conflicted on whether the child was innocent, or if he or she would've grown up to be like their parents. In any case, I think you already know if Jay did or not. If these people were monsters in both of your eyes, I don't think Jay is the type that'd allow a potential little monster to become a big one that could harm either of you," she heard Rayya reply.

"The one holding the kid is the mom, and the one in the golf cart is the father, they were from hell itself, trust me. All three were killed, kind of by one bullet, but I don't know whose bullet. I told Jay if he was the one who took the shot, that I'd still love him for being able to do that," she whispered.

"I...sweetie, aren't you and Jay both monsters? Haven't both of you done worse? Aren't you both child killers, and parent killers of people neither of you considered monsters? If

Jay did shoot this kid, I don't get why you care. What's the difference between shooting a kid, or filling up a house full of drugs and weapons? What if it was the drugs from your Cartel that killed the 'lil' girl and her parents in the cabin?"

"Lil' girl in the cabin?" she whispered, feeling zero remorse for said girl, even if it were her drugs that killed her.

"Yes, a 'lil' girl. She'd been accidently low dosing herself by touching and using spoons her parents used to shoot up with. She was on death's door, and when we arrived, she walked through it," she heard Rayya reply.

"The difference is nothing, and the difference is everything," she said, raising her hand, forming it into a mock gun, pointing at the AI's Parrot avatar before saying, "Poom! I have taken this life by a direct choice."

After doing that, she looked at Rayya and said, "You love coffee yes?"

"Um," she heard Rayya reply sounding confused.

"Si or no Mami? Of course I'm asking rhetorically cause you're an addict."

"Yes, I love coffee."

"Coffee is a drug. Different distributors sell that drug. If one of your distributors stopped selling cause they died and got their territory taken, you'd just find a different source. You'd probably not even know the main distributor died, and got their territory taken over. The only time you'd notice is if the store in your hood moved around a 'lil' too much, or the quality changed. You want the coffee, you are hooked to the coffee, you will do anything for that coffee, and you don't give a fuck about yourself, or the people around you to get that coffee. You will pay the price for this coffee, you will seek out this coffee, no matter what. And I am the person who can supply it to the stores, and if I disappear someone else will take my place."

"I get your point Karman," she heard Rayya say.

"Do you? Then you get what I mean, the difference is nothing, and the difference is everything. And I'm afraid if I know the truth, I'll be a liar. I'm afraid I'll let my husband down because I wouldn't be able to back up my words. He loves me so much, so, so much. I know his heart; I know it beats for me. So, I don't know why I care so much if he's the one who pulled the

493

trigger. I don't want to know, but I really want to know. Am I being unreasonable?"

"Yes," she heard Rayya reply, shocking her.

"Don't look at me like that Karman, in my opinion, you are. Your mind keeps bringing this up for you to address it. So, look at the damn treehouse and find out, or make your peace with not knowing. And yes, I'm a hypocritical bitch who can't solve her own problems," she heard Rayya say as she came behind her, wrapping her arms around her breast, pulling her close.

"I'm here, I'm here for you either way," she heard Rayya whisper in her ear, kissing her on the cheek.

"I don't even know if looking at the treehouse will even show me anything more than what I've already seen. What if I just see the kid get shot all over again? I don't want to see that again," she replied, gazing at the tree, seeing it begin to illuminate which caused her to look down.

"I 'dunno' Karman, I'll just hold you, just take your time," she heard Rayya whisper.

All around her, the landscape was changing, wilting to dull greys and greens. In the back of her mind, she'd been observing everything, absorbing all the data she and Jay's AI continually uploaded, showing her that the Nanites were being bested by her and Rayya's immune systems. Staring down at her feet, she could see Jay had been busily categorizing, and Rayya had been able to work out how the Nanites were communicating with each other to some degree, and that with their minds are all working together, they were on the brink of creating digital vaccines that could be used for future mutations of the Nanites.

Closing her eyes, she mentally tapped her husband and asked, "If I look at the treehouse, will I see your memory?"

"Yup," she heard her husband answer nonchalantly.

"You ass, don't be like that. Do you want me to see?"

"Yes, but not because of the dead kid," she heard her husband say without remorse, causing her stomach to tighten.

"Do you even care how I feel?" she snipped.

"Always, I literally always care how you feel. And you wouldn't even be able to feel if hadn't saved you. Do you even care about how I feel about that?" she heard her husband say, seeing a glimpse of his memory open up in her mind where he was walking slowly through the jungle with his Rifle raised.

"Right, I'm sorry. Forgive me, I'm 'kinda' ungrateful. I'm being selfish, holding you hostage to something you might've done to save me. I'm not being fair, you deserve better than this," she replied, retuning back to herself, opening her eyes, looking directly at the treehouse.

In that instant, the landscape completely illuminated and returned to the way it looked on that day.

"Damn hubby, y'all were 'kinda' far behind me. Not even in sniper range," she whispered, seeing that the AI linked factual reference such as time and distance from the shadows and other references so that she could see both her memory and Jay's together at the same time.

A kiss on the cheek and a small squeeze from Rayya gave her an added boost of encouragement, and with it, she and Jay's memories played out in unison. As she watched, she heard Maydays' calls play out faintly in the background. At first, she thought the calls were like the others, but then she realized that she was hearing it from Jay's ear piece.

"Those creepy Mayday call are the best. It's like what I heard before, the computer material 'thingymajiggy' is for sure in that treehouse...that and sweet vengeance. Yup, yup, we're close," she heard Jay whisper.

"Bro, why'd I let you talk me into this? Especially since the last time you touched one of these things, you came home to find your crew dead," she heard one of her husband's teammate say.

"Bitch, cause you love me," she heard her husband reply.

"Karman, this Mayday call in your husband's memory is very unique. I can see and feel a difference in its vibration. I'll have the AI layer that in here," she heard Rayya whisper as golden, tendrilled webs spread out from the treehouse to places within the forest and far beyond.

"Fuck!" she heard her husband whisper, seeing him raise his Rifle, then bring it down.

"Sup fam?" she heard one of her husband team member say, raising his Rifle before saying, "I don't see shit. Oh wait, one of your weird gut feeling things huh?"

"Yeah… I, fuck fam, this is no bueno," she heard her husband say, seeing tears run down his cheeks as he raised his silenced sniper Rifle and fired.

"Oh, I know whoever that is, is dead," she heard her husband's team member whisper.

"Fam, I just crossed a line I can never uncross, but just now, if I 'ain't' do that, I felt like my heart 'woulda' been gutted," she heard her husband reply.

She could see Jay's teammate shake his head, then touch Jay's cheek with his gloved index finger.

"I 'ain't' never in my life think I'd see you cry fam…team A, when 'dat' bullet hit, open fire," she heard his teammate say, starring at his finger, before bringing it up to his lips, tasting her husbands' tears.

"Word, it hit like a 'lil' bit ago, we started 'da' killing figuring that was the cue," she heard a man say, hearing what her husband had heard through his coms.

"Word," she heard another of Jay's team member say over the coms.

"Word, Jay is 'thorough' as fuck! He popped a 'lil' one and her mom at the same damn time. Then, they fell onto the golf cart and killed the pop! Shit was wild! 'Yo'! Did he use that creepy shit to aim at 'dem?'" she heard another of her husband's team members say over the coms.

"Yeah 'fam,' he used that creepy shit," she heard the team member standing next to her husband respond, clasping him on the shoulder, before saying, "Let's go find out who was worth you popping a 'lil' kid for. If it's a dude, you gay. And 'fam,' if you gay, then shit, let's play."

"Fucking Libras," she heard her husband mumble, shaking his head, raising his Rifle, walking towards the treehouse.

The imagery shifted, and she could see her husband firing his Rifle methodically towards the treehouse, yet seemingly without aiming. Then she saw him standing somewhat behind, but next to her and her sister, followed by an explosion coming from the direction of the treehouse. In slow motion, she watched tendrils of energy begin to engulf the entire area, touching everything - except for an area about two meters around her husband, which in turn protected both herself and her sister from most of the blast energy.

"What the hell? How's that possible?" she heard Rayya whisper as the background changed to one of a beautiful meadow with rolling hills and short grass.

"I have no clue. I've always asked him how he didn't get hurt. Seeing this, I still don't understand," she replied, watching as tiny, red peddled wild flowers spread out from where she and Rayya stood.

"Crazy," she heard Rayya whisper.

"Very," Karman replied, gazing down, seeing that where her and Rayya's blood touched, the greatest concentration of flowers grew.

"Look Rayya, the work we were doing in the background payed off. Now the AI is implementing it. It looks like each plant is an evolutionary prediction of an individual Nanite, and each flower peddle would be the vaccine."

"Karman? Don't do that? Don't hide behind the science shit and shut out everything that just happened," she heard Rayya whisper.

"But I can't deal. Even after seeing it, I just can't deal," Karman whispered, feeling a rage stir up from somewhere deep within her.

"What do you mean you can't deal Karman? Jay cried! Your husband didn't want to do it. He said so himself that he crossed a line. I don't know the back story. What would make him need to do that? He said if he didn't, he felt his heart would've been gutted. Why? And you were aiming at the woman, why? You said they were monster. So you were there to kill them? And your sister was there. Actually the AI is telling me the story. I guess I'll hear it from the computer and not you!"

"Rayya, cut it off. I'll tell you."

"Fine, I muted it...for now."

"Rayya, I was dead to rights. The person he shot, she and her husband laid a trap for me. They knew I'd stop at nothing for revenge, especially after what they did to my family and I. They mutilated my parents and brother, and made my sister and I watch them bleed out as they...took advantage of us. While the took turns on us, they cut into us...I know you saw the scars

497

under my breast. And the ones in my inner thighs. They, they are the fucking reason my sister and I are La Tunda! They made us who we are! Fucking Americans! They came to my country and started just conquering everything and everyone! Getting families to betray each other, getting them to steal each other's land and shit! My parents where in charge of my tiny 'lil' jungle town that just so happened to be sitting on top of a lot of jade and other fucking minerals 'n' shit."

"These two fucks wanted it, and started choking off resources to the town. So my parents had people in the town plant drug crops weed, and all the other shit so we could stay afloat. Then these two fucks were all about the drug money too, and got super insulted that my parents were giving them the slip. So what'd they do? They bribed and manipulated my parent's brothers, sisters and their kids to betray us and the whole damn town. My parents own brothers and sisters served us up like a meal! Let them in our house while we slept! The only reason my sister and I are alive is because the town elders stormed in, then there was this bright light. I don't know the rest of what happened. I woke up in a bed like a week later, both breast infected, pussy all fucked up and infected from abrasions and from, luckily curable STI's. Rayya, bitch! They were it! They were the beginning of my sister and I! We decided no more fucking being nice! Once we healed, Oh! We hit the streets and the jungles hard! And we took and took and took and never stopped taking!

"And the only thing at the time that was still standing in our way was that those two fucks were getting stronger and stronger. This day, this day right here! Well I had info that if I didn't try and kill them right then and there, they'd gain enough power and become out of reach. They had some 'kinda' deals going down that were making them richer by the second. So, I went alone in the jungle to go kill them. Haha, but they knew, they knew I'd come, they had trap after trap ready for me…but like I said, I went alone. I slipped past all of them, right up until I got to the kill shot. Then this bitch picked up her kid! Out of everything, she had that kid in her arms, in my face. I wanted to squeeze the trigger, but I just couldn't! I put my gun down and then boom! I had a Jay moment!"

"You know, that crazy sixth sense 'kinda' feeling? I mean I'd get those feeling from time to time before, and they'd always saved me. But like it was a big one…a big one that could do nothing for me. I could tell I was surrounded. I'd slipped past everything, only to get myself gulped like a 'lil' fish. I 'dunno' how they knew where I was, but they were on to me. Then everyone started dying around me. And now I know, now I know it was really hubby who started it. Him, I knew he did it," she said, feeling mentally and emotionally exhausted, yet still angry at her core.

"Karman, as you spoke, I saw…I somehow saw a lot of those memories of what they did to you. I'm so, I'm so, so, so sorry you went through that!" she heard Rayya gasp, hearing her begin to sob right after.

"Stop crying! stop it!" she growled, pulling away from Rayya's embrace, staring defiantly at the treehouse.

"I waited years for revenge! Years! We became monster to survive among monsters! There was no one we could trust! No such thing as family, or friends! We already knew everything there was to know about that."

"Karman," she heard Rayya say, in a tone she knew was to try and calm her down.

"What!?" she snipped, looking at Rayya's face, seeing a deep pain that somehow hit her heart.

"You've got your truth and now you're…" she heard Rayya begin before she cut in and said, "I got the truth and I'm still angry!"

"Angry?" she heard Rayya ask, sounding confused.

"Yes, angry! Angry because nothing is clean! Once you get your hands dirty, you can't go back. Angry they pushed my parents into that 'kinda' life. Angry they pushed us to feel like it was the only way! Angry because every time my sister and I even showed a tiny drop of remorse or kindness, we almost lost our lives and the rest of our dignity for it! It's awful trying to rebuild your dignity after it's been stripped away! I'm angry because becoming monsters…seemed like and still seems like the best decision we've ever made! That them brutalizing us, was the best that thing that could have happened to us!"

"And I'm angry I could not pull that fucking trigger! They were mine to kill! Mine! I'm angry because Jay had to clean up my mess! He had to take care of my responsibility which was to wipe those people off the face of this earth! Was I not monstrous enough to pull the fucking trigger after what they've done!? And then, I find myself wondering, if what they did to me, well, was it really that bad? Honestly, I've played out my life to its conclusion. If they hadn't come and fucked us up, in four years' time, I'd have been a mine rat! Yeah, a fucking mine rat, 'cuz' my tiny 'lil' town got swallowed by a huge, part American, part Chinese company that enslaves all the people to work in the fucking mines.

"This all happened while my sister and I were in the main cities gaining power! This happened to my town, and all the other 'lil' ones around it! These fucks gave me and my sister life through fire! I'm wondering if at the time I felt like I owed her for making me become one bad ass bitch. It has to be that! Or I was too weak to pull the trigger?" she said, feeling waves of emotion flow through her.

"Karman!" she heard Rayya say, this time in a voice that demanded respect.

"Bella?" she replied, turning and fully looking at Rayya, who'd stopped crying.

"Pull the trigger now. Take your kill shot and wash your soul clean with blood," she heard Rayya say, seeing the same Rifle she'd had with her that day appear in Rayya's hand.

"Why? This isn't real," she replied, taking the Rifle from Rayya's hands, feeling an odd calmness overtake her, then another wave of rage.

"This isn't real Rayya! My husband already took revenge from me! Because I was too weak! And I was too dumb and got myself trapped!" she snarled, turning towards the treehouse, raising the Rifle, looking through the scope.

Around her, the settings changed and she was now in the exact position she'd been when everything had been real.

"Fuck," she whispered, seeing the exact image of her target picking up the child just as it had been before.

"I think you didn't want to pull the trigger because, you felt that once you killed them, there'd be no more reason left for you to be a monster, that you'd lose your strength because there would be nothing left to hate. I think you were also thinking, if you were to kill them and be free, well that you wouldn't be able to feel that way, having killed that child directly on your hands.

"Huh? Maybe?" she whispered feeling Rayya's words resonating.

"It was your wording, 'Poom, I have taken this life by a direct choice.' You hate killing in general. You disassociate from the death you and your sister bring by rationalizing it as, you're a tiny cog in a wheel of weapons, drugs, and death that would keep on turning even if you two weren't around. But in actuality, even if that's true, you have the sweetest heart."

"Do you know how many people I've killed directly for you to say that I have the sweetest heart?" she whispered, because it was true, and to give herself a boost of strength to pull the trigger.

"Good then, you have no reason to hesitate, pull the trigger. Plus, like you said, it's not really them. You have nothing to lose, and everything to gain if this clears your conscious," she heard Rayya say.

"Wash my soul clean with blood?" she whispered.

"Yeah," she heard Rayya reply, feeling Rayya's hand touch her bare back.

Karman took a deep breath, and truly focused while she continued to look through the scope. Her target had been on pause as she and Rayya had spoken, but was now moving the way she'd saw just before she had taken her finger off the trigger in real life all those years before.

"Okay, I like the way that sounds," she whispered, pulling the trigger of her silenced assault Rifle, keeping her eyes open to see the bullet connect.

Yet, the bullet connecting is not what happened. Instead, a bright blue-white light flashed and illuminated her and everting thing behind her in a wide swath.

"What the fuck?" she whispered, almost in unison with Rayya.

"AI is receiving further information from the unknown data source. AI can see that the computer module your husband was searching for was a combat module. When your bullet was fired, an energy perimeter that detects weaponized kinetic energy, as well as concentrated energy sent instructions to multiple energy weapons inlayed within the treehouse to fire on your location, as well as all the area around you for safe measure. Had you fired on that day, you would've instantly been disintegrated," she heard her AI say nonchalantly.

"What the fuck! Just no! Then how'd my husband's bullet hit?" she blared.

"Your husband was recognized by the devices' 'friend or foe' detection system, and deemed him as a 'friend.' It allowed his bullet to pass. When his bullet killed all three principle operators of the device, his comrades were then safe to fire their weapons. Had they fired first, they would've been disintegrated. Once the principle operators perished, a self-destruct sequence activated. However, as the device still recognized your husband as a 'friend,' it manipulated its energy away from him, and consequently away from yourself and your sister. To make a pointed note, as AI knows you've been studying and trying to replicate this self-destruct event multiple times – AI now understands that the event was not an explosion, but a controlled energy spread."

"So, her being out there was a trap too? Then how 'bout' the kid, did she pick up the kid to taunt me, to see if I'd stoop low and pull the trigger and get turned to ash? Would this bitch use her kid as a taunting shield? Or was she feeling pity, not wanting to have a passive aggressive death, knowing I'd for sure not pull the trigger? Maybe she thought it'd be best I die by the more conventional means."

"AI, you said all three principle operators? So the child was considered one?" she heard Rayya inquire.

"Yes," she heard the AI respond to Rayya's questions.

"Yeah, I picked up on that too. Maybe they were grooming that kid to become a monster after all. In any case, my hubby literally saved me through and through," she whispered, feeling raw and drained, yet lighter.

"Holy shit, I'd been bottling all that up to the max," she whispered, watching the treehouse disintegrate, leaving a jungle that was quickly becoming only the plant life that represented the Nanites and vaccines.

"I'm happy you were able to face that," she heard Rayya whisper.

"Thank you, thank you for being there for me. For getting me through that," she replied, finally beginning to feel weight lifting off of her conscious.

"No problem Habibi," she heard Rayya reply, feeling her come from behind, hugging her, and kissing her on the cheek.

"Rayya, your wall…is getting bigger," she whispered, having not realized it till now.

I see why you two made this place, it's not just to work in secret, it's to free yourself from body limitations. Like if you're tired or sick, it won't matter in here. In here, you can work with just your mental strength," she heard Rayya deflect.

"Yes, that's exactly it," Karman replied, before whispering, "girl, you've 'gotta' clear that wall."

"I, I don't know how to," she heard Rayya reply, seeing the wall grow even larger with Rayya's confession.

"You just helped me, let me help you," she replied, breaking free of Rayya's embrace, going behind Rayya, hugging her the same way.

"You don't understand Karman, I physically and mentally can't," she heard Rayya reply, trying to break free of her grasp.

"No, keep still. That wall is getting out of control. It's my turn to be there for you," she whispered.

"No! She will get me! She will get me!" she heard Rayya gasp and scream, sounding panicked.

"Who will get you!?" she asked, releasing Rayya, who was covering her face and eyes, and immediately dropping to the ground in a squat, keeping herself in a tight ball.

"Rayya!? Who will get you!?" she asked.

"No! leave my problems alone. You just dealt with yours, focus on that!" she heard Rayya say, sounding muddled from her face being tucked between her legs.

"Really! How can I feel at peace, seeing you like this Bella?"

"I don't know…I don't know," she heard Rayya whisper, looking up with tear filled eyes.

"Hey, there we go, hi sweetie," Karman whispered.

"Why, why don't I feel the pain?" she heard Rayya mumble.

"What? What pain? This places blocks...wait, it hasn't been doing a good job of blocking anything. I feel fucking everything, so back to the first question. What pain Mami?" she asked, almost being head butt by Rayya as she shot up from her squat, looking left, then right, then at the wall.

"The pain my mother brings if you dare even think of her for too long," she heard Rayya reply, turning her head sideways like a curious animal.

"Chica, you've always been weird, but you're adding to it," she whispered, seeing black and gold vine like patterns begin to appear all over the wall, rung down to the ground.

Once touching the ground, Karman watched the two types of vine like substances rush towards her and Rayya's position, with many of the same type merging together, forming thicker strands, while others integrated, forming black and gold helix shapes.

"Earlier, I told you that my wall is made up of too much truth. And then that makes you wonder why I wouldn't be free, since supposedly the truth is what sets you free right?" she heard Rayya whisper, watching the thousands of gold and black vines rush towards her and Rayya even faster.

"Rayya, AI, what the fuck is this?" she gasped, feeling butterflies in her stomach, seeing and feeling the vibration of the vines now running under her feet.

"Umm, the best way to describe it, it's energy, thought energy and vibration. This is energy behind mental connection," she heard Rayya say, watching a golden and black energies begin to swirl beneath Rayya's feet.

"Have you ever wondered why I chose to study quantum entanglement? It's because I was born understanding it. From the time I can remember, I saw the deeper connections in everything. In the same way you've always understood the materials you work with. Or just like Jay, who always understood electronics and magnetics. What you see below our feet, these forms of energy. This is what my mother uses. This is her domain. This is how she manipulates everything around her. And for my whole life, up until now, this is how she's kept me in check. But somehow, in here, I don't feel her fully connected. Don't get me wrong, she's still strong, but it's something I can

504

take," she heard Rayya say, seeing and feeling a pulse come from the center of her forehead, running down the length of her body into the swirling center of black and gold energies beneath her feet.

Almost within that same moment, Karman watched the pulse travel out from the center through the tendrils of energy, slamming into the wall which instantly began to crack.

"Finally," she heard Rayya whisper, sounding relieved.

Then she saw a pulse resonate from the wall, and felt hate beyond her wildest dreams aimed directly at Rayya. Without thinking, she ran behind Rayya, hugged her, and whispered, "Never will I let you hurt her."

Searing pain slammed into her body, but instead of giving in, she allowed her mind to swallow it whole, which was a trick she'd learned during countless hours of torture by both the couple that'd began her career as a Cartel Leader, and from a few sticky situations she'd gotten herself into on her climb to the top.

"Shit! I should stop! She's found me! I should give up! I thought she wasn't here!" she heard Rayya gasp.

"No! Fuck that! I'm here! Fight her!" she said through gritted teeth as the pain intensified.

"You see Karman; do you see what the wall is really made of! This is my mother, my mother who hates me, my mother who thinks of me only as a tool. I've watched her my whole life sit in front of one T.V after another, sending her commands through the frequencies!"

"She trapped my father into loving her, created me with him. It's not out of love I was born, she made me so that she can have a replacement! She didn't know that I knew, she thought she was being careful hiding it from me, but over the years, I could hear, see and sense her intentions through the energy webs!"

"You see, I was born with the same gift as my mother and have the inherent ability to interact with these forms of energy. From the moment I picked up mal-intent from her, every day I painstakingly try to learn how interact with the energies so that I could evade her detection."

"Karman, I was there on these webs when she sent the order to ensnare my father into his life debt. It was her way of punishing him for loving me too much! She saw him as a threat! He was messing up the influence she had on her replacement tool. She wanted him gone, trapped in a lab somewhere so she could lock me up in the house and brainwash me!"

"Then, on the day my father was killed, he passed his life debt to me! After learning what a life debt was, I had thought he was just as evil as my mother for giving me such a burden. But later on, I think I understood why he did what he did. I think that somehow he must've known mother's intentions. You see, I didn't know this at the time, but on the day my father was killed, it was the day she'd fully given up on wanting to use me as a replacement tool and had decided she wanted me dead."

"At the time, I had zero clue. The Israeli invasion scared the shit out of me and she was being extremely careful to mask her intent on the energy threads. The awful part was that after I almost died with my father, she did something extremely odd, which was to show her emotions. She actually did what a normal, hateful person does when they wished you dead. In this case, it was throwing my father's artifact, which represented the life debt he passed to me in my face the moment I woke up in the Lilith healing facility."

"I was mentally whiplashed at her mindset change and wanted to know what the hell was going on. It took me almost a year of honing my energy interaction skills before I could get close enough learn why."

"On the day she decided she wanted me dead, it was also the day I lost my virginity. With the invasion going on and Ilias being Ilias, wanting to go run out there and fight, and those bombs dropping wherever the hell they dropped without discrimination, we didn't want to die virgins. It was also the same day, my father said he'd tell me his pride and joy of secrets. And all morning, he was like doing this really sweet, over the top presentation before he did his big reveal. My mother, she just snapped."

"She must've saw then, that I would choose to love and be loved, and would never be the kind of person she was, and be her replacement. If I were to follow her path, I'd lead the life of a zealot who hate all who were not Muslim. Hates all who do not follow the purest of Muslim tradition. One who views myself as a lowly woman, below all men. And the list of pure oppression goes on and on. My mother, on that day must've realized that I had a spirit that she could not contain. So then, yeah. Fucking ironic isn't it? My father took my freedom in life to spare my life. He knew my mom would be forced to honor the life debt to Lilith no matter how much she hated it."

"My God," she whispered, feeling Rayya's emotions course through her, soothing her body from the pain her mother was continually inflicting.

"Right!? Who'd want a life of oppression right!? I wanted her to love me, not trap me. I wanted her to be proud of me, not look down on me. I knew she was incapable of love, but how could I actually accept that!?" she heard Rayya scream.

"Good, let it all out," she whispered.

"This pain, this truth! Her not loving me, not even a drop! Me not wanting to really know, to accept it! How can I accept my life like this! This is what this wall is made up of! How could I accept that I was made to be a tool!? How do I accept always being hated, and other people, not just my mother, always wanting to discard and belittle me like trash!? Who'd want to accept this as their reality?" she heard Rayya scream, feeling an enormous pulse rush through her body just as the hateful energy from Rayya's mother clawed deep in her mind, trying to make her re-live her memory of the child being shot, and trying to make her hate her husband for striping her from taking revenge.

"No bitch! I'm over it, he's my partner. We're one in the same. That's what real love is. And guess what, I love your daughter, and she loves me. There's no space for you here," she said, squeezing Rayya tighter, hearing her gasp, followed by her body trembling as she began to sob.

"Love me? You, you really love me? Karman, I love you too. I love you and Jay just as much as I love my own husband," she heard Rayya whisper, feeling a pulse stronger than all the rest resonate from Rayya's body, sweeping aside the pain and negative energy Rayya's mother had been using to attack them with.

In front of her, she watched the wall crumble, break off in huge chucks.

"Rayya, my Habibi, accept the duality of humanity, embrace the blessing and the curse of life. Embrace the fact that there needs to be evil to maintain good, and good to maintain evil. Embrace these facts the same way you embrace that light is a particle and a wave at the same time, and that light is energy but can be of many different wavelengths. Make sure you see the world this way before you call it cruel, or feel unloved. Live as an observer, creator and destroyer. And live deeply within each space," Karman heard a man say, with a choking death rattle, at first in Arabic, quickly and seamlessly changing to Spanish, allowing her to understand.

"Allah, thank you for the gift of his voice again," she heard Rayya whisper, feel Rayya's body rack as she began to sob heavily.

"You father?" she asked, rhetorically, having known the nurturing sound of a father's voice.

"Yes, this is the last thing he said to me. But I couldn't remember because I had blacked out from blood loss right after," she heard Rayya whisper in a shaky voice.

In front of them, the wall was now breaking off in huge section, and as it did so, the image of a women she couldn't recognize in an Israeli military uniform appeared in the dust.

"Rayya, bella, who's that?" she asked, hearing Rayya gasp and go ridged.

"Bella? Mami?" she asked again, feeling all of Rayya's sadness vanish into cold resolution.

"I see you...I finally see your face after all this time. And I finally see why my mother was able to hide her intentions so well that day. You were the final answer, and it was just so simple. You were evil and selfish enough, all on your own that all she had to do was mentally tap your shoulder so you'd be curious about our house. Then all she would had to do is sit back and let you do the rest. Just neither of you were counting on my father passing on his life debt to me," she heard Rayya say to the image of the woman, who showed no signs of hearing her, seeming to Karman more like the image of a memory.

After Rayya spoke, the image of the woman vanished with the billowing dust of the disintegrating wall, which now had an enormous hole through it in front of where they stood. Looking through the hole, Karman saw an ocean with a tiny wooden ship anchored right off the shore. After seeing this, she saw a blur and felt a belly rush. Almost in that same moment, she then found that she and Rayya were now standing on the very deck of that ship, with her husband's nude form holding a dark, black wooden wheel, with numerous broken spokes.

"Hey, you two, welcome back, are both of you feeling better?" she heard her husband say, turning to look at her, then to Rayya with a head nod.

"I…don't…know. Wait, well… actually, yes. I do feel much better. Hubby, it wasn't right for me to question your heart, or your character. Do you forgive me papi," she replied, wanting to take full onus of the way she'd treated him.

"Forgive you? Silly ass Eggy, I didn't blame you. I 'shoulda' just explained that I did the weird thingy, and killed the kid. As for the explosion situation, I really didn't know why I didn't get hurt till just now when both of you learned why as well. When it happened, my first thought was, 'fuck, I'm dead.' Right after that, I felt like I'd be okay, and the blast energy didn't touch me. Since I know that those artifacts are way more advanced than the things we could come up with, I just 'kinda' smiled at the fact that I was alive and let it be. Seeing that the very first artifact I had messed with communicated to this one, and called me a 'friend' is weird to me, and is the only good that ever came from it," Karman heard her husband say, coming to her, giving her a tight hug and kiss on the lips.

"I see. I just feel guilty. I gave you way too much grief, and I feel you're forgiving me too easily."

"Love is about growing. We're not perfect. You had every right to feel the way you felt about me," she heard her husband respond, stepping back, giving her a warm smile, before walking over to Rayya, giving her a hug and kiss on the lips, that made her heart leap for joy.

"That was some deep shit going down with 'ya' mom. This stinging feeling, randomly hitting our bodies, 'ya' mom is literally smashing into here any chance she gets. You're so strong to have lived with her, to have escaped her. Don't feel any shame around us about your wall, your insecurities, about nothing. We're both here for you, just like you were here for us," she heard her husband say to Rayya, melting her heart, causing her to come hug them both.

"Thank you," she heard Rayya whisper, breathing a deep sigh of relief.

"Mayday, Mayday, Mayday," she then heard, followed by a sharp shooting pain in her chest.

"Your mom is really a bitch, she won't even give up," she whispered, steeping back, rubbing her chest as she looked herself and the other two over, seeing that both herself and Rayya were still heavily menstruating, with bright red blood flowing freely down their legs onto the deck of the ship, with some spots already turning into dark green plants with red petals.

"Crazy, this place is crazy. It's using so much of our mental energy to form this, everything is so real, but not," she whispered, watching her husband let go of Rayya, looking down at the growing plants on the deck, with his face changing to dark and serious.

"What's up hubby? Why the look. You think these vaccines are not enough to outpace the Nanites? You think we're still not 'gonna' make it?" she asked.

"I have no idea. But at this point, like I…you know how we said if we die, we just die and leave things undone, 'cuz' we're dead and who cares. Well I changed my mind, I want to send the recruitment message to those people. We picked them for a reason, I think it'd be dumb not to."

"Recruitment message?" she heard Rayya ask, seeing her rub her lower belly, then her chest, shaking her head with a 'these situations are fucked' smile.

"Yeah, recruitment messages. Rayya, I have a favor to ask you. With your help, you'll see them," she heard her husband say.

"Of course, of course I'll help you," she heard Rayya respond without hesitation.

"Thank you! Thank you so much! Okay, look, while working on the vaccines, I saw we all had strengths and weaknesses. Rayya, I saw how you made the larger connections, tapping into those energy webs, helping send the information to the Lilith base. So that being said, I, or I should say we, need your help to send the recruitment message on both that darker energy river, and the golden threads. What do you think? Oh and I've already begun mapping out some of the places in the energy currents we'd want the message sent to," Karman heard her husband say as images of both the gold and black energy currents appeared with different annotations.

"Wow, this is a lot of planning. Jay, this level of detail, how'd you know the energies are made purely of thought? I know you're brilliant, but like what gave it away. Just inherently knew, or was there a tell?" she heard Rayya whisper.

"Both, a gut feeling and some tells. Like this one," she heard her husband say, raising his hand showing miniature images of both Rayya and herself.

"I was watching both your vitals and body functions with something like this, and to my surprise, it showed me both of your Chakra's functions. When we began creating the vaccines, this is what happened," she heard her husband say, seeing a violet then golden light rise up from both she and Rayya's head, while dark black energy erupted from their feet.

"Anyone who knows even basics of chakra, knows of the crown chakra. Both of you are so gifted, so tapped into nature and in tuned with what you're doing that y'all were literally manifesting and understanding everything, it was the only way it was even remotely possible we've outpaced the Nanites evolution. You, my material scientist wifey, and you, my quantum entanglement expert, who know how things communicate, playing intercept, getting the jump on them as they spoke, and tried to adapt as well as tying us into this network of energies in the first place, you both are simply amazing," she heard her husband say, smiling at them, with his eyes flicking to the black energy.

"And black?" she asked.

"Black would not be the Chakra, black would be survival thoughts and…'kinda' like human and other sentient beings' beginning of life coding. Like when a human baby is born, they have pre-coded DNA. As they grow, their DNA tells them what to think in regards to survival, and based on their personality, they act on it. Like wanting water, but, there is not enough of it. When the said child grows, does the child kill the opponents, share or dig a bigger well, etcetera, that is the black energy. Well this is my interpretation of it… actually ask Rayya," she heard her husband say, tipping his head at Rayya who she could see was looking at him in amazement.

"Rayya?" she asked after a few more seconds passed, laughing when Rayya moved her mouth to talk, only to smile and shake her head.

"Karman, I'm not amazed he knows this. You can go online and see references to all of this. I'm amazed that I can sense him here now. I can tell he's never touched these energies directly till today and now...he's blundering around, making a lot of noise, running into my mother way more than anyone should be. What the fuck Jay, how can you learn so fast?" she heard Rayya whisper.

"Because I'm desperate to send my messages. I had my own crown chakra awakening. So, let's do this! And thank you again! Beside my Eggy in my life, me completing this means the world to me," she heard her husband say, somehow breaking her heart.

"Baby what? You always made it sound like this was just like a job. An important job, but still just a job your organization was making you do to prove yourself. But just now, I felt your loneliness," she whispered.

"I told you, without my crew, I would've lived a life worse than death. Then, then, they were just gone, stolen from me, like everything else. I owe it to myself to rebuild after being adopted by another Captain, another crew. They sacrificed for me, and suffered. All because I have some 'kinda' curse, a curse they were willing to accept. I have the means and strengths to make it right because of your support," she heard her husband say, summoning she and Rayya to come behind him.

"Thank you ladies," she heard her husband say, as she and Rayya placed their hands on each of his shoulders.

"To the many that are lost at sea, to the many that are lost in the jungle, hear my call. My name is Captain Jay Sao...," she heard Jay say, with his voice resonating in her soul.

As her husband spoke, she saw clouds beginning to form and spin, and within seconds they were in the dead center eye of a hurricane.

In her mind, she heard him say, "it's time we made a proper crew."

With his words, she felt their souls anchor together, and as they did, she felt a new portion of herself come alive, while the other began to die.

-Within the Lilith Corp base-

Karman felt different from the moment she woke up. Her body had just won a huge war in which each battle had to be won or else it would've been her last. The fear and inner turmoil she'd held onto during her life were disappearing so fast she couldn't even remember what it'd been that'd been bogging her down.

"I'm so hungry!" was now a permeating thought, but when she thought of any foods she liked, her stomach turned.

Inner peace swallowed her whole, and made her want to fall back to sleep, she felt like she was in no danger whatsoever when she was told to get out of the SUV.

"I have them with me," Karman thought, hopping out, feeling a flash of annoyance just for a moment that felt way too intense before she calmed herself.

"My hip doesn't hurt, my big ass boobs aren't hurting my back, my stomach doesn't hurt, I'm hungry, all three of them smell so good! I want to bite the fuck out of them. Hurry up and heal hubby, hurry up and heal Nate! I smell your breaths, both of you are healing by the passing second! Just too slowly!" she thought, feeling a flash of confusion.

"Not normal thoughts!" she thought right after, snapping out of her lazy hazy feeling, delving into everything she was sensing.

"I feel like I'm trapped within my own skin," Karman thought, when the battle erupted all around her.

As women began to fire all around her, all she knew was that her husband needed exactly thirty more seconds before he'd change into …whatever she and Rayya had changed into. Without hesitation, she ran directly in front of her husband, allowing everything that was meant to strike him, slam into her.

"Freedom!" she thought, feeling her husband catch her in his arms as she fell.

"I love you," she heard her husband whisper.

"I love you more," she forced out as everything went black.

Jay could tell he was holding on by a thread. When the Nanites invaded his body, his mind had done something he'd only seen once before, which was to plunge him into a type of control center where he could see all his body functions.

When the Nanites tried to shut down his respiratory functions, he overrode them and forced his every breath. When he saw them change his endocrine system, he commanded a plethora of reactions to counter it. When his body received information from the women on how to combat the vectors, he micro managed every portion of the fight, locking different Nano vectors in different parts of his body so that each antigen could work directly on the problem area. It was still way too much for him to handle, and Jay truly understood that no matter what, his end was near.

<**Jay to da A:** Eh, AI, when I die, make sure the rest of the recruitment messages are sent the ways we've set it up.> Jay commanded, mentally examining the digital package he and his wife hand painstakingly created.

A burst of white light flashed before him.

"Holy 'IT'! Just like in the jungle!" Jay thought, seeing a message in his View-Tech's before feeling and seeing it appear in his mind's eye.

"In your time of mortal crisis, do you wish to continue to learn?"

"Yes," he responded without thought or hesitation.

"Probation passed. You're now instated with the full duties and responsibilities of a Tier One Tet operative."

"Probation passed? What the fuck is a Tier One Tet operative? I never applied! I'd joined Nammu to get closer to Tet's inner circle and ended up inside an information stagnant fish bowl. So that's what that alert message about the space elevators was about! That was their way of showing me a deeper glimpse of them, their way of testing my reaction," he thought as he replied, ***"What are my duties and responsibilities? Is Tier One low or high in rank? And hey, I have an inner promise I must fulfill, will your duties clash with my own?"***

"If you were told you could not peruse your goal any longer, what would be your response?"

"Kiss my 'Blasian' ass," he replied.
"If you were told it would clash?"
"I'd find ways to do both."
*"Then your title stands. May all that you illuminate
bring encompassing darkness. And may all that you cover in
darkness bring encompassing light."*

After reading this message in his mind's eye, Jay then saw
oily black droplets smack into the windshield. Inside each
droplet, he could see lines of golden threaded connections going
off in every direction. As he tried to follow them, another bright
white burst flooded his vision, and where he'd saw golden
threads, he now saw thick black rivers of pulsating energy, all
coming from a center point.

*"So, this is how there are still signals, yet none at the same time. This
energy or whatever it is, eats everything, but will also spit it out. Ah, I see,
but whoever sends a signal through it can't rely on it being secure. That's
probably why the Admirals still haven't initiated contact. It's all good
though, I don't have much I want to say or hear from them anyway. Hey,
hold up, I'm starting to understand this. I can see Rayya in here, connecting
things! Maybe I can use this to send the first wave of recruitment message,
while I'm still alive,"* he thought, studying the two different
information highways, understanding how and why the signals
were being carried with greater clarity with every passing second.

By time Jay figured out how to send a not so easily
retractable message, he saw that his wife had finished her mental
journey.

"And now she knows how it happened," he thought, feeling relief
and deep shame, knowing that although she understood how it
had happened, it did not change the fact that he'd made the
conscious choice to kill a child.

Hearing his wife say she understood and hearing her
apologize for questioning him made him feel even more guilty,
but the moment of shame passed just as quickly. His liver was
failing and no matter what he did, he could not clear the toxins
fast enough. It was in that vulnerable moment, he opened his
mouth and blurted something that in truth he'd never wanted to
confess. Jay was always keen to face his demons, and he was all
too aware that he had abandonment issues. But to Jay, this was
not the demon you could just face, it was the demon you had to

make love to, to cuddle with and get used to, because any show of force and loneliness, that demon would thrive on it. Now, with both his wife and Rayya behind him, and the presences of Nate's mental energy as his ship, Jay felt complete.

Mentally touching the invite messages, he and his wife had created, Jay gripped the wheel of the ship and said, "To the many that are lost and adrift at sea, and to the many that are lost and alone in the jungle, hear my call. My name is Captain Jay Sao of the lost Long Island crew. Many years ago, when I returned home to find my crew slaughtered, I felt swallowed by a loneliness that was incomprehensible."

"Born to a mother and father who'd been killed shortly after I'd been born, I had no one until my crew took me in as one of their own. I'd never understood the true essence of companionship until them, and just like that, another family had been taken away from me. I don't believe in a Sky Daddy, but I do believe there are higher powers at work that both try to protect and try to destroy us. I say this because without this horrible experience, I would not be hailing you as I am now. I want you to become my crew."

"Correction, I want you to become my fleet. And to do so, you must be willing to sail, and walk into the uncharted, use your expertise, and most importantly, rely on one another to help you overcome your shortcomings. It will not be easy, and many times you will fail. But the reward will be far greater than allowing yourself to be as you are at present. I speak under the assumption that every single one of you will accept this invite regardless of not knowing or understanding who I am, or what I'm asking of you. Within this invite, I give you privy to my wife and I's encompassing plans, which we named, 'The All'. Wishing you fair winds and following seas."

Satisfied with his opening message, Jay sealed the digital message and mentally passed them to his wife, who shaped them to slip into the dark energy river and then into the tiny, golden energy webs. With a mental head nod from Rayya to both he and his wife, he watched Rayya take hold of both forms of energy. Then, with a great expense of Rayya's own energy, send the messages through the streams.

"Done!" Jay thought, feeling closure for the first time in his life.

With that closure, Jay felt his body healing just a little bit faster, and when he mentally inquired further, he could see that both he and Nate were not doing as bad as they were before. Withdrawing himself from the Mind Lab, he could see that Nate had been resuscitated and that this time he was not slipping right back into death.

"Thank 'It!'" Jay thought, squinting at the distorted circular lines looping from Nate's body.

"The AI is telling me that my brain is seeing magnetic signatures. And that the Nanites and that crazy Mayday signal traveling through those two energy channels are triggering my already sensitive brain to see them even clearer. This is some freaky ass shit!" Jay thought, seeing the lines in Nate settle and grow stronger, followed by his AI showing him that Nate's body signature had not just changed, but went back to 'relatively normal' for a human male, where as before, there had been something impeding him, both from a chemical reaction in his blood and from a mental barrier Nate must've been holding onto.

Asking what the AI meant by relatively normal for a human male, the AI showed that Nate's blood stream had been filled with estrogen, and that the Nanites had dissolved all of it. With that, Nate's energy showed up as a male, and not something in between. Feeling that he very well might survive the Nanites, Jay's priority became solely to get the hell out of the Lilith base as soon as possible.

~ A few minutes after entering through the 'Cervix' ~

After the Mayday call that had played during their drive through the 'Cervix,' Jay felt his consciousness fully return to his body from the Mind Lab. Upon his return, his AI showed him that copious amounts of unsolicited data from the Lilith base, as well as from unknown locations were pouring into his Mind Lab, directly begging for he and his AI attention. It was like the data was alive, and more nerve racking still, behaving in a respectful manner. He saw that whenever his Mind Lab, along with his own brain, felt like it'd be too much information, whatever was pouring through would stop, giving both he and his AI time to adjust before flowing in again.

"*What do I do? A lot of this data looks the same!*" he thought, feeling the gloved hand of a woman that his AI identified as Estris, around the back of his neck.

"*Mayday call after Mayday call. And what the hell is this?*" Jay thought, now seeing the images of two people making love inside of an orb of fluid.

From the image, he saw that the two people were the source of the Maydays' signals, and both forms of black and gold energy.

"*What the fuck!*" he thought, as he felt the presences of the two people turn towards him.

"We are Darren and Serena. Hello Jay," he heard them say in unison, now finding his inner consciousness in a place of darkness that he could somehow still see within.

"Take the others here before it's too late," he heard them say, followed by a presence that was both malicious and loving.

"Help me cleanse the impurity! Help me cleanse the impurity! The filth! It's God's will!" he heard a male voice say in his mind.

"Na fam, I don't cuck for Sky Daddies' wills. I do my own thing," he replied.

"So be it," he heard in his mind, sensing the man who'd spoken heart actually break in sorrow, followed by the intent to wipe him from existence.

By the time Jay snapped out of it, a full-blown battle was happening right before his eyes.

"Baby?" he whispered, watching his wife run towards a weapon.

"Take them there now!" he heard in his mind from the couple within the orb, while simultaneously feeling he and his wife's energy tethered together.

"*This feels real, she's here with me. This is like a trillion time stronger than what it felt like in the Mind Lab,*" he thought, watching in horror as his wife was cut down by weapons of fire.

"*No! No! No! Not ready for this! Not ready for this!*" Jay thought running to his wife, catching her as she fell.

"I love you," he whispered, staring at his wife's eyes, whose light was quickly fading.

"I love you more," he heard his wife whisper, now feeling her hand on his shoulder, in the dark place where they were tethered.

"This is the horrible feeling I've had all morning. Just fucking doomed!" he thought, enraged, seeing, feeling and smelling his wife's blood and burned flesh.

"Lay me down, let me go baby," he heard his wife say in his mind, sounding just as upset as he felt.

"No, I want to hold you! Hold you for as long as possible. I want to…" he whispered out loud, stopping when pain shot up through his feet, into his body.

"What is this stuff?" Jay thought, seeing vicious fluid spraying out from the orb, oozing all along the floor.

"Jay, nothing happening here is of any of your concern anymore," he heard Darren and Serena say in his mind in unison, followed by a pulse of light.

The real world fell away, leaving him standing in the place of darkness, with his wife whose face bespoke of shock, sadness and an odd sense of liberation.

"Take your wife, and the other two here, in this realm before it's too late. We will stay, we are stronger, we can maintain," he heard the couple say as a beautiful landscape of greens and blues opened up beneath he and his wife's feet.

"Why should I just rush in!? I have no idea what's going on to act so reckless," he thought, looking into the realm, getting a data burst upload, explaining time, date, and scenario, which lead him to look further out into the distance.

"Shit! This, this is the real deal! No wonder everyone's so confused about humanity! Who the fuck would believe this!?" Jay thought, feeling utterly shocked to the core.

In his peripherals, he saw Nate and Rayya arrive, and looked up to visually greet them.

"Will I continue to learn, Tet Corp. asked? And now I'm being told to jump into this place. And it's not like I have a choice," Jay thought, feeling his flesh and blood body stop functioning.

"And, that's that," Jay thought, almost feeling sorry for himself before he thought, *"fuck it, this is still life if I'm here right now!"*

As he spoke to Nate and Rayya, preparing them for what they were going to see, he thought, *"will I continue to learn they asked, to then to see a place full of answers that'd force me to ask a billion more questions. It was like they knew I'd end up here, which raises even more questions. I really want to know how I was accepted into Tet's inner circle. I must've passed some sort of evaluation. It'd make sense, 'The All' message wifey and I created is one big evaluation to weed out the weak and those who'll not bond together. By the time someone's finished and heard my full offer and plan, they'd simply accept because they wouldn't have gone through all the trouble in the first place."*

Observing and hearing Nate's reaction after he'd seen the silhouettes within the realm, Jay smiled and thought, *"I can't believe it either, and I believed in a lot of crazy shit about humanities' history."*

Not wanting to hesitate any longer, Jay then mentally shoved all four of them through the threshold.

Landing onto the soft grass, Jay thought, *"I wish the Admirals would've found a way to speak to me. It would've been nice to have a pat on the back for …for finally trying to rebuild my house after all this time being Captain without a crew."*

Taking in his surroundings, he smiled at everyone's shell-shocked expressions, then mentally began to force thoughts of his old life away. And that's when he heard, "Fair winds and following seas," from both men and women in solemn yet prideful voice.

Above them, the threshold they'd entered closed and with it, he, along with his wife, Nate and Rayya were now fully present to the full sights, scents and sounds of the realm.

"I thought I'd know my limit for what I'd consider overwhelming, but this situation is not easy to wrap my mind around," Jay thought, now hearing Mayday calls from every direction, tracing many of them visually, seeing kilometer's long blood stains stretching from the forest to the ocean.

"I said I wanted to keep learning…And now, here the fuck I am," he whispered to himself, finding himself completely inundated by the thick, repugnant smell of blood, death, and heated ozone.

Epilogue

Remember the Tower of Babel!

Date: Sunday, April 15th 2017

Time: 7:45 am

Location: Tel Aviv

"What the fuck was I thinking!?" Lailie thought after hitting rescind, looking at her device like it'd betrayed her for allowing her to transmit the message in the first place.

"I think I would've puked if Nate wrote me back, saying he loved me," Lailie thought, swallowing down bile from the imagery of her son showing affection to her after all the hell she had and continued to put him through.

"Madam Lilith, a woman keeps calling on our main channel, she says it's an emergency," she heard her new number One say, sounding annoyed.

"I'd completely tuned out the vibrations of the calls," she thought, panning the screen on her wrist device, seeing the name Saraswati and 'missed call', with a ridiculous number denoting the attempts.

Tapping 'call,' it connected instantly, and in her earbuds she heard, "Lailie! Since when do you not answer on this line right away? That's not like you at all!"

"What? What do you want? Why have you been calling me so much? We're not friends, I don't even slightly trust you as a business partner, and last but not least, I simply just can't stand you," she replied, moving Saraswati's image from her wrist device to her View-Contacts.

"Did you look at the thing I sent you? It's important. It may hold information about our predecessors," she heard Saraswati say.

"Saraswati, I'm hanging up."

"This is important! It truly may hold revelations about our bloodlines!"

"What's your obsession about our bloodlines? It's not confirmed, but I know it's your teams hacking into my systems, digging into my archives! And I know it's your teams doing those fast excavations, stealing things from our artifact sites. I give props to them though, they do a really good job. Look, the more information you want from me, the more I'd never tell you a thing. Any significant upper hands you've ever gotten from those who've helped you, you've ruthlessly pounced on and destroyed. I'm not interested in being one of your foolish victims."

"Lailie, today is the day of our rebirth, the day that the last transitional energy oscillations end and become steady. I know you can feel that the true age of Aquarius has begun. Let's start fresh," she heard Saraswati reply.

"I like how you didn't even acknowledge what I said. The way you just ignored me, is exactly how I plan on dealing with whatever it is you sent me. Humm, wait though, I think you've got the right idea about starting fresh! I shall start fresh!"

"Really!? Okay, then please take a look at the...," she heard Saraswati begin.

"Yes! As of right now, I never want to speak to you again, don't call me ag...," she replied, about to cut the conversation when she heard Saraswati reply, "sure," in the most deadpan voice ever.

"Fuck me! She was done with me! No one gets to be done with me! Now I will end this conversation when I'm done with her!" she thought, seeing Saraswati stare at her with a solemn look.

"What?" she asked in a neutral tone, feeling proud of her self-control being that she wanted to snap at her.

"I know you know, that in this new Era, it'll be sink or swim, and that we won't have a lot of opportunity to make sure we're above water. Our rivalry is just as important to me as it is to you, but I hate not knowing the full story of who we are. And I know you hate it too. We both pride ourselves on wanting to beat each other without a terrible fall out and slow demises, which is what would happen if we truly go after each other. It's a hell of a gamble to unlock our past, and find strengths, weaknesses, or possible reason for a friendlier relationship. You sitting on your hands with the stance that you don't want to help me, even at the cost of helping yourself, is small minded and cowardly," she heard Saraswati whisper.

"You're saying all the right things to trigger me, I'll give you that," she replied, feeling her right eye begin to twitch.

"Good," she heard Saraswati mumble.

"Nonetheless. My hands feel good under my ass when it comes to dealing with you."

"Of course!" she heard Saraswati blare.

"How can you blame me for being as cautious as I am? For thousands of years in this seventh Era, we females have struggled in the toxic masculine energies of the Pieces, making it way harder to gain the same respect and opportunities as men. It's honestly surreal that I get to be alive during this transition, to feel myself growing stronger with each breath. The funny thing is how much I didn't know how asphyxiated of energy I was until today. I only had a clue of the depravation from how my mother, my grandmother and all the females in my bloodline had to lead this Order. I saw that for centuries, the world truly does not see human females as the figure heads. That they only see the powerful, ruthless and seductive imagery of Lilith."

"And actually, even with her imagery, sometimes it wasn't enough. That to gain audience, we had to stoop low and rely on males as spokesmen. The utter disgust I feel knowing that for generation we leaders of our Era never truly felt strong enough to show ourselves, fearing that once males saw our bodies, curved and soft, they'd dismiss and undermine us. Today is the first day I feel strong enough to absorb and redirect all that oppressive force. If I feel this way, then I know for certain that you're feeling up to new challenges as well. I think you're hiding behind your candor and are actually ready to do what you were just saying. I think you're ready to pounce, to take me out fast. All you'd need from me is a slip-up, and the perfect bait is to finally get me way too curious about that thing."

"I do feel stronger indeed. But honestly, this makes me want to be even more careful than I have ever been before," she heard Saraswati reply.

"Yeah un-huh," she mumbled.

"As of right now, I would not move against you until I've felt that I had the proper time to gauge our strengths. What I'm asking requires no compromise from you other than to look and see what you find. What if you learn something that can only benefit you and not me, is it not worth it?"

"You're the Queen of double talk. Saying she'd be careful, while trying to goad me by telling me I'm not brave enough to check that thing. You truly are unbelievable," she whispered, shaking her head.

"Lailie, I know that you're about to do the press conference, but I think that you should have someone with less new energy coursing through them speak on your behalf. That or you shouldn't stay on stage too long," she heard Saraswati say – not acknowledging what she'd just said, causing her eye to twitch even harder.

"You think you're the master at that mental game where you don't acknowledge the other person, leaving the topic dead in the air, then shifting the conversation! Look, your little twisted, mind gaming, internalized misogynist piece of shit. Don't play mind games with me, telling me to lay low as you grope and grab at any tendrils of power you can get your conniving hands on."

"Do you know how obvious it is to myself and everyone that you're always trying to find the ancient bloodline activated weapons? I know damn straight somehow, me studying this thing, learning anything from it, will somehow benefit you!" she replied, stopping when she realized she was all out growling and snarling with rage instead of just being snippy.

"Uh-huh, and you want to hold a press conference. Those journalists are going to have a field day if you lose your temper. Listen, although the energies of Aquarius are now in our favor, it doesn't mean we can wield them assuredly. Taking time to learn how to deal with this is very important. Aquarius energy is legendary for being the most passive aggressive and destructive. Also, you have to take into account the fact that male energy from Pieces has not lessened, but also moved into Aquarius. Male Aquarius energy is known to be just as dark and deceptive as the females. If you're not hyper aware of the energy you project into that crowd as you speak, you could easily become the cause of any problem. Essentially, what I'm saying is that, besides the elemental energies of water, you don't know what's in that pot Aquarius carries."

"All energies can have destructive tendencies, and ways to imbalance them. What the hell are you, the newspaper? I don't need a generic doom and gloom reading that pretty much tells me not to go out there and disturb the sheep. I give you credit though, your logic is perfectly twisted to unsettle me, telling me that I might provoke chaos while I try to preach continued resolution. Devious, as always."

"You love it. If there's one thing I know for certain about you, is that you love conflict, and love having enemies. I bet you're going crazy right now because there's no rockets being fired, no Iron Curtain horns and alerts. I don't even know why you try to pretend."

"Humm, everything you say is true. But you are a bit special, you're an enemy that somehow exhaust and kills all the thrill. It's one of the reasons I avoid you at all cost. If I'm to spend time doing mental gymnastics, I prefer to be someone else's problem."

"Well, you can't always have your cake and eat it too."

"Most of the time I can. While soul searching, I realize the reason you irk me so much is because I deep down genuinely wish you'd go use the same conniving energy you use to try and gain the upper hand with me on the males in your society. I honestly think if you redirected just a little more time to that, you could rally power and take the country back under female rule. That entire landmass was under Matriarchal rule at its birth, and yet it remains poisoned by men, with women still being the subservient. You know what, it's not just you who frustrates me...I just don't get your society whatsoever. Why are there so many women like you who hold power and influence, yet not taking full control? And why are so many of you worried about everyone else, and not focused on yourselves?" Lailie said, taking a deep breath right after, wanting to make sure she regulated her tone and temperament.

"You often call me out for contradictions. It must be because you recognize yourself in me easily. You ask why females in India don't take back power, yet admit hiding behind the legend of Lilith and the face of men. You have no clue what you're asking us to do, and if you do, then you're even more malicious than I've ever given you credit for. The unbalanced energies, the lack of resources, along with the complications of being the true face of power. Just no, you'd be destroyed by just one of the problems if you ever stepped foot in my lands. You're too narrow minded in the power of pure femininity to ever understand how to maintain true power! Lailie, you don't get to have an opinion on India!"

"I don't get to have an opinion on India? Haha! Your lands are a cesspool, that's a fact," she remarked, wanting to sting Saraswati.

"Coming from you? Coming from a bloodline of people who single mindedly thrive on dividing and conquering anyone and everyone around them, all to reclaim your supposedly sacred lands between the Nile and the Euphrates rivers?"

"Touché," Lailie replied dryly, watching Saraswati hold her belly, laughing hysterically.

"Sorry, that was too funny. Lailie, listen to me. On any other day, yes, I'd be trying to pull one on you. Today, I called you with a genuine warning to be careful with this new energy. And if you want to know what I'd get out of it, is that I don't want you doing anything that has a harmful butterfly effect. My supposed cesspool country is where a large majority of the tech innovations to create the space elevator will be coming from. And get this, a lot of the scientists and engineers are females. If you want reclamation of power for women, don't fuck this up."

"Un-huh, what else do you gain from it? And having a population of one point five billion people, your country better be one of the top providers of human resources," she mumbled.

"Well, I've been having bad dreams about our future, and you were in many of them. So for now, I'm trying to mitigate my perceived danger," She heard Saraswati reply.

"What if you meddling with me, inciting my wrath, is that danger?" she asked.

"Well then, vicious premonition cycles it'd be. But I'm willing to take that chance. I guess I have control issues. With warning you, I feel like at least I tried. Yeah, at least I tried to take control. Hey umm, speaking of our future, rumor has it, Tet will have two stand-in reps for our meeting. This is to greet a new Era, and still, they won't show their true faces. I can't believe it."

"Well, they were betrayed and hated by so many, including our own bloodlines. They make sense, as they were almost wiped from the face of earth by everyone else attending the meeting," she replied, seeing amber icons in the corner of her vision, reading, <Emergency, there are Makers in distress. And one has expired. The cause seems to be from a stress induced brain hemorrhage.>

"Did you just get news on something," she heard Saraswati ask knowingly.

"Nosey huh?"

"Yes, I want to know everything, hence my mother named me Saraswati. Anyways, keep your news a secret. I'll see you later."

"You just love having the last word huh?"

"I just love annoying you," She heard Saraswati say, disappearing.

"Bitch! What a Bitch!" she whispered, hating and loving the way it felt to have a push-pull relationship with a woman of power.

"Madam, are you ready?" she heard her number One ask.

"Let's do this," she replied, feeling a flash of apprehension that genuinely startled her, causing her to think, *"I'm no fool. That feeling alone was far more than enough to tell me her warning to tread lightly within these new energies is legitimate. But to what end? How do I save face? I'd only trust my daughters to do this, and I've hidden my children's existence this long, I'll be damned if in this new Era, I hand their faces out to the world to be targets. Damn, what do I do? If I play the humble sheep herder, I can already tell from the energy in there, some will get braver than ever before towards Lilith's voice of authority. If the others see that, it won't be good. How inconvenient and frustrating it is that bad feelings don't come with the exact rectification feelings attached to them as well."*

"Madam?" she heard her number One ask, steeping between herself and the door as if he'd heard all her apprehension in those few seconds.

"I'm fine, get out of the way and open the doors, and where's the Rabbi?" she asked, seeing the man in question calmly walking through the glass doors just as they opened, giving her a bright smile.

"Lailie, how are you?"

"I'm fine Adam. Look, I want you to sit this one out. Talking to the world with you next to me would look like I'm just talking to Israel and Judaism, and I can't afford to rub salt into the wounds of the prideful, sexist, sheep men following the opposing Alt Percept Order."

"I was actually thinking the same thing. Hey, I need to run something past you. But Later," she heard Adam respond.

Seeing the glass doors fully shut, surrounded only by her guards and Adam, she looked him in the eyes and said, "What? And since when do you ask me anything? Since when are you being cordial to me?"

"Since today. Today you and I are not who we used to be. I think we both know with this new energy, we no longer need, and or, can benefit from each other. I think it's best I continue my duties as a limiter, but only for your son. This is what I wanted to run past you, I was thinking I'd join Nate's shadow guard," she heard the Rabbi say, with a warm smile that made her inwardly cringe.

"What? That doesn't sound like a good idea. You've always been here to keep me pinned up, keep me in check. What the fuck is wrong with you? It's been generations that our two bloodlines have done limiter parings. We were matched to only limit each other since pre-birth! How can you even breathe words of a split!? The outcome might be complete degradation of our bloodlines hard work to manage the sheep! Not to mention, none of your Elders, or my board would allow for this! Wait, are you thinking to run this past everyone at the meeting? Is this why you're telling me this now? You are, aren't you!? You've lost your mind after your death, haven't you!?"

"Yes and no, look, we'll talk after you finish this, okay?" she heard Adam say, giving her a reassuring smile.

"To this day, as fucked up as you are, I never know how you make your smile look so genuine. It's making me nauseous, stop it at once!"

"It is the smile of a man who always knows his true purpose and place in life. I am happy to do God's work."

"Disgusting, don't use Alt Percept methods on me! I'm all for believing in a being or beings of a higher power, but I'll never allow that methodology your Order uses to ensnare people, to spool me up into becoming like one of the sheep! I swear, I'll never get used to how fundamentally twisted your Order is," she replied with a chuckle, thinking, *"Yet, I put up with him and his organization's presence, while denying myself the love, affection and attention of my husband and children. My mortality has always made me fearful. I'm terrified to be weakened by love, and a need to need someone. I cast it out, beat and betray it. But here I stand, knowing that what I've always feared, I've somehow managed to do to myself."*

"Self-preservation, I always called it, and yet, all I did was betray and hate myself. Feeding my soul, loneliness, despair and agony. I shouldn't say I don't understand the Alt Percept Order. It is clear as day that their source of power is the most simplistic and easiest of all human emotion to manipulate - the perception that they can fill the hole in the heart that one creates in themselves."

"Haha, let's take a break and stop reminding each other of how much we hate each other. You're at six times this week, I'm at ten. And we've said we'd stop wasting our breaths on each other I think equal amount of times. So, with that being said, go, go do the press conference. I'll be around when you're done."

"Why? Why do you want to guard Nate? What makes you think you'd pair well with him?" she asked, wanting to hear what she had already assumed.

"Lailie, you already know why. All the years you and I have spent weakening him with mental and hormonal inhibitors are already quickly starting to wear off now that we are fully within the energies of Aquarius. Let's be realistic, I won't be able to manage you or your daughters at the rate that they are coming into their energies. This morning, when all four of you woke up from your deaths, I felt all of you on an individual basis push past me, and I know all of you felt the same. With Nate, who has no clue of this Era, who has not gone through transition due to our inhabitance... I can still maintain some form of limitations as he grows into his power."

"And, the other reason is...you'd kill him if he goes astray," she whispered, feeling oddly calm – just for a moment.

"Of course," she heard Adam say, in a tone that for the briefest moment almost sounded acceptable.

"I wonder if we overdid inhibiting him? Do you think it was wrong to prevent him from experiencing the death and rebirth? Having a male child, I just, I had no idea what to do with him, and there wasn't much guidance from my bloodlines'

529

memorandums on how to deal with the extremely rare, male offspring…other than, of course to limit them so that they don't become a scourge to earth."

"Well, you and I weren't living blindly by your bloodlines' historical text to limit the male offspring. We saw how he was behaving as a child…and if we didn't do something…he very well might've become the scourge the moment he hit puberty. It took a long time for me to make him think his rampages, killing those guards and people, were bad dreams…and even longer to make him feel shame for …dreaming it. So, as an adult, for him to experience the metamorphosis, I can't imagine what he'd become. And, from what I can tell from just checking in with him is that he might very well be having a delayed metamorphosis. During the last three days, he was extremely ill, very near death. Awakening today, I can see that the rate of healing, and the strengthening of his mindset has already begun to increase past where we'd meticulously engineered him to be. I'd either want to prevent this, or bring him into the realization of his new strengths as slow as possible," she heard Adam whisper in a warm, reassuring tone.

"Yes, I understand," she replied, eyeing Adam carefully.

"Lailie?"

"You're too humble about your own growth when you say we surpass you. Your words, your temperament, for less than a second, you owned me, making me feel comfortable with you needing to kill…to kill my son. To have that kind of control, to make a mother accept and understand the need to murder her child for any reason…is telling of your true power. I can see now why you want to separate from me. If we were to clash, we wouldn't be recoverable, would we?"

"Yes, we'd slip into a maniacal state of fighting over what we'd think is righteous, and it'd be akin to two nuclear reactors melting down at the same time," she heard Adam reply, bobbing his head in self-affirmation.

"I see," she whispered, thinking, *"I understand we are absorbing the new energies, but how, even for that mere moment in time, did he do that to me? If he could do that to me, I can only imagine what he could do to the sheep. How strong is he really? And what's with that guiltily look on his face? It bothers me more when he actually cares about something!"*

"What? What's with that face!?" she finally asked, seeing that Adam was not going to speak.

"I think I could've done a better job giving Nate an out. I told him he was a good person a little too much. I think I should have told him that the horrible things he did in his quote on quote dreams, and from the things he remembers doing, weren't favorable to God, so that he'd fight hard for God's love. Instead, I made him feel too loved and not deserving of it. Now his decision-making skills, especially when it comes to carrying out missions that require mercilessness, he hesitates, already burdened with the idea of being too loved and not worthy."

"I mean, what'd I done was good when our goal was to emasculate him as much as possible because we could reinforce his fragility by stinging him for not being merciless, while at the same time, passively and silently forgiving him for not being so. But now, with this new energy, if he does anything merciless in the name of following our orders, it'll boost his ego, and he'll feel much more capable, without needing our assurances for any of his next missions. We will now have no justifiable reason to tell him to restrain himself and he will have no more reason to come to us crying, asking for guidance so we can give him contradicting advice that makes his mindset weak and malleable. In the coming days, he'll become much sharper, and he'll soon catch on to what we've done to him, and then he'll hate us, and hate God. And I predict, his final decision will be to completely cut ties with us. What a fool I am to have not thought of what could happen in the future if he did get stronger. I was too prideful that what we did and would continue to do to him would always work."

"Strong statement. Since when are you an oracle who sees only doom? When you say cut ties, I hope your gloomy thought process is that he'll sever relations with the identity Percept deity of your House of Juda, and not me," she replied.

"Well, where will he fit in, if he gets stronger? He has no place in your female oriented cast system, and with all the female energies you channel in and around your buildings. The stronger he gets, the further he'll be pushed away. I have a suggestion you won't like, which is to allow him to grow closer to his father. No jealous power trips, keeping him from visiting, etcetera. His father is a very strong male figure who has a natural guiding energy that's not too overwhelming or biased."

"Huh, I thought I've gotten subtler about my sabotaging of their relationship. I absolutely hate your advice, you're right. You know he blames us for Nate's bi-sexuality."

"He loves Nate; he doesn't care about his sex life. He is annoyed on the principal that our manipulation might be the cause of it, which would've robbed him of the opportunity of making the choice on his own, that is all he said. Anyways Lailie, stop delaying, go in there and do the press conference, we can talk after," she heard Adam say, now sounding short of breath.

In the last few seconds, she'd felt her annoyance and frustration at her present situation project out, infusing into Adam. But in the same breath, she felt his energy flow into her.

"I feel disgusting ...and so fucking turned on!?" she thought, wanting to scrub herself clean, even as her pussy began to throb at thoughts she'd yet to even perceive.

"How? How are we projecting so easily?" she whispered, taking a deep breath, now purposely channeling her body energy into Adam, hearing him let out a small gasp of air.

"Interesting reaction," she whispered.

"Don't play with me, you won't like how I handle you. I'll be on the helipad,'" she heard Adam say, seeing him move his foot back like he wanted to leave, only to see his face turn bright as his body fought to stay in her presence.

"But what if, what if you like it, should I stop?" she replied, inching back, making eye contact with the Rabbi, smiling when he kept it.

"I told you to stop," she heard him reply in a dark tone, feeling all of the magnificent energies of lust and desire turn to utter disgust to the point where she would've peeled her skin off to get rid of the itch.

"Do you understand now?" she heard Adam ask as he turned and walked towards the helipad placed on a secondary landing of her rooftop.

"Deceptive and volatile energy," she whispered to herself, now feeling nauseated from the contradictive states of energy that'd just passed through her from his push back.

"Madam, is there anything you'd like us to do to calm the restless sheep?" she heard her number One say.

"Blow in more of the Lavender scent, lower the lights a little more. Make sure they're all sitting in those comfy chairs, offer more of those tiny, delicious cups of Moroccan tea, then tell them I'll be there shortly, and that the delay is that I was receiving an update from Tet regarding the project. Honestly, I just have one last thing I need to do," she replied, sending a call.

"Lailie?" she heard a soft voice reply almost immediately.

"Mrs. Sarah Maclear. Tell me something, how can you be the President of the United States, yet still allow Tet to hold you by the ovaries?"

"What? What would make you think that?" she heard Sarah reply, sounding genuinely surprised.

"Don't what me. What do they have on you? Let me try and help you!" she replied, as she thought, *"She's always felt slightly controllable, but just out of reach. Tet has probably had their claws in her for a long time. And knowing them, they allowed me to control aspects of her because they didn't care what I was up to. I hate their way of doing things. It's unmeasurable."*

"Ha, you can't help me. No one can. But it's not Tet you should be worried about, it us so-called leaders of society."

"I need to press her about Tet regardless. If I leave her to struggle, I'll never know the depths of their control, and I damn sure need to know what's coming from her and what's coming from them," she thought as she said, "Bullshit, my sources say you've been with true Tet agents! Did they force you to do some kind of Alchemic Working?"

"It's the only thing that'd be strong enough to make this world peace bullshit sticking long enough to make the war horns go silent! No war whatsoever since you made the announcement on March Fifteenth. This is beyond unreal unless you used the 'Ides' energy in a 'Working.'"

"You want not normal? It's you, having this kind of conversation on these coms. Normally you bring me to a dead room when you have your wild theories!" she heard Sarah retort with wide, accusing eyes.

"Dead rooms can be bugged! Last time I was burned was in a dead room! And at this point, I don't care!" she replied.

"It's still harder to bug a dead room! So I care! Risk yourself, selfish bitch!"

"You know how I know you want my help!?" Lailie pressed.

"I really don't want or need it, trust me!" she heard Sarah reply instantly.

"You would've hung up! You want me to dig!" she replied, seeing a strange expression between hostility and acknowledgment play across Sarah's face.

"Exactly," she whispered after hearing nothing for about ten seconds, "You and I both know this so-called peace is a patch on a wound that'll soon become festering and gangrenous. Humans need to fight it out, just as much as they need to fuck and make up. I don't get why suddenly you jumped the gun on this! We all know the Space Elevator project needs to get done, but after seeing everything that could go wrong with those calculations, we all agreed to wait at least twenty years!"

"Even with the latest calculations done, we're nowhere close to hashing out the problems our ancestors overcame, and we don't know if they were doing those calculations to see if they could build one, or if they accomplished it. Now I must stand on stage and get these sheep all riled up so they can be even more unified. I really can't put into words what I think the aftermath of this collaboration will bring," she whispered.

"I had no choice, I had to do what I had to do the moment I found out what I did. It was either this, and let everything go to hell while we survive as a species, or we literally don't make it," she heard Sarah reply in a dead pan voice. ·

"What?! What the hell are you talking about? Have you found evidence that one of the Prophecies from the Living Scripture will come true in this new Era?" she asked, feeling her stomach tighten in apprehension as the Prophecy that her bloodline had chosen to live their way of life by had always focused on its arrival at the time of a new Epoch.

"Lailie, you know damn straight I no longer acknowledge any of those so-called Prophecies spewed from that Fountain, or any other supposedly sacred site. Remember in two thousand twelve, when all of you were freaking out about the coming of a new Era? And then I sent evidence that that so-called Living

Scripture Fountain may have very well been a sixth Era data node, and or maybe even a damn public library."

"Now, four years later, all of you are still secretly freaking out about some Nefeshka person, or what's the other one Saraswati and those other Yoginis talk about? The return of some Lanying person. And worst of all are the damn houses of the Alt-Percepts, who seem to have fallen victim to their own manipulations, scared of every name in every supposedly holy book returning for some kind of vengeance."

"How dare you mock Lilith! Your tone suggests my bloodline flocks at stories like the sheep! There are reasons, based on fact for all of our actions! Sheep need and use Deity ideas to best serve their own holes in their heart, and for reasons to turn a blind eye to personal responsibility! My bloodlines' preparation and vigilance come from fact, pure fact!"

"Says the person who does not acknowledge all the other stories that've come from that Fountain or any other scared site as real, really!? Including one that is literally called, 'The book of Nefeshka?' You don't even want to acknowledge it, all because a different bloodline that grew under the lead of a different Alt-Preceptor house fought over land with your own bloodline and chosen 'Alt Percept' house! Really!? You don't think that's absurd?"

"We acknowledge that their book is our book! We don't say we don't believe! We are pissed because their Alt-Perceptors used powerful workings to splice lies within the original books to fit their purposes! And we wanted to share the land, they wanted to steal it! They spun it to make it like we left Egypt on a quest to steal it! Bullshit! Everything was peaceful till they began getting greedy over the use of 'Ether!'"

"Classic he said, she said shit! The way humans are, we both know it was just plain old tit for tat, greed and selfishness done on both sides! And it's clear to see why, because you're showing how hardnosed, unwilling to accept another scenario you are. You also don't believe in the return of Lanying, when Lilith and Yogini bloodlines are almost the exact damn thing! And the story came from the exact same place! To me, all of you are insane and twisted in many ways. All of you are stuck on one story, and I think if you can believe one from that Fountain, then you should have the capacity to believe them all. Or more rationally, if you can see a bunch of stories came from one place, and you know the cycles of humanity, then you can bank on the source being a simple, mundane, data node center or public library!"

"Your proof was a poor audio-visual of a woman, possibly singing a nursey rhyme in front of children, displayed in a very off looking emerald tablet. No one who's seen it thinks it was authentic. Hardened fluid from the Fountain is always perfection, such as the books of Lilith, that are beautiful, translucent, yet emerald in color, without cracks or warpage in any of the surfaces! Whatever you showed, it looks beat up, looks like you tried to make it in a lab and failed!" Lailie replied.

"Lots of things could've explained why it looks beat up, gee, I 'dunno', like war! That, and you know damn straight a lot of our ancestors had self-destruct fetishes for their technology! Also, you're acting like that Fountain and the fluid running through it is perfect. If it was, it'd still be working one hundred percent, not belching out intermittent burst of energy of which you then selectively choose to listen to and deem important. Let's just be practical, that Fountain is just tech built to last a long time. And finally, after thousands, upon thousands of years, it's showing its age."

"Well, we all asked you to let us study your supposed artifact to see if it had the typical marks of a failed self-destruction situation! You won't let anyone near it!" Lailie blared.

"Y'all would hide or destroy it to make sure your hardline ideas last for another era! It's actually laughable to me now, that what all of you are dead set in believing in - this Living Scripture Fountain - could be spewing sixth era's greatest fantasy war novels, and or, wars that had gone on during the time. Hell, it could even be older than the sixth era. Can you imagine that? If that's true, it'd be even more amusing to me. It's sad too in a way. All of you do a good job making the world feel mysterious, and make people such as myself, work way too hard to win both the sheep and yourselves over."

"Making me pose and posture, and sometimes even truly believing in all this mystic Prophecy bullshit. Then one day, after climbing so far, I realized I'm not thinking for myself. So now, I'm using the power I've gained to get practical answers and find out who humanity was in the prior eras. And almost all the answers I've been getting thus far, have been relatively simple. During each era, we've become so 'Teched' out, that when we've gone to war, the destruction has been so overwhelming, we kept sending ourselves back to the dark ages. And now, here we are again, standing at the beginning of the eighth era, looking like we're close to doing it all over again…but this time," she heard Sarah say, giving her a crooked smile.

"Go on, this time, what?" she pressed, followed by, "I'll confide something that I'm sure you and many others have already deduced about me. I'm not like my predecessors. I try to be, but I'm way too curious for that. I look for answers, just like you. And I've made some very simple deductions based on the information I've retrieved, just like you. It's why I'm so lenient with my children, and why I genuinely work together with so many other people that my predecessors would have never interacted with on equal terms. For example, my bodyguards, that I trust with my life, are all from Lebanon."

"Umm, all done with biases. And all done to boost your ego, where you make yourself feel benevolent. Once you feel good about yourself, you then feel your bloodline was right and stop thinking any further. Oh, and please spare me the work together statement. That war in Lebanon during two thousand – six, was a huge sham started by you to get artifacts you found out were buried under downtown Beirut. And you wanted to get your hands on that scientist, but one of your Lil-Guard had so much brainwashed hate pumped into her, she maliciously pulled the trigger, forgetting her mission was to apprehend," Lailie heard Sarah say with a sarcastic snort.

"Yes, Estris…I sharpened her a little too much. That was my fault. And you misinterpret, that war was staged on both sides. Al Babadur and I both needed to take lives for a 'Working,' and we both needed the artifacts dug up. The artifacts were buried deep, and a seamless, without question excavation would not have been possible, as sheep are not as dumb or unaware as we would wish them to be. So, we had Alt Percepts instigate any minds that were already agitated and wanting to fight. Once they were stirred up, we bombed them and the artifact sites, knowing the artifacts would not be damaged. In the chaos, both of us took the artifacts we desired. I thought you knew that. Well, if you didn't, add this as bonus information while I'm confiding," she whispered.

"I am a little shocked, my intel did show that both parties got their hands on artifacts, but I thought that was what y'all were fighting over. It all looked one sided. Like you were attacking, and that they were trying to keep the artifacts already on their land. Not that both of you agreed," she heard Sarah reply.

"You have no idea how good Al Babadur is at making it look like that. They've been using and perfecting that technique for countless centuries," she whispered.

"And I can't believe that man selfishly passed his life debt to his dying daughter. Why did you go through with saving Rayya? I know you have obligations with Al Babadur, but you break them when you want to. Rayya is not even a good Medium. I watched you try to awaken her mind with those ancient space elevator equations. But she often under performs. I had hopes she'd solve those tether issues," she heard Sarah say, giving her a questioning look.

"Why? Well I am benevolent after all," she replied, with a soft chuckle before saying, "And, I hate to defend her, but those equations are not really her strong suit, she does wonders with quantum entanglement," she replied.

"Umm, she's okay. I have Mediums that think circles around her in the pentagon," she heard Sarah reply, folding her arms.

"Can they walk across the lab without being wrapped in bubble wrap? Can they communicate their works for the rest of us to understand, or sometimes do you find yourself thinking they are so disconnected from reality, you think they are Makers themselves? Don't even bother answering," she replied with a smile.

"Fair enough. Still, I don't see what Tet saw in her to hire her. It was odd for me to hear reports of them touching her, knowing she was owned by you," she heard Sarah whisper before saying, "Changing topics… One thing about you that really does surprise me. I mean you did say you're lenient with your children, but to allow Nate to read the book of Nefeshka, I thought that was forbidden?"

"Oh please, that shell company of theirs is operating without even a single true Tet agent there to investigate her. Those sheep in Nammu Tech don't know who she is. Speaking of Tet agents, you're the only one in a long time I've actually seen spending time with them. Tell me, how do they behave, other than aloof," she replied, tilting her head as she said, "As for Nate, well, I told you, I question things. In this case, I allow my son to do it for me. And no one dares to tell me to reprimand him. They know I'd gut them."

"I see," she heard Sarah whisper, with a look that made Lailie's stomach twist.

"Your facial expressions annoy me. My body reacts to your distress. You should take more emotion hiding classes, you still show every tell," she said, gritting her teeth, seeing more distressful looks play across Sarah's face as if she were wrestling with something.

"What?" she whispered.

"Look Lailie, you're right. I did rush this form of peace with a 'Working,' but not with Tet, they came after I did what I'd done."

"I knew you did a Working! What kind of Working!? Blood? Life sacrifice? Sex work!? Technological? Mediation!? Astro planning?! Please tell me you chose one you are very, very familiar with! Friend-enemies or not, you should have called me, Saraswati, or any of the Yogini's to help you if it was a Blood, Life Sacrifice or Sex Working!"

Lailie saw Sarah's face scrunch defensively.

"Your face again. I knew the Working you did to make a peace like this would require one or a combination of the three. And I know you, you're no good at those kinds of 'Workings' whatsoever! Tech, Astor, and Mediation Workings are the only thing I'd trust you could do alone! So, please tell me you had someone I somehow don't know about to help you!"

"I did the Working on my own…I won't tell you what kind because I don't want to be scrutinized. I'm telling you to explain how desperate I was, that way you understand that when I found out what I did, I instantly reacted. Like, instantly…do you get me?" she heard Sarah ask, sounding nervous.

"Yes, you were flustered, then you acted recklessly. Now we're in the midst of your Working and don't know what the true cost of it will be. People wanting to kill each other, finding themselves unable to act, means they're bottling up an incalculable amount of resentment. When the energies of your Working begin to break down, people's hate will erupt like a volcano."

"Lailie, I said, instant! Grr, you're not getting it…Trust me, there won't be an eighth era if we don't try to do something now!" she heard Sarah snap.

"What do you mean! Do something about what?"

"The state of the world! The exact reason of my Working! All of us have lied to each other a little too well on how bad everything is. Our resource reports have been fraudulent for decades. Same for our toxicology reports for both the land and oceans. How much fish left in the oceans, lies! How much potash, lies! We've already driven ourselves off the cliff to extinction already. I know damn straight how dangerous this Working is, but if we don't try reverse our situation now, we're going to just free fall!" he heard Sarah respond.

"All lies, for decades? No way. Agreed, we do try to trick each other, but none of us operate without watching the other's every move. Not to mention, what you're saying implies the organizations bent on reducing human population have somehow bested all of us. That's insulting. We are all monitoring each other to the extremes. Hell, I have people so imbedded within your ranks, sometimes I've known if you've even sneezed, while you're actually still sneezing. Ha! As a matter of fact, I know how many times you wipe your goddamn ass, and that you waste paper by not folding it. This is our norm! I expect you and everyone else to do the same to me."

"We can talk about what we know about each other, but you didn't know what you didn't know, right? For instance, all of you were watching me so closely and had no idea I'd done the Working, right? So, so what about our spies? Realistically the more we've spied, the better we've gotten at hiding from the things we should've been most accountable to each other for.

Go do the press conference, try to ensure the world remains unified. I'm not about to do what I did once more to make this kind of peace happen again. I'll see you at the meeting," she heard Sarah say, knowing she was about to cut the com.

"Hey, just curious, well, this is embarrassing to reveal, but I still don't know what Rayya's mother name is. Do you have any clue?"

"Zero clue," she heard Sarah reply quickly with a 'please shut up look.'

"That face you just made. Does the same thing happen to you as it does to me? If you try to think of her face and give her a name, do you begin to get a panic attack? Well, I used to feel that. Haven't tried since my reawakening. Have you tried to do anything you had trouble with before and find it easy since your reawaking? You did, you did die for three days, right?" she asked.

"To my knowledge, no one knows her name, and she gives panic attacks to anyone and everyone for any reason she wants. I had a few teams experience very weird tragedies getting too close to her, so I give her, her space. What I do know is that your Estris killed her husband, and him passing his life debt to Rayya has made her one dark, pissed off bitch. She sits in front of that T.V. all day with her Alt-Perception energies traveling along all the frequencies. She moves people around like puppets when she wants too. And um, as for your other question, mind your business. Look, you've literally made the audience I'm asking you to address wait for almost an hour. Goodbye Lailie, good luck with the conference."

"All the resource reports she says are lies," she whispered to herself, thinking, *"How? And why? It doesn't make sense. We're all greedy, but except for the organizations that want to downsize humanity, who else would allow for us to run out of resources?"*

"Is she lying to cover her ass for doing what she has done?" she mumbled, feeling eyes touch upon the side her neck, causing her to look to her left at Adam who was now on the helipad, but standing at the edge facing her.

"Leaving me, after all these years. I honestly never thought it'd happen. And whenever I've mused what that'd be like, for sure, I thought I'd be happy," she whispered to herself, hearing Saraswati's voice in her earbud saying, "Hi Adam, touching down soon, thank you for having me over. Tel Aviv is so beautiful and so is Lailie's building."

"Madam, I hear someone's coming to meet you and the Rabbi over the coms. The rest is encrypted. I take it you may not have heard, as I noticed you were…dealing with other situations," she heard her number One say.

"That your Madam is all over the place, which is very much not like her right?

"Uhhhh," she heard her number One reply cautiously.

"Yup, okay, noted. And I heard the message. It's nothing I need to deal with as said visitor is coming regardless of whether I want them here or not. Okay, open the doors, let's do this," she replied, nodding her head to her number One, and then to her other guards who quickly opened the doors for her.

In calm strides she walked in, forcing herself to breath in the warm, Lavender scented air, thinking, *"this is the worst! As much as I lie, I hate this kind of dishonesty. It goes against everything I believe in."*

"Our hack feeds will be coming through to your contacts Madam Lilith, you should be able to see all communication from the journalist, this way you'll be able to ensure none of them can catch you off guard," she heard in her earbud.

"I have to keep them unified for the greater good," she reminded herself, walking up the three blue carpeted stairs onto a comfortable blue and white carpeted stage.

"Good evening everyone," she said when she reached the center of the stage, staring at the multitude of men and women who'd shot up from their plush, body forming seats to great her with curious, yet somewhat aww struck eyes.

"Any individuals I should look out for? Where are their messages? I don't see any flag details," she mentally said to her intel team and AI.

"There was a lag in the data, we're assembling everything now. Should be done in a few more seconds."

"Lag in the data my ass. I'm no fool. Later, I need to go talk to the head of Intel and find out how bad we were just hacked," she thought as she said, "Please take your seats. Thank you for the honorable greetings. I've called this meeting to reiterate Lilith's support for the space elevator project. As we all know, humanities resource

542

consumption is climbing too fast to keep up with our growth. Although we have enough natural resources to survive for the next twenty to fifty years, with each passing year, it will increasingly grow much more uncomfortable, not to mention we cannot take the risk of running out whatsoever."

"It's time to reach out into the vastness of space and bring back what we need without constantly having to launch vessels into space as we cannot risk losing more and more valuable resources such as metal to the void. Now that I've reiterated our common goal, I want to answer as many questions as I can in the short window of time we have to talk. Okay, what questions do you have for me?"

"Intel team, I know we handpicked some of the biggest nay Sayers on the globe. However, there's a fine line between a tough question and someone landing a damn haymaker. Stay vigilant! Okay, let's see what we've got," she mentally commanded.

"Yes Madam Lilith," she heard a monotone voice reply as color coded icons appeared above people's heads, along with visualizations of the message they'd sent back and forth between colleagues, bosses, and friends.

"Maybe Saraswati was right. Maybe I should've laid low. There's this taste of extremely toxic energy in here, and so many damn haymaker questions, it's ridiculous. But at the same time, this is actually what I wanted, isn't it? Maybe if this all goes to hell, everyone will go back to fighting, with a side dish of working together," she thought, pointing to a young female journalist whose icon stayed a steady red as she scrolled down a list of hard hitting questions she'd saved in her notes, stopping at one that read, 'ask first.'

"Trying to go straight for the kill. May your veins flow with warmth," she thought as the woman said, "Hi, Madam Lilith. I'm honored to be chosen first."

"The honor is all mine," she replied, gesturing for the woman to continue with her question.

"Madam, I'll get straight to the point. The math doesn't add up no matter how it's presented. We're being told the space elevator will create jobs. And... okay yes, there's been a big uptick in the technology job sectors. But it's easy to see those jobs are finite. Once these new and old tech companies settle and get into some form of rhythm, that'd be it for all the rest of the people waiting at their doors seeking employment. We all know how the job market goes these days, so whoever did make it in, they'd better milk their jobs. It's now common knowledge that if a person comes up with solutions too fast, they work themselves right out of a job and back into pure instability."

"As of current, the data is showing that four hundred thousand people worldwide will be directly and indirectly employed during all phases of this project. Which, if all goes correctly will be complete in twenty years. That's a drop in the bucket for the eight hundred million to one billion jobs that will be lost to automation in the next ten. I'm sorry, world peace is great, I'm quite enjoying it for the little time it'll probably last. But, what are we really doing? By the time this elevator is done, robots and AI systems will be able to do everything better than we can."

"Thank you for your question. I can genuinely appreciate your concern. Please allow me to explain. With new resources from the asteroids, and new 'breakthroughs' in the sciences, we'll be able to better exploit these resources, humanity will have a major shift in all of its job sectors. These shifts in the job sectors are extremely hard to quantify with words as we're just beginning to take such a huge step forward. But believe me, with a fresh flow of tangible assets - such as the precious metals within those asteroids, there will be a lot more jobs, allowing people to add value to their community and the global society."

"It's easy to stare at the future and say that what we are as of current will not work, but that's because it's the future. When steam and electricity took thousands of jobs from people who did manual labor, that was not their end all. But for those people at that time, it might've seemed like they were going to live without purpose. Obviously, those people readapted and created following generations, or we wouldn't be standing here today. Also, with the new resources we gain, there will be a great influx of wealth. Wealth that we can use to fund an everlasting 'Universal Income' for those who find themselves forced out of the labor market, needing to be retrained in a new skillset so that they may return and aid to our global societies' development," she replied, pointing to a man of which her intel team had just flagged as, 'Possible Haymaker.'

"You?" she asked, pushing the warning to the side as she mentally replied to her team, *"There's no longer a need for warnings. Everyone here is locked onto me like a shark in blood filled water. The young lady's question has opened the door for them to truly lay into me. I know all of you can see that anyone who'd been an easy green has now closed their notes."*

"With all due respect Madam, I'm staring at the future right now, and can confidently say that the everyday person won't fit based on what's already happened. I'm from Singapore, my father is...was a taxi driver. My mother is... was a clerk at our local supermarket. Now, self-driving cars are all our taxies. And a scale and basket laser now auto ring up everything in the store she used to work. This job I'm doing can honestly be done by a drone or a robot. Well now it, it's the only thing paying all three of our bills."

"Madam Lilith, do you think it's safe to proceed to take further questions?" she heard in her earbud.

"Yes, it's fine. As a matter of fact, I just thought of an approach that might be useful," she mentally replied, as she said, "Yes, I see your point. Okay, I'll take the next question from you young lady. I saw you raising your hand very rapidly when I'd first asked if there were questions."

"Madam, oh, excuse, I thought you were, weren't you going to answer his first?" she heard the young lady she'd selected ask.

"You came all the way here, just to ask that?" she replied flatly, giving the woman the most dead pan, 'are you serious look' she could muster.

"Madam, I came here with the shared concerns of many who are in front of you. I heard you mention 'Universal Income' being funded by the resources we'll bring down from space. That's indicative of you already knowing millions or even billions of people will not have the ability to work for income due to automation."

"Young lady, I said 'Universal Income' will be the cushion we'll use to retrain the people who've lost their jobs due to automation."

"Right, I did hear you say that. But from the way you said it, I can't help but wonder why more companies such as yours haven't already begun to work with governments worldwide in regards to putting the people that are at risk of losing their jobs in the near future on Universal Income? To build the space elevator, humanity will have to innovate and implement the most top of the line automation and Artificial Intelligence technologies, which will then easily sweep aside the human factor. I don't understand why we're rushing to this future without a cushion. Why are we waiting for the resources to come out of the sky before we protect the people?

"Also, when you say Universal Income, I feel that, well, I feel that the world is not all on the same page. You've used the term global society, and you said it quite naturally, which indicates that you truly feel this way and have not scripted this for our ears. With that being said, I think you're biased in regards to who the leaders of this global society are, and simply mentally omitting counties that are not. Madam, I feel you should advocate the implementation of Universal Income to every nation. In my country, the Philippines, our government not only never mention Universal Income, but if we bring it up, telling them a few countries such as Finland are testing this, they shut us up, sometimes by making the loudest advocates go missing. In the call to build the elevator, all of humanity is supposed to be working together, but afterwards, it seems like some countries are not going to be included in the reward. If we work hard now and get cut out of everything, what will the people of Philippines do?"

"We picked up burst signals, they've been recording with View Tech's and View-Contacts, and are now attempting to live stream. Please advise as you had wanted this air tight and edited before publicized."

"This really might cause an ugly reaction by the public, but it's better now at the beginning, then later on!" she thought as she mentally replied, *"yes, of course they don't want us to edit and make ourselves sound perfect. Okay, let it through. If we block it,*

they'll show it, and that would make it look like we have
something to hide, everything would only get worse."
    "Understood."

"I'm good friends with your President, I will speak to her about her plans to implement Universal Income. As a matter of fact, I'd like to form a rep team with you being one of the leads for your city. Leave your information with one of my staff. I can hear from your accent that you're from Cebu? Am I correct?"

"Uh, wow. Yes, Madam," she heard the woman reply, giving her a doll eyed, shocked look that made her want to laugh.

"Perfect," she replied, pointing to another woman, saying, "yes young lady, what question do you have for me?"

"I'm from Colombia, and I think I speak for a lot of my people when I ask, how can they be digging anchor points when there's no blueprints for the elevator yet? And everyone is discussing automation, but in our case, we Colombians don't understand why you need so many people to go to the sites when there's so many self-guiding, digging machines? Adding to this, I've gone to the space elevator meetings in Seattle before. Many have said it's best to do this on water, so I just don't get why this is being done on land. To be frank, it looks like Colombians are going to labor camps and never coming back, plain and simple."

"And as far as my intel goes, it looks that way too. None of my spies have returned to tell me what's going on. Where the hell are those people? How the hell can Tet make so many people disappear in front of everyone's eyes so passive aggressively?" she thought as she said, "Ah, young lady. Great questions. Well, this operation is being spearheaded by Tet Corp., so I don't want to speak out of turn for how they run things; however, this topic was why I was tardy for this conference."

"They've disclosed to me that the anchor points will mostly be dug by machines to prevent unnecessary casualties. While the surrounding facilities, such as the refinement and waste conversion plants, will mostly be built by a human labor force. As there will be many facilities surrounding the elevator, it would of course need a sizable human labor force.

"Now as for why the anchor points are being dug right now, well it all boils down to the research already done. For many years, extremely complicated math and physics equations

547

have been worked out, solved and checked over and over again. These equations are based on what used to be theoretical materials that are now, day by day becoming a reality due to breakthroughs from the hard work of scientists around the globe."

"Trust me when I say this, but I understand your concern young lady. And I see and understand the concern on everyone's face. But rest assured, the build plan on the Colombian equatorial line is not being overzealous, it's based on the information and technology we have. It may seem like everything is moving too fast, but understand that all this movement is actually us doing our due diligence. Apart of digging the anchor points, there is the constant check and recheck, ensuring everything will be stable once the elevator begins to rise. Okay, you sir, and you're going to be the last because I've run out of time."

"Thank you Madam for the opportunity to speak. Okay, so they're building the potassium and rare metals' processing plants before you even get the material needed to erect the elevators? I ask rhetorically and seriously, because it doesn't make sense. The completion date for the elevator is set twenty years from now. The processor plants will be done, well they haven't set a date, but common sense says it doesn't take twenty years to build them. Even a far-away guess would be, I 'dunno', I'd say max five years. Also, this whole you, Tet and other companies working together thing, seems way too convenient."

"Right when a burst of private tech and resources' companies began to grow up and spread their wings, a huge plan to get the proverbial 'pot of gold' comes from the 'big dogs.' Seems contrived and sounds like all of you got desperate to not be eclipsed from the loss of control of all the tech and resources. I think it's a move based on fear. All of you are starting to see that the everyday folks don't need y'all anymore, that the everyday folk can create Three D printers and use them to create all sorts of things. All of you can see that the everyday folk can create cheap tools that allow them to monitor the true nutrition of their fruits and vegies, finally able to tell if the crops they've bought are grown on those mass production zero nutrient farms."

"Sir," she began, seeing the man eyes harden, causing her to hold her tongue, not wanting to seem overeager to shut him up - which she was.

"Sorry Madam, just speaking my mind. This space elevator project screams large corporation desperation, and since all of you already have the money, power and influence, all that you all's needed to do was to have a practical, but crazy goal that'd allow us common folk to need you again. I feel all the rivalry stuff was just a play by play farce to have the world watch y'all, like cooperation wrestling entertainment. The perfect script would be for us folk to see conflict resolution, then y'all think we'll feel sympathy and unity, and feed our idiot selves back to you. Oh, we're so sorry big companies! What were we thinking, doing everything ourselves!? Thinking for ourselves!? Yes, please, put us back under your thumb by making us march to a common goal of wealth bringing convolution!"

"And I know why, it's because all of you don't want us to know we can take care of ourselves, that we can come off the grid with self-sustaining farms and energy! Back in the day, y'all would sabotage any and all attempts of the common folk trying to do this, but the average person making up the masses wasn't smart enough, or desperate enough to want to break the pattern. Then y'all got cocky and greedy, made a mistake by creating your streamlined money making schemes, kicking brilliant people out on their butts with no employment, leaving them drowning in life long debt, bad credit, and homelessness."

"Yeah, that 'kinda' ruthlessness is pure lack of foresight on y'all big boys. Y'all were too busy rolling in the money and your perceived power, thinking you left them too crushed to recover, and didn't see them springing up so many private ventures, bringing their neighbors on board, sharing not just the products they were building, but the baseline knowledge that can't be destroyed or silenced by death via a magic car accident, blocked patents, shut up money or NDA's. Nowadays, as my teenage kids would say, people are becoming woke A.F. Ha ha-ha. That's a good one, just figured out the A.F. part just now."

"Sir, is this a question, or…what?" she asked, watching the chubby, bearded man furiously chew his gum, feeling her eye twitch, reflecting on the fact that he'd used the term 'big boys' in his grouping of the large companies.

"Well Madam, it's a question-statement. The best way to convey a message is by telling a story. Why, do you want me to stop? Is this too much? My wife says I ramble, am I rambling?" she heard the man ask, with a wicked smirk that made her want to fly off the stage to behead him.

"Yes," she thought as she said, "no, just clarifying what it is you want me to address, you're covering…a lot," making sure she used just a dash of condensing tone to gain support of any who simply hated people that did not use words to directly get to the point.

"Well, while I'm at it. Let me touch on this Tet Corp. Itself, like how is it so large, but remains so low key? It's a little weird for it now to be the face of this project. This to me is a dead giveaway that Tet Corp. is all of you put together from the very beginning."

"Born and raised in Boston, spent the rest of my adult life in Philly, I know shady things when I see 'em'. For instance, this supposed Tet, openly using bankruptcy protection shells like Nammu tech and O.L.O. engineering. Also, I'm forty-seven, never in my life have I actually heard from someone directly from Tet, if that makes any sense, someone is always saying on behalf of Tet. It's all BS, it's the way to hide legally in plain sight. It's the same practice the movie industry uses. Opening a new company for every movie or T.V. show, so if something goes wrong on that one movie or set, they can just take the hit there, like cutting off a dying limb from a tree. If I'm wrong, then explain why you're the spokeswoman."

"Keep going, you look like you have more to say. I'll do my best to touch on everything after," she replied thinking, *"Many of the things he says, of course have merit. The funny thing about sheep is that they think we shepherds think they're dumb and that we take advantage of it…when the truth is that it's their brilliance that allows them to understand why they should fear so many things. They all know an unguided future ultimately traps them and caps their abilities. No sheep nor Shepard has ever been known to have full resolve for a truly free, technological advanced society. Humm, my lesson to my guards about sharing the same air has new layers of meaning for me …the medium or air we all share is 'fear'*

550

in all of its forms - loss of control, isolation, loss of guidance, loss of the ability to dump twisted and selfish actions onto their leaders."

"Thank you Madam for your patience. Like I said, I have a lot on my mind and had a lot of time to think about it. For instance, my whole life, Lilith Corp. has been one of Tet's biggest rivals. Now, now they let you speak on their behalf, conflict resolution or not, it seems like a huge leap of trust from the way y'all were fussing it out with legal battle after legal battle, and one espionage attempt after another. It's hard to forget whistle blowers on both side dying in car accidents and mysteriously vanishing before trials. I guess my point is, we need a little bit more transparency on how all of you are working together right now. And many others are feeling the whiplash after seeing all this drama playing out," Lailie heard the man say, with his city accents meshing perfectly.

"He speaks perfect English, but using his backgrounds and accents to gain the attention of those two locations. I haven't done enough to crush intelligent, manipulative men in this patriarchal world, have I? I will put my thumb on him and press just a little to show women everywhere to never let men like him have his way," she thought as she said, "Sir, this should not give you insecurity, but surety. This is how dire our situation is. Rest assured, we are still rivals! But we want to live on earth comfortably as a still thriving species! For that to happen, even the worst of rivals need to cooperate. Tet can mark my words; Lilith will always aim to be number one. But with that declaration, my aim is that Lilith be one of their strongest allies when it comes to the space elevator project!"

"Yeah, like I said, sounds more like drama for us to gobble up. Makes sense why the movie industry and you big corporations would use the same practices. They feed us fictitious BS for us to gobble up for entertainment, and y'all feed us the same, but the price all of you charge is not just movie admission, but our lives," she heard the man say with a dark tone that sounded personal.

"You want life painted in transparency, but when things are crystal clear, mud would be thrown on it by the masses and then named convolution. Yes, the feuds we have between each other look nasty and drawn out, but ask yourself as a journalist, ever get your story looked at without that editor's flare? Your job requires you to make everything look interesting even when it's not. So now I wonder, are you just saying all of this to make this sell you? To show that you've stood up to Madam Lilith herself...or do you believe we're really doing all of what you say? If you really do believe that big corporations such as my own are this convoluted, I advise you to stop drinking so much of your own media flared medicine. As you know from all the times you've needed to make something sound way more interesting than it really was, that most of the time, life is, just what it seems to be," she replied, glaring at the man who was now gazing down at the floor.

Satisfied at his reaction, she looked out at the crowd and saw many conflicted faces.

"He's looking down because I'm pissed at him, but his words have unified them. Interesting, it means he's watered the seeds already their minds. I had no idea...I've kept myself a little too far removed from hearing what the sheep think. Lesson well learned," she thought, watching as a blond hair, blued eyed man's hand slowly rose, giving two quick waves.

"All questions are closed," she replied sharply.

"Mam, it's not a question. Sorry for speaking out of turn," she heard the man say in a thick, German accent, giving her a pleading look.

"Yes? Continue," she replied, surprised at her own curiosity, which somehow surpassed her hatred of the bloodline he represented.

"I just want to go on record and say that it's amazing to see humanity working together. I mean, this form of peace is unprecedented. I think the world is so much closer because we all can unite under one common language," she heard the man say.

"Um, sure. Look, no matter what language we speak, we have the commonality of needing to survive, while maintaining a high quality of life. In order to survive as a species and make sure every person on earth is, and will continue living in quality, we need this project to be successful," she said, pausing and looking over the crowd.

Seeing small nods of approval, she smiled as an idea came to mind, then said, "I have a question for all of you, and to the world. Do any of you genuinely want to go back in time, technologically? Can any of you really live without your laptop, cell phones, View-Tech's? For those of you with diabetes or have family with diabetes, those needleless shots that just came out are great right? And let's talk about sex, the new affordable anti STI, anti-pregnancy treatments, are saving lives, and saving moral and mindsets, right?"

Everyone's eyes were locked on her and there was this absolute stillness, and she could tell that everyone was picturing living life without what they had now.

"Perfect, now to herd them further," she thought, as she said, "hard to imagine looking back huh? Everything we have now seems to fit seamlessly as necessity in our lives, yet now we stand here afraid of the future, with doom and gloom at the forefront of our spoken words. Doom and gloom can come from anything and we know this, but we like to quantify that fear as the unknown. Even I, myself am guilty of it. Young man whose dad lost his job driving the cab, let me ask you how many late-night shifts did you almost lose him to exhaustion? Or maybe how many times has he almost be caught and drown in one of those nasty Singaporean flash floods?"

"Uhh, a few times," she heard the man whisper, sounding ashamed.

"This new change might be taking his employment, yet be saving his life. And now he can do something safe and still be with you. I get the resentment, as yes, many places in the world have let the ball drop and let its people fall into unemployment without purpose and guidance. But this is why we need to stay unified. This is a new world we're stepping into, and there will be a lot of growing pains we need to process and mitigate."

"What I want to stress as we move forward into this future, is that we maintain and reinforce our human connection. Caring about each other as we move forward, step by step, we remain responsible, and we make sure no one is left behind," Lailie said, keeping her emotions calm as she studied the crowd, seeing if her words resonated with the journalist.

"Something's off, the mood in here is even more distrusting and agitated than when I first walked in here. And now, the sickly energy I had picked up earlier is getting stronger, moving through the crowd. I can taste it

at the back of my throat, yet I can't find the source," she thought, seeing the man who'd said he'd wanted to go on record about being happy that everyone was working together, smiling with his hand up.

"Yes, this is all the time I have left," she said, now growing nauseous from the toxic energy scent.

"Madam please! We're all speaking the same language! Please address all of our concerns! You didn't discuss deeply one of the very first things brought up."

"What?" she asked in a flat, controlled tone, feeling her temper beginning to flare.

"Well automation, of course. Gives us more surety! What happens when Three-dimensional printers can easily make and assemble the elevator without one human touching it. What happens when the same Three-dimensional printer creates robots that fix itself and themselves!?"

"And with machines speaking and learning from one another, they're learning faster than they can learn from us. Our aim is to build an elevator to ensure our future with abundance of resource, but the cost would be to make ourselves obsolete! What would we be needed for!? The hundreds of thousands of jobs this project is supposed to ensure are not even going to be at one time! Just small contract jobs to finish making the machines that build the elevators and process the raw materials. Then back to joblessness!"

"Everyone's beginning to wreak equally! But I'm sure it's coming from him! What the hell is going on!? How's he doing this! Aquarius energy is proving to be ridiculous!" she thought, as she said, "you came on record saying you were happy we're all working together, only to double back and bash the project. How do you want people to take you seriously if you flip flop so quickly?"

"I am, but I'm also afraid! I mean, why else would there be a story in the bible that depicts this! Remember the tower of Babel! God didn't want us reaching into the heavens! God wanted us to stay on earth! Speaking the same language brings us closer to God, who communes with all beings. He didn't want that from us! Take a closer look at what we are doing and see why it is wrong in our Lord's eyes!"

554

"First, we made English a world standard language, next we made computer coding the world's strongest standard language. Now we're building things that make us obsolete so that we can reach into God's domain to take from there what we've used up on earth! You're a heathen Lailie of Lilith Corp! I'm here as God's warrior! I'm here to fight back! I'm here to say, just because we can do it, doesn't mean we should! Everyone, remembered the tower of Babel! It was not meant for us to reach the heavens! And our Lord and savior stopped it once! Can't you see!? We're creating our literal doom; we're inciting God's wrath! We are inciting God's wrath! Remember the tower of Babel! Remember the tower of Babel!"

"Mam! Bio magnetic wave lengths from him have now spiked, but are not as strong as they'd be if he were from one of the Perception Alteration organizations," Lailie read in her View-Contacts.

"Is he being manipulated, or is he a potent novice unleashed. And is he alone, or...," Lailie began to ask her security team, when a woman next to the man, wearing a Hijab, looking to be of Malaysian or Indonesian decent began to scream, "Hallelujah! Praise Jesus! Praise Jesus! Remember the tower of Babel!"

"Jam all signals, for fucks sakes, jam it all and send Alt-Perceptors to all locations where people have viewed this. As for the footage, I want an editing team to make this look amazing. You know what, none of these people are leaving the building. Use the leverage files, buy them, buy their families, and send a team of Alt-Perceptors in there to untwist them if possible. If not possible, arrange a long list of inconspicuous accident deaths. Oh, and avoid car crashes as much as possible, everyone uses that too much," she mentally sent her intelligence team, thinking, *"twice have I ever seen people get their wires crossed like that, and the bitch who did that to my spy team, my son finds a way to fall in love and marry her daughter."*

"Remember the tower of Babel! Remember the tower of Babel!" Lailie started hearing more and more people in the room chant.

"If I extended my energy into the crowd just a little…yes, I can see what he's doing. I have the power to stop this on my own, but should I? In my entire life, I've never shown anyone I could touch the same energy threads as the Alt-Perceptors. Is now the right time to do it? Any spies watching would know it was me. No, I shouldn't, I've already called my teams into action."

"They're way more adapt at editing a situation like this with a feather's touch. If I start touching these people with my energy, I know I'd want to kill everyone on principal that I've lost control. I need to be mature, I'm the one who'd chosen them, knowing they wanted to hand me my ass. Yeah, now is not the time for flexing just because of my ego. And what the hell is wrong with my inhibitor? It's hot as hell, like my power is overwhelming it," she thought, gazing down at her wrist, at the device that was for both communication and for inhibiting her natural body energy.

"Teams in place Madam," she heard in her earbud.

"Perfect," she mentally replied, calmly gazing at those who wore religious items and effects.

"Classic material reinforcement mindset manipulation, but the new ambient energy is so strong, it allowed cross contamination," she thought, studying the journalist without religious effects, who were now looking at their fanatical peers with disgust and shock.

"Listen, okay, I understand everyone's fear, but I'll be frank, humanity flat out failed ourselves and mother nature already. Our fear of this should've been used for the real problem we already knew was coming but let happen anyway. We over used and abused earth, and if we don't do something now to retrieve materials at a relatively cheap, consistent rate, everything will collapse. The sad part is that even if everything collapsed economically, all the census data shows that the global populations would still increase for a while until we are at ultra-critical, meaning we'd be at a point where we literally couldn't feed another soul, and then we'd all die.

"So listen, we either ask our respective God or Deities to forgive us and allow us to reach into the heavens so that we can save ourselves, or, or we behave like primal rats who've overpopulated a contained area, where we begin to eat each other to survive, which I'm sure all of you know is already happening in some places. If our Deities are as good as the scriptures say they are, then we all know they do not want their blessed creations behaving in such manner!"

"If any one of you believe their Deity wants us to fail at this project, then ask yourself. If your Deity has given every person the ability to reason with each other, and unite with love, respect, and commonality, then why now are you chanting for pure segmentation of religion and people!? And well, well, that'd be hypocritical huh? And counter intuitive of what many of your Deities ask of you, which is to spread the word! You don't want to speak the same language! You don't want a common tongue to commune with!? Well then, you would've to stop sending missionaries to spread the word! Right?"

In an instant, all the hysterical people fell silent, yet the smell of toxic energy intensified.

"Ah, the terrible scents of hypocrisy! With this silence, they're actually screaming louder. Still, I'll enjoy this. So desperate to crush this idea, they made their own trap. But I guess it makes sense…I'm dealing with the purest forms of hypocrisy, logic need not be sought after," she thought, as she said, "Okay, good night everyone."

Still, everyone remained dead silent, with those who'd be hysterical, wearing looks of deep consideration and confusion.

"It's sad, now I really want one of them to be brave enough, and or angry enough to open their mouth. Argue against me, and argue why your religion should spread. Argue and hammer nails into your religion. Please, argue and make everything you stand for a fallacy!" she thought, seeing in her contacts the timer for her intervention teams to arrive hit forty-five seconds.

Turning to the right, she calmly walked off the stage and out the double doors her guards opened for her.

When she was far enough away, and the doors closed, she laughed and said, "did you see how quite they got? Ha-ha, I actually enjoyed that last part way too much," to her number One, Two and Three, who took up protective positions around her as she began to walk towards the helipad, where a helicopter was just rising up and departing, with Adam and the familiar figure of a woman rocking in the gust of the down washed wind.

"Annoying, she's so annoying. More so because she's actually really sexy. It's hard enough not wanting to just stare at her through the coms. Seeing her in person, now I have to

557

ignore myself or she'll honey pot me," she whispered, stopping in her tracks, watching as Adam and Saraswati came down the stairs onto the main level of the rooftop.

"Daily, I grit my teeth at having to deal with Adam, and now you keep popping up in my life...I'm not..."

"Lailie, where is the gift I gave you? Did you look at it?" she heard Saraswati cut in using a soft nurturing tone.

"No, I've been busy," she replied, remembering not trusting or even going near it, having her guards take it to one of her hundreds of sealed off, empty vaults she had scattered throughout the world.

"You had it shipped off, you didn't even glance at it huh?"

"Huh?" she mumbled

"Unbelievable! You're always too suspicious," she heard Saraswati say.

"Would you trust you? No, because you don't even trust you. As you breathe, you lie, scheme and deceive. You have zero honor, and you want me to open some box you gave me. I thought it was a damn bomb or something. Why are you here? Adam, why'd you bring her here?" she asked, glaring at Adam.

"We all need to talk, and I knew you'd say no," she heard Adam say.

"This could've been done over coms," she replied, staring at Saraswati, beginning to grow flustered, loving the see-through red and gold Sari she wore.

"She's stunning, head to toe, just absolutely stunning. If her malice didn't mirror my own, I'd want to spend hours exploring her body. But I know she'd destroy me the moment she sensed weakness. Hell, I know I'd do the same."

"Over coms!? You always want to hang up!" she heard Saraswati reply.

"It's you, she has good reason to be honest," she heard Adam reply flatly.

"Anyways, Lailie, let's go to one of your private chambers, one that you have sealed off from everything. And I was thinking, we should all go to the meeting together," she heard Saraswati reply.

"I don't want to be alone with her, and I sure as hell don't want to go to the meeting with her! What's she up to? We don't have time to go chat,

558

we need to be leaving right now. So, does she want to see my route and mode of transportation to the sacred site? Why though? What would she gain? As fundamentally amazing as it is, it's also simply mundane," she thought in frustration when a warm, sweet summer breeze wrapped around her, offering her Adam and Saraswati's scents.

"What the hell? For the first time in my life, their scents are not making me nauseous?" she thought, folding her arms, staring at Saraswati, who was just a hair shorter than her, before looking up to Adam who stood at just under one hundred eighty-three centimeters.

"Why are you being indirect? We all know we don't have time to go chat somewhere."

"Well then, that settles it," she heard Saraswati say with a small smile spreading across her lips.

"So, you came here to force me to take you to the meeting? This is childish."

"You can always say no," she heard Saraswati reply, biting her bottom lip, seeming anxious.

"Stop that!" she thought, feeling her nipples grow firm as she said, "What if I said no? How would you get to the meeting? You're a long way from home and…Humm, you would've never left yourself without an out. Have old nodes reactivated in the energies?" she asked, studying Saraswati and Adam's for tells.

"If you're going to say no, say no now so I can be on my way. If yes, let's talk in transit, I'm sure it's just as secure as one of your rooms, if not more so," she heard Saraswati reply, looking at Adam, then to her with a victorious look on her face.

"Ridiculously childish, yet, yet I'm won over. No wonder we don't kill our annoying offspring, their simple manipulations are so ridiculous, it works by default," she whispered, enjoying every moment of the breeze as it kissed her skin, turning and walking to a small door tucked in-between the helipad and the main doors of her penthouse.

"I feel like I don't know myself today. Am I doing this because I no longer fear her, or because I secretly just want her to try something, so we can fight it out once and for all?" she thought, steeping in front of the small door, mentally commanding it to open before making a small hand gesture for Saraswati and Adam to enter.

Watching them enter, she could see that both seemed puzzled and smiled as she turned and looked at her guards who'd fallen back to give them privacy.

"I have that meeting, go take care of your personal matters, the ones we were discussing earlier. I know I said to just go do it, but all of you know I'm fast, fast, fast. In reality... I'd say take your time, give yourselves time to enjoy every aspect. It will not be realistic if they lay await with legs open. Go and try to win a lady...or a man over," she said, steeping backwards through the door, seeing her guards all giving her sidelong looks of apprehension.

"Enjoy?" she heard Saraswati ask when the door closed.

"Yes," she replied, mentally sending instructions to her HR team to go speak to the women that'd congregated at the ice-cream stand.

"Interesting choice of words," she heard Saraswati whisper.

"Why? Am I not allowed to say happy things?"

"It's you," she heard Adam remark just as dryly as he had when he'd said the same regarding Saraswati.

"You can no longer use that logic," she replied with a chuckle.

"Why's that?" she heard Adam reply sarcastically.

"I don't feel the same since rebirth. Think about it, would either of you ever think I'd turn my back to Saraswati in a confined space? No, right? But if you want the other me, then I'm genuinely surprised I don't feel a knife in my back, and my throat being slit," she replied, turning around as the chamber expanded, with the walls turning translucent, revealing that they were traversing in a pod through a tunnel deep beneath the Mediterranean Sea.

"I've looked for this for years, but nothing shows up when I've sent people to find it," she heard Saraswati reply, looking around, touching the walls in what looked to her to be false curiosity.

"My parents and my Order discussed this, telling me to keep my eyes and ears open for this when Lailie and I had been paired. I'd spent countless hours roaming this building and the surrounding ones, and found nothing. Then on my twentieth birthday, to my surprise, Lailie took me on here. I, of course reported it to my Order, and they told me to investigate further. I wonder if that's their form of a humorful request, because I can do that all I want and get nowhere, nor can any teams they've sent to help me. If she doesn't take me on here, I can't access it. When that door opens, it's just an enormous tunnel that goes down as far as the foundation, and that's that," she heard Adam say with a snicker.

"Why does this interest either of you to such a caliber? All of our bloodlines and organizations have something similar for modes of transport to the sacred sites," she replied, feeling an odd, being watched or studied sensation travel through her body from somewhere in the distance, causing her to genuinely look towards the ocean in search of who or what it was.

"Sometimes, you surprise me with your assumptions, do you have evidence of this?" she heard Saraswati whisper.

"No, you're right, I assumed. But I make this assumption based on how I know this one works. From that, I never bothered to look into how the rest of you move about to the sacred sites. Our ancestors seemed to have worked very hard making these transport methods as elusive as possible. I don't like wasting energy on looking for something that moves a person, when I can just wait a little while, and find the person when they are more exposed...Utterly beautiful," she replied, staring into the depths, surprised at her appreciation for what she was seeing, as it'd always been just background to her.

"Humm, is that so? In that case, how would you say this works? And yes, it is beautiful," she heard Saraswati reply.

"I'm just realizing that I always liked coming here, that I'd leap at the opportunity to do so. My husband recognized it though. And when he'd try to cater to it or bring it up, I'd rip his fucking head off. I now find it funny how I've guarded something seemingly so small," she replied as the sensation of being studied moved behind her, changing to one of being hunted with malice.

"It makes sense why you'd hide small parts of your heart. Um, just wondering, can this thing move any faster?" she heard Saraswati whisper.

"So, that feeling was not just my imagination? Interesting, I didn't imagine you as the type to be afraid of anything," she replied, turning directly towards the sensation, daring whatever it was to reveal itself.

"Fear, no. Uncomfortable, yes. That sensation was new to me," she heard Saraswati mumble, looking toward Adam who nodded his head in agreement.

"Well, we're going as fast as it can go," she replied, forcing herself to ignore the feeling, focusing on Saraswati.

"What?" she heard Saraswati ask, following her eyes as she looked her up and down as if sizing her up.

"While you're, I guess, sizing me up. I have a question. What's with your Sari? Not very traditional for your culture. You look more like a belly dancer with those see-through parts," she replied.

"I wanted to wear something more reflective of how I feel today. I want to show off how sexy I am. When I get home, I'll just have my guard dog, Alt-Perceptors, make everyone else see a regular Sari," she heard Saraswati say, looking into her eyes, then past her in the same moment the sensation of being hunted vanished.

"Guard dogs? Pfft. I can confidently speak for all my Order, no matter which house they belong, the symbiosis with types like you two is awful. The imbalances you both represent is full blown disgusting," she heard Adam say in a dark tone.

"Being around us just makes all in your Order painfully aware of your own imbalance. True to your kind, you Alt-Perceptors are the only ones who can trick even themselves into believing they are stable. At least with us, if we're not being babysat by your Order, we'd revert to our true forms. I don't think anyone, including yourselves know who you are or what you'd become if y'all didn't have our energies flowing within you from symbiosis parings," she heard Saraswati say, giving Adam a nasty look.

"Speaking of pairings, Saraswati, where are your handlers by the way? Is their absence the reason you don't smell disgusting? And Adam, why do you not smell like trash as well? Since our pairing, you've always had this sour smell coming off of you."

"Humm," she heard Saraswati reply, giving her a questioning look, while Adam looked away from her.

The view outside began to turn ever so slightly dark, ten seconds later, everything went pitch black, less the soft red glow of the pods' internal lights.

"Are we here, does this mean we've arrived at the sacred site?" she heard Saraswati ask with a mirthful smile spreading across her lips.

"Neither of you going to answer my question?" she replied.

"Lailie, since this morning, we've outgrown each other, just as you've outgrown Adam. I've quickly accepted it, whereas you seem heartbroken that Adam will be leaving you," she heard Saraswati reply.

"Adam, you spread our business so fast!"

"Oh please, don't blame Adam, he never said a word. I just know longing; heart aching looks when I see it. I figured he must've told you he's leaving. Humm, I wonder if your dependence on him is due to your Lilith bloodline being weaker than my own."

"Not this shit again, for the billionth time," she whispered.

"I want you to accept truth that we Yogini were the originals. All of Lilith bloodline find that hard to accept. We have stories depicting that even the first Lilith herself went around trying to destroy all proof of this," she heard Saraswati say with a snide smirk.

"If Yogini are the originals, then why allow us to exist, why have none of you ever brought the fight to us and tried to wipe us out? Right, because stupidity or your culture made you fuck like rabbits and dilute your gene pool, and now it'll take hundreds of you Yogini temple bitches to take me on, and that's with my limiter on. Dare I take it off," she said, chuckling darkly knowing that her boast was only half true.

"Triggered so fast over smack talk, relax would you," she heard Saraswati reply with a chuckle.

"You weren't smack talking. You always spew that garbage. Look, what the hell do you want? We've used the transport, big whoop. We're in private, discuss what it is you'd wanted to discuss. If you really don't have anything important to say and everything was just to ride this thing, then don't just fill the air with bullshit, just shut the fuck up and let's go to the meeting in silence," she replied.

563

"I am discussing things I wanted to discuss. Lailie, you're losing patience with me so fast. Faster than normal I should say."

"Because this is some of the same old bullshit, no need to be private, no need for you to be here," she replied.

"Well I had already asked you about what I'd sent you. You said you know nothing since you're saying you didn't look, which I think is a lie, I'm sure you did some form of check. So that's still something I want to talk about. And there's something obvious that I think you know I want to ask you, and for sure I know this topic should be private," she heard Saraswati reply.

"Like?" she whispered with a sigh.

"Like the changes you've experienced since awaking this morning? And if you, you remember the last three days prior? I, I don't remember anything," she heard Saraswati say without a stutter, but with enough hesitation it made her grit her teeth.

"She lies for lies sake! It's why I cannot stand her! And what's her gain in knowing anything of my death and rebirth? I don't remember anything! I just woke up this morning, feeling vibrant and refreshed, but not fully my old self," she thought, studying Saraswati and Adam carefully.

"I really don't remember a thing, and I'm sure it's as it should be. You don't remember things when you're dead. From your tone, I think you're lying, and that maybe during your death you had some 'kinda' spirit journey that you remembered small bits and pieces. I can't figure out why you care about what I'd experience, and I pride myself on being a strategist."

"I'm genuinely curious of course, and of course, it helps me size you up. Why are you not asking me questions to do the same? Or have you taken on the assumptions that everyone experienced something similar?" she heard Saraswati ask.

"I just don't care. I'll start seeing how everyone has metamorphed very soon, and then I'll act accordingly. After this little meeting, depending on how it goes, I'll begin my test, and undoubtedly, everyone else will begin theirs as well. I see no need for private interviews," she replied flippantly.

"I maybe your adversary, but I also want to help you as it doesn't benefit me to ever completely destroy you or your bloodline, even if I had the means and method. If anything, us talking right now, I seek information that may reveal both weakness and strength in both of us," she heard Saraswati reply.

"Really?"

"Yes, really. Our bloodlines are like the Polar and Grizzly bears. Different enough, but at the core, the same enough where they can mate and have fertile offspring."

"Well in general, somehow, we've all been diluted by the Homo Sapien bloodline, your argument is…well never mind, I get what you're saying. Okay, I'll humor you," she replied, as a soft chime went off followed by a neutral voice saying, "Depressurization and detoxification complete."

A door opened behind Adam and Saraswati, and a warm, sweet, salinized breeze she loved rushed in to great her.

"After you," she whispered, gesturing for Adam to take the lead.

"Sure," she heard him reply, giving her a strange look of consideration before stepping into the dark chamber, aglow with light that came from the smooth dark brown surfaces of the almost perfectly circular chamber.

"This is …interesting," she heard Saraswati whisper, shaking her head left and right behind Adam as they stepped out of the pod.

"Maybe I do assume too much, I for sure thought your transport would look similar, but you seem like you're totally unfamiliar with this," she replied, watching Saraswati touch the dark brown wall then look at her hand, titling her head in curiosity, whispering, "it's growing warm."

"Is it?" she asked, touching the wall, feeling a warmth she'd never felt before.

"As much as you assume Lailie, I'm surprised you don't fail way more often,"

"I barely blink at failure and keep moving forward so fast. I make my goals a success no matter how many failures I face, plain and simple," she replied, trying to give Saraswati a hard look, to no avail as she was still with her back to her, running her hands along the walls.

"So Lailie, since you're willing to humor me, you say you've noticed Adam and I's scents like they were part of your norm, is it? From what my spies have told me, only for brief movements in time during your childhood, or very, very brief moments during your cycle as a young lady were the only times you've ever caught the scent you're describing, am I right?"

"I've always had the ability to pick up body energy scents. And even more so, real scents. Without Adman's impediment energies, even the tiniest non-organic chemical scent, like inks and dyes for clothing would make me so nauseous I'd want to kill myself. To be honest, even with Adam always around me and my limiter working at full strength, I've always had the ability to break free and tap into the abilities afforded to me by my bloodline. His energy and presence has always made me…I don't know the word, not be deeply interested in doing so, whereas now I feel like …I'm more inclined, but hesitant. I want to be responsible for my actions, and I want to make sure what I do, I'd be in full control if Adam were not here."

"So, with this new energy, what will you do? For centuries, your bloodline has been trying to completely take over and maintain control of the land between the Nile and the Euphrates. You just backed up the stance for world peace, but don't you want to tap into your power and make that dream of your bloodline a reality?" she heard Saraswati ask, turning to her with a pensive look on her face.

"You don't know me as much as you think you do," she whispered, seeing both Adam and Saraswati give her a sarcastic look, causing her to say, "well, the ambition is right, but you don't understand the actions I took towards them. Trust me, I've taken into consideration why my parents chose to link up with our opposites after the Holocaust. Choosing to slowly absorb Palestine and the lands around them is absolutely tedious, and cause abrasion between the populaces."

"Yet, doing things without using brute force has yielded more gain for my bloodline than anything else. The Holocaust was proof that if we move with reckless abandonment, it draws too much attention. The same can be said about the Alt-Perceptor house who created the Nazi regime to wipe out my bloodline as well. Them rallying and manipulating people to do such a huge purge and conquer, led to a good number of sheep evolving to the likings of the ruling class predators, all just to restore balance. It's a good thing most died in battles by the end of that war, or as we all know, there would've been another war between us Shepard's that would've destroyed everything."

"Y'all are strange to me Lailie. Always, this part of the world is in chaos because of people having too much opportunity. This is laughable for me. In India, we make sure our people know what class system they belong to since birth, and to stay in their place or else suffer the worst of consequence," she heard Saraswati say.

"Yes, I heard you had a man of a lower class beat to death for owning a horse, when he shouldn't have been wealthy enough to do so," she replied, raising her eyebrow at Adam who shook his head in an – 'that's ridiculous' manner.

"Yes, yes I did. His death, and any like it, is necessary. That way, even when my people move abroad they can't escape their mental prisons. We've ingrained into the fiber of their being a reminder of who they are at every moment of their life, or else. Every action they take, someone, somewhere, somehow reminds them of who they are, where they fit, what is acceptable, and what isn't. And as much as some fight this, most fall right back in, becoming another reinforcement of what is and what isn't, forcing their kids, cousins, lovers into the fold."

"From my peoples' study and my own, the three Alt-Perception religions used to control this region are too contradictory to the inner energies of the populace. I'm not saying the religions do a poor job of oppressing and mentally subjugating those who follow it. If anything, I'm saying it works too well. The three religions allow people to fall into hopelessness while receiving absolute love from their Deity, giving them the ability to ride waves of natural blood lust and self-preservation, with the religion that is supposed to be pacifying this as fuel.

"In India, we replace hopelessness with absolution by establishing cast of life and status. We make sure everyone is way too busy caught up in the constancies of this to fall into hopelessness or hopefulness to ever evolve. And of course, we kill and utterly brutalize the outliers and their families as 'back of the mind' reminders to further trap people who even think of freedom from the rat race," she heard Saraswati say.

567

"Good for India, what do you want me to say?" she replied, smiling, remembering her eldest daughter, sarcastically slow clapping at one of the LiL-Guard recruits for answering a question, wanting to do the same.

"Nothing, just saying...I disagree with you parents and your methods. In my eyes, you are failing. I think it's absurd that you believe you're winning by the tactic of erosion and absorption. In absorption, factually, you're becoming a blend of something else. That was not the way of the Lilith bloodline. I think you should ingrain better social class structures within your people, and then complete the ownership of the land you want. On your opposition's side, they are losing control of their people, but are quickly regaining it with hardliners. Syria and Iraq are great success for your opposition. If you can take over their lands, you can harm them, and help them. They'd be able to take advantage of the chaos, take deeper control of their peoples' mindset, and you can fortify your new borders," she heard Saraswati reply.

"Fuck yo...never mind. I think right now, a lot of what we're doing is pointl...I think we're all painting canvas after canvas, and the paint dries, gets old and cracks," she whispered.

"Huh?" she heard both Adam and Saraswati reply, sounding winded.

"Nothing, nothing," she replied, feeling her rage grow as Saraswati's verbal slaps began to resonate deeper.

"You little...," she began when Adam stepped between them and said, "I found something very, very important. I gave it to Saraswati first, and that's what she sent to you. And of course, you shoved it in a vault without looking."

"Oh, for fuck sakes! I opened the box, I glanced at it, it gave me a bad feeling. And the color of it. If that material is what I think it is, I'm intrigued but not foolish or curious enough to mess with it. If it's a forge, then to me, it's still a trap," she said, glaring past Adam to Saraswati, who smiled at her, mouthing, "If you react in anger, shame on you, not me."

"What a mindset! They shield themselves from being destroyed by the irritation they cause by turning your loss of temper into a statement that you have lost control due to their ability to manipulate your emotions! Damn it, that's even more infuriating!" she thought, now feeling even more

inclined to lose her temper, only to yet again become trapped by the paradox of Saraswati's words.

"I knew you looked! But I don't get you looking and not doing anything!" she heard Saraswati reply with her voice raising an octave.

"I like you sounding choked. Yes, I did nothing, please say something to sound desperate again," she said, seeing Saraswati's light brown face grow red in frustration.

"Lailie, I know you know that material is authentic. When seeing it like that, it's absolutely unmistakable. And I know you saw it had depictions of Vajrayogini and what looks like a Lilith as well. I know both of your bloodlines have always been looking for hard proof of what's what. So, you had a bad feeling? Really? Because if you're not lying, then still, I would think you would've done more. You never were the type to sit on a bad feeling without action," she heard Adam whisper.

As they talked, they'd walked, and were now standing in front of an almost six-meter-high circular, translucent structure, with ridgelines running through it and a circular hub almost directly in the middle.

"Where did you find it?" she asked, thinking *"Why are they surprised about my caution? If that's true crystalized material from the Living Scripture Fountain…why in all hell would they share such a thing without there being a dangerous catch?"*

"I took it directly from the ruins of Babel," she heard Adam reply flatly.

"The ruins of the tower of Babel! What!? No! No! No! No! No! You're very young in your Order, they would never, ever let you near there. Just no! The Houses in your Order rarely ever get along, but the one thing they all stand unanimous on, is the rules of that sacred ground. And dare I infer the incident just now with the journalist, would that have been your doing? If not directly, then via a person or persons of your Order meddling. And, what are you doing trying to help Saraswati or I find out anything about ourselves? If we learn anything, it could give us the upper hand. Why did you risk throwing off the current balance of power?" she said, feeling chills run up her spine as she thought of the implications of different Houses among the Alt-

Perceptor Order aiming the full brunt of their disgusting, self-righteous wrath at her and everything she'd built and stood for.

"Well, I don't know what I'm trying to accomplish, other than to learn what's going on! I haven't been taking the balances of power into consideration because on my end, there is no longer a need to protect what isn't there! The only two people I even slightly trust is you two!" she heard Adam blare.

"What? What do you mean?!" she asked, backing up and steeping sideways to study Adam and Saraswati's body language more clearly.

"Many of the Houses in the Order of Alt-Perceptors are no more," she heard Adam reply, sounding shaken.

"Uh, no! Excuse me!?" she gasped as a feeling of loss and dread began to engulf her.

"December twenty-first, last year, some of the strongest Elders began to recluse themselves, no longer sending direction to any of us. At the same time, the Houses controlling Christianity and Islam stopped squabbling. They literally didn't have even one argument. There was just silence, without energies to even show if the silence was founded on peace, grief, or resentment. My House of Judah and House of Islam held a meeting. Afterwards, House of Islam met with House of Hindu and House of Buddha. Then, all the Elders of every House met. I have no idea what took place in those meetings. All I know is that by December twenty-fifth, almost all of the members in the House of Christianity just simply vanished, leaving only the Pope and a few young ones. After this, on each one of the Houses' respective founding dates, all would vanish, less one elder and again a few young ones…such as myself."

"Do not disrespect me! I would've sensed weakness and marched my army to Babel! For far too long the Alt-Preceptor Order has maintained control over far too many artifacts and documents of all of our origins!" she screamed, shaking in anger.

"We have lived side by side as adversaries since our paring as children. Do not disrespect me, claiming I wouldn't directly insult you to your face! When I want to use words to smack you, I smack you, true or false!" she heard Adam retort, raising his voice to a level she'd never heard before.

"*True. He never misses a beat to mock me for any of my small overlooking's, let alone any of my larger failures. This look on his face, this power I feel rushing from his core, it's immense and dominating! I'd throw myself to him if it didn't also make me hate myself!*" she thought as her cheeks began to burn and nipples began to harden.

"I said, true or false?" she heard Adam press, causing her pussy to throb.

"True," she replied, looking at Saraswati, who appeared just as flustered and aroused as she felt, seeing her look down to the floor, with her light brown cheeks flushing red.

"You felt no power vacuum because, well, because much of it transferred to everyone who remained. The rest, the rest that we could not absorb, it's being absorbed by people all over the world. That situation during your conference, is that ambient energy playing havoc."

"I felt your strength increase, but it should be much more if you absorbed what you're saying you have! Shit! What you said about the conference does explain why that scent was traveling around like a gas," she practically growled, balling her fist.

"Well, I've absorbed energies I don't know how to handle, so with my last remaining Elders' help, I've inhibited myself. It's the only responsible way. I can't risk losing control," she heard Adam respond.

"I'm surprised you haven't challenged me, even a little," she whispered, trying to put herself in Adam's position to understand why he'd chose caution and reservation.

"I just told you why. You, being yourself, suffer from cognitive dissonance," she heard Adam say.

"Excuse me!?"

"You always speak of action, and yes, you act rashly, but only to an extent where everything you do damage wise is manageable. Same can be said of your daughters. All four of you know that the strength you have individually could surpasses thousands of weaker ones of my House. This is despite my up close presence, and with y'all are wearing powerful Alt-Percept inhibitors. The cognitive dissonance you have when you speak of action is that, it's your nature, as well your daughters to actually to be mindful. All four of you, honestly respect power balances, but then act surprised when others do as well," she heard Adam

571

say, with his eyebrows raised in an, 'this is really the way it is' look.

Lailie stood still and visualized everything Adam mentioned, then said, "Yes, I see, this further reiterates your decision regarding Nate,"

"Yes," she heard Adam whisper.

"Still, I didn't like that cognitive dissonance comment, or the fact that earlier you tried to make me feel okay with possibly needing to kill him," she replied, glaring at Adam, finding him now somewhat checked out of reality.

"Damn it," she heard Adam say after a few more seconds where he'd stared off in space, mouthing something inaudible to himself.

"What?" she asked, placing her hands on her hips in impatience.

"We were talking about the artifact, then we got side tracked," she heard Adam reply.

"Yes, of course we did, you just told me the craziest shit ever. And it was not all the way off topic, everything's related. Okay, so… what about this artifact do you want to discuss?" she asked, thinking *"I don't want to leave here. I don't want to stop talking. What's this feeling? Am I afraid? No, I'm not! Am I? I feel like I can't even think about the meeting. I know we should get to the next transport area. And it's not just me, I can tell they want to talk as well. Are we stalling?"*

"You tell us what you think we want to discuss, you saw it and…" she heard Saraswati begin, when she cut in and said, "anyways, Adam please continue."

"Well, I found it laying on the floor, next to many others lining the floor on the way to Living Scripture Fountain," she heard Adam reply with reflective look.

"Were they similar shapes, sizes, colors, or like different kinds of artifacts? Were they lining the floor like gifts? Or were they positioned there with some form of purpose?" she heard Saraswati ask, stealing her similar line of questioning from the tip of her tongue.

"All were teardrop shaped like just like that one. Sizes were largest in the outer most row where I'd found it. Colors, all the same as well, appearing to be made up of the crystalized Fountain

572

fluid. Also, all of them had art like engravings, along with the perfect centerline indentation band," she heard Adam whisper.

"They all sound similar. So then, what, you just picked that one up?" she asked.

"To be honest, I had strong visions of those things when I was a child, and I never knew where or really what it was. In my dreams, this one's exact engravings were always there, yet oddly enough, finding it was very lack luster. I'd walked into the chamber on a mission to finally see the Living Scripture Fountain with my own eyes, and when I stepped in, there were just rows and rows of those things on both sides of the floor. None of them called to me, and my dreams from childhood were far from my memory. I wasn't interested in them whatsoever, and just wanted to focus on the Fountain."

"Then on one of my trips, my eyes rested on it while I was thinking about the Fountain, and that's when I remembered my dreams. I mean like you said Lailie, they're all similar, but something about those engravings hit me just right. Actually, truth be told, even after recognizing the images, I had to push past dismissing it as a coincidence and force myself to go examine it. But, when I touched it, I had a vision of us three standing together. When the vision ended, I truly looked at the image of Vajrayogini and realized I'd not given enough attention to a symbol placed in line with the crown of her head."

"It's really, really faint, in my defense. Anyways, after a few reference checks, I'm certain it translates as, 'lighthouse shrouded by fog,' and well the other meaning for it is, 'shrouded' or 'hidden castle.' In Alt-Perceptor history, this was one of the original symbols representing the entire Order, when there were no separate Houses. On the opposite side of that symbol and Vajrayogini, there was an image that seems to depict the original Lilith. The only thing was that the wings looked a little off to me, but the state of the engravings, well you saw it, the engravings seem, worn down, faded. As supposedly robust as the material is said to be, being immensely difficult to harm once formed, I don't know if the artist made vague drawing and symbolic inscriptions on purpose, or somehow back then, our ancestors had the means to wear it down. Either way, I definitely wanted your opinion of the image Lailie."

"As for your question Saraswati, my first guess is that they're gifts, and that the images etched on them represent a truce our ancestors had during the construction of the tower. Lailie, the center indentation lines on them give me the feeling there's something inside. I tried to pry all along the indentation with tools, and as legend said, all my tools broke almost instantly. Next, I sent my body energy into it. To my amazement and surprise, I saw small movement around the indentation, as well as a very, very faint glow from deep within, lasting less than a second. For a few more days, I tried to do more with my body energy, and noting. Annoyed, I realized, if there were three separate bloodlines, why not ask you and Saraswati to examine it. I chose to ask her first, explaining that she should try sending her body energy into it. When she received it, she tried it and the shape changed again, this time with a much more noticeable difference."

"It confirmed my suspicion that it's bloodline specific in activation. So then, next was your turn, but both Saraswati and I had a feeling you'd do what you did, so we knew we would need to talk to you in person. And well, here we are now, telling you this story, as well as to ask you, once we're done with the meeting, let's go try to open it together. I have hopes it has answers to how to best work together in this new era, whether it would be stories of our bloodlines' peace or maybe failures, so we don't repeat them."

"He says he's inhibiting his power, but still, he should be exuding the power of an Elder because they can barely keep a cap on so much energy. Anytime I've ever gone near an Elder from an Alt-Perceptor house, their aura has almost been unbearable. Why can I stand next to him right now without feeling like I want to scrub myself clean for being a filthy animal. And he says he's visited the Living Scripture Fountain itself, yet chooses to discuss this artifact more than the Fountain!? One of the three main prized possessions of every Order, he has card blanch access to, and he treats it like it's mundane? Something's way off about this story. And we're still just standing here...why haven't I taken the lead and ushered us to go to the meeting. Am I afraid? I don't feel afraid...do I?" she thought, trying to digest what Adam said, picking apart everything he said, piece by piece.

"Lailie, are you listening to me?" she heard Adam ask, sounding agitated.

"Yes, maybe too closely to be honest. Pardon me, but you're telling me you have free access to roam around the sacred ruins of the tower, and free access to the Living Scripture Fountain, and zero excitement comes from you? What of others in your Oder? What else are you finding in what used to be one of the most guarded and sacred of places? Surely, there are way more significant things in there other than this artifact we're discussing!" she said, realizing she'd begun to shout.

"We all swarmed that place and quickly grew bored. All the stories of places to explore, hidden chambers full of knowledge, yeah, there's nothing. You walk in, and maybe twenty feet from the entrance, there's the Fountain. Literally, that's it to that place. I wish to hell there was more," she heard Adam reply.

"Oh, for fuck sakes. Fine then, what's the Fountain look like? Is it at least like the stories say, or is everything bullshit?" she asked.

"Umm, well, I don't want to call bullshit. But it doesn't look like what the stories describe. In the stories, it makes it sound like there's a center pieces with the emerald fluids of the Living Scripture coming from it. It's actually more simplistic and elegant. It's an eight-foot-wide, perfectly cut circular indentation in the ground, with the max depth, nearest the Fountain orifice being five inches. The orifice is a perfectly circular, two-foot hole, where you can see a small up current of the Living Scripture Fluid rising."

"So, there's an up current, but the shallow bowl, it doesn't overflow and flood the chamber?" she asked.

"No, the fluid stops dead on the line. And get this, other than that up current that's already barely perceivable, there's no ripples in the fluid whatsoever."

"Tell her about the beauty of it, and the scent" she heard Saraswati say, giving her a smug look.

"Beautiful, is it now?" she replied dryly.

"Yes, it's a perfect emerald green, that smells of both the purist toxicity, and the most lavish fruit. The ultimate, getting high off of paint or gasoline smell if you will. But the intrigue ends there. There's no words or sound appearing in it like the legends say. Many of us gave up on it being anything but what it looks like after only a few visits. And before you ask… yes, we sent probing body energies to do the measurements, and to see if anything reacts.

"And?" she asked.

"And, Lailie, there's a foreboding sensation the longer we'd done it, so we stopped. Body energy probes is where the studies ended. Even thinking about physically touching the liquid gave us all varying degrees of panic attacks," she heard Adam say.

"So, it's in communication with y'all, at least to tell all of you to respect it. Interesting, I want to see the Fountain with my own eyes. As for that artifact, I, still don't want to go near it. I know both of you have seen the uptick in artifact self-destructing since two thousand twelve, some have gone off rather violently. I honestly thought that's what you were up to Saraswati. Figured maybe you wanted to passively aggressively bomb me, killing the curious cat," she whispered.

"I'm shocked, shocked you don't invite me to come to the Fountain Lailie," she heard Saraswati reply – with a tone that said, 'why should I deny your accusation?'.

"That's because I don't want you to come, well unless you allow me to push you into it and see what happens," she replied, smiling at her reply, reflecting on what Adam said about the imagery of the wings, mentally accessing her vault machinery and cameras, moving and scanning the artifact carefully before saying, "Saraswati, my mother has always taught me, and shown me evidence there were seven variances of humans such as us. One for each of the seven era's. She, of course says, we were first, and that your bloodline came in the second era. She said the tell was that your bloodline was the only variant without wings, which is well documented in all second era's artifacts and writings."

"What are you getting at?" she heard Saraswati ask, sounding annoyed – which was somewhat her goal.

"Well, you're a knowledge gatherer by nature. And I admit, we Lilith are prideful and like to hone in on records that reinforce our beliefs. But having done my own extensive research, I don't necessarily agree there was one variance for each era."

"Are you sick Lailie?" she heard Saraswati ask, sounding shocked.

"No, not sick. Changing," she replied with a smile, before saying, "The issue our bloodlines have of course comes from the story of 'Garden of Eden.' It is well recorded that Lilith was Adam's first wife. Both our bloodlines agree with this is fact. The thing is, I've been wondering, would the story of Adam and Eve constitute as the first era? I wonder if your Yogini bloodline could have come in the time of people's before Adam and Eve. And that we are arguing over semantics. This situation and many others are causing me to reevaluate my strong bloodlines stance."

"Lailie?" she heard Adam and Saraswati both whisper, sounding shocked.

"I recorded both of your reactions. I'll masturbate to it later," she said in a flat tone, wanting to laugh, but also keep as serious as possible to make the moment as awkward for the two as possible.

"You, I just can't even believe my ears. You, who thumps her chest about her bloodline, say this!?" she heard Saraswati whisper.

"Shut up Saraswati. And Adam, please, are you really shocked?" she sniped, watching Adam shaking his head.

"Whatever, to both of you. As head of my family, my job is to be the chest thumper. In any case, I blame my failing narcissism for my bloodline on the dilution of my gene pool due to way too much mixing with the Homo Sapiens. With their weakness coursing through me, I question things I was told to believe with blind faith. Thus, I've been breaking into the sealed artifact vaults I was told to never open, discovering things that cast much doubt on not just the hardline stories I was taught about my bloodline, but all of ours."

"Doubts, that make you say you don't believe in bloodline segregations per era? That's probably the only thing any of us had ever agreed on," she heard Saraswati whisper.

"Well, I break down my thoughts in steps. As you both know, when the Lilith bloodline had been purer in nature, we had feathered wings. Saraswati, your bloodline had the extra set of arms, while the people of the South and Central America had scaled or skinned wings, supposedly at third and sixth era respectively. Yet, some of my most recent discoveries depict stories that the first Lilith herself met with those of scaled and skin wings. And at both of their meetings, they feasted on the blood of what they called the 'food source' - Homo Sapien."

"Then, after their feast, they had passionate love making sessions. If these records are true, and it was the first Lilith herself that was meeting these people, then none of the era timeline stories we've been taught and fussing about are true. Whether the original Lilith was from the first era, like my bloodline believes, or the second era like your bloodline believes, it is well documented she was no longer around before the third era as she had left the normal domains of earth to be with her lover of poisonous death. There would've been no way she could've met the scaled wings of the third era, or the skinned wings of the sixth era."

"I see," she heard Saraswati whisper, with an odd smile on her face.

"I'm sure I'll hate your answer, but what's that smile for?" she asked, gritting her teeth in anticipation what she was sure to be an annoying response from Saraswati.

"I wonder if the burning question that really caused you to break into your forbidden vaults is, why would the first Lilith wander into the 'Garden of Eden,' meeting Adam and choosing to have children with the Homo Sapien, the supposed prey species? I'm not saying that to be condescending, I'm saying that because, that question, among many others are why I've been breaking into the forbidden vaults of the Yogini. I want to know why our predatorial bloodlines all started intermingling with our food source, diluting us to the way we are now."

"Hum, yes, you've got me there. So, we are sometimes similar," Lailie mumbled.

"Well, of course we are. It's frustrating for us to be taught they are a prey species, yet now all of us, no matter what variance, are ninety percent just like them," she heard Saraswati whisper.

"Yes, so many chunks of history, missing. So many lies taught and gobbled up blindly," she said, reflecting on the one-way conversation she'd had with God.

"Well, there were seven fallen era's, as well as the seven rising. So off course there is a lot that would be lost. Why do you think we're discussing this artifact with you now? If it can be opened, we want to find out what's inside of it, past knowledge is power," she heard Adam say with his hands raised in a manner that said, 'what the hell? Do you not understand my reasoning!?".

"A seed well planted then, I feel swayed to help," she replied, hearing Adam chuckle, placing his hands down to his side, now giving her a 'ha-ha' smile.

"Go to hell Adam. I hate when you think you've beat me. Anyways, I'm mentally synced with the vault holding the artifact. Right now, I'm looking over the images, putting aside the worn-down look, you're right Adam, the wings do look off. You wanted my opinion, well I think this is a twisted rendition of her, or it's not the original Lilith at all as her wings and feather patterns are very distinct, and on every other artifact I've seen, the persons or person capturing her image were sure to show them off."

"I'm going to go with twisted rendition because her face looks just like Lilith," she heard Adam say, raising his eyebrow, which she knew was his way of saying, 'you're not really helping me'.

"Interesting times we're in. This would then be the only artifact I've ever seen like this. It's just way too odd. Actually, it still has a feathered look, but smoother, which makes me think they're scales…shaped like feathers," she replied, all of a sudden felling a strong urge to continue her journey to the meeting, followed by her knees going weak for just a moment.

'I am afraid! Why am I afraid to go to the meeting!? And what was that pull just now? It felt like it came from an Alt Perceptor!' she thought, feeling her legs quiver as she tried to take a step in the direction of the next transport node.

"Choosing to stay trapped in fear is an interesting behavior for those who consider themselves the Shepard's of the Sheep. All standing with their toes dug in the proverbial sand, discussing things, just to discuss them, planning things just to plan things, and posturing as if your power dynamics still matter. Not one of you believed your mundane actions would be able to carve out a reality where you'd remain in control of your fate. You all know you must come to this meeting, yet you all still tried. Since not one of you has come first, then all shall be led by the hand," she heard a stern, yet calming female voice say, resonating through her entire being.

"No! I'm not ready, not yet!" she heard Adam gasp, with his face turning pale as he gripped his chest.

"*Nor am I! Fuck! I thought so highly of myself! I've always looked down on anyone who's hesitated! I teach and preach facing fears, yet I allowed myself to stall over and over again!*" she thought, feeling shame and anger, seeing a similar reaction mirrored on Saraswati's face.

Below her, the ground grew hot, and as it did, she could see a type of softening and vibrancy in the surrounding surfaces. On her left, she heard a deep thudding sound of a drum, followed by the sight of rippling energy surrounding all three of them.

"*This looks like the same energy that envelopes me when I'm at the finally transfer node, but we're still a good five-minute walk from it! How's this possible?*" she thought, watching the rippling energy begin to smooth, leaving her standing in ankle deep water, facing a beautiful beach, with stars above so bright she instantly lost her breath.

"*Where is this!? Is this…? No, it can't be! But the star alignments! It has to be! This place has to be 'Peace!'*" Lailie thought, feeling and seeing her electronics, clothes and wrist inhibitor turn to beautiful, baby blue dust, floating away and vanishing, leaving her completely nude.

"*No inhibitor?! I've always wore one! What will happen to me?*" she thought as odd vibrations and sensations of hot and cold traveled along her body.

"This is…this must be 'Peace!' How can this be? And our positions! Unbelievable!" she heard Saraswati whisper, followed by Adam softly sobbing, whispering about the loss of his inhibitors and feeling disgusted that he was nude.

"Unreal," she whispered, looking around, seeing that she and thousands of others were standing in pattern, forming a trident.

"*Holly shit! I'm positioned as the spear tip of the middle spear head!*" she thought, seeing that Saraswati was slightly behind her on the left, facing the left spear head, which represented the Orders of Logic, Studies and Technology.

While Adam was slightly behind her on the right, facing the right spear head, which represented the Orders of Perception.

"All of you have awoken from your death's, knowing it was now time for ascension. The stories you've been taught since

580

birth were to prepare you for this. Resurrection and ascension means you are no longer welcome on earth! Yet, none of you capitalized on the days and hours you had to say goodbye and put your affairs in order. All of you chose to move about as if you had more time. Now here all of you stand, in fear and incompletion. Well, let those negative emotions go, as the time you've wasted, you cannot reclaim," Lailie heard a man say in a somewhat unsure voice that seemed to come from all places at once.

After the man had finished speaking, she felt so much fear and resentment, she could barely breath or see straight.

"I sense no release! Still only fear and uncertainty! Listen, all of us are here due to the Great Workings of our ancestors in the eras prior! And all of you are here to do a Great Working to welcome in this new era! Your Great Working will water the seeds you and your ancestors have sown, so that the human race can continue to thrive and be successful!" she heard the man say, now sounding extremely fearful himself, with his voice having broken and cracked at certain parts of his speech.

"Fuck you! You sound like a coward yourself!" she thought, now seeing a nude, muscular, male figure, with honey-brown skin, long, nappy, orange hair and blue-green eyes appear atop of a high sand mound which would allow him to overlook those who stood below him on the beach.

"Who are you!?" Lailie heard some from the crowd blare, while others screamed, "he must be a Tet rep! Kill him! Kill anyone Tet!"

"Silence!" Lailie heard a woman's voice command, seeing a beautiful nude female figure appear next to the man.

"The voice of the person who'd spoken before we were transported here," she thought, feeling self-conscious for standing in the very front, remembering how it felt to be called out by the woman for being afraid.

"Why'd she not speak first? The misogyny! It's traveled into the new era!" Lailie heard hundreds of women in the crowd say in perfect unison, realizing only after her mouth had stopped moving, that she'd also thought it and spoken the concern as well.

"Let's escape! Run! We cannot be held here! I've studied scriptures that speak of this day! It says there are ways to escape this!" she heard one man say, followed by many people asking, 'how,' or shouting, 'let's go!.'

"Filth! Why are we nude!?" she heard Adam and many of the other Alt-Perceptors scream in unison.

"This is the true voice we who call ourselves world leaders. It is sickeningly obvious that we're all just a bunch of conniving, petty cowards!" Lailie thought, feeling tears welling up in her eyes, forcing them to stop, hearing more and more people scream obscenities or try and convince each other to run.

"Good! I can at least slightly get a hold of myself and control my emotions," she thought, now taking in the details of the woman standing on the sand mound, noting her Pacific Islander facial feature, short, muscular frame, almond brown skin, and long and black hair, which ended at her ankles.

"Young, beautiful and commanding! She makes me proud to be a female!" she thought as she opened her mouth and yelled, "she said to be silent!" feeling a powerful wave of energy leave her body, rippling throughout the crowd.

"Good! Much better!" she thought as everyone fell silent, giving her peace, where she was now staring into the woman's light brown eyes, which seemed to hold every stars' light within them.

"All of your earthly concerns, such as who speaks first, where to run, or who to sweet talk to, to gain a favor from…none of it matters anymore, just let it all go," she heard the woman say in a calm, cool, collected voice.

"Shut up!" Lailie heard people scream, followed by raging outburst, all accompanied by shockwaves of energy that felt like hurricane force winds.

"We understand the anger and fear, but just let it all go. In this new era, an old tax humanity owes to itself must be repaid, and all of you here will be the currency. For those bloodlines who have prophecies, such as the return of Lanying, Nefeshka, Takumbo, the Master, the Makers and so on and so forth, their truths shall be reveled," she heard the woman say, with a tone of absolution.

Lailie was floored. The Prophecy was the fear that had always imprisoned her mind. Even during her death ritual, she had the Book of Lilith in hand, as she'd been looking for signs of Nefeshka's arrival and methods to protect her children.

"Be calm," she heard the woman say in a firm, controlled voice.

"Holy shit, what'd she just do?" Lailie thought, feeling all the limbs in her body go numb as if each had restricted blood flow.

"All of you, listen carefully. When Tet was all but destroyed two-thousand-seventeen years ago, the three Orders of the Trident were unable to, or chose to no longer be accountable for their responsibilities," she heard the woman say.

"Nefeshka! Talk about Nefeshka! Tell me!" she thought, feeling a pressure in her mind, followed by her fear floating away.

"Did you hear what I just said? Lailie, you're normally focused," she heard the woman say in her mind.

"I want to protect my children! I want answers! She wants me to listen and focus, but I want...Wait, what!? Wasn't Tet the first of all Tech Advancement Orders? But the way she just worded it would mean that Tet's is not a part of the Orders of three in the Trident!"

"I see that all of you are focused and have now understood my implication clearly. There has been much confusion and misinformation handed down to all of you for generations. Tet was never, and never will be an Order of the three. Those who are truly of Tet are the extract, or refined product of all three Orders. We are the personification of the Alchemic yields of every Order."

"As in Alchemy, the product of any work is always used. In the seventh era, technology was far behind where it needed to be in order for humanity to survive, therefore, true Tet agents worked tirelessly to have humanity pick up its pace in all advancements. Our final push, being the instigation for the development of the space elevator. Yet in seventh era, many dragged their feet in the sands of selfishness, that only till the cusp between the seventh and the eighth era, did any of you begin to accomplish work on this project in earnest. Humanity must hurry in the reclamation of the Ether. Now that everything is set in motion, it is time for the next phase."

"*Reclamation of the Ether? Her wording again, but in what capacity does she mean? Many text and artifacts have shown me that humanity had already achieved space travel at least once per era. But from the many I've studied, none show to what degree. But her emphasis on the word reclamation…sounds like, we did much,*" Lailie thought, feeling her mind being pulled into darkness, before seeing an orientation change where earth was sliding away from view at immense speed.

"Why!? Why not let humanity stay beings of earth!? There's no need for technology! Technology has only ever led to our near extinction! Let humanity of this new era cast down all technology and live in faith, where they love nature and worship something of ultimate divinity!" Lailie heard many voices of the Alt-Perceptor Order say in unison.

"Tet wants humanity to live free, and if we do not fulfill our promise and our purpose, humanity would be forced into a fate of pure suffrage, due to the tax we've imposed on ourselves. Picture humanity as an exploding star. The gasses and shedding materials would be all the amazing, relevant, beautiful things forming a nebula, that could one day form new stars and planets. Now envision pure selfishness as the mindset of billions of people. Imagine that this selfishness is the exploding stars' gravity, that will pull in everything around it."

"In this case, the selfishness would be pulling in even more people, making them pure selfish and hateful as well. If mass, or in this case, toxified people are not moved away fast enough, a type of black hole will form. This is a critical time for humanity, for unlike past era's, due to a great many events unfolding, humanity has zero time to recover and work on bettering themselves. In truth, humanity does not even have the luxury of making itself go extinct, and not suffer from the consequences of their prior actions," she heard the woman say.

"What!?" she heard herself and all the others ask in unison, along with a unified shock wave pulsing out, which somehow stopped short of both the man and women standing on the sand mound.

"The energies of Aquarius have now begun resynchronizing the nodes of our ancestors. Earth will now become re-known to all throughout the cosmos. Vengeful, impatient, long ago

584

weakened parties, who have now, or are currently looking to gain strength, are now wanting payment and retribution. All of you must be the buffer," Lailie heard the woman say, parting her legs, reveling dark red blood running down from her pussy.

"No! Let us out! Let us out of here then! There's so much more we can do! We have data networks that still need to be set up! We have patents for spaceships! We have patents for Nano-Technology! We have! We can!" Lailie heard people from the many houses of the Tech Order beg and plead.

"All Orders, listen to my warning! Do not go back to the place you've poisoned. You will find that you will not be able to bear your own toxicity. Staying here, becoming the buffer, and the first payment of a large tax debt humanity owes is the fastest way humanity can even be slightly ready for what is to come," she heard the woman say.

"Known throughout the Cosmos? And not have the luxury of making ourselves extinct!? Excuse me!? What are you implying!? Clarify that!" she blared, trying to stare down the young woman, feeling herself balk in apprehension, redirecting her angry look toward the man who was looking around at everyone, seeming jittery and nervous.

Then the man's whole body jerked erratically, as if he were being struck multiple times by a powerful, invisible force.

When the man stilled, he then calmly returned her gaze and said, "take a look for yourself," with his attitude changing to one of fearless dominance.

'Look at what!', she was going to say when a burst of images and voices began to play in her mind's eye.

"*Oh shit!*" she thought, realizing she was now connected to all six thousand, sixty-four people forming the trident along with the man and woman who stood in front of them.

"*This is too much! I want this to stop!*" she thought, feeling smothered and ripped apart by so much anger, hatred and unyielding beliefs, smashing into her.

"All of you are fighting it of course," she heard the man whisper as the images and sounds became even more erratic.

"*Who are you two? Who were you two before you became Tet?*" Lailie thought, suddenly finding herself pulled into the woman's mind, now feeling herself floating in water, staring up at a starlit, night sky before jumping into the man's mind, seeing flashbacks of a life filled with joy, despite him and his family being utterly destitute.

She then saw and felt the man's joy change to that of fear and confusion as suddenly him and his family had been rounded up at gun point, and placed on a bus. Through his eye, she watched him and his entire family being tied up before a bag was placed over his head. Pure silence, a command from one of the soldiers who'd tied them, then searing pain for just a moment, then nothingness.

"That last part, that's what just happened to him right in front of my eyes! He's from Papua New Guinea. He was just purged in one of Indonesia's land grabs. I can't believe it. I just literally watched this man die. The way he was speaking and behaving. The fear, the shaky voice, it all makes sense. He was in two places at once. So then, how's he not fully dead? How's he here?" she thought, hearing the man say in her mind, **"you've seen my life, and I've seen yours. Besides losing your children, it seems to me that you fear yourself more than anything else. Now is the time to address that, or you'll destroy yourself and all around you, which in turn will hurt all of humanity. You are the tip of the first spear head, you are supposed to be their leader. Start off by taking control of yourself."**

With his voice calming her down, she took a deep breath, and stilled her mind. Everything went dark for a moment, and she felt at peace. A few moments later, she saw the glowing ethereal form of her nude body appear in the pure darkness. A few more seconds after that and the darkness began to fill in with color until she was standing in the most beautiful garden she could ever imagine. Darting through her ethereal form, a nude, extremely muscular, mocha brown skinned woman appeared.

"Lilith! She's the original Lilith! I've seen her pictures in the artifacts a billion times! This is her!" she thought, watching the woman turn towards her and dig a small hole, before dropping an apple seed within.

"What's she doing?" she thought, watching the woman squat over the hole, seeing her make a face that looked ready to kill as bright red tears ran down her face.

"She's doing blood alchemy!" she thought, watching menstrual blood drip down onto the seed, seeing a sapling rise from the ground in that very same moment, almost impaling who she thought to be the original Lilith's vaginal entrance.

"They must know. They must know to never repeat the same mistakes again," she heard the woman mutter.

The image blurred and all Lailie could see were people in cages, some with bars, others completely sealed with thick, clear window ports, while others looked like luminous energy beams, keeping hundreds suspended in midair.

"This was our fate, seven times before. Each time, there was a promise to never let it happen again. Now, due to the tax we placed upon ourselves, a short term, extreme form of what you've just witnessed must happen again. It's that or humanity will be trapped with this fate for a very, very long time," Lailie heard the woman say, resting her hands over her ovaries.

"Why'd seeing her place her hands over her ovaries just break my heart?" Lailie thought, feeling her vision begin to blur from tears she could not control as tiny golden orbs burst through the woman's hands, followed by golden specks of light erupting from the man's testis.

Before her tear-filled eyes, Lailie watched the golden specks of light from the man's testis mesh with the golden orbs from the woman's ovaries and felt her body almost shut down from a sensation of dread and awe.

"Oh wow, there are even more awaiting to come through. Things must've gotten worse," she heard the woman whisper, seeing even more golden specks and orbs erupt from both the man and the woman.

"No! What have you two done? I can feel her coming! I can feel all of them coming! My children! They don't deserve this!" she choked out, feeling powerful eyes on her, coming from every single one of the golden orbs.

"She will turn the oceans red with blood. She will emulsify her enemies! Enslave all she finds fit for her purposes! She enjoys giving gifts of pain and suffrage. As do her lesser, all of which are 'Masters'. Those with great technical aptitude, and void of heart will join her side. They will be here 'Makers', and shall build whatever she bid," she remembered reading

countless time from the book of Lilith, wanting to run with all her strength, yet still completely unable to move.

"Do not run," she heard both the man and the woman say in unison as the orbs began to grow, and silhouettes of women began to appear.

"I can't run, even if I wanted to," she gasped, feeling energies of blood lust and disgust rushing out from every orb.

"Yes, you can. All of you can run if you wanted to. But do not go back, stay here," she heard the woman say as an orb floated directly in front of her, stopping two meters away before growing larger.

"What!? I can't run! My body won't move!" she thought, seeing a familiar, hypnotically beautiful figure step forth from the golden orb.

"Nefeshka," Lailie gasped as she tried to comprehend exactly what she was perceiving from the woman before her.

"In the scriptures, her images hypnotize you, leaving you feeling insanely horny yet almost blind with fear. In person, I don't feel turned on whatsoever. I feel dread, like she's going to eat my soul. But then again, I can't even feel my body to know if I did get turned on. I don't even understand how I'm even seeing her, she glowing with too many colors I can't really perceive, it feels like my brain is going to explode trying to understand, but I can't look away," she thought, staring at the intricate, soft colored, glowing patterns of sacred geometrics and solar systems inlayed into the darkest, somewhat reflective part of Nefeshka's black body suit.

"Lailie, I understand you think you know me from the things you've read," she heard Nefeshka say in her mind, tipping her head at her in a greeting.

"She's so beautiful. Looking at the book, it takes a long time of staring before her face is perceivable, but somehow I see her clearly! And what the hell! Instead of evil, she actually looks kind!" she thought, having moved her eyes off the body suit to Nefeshka honey-brown face, seeing soul piercing, luminous, green eyes, dotted with what she considered, extremely acute pupils.

"As a child, it was ingrained in me that one day you and the lesser 'Masters' would come. When I found out it might be in my timeline, I did my best to prepare. Upgrading as much technology for my LiL-Guard as possible. Using both artifacts and technological breakthroughs, I also did my best to kill or enslave more Makers and Mediums than any other in my bloodline. I wanted to do my very best to have a technological edge, and to ensure you had as little allies as possible. In addition to that, I've taught all of my LiL-Guard how to tap into and control their body energy, ensuring that their metaphysical abilities would cover any lack's in our technology compared to your own. Yet, now here I stand, disabled, no technological weapon to aim at you, and too afraid to dare make a move against you with anything metaphysical."

"Not that I think it'd matter. I'm well aware that any...Human? Coming back, or from someplace unknown, and never mentioned, would most likely have both the technical and metaphysical capabilities to sweep aside anything awaiting them. Seeing you now, feeling your aura, feeling the blood lust, and aggression from those who've come, and are coming through, these...energy nodes? Well, it's apparent to me that we're mere ants to all of you. However, it was my job and my bloodline's job to try and make sure we stung. The rest of the time when I was not preparing for your arrival, with the power, money, influence and technological advancement at my disposal... I, like my predecessors, genuinely tried to keep the world from becoming completely out of balance."

"I'm human, all who've come with me are human," she heard Nefeshka respond in her mind, giving her a soft smile, before turning and preening her thick, curly hair that was so long it lay curled in the water.

"I heard the term cosmos earlier. I'm hung up on the lack of explanation of where you and your people come from, had gone, method of returning, etcetera. So much history has been lost in wars, hidden, or spliced with lies. I'm no fool to think humanity would be the only intelligent species. It's crossed my mind many times that maybe, you and yours were not an actual human species, but maybe visitors that lived alongside our ancestors", she said, seeing Nefeshka's face turn slightly sour as she moved her hands through her hair.

From Nefeshka's reaction, Lailie felt herself panic, instantly feeling pressure squeezing the inside of her head, chest burning and clenching to the point where her breath was stolen. As she

589

forced herself to breath, an odd, numb, releasing sensation took place in her bowels and bladder.

"Unreal! This can't be happening! How can fear be my presiding emotion? Especially since I've just experienced death and know that all there is, is nothingness! What am I reacting to? Do I fear enslavement? Being tortured? I have never been this afraid to understand this!" she thought, trying to inhale, feeling her fear response block her right away, followed by a deadening of her sense of smell, where she could no longer pick up the scent of her stool and urine mixed with the ocean.

"What's happening now!? What are they doing to me?" she thought, now seeing two vastly different looking women wearing the same skin tight, oily black body suits, inlayed with different forms of glowing, sacred geometrics come up behind Nefeshka, nuzzling her, kissing her cheeks and lips, before taking her hair, combing it with their fingers.

Grunting in frustration at her predicament, she watched Nefeshka raise her hand and roll it in a lackadaisical gesture. In that moment, even with the numbness in her legs, Lailie felt water reach up, spin and drop down. Afterwards, one of the two women, who was shorter, stockier and much more muscular than Nefeshka peered from behind Nefeshka's hair, reveling an almond brown face with freckles.

"She wants to stare at the person who just shit themselves in fear...bitch," she thought, staring at the woman's short silver-grey hair, and almost glowing red eyes in an attempt to regain some form of respect, only to receive a dark, conniving smile, followed by the other woman peering from behind Nefeshka's hair.

"Great!" she thought, wanting to ball her fist, now trying to stare down the tall, thick and curvy, pale skinned woman, who she could see was ignoring her challenge and instead, looking her up and down in the way one does when assessing aesthetics.

"What could I even do to defend myself?" she thought, now watching the taller woman roll her head, swinging her long, curly red hair completely behind her shoulder.

"Nothing...there's nothing I can do!" Lailie decide, finally locking eyes with the taller woman, instantly becoming lost in their bright blue depth.

Not knowing what to do next, as all the fight in her had quickly drained out, she tipped her head as a, 'Fuck it, hello,' and to her surprise, she saw all three women begin to laugh.

"They remind me of a pride of lions, who preen and coddle each other, as they hunt, torture and kill their prey," she thought, watching as the taller woman placed a chain around Nefeshka's neck that had a gold and silver Ankh medallion, followed by another chain that had a gold and silver Trident medallion.

She then saw Nefeshka take a deep breath, seeming relieved. Right after, she saw the shorter of the two women wrap a thin, golden belly chain around Nefeshka's waist. When in place, she watched an almost translucent, liquid orb form and hover just under it. Again, she watched Nefeshka breathe another deep sigh, this time hearing it come out sounding like the most relaxing melody she'd ever heard, almost sending her to sleep.

"Pardon me for earlier, I had just received troubling news, and then I had to ask permission to..." she heard Nefeshka begin to say in her mind when the tall, red hair woman whispered in Nefeshka's ear.

"Pa...Pa..Par...don? Excuse? I, I never, use my..." she heard Nefeshka stammer, then pause, looking back, pecking the taller woman on the lips, laughing hard, revealing eight fanged teeth.

"Are those Yogini bloodline fangs!?" she thought, trying to process what it meant in regards to Nefeshka's two upper canine, two upper incisors, two bottom canine and two bottom incisors being over elongated, just as all ancient Yogini bloodlines had.

"Pardon me, I never use my voice anymore, and frankly I was being too lazy to learn the nuances of your language. I would also like to ask you to please pardon myself and my crew for our mistakes," she heard Nefeshka say in perfect Hebrew, chuckling as the shorter woman pointed towards her and shook her head at Nefeshka.

"Oh, Akalia just told me that I should address those mistakes I wish you pardon. It'd mostly be for our poor body energy management, which is what's causing you and your people to experience hyper active fight or flight responses. We don't mean to cause this. It's just that my people and I are very ill, very exhausted, and very aggravated, making it hard to maintain our energies to what would be a comfortable level around all of you," she heard Nefeshka say, giving her a warm smile.

"Very ill? Very exhausted? And very aggravated?" she replied, staring at Nefeshka and the two women behind her, not seeing or sensing any signs of discomfort.

"Yes, never in our life would we have guessed this illness could affect us to the level it has. As for our exhaustion, we've just come out of long, and heavy combat and have not had the time to wind down before arriving here. And here, this place has a lot of rules that are keeping us feeling pent up. We really don't like being nude," she heard Nefeshka say, tilting her head in curiosity, undoubtedly because she was now staring at her as if to say, 'what the hell are you talking about?'

"What?" she heard Nefeshka finally ask.

"Nude?" she whispered, squinting and staring hard at all three women's skin tight body suits.

"Oh wait, translation error. It seems like the normal way for using the word nude for many of your cultures would mean, clothing-less. In our case, nude means without our weapons, which for many of my people, would be this orb hovering below my belly chain, our Ankhs, which we use for energy works, and if we're so honored, a command chain, which is always shaped in the form of a Trident. Our people do not have or wear clothing. What you see covering us is actually armor made of Nano-material. If we're not in combat or alert status, we're always what your culture calls nude, as we simply withdraw our amour within our bodies. Now that we will be leaving this place of rules, as you see, I am no longer in my form of nude," she heard Nefeshka say, giving her a bright smile that showed genuine relief.

"Umm, okay, good to know. Umm, curious, why do you want to subjugate, kill and do all those horrible things it says in the scriptures? Also, how could you be alive after thousands of years? Technology? Like Cryogenic sleep? Some form of powerful metaphysics? And, I have to ask, what bloodline are you? Your teeth are like that of bloodline Yogini," she asked in a rush, wanting to get everything out before she felt too afraid to say it.

"Give me just one moment," she heard Nefeshka say, seeing her eyes flash red, feeling a sense of vertigo as the stars changed orientation and grew brighter.

"What just happened?" she asked, seeing an enormous dark orb growing smaller and smaller with each passing moment.

"Okay, to answer these questions, all of you will need references, and perspective, and so will we," she heard Nefeshka say, taking hold of her Ankh, seeing an indigo glow surround her body right after.

In that very same moment, Lailie saw thousands of images float up from Nefeshka's body, filling the sky. Right after that, Lailie then saw hundreds if not more of Nefeshka's people appear behind Nefeshka, all glowing indigo with their Ankhs in hand, followed by more images floating up in the sky.

"Holy shit! Is it possible that I'm still dead and that this is a spirit journey?" she thought, feeling butterflies at the base of her belly, now feeling the memories of Nefeshka and her people pouring into her mind as she looked up into the image filled sky.

At the same time, Lailie felt Nefeshka and her people, mindfully peering into her mind, carefully opening up memories, studying them, then moving on to the next.

"Ah, we now see where the confusion of your people has arisen, and it's very well warranted," she heard Nefeshka say, stepping forward, before whispering, "we gave all of you our memories so that as question come up and we explain, all of you can then see our experiences. Lailie, this may come as a shock to all of you, but we've never been here before. And before we were sent here, we had no idea here existed. This may be difficult right now because you've just absorbed them, but try to look at some the memories we've just shared."

"What!?" Lailie gasped, hearing many of the others in the meeting say the same in response to Nefeshka's confession.

"Just focus on my memory, do you see and feel my shock hearing about earth, and about actually finding it?" she heard Nefeshka ask.

"It's, it's blurry. The person telling you to go, it's just a shadow, but bright, almost blinding. But yes I feel your shock. And a feeling of optimistic, hopelessness," Lailie replied.

"Yes, optimistic hopelessness is a good way to put it. None of us ever believed we'd find this star system. After being sent here, we assumed earth and its people were, what we are to you, a prophecy that will never happen," she heard Nefeshka say, shrugging her shoulders.

A commotion began where almost everyone attending the meeting both verbally and mentally began screaming at Nefeshka and her people.

"Let's go someplace quite," she heard Nefeshka say, seeing Nefeshka's eyes light up a soft green.

In that same moment, she found herself standing alone with Nefeshka in an almost pure darkness, less the soft, multicolored luminesces of the body suit Nefeshka had called her armor.

"This is much better. As we speak, your mind sort out the memories we've shared with you so that you have lots of answers and perspectives," she heard Nefeshka whisper, raising her hand, gesturing for her to speak.

"Well, you're here. So there's merit to the prophecy to some degree. I want to know the facts from the fiction. Like I asked you earlier, I want to know your intentions. Just before coming here, a friend, enemy of mine had just told me that the source of the book of Lilith might just have come from a library or data node and that pretty much, it could've just been a fun Sci-fi novel at the time," she replied, suddenly seeing Sarah standing in the position of the spear tip which represented the leader of the entire Tech order before her vision retuned back to normal.

"Ah, the place that many of you call the 'Living Scripture Fountain.' From what my people and I have just learned, it served as many things, during many times," she heard Nefeshka say, stepping closer.

"Okay, that was a not so cryptic way of saying, 'yes, at one point it was a library, data node'. Well then, I just don't understand. You say you've never been here, and say you did not even know we're here till you were sent. So, how did my ancestor know you were coming? You look just like the images in the book of Lilith. My bloodline and I have done a lot of cruel things, extinguishing a lot of lives all just to make sure we were ready for your arrival. Was it all for nothing? Hum, and now I'm wondering whose hair it is we're studying if it's not yours?" she replied.

"Yes, I saw. I know all of what you and everyone else has done. I understand the extreme lengths all of you have taken in regards to your respective prophecies, as many of the stories about myself and my people's travels and wars are true. The only thing is, that none of it took place on earth."

"Then…the book of Lilith is also spliced with lies?"

"I'm going over your planet's historical records even as we speak. There are many stories of powerful Nefeshka's, it seems like it was a popular name. And, well yes, I see many of your ancestors mixed in the stories of those Nefeshka's with my own to create the book of Lilith. A lot of them did not want to acknowledge where I come from, who sent me, and so on and so forth. Back then, when your book of Lilith was created, my people still had very small ties with those on earth, but not the friendly kind. Tell me, are you able to see the memories of our travels in your mind yet, or is it still mostly blocked and scattered imagery?"

"Too much, everything you're saying, is just too much. And yes, scattered imagery. Jumping from too many people's points of view about the same topic. I feel overwhelmed, then luckily my mind just stops it," she replied, happy that the experience she was describing was not painful or overly disorienting.

"I share your shock as well. My people had experienced much misunderstanding and loss of history as well. Arriving here, everything began to quickly make much more sense in terms of how my Empire was formed," she heard Nefeshka say, plucking a long strand of hair from her head before saying, "that being said, now that I have access to much of your worlds history, I have to clear up your time frame confusion in regards to what is actually considered an era, but I'm unsure if you're ready to hear it."

"As overwhelmed as I feel, I'm still more than ready for answer. Also, I know you know my body still can't move, why are you taunting me to take your hair?" she replied, seeing, *< Symbiosis on Standby: >* in her mind's eye.

595

"What was that?!" she thought, hearing Nefeshka say, "oh, you can move. You have not chosen to fight this state because you haven't finished assessing my character. If you deem me too strong of a threat to run from, you'll allow a powerful stress response to overload you, killing you so that I don't have an opportunity to torture you. You're mostly doing this without thinking about it. Almost all of you are doing this, less those who are referred to as the Tech order."

"True to individuals of their nature, they are currently living by cold, hard logic. Their idea of fear response was to sync up with my ship as fast as possible, allowing their bodies to just be there, while their minds transverse the data. I love and envy people with this kind of personality, as they have a huge role in propelling our species forward. If not for them, then risky, beneficial discoveries would rarely be made," she heard Nefeshka say with sinister grin, before flicking and blowing the strand of hair in her direction.

As the strand of Nefeshka's hair reached arms distance, feeling in her limbs began to return, so carefully she reached out and grabbed it.

"Good, you're adjusting to our presence," she heard Nefeshka say.

"You said the people of the Tech order synced with your ship? Would this symbiosis prompt I just saw have something to do with syncing to your ship? And, um what ship? I, did not see a ship," she asked, hearing a soft chuckle from Nefeshka.

"What?" she snipped, feeling annoyed at being laughed at.

"Just curious. Where do you think 'Peace' is?"

"Peace is a sacred site in the Antarctic, heated by geothermic energy, said to be closed off by ancient earthly energies and a powerful metaphysics working. The constellations that were above aligned with the scriptures," she replied, annoyed at Nefeshka's condescending smile.

"Halfway right," she heard Nefeshka say, pursing her lips with a dubious look on her face.

"Just spill it," she responded with a sigh.

"Well, you're on a ship. Peace was on earth, where you said, then it moved to the last outer planet of your star system. It was the black dot you saw getting smaller and smaller when we launched. Remember, I had told you we were leaving the places with lots of rules that made my people and I feel pent up because… well for one, we had to be nude."

"Oh…shit," she whispered in shock.

"Lailie, back to what I wanted to tell you in regards to what your people are calling eras. Well, it's not correct how you all are counting them."

"Then please explain," she replied, still in shock from the last thing she'd learned.

"The earth cycle you refer to as two thousand twelve, was actually the end of two forms of eighth eras, a minor one and a major one. Also, your current people's entire count of the minor eighth era, is off by one full era. So, actually, this is now the beginning of the ninth major era in Homo Sapien history."

"Excuse me?" she whispered.

"Your people are currently counting the first, minor era, starting from twenty-one thousand, eight hundred seventy-five earth cycles prior to earth cycle two thousand twelve. I'm saying this would not be the first, minor era, but would be the second, minor era. The count is off by three thousand, one hundred twenty-five cycles, as this is how each minor era is divided to fit within each major era, which is twenty-five thousand earth cycles long. I say this, because looking at the history of what all of you are considering the first, minor era, both Takumbo, and I had already become lore."

"Now, hear me out. The first scouting party my Emperor and Empress sent to earth, was twenty-five thousand cycles from the earth date, two thousand and twelve. My departure to be Takumbo's reinforcement was also twenty-five thousand cycles from that date. In earth's time frame, she would've left in January, and myself in April. How could we have become lore without some time passing by? Which it did. That means the people of the first, minor era had metaphysical and technological abilities to pick up both Takumbo and I as we travelled the ether in search of here."

"A few hundred years before the end of the first, minor era, what you call the book of Lilith was created. But at the time, it wasn't called that. It was just simply a log book of our travels. When the civilizations of that first, minor era fell, and second, minor era began, it's when your ancestors started tweaking the log book for their own purposes, adding in lots of stories from the other major eras to cause confusion, and to fit their individual purposes."

"That's...this is a lot to take in. Eight major eras, with eight minor eras within each of them. Fuck, we had it all wrong," she whispered, suddenly feeling her body return to normal, minus a dull, itching ache between her shoulder blades.

"Your ancestor did a very good job of destroying all the evidence, and distorting the truth of things they couldn't hide. At your peoples' current capabilities, both technically and metaphysically, there's almost no way any of you could've known this information, as it is not easily assessable, not even for my people and I, and we have many ways to view...situations," she heard Nefeshka say, smiling at her knowingly as she reached behind her, scratching between her shoulders as best she could before giving up.

"Why did they do such a huge purge of history? They must've been panicking. Doing the math on what you said...you can see back, two hundred thousand years, huh? Tell me more," she said, all of a sudden feeling extremely energized, light weight and refreshed, with her only annoyance being the aching itch between her shoulder blades growing more intense.

"I can see back further than two hundred thousand earth cycles, I can see back three hundred thousand, when there were a number of other human species living alongside our own," she heard Nefeshka say.

"Just, wow. Three hundred thousand years. Well, hearing it, it makes sense, as there's plenty of archeological evidence showing that Homo Sapiens emerged as one of the only remaining species around two hundred thousand years ago, with anything older showing that we did indeed walk alongside other human species. It's just... the way you're saying it, it's like...are you saying what I think you're saying?" she whispered, tugging the strand of Nefeshka's hair, not feeling it give no matter how hard she pulled.

"Yes, I'm saying that Homo Sapiens, by themselves, in a two hundred thousand cycle time frame, from the date you call two thousand and twelve, rose and fell technologically and metaphysically, a total of sixty-four times," she heard Nefeshka say in a flat tone.

"My god," she whispered.

"Yes, and prior to that two hundred thousand cycle time frame, there was a one hundred thousand cycle time frame, where the many different Humans species lived together, forming civilizations that rose and fell eight times. At the end of that one hundred thousand cycle time frame, that is when Homo Sapiens rose to the top as one of the last surviving human species along with Neanderthal's. From the records I'm currently going over, we Homo Sapiens were fierce beyond all measure, and still are," she heard Nefeshka say, pursing her lips, seeming genuinely sorry for turning her world upside down.

"Where are you getting all this information? What records?" she asked, opening her fingers, simply dropping Nefeshka's strand of hair as she mulled over everything she'd just learned.

"We're accessing all the data every civilization has ever left behind, and as we sift through it, we're cross referencing to make sure we extract as much of the facts as we possibly can. What do you think of us? You think I'd just make this up?" she heard Nefeshka say with a soft giggle.

"I don't know? You're speaking to me like I'd know your personality. And if those stories about you are true, but just not on earth, then shouldn't I expect the worst from you? Why should I think you'd be honest with me? Why are you here?" she asked.

"I told you, my Emperor and Empress sent me," she heard Nefeshka say, waving her hand, showing her that everyone from the meeting was still currently standing in the position of the trident.

"All of them have just learned what you have about humanities' history, and many are not handling it well. They do not believe humanity, whether it be Homo Sapiens or the other species could've formed civilizations capable of interstellar travel seventy-two times before going back to, what many of you are term 'the stone ages'."

"Well, it's a tough pill to swallow, go figure," she whispered.

"In this star system alone, we have all the necessary proof to show all of you that that's exactly what happened. Plus, there are thousands of human civilizations and Empires beyond this star system. I find it interesting how many of you seem to honestly hate reality, and call truths tough pills to swallow, when truths are, simply…it is what it is," she heard Nefeshka say, giving her a beaming smile – that made her feel deeply uneasy.

"So those names, the names of the people you were crushing in the stories, are they from some of the thousands of Empires and civilizations you've just mentioned? If so, then you really don't seem to get along with anyone," she said.

"I've just told you, there is so much more than this tiny dot of humanities origin, and you don't spend time in wonder of that? Only choosing to wonder how I've dealt with my enemies? Why do you mind the business of those no longer in their first life? What a miracle and an honor to be human in this first life. To know and share in the honor of having rose and fell seventy-two times is a testament of everything we are. I honestly, really love our species. I've seen so many unique beings, and still I'm a narcissist who thinks we are one of the greatest that've ever come and ever will be."

"How small minded do you think I am? I am in wonderment. Yet, the practical questions still remain, my main one being, are you going to do anything to harm my children?" she said in a low voice.

"Lailie, does anything about me speak of hesitation? If I wanted to harm your children, or you, I would've done so."

"You could be toying with me? Maybe gaining strength before you attack, I recall you saying you're sick," she replied, hoping to hear a revealed weakness.

"Yes, my crew and I are extremely ill, but that makes zero difference on our ability to do great harm to everyone on your planet. Anyways, I have something to show you. It's regarding what the people of Tet said about the tax humanity owes. They were not over exaggerating how problematic humanities situation is."

"Oh-kay," she replied, feeling mentally winded at how easily Nefeshka shut her down and moved the conversation.

"To show you, the Nano-Material that is this ship is created of and that dwells within myself and all of my people, requires your full permission to merge in symbiosis with you. And once given, it's not something you can easily retract without great consequence to both your body and your self-worth."

"Sounds like a normal life choice," she replied.

"My crew and I are asking the same permission from all that are assembled here, and many have not answered like you have. We believe and are deeply worried that many of you will run away and renege on the symbiosis once formed. If many of you run away and do not help us take care of the situations we reveal to you, we'll have to do it ourselves,"

"Well, I'm not weak like many of them," she replied.

"Yes and you pride yourself on wanting to protect your offspring, your legacy, and so forth. So, here's your chance to prove it. Please do not run away after you've accepted the symbiosis and learn further truths," she heard Nefeshka reply.

"Just show me, I don't even know where the hell I am to run away to. You said ship, I thought I was in the damned Antarctic. If I don't even know where the hell I am, I obviously can't run away, can I?" she replied.

"So, you're giving full permission?" she heard Nefeshka say, giving her a deeply concerned, questioning look.

"Yessss," she replied.

"Great, I'll set it up so that you learn in stages. Also, as you learn from the symbiosis and from us, do deep evaluations of yourself. Once you being this new life with us, you'll be dealing with one superior problem after the other, many without easy answers or actions you can take," she heard Nefeshka reply, seeing her body suit begin to ripple like a fluid before covering her face and hair.

< With your permission, symbiosis will take place and full activation of recessive, stress response genes will begin.> Lailie saw in her mind's eye.

"Why are you hesitating? You had verbally confirmed with me that'd you'd say yes, back up your words with actions!" she heard Nefeshka exclaim.

Yet Lailie was distracted, thinking *"what the hell are you doing? Have you lied to my face? Why have you drawn your weapon?"* watching the clear orb Nefeshka had called her weapon float free from her belly chain, forming into a sinister looking Trident with an eerie pink glow coming from the tips, which appeared to be made up of crystal.

"Where are you going?" she asked, watching Nefeshka raise her hand, seeing a patch of darkness change shape, followed by a rush of air blowing past her that smelled of pure, rotting flesh.

"You'll see, when you actually give permission," she heard Nefeshka whisper, looking at her and then the dark patch where she could hear a woman's voice, calmly saying a word over and over again in a language she'd never heard before.

"Still not ready huh?" she heard Nefeshka ask before whispering, "Nanites, translate for Lailie."

"Mayday, Mayday, Mayday," Lailie heard right after.

"You understand? You're going to need the Nanites, but they'll need permission to merge with you," she heard Nefeshka say, looking away from her, walking into the shroud of darkness – seeing the distortion go back to normal right after.

Minutes passed by, and Lailie stood in darkness, going over the pros and cons of her situation, before finally saying, "I give my permission"

< Merge complete. Recessive genes activated. > she saw in her mind's eye as pure ecstasy, and horrific pain coursed through her body.

Falling to her knees, she watched black fluid ooze out over her hands and arms, all while feeling her shoulder-blades tearing open. At the same time, in her mind's eye, she saw a couple hiking in a forest, going into a cave.

"I love you Serena, I brought you here to tell that. I know you wanted to get away from school. I figured a road trip and a hike to the middle of nowhere would help take our stress away. Distract us from the fact that everything we went to school for, well… that is was for nothing, since there's barely any jobs in those sectors anymore."

"I love you too Darren, and when you bring someone to a place to relax, you don't bring up the painful situation, you idiot. Now use your mouth for something more useful, and eat my pussy," Lailie heard, the woman respond, seeing her lean back on a rock, pulling down her leggings.

"Mmm, I think you staged this, baby almost every time we fuck, you're on your period," she heard the man named Darren say, followed by the images shifting where she could see the rock the couple was having sex on engulf them.

"What the hell?" she thought, unable to understand or see more as the images shifted, now showing her a man typing on his laptop.

"What is this!? What does this mean!?" she thought in frustration, seeing the man press, 'control', 'find', then 'replace', changing the name Kira to Nefeshka in his manuscript.

The image shifted again, and she could see the man staring at the title, called, 'Before the Williamage'. Behind him, she saw a thin, but shapely Asian woman aiming a weapon at the back of his head.

"Baby! I just finished the new Seri...," as the man said series, the woman pulled the trigger, but just before she did, she moved her aim to his shoulder.

"This makes no sense! What's happening?" she thought, hearing the man groan in surprise and agony, watching tears fall from the Asian woman's eyes, hearing her say, "shit! Shit! I have to, finish this!" before aiming at the man's head.

"Baby? Baby!" she heard the man scream.

"I, I still love you," she heard the woman whisper, pulling the trigger, but instead of hitting the man in the head, it hit him in the center of his chest, because in that moment, the man had jumped up and moved incredibly fast as he had reached out for the gun.

"Why? Why'd I have to do that! Why'd they make me do that!?" Lailie heard the woman sob, watching her crouch down next to the man's lifeless body, then whisper, "fuck this," placing the gun to her heart, pulling the trigger.

The image shifted again, and she could see her three daughters arguing in the kitchen of her eldest house.

"We cannot tell anyone that mom is missing!" she heard her eldest daughter say.

"It's been a month! What do we do!? Artifacts are reactivating all over the world! And people are starting to write portions of the book of Lilith! All our Makers and Mediums are dead or missing! And what do we do about Tet's proposal, forcing us to work with Al Babadur to build a second space elevator?"

"Who cares about all of that? Why haven't we told Nate about mom?" she heard her youngest daughter, Hila exclaim.

"He's too weak!" she heard her eldest say.

"And you want to maintain control over him? Don't make that face. I agree, with maintain control over him too. So then the right thing to do is to at least fake that she's still here," she heard her youngest say.

"No!" she heard her middle daughter say.

"Yes, I'm hacking mom's com channel. If we're not telling him, then we need to maintain her presence and send him mom type, fucked up things. We 'gotta' threaten Rayya, and then offer them a mission, and 'thennnnn' hint to them about wanting grandkids, but say it in a way that makes them think that if they do have kids, they'd be put in an underground lab like what we do the Makers and Mediums. We 'gotta' be fucked up and loving just like mom!" she heard her youngest daughter say.

"My babies! What do they mean I've been gone a month!?" she thought, trying to hold onto the image as it began to shift, now seeing everyone who'd been at the meeting now on their hands and knees, with the same black substance coming out of their skin.

"She called this armor? Why does it hurt, yet feel so good!? she thought, feeling the flesh up and down her back rip open, along with an extra weight that grew heavier by the second.

Gasping, she looked to her left and saw a silhouette of wings coated in black.

"Shit!" she grunted, somehow belated at the sight, while in her mind's eye showed her two arms bursting out of Saraswati's back, along with a shroud of energy bursting out of Adam, forming a golden Halo and wings formed of pure, white and blue energy.

"The filth!" she heard Adam exclaim, standing up, revealing his nude muscular body covered in black, with a bright, baby blue energy circulating around him.

"No! It's you who is the filth, and no one else! You hate yourself, you maggot of contradictions! All of you should've been the ones purged! I've seen the things those in your Order

604

have done!" she heard Saraswati growl, dodging a fast kick from Adam that would've struck her on the side of her head.

"What the hell! She must've had truths of lineage revealed to her …while I'm seeing skipping, damn near incoherent images!" she thought, watching Adam and Saraswati begin to throw blows, with shock waves of energy coming out after each strike.

Gazing up through her own eyes, she could see black liquid flying everywhere but heard no sound. Then another shock wave came, and she could see a hole tear into the black liquid in front of her. Through it, she could see everyone from the meeting, with many fighting just as Adam and Saraswati were.

"I must stop the imbalance from spreading!" she heard Adam say in her mind, seeing his energy grow stronger before he slipped down through the floor.

<Energy channels repairing. Stand by:> Lailie saw in her field of vision right after.

<Standby:>

<Standby:>

<Loading:>

Lailie had a very limited memory of ever having fun. The only feeling she'd ever associated with fun, was the belly rushing, butterfly sensation she'd gotten from going really fast. As lifetimes of information poured into her mind, that same excitement she'd had when she was young surged through her body a hundred-fold, causing her to feel an incalculable sense of ecstasy.

"I'm learning everything! Everything! Oh no! Is this, is this what happened!?" Lailie thought, overwhelmed with so many truths revealed.

"And wait, so then what!?" she thought right after, realizing that so many answered questions, led to even more complicated, unanswered questions, and that there were data paths from individuals seeking those answers spanning back for centuries.

"If I give in, I can lose myself. I need to focus on what's relevant to the here and now!" Lailie thought, taking control of her minds wander lust, focusing in on what it was that'd entered her body giving her the ability to witness everything she had.

"Biological base line – but not alive. It's been manipulated to make Nano technological and it makes up the entirety of this Orb-ship, with its

605

substance flowing in and out of the crew members in a form of symbiosis. Fuck, both the crew and the ship are sick. And now so am I. But after the information upload, I can see I was damned either way! The Lilith imbalance within me was going to grow faster than I would've been able to control it. I would've sprouted these wings and went crazy for blood, so much so, that I might've blindly sucked dry my own family or staff. It's just shit luck that this Nano-Material is weakening by the second! It's like taking poison to cure my hereditary defect. Sooner or later both things are going to do me in!" she thought, feeling her stomach sink in despair as she had hoped that she'd have a long life after the symbiosis, consider the fact that Nefeshka and her crew had been alive for over twenty-five thousand earth years.

"I want to protect my family; I had thought I'd known what horror was!" she thought, feeling the Nano-Material react to her subconscious thought, bringing up real time visual and audio of all four of her children, along with her husband.

"Fuck!" she grunted, seeing her entire family in various forms of distress.

"Sarah's Working is going to collapse, and all that hate that's bottled up is going to overflow! And just as I was planning to strike after reawaking, so was everyone else! But now, the head of each Order is up here, unable to mitigate the intensity of the conflicts! Our young ones will go too far and destroy the power balances! I refuse to let this happen!" was her first instinctual thought, feeling and seeing her body energy and the Nano-Material wrap around her like a cocoon, before instantly being launched out of what she could see was a fluidic, Nano-Material, orb ship.

Gazing down at the earth as she plummeted towards the surface, she felt utterly fearless in her choice. If anything, she was over eager to connect with the atmosphere, to see and feel the friction of the decent - for it'd match the rage she felt about the pressure cooker situation she could see her family placed within. There was just one problem, data was still pouring into her mind and she was constantly seeing each and every choice Nefeshka had to make on her journey to earth, as well as the corresponding emotions behind them.

"I'm making a mistake," Lailie thought, extending her body energy, knowing from her symbiosis with the Nano-Material,

exactly how to manipulate it to change her decent into a stable orbit.

"It's time I force myself to do something I've never done before, especially since it's already been this long," she thought, knowing from her symbiosis data that the earth date was now June first, twenty seventeen, and that everything she'd been perceiving as linear time had been because of the speed she'd been traveling on the ship, along with all the times she'd lost consciousness, awaking on her feet, seamlessly caught up by a mental synch Nefeshka had maintained – in what she assumed was an attempt to spare her, along with the rest, embarrassment for constantly checking out of reality due to fear response or nervous system overloads.

<Show me Sarah's Working. Show me the actual departure of Nefeshka coming to earth through her eyes. Put me in an orbit where I can intercede with Adam if he…Actually no, do the opposite, move me somewhere where I can do nothing. Just let me know the distance he's shadowing Nate. And all the small details in between. Show me what Saraswati's doing. Show me where Nefeshka is, show me the crew, give me relevant information, and help me streamline my thought processes. And finally, unless I'm utterly about to die, do not allow me to intervene in anything. No matter what I say,> she commanded the Nano-Material.

The response was seamless, with the Nano-Material adjusting her body energy, changing her orbit as well as organizing all her thoughts in forms of priority.

Beautiful patterns came into view in colors she'd never seen before, emotions coursed through her giving her both heartache and great joy. Having always been the person to preach that an individual needed to observe deeply before making any big decisions, or that an individual should take time to know thy self, she often never did so herself, nor through her abrasive nature allowed anyone in her company or sphere of influence to do so as well.

Date: Tuesday, June 20ᵗʰ 2017

Location: Destroyed Lilith Base, Beneath Ellsworth Air Force Base

Staring at the Nano-Material covering her arms, Lailie then looked within herself, ensuring that the Nano-Material now living and multiplying within her body had not suffered new forms of degradation from the illness they both harbored, and that she was still perfectly cloaked. Seeing that there'd been no new degradation and that her cloak was still active, she breathed a small sigh of relief.

"God, I had asked you how you do it. Now, after seeing so much, I slightly understand what kind of paint you use and I'm grateful that you've tried to answer my question, grateful, you do reply," Lailie thought, gently running her hand over the petrified remains of her son's face.

Looking away from the dark brown, blood colored substance her son, his wife and almost everyone in the chamber had been coated in, Lailie watched Lilith Corp. and Tet Crop. teams move about carefully in full, combat ready hazmat suits, all lead by her youngest daughter who sat nude and impatient in quickly erected isolation area next to an equally nude woman named Grace.

"These feminist militias have cost both of us a lot and will continue to if we don't find out who's leading them. I thought joining a group and climbing the ranks, I'd get closer. But I quickly realized that it wasn't going to happen when I was injected with Nanites that can track your movements, among other things. So, then I stayed to see what 'kinda' life they lived. You see, I kept losing women I was choosing to build my house with to these feminist militias. I know you know of my Order, so you know how important it is that I build my house. I hated the feeling that my foundations were being stolen. I wanted to see if these women were going to live a better life than the one I was offering," she heard Grace say to her daughter.

"They weren't stolen. You can't lose what you didn't have. I'm not condoning this situation. But the women you chose, did not choose you. You were not picking women whose goals aligned with yours, and I can understand them in a way, as your Order ask females to respect men at equal value and that's unfathomable in my eyes."

"First of all, you don't know how our prospecting works. For them to, to just change like that, it's fucked. Speaking of that, your brain is fucked. I'd heard you were the most even headed of all three sisters, and if that's true, then I can't even imagine your sisters," Lailie heard Grace say to her daughter.

"My sisters are dead; my mother has been missing for months. I'm all that remains," she heard her daughter reply in an even tone.

"You left out your father, who's alive and well. And you mind speaking off your loss like you care? Mind sheading a tear? What the fuck are you, a spider? You know what? I want another one of these lab rat jails put up from me before I get mentally infected hanging around you," she heard Grace say, flagging down someone in a Tet suit.

"You have the reputation of being cold hearted Grace. I've heard that people don't get to live long enough to spread too much information about you. You, the same person that's claimed over a thousand lives, dare ask me to cry? You dare support the patriarchy's label for women, that we are emotional and should cry!" Lailie heard her daughter say, shooting up from a foam chair, holding her stomach right after.

"Patriarchy? What? Crying is being human. And you calm your tits, if you know who I am, then you best believe I'll not let you disrespect me without repercussions," Lailie hear Grace say, with her face changing from twisted and annoyed to concerned.

"Hey, you okay?" she heard Grace ask after a few moments, where her daughter just stood there, moving her hand over her belly with a look of disdain.

"I feel nauseous, and something else, I feel weird," she heard her daughter whisper, looking at Grace with concern.

"Sorry, you're glowing like a candle, I shouldn't be annoying you, raising your stress. However, you and I are in the same boat, and I can't really control my emotions either, it's probably why I'm talking about crying," she heard Grace say with a chuckle.

"What?" she heard her daughter ask.

"Girl, are you in some 'kinda' denial? You gonna tell me you don't know you're pregnant?" she heard Grace say, chuckling even harder

"Oh shit!" she heard her daughter whisper, placing her hands over her eyes.

"Yup, that'd be that flashback where you remember him cumming in you. Trust me, I had the same flash back on June forth. What alerted me to my pregnancy is because I had to use body energy to stop this single mind chick named Sabrina. She was determined as hell to kill Karman, the chick that's dead as hell over there by the car. She went out into the forest to wait for the perfect opening to snipe her. I would've just followed her out there and broke her neck for even having the thought of killing one of my shipmate's wives, but as you know, the Nanites inside us monitor everything."

"Anyways, long story short, I kept doing small body energy pulses to fuck with her mind, fuck up her resolve by casting doubt because she'd already received orders from the tippy top not to do anything to Karman as well. But this bitch finally decided she was going to do it anyways! I felt the kill intent clear as day! So, right when she was about to pull the trigger, I did a pulse to mess with her eyes, but yeah, it came out, different. Different better too, then I felt this crazy connection. Like I wasn't alone. There was this deep, unconditional love rising up from my belly, and yeah, that's when I realized that I had a baby in me."

"Well, congrats to you too. Now, back to business. You want to share info? Well, care to tell me why you used your Order's technology to help those women you joined identify my brother? Nanites or not, there would need to be a record of Nate available. Your Order would be one of the only ones that'd know his identity. And what else did your body energy pulse touch. Did you go after my brother's LiL-Assault Rifle? My reports are showing the power source overloaded, and luckily the material was able to withstand and redirect all the force before blowing up the room.

"That weapon Sabrina was using would've killed everyone in that room. I know it doesn't mean much now, but at that time, I was the one that had saved them. And no! I didn't touch that Rifle with my body energy. As a matter of fact, that power source, is, was, well, it didn't feel right. Even with my body energy not extended, I felt it kick to life, and I felt it ring out with

610

what felt like celebration when it fired its projectiles into Sabrina. Listen Hila, I'm not your enemy, if that's your mindset, I feel sorry for your babies' father," she heard Grace whisper.

Shaking her head in sadness, Lailie walked away from her daughter and Grace, towards the cracked orb, where she could see Nefeshka staring with deep consideration.

"What was the deciding factor that made you stay up there and watch?" she heard Nefeshka ask as she came closer to the orb.

"You can go into my mind and see," she replied.

"I didn't need to go into your mind to know that you'd say that. In any case, as you know from what you've learned from symbioses, all our thoughts when they begin are still private. We still have the luxury to only share if we want to share."

"Yes, I remember. And I remember there are people who can shatter all forms of thought, like Adam, and his twisted mind," she whispered, feeling tears forming in her eyes.

"I tried to look into his mind, and the whole time, I had zero idea what he was feeling or actually thinking. But, in the end, knowing what I know now, how can I blame him at all, even as much as I hate it," she whispered.

"Okay, that's too much of that," she mumbled, crushing her sadness, looking into the orb, focusing on the petrified, nude remains of Darren and Serena before looking back towards her son and his wife, then towards Nefeshka with a head nod before saying, "I'm hopeful."

"Good, because just now, I've just confirmed that they all made it to…'

"To?" she asked, pressing into Nefeshka's mind trying to see what she saw.

"Well, that will take some time to figure out," she heard Nefeshka say, feeling her, in a kind way, push her out of her mind.

"I figured you'd say that. I saw thousands of pathways, if not more. And I saw just as many Entanglement blockers. God, to make so many countermeasures after making it so easy to travel so many places!" she said in frustration, quickly reentering Nefeshka's mind, peeking behind her eyes, watching as she cast her energy through one Entanglement node after another, attempting to spot her son's DNA, only to see the blockers activate, thwarting Nefeshka's attempts.

"Thank you for looking for them," she whispered, now smiling, realizing that she had the answer to Nefeshka's question.

"Yes, you have an answer for me?" she heard Nefeshka ask knowingly.

"It was a mix of things, beginning with when you told me that you'd share once I gave it permission for symbiosis, suddenly, I had this safe feeling. I had wanted to desperately push that feeling away because I was having glimpses of those memories all of you had shared with me. The ruthless way y'all conquered solar systems after solar system, crushing humans and sentient beings like they were bugs. And then I thought about what kind of mother I am. I thought about the conversation I had with Adam about Nate. I thought about how I treated my daughters. I thought about who my daughters had become. I realized, they were more me than them, and that the little that was left of them, was still filled with contradictions and negative energy."

"As I was realizing this, I was also learning from the symbiosis, that people here on earth have no connection to one another, and is a huge part of what's making all of you ill. Then that's when I realized, I'd done far more than enough on earth. And the worst part of it was…that I took that step back, unsure of what you'd do, or if others like me from the meeting would go down and head straight for my kids."

"The thing was, I'd literally just had enough of myself and I wanted to step out of my own way, my kid's way, my husband's way. I wanted them to live their life just the way they would live it. Of course, what do I get for it? My eldest daughter has been turned to ashes by a raid from Saraswati's people. My middle daughter, crushed to death in the depths of the ocean because she wanted to track down and eliminate Karman's sister, who she knew was just dangerous as anyone could be. And then there's my youngest daughter. Don't get me wrong, I'm over the moon with joy she's still alive, and I'm proud of her female pride – but at the same time, I'm terrified for her because I can hear her going way overboard," she said, now looking at the petrified remains of her son's 'friends', shaking her head in disdain.

"From the data my people and I have gathered, I can see that your two oldest daughters would've still been killed even if you went down there. It also shows me that if you went down there, there'd have been an eighty-six percent chance you'd have gotten Hila killed as well," she heard Nefeshka say, causing her to look up, wanting to study Nefeshka's face, finding that she was staring at Jay and Karman's petrified remains just as she had.

"Whenever you look at Jay and Karman, I hear you think of a historic reference called, 'seeds of war'. And whenever you think of it, you always get this tiny, creepy smile. Why is that? Are they like the people in that story? I haven't had a chance to look it over yet."

"Creepy smile? Really? What do your people say to return an insults? Go to, go to hell?"

"Yup, that's a good reply," she replied with a snicker.

"Anyways, I'm smiling for two reasons. One is because of the reason you gave me for staying still and not intervening. And the second is yes, Jay, Karman, that woman, Grace, and of course Tet Corp., remind me of my own people and remind me of certain stories during a war in my Empire's history called 'seeds of war'. I know you are overloaded, but when you have time, take a look at everything that had happened."

"I for sure will," she whispered, asking her Nano-Material to do character references from the history of the 'seeds of war' to see who Jay, Karman and Grace reminded Nefeshka of.

"Nefeshka?" she asked, feeling an odd emotion come from her.

"You're picking up our moods faster and faster, quickly integrating with us. That feels good, and promising," she heard Nefeshka whisper.

"I don't know what the emotion meant. Just know it felt like fogy, cold air. And had an acidic, sour scent," she replied.

"That is me being disappointed. You heard what my Emperor and Empress said, yes?"

"Yes, well I heard, your Emperor, your Empress just smiled, and head nodded. In any case, he sounded like he wanted you to hurry, to get here."

"We believed his urgency was his way of telling us he wanted us to protect earth. Arriving here to find that humanity has fallen below a Tier one civilization is disappointing. I had assumed we were going to meet a human society more superior than our own. In my mind, I'd envisioned that we were being sent as earth's reinforcements, that we'd be cannon fodder as many of your people call it, and I was honored."

"And now, not so much?"

"I'm honored, but in a different way. Since earth is the origin of humanity, my main thought is, who am I to touch too much? Who am I to spit in my ancestor's faces? I would not be who I am, nor would any Empire or civilization be who they are without our species going through this kind of up and down cycle."

"Okay, you say that. And I see you really clamping down on this 'don't touch' rule you have going on. But how do you plan to stick to that? All kinds of shit has hit, and continues to hit the fan, with the shit breeze, blowing all over the world. No disrespect to your authority and your methodology. But, we both know the power of observation alone can cause and change outcomes. So, the only true proper way not to touch is to leave and not even look."

"If you're not leaving, which I'm sure you're not. Then where will you draw the line in, observing, or slightly helping, versus frankly assimilating everyone. Your Nano-Material alone, as weakened as it is, could easily form symbiosis with everyone on earth and bring them up to speed. You can conquer earth, just like you conquered those whole lot of other places. You can try to work on healing yourselves and the Nano-Material, while everyone on earth gets on the same page. Damn it, I just reminded myself of Sarah," she said, whispering the last part.

"Humm," she heard Nefeshka mumble.

"Yes, you think, while I come to terms with…holy fuck! I'm going to be a grandmother. I'm standing right here, and my daughter can't see me! And God, I want to tell everyone to take those ridiculous suits off!"

"Lailie," she heard Nefeshka whisper.

"Yes,' she asked, seeing Nefeshka face darken.

"When you saw us conquering those worlds, we were all healthy and we were working with the Nano-Material seamlessly. There is too much risk merging people with it right now."

"Uh, okay then, never mind I guess" she said, watching Nefeshka's face turn predatorial, feeling a tinge of fear.

"Is this fear from me reacting to her look, or is this her passing fear into me?" she thought, trying to probe into Nefeshka's mind, feeling resistance, now seeing her shake her head, rolling her tongue in her mouth, over her teeth.

"Searching for your son just now, I just saw something that makes me want to risk integrating the Nano-Material symbiosis with the people of Earth. Yeah, there's no longer much to lose. Come, we need to explore all the pathways to heal ourselves and the Nano-Material."

"Okay," she said, in a dead pan tone, sending her energy outwards, trying to see what Nefeshka's was seeing.

"And Lailie, never think my people or I would keep you out of the loop, we are not like that whatsoever, any resistance you feel, is not from me, it's your body and your mind warning you that you've had enough. Make sense?" she heard Nefeshka say, taking hold of her.

"Ready to go?"

"Yes, sure," she whispered.

"Good," she heard Nefeshka reply, feeling a soft, odd, yet energetic tug, seeing her vision go dark for less than a second before finding herself standing within the now familiar oily, black colored Nano-Material.

"Wow, that's beautiful," Laila whispered, as the Nano-Material turned translucent, where she could see they were traveling about twelve meters below the ocean.

"And look," she heard Nefeshka say, pointing to a large pod of Orca.

"Yes, they are amazing. I've recently come to terms that I love seeing views like this, thank you," she whispered, smiling at the Orca who were now swimming next to the ship.

"No need to say thank you. We must enjoy everything we love while we can," she heard Nefeshka whisper, seeing a portal open up in front of her.

"Just curious, where are you heading now?" she asked.

"To...observe," she heard Nefeshka say hesitantly, giving her a mischievous smile.

"Oh, okay. Wow...haha, I just caught on. I'm honored that you'd listen to me. How can I help you gather people to introduce to symbiosis? Do you have specific types of people in mind?" she asked, getting a beaming smile from Nefeshka.

"I do, and so do you. We'll discuss it a little later. Stay here for a bit, enjoy. When you're through, use your horrible Entanglement skills to meet me," she heard Nefeshka say, giving her a warm smile and a head nod as she stepped through the portal she'd created.

"It's not that bad," she mumbled, mentally beginning to form an Entanglement portal, that collapse·over and over again.

"Shit, she's right, I'm not stepping through that thing. If this ship won't take me, she's going to have to come back and get me," she said under her breath, cracking up laughing at both her shortcoming and the Orca at play.

The End

Foreshadows

(Walks into the movie still playing in your head, with a smile on my face)

Hi, it's O.M. Wills. Welcome to my realm. It's not even close to being over.
Here's a preview of things to come.

Date: Tuesday, June 20ᵗʰ 2017

Location: A Polynesian Island

Situation: Tet's first official meeting since it's near destruction, two thousand seventeen years prior.

"The tides and winds of energy have returned in our favor! It's time to rebuild our Armadas! Before our shipmates' departure, they set out a course for our Order to be reborn! It's our duty and responsibility to carry out their wishes. This means that we cannot allow 'The All' initiative to fail! Let none who cross our path know mercy," Ihi heard Haumea say in a warm, yet powerful voice, filling her with resolve.

"Ihi, have you looked to the stars and charted your journey?" Ihi heard Lono ask, with his voice low and commanding, yet somehow reassuring, reminding her of watching a thunderstorm with hot coco in hand.

"Yes Elders. I travel to Guam on the summer solstice. I plan to work with a newly established Lilith Corp. recruitment outpost. They are seeking strong females for both the space elevator project, as well as to rebuild their ranks from their most recent losses. My goal is to prospect and possibly recruit females that have already passed Lilith scrutiny," Ihi said, feeling goosebumps rise all over her body, feeling both excited and honored to be allowed to choose her own path by the Elders.

"Fair winds! And Following Seas!" Ihi heard the entire assembly say, standing, placing their fist to their foreheads then hearts, wishing her farewell.

Standing, Ihi returned their salute, feeling more goosebumps of pride rise all over her nude body.

"Your blessing is the wind that powers my sails," Ihi said, in her humblest voice.

Ihi then faced, and walked directly out of the large palm hut, making a sharp right, going directly into another smaller palm hut where four tattoo artists sat awaiting her arrival.

Date: Tuesday, June 20th 2017

Location: A Polynesian Island

Situation: Karman's sister, Rosa, wants to crash the Tet meeting on the Polynesian island, so...she does.

"Weeee!" Rosa bellowed as her submarine tilted close to perfectly vertical, shooting out the water like a breaching whale, slamming into the water with a relatively quiet smack due to its sleek and slender shape.

"Get us closer to land! Like right here, move us there," Rosa said excitedly, studying the structure of the island from her monitor, pointing to a group of jutting rocks as she unstrapped herself from her command chair,

"Aye!" she heard her two Helmsmen reply

"Okay, yes! Let's go," she mumbled to herself, smiling brightly as she hoped out of her command chair, quickly walking through the bridge's a watertight door that her subordinates had already opened for her.

Within two minutes of walking through her submarine, chatting with her crew, building moral, Rosa was now climbing a short ladder to the outside world.

"Ahhh!" she sighed, arriving at the top of the ladder, climbing up and out into the open air, watching as her submarine moved closer to the rocks she'd chosen.

"Here is good," she said, with her mind, commanding her bullet and knife proof, neuro-link wetsuit to transmit as she walked along the 'sail' of her submarine.

"We're picking up two heat signatures coming from one of the smaller huts," she heard a female voice say in her mind.

"Mmm-hum," she replied out loud, mentally commanding her wetsuit to transmit as she gazed down at the crystal-clear water below, marveling at the depth of which she could see before it turned to dark blue.

Feeling and watching her submarine slow as it inched towards the rocks, she used her View-Contacts to zoom in, seeing two nude, tattooed female figures staring in her direction with arms folded.

"Helm, all stop. I'll swim to the rocks from here," she said out load.

"Aye! All stop!" she heard, feeling her submarine slow further, then completely stop.

"Okay, stay alert, I'm off," she said out load, moving to the lip of the 'sail,' diving into the crystal-clear water.

"Wow! This is perfect!" she thought, loving the way the warm water felt against her face – as it was the only place the water actually touched her body.

Keeping her face down, she swam slowly, having spotted flicks of movement from what she thought look to be an underground cave on her far right. Moments later, the movement grew more distinguishable. Using her View-Contacts, she zoomed in and clarified, seeing a pod of Orca emerging from an opening at the bottom of the island, almost directly under where the women on the beach were standing. Stopping, she lifted her head, took a measured breath, then placed her face back down in the water to watch as the pod of Orca swam towards her.

Roughly two minutes passed where she just lay floating, breathing, listening and watching as the Orca came closer. Now, to her delight, they were swimming directly underneath or beside her. Smiling, she took a deep breath and looked back into the water to find an Orca spinning in tight circles directly beneath her. Suddenly it straightened, and begin to swim up towards her at an extremely fast pace. Without thought or hesitation, she calmly moved her arms in the water, propelling herself backwards as the Orca breached directly where she'd been, with its belly almost touching the crown of her head.

Hearing it let out a breath, she positioned herself upright, and watched as it slowly inched down.

"Hey, nice to meet 'ya'. I'm Rosa. And when you say it, you 'gotta' roll the 'R.' And when you say the a, you 'gotta' say with it like, 'ah', like you 'screamin'. Like this, 'Rrrro-s-ah,'" she said, looking towards the beach, then back towards the Orca.

"You 'gotta' name?" she asked, hearing another breath right after.

"You 'a' sassy one, huh? Hey, Mami or Papi, can you take me over there please?" she asked, smiling at the quick head jerk the Orca made right after, mentally personifying the movement to be one of 'shock' at her question – even though she had no clue what it truly meant.

In that same moment, Rosa felt a profound peace overcome her. Breathing deeply, she allowed herself to enjoy something she never knew existed. As she continued to live in the moment, she watched the Orca sink below the surface, bringing its body underneath her. Then ever so gently, it rose up, placing her onto its back.

"Thank you," she whispered, removing her gloves, allowing them to hang free via a flex-cord connected to her wetsuit, before running her hands over the Orca's back.

After her words and touch, the Orca then began to swim towards the direction she'd indicated. With every passing moment that she grew closer to her desired destination, the peace she'd been feeling became replaced by a joy so powerful her cheeks began to burn from smiling. A few minutes later, the Orca had brought her as far as it could go, which was right in front of a sea cliff's edge, where the shallows of only about one-meter depth would begin.

"Thank you again she said," sliding off into the water, feeling the Orca pull back ever so slightly, giving her a soft nudge pushing her a little past the cliff's edge, ensuring she was in the shallows.

Turning, she smiled to thank the Orca again, but it'd already turned and begun to dive.

"Amazing," she whispered, turning towards the two women on the beach, who were staring at her with looks of curiosity and mild shock.

"Que?" she asked, as she trudged through the shallows, hearing no response from either of the women until her feet touched the dark black sand of the beach.

"Take off your wetsuit and anything underneath. Bring them to the smaller hut there, then go into the larger one, she heard a woman she recognized from her intel as 'Grace' say.

"Cool," she replied, reaching out her hand before saying, "hi, you're Grace right? Nice to meet you. My intel says that recently you got promoted to Admiral. Congrats, I know that's a big deal for your people, right?"

"Yes, I'm Grace," she heard Grace reply, taking her hand between both of hers, then letting go, which was a warm, welcoming gesture she'd not expected from someone with such a cold, aloof demeanor.

"And you, I don't recognize. Jay was very good at keeping his data away from me. I only know about Ms. bella Grace because of the day all the weird shit happened. Her basic info popped right into my tablet, then vanished, which I know... means he gave it to me. In any case, it's nice to meet you...and you are?" she asked, moving her hand towards the other woman.

"I'm Ihi, and as of a few hours ago, I'll be acting as Admiral Grace's eyes and ears, as well as her recruitment officer," she heard the woman reply, taking her hand, squeezing it with the perfect amount of pressure that bespoke of warmth, sincerity and I'll crush you if you cross us, before releasing.

"Right, of course. You 'gotta' keep your girl from working too hard. Especially with the baby on the way and all," she said, smiling at both women as she sent a mental signal to her wetsuit to undo its inner fasteners, then striping nude the moment they were undone.

"Thank you for not protesting about taking off your clothes," she heard Ihi say.

"Why would I?" she asked, staring down at her pussy, comparing it to the other two women, seeing that theirs were both shaven bald, unlike her, who hadn't trimmed or shaven in three months.

"Alicia said that you're a pain in the ass. I had assumed it was because you're a bitch, but now I can see that it's not the case at all. I see what her issue is with you though," she heard Grace say with a soft chuckle, running her hand over her belly.

"Yeah, I'm no bitch, I'm chill. So uh, what issue would that be?" she replied, stretching, enjoying the warm evening heat, the puffy white clouds, the scent of the ocean, and the feeling of being nude and free.

"You're very different on the spectrum of people. For example, how'd you find this place, this place is protected on many levels that should've kept you out, yet here you stand. Or how'd you ride a wild Orca? Do you know that the one you rode, she's the Matriarch of her pod? Do you know what the significance is of her allowing you to ride her, as well as what it means for her to directly bring you here to us?"

"Uh, I looked for here. I found here. I asked her for a ride, she gave me a ride. She's a lady huh? The main mami, huh? That's cool. Well I 'dunno' the significance, I mean it could be very simple. I mean Orca got good vision and can see through me with sound. She saw my anatomy; she knows 'Ima' chica too. Maybe she just wanted to help out another chica of a different species. My dumbass wanted to climb on the rocks to get on the beach, and then walk all the way the fuck over here - thinking at the time, I wanted to take a fifteen-minute walk. In the water, I realized I exercise enough, and didn't need or want that walk."

"Yup, see. You're just...yeah. So, why are you really here?" she heard Grace ask.

"Umm, revenge. Alicia said she was going to an important meeting and that it could help her get revenge for Jay and my sister. So, yeah."

"Revenge?" she heard Grace say, smiling and shaking her head.

"What? That's a damn good reason! Is it not?"

"It is, I didn't say it wasn't," she heard Grace reply still shaking her head, silently laughing.

"So weird, you just laughing at me like that. Anyways, do you think Alicia loved Jay? I felt like I was in a Korean drama back then. She'd be staring at him when he wasn't looking. Watching his back always, AKA passive aggressively threatening

Karman and I nonstop. Not talking to Karman for like a year after she got married to Jay, it was cute. Oh, and personally I think she moved some of her operations from Singapore to my country because of him. Crazy huh? A real life Korean drama. She loved Jay, I loved Jay, my sister loved Jay. He loved my sister, used to love her, till he realized she was way too 'cray cray.' But then he still wanted to sleep with her, with my sister. And...he wouldn't even touch me, and I always let him know I was down to play. Yeah, those were good time, we should've made a show. Oh and where's Alicia by the way? This is the meeting place right?" she said, looking down at Ihi leg, seeing lines of sweat, blood, and oil mixed with red and black ink running down.

"Fresh 'tat' in the sun? I know it's oiled up, but is that safe? Can I see it?" she said.

"Sure," she heard Ihi reply, turning around, revealing a portrait covering her entire back and ass, depicting an owl, soaring over the island they now stood in a night time setting, with a moon reflecting off of the water and a pod of Orca swimming in the ocean.

"Nice!" she whispered, now studying Grace, who was covered neck to toe in tattoos.

"Thank you," she heard Ihi reply, turning around, facing her with a prideful smile.

"Grace, you still have this, confused look," she said with a giggle.

"It's just you being here. When we picked up your submarine, even my elders were surprised...and it takes a lot to make them surprised. They're very well informed, and very attuned so to speak with their surrounds, yet, somehow you're somewhat of an outlier them," she heard Grace reply.

"I never think too deeply about anything. When I want something, I simply act on it with the best of my abilities and try not to get dead. Sometimes I fail and don't get what I want, sometimes I almost get dead and people need to save my ass. Other times, I get exactly what I wanted, or something better that I did not know I even needed. I found here because I wanted to be here...because I think this is where the meeting Alicia had mentioned would be."

"Yeah, but how? We're not even on the map. And this place is hidden, technologically and by other means," she heard Grace say.

"Really? Well, I just aimed my sub to the last known sightings of some of y'all ships and subs. Specifically, those of Alicia's fleet. Then, I started to narrow it down where to aim my sub by gut instinct, and by asking my crew what their thoughts were. Since their suggestions all seemed valid, we did them all. Then just a bit ago, we ended up in some random, extremely beautiful spot in the ocean where we could see four tiny islands filled with jungle life. As we were checking the islands out, we saw a pod of Orca and wanted to follow them to watch them play, 'cuz' we were all bored, tired and needed a break.

"When we started following them, they all vanished and it made us curious how the hell they could outswim a sub. As we came closer to their last known location, well then, this island showed up out of nowhere. Since I know y'all are secretive as shit, and probably did hide this place with all kinds of tech gadgetry, I figured this must be the place. I figured y'all got tired of watching me sail around in circles looking for this place, and just turned off whatever it was keeping me out and just let me in. I was thinking that or it was just a fluke of good luck that I slipped past a downed defense or something."

"Amazing," she heard Ihi whisper, giving her a warm smile before looking out into the ocean.

"Yeah, I guess. Hey, is Alicia here? If she is, I want her to cook that Singaporean fish she always makes for Jay! It's stinky as all hell! But it's good!" she said, walking past Grace and Ihi, towards the smaller hut, feeling their 'what the fuck' looks all over her back and neck, causing her to laugh.

Date: Tuesday, June 20th 2017

Location: A Polynesian Island

Situation: Tiana wants to speak to Grace, but Nefeshka has forbade direct contact.

624

Cloaked, via the Nano-Material that now lived within her body, Tiana stood motionless, no further than thirty centimeters away from Grace, Ihi, and a woman named Rosa, who'd just arrived.

"I could've been standing there with Grace, but I betrayed her. After everything she'd done for me, I couldn't see her vision. Grace wanted balance of power in her house, but I was born and raised in Guam, trapped in that church. I was certain at the time that men would never share anything! That they'd just take, and take, and take! The feminist movement made more sense to me and I felt much safer. Grace wanted me to embrace my sins and become a full blown criminal. I was horrified that I was easily becoming that person. I felt like I could save my soul and have a meaningful purpose in the feminist movement. And I felt like I could save Kaysha, and all the women that were treated like shit by men," Tiana thought, realizing she'd unconsciously placed her hands on her belly when Grace had.

"And now, because of me, her lover is dead, and her child will grow up fatherless. Because of me, what she tried to build and all those people's lives are destroyed. I did not see what I'd become after falling so deep within the feminist movement. Well, not until I was left all alone, dying in the ocean with my neck slit ear to ear, and stabbed up like a pin cushion," she thought, sorting through her memories, using the Nano-Material symbiosis to play out her actions, seeing when and where she could've done something different, realizing that she had all the time in the world to change her course, but instead, had only chosen the path of maliciousness.

"How long, how long till you let this go?" Tiana heard Nefeshka say in her mind.

"How do I let it go? Seeing me, it makes me hate me. What the hell was I even doing? How'd I get into so much shit? I was like the scourge of Guam," she mentally replied.

"Scourge? Haha. You've been going through the history, picking up some of the common terms huh?" she heard Nefeshka ask now speaking into and through the Nano-Material.

"It's true, I was a nightmare," she whispered in reply, using the same method of communication.

"Well I love you. You saved us during your darkest time. And out of all the women who heard our distress call, it was only you who was selfless enough to reply," she heard Nefeshka whisper, feeling her arms wrap around her, followed by a warm kiss on her cheek, that she felt through her Nano-armor.

"I did that in spite. I saw rage and anger from all of you and I thought, is this hell? Because if it is, I'll help hell arrive, and make people suffer. Think about it, I saw clearly what the cost of bringing all of you here would be, and I still didn't care. Think about what kind of person that makes me. Until that woman on 'Peace' told me everything, well enough of everything. I would've just acted on the thought that I was just bringing pure evil to earth before completing the works to get y'all here," she said, wanting to cry.

"You didn't need to hear it from the Guardian of Peace to know we were not what your people consider hell. It was clear to you that we called out mayday because we were in distress. I felt your heart when you sent out your energy to guide us here. You were purely concerned. Don't try to talk tough."

"No! Nefeshka! I was thinking and wanting both at the same time. I know you know that! You're being loving and lenient because you feel you should be kind and understanding because this is the birth place of humanity. But don't be! Be yourself! I saw who many of your human enemies were before you came here. I saw that they were all infected with the twisted thought processes that destroy both your physical body and life energies at the same time... just like the people here on earth."

"Yes, you're right. I know you were thinking both," she heard Nefeshka admit, causing tears to well up in her eyes.

"You're being way too kind and not cleansing this place is making all of you even sicker. I saw the Versus ships your Emperor and Empress created in order to cleanse this illness. And I agree with how they ordered y'all to eradicate the people the process did not work on! The cost of allowing them to live, well I saw the maps of how this illness is spreading. So many sick minds, sending out so much twisted energy, how could it not? I think, if you have the means, you should create a Versus ship and try to cleanse the people of earth, before you get too sick and can't do it."

"My love, duality is a trait that's inherent to many individuals of humanity. It a part of our growth as the more information gained about the nature of things, the more we need those types of thought processes to gain understanding of what we are seeing. This illness that's spreading, yes, it's praying on the very aspect of what helps us see and learn from all different angels. That is why it's so hard to contain. You cannot just attack it. And creating even a small Versus ship is not only extremely difficult, but the outcome if we make even a small mistake, if there's word beyond dangerous…apply it here," Tiana heard Nefeshka say.

"I think you should apply the word for, 'beyond dangerous' when you don't try to help, then get too sick to help when earth gets a billion times worse," she replied, mentally pulling up the historic records she'd just studied regarding the illness.

"Nefeshka, I know you were sent here before you got to personally see the inversion of the Sai'nct and Cen'tia systems with your Emperor and Empress' Versus Ships, but like, I'm not you or your people, and seeing these people, how far they went haywire, it scares me to no end. I already see pockets of their behavior all over Earth. What's worse, is that while studying them, I'd found myself understanding and deeply sympathizing with their mindsets as well. Studying this war, studying these people, I was left feeling dirty for hours, feeling like I smelled like rotting fish come from my pussy. Feeling the urge to hate men, way more than I even thought possible - on a level of like revolution. The amount of contradicting thoughts I had meshing in my head that I soon felt were normal thoughts… Nefeshka, it was fucked. Fucked like, a lactose intolerant person pouring orange juice into their milk, downing it, then hating that they then have the shits."

"Interesting reference. And thank you for your warning and suggestion. You are among many who have said the same thing to me. In regards to what you said about becoming easily influenced while studying the historic records - when we get back, begin working with us on strengthening your mental reinforcement loops. We will show you how, although weakened by this illness, we have not succumbed. I want you to see the greatness, beauty and strength in a human's ability to perceive in duality."

"I look forward to it, because all I see from duality is the meaning of cognitive dissonance. Smart enough to become beings who can travel to different galaxies, terra form and populate millions of worlds, yet… in the same breath, think playing with our dicks or pussies summons demons that drag them down to hell," Tiana whispered.

"Yes, but some made up stories such as being in the heavens was enough to intrigue minds, causing people to actually find ways to go seek. Some using technology, while others using mediation, thus learning to use their body and ambient energy to do energy Workings such as astral projection, where their range of travel maybe even infinite as they wouldn't be tied down by technical and physical limitation," she heard Nefeshka say.

"Yeah, yeah so true. Damn, thinking about this is giving me a headache," she whispered.

"You're getting a headache, as well as heartache, because you keep looking in the past and keep picking the saddest parts. You have no idea how thankful we all are for your sacrifice. I love both sides of your mind, body and spirit. Come, leave here my little scourge of Guam. Let them live their life, they have much to do. If you're wondering why I'm not deeply interfering with people on earth, minus the people Lailie suggest I look after, it's because I want people here to develop as natural as possible."

"I want them to find their own cure for the illness and I want to sit still for once now that we're here, and take care of our own illness before we even think of planet wide curing attempts. Doing it any other way would simply make us 'Conquerors of Earth.' I didn't come here to conquer the birth place of humanity. I simply refuse that outcome," she heard Nefeshka say, feeling Nefeshka place her hands over her ovaries – which no longer held even a single egg.

Feeling soothed by Nefeshka's embrace, she leaned back and whispered, "I wanted both. I wanted the life Grace offered me. And I wanted the life the feminist movement offered me. Guam is a tiny place, with almost zero opportunity to grow and thrive beyond that isolated life. To be taken under Grace's wing, to travel with her, to learn from her, it was the best! But when I was home, in Kaysha's arms, that was the best too. Funny thing about my selfish ass is when both Grace and Kaysha kept giving me space to chose one life or the other. I'd get even more spiteful, and fuck everything up on both sides because I was scared it'd end to cleanly, and that they won't feel the loss of me being gone from their lives. And those silly loving bitches, still kept forgiving me. Crazy huh?"

"They saw something special in you, like I do," she heard Nefeshka whisper, feeling another kiss on her cheek.

"They didn't think that I would flat out, fully betray them," she whispered.

"Remember, I brought up mental loops?" she heard Nefeshka whisper

"Yeah," she replied.

"You're build one right now. I can see it in your mind getting bigger and bigger as you reinforce your stance that you're evil and unforgivable. Humm, part of Working with mental loops is all about time management. Right now, you have all sorts of things you could be doing. But you are using your time to relook at your memories and recreate yourself in the worst images. Do you see why technology or ethereal abilities does not make us more than who we are? That you have to continually be aware of your own mindset?"

"Fuck, I am digging my own hole, huh?" she whispered.

"Yes, yes you are. I have a suggestion of my own since you brought up the Versus ship. Why do you go through the full process with us as we begin to heal ourselves? I'm actually having a relatively small one created as we speak. When it is complete in a few months, as you call it, you can be one of the first to enter. And well, before that, I suggest you begin practicing our normal customs and recreations that we use to remind ourselves to live in the present moment."

"Wait, is one of these reminders when y'all...um, no, pass," she replied, feeling herself smile and cheeks flush as she thought what she'd saw the times she'd been invited before.

"Sweetie, you run every time, but I know you want to come," she heard Nefeshka say, feeling her Nano-armor give under Nefeshka's touch, feeling her soft lips touch upon her neck, while her hands caressed her breast.

"I refuse to admit this. I'm a freak, but the way y'all get down, I don't know if I can handle it," she whispered, hearing Nefeshka giggle, feeling her left hand grip her breast tighter while the other moved down her belly, to her pussy, massaging her clit.

"Yes, yes you can," she heard Nefeshka whisper, feeling a tug of energy she'd grown accustomed to, now finding herself in a semi dark chamber filled with the glow of soft alluring light.

"Oh, fuck," she whispered, biting her bottom lip, seeing hundreds if not more, nude forms in various acts of passionate love making.

"Yes, that's the idea," Tiana heard Nefeshka whisper, feeling her arms wrap around her belly and breast, then one hand slide down to her pussy.

"Um, but I 'dunno' if I can," Tiana whispered, tilting her head to the side as Nefeshka's cheek brushed against hers, inviting the soft kisses she was now receiving upon her neck.

"But, Fuck," Tiana gasped, parting her legs, allowing Nefeshka's fingers more room to play, feeling her already wanting pussy ache to be pressed and filled even more as Nefeshka continued to lay kisses upon her neck.

Date: Wednesday, July 26th 2017

Location: Jerusalem, Israel

Situation: Hila, the sole remaining Matriarch of Lilith Corp, is waiting for true Tet Corp. representatives to arrive after receiving a message, asking to meet.

"I have butterflies because of this baby, not because I'm nervous to meet them. Yeah, it's because of this baby," Hila tried to convince herself, catching a whiff of meatballs, instantly wanting it with yogurt, then wanting to throw up because the scent of meatballs grew just a hair too strong.

"And why here?" she thought, gazing around the 'hole in the wall' restaurant the true Tet representatives had asked to meet within, shrugging her shoulders at one of her guards whose face twisted up when a group of mating flies buzzed past them in a mid-air orgy.

"I want to go home to Tel Aviv where there's a damn breeze! The Alt percepts can keep this landlocked city," she thought, hearing sirens go off for what she considered the billionth time that day,

followed by the hiss of her countries countermeasure rockets, then shockwaves as they intercepted whatever it was that'd been launched towards Israel.

"My mother would have found an excuse to go outside just to watch, risking death by shrapnel just to see the rockets intercept," she thought, watching people rush into the restaurant with startled eyes, only to be instantly detested by the dinginess, demarked by the fact that all six individuals who'd entered then opted to risk death by going back out, quickly running into the much cozier, cleaner shop right next door.

"How's this place even open?" she whispered to herself, gazing at her four guards dressed in plain clothes, noting that all of their expressions appeared to agree with those who'd just left.

Through the chaos of panicking people, she saw two individuals dressed in very casual clothing, stroll calmly past one of the restaurant's front windows, then towards the door.

"They utterly fail at blending in! Who fearlessly strides through panicked people?" she thought, gritting her teeth in disgust as the man open the door for the woman, gesturing for her to enter.

At that gesture she became so infuriated she saw speckled burst of blue-white in her vision. Holding her breath, she pressed a smile on her face and casually leaned back in her chair as the individuals approached.

"Hila, hi I'm Ahmad, and this is Lina," she heard the bald, light brown skinned man say, bobbing his head, keeping eye contact with her as he pulled out a chair from underneath the table, gesturing for Lina to sit down.

"Thank you for meeting us so informally. And thank you for sparing us the pat downs and everything else," she heard Lina, who was short, light skinned, green eyed and curvy say, smiling at her as she sat down.

"One thing I know for certain about you people... is, if you wanted me dead, I'd be dead. Since we're being informal, let's cut all forms of small talk and posturing. I want to know, what would this meeting be regarding? And, I'm sorry, I'm not sorry...why do you let him control you? You can open your own doors, pull out your own chairs. Who is he, to be leading you by gestures? Just...no," she said, keeping her tone even.

"We are here to tell you in person that you will stop all your technological impediment procedures. And that you will also halt the process of fully trapping and enslaving people that are commonly known as Mediums in your facilities. If they are already in, or make choices that cause them to become a life debtor, that'd be as low as they go. This will be very small changes in their overall treatment that Tet Corp. has decided will make big beneficial gains for humanity," she heard Lina say without any stress in her tone to indicated she was fazed by her words.

"What! No full capture and keep protocol? We have no Mediums left after all that craziness! And you want me to do what!? I need to rebuild my scientific force! And that means finding new Mediums and jamming their brainy barely socially adept asses in a goddamn lab under twenty-four-hour surveillance so I can milk every drop of smarts they have," she said in a low snarl.

"Listen, don't speak. If your recruitment or search teams do find Mediums, instead of fully enslaving them, we want you hire them with salary and vacation. Treat them like normal citizens, with of course longer hours. The nature of work they often do, that would normally go without say anyway. We do not, I repeat, we do not want to find out that you have them buried in labs, missing, and away from their families," she heard Lina say, with only a slight threatening edge coming to her tone.

"This is! Utter!" she began.

"We of Tet are now personally spreading the word to all Tech Conservative Orders, and all balancing Orders such as your own that we will no longer allow any more Technological limiting protocols. This means, no censoring, no car accidents, no patent buys and buries, nothing. If a person makes new technology, it's made. If they release it to the public, then that'd be that, it's out to the public. If we find out you're violating our mandate in any way, we will apply specific punishments to you and those responsible in your company, as well as hastily develop and release the technology that you were trying to suppress," she heard Lina say.

"I know full well we are on the brink of a technological exponential increase, especially since your Order has forced this elevator down the world's throat, but I still strongly believe some moderation is required," she said, keeping her tone low.

"Why? When in nature do you see things that do not follow the path of least resistance? We've calculated that even with all the inhibitors, many companies, such as your own would like to put in place, that humanity would still be able to achieve the first stages of useable fusion energy within the next fifteen years. Without inhibitors, the data is showing that we will achieve usable fusion energy within the next seven to ten years. You see? There is no longer any point trying to silence or block anyone. There is already too much forward momentum, and interference will not change it. All interference would do is waste good minds to death and too much stress," she heard Lina say, giving her a dead pan look that made her feel small and stupid.

"Fine, maybe I'll stroll down to some vaults and pass out some artifacts and let the public have their way with it. As a matter of fact, I think I have a whole cockpit of an ancient battle tank freshly stolen from the Yogini bloodline. Yup, it was buried in the sand next to 'Adams Bridge' in Sri Lanka," she replied, smiling bright, feeling she'd stabbed them in the face with their own reckless logic.

"That's a great idea! It is good you see it our way!" she heard Lina exclaim, returning her smile – seeming genuine and enthused.

"This bitch can't be that simple! What the fuck is going on?" she thought, clenching her teeth when she realized her mouth was opening and closing like a dying fish.

"Oh, you were being facetious," she heard Lina say after a view more seconds.

"No shit," she whispered.

"Look at the big picture Hila. It's already well known that salt water can easily be converted for power, with little impact to the environment. Our AI systems are growing smarter by the day, not the year. Humanities collective intelligence can no longer be limited even with every inhibitor tactic put in place. Therefore, there's no longer a reason to focus valuable time and resources on control protocols. At the current growth rate of human consciousness, for every person you stop from inventing something, one thousand more will invent the same thing or something similar within the same time frame. It's time we just let everyone be and focus on being prepared to mitigate tragedy with whatever new technologies we have at hand. We must police ourselves by allowing the whole world to feel the impact of each new thing that arrives. We must adapt to our own pacing, the same way marathon trainers' muscles begin to regulate and adjust the further the person pushes their body," she heard Ahmad say.

"Listen here," she began.

"This is not a discussion, do not break our mandates. We think you're a borderline good fit as head of your company. Do not forces us to reconsider that border. With that being said, start hiring and giving purpose to all those who've suffered from the technological impediment initiatives your company and many others have implemented over the last few decades. Goodbye Hila," she heard Lina say, standing and stepping back, with her eyes locked to hers.

Once Ahmad stood, she watched them turn their backs and walk away.

"How? How can I hire people that will work themselves out of a job faster and faster per project, and their product efficiency increases exponentially? Are you fools blind? Tough talk is part of Lilith's persona, but let's be real. We weren't locking Mediums up just so we could milk them for their smarts. We did it to pace them, and to keep them from realizing how fast they'd outpace themselves by bird feeding them the next project. When you say hire, now I'll have these extremely intelligent people, who are too selfish and too headstrong to ever work in a team, knocking at my door asking for top dollar, sucking my company dry, then leaving and remaining unemployed for a long damn time because their projects worked too damn well," she whispered while Lina and Ahmad were still in earshot, hoping they'd turn around.

"If that's the way you feel about humanity, then you're thinking way too small, and you'll fail, and be replaced. Time erases almost all, but in this case, in a very short time, no one will even remember your name," she heard Lina say, stopping in front of the door, waiting for Ahmad to open it before stepping through.

"Who do they think we are? Do they think we're fools? We've run countless card blanch test scenarios where people could build whatever they wanted and introduce it to a controlled public. And every time, it was like opening a portal to hell. The last time, there was no one even left to kill, to make sure everything stayed silent," she whispered, having flashbacks of walking through a 'card blanch' project city in the Lebanese mountain range, where the whole town had been scorched and turned into a form of light blue glass no one had ever seen before.

"Madam Hila! Madam Hila, we can tail them and then snip them!" she heard one of her nearest guards say, leaning on the table in front of her with a ferocious look in her eyes.

"I know you want to get revenge for my honor, but true Tet representative, unfortunately, are not individuals you even entertain the idea of trying to kill. You see, they are 'sorta' similar to our enemy across the border. They don't care if they die, and will move like a force of nature to achieve their goals. If you shot them dead right now, new reps would be called to take their place. And then, the leaders of Tet would send out an order to kill your entire family and almost all of your friends, while leaving you alive."

"Then they'd send follow up agents to me, to make sure I did what they've asked and to see if you learned your lesson. They'd then ask both of us to re-tell the story of how they punished you to any and all we came across, ensuring that we put fear in the minds of anyone who might be considering to cross them. And listen to this, if I really started to grind their gears, they'd let me get near birth, then take my baby from me and raise it as their own, with the added bonus of raising my child to hate me. They've done things like this, since...since always. That's the kind of people they are. And in this world of predators and prey, even in their scarcity, they're still at the very top of the food chain."

"How about wiping them out? You've told us it was close to being done once before," she heard her guard press.

"Haha, I see I talk too much when I'm...nervous. Yes, it was attempted two thousand seventeen years ago. With that attempt, a different form of pain came in the form of an illness of sorts that spread among humanity. Going unchecked because, well, they were the only buffer strong enough to stop it."

"Illness? Like the plague?" she heard her guard say, with her face softening.

"It's a plague alright. But it's often not perceivable to people's eyes. It a toxic energy from people's mindsets that goes unchecked. Negativity energy loops that our minds get hooked on, and when that happens, well our bodies die faster, and we as a species, run each other down to the ground, but can tell we're doing it because we are thinking our fucked up thought are normal. You ever heard of those stories where people have clarity during death, it's because their bodies and brains are dying and not functioning well enough to keep latching onto the twisted energy loops," she replied, seeing her guard begin to sweat.

"We are all sick with it now. Why do you think human life is so short compared to the stories in the holy books? You're Christian right? How long did Noah live? Nine hundred fifty years right?"

"Yes," she heard her guard whisper.

"Haha, and now we can barely make it to one hundred with fully functioning bodies," she said with a dark chuckle.

"But, I thought after the event in June, you detest every holy book? Why do you bring up Noah?"

"I do detest holy books, prophecy books, all of it. After going through that hell in June, I've learned a lot of truths about how the Alt Percept houses formed religions, as well as how those prophecy books were created. The crazy thing though is that a lot of the people referenced in those stupid stories were real people, including the parts about their lifespans. Noah, was a real person, he really did live that long. In any case, when it comes to this illness. Well, I'm sick as hell from it recently, and as strong and capable as I am with use of my mental and body energies, well it uses that strength against me, keeps me from locking in on it. For you all of you, well none of you even see or notice it, it just incorporates itself in your daily life almost seamlessly."

"But, what? Why? If you're identifying it? That means you can see it," she heard her guard whisper.

"No, well yes. Fine, put it like this, we can all see it. Almost every single person on earth feels something is deeply wrong. Example being the massive upsurge in anxiety and depression. Or our deep hatreds and biases that we can't fucking shake even though many of us know deep down inside it's really dumb to hate someone for their skin color or if they're the opposite sex. For example, how I hate the Tet rep Ahmad for simply being a male. How I hate him for opening the door, or moving the chair for Lina. Right now, the other half of me is asking, why Hila? Why do you even care? Who gives of shit who open the doors for who. And then the sick side of me is screaming and fighting, calling myself an internalized misogynistic bitch. In this battle, unfortunately the negative mindset begins to take over all of us. And for those who prevail and become positive, the populace singles them out and treats them like garbage till their mindset gets beat down and become negative again. Or they're simply hated and killed."

"Holy shit," she heard her guard whisper.

"Yes, almost all the really fucked up shit you see people do to each other, purposely as well as mindlessly is because of this illness that spread the day that Tet was almost eradicated. This is the true story of B.C. and A.D. In all actuality, it's before and after Tet. Don't worry... I was, and still am just as shocked as you are right now as this information was yet another one of my eye opening, June lessons," she whispered, head nodding her other guards, who'd all gotten closer to hear her speak.

"Why are you telling me, I mean us this? Aren't we just expendable guards? You haven't even given us names or even numbers yet," she heard the guard in front of her say.

"I've been reflecting while sitting here and realized since choosing all four of you as my new guards, that I've been talking a lot, spilling information that I never discuss with anyone else other than the Lilith board members. Even just now, I was kind of scalding myself for talking to you about Tet, and this illness. But upon completion of my reflection just now...I've come to the conclusion that guarding my life does not only mean protection from outside forces, but from myself as well. None of you can or would be able to do that if I don't show you who I truly am, flaws and all."

"It also means I must teach you almost everything I know so you have information at your disposal so that in the event I'm sick or hurt, one or all of you can make important decisions that could save my life, and my dignity. I whole heartedly believe in sisterhood and solidarity; therefore, I'll be holding myself accountable as a Matriarch who leads by example and ensure she opens up and builds those bonds first. It has only been three full weeks since we've been together, but yes, I think I do have names, not numbers in mind for all of you. You in front of me, are the bravest and bat shit craziest. Coming to me with suggestions such as to kill two true Tet reps whose auras wreak of fearlessness, strength, death, and destruction. I name you Nur. And you, who silently nodded her head in agreement with Nur, who kills those creepy centipedes in the tub for me before I get there…I name you….."

Date: Tuesday, August 1st 2017

Location: Chicago, Illinois

Situation: Hila meets her father Betzalel, who runs one of Lilith Corps greatest Research & Development labs.

"Hila, we've never seen anything like this before. I really don't know what to think of Jay and Karman. I would've liked to have met them, but I'm happy they're no longer around," Hila heard her father Betzalel say, pointing to a whole bunch of different holograms displaying data.

"What are you showing me? And what are the implications? Be clear with me, were they functional Makers?" Hila asked, staring through several layers of clear, ultra-strong Meta-material, gazing into the 'Scan lab', where the SUV, weapons and other content belonging to the couple had been placed for study.

"My gut feeling, and short answer is, yes. The long answer is, maybe… not so much," she heard her father respond, sounding hesitant.

"It's a yes or no question," she replied, turning around, studying her father who was dressed in a white, with silver accents Thawb that set her nerves on edge, not because of what it represented, but because she knew he was doing it just to test her, to see if the illness she was now suffering acutely from, had dug into her self-conscious to the point of making her biased over clothing.

"Well, because of what they've done, and how they've done it, they would not fit the specifications of what we consider a Maker," Hila heard her father say as he turned away from her direct gaze, giving her a sarcastic, sidelong look as he peered into the 'Scan lab'.

"What do you mean?" she sniped.

"Why, why after all these years, why are you here, talking to me? You could've used another lab," she heard her father ask, with a slight crack in his voice.

"Why do you sound like you're going to cry? That's very weak," she whispered.

"I love you. You're all I have left. I've missed you," she heard her father reply, still sounding like he was on the verge of tears.

"I see. Mom must've left you here because you are indeed very weak," she whispered, seeing her father turn and face her again, with a small streams of tears running down his cheeks.

"What the fuck is wrong with me!?" she thought, instantly feeling her heart sink, causing her to turn away.

Keeping her eyes locked forward, staring into the 'Scan lab', she watched as machine arms picked up one of the Rifles Jay and Karman claimed they'd made, seeing a soft burst of light at play along its surface.

"My Halo, when Jay and Karman told your brother and Rayya they had help creating everything, they weren't lying. They had a great deal of help. The research and cross fields of study to accomplish even making the outermost layer of those Rifles or those Machetes would've cost billions of dollars. Doing this on their own, they would've stood out the moment they started spending money on a lab, and equipment. Spending money for things like that, as you well know, is the 'M.O.' of a Maker."

"You know when they get that bug in them to create, nothing stops them, and they begin syphoning funds from any and everywhere so that they can build a functioning lab. And once their lab is up and running, they go from secretive to no longer covering their tracks the further they get to realizing their goals. This Jay and Karman, these people literally outsourced almost every aspect of the work, but then somehow, they did a full assembly of everything at the end," Hila heard her father say, sounding envious.

"If they were functional Makers, then that means there could be more. It means we could lose complete control of technology. If we lose control of technology, Lilith Corp will become obsolete. Everything here, all the things we've ever done to maintain control, it'll be lost. Our technological advancements and our ability to manipulate our body energy has been our foundation, and has always kept us above the sheep."

"And since the gap in technology is already closing fast enough without having functional Makers walking around, I don't understand why you just sounded so envious. And need I remind you, since this Reggie movement, there's been a spike in his followers and that those followers are now able to manipulate their body energy to the same levels as us! They are doing this without training! The two things that are core of our strength are now becoming a norm for the sheep!"

"I know Hila," she heard her father whisper

"You know, yet your tone just now, it's as if you seem happy we are facing Lilith's last breaths. Do you really hate mom, and women so much you want us to fail?" she whispered, clenching her fist.

"What do you want me to say Hila?" she heard her father ask.

"Say you care! And act on those words! I just want things to go back how they were! I want to seek and destroy Makers and capture Mediums and make sure there's a damn balance to civilization! And this Reggie movement, I don't like it, it's too good to be true. It's actually really helping women all over the world! It's really empowering them! Ra! It's disgusting and, and, and hypocritical that this kind of movement was started by and is still being led by a disgusting, vile male" she growled.

"Did you ever consider why Tet told you to stop hunting Makers? Or to treat any new Mediums you find with respect?" she heard her father ask, closing the six-foot gap she'd constantly maintained since entering his private study chamber that over looked the 'Scan lab'.

"Yes, they want Lilith to die a slow death," she replied, seeing no other reason.

"Halo, they told everyone… literally every company who has similar practices as we do to stop. Also, they could've killed you and I at any time they wanted. We both know if Tet wants to replace us, they'd do it. And we both know that if Tet wants someone or a company to suffocate, they'd be much more sadist about it. Knowing them, they'd probably send two official Tet reps with sociopathic smiles to stop by, asking detailed questions, ensuring that they record each one of their victims gasping breaths."

"They were sociopaths! Even I don't stride calmly under fire of a rocket!" Hila replied.

"My Halo, they were just giving you a warning and left you to do as you will. Which, I admit for those of a too head strong will and want to dare them, is like leaving one with the proverbial rope to hang oneself with. Nonetheless, you and I both know that this was not in any form, a kill strike for you, because as head strong as you are, you're not the type not to ignore their warning," Hila heard her father say, laying his hand on her shoulder.

"Then what do you think they really want or are trying to accomplish?" she asked, turning and looking into her father's eyes, which were still red, seeming like at any moment he'd cry again.

"Hila, I think humans are inside ourselves a little too much. We know we're animals but forget at the same time. My love, think about how long quote on quote 'Makers' have been hunted and Mediums enslaved. If an animal doesn't go extinct, they adapt. If you're willing to listen, I'd like to share with you a project I've been working on since your mother returned to Israel."

"Project?" she asked, feeling butterflies in her belly.

"Hila, there's evidence that in one single generation, humans can and have evolved from Homo Sapiens, to something else much more intelligent and functional. From my research, the change is brought on by extreme stressors. I mean very extreme. Humans being hunted by other humans would be a perfect example of that kind of extreme stressor. For all we know, Tet could be trying to prevent the evolution of new types of Humans by reducing the stress both Makers and Mediums go through by our hands," she heard her father say, giving her a flash back, recalling what the Tet agents had told her in regards to treating people like employees, and not a captured slaves.

"I'm here because my illness is getting worse by the day. My bias towards males has become pure hatred, making me no longer even recognize myself. Hearing your voice, being around you, suppresses my illness long enough for me to somewhat think clearly so that I can hear reasoning. For too long, I've not been able to listen to any of my male staff. And the more I listen to only female board members, and my female companions...my company goes to shit. Many of these women are Jealous of me and are poisoning me with smiles, and politics, all while bonding with me based on my mutual hate for males. I can see the toxic spiral clearly, and so can the rest of the world."

"Where Lilith was once respected as forward thinkers and role models for women around the world, we are now seen as purely misogynistic. Now, male led companies that Lilith needs in order to keep things flowing, are running away from us with every excuse under the sun. Making things worse, I've yet to rebuild my science and technology ranks after losing so many to the June events and intra company wars. It's just that I have no idea how to rebuild while I'm sick like this! I can't even think straight! I need your help dad, but when I think of asking you, I hate the thought of humbling myself to a man so much that can barely breathe."

"Hila?" she heard her father ask.

"Yes?" she replied, feeling dizzy the more she tried to think about asking for help aloud.

"Are you okay? You're turning pale. Come, let's eat, the baby is taking all the nutrients it needs from you. It's your responsibility to put those back," she heard her father say, taking her hand, calming her.

"Dad...Sorry for calling you weak. It takes strength to show emotion. Dad...I need..."

For a moment there was only darkness and the world fell away, swallowed by pure hatred of every male on earth, every male that had been, and every male that ever would be.

"I love you," she heard her father whisper.

"I...I Need your help dad. Need your help to rebuild. I need new, competent staff. People eager and willing to give it their all to try and outpace the sheep, both technologically and metaphysically," she forced herself to say, feeling a literal heat rush out from her body, mostly pouring out her mouth, ears and nostrils.

"Of course, I'll help you in any way I can," she heard her father reply, embracing her tightly.

"Thank you, thank you," she gasped, hearing a soft chime go off, then another and another, and another.

Breathing deeply, she felt her body begin to tremble, then she felt the need to urinate right then and there as if she were a child, not even wanting to go to the restroom.

"Is this a symptom of the illness? What the hell is wrong with me now?" she thought, feeling her father squeeze her tighter, followed by another burst of heat, causing her to sweat so much it instantly oversaturated her dark blue jumper.

The month of April came into mind, with the memory of her watching T.V. nude in her recliner. She remembered drifting off to sleep a few times on the same day, then waking up three days later, siting in the same recliner. More chimes went off, and she could now hear Jay's voice...and she recognized it was the message he'd sent where he was asking for his house to be rebuilt. She then felt her father who'd been ever so slightly rocking her go ridged.

"Dad?" she asked, feeling him release his embrace, waving his hand, stopping the chimes as new holograms with flashing icons and data appeared.

"I'm not going to lie; I was not sure how I was going to help you rebuild till just now. But now I have an idea," she heard her father whisper.

"Really!? How!?" she asked.

"Well, one thing is to keep doing what you're doing. I like the way you've begun your recruitment process," she heard her father say.

643

"What? Even in my eyes, it's too biased towards females. I'm losing the confidence of any woman with a husband or son, as well as any male who has even the slightest dignity," she responded, feeling pressure in her head as the dark part of her mind hated her father for being a male who'd come up with an idea to further segregate males – feeling that he'd stolen the honor of crushing males away from her.

"Well yes, you're being a little heavy handed. But that's fine because as you grow, it'll for sure tone down. Think about it, this heavy hand is you rekindling the inner spirt of Lilith Corp., rekindling the strong Matriarchal, female orientated foundation! Do not look at what is happening as short comings! Those that are crumbling under you are the weak branches that would not stay when times get hard either way!"

"Yes! Yes! Okay! Right!" she replied, staring to feel revitalized by her father's words.

"Good! Good!" she heard her father say, giving her a bright smile.

"But, okay! Still, what's your other idea, it can't be to just do what I'm doing," she whispered, moving closer to her father, feeling heat rush out from her body again.

"Um, well I just heard Jay's message again. Did you hear his message as the chimes went off?" she heard her father ask, inching back giving her a confessed look.

"No, not just now…I heard…well saw something else. What's going on? Dad, I really don't feel good," she whispered.

"I know baby. Look, I have a plan to help you with that as well. As for your other question on how to help you rebuild your company…Then it's all about the message. I strongly suggest you help Jay…which is actually …helping Tet, rebuild," she heard her father whisper.

"What? Why! And how even!?" she asked, shocked at what she was hearing but too weak to really be angry.

"From the data I just received, I'll be able to have a list of people Jay and Karman's message was sent to. If you want some form of balance and talented people, send all your strongest, most personable female HR Managers to go out and recruit those people to either be a part of our main company, or a shell addition. Now, come, I just been notified preparations are complete. I need to take you to be healed. Your unborn son and the love you have for me as your father is all that's tethering you. Without us, the imbalance this illness is causing you would make you actively try to destroy every man on earth."

"I just don't understand how, how this imbalance has been triggered. I was the last of my sisters to feed into mom's man hate delirium. And as thankful as I am to be pregnant, do you have any word on how the Nil-Venusian failed to stop this from happening," she replied.

"I...Hila, the Lilith bloodline death and rebirth process, is very not very well documented to be understood. So far, from what I've learned is that what dies with you becomes reborn again with you. Also, when you died, a large majority of the Nil-Venusian began to be absorb in your decomposing womb, keeping it from attacking the sperm which can live up to five days. Since you were only dead for three, when you were reborn, and your egg was revived, the sperm must've fertilized your reborn egg. And if you're wondering why the remainder of the Nil-Venusian didn't kill the sperm or the fertilized egg when you were reborn, well, it appears since your rebirth, your body is now a huntress that kicks out all foreign objects."

"I still think it should've stopped the pregnancy," she whispered, having another flashback of watching T.V. in April, along with a dark, twisted ominous feeling.

"Anyways, what do you mean take me to be healed? Is it possible? Because, these thoughts are so strong, I'm actually starting to consider that I might genuinely be mentally ill," she whispered

"Yes, it's possible and the sooner you go, the better."

"Go where? With who?" she asked, picking up on her father's awkward tone.

"I will have you meet the person you were just complaining about. Reggie and a very large group of his followers are here and have set up in the penthouse where they will or all of you will...participate...in a... umm, powerful Working. So...umm, while you're with them, I'll start working on that list."

"Reggie? A Working? Dad? What! What kind of...holy shit! Are you serious!?" she asked, wobbling where she stood, holding her belly, staring at her father who would barely make eye contact with her.

"Trust me, trust me I hate the thought of it. But from all my understandings of how the imbalance works, it's, it's one of the only ways. And like I said, you have to do it soon or you could be trapped in the thick of your imbalance for a very, very long time," Hila heard her father say, giving her a tight embrace.

'Life is crazy. My brother and his wife, with their need to have fun, created Reggie, who created a following of people just like...them. And now people like them...and the things...the things they do are possibly the only thing that can save me! Crazier still, is maybe I would never have found any of this out it if I hadn't confided to my bodyguards that I felt this illness the other day, if I hadn't acknowledged and confided to them that I'm afraid, and feel lonely, and that I missed my father. I asked them to protect me from my self, and those crazy bitches...tied me up and took me through a transport Node...delivering me to my father," Hila thought, mentally tapping into her View-Contacts, calling up an image of Reggie and a manifesto of the followers he'd brought with him for the Working, feeling the horrible pressure in her head, negative thoughts of all men needing to die and be crushed by women, already begin to ease.

"Oh shit! If I'm already feeling this good from just looking at them, and...is his dick curved to the left, oh yes please! I love dick curved like that! And look at her body, she's so fucking sexy! And...are those boxes of toys? Wait! Are those nipple clamps inside that one box? I've always wanted to try those! And, oh my God! Reggie brought rope! Okay, fuck shame! Yes please, time a billion!" Hila thought, feeling another rush of heat pour out from her body, but this time, the sweat and her scent were all comforting and welcoming to her.

"Dad, I umm...you don't need to walk with me. I'll, ummm...I'll just go meet them myself," she said, trying to make sure she still felt awkward and ashamed that it was supposedly the only way.

"Yeah, go, I'll be here," she heard her father say with a look that agreed with her statement.

"Okay, okay," she replied, awkwardly bowing, slash bobbing her head at her father as she walked towards an enormous round blast door that silently rolled open, allowing her to come out of the 'Scan lab's' 'safe study' room.

"Lilith AI! Block my father from seeing me run, I don't care what you have to do to make it happen!" she commanded, taking off towards the elevator, running into it saying, "Doors close! Penthouse! Go to the Penthouse now!"

In seconds, the Lil-hov-elevator arrived at the penthouse, denoted by the doors opening and the scent of warm incenses and candles rushing in, along with the sight of warm alluring lights.

"I am of Lilith bloodline! I'm supposed to be the embodiment of all carnal desires! This is supposed to be my bloodline's natural element! I see now that this illness has even stolen this from me! Making me always feel like doing something like this would be disgusting, making me hate something that can cure it, with all my heart! Well then, it's time to fix that and become the powerful woman I'm truly supposed to be!" Hila thought as she looked herself over in the elevator mirror, taking in the details of her now fully grown out, long, thick, black, curly hair.

"Yes, I look good!" she whispered, now staring at her plush lips, lined with red lipstick, then to her golden earrings and jewelry, that matched perfectly with dark blue Jumper.

"Oh, yes! Even with the sweat here, I still look good! As matter of fact, I think I'll keep it on till it's completely drenched or they rip it off of me," she whispered smiling at the dark patch of sweat on her back and under her breast.

"Madam Lilith, we're await your beautiful presence," Hila heard a male voice say in a warm tone.

"God, his voice is sexy! Yes! Time to go!" she thought, puckering her lips, giving herself an air kiss, then strolling out the elevator to find Reggie standing nude with a warm, mischievous smile on his face…and red rope in hand.

-At the same time, one level below, inside 'Small Items' scan lab number 2-

"I'm happy my design is protecting people. Yet, I still feel it was a close call. Reviewing the blast data, shows that if Nate had been one foot closer, the lens material would not have had enough time to disintegrate, and would've gone flying into his eyes. Damn it, it's so hard to make battle ready View-Tech lenses! Balancing when they should stay firm, or when they should disintegrate, feels like an impossible task! One day, the lenses staying firm

647

might be perfect, the next, there goes their eyes, or worse their lives," Hyun-Shik thought, pressing *{Re Sync to View-Tech's}* on his control console, before looking up, staring at the remnants of Nate's View-Tech's in the actual 'scan room' itself, which was a relatively small chamber, separated by ultra-strong layers of clear, meta material, filled with machine arms and various apparatus, such as laser, and spectroscopes.

"This is difficult, but it will be worth it when I finally make them perfect," Hyun-Shik mumbled in his mother tongue of Korean, seeing a green icon indicate that Nate's View-Tech's had now synchronized with the scan labs, Lilith Corp AI.

Pressing *{play}*, sound wave oscillation data from the blast that occurred within the Lilith Corp. base appeared in a hologram in front of him. After two hours of studying the data and tweaking his mixture of material for his lenses, with no avail in terms of balancing them to shatter sooner, without compromising the structure to hold for weaker forces that realistically would not require them to disintegrate, Hyun-Shik, grew frustrated and smacked his hand on the console.

"AI is receiving a message from a visitor named Reggie, would you like to connect?" he heard the Lilith AI of the scan lab say in his ear bud.

"Reggie? Like, the pervert Reggie? How would he even know I exist? How would he…Ah, whatever. AI, patch him through," he said aloud, too tired and frustrated to think too much, and with the thought in mind that he'd get more answer, just accepting the call.

"Hi, upon my journey in the astro realm, I very briefly, visited with Nate, Rayya, Jay and Karman. Your frustration in regards to the lenses was somehow reaching them and they wanted me to be their medium to speak with you. As you know from your briefings about the events that transpired. Karman, is a material scientist, with an aptitude as great as your own. She and her husband, Jay, would like to grant you access to a certain place where you can possibly work out your problems. Additionally, I've asked them for permission to share an intimate moment between all four of them, with hopes to relieve your stress, and to awaken parts of you that you've long suppressed," he heard Reggie say in a deep, warm tone, that somehow made him feel comfortable, yet ...highly alert.

"Astro realm? So, are they fully passed or are they somewhere else? My colleague is at a loss scanning all four of their remains. She's under the impression it's not actually them. She's hypothesizing what's she looking at, is like a shell of them. Like they've shed their entire bodies the way an arthropod would. Is it possible that if I mediated well enough, I could go speak to them myself and find out?" he replied.

"I figured you'd ask that. In order to mediate to such a level, you'd need to un-suppress you lower two chakras. I can sense that they're highly starved," he heard Reggie reply in a perfectly neutral tone.

"I don't want to. Too many people think with just their lower two energies. You're a perfect example of what I see wrong with the world. You've even turned it into a way of life," I value being conservative, and value not trusting anyone.

"You want to fuel your mind body and spirt, but don't want to fully nurture your roots. It all starts from the base, Hyun-Shik, you know that. In any case, on their behalf, I've unlocked the encrypted files where you can watch their intimate experiences, as all four of them were wearing View-Tech's during their love making session together," he heard Reggie reply.

"Why would you chose for me to see them instead of just watching porn?" he asked.

"Because, like you said, you want to go speak to them yourself. They are very deeply in love with each other. I think, to get your mind, body and spirit to resonate with them so that you can better find them in the astro realm, you should get to know them in an intimate way," he heard Reggie reply.

"Hummm...I've had my heart crushed by intimacy. I don't like this idea whatsoever, but I'm highly tempted. Speaking to all four of them would be valuable beyond words. In regards to my other question about if they're fully passed or not...wait, you're going to say...I should go ask them myself, aren't you?" he replied to Reggie.

"The four intimate files are unlocked, as well as Jay and Karman's special place. Inside of that special place, you'll also find an invitation from them as well. Oh and if watching them further motivates you to rebuild your base chakras, I'll be here for a few more days to assist you. Madam Lilith is here with me now, and grants you and anyone you chose to bring, to come join us as well," he heard Reggie say, followed by silence.

"Madam Lilith herself has granted me, the person she's been calling a lowly, male scum, scientist, to come participate? In my opinion, this is now no longer even an ask or a suggestion form anyone else, but her. My life and livelihood depend on her opinion of me, and even her supposed suggestion, I best do, or else risk the chance of further falling out of her good grace. I can't afford that. I value my family and my life way too much to be a prideful fool that doesn't conform," Hyun-Shik, thought, seeing two icons floating in the hologram projected from his control consol.

Pressing open for both, he felt his body go heavy in his seat, then his mind pulled somewhere that felt like he was living within a dream. In front of him, he could see the forms of Nate, Rayya, Jay and Karman's appear. Then, from each of their viewpoints he watched them flirt, tease, taunt, and finally make love together. At first he felt the same numbness he always experienced when something sexual or intimate would come up in his life. But after a while of watching the two couples, genuinely enjoying each other, the numbness slowly began ebb away, and then parts of him that he'd long closed off, finally began to reawaken.

News Reports

From: March 13th to June 21st, 2017

Date: Monday, March 13th 2017

News Reporter: "This is a very ugly storm over Washington D.C. Snow, hail, strong wind gust. We recommend staying indoors unless you have to be outside."

Date: Tuesday, March 14th 2017

News Reporter: "The storm has intensified, but instead of staying inside, looters are out in the streets of D.C. There have been thirteen homicides and forty-four storm related deaths."

Date: Wednesday, March 15th 2017

News Reporter: "The Opioid crisis in the United States of America is still going unchecked and is even worse than we thought. This horrible storm slamming into D.C. seems to want to bring this to light by opening up abandoned houses, exposing whole entire complexes of people who've gone in and unfortunately died from overdose. Essentially, these houses have become drug dens of death.

Date: Wednesday, March 15th 2017

News Reporter: "Tonight, we're reporting a global phenomenon where billions of people are reporting that they've been feeling off kilter. The main physical symptoms people are expressing is dizziness, headaches, nausea and seeing colors they've never seen before. We are also being told that this off feeling is curing people's sex life problems, while others who never had a problem are saying they don't feel safe, confident or comfortable any more. Finally, there are reports that are a little bit harder to believe, where people are saying that they've been feeling and or hearing other people's thoughts. The progression symptoms were that everyone had felt something similar at the beginning of the day, and then from there branching out to the other various symptoms as the day progressed.

Date: Thursday, March 16th 2017

News Reporter - Kelly: The president of the United States has just delivered a moving speech on why all of humanity should work together on building a space elevator. Shocking the world with the ice-cold reality of how humanity is living in a time of crisis. But with her message, many cried tears of hope and joy.

News Reporter - Kelly: Not only is today a landmark day due to the President of the United States speech, today is also the first day in recorded human history where worldwide, no one has reported any form of killing a person whatsoever. But get this, there were still arrest for attempted murders and that's what makes this story so much more, well…humbling. Let's take a look, we have Paula who will be broadcasting live from Saint Louis.

News Reporter – Paula Banks: Hi, thank you Kelly, this is Paula Banks and I'm here, live in Saint Louis, at the site where a raging gang war would've taken place, except the two parties involved both said they physically could not go through with it. Here is one of the gang leaders, let's take a listen.

Interviewee: 'Yo', I was strapped up, had the chopper out and aimed at dude's melon, and 'yo', I couldn't clap him up for the life of me, you heard? Like I want to blow dude's head off right

652

now, like right, right now. But, I can't do it. I don't care who hear this, the judge, the jury, the world, that dude killed my lil brother in cold blood. He came up to my house, rang the doorbell, put his gun to the peephole and blew his head off. My brother and I were not even in the game, dude just picked the wrong house and killed the wrong person, and afterwards, just no apology. So, I gathered a clique that's tired of this dude and his crew snuffing us innocents out without remorse. We figured its finally time to fight fire with fire, vigilante stuff, 'ya' heard! We da vigilantes!"

News Reporter – Paula Banks: So, y'all are called the vigilantes? So what made you not be able to take action? Did you have second thoughts because being a vigilante is still a crime?

Interviewee: Fuck it being a crime! Living with no help for the police of government stopping these fools is a crime! It's just, I literally could not pull the trigger. Like I tried. But the harder I tried, the more my hand would lock up, then I had a small panic attack and you, I started crying, I never cry, even when I saw my 'lil' bro with his top blown off, even after I buried 'lil' man, I 'ain't' cry, so why would I cry about killing this fool? This is some 'kinda' government mind control voodoo shit. I've seen them chem-trails over our neighborhoods, and I know they putting stuff in black people's water."

News Reporter - Kelly: Thank you Paula for your report in Saint Louis. Next, we have Yousuf Khan in the West Bank.

News Reporter – Yousuf Khan: Hi, thank you Kelly. I'm standing with fighters who've attempted to fire rockets into Israel today. They said they could not bring themselves to go ahead with the attack. Let's listen to their testimonial.

Interviewee (Translated): The infidel spread, taking our lands and taking our way of life. We, like all other days, come to resist, to fight - bless Allah, our God. Today, bless God, we could not fight. Today, bless God, he said, be still. So today, we are still. We, bless God, trust and will fight with his plan.

Date: Saturday, April 15th 2017

News Reporter: All over the world, it's been a quiet three days. And many are saying, a little too quiet. Questions are arising because prominent corporate and government leaders across the global have all seemed to recluse themselves, stating that they're having meetings regarding the space elevator and the future of the world. But there's a lot of buzz, with people saying that no meeting is taking place, and that the leaders have not been seen leaving their respective homes since April thirteenth. However, Madam Lilith this morning did announce that she would be holding a conference tonight in Tel Aviv regarding the space elevator project. To me, it just sounds like they've been having teleconference meetings at home during the last few days.

News Reporter: It's been almost one month to the day, and there still hasn't been any reports of someone killing another person. This means no murders and no prisoner executions. That doesn't mean armies are not practicing, staging and posturing. But no shots have been fired. No one is actively moving to kill each other. This phenomenon is on the tip of everyone's tongue because no one knows really what to think.

Date: Sunday, April 16th 2017

News Reporter - Joel: It is with a heavy heart that I must report that killing, in all its horror has begun again all over the world, literally one month and one day after it had all ended. The oddity and only slightly positive news is that the violence did not last long in any one region of the globe. As quickly as it had begun, it had ended. No one knows why the violence had ended, and no one knows why it has begun to return. Now, at the end of this day, all seems to be calm again. We ask you please give your thought and prayers to the many that have lost their lives.

Stand by as we connect you to Clarissa, who's in Guam, where it is thought that the first of the violence began.

News Reporter – Clarissa Stafford: Hi, this is Clarissa Strafford, we're in Guam where like Joel said, is thought to be one of the first places killing has begun since last month. The violence that took place here is on this medium sized yacht where twenty-one people have lost their lives. We're unclear of the circumstance as all thirteen women and eight men are known to the public as mischievous, but otherwise kind and helpful to the people of the community. Adding to the oddity of this story, is how this scene was found in the first place, with witnesses for hundreds of miles seeing a spectacular light show, displaying furious bolts of lightning in an utterly cloudless night sky, along with aurora borealis above the location where the heaviest concentration of lightning was taking place.

Many were thinking it could be a new volcano forming and rushed out to the scene to find this yacht, filled with the deceased, who were all nude and suffered from deep lacerations and stab wounds all over their bodies. Now the oddity does not end there. Witnesses say that the lightning was not coming from a volcano, but from the close proximity of the body of a woman named Tiana Masga, who was found floating a few hundred feet away. Still now, hours after Tiana's body has been discovered, it's yet to be recovered. At first, it was because the lightning concentration and frequency was too much to deal with. Then, as the lightning died down and the recovery teams got closer, one of the largest gatherings of Orca ever known appeared and surrounded her body. I'm talking so massive of a gathering that it's even larger than what is seen when they are hunting the Blue Whale. Any time the recovery team has tried to get close, one of the Orca move her body further away. Also, whenever one of the Orca touch her body, it seems like bolts of lightning begin to strike really close to the recovery team's vessel. We will be back with more as the story unfolds.

News Reporter: Stocks had been going down every day and have now hit resistance, and then for the last two days we've seen this level out. Economist worldwide are puzzled because they've never seen the global market stay in exactly one place for two days. It literally looks like a flat line. We've been hitting this story hard, and everyone is saying they are trading…but nothing seems to be happening. IT specialist are checking trade software; we have investigators looking into all sorts of different aspect of this.

News Reporter: Killings all over the world per day are increasing. Although tragic, the killing are not nearly to the level they had used to be on a daily basis before the no killing phenomenon started.

Date: Tuesday, May 16th 2017

News Reporter: While the world was focusing on the phenomenon of no, or reduced, homicides and executions, it seems the world neglected to bring up the number of increased suicides and mass attempts and successes of self-harm, which are quite frankly staggering. In the U.S., suicide by OTC drugs alone are hitting small town and large cities hard. On just this street alone, in Cleveland, Ohio, there have been fourteen fatal overdoses in the last month. In San Francisco, there have been one hundred people who have jumped, with only one surviving. If you want to take a quick peak at the world, we can look at Brazil, where we have people have been purposely contracting sexual immune deficiency viruses. They are saying it's the only way to save their people, by reducing the population. In nations with very limited water, people are refusing to take their allotted rations and are opting to just die. In Japan, there have been what looks to be suicide packs between office workers and their bosses, where they've all collectively ran onto the train tracks, eaten the poisons parts of puffer fish, or taken trips to what the Japanese call the suicide forest, where none are ever to be seen again.

Date: Saturday, May 20th 2017

News Reporter: We bring you sad news tonight from Seattle. An up and coming Sci-fi Author was killed in a murder-suicide by his girlfriend of just three months. Family, close friends and fans of Author William Brown and Vivian Chan are extremely heartbroken and shocked. Everyone is saying that Vivian is not even the type of person who'd kill even a fly, saying that she'd spend time and energy chasing them out of open doors and windows. Investigation so far show no signs of dispute. William was found on the floor in front of his laptop, his novel just saved as complete, with the ending stating, 'kill all those who know of Nefeshka'. Apologies, I'm just getting notification that, that ending wasn't actually in there. We will now go for a short break. **(Later that night and for weeks after, just that portion, "Kill all those who know of Nefeshka," played thousands of times under the pretense of; 'making fun of... or learning from a Journalists' error'.)**

Date: Sunday, May 21st 2017

News Reporter: The question is, why has company and government leaders been so absent. Ever since April, there has been almost no signs of them. And any small sighting people report, are being disputed by people who are saying that it is in fact stand in, doppelgängers meant to be seen so that we don't suspect that they are actually missing.

Date: Monday, May 22nd 2017

News Reporter: Lilith Corp, say trials of their all in one anti STI and pregnancy treatment they call Nil-Venusian has passed all trials and will soon be made available worldwide. Nil-

Venusian is a gel with Nano technology that is placed inside the vagina, and or on top of the penis. The Nano Technology then destroys virus and bacteria before, during and after intercourse, as well as destroying sperm and egg cells to prevent unwanted pregnancies. It is meant to act as a treatment for those who already have STIs, as well as a preventive measure for those who do not, but are planning to have intercourse with someone who has STIs. Lilith Corp boast that Nil-Venusian does not have any form of unwanted side effects and that it's perfectly safe to use for an indefinite amount of time. They also boast that Nil-Venusian will have a huge historic positive impact on human society, and that this positive impact will be felt very, very shortly.

Many people such as those in polygamous relationships, swingers, porn actors and actress, as well as sex workers had been chosen to use it for trials and swear by it that it works at a ninety-nine percent rate. And during interviews with the people mentioned, all seem over the moon with joy. Stating that their overall quality of life will and has already increased.

Date: Thursday, June 1st 2017

News Reporter: If you are receiving this message. (Coughs) Excuse me. I meant to say this is New Rapid City ...

(This blunder happened all around the world in every language and when questioned. It was actually taken seriously. Journalist were then interviewed on what they saw, felt and heard before making that statement. But the thing was that no journalist remembered experiencing anything odd. In the end, well...there was nothing else that could be done.)

Date: Friday, June 2nd 2017

News Reporter: We have heard rumors that Tet Corp. was putting pressure on other companies for the construction of a second space elevator. Tet Corp. said they will make an announcement soon to address these rumors.

Date: Saturday, June 3rd 2017

News Reporter: Rumors that companies are sending their private armies to fight each other have been verified with video proof of their raids on each other. However, every person who has shared such videos now say their entire family has somehow died within the subsequent days. Many of them have then shortly after committed suicide. We journalist understand people wanting to get the truth out there. But, even from our point of view, we journalist around the world plead to you and say, that maybe somethings…are better left unsaid and unproven.

Date: Tuesday, August 1st 2017

News Reporter: We are live with the man who has started the first legal sex religion in the United States. Reggie, please tell us how you came about this. And how you've managed to get your religion protected, when all other sex religions have been fought and blocked within the United States. And we have also heard your worldwide followers are also opening up their own temples and that they are being approved by their governments as well, how are all of you doing this?

Reggie (Standing calmly with a knowing smile): Samantha, you're an investigative reporter, right?

Samantha: Yes.

Reggie: Well, step into my temple, and find out the truth for yourself.

Samantha: I know what happens in those temples. I'm married. No thanks.

Reggie: I understand. I respectfully ask that you bring your husband. All truths are revealed with your loved one. I never ask for money. You don't need to stay any longer than either of you want. Or ever come back if you do not want to. Our practice is about mindfulness and shared experience of the body. When you and your husband come, there is no one to pressure either of you. You would come in and do as either of you see fit. We provide the light, the people who enter, then for the most part guides themselves.

Samantha: I...I. Um. Well it looks like what's separating Reggie from all the other religions that quickly get considered cults and outlawed, is that he asks for no monetary supplementation. Reggie, what put you on this path.

Reggie: The warmth and love of two beautiful people named Rayya and Nate. May their journey, and that of their friends be blessed.

Thank you for reading!
Please take a look at my other books!
They may contain answers to question you may have about my realm!

Website: Omwills.com

Made in the USA
Monee, IL
22 July 2020